M000235612

# THE OTHER MAGIC

## PASSAGE TO DAWN: BOOK ONE

### DERRICK SMYTHE

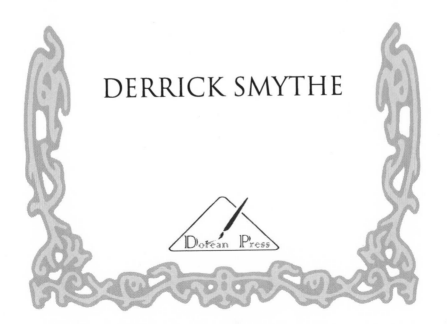

Dorean Press

*The Other Magic: Passage to Dawn Book 1*
© 2019 Derrick Smythe, All Rights Reserved.
Published by Dorean Press, Cicero, New York

ISBN 978-1-7340953-2-6 (hardback)
ISBN 978-1-7340953-0-2 (paperback)
ISBN 978-1-7340953-1-9 (eBook)

www.derricksmythe.com

This book contains an excerpt from the second book in the series, *The Other Way*, by Derrick Smythe. This excerpt has been included for this edition only and may not reflect the final content of the upcoming book.

This is a work of fiction. The events and persons are imagined. Any resemblance to actual events, or to persons, alive or dead, is purely coincidental.

Without limiting the rights under copyright reserved above, no part of this publication may be reproduced, stored in or introduced into a retrieval system, or transmitted in any form or by any means (electronic, mechanical , photocopying, recording or otherwise), without the prior written permission of both the copyright owner and the above publisher of this book, except by a reviewer who wishes to quote brief passages in connection with a review written for insertion in a magazine, newspaper, broadcast, website, blog or other outlet.

Publishing consultant: David Wogahn, AuthorImprints.com

# ACKNOWLEDGMENTS

**T**O MY PARENTS, WHO INSTILLED in me the virtues of faith, respect, discipline, and integrity that formed the core of who I am today. My mother fostered a love for the written word early in life, then later demonstrated that you're never too old to start something new, even if that new thing is marathon running. My father has been an inspiration to me and my siblings with his own brand of tirelessness, putting in countless overtime shifts in order to give us the best chance in life possible, never voicing a single complaint along the way.

To my older brother, who managed to captivate an easily distractible audience with his epic childhood action-figure productions equipped with space crafts, backstory, and a long cast of characters with plot twists designed to cause us, his two younger brothers, to cry at the deaths of our favorite heroes.

To my eighth grade English teacher, Ms. Ryan, who likely had no idea how inspiring she was to my confidence as a writer, yet proved a pivotal hinge in my writing life in the years to follow.

To Wayne, who asked the kinds of questions that made me realize just how much I didn't know about my own world in the early stages of my work and connected me to a local writing workshop where I met an author who encouraged me to join a writing group. Through monthly meetings, this writer's group slowly eradicated the worst of my writing habits, and encouraged me to continue working toward publication over the years. They're a quirky group, but I'm forever indebted to them.

To my best critics, who not only saw the good in my early drafts, but also weren't afraid to tell me what needed to be done in order to make them better. Alex, Lynna, Dee, and Foster, all of whom read multiple drafts and provided valuable feedback for each. Matt, my consultant on everything magic; thank you for the discussions on magical theory that would eventually give birth to the world of Doréa.

To Dr. Dawson, who treated my manuscript as if it was one of your students' dissertations, dissecting it to the core, identifying weak points, and providing suggestions that helped bring the story to a higher level than I could have ever done alone.

To my editor, Carolyn, whose remarkable attention to detail provided the critical polish prior to publication. To put it simply, a writer without an editor is like drywall without paint; and not all paint is created equal.

To my wife, Kelly, whose editorial expertise transformed my writing from an unpalatable jumble of ill-advised commas, and, heaven forbid, sentences ending with prepositions, to something I could share with others without losing their respect on the first page. Kelly's frank critiques, and enduring patience with me, not only as a writer but as a husband cannot be overstated, or over-thanked.

And finally, God, whose subtle nudges encouraged me to begin this journey in the first place, and who keeps me far from despair whenever things don't go according to my plan.

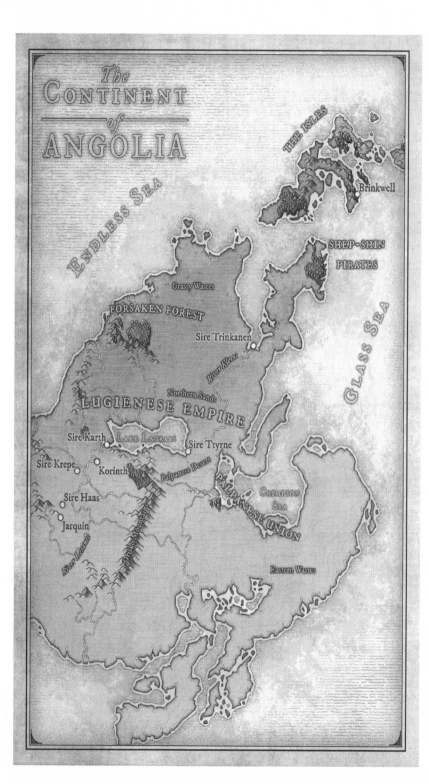

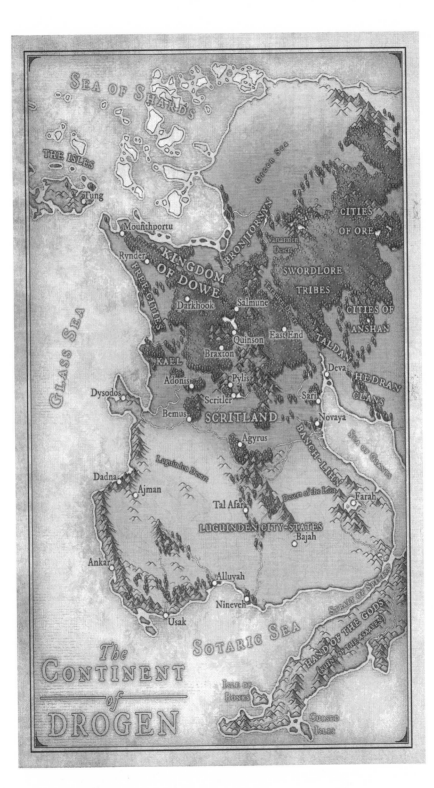

# THE
# OTHER
# MAGIC

## CHAPTER 1

# KIBURE

KIBURE SAT UP, RUBBED HIS face with his hands, then rose to his feet, frustrated that he could no longer sleep. The glow of the two moons illuminated the room enough for Kibure to see his way to the door of his slave hut. He tiptoed carefully to avoid waking the others who claimed their own crammed spaces along the floor; he would have hell to pay if he caused a disturbance that woke one of the elders in his hut.

Pushing gently, he cringed in anticipation of the squeak that, surprisingly, didn't come. *When did they oil that hinge?*

As Kibure stepped out into the night air, he noticed another oddity. The light he saw coming from the moons was, of course, limited; but even that partial lighting lacked the slightest semblance of color. He blinked, then reached up and rubbed his eyes; something felt wrong. Confused, Kibure swallowed hard and realized how acutely dry his throat felt. *Water. I need water.* He felt his heart thump, and started toward the nearby well.

He would have to be extremely careful to avoid waking one of the overseers who lived in the cottages beside the estate. Kibure stopped when he was only halfway there. The penalty for stealing a strictly guarded commodity like water was no less than twenty lashes, and yet he resumed his movement toward the well.

Once there, he took hold of the rope and pulled nervously, and slowly, so as to avoid causing the pulley to squeak. He looked over his shoulder as he did so, making sure he remained alone. Slowly, slowly—the rope slipped from his hand. *Noooo!*

The pail fell and Kibure scrambled to catch the line. He didn't. The heavy bucket landed with a—silent—nothing. No sound whatsoever. Kibure looked from side to side, then leaned over the well. Something was very wrong here. Then it hit him like a lash to the back: his breathing, heavy as it was, made no sound, the door had made no sound, even his footfalls had been silent. He brought his hands up and clutched his ears. What was wrong with him? He turned and ran back to the slave shack as fast as his twelve-year-old legs would take him, his fear of retribution from the other slaves gone.

He threw open the door and ran to the closest thing he had to a mother, Berta, then stopped just before her bed. It was empty. Scanning the room, he recognized that he was completely alone; there was not a single soul in the room. He fell to his knees, closed his eyes, and cried out; only his cry was as silent as the pail of water at the bottom of the well.

Kibure shook as he knelt on the ground, uncomprehending and afraid. When he opened his eyes again, his vision was blurred by tears. He gasped; a rush of sensations returned, primary among them sound, and the sound was him screaming. But he was no longer kneeling, he was on his back staring up at the ceiling. So satisfied was he to hear his voice that the hand gripping him had almost no effect. Then a second hand slapped him, and he quieted.

"Kibure! What's wrong?" whispered Parvel, trying to cover Kibure's mouth with a hand. Parvel, who slept beside him, was a few years older, and much bigger. Kibure's face grew warm where he had been hit. He didn't care.

"I—I—" What could he say: *I was walking around outside and tried to steal water when I realized I was seeing no color and hearing no sound?* Parvel would think him mad. *Maybe I am.*

"I think I—" Understanding dawned on him. "I think I had a bad dream. I'm—sorry."

Grumbles sounded throughout the shack and Kibure did not dare move or speak again for the rest of the night. Neither did he dare return to sleep.

Kibure's concern over his nightmare faded with the resumption of labor the following day. It was difficult to worry about much of anything once back in the familiar monotony of exhaustion and routine. After a brief lunch, Kibure started back at his work, cutting the heavy, greenish-red drogal fruit from the stalk with the dull wooden tool barely sharp enough to do the job. He fell into a familiar rhythm of work and song:

> *Toil, toil, in the field,*
> *To Klerós we are bound,*
> *Cut—THWACK—*
> *Cut—THWACK—*
> *The thin spot, don't bruise the drogal,*
> *Crack, crack, goes the whip,*
> *Pick up the pace,*
> *Cut—THWACK—*
> *Cut—THWACK—*
> *The thin spot, don't bruise the—*

"Hey, what I tell you about that rippin' singsong stuff?"

Kibure looked up to see Jarlax, a crotchety old slave, just a few trees away. "Sorry."

The slave shook his head. "Yeah, always sorry, but still always singin'. Just shut it, already!"

The other slave returned to his work, mumbling under his breath. Kibure resigned himself to labor the rest of the afternoon in silence, *mostly*. He hummed the tune loud enough for only his ears. As the day progressed, Kibure worked his way along the edge of the field, away from the others, filling his bag with fruit ahead of schedule for once. He carried his bag to the next tree and set it down with a satisfying thump. The bag, nearly full as it was, caused him to lose his balance in the process.

Kibure landed atop the bag, then slid down to the ground and rolled over so his back leaned against the bag of hard fruit. Sitting there, he let out a loud, satisfying breath, then he yawned and his eyelids drooped, pulled down as if by some unseen force. *Should stand up before I—*

He did not stand up.

Pain exploded across his thighs and Kibure's eyes snapped open, his heart instantly pounding as if he had just sprinted full across the field.

"Sleeping on the job, are we?" Musco Zagreb's thick, full-figured body towered over Kibure's lounging, diminutive form.

Kibure could feel the burning heat where the whip had lashed his skin. There would be a welt, and perhaps a few spots of blood. He didn't dare look. He also dared not speak for fear that whatever he said might make things worse.

Zagreb shouted gruffly, "Up! Now! You know the penalty, and that first one don't count."

Kibure did know the penalty. Fifteen lashes—no small sum where Zagreb's heavy-handedness was concerned. But Kibure rose to accept the judgment. He had no excuse, and Zagreb would have heard none, anyhow.

Kibure removed his tattered shirt.

Zagreb did not waste a moment, and Kibure shuddered as the rough whip sliced his scarred back. Kibure bit his lip to keep from screaming, knowing that Musco Zagreb believed silence a penance, a revered act for a slave. Kibure remained in fixed a standing position for the next ten lashes. But with such effort fixated on keeping quiet, he faltered.

An attempt to regain his footing failed as another crack of the whip reopened old wounds.

His face crashed into the sand. *Now I've done it.*

His weakness would only serve to ignite Musco Zagreb's rage. The whip struck again.

"Don't count if you on the ground!"

Kibure worked shaky muscles, urging them to cooperate with his will, and managed to secure a kneeling position. He paused as he spotted a boy his age, one of Zagreb's children, a true-blood. The boy was cutting away at weeds with a stick along the wall of the estate.

*Freedom*, thought Kibure as he spat jealously. It was almost unfathomable, and still he tried to imagine it, wondering at escape, though he had no idea where he might go. As far as he knew, there were no free-folk within the Lugienese Empire besides those of the true-bloods. Kibure imagined a faraway land where everyone smiled and no one used whips. Could such a place truly exist? He shook his head. He wouldn't survive more than a few days alone.

The next blow returned Kibure to the sandy soil, and the present. His back became a cauldron boiling over with pain. Kibure turned back to his musco, eyes pleading him to stop, but he knew the man wasn't finished. A slave's weakness was defiance. His musco raised the whip even higher. Just as he readied to strike, a flash of movement above caught Kibure's attention, followed by a thick white substance, which suddenly oozed down Zagreb's face. If the man's previous expression had been one of contempt, this new one was pure malice. The man wiped his face, then looked at his hand, recognizing the pungent white goo for what it was. He turned his attention to the sky. Kibure breathed a sigh of relief. His master's anger had been redirected. This might just allow Kibure a chance to rise again and return to work, forgotten.

Zagreb scanned the sky where the flying lemur, a raaven, circled, cooing and cawing its approval at having hit its target.

*Slowly, now. Yes. Still distracted.* Kibure slowly crept beyond reach. *Yes, that's it.*

"Blast you!"

Kibure froze. *Oh no.*

"Dagnammit, you baggin' winged rat!"

Kibure blew out the breath he had been holding. *He's not talking to me. Keep moving.*

"When I get my hands on you, I'm gonna break every rippin' bone in your body, then leave you strung to a post to rot! You maggot-laying, roach-infested, flying little grumpkin!"

Kibure was surprised at the creativity of Zagreb's insults while the raaven disappeared beyond the walls of the estate. But he was mostly just glad to no longer be the object of Zagreb's ire.

The young slave watched out of the corner of his eye as the winged, black lemur drifted out of sight, jealous of its freedom to come and go, something Kibure the slave would never know. He smiled nonetheless, imagining himself soaring through the sky, teasing the wicked, like Zagreb, just for the fun of it.

The raaven had been a fixture of the estate for as long as Kibure could remember, stealing whips and other tools as well as getting into the food stores. It was no secret that Zagreb hated the thing.

The slave master mumbled as he wiped the slimy, white substance from his brow with the rag he carried at his waist to dab away sweat. Then he turned back and spotted Kibure, who froze at the man's stare.

"Thought I'd forget on account of your little friend's distraction, did you? Come on back here," he barked. "We need to finish your punishment, else you'll never learn."

Kibure felt blood running down his back from the most recent gashes. He returned to stand before his master.

"Only thing I forgot was where I left off." Zagreb grinned. "Guess I'll have to start over."

"Twelve while standing, sixteen altogether," said Kibure without looking up.

"What's that, now?"

"Struck me twelve times while standing, and another four while on the ground."

Zagreb tilted his head. "You trying to be smart, but it's coming off real stupid. Gonna be twenty for you now. Any more numbers you wanna say?"

He lifted the whip to strike, not seeming to care that Kibure was still facing him. He swung, the whip taking Kibure full in the chest. This time he did cry out. And by the time the second strike came, Kibure had turned his back, his chest stinging intensely. But there was something else, too. Feelings Kibure didn't even know existed bubbled to the surface of his consciousness and poured through his veins. And not just feelings.

*Something* was happening to him.

He set his jaw as another connection was made between the leather whip and his bare back. Kibure stood more upright, teeming with alien emotion, and *something* more. Zagreb paused, confused by the change in posture.

Another sense awakened in Kibure, a sense of certainty, and a sense of—defiance. Kibure squeezed his eyes shut. *No! No more.*

He felt himself straighten completely. Then he opened his eyes, slowly, resigned to allow his emotions to take control. His mind pulled away. He did not try to stop it. His body went numb, replaced by a deeper, nearly overwhelming sensation, as if he were suddenly connected to every particle of orange soil beneath his bare feet.

An instinctual awareness overwhelmed him and his body became an unfathomable vessel, acting of its own accord. *I'm going to do something very bad.* He shook his head again. *What do I care? I have nothing to lose.* He turned to face his master, who raised the whip to deliver another blow. Kibure's body quickly closed the gap between himself and his master. Time seemed to bend as he moved, the seconds becoming hours, nothing going unnoticed. He saw the whites of Zagreb's teeth as his grin became a snarl. He saw the dirt beneath Zagreb's nails as he gripped the handle of injustice, preparing his swing. The man appeared still unconcerned about the frail slave who flowed toward him.

Kibure could hardly believe what he was doing. He narrowed his eyes and drew back his fist. Considering his small, slight stature, it was a vain attempt, but he was done caring.

His arm swung to strike the much larger, much stronger man, who looked down at him bemused. Zagreb's inevitable retribution would come later, Kibure knew. But with shocking speed, Kibure's fist moved toward the target, Zagreb's chest.

A wave of heat washed over Kibure as his fist continued forward. But as his closed fingers approached Zagreb's body, a surge of—*something*— pure energy?—shot out from that very same fist. The strike never directly contacted Zagreb's body, but the energy sent the slave master hurtling fifteen paces through the air. Zagreb's scream radiated both shock and pain as the air was forced from his lungs. Then he slammed into the hard desert floor. Displaced dust floated into the air around his body.

All was still and for a moment, Kibure thought he had killed the man. He let out a breath when Zagreb groaned and rolled to his stomach, calling to the overseers for help.

Kibure stood there somehow buried to his calves in the rock-hard sand, which had become more like overripe drogal fruit, thick, mushy, and malleable. He pulled his legs free then fell to his knees. That was where he remained until two of Zagreb's true-blood overseers approached cautiously from either side to take hold of him. Kibure spotted Zagreb a safe distance away, holding his chest, hatred oozing from his expression.

The men secured the shackles slowly, hesitantly, but Kibure did not resist; he couldn't. Whatever otherworldly power had come over him in those moments of passion had fled his body the second he realized what he had done.

## CHAPTER 2

# GROBENNAR

GROBENNAR'S EYES FLEW OPEN AS a loud boom rattled his bed-chamber, rousing him from sleep. He immediately drew on the powers of his god, Klerós, prepared to vanquish the source of the distur-bance. Then it came again: *THUMP-THUMP-THUMP.*

He sighed and relaxed, extinguishing his god's magic as he rose from the bed. Just a messenger. "Coming."

Grobennar instinctively snatched up the red-ruby pendant on his way to the door.

*"Ooooh my. A missive so early in the morning? Whatever could this be?"* came the familiar haunting voice in Grobennar's head, from the spirit trapped within the pendant, Jaween.

"I suspect we'll learn shortly." He shook out stiff limbs as he approached, rubbed his still sleepy face, then pulled open the door.

A palace soldier stood at attention, waiting respectfully for Grobennar to speak.

"Yes?"

The soldier gave a dutiful bow, face nearly touching the stone floor, and rightfully so in the presence of the High Priest. "The Lord King wishes to see you in his chambers at once, Your Grace."

Grobennar glanced out his bedroom window to confirm that it was indeed still dark outside. *A summons before dawn?*

Turning back to acknowledge the soldier, Grobennar grumbled, "Very well."

He strode across the room to his chest to retrieve a suitable robe, the one with the yellow embroidery, a subtle reminder of his position as Fatu Mazi, greatest among the priesthood. The God-king knew this, of course, but as his spiritual leader, Grobennar felt it necessary to always model perfected etiquette. The Lord ruler's endowed magical abilities were frighteningly powerful, but he lacked any feel for the formalities that came with leading the Empire. He had grown increasingly defiant in recent months, and Grobennar had resorted to simpler, indirect teachings through example.

*"With the God-king's indignant mood as of late, perhaps it would be wise to stop at the kitchen for a pastry? Humans like pastries."*

"Quiet," hissed Grobennar.

*"Fine. Fine. I'm only trying to help. You know how much I like to be helpful."*

Grobennar scurried down the narrow corridor toward the God-king's chambers, still dark but for the mystic flicker of red flames on either end. Grobennar's joints had shrugged off the stiffness that came with his thirty-seven years by the time he reached the guards outside the chambers.

The two men bowed deeply, then opened the massive oak doors to Magog's bedchamber, their expressions intense as they regained their positions at attention, prepared to dispatch unwelcome guests.

Grobennar entered and saw Magog seated at the edge of the bed, his bronze skin shaped by an imposing muscular body, shimmering with sweat, nude from the waist up. The God-king's long translucent hair hung wildly about his head, taking on the color of the flames around the room.

Grobennar bowed with minimal reverence, then continued his approach to stand before his Lord. "You requested my presence, Lord Magog?"

Magog's topaz eyes became narrow slits. They were surrounded by an increasing number of red scale-like growths mostly around his left eye, though a few had started around the right. These scales, reminders of his unusual birth and his growing power, were disconcerting and comforting at once.

He said, "I observed the crescent and the full moons crossing Lesante's gift this night."

Grobennar understood the implications of such signs. The founder of their faith, the last prophet, and her seers had foretold the Renewal, a purge of the unsaved world through force. This sign was said to mark the beginning. The crescent moon crossing its smaller counterpart at the center of the most well-known constellation was representative of the Lugienese Empire stretching their dominion to the ends of the world.

"You are certain of this?" asked Grobennar, skeptical as always. This astrological occurrence had been observed before, but the scholars had dismissed it, believing the location in the stars not centered enough within Lesante's gift to pass scrutiny.

Magog let out a breath of frustration. "Of course I am certain. The enemy has stirred. Last night I felt a presence, a *wrongness*. It was faint, but combined with these signs, the truth cannot be ignored."

Grobennar did not like the sound of this, for he had sensed nothing. "How can you be certain of what you felt? Perhaps your stomach simply did not agree with your evening meal."

Magog's frustration leaked through his voice. "I am certain! The Dark Lord's agent stirs; it is time to act!" He glared at Grobennar, daring him to disagree.

Grobennar knew better, yet the idea of rash action did not sit well with him. He was a believer. After having seen Magog's birth with his own eyes, how could he not be? And yet, these prophecies had been twisted over the years to fit situations that later proved imprudent. Grobennar remained straight-backed, knowing the importance of posture in projecting the credibility of his advice, something Magog had been less inclined to accept as of late.

"You are right to be prepared with the knowledge of the prophecies. You are, after all, the prophesied redeemer. Yet do these very same prophecies not speak of caution? Do they not speak of the importance of our preparations? I do not doubt your sincerity, of course, but perha—"

The words died in his throat as he felt the tingling sensation of magic, Magog's magic.

*He wouldn't dare, I'm his—*

A wave of power struck Grobennar like a line of fists and he careened into the stone wall across the room. The impact knocked his wind out.

Magog's booming voice followed—"I am done waiting! I am the God-king!"—penetrating deep into Grobennar's throbbing head.

Grobennar coughed and sucked in a deep breath of air. He crawled to his knees, angry at being attacked by the boy he had raised and trained from infancy. He began to rise to his feet.

"How dare you! I am your—"

Another blast of energy split the air. Grobennar used his own powers to deflect the blow, but the sheer volume of energy was too great and he was still thrown back into the wall again. He landed with a thud, then groaned.

"You are my servant!" Magog's voice became a growl. "I am not yours to command. You have forgotten your place."

Never before had Magog lashed out like this. His powers were as of yet still manifesting, still growing, but already he commanded strength unknown to any mortal man. Magog could easily kill him if he wished, and Grobennar now feared that in his anger, he just might. He forgot the physical pain of the attack on his body, and the great blow to his ego.

"I—I am sorry, My Lord."

The voice in Grobennar's mind interrupted his already strained thoughts. *"You're not alone with the God-king. I sense the life-essence of another; a wielder."*

Grobennar collected himself and rose, forgetting the danger posed by the unpredictably obstinate God-king. It was still Grobennar's duty to serve and protect. Perhaps the God-king was right about the coming of the Dark Lord's agent. Grobennar drew in Klerós's power. Then he spotted movement to his right. He summoned more, ready to strike—

"What are—how dare you!" Magog yelled.

Grobennar ignored the oblivious Emperor as a form materialized from the shadows cast by ceiling-high drapes in the corner of the room. Grobennar shouted, "Get down!"

Grobennar extended a hand, readying to strike. Just before he released a bolt of searing energy, the shadowy shape stepped into the light and spoke. Grobennar recognized the voice with revulsion, relaxing his magic with reluctance.

*Mazi Rajuban.* A member of the High Council and long-standing opponent of both Grobennar and his more conservative faction within the Council. "Peace, brother. I was asked by the God-king to be in attendance for today's meeting."

Jaween spoke into Grobennar's mind, *"Have I mentioned that I do not care for this man?"*

*Nor do I*, thought Grobennar wryly to himself.

His own anger reignited. *That's what Rajuban wishes.* Grobennar forced himself to relent. "Of course. The God-king is wise to seek the wisdom of a member of the High Council. Yet perhaps this is a matter for the collective wisdom of the High Council to discuss in its entirety."

The God-king bellowed, "The High Council is fickle, paralytic, and incapable of action!" Lowering his voice, he added, "You are right about assembling the Council. But it will not be to initiate discourse. You will *inform* them." He raised his voice once more. "You will inform them that the time has at long last come to begin preparations for the Purge. The enemy stirs! We too must shed our idle position."

Grobennar knew better than to disagree. He had somehow lost favor with the God-king, and Rajuban's attendance here served as an answer to the question of how.

"Yes, Lord. It shall be done."

Rajuban smiled. "You are wise to see the wisdom of the God-king's words. He has been tightly leashed for far too long. The time has come for him to realize his true destiny as avatar to Klerós, praise be his name."

*"Oh he's good. I can't help but hate him, but his politics are praiseworthy. Perhaps we might torture and kill him later?"*

Grobennar ignored Jaween, instead looking to Magog, nodding. The decision had been made. Rajuban had defeated him in this bout.

"Of course. This is well. Klerós guide the both of you."

That *snake* had maneuvered behind his back to gain the ear of the God-king. He would need to tread very carefully.

Grobennar bade the God-king farewell, refusing to acknowledge Rajuban, then stalked out of the room as quickly as possible. He considered his next course of action, though there wasn't much to consider. He had no choice but to call a full assembly as instructed.

Grobennar entered his own chambers and melted into the chair beside his bed, mentally exhausted.

*"So. This purge. That means war, right? I will be able to persuade our enemies?"*

Grobennar picked up a quill and ink from the small table to his left to begin writing out a list of preparations. "Yes, the Purge means war. I suspect you'll have plenty of chances to persuade, you might even see some killing."

*"Ooh-ooh-ooh. Yes, persuading and killing! I know your mood is a touch soured from earlier, but this really does call for celebration. A small feast, perhaps? That might lighten your mood, as well."*

Grobennar ignored Jaween.

*"Did you write that down?"*

Grobennar continued to work on his list.

*"Are you ignoring me again? You know it hurts my feelings when you ignore me."*

Grobennar reached up and removed the pendant from his neck and tossed it onto his bed a few paces away, limiting the strength of the spirit's connection to him. "I need to think," he said through clenched teeth.

He wondered if perhaps secreting the forbidden spirit from the debris all those years ago had resulted in more trouble than it was worth. He heard a sound in his head that was disturbingly not like weeping, yet he knew from his time with Jaween that this was precisely what the spirit was intending to communicate.

He sighed. "I'm not ignoring you, Jaween. You can stop the crying. I just need it quiet in order to think."

Jaween's mood elevated. *"So that sounded like real crying this time, didn't it?"*

Grobennar rolled his eyes. "Closer than ever before."

It was going to be a very long day.

## CHAPTER 3

# AYNWARD

"THERE. THAT'S THE LAST OF it," Aynward said to his servants as they finished packing up his things for the long journey.

"Make sure you put my dice somewhere I will not need to dig for hours to find. I suspect I'll have need of them the moment I hit shore. In fact, wait." His gaze went to the ceiling with the quick thought. "Put them in my satchel. Perhaps I'll be able to coerce a ship-hand to play at chances with me along the way."

Aynward's only sister rolled her eyes at the youngest of six, fifth in line to the throne of Dowe, the most prosperous, arguably most powerful, kingdom on the continent of Drogen.

"Truly? You can't go a few weeks without dicing? Do you honestly believe the voyage will be so terrible?"

"I'm to be stuck on a ship with Counselor Dolme, no friends, and likely very little ale to top it. Gods know he'll try to stifle any and all attempts at fun along the way. So yes, it will indeed be quite terrible."

This time Dagmara's fluttering eye roll was accompanied by an exasperated sigh at her younger brother. "You're far too critical of the man. Considering your . . . appetite for foolishness. It's a wonder he hasn't lashed you far more than he has. If anything, you owe him your thanks for how much he's shielded you from Father's wrath."

Aynward waved away the comment with a hand.

"No, seriously. Consider last high harvest. You and Fronklin were found, gods only know how, passed out on the south square stage, clothed like jesters, with empty bottles of apple brandy in your hands!"

Aynward acknowledged that story with a grunt, and his head hurt at the mention of apple anything.

"Well? Did Dolme make Father aware of this little mishap?" She answered his silence for him. "No. He made you repay the spirit holder from whom you'd stolen it, and scrub the stage for a week, but he didn't rat on you to Father as he probably should have. He really does mean you well, Aynward. It's just that you don't always seem to mean well for yourself. You're your own worst enemy much of the time."

With an edge to his voice, he replied, "This coming from the girl who secretly learns of the sword, a crime punishable by no less than fifty lashes if discovered. Not that Father would ever see the punishment through on his one and only little princess." He snickered.

She narrowed her eyes. "That's totally different and you know it! There's actually a practical use for that."

"Yeah. I'm sure your talents with the sword will really come in handy the next time you need to cut your way through a contingent of sworn Kingdom guards in order to escape the perils of the palace. Oh wait . . ."

Dagmara stammered then let out a cry of frustration. "You're impossible!"

Aynward laughed slightly then relented. "Listen. I'm all for it. If I wasn't, I'd not have endangered myself by indulging this *interest* of yours in the first place. In fact, if anyone were to receive your fifty lashes, it would be me for teaching you. All I'm saying is that you don't get to sit all high and mighty while you cast judgment on my choices. I've just celebrated my sixteenth name day so in accordance with Kingdom law, I've been a man for three years. You may be two years older but, according to this same law, you just took womanhood only two moons past. If anything, it should be *me* giving *you* advice on life."

Dagmara took in a deep breath and opened her mouth, then breathed out a long sigh in disappointed consideration. "For one thing, I can't even believe you'd use such a vapid argument as Kingdom custom to justify one's ability to make sound judgment. Wasn't logic supposed to be one of your strong suits? Oh yeah, that's right, you dazzle people with your snide language to make up what you lack for in validity. Nice trick, but you've not fooled me."

Aynward started a retort but she cut him off. "Secondly, I think perhaps you and Tecuix might need a little reconciliation as far as the nature of this *enjoyment* you speak." She immediately pointed to her heart and then the heavens, a ritualistic show of deference at the mention of Tecuix. She continued, "Our Creator's word is very clear about the overindulgence of fermented beverages—or *any* abuse of intoxicants, for that matter."

Her referral to the Creator in such an even tone, with such nonchalance, placed Aynward teetering between fury and laughter. She spoke as if Tecuix actually cared about the goings-on of anyone, and furthermore, as if she'd be the one to know if he did. Like speaking of an old friend. Aynward sometimes forgot how *religious* she was. Not that he wasn't religious, per se. He just wasn't quite so devout as she, or most others.

He realized she was waiting for a response. "Um—well—I'm just trying to keep all the gods happy. Tecuix gets praise enough. I'm a little more humanitarian in my respect for the gods. I feel like good ol' Kitay doesn't get enough appreciation, and Kitay and I seem to connect on a much more intimate level with a few mugs of ale between us."

"Oh yes, I'm sure the Goddess of Luck truly appreciates your drunken patronage."

*She won't even give the Goddess of Luck her due respect of name.* Dagmara was real elitist when it came to worshiping the gods. She really was intolerable sometimes. Yet his heart sank as his mind snapped back to his impending departure. No matter their differences, he'd miss his sister. Their witty squabbles most of all.

But good-byes wouldn't get any easier the longer he waited. A clean break was always best.

"Dagmara, I must be off to say my official farewells to Mother and Father."

"Tonight? So early?" She gave him a puzzled look.

"Well, with such an early morning exodus, I plan to sleep onboard the vessel this evening. I'd hate to keep the ship waiting, you know, in case I oversleep or the servants forget to wake me. You never can trust these things. Or what if some illness befalls me, and travel to the harbor becomes difficult? This way I'll already be there when I wake, floating gently down the river. Father would send someone to lash me if he ever caught wind that I delayed our departure."

Dagmara eyed him for a moment, suspicion on her face, then looked down as if she'd accepted his story. A few seconds passed, then her gaze shot back up to meet his, skin tightening around the edges of her eyes. "You! You little rat. You're going out tonight, aren't you? One last hurrah before you go. You don't care about getting to the ship on time, you just don't want to have to see Father early in the morning after a night on the rampage. Figure you can just stumble onto the ship tonight, or in the wee hours of the morning, rather, and pass out there? That it?"

His stoic card face shattered, replaced by a wide grin. "You make it sound so much worse when you put it like that, sister."

"Aynward Dowe! You had better not. Tecuix bless us all, please tell me this is a joke."

"Gods above, you speak like I'm planning to do murder. I'm just going out to have some fun with my friends on my last night in Salmune. I won't see them for at least two years. And by then we'll all have *responsibilities* and *expectations* to uphold."

She spoke almost to herself. "Dolme's right, some babes just can't learn to stay away from a hot pan without first burning themselves on the iron."

"Huh?"

"Oh, nothing. Just something Dolme said." She sighed. "I'll leave you to the rest of your good-byes."

*Why has she been talking to Dolme? Well, never mind that.*

She stepped forward and opened her arms for a hug and he did the same, taking a tight hold of his sister. It lasted only a few moments, but the sincerity of her embrace melted away his sarcastic facade, if only temporarily. They separated and stood quietly, looking out at the view from his bedroom's vast balcony, which overlooked the harbor of Lake Salmune. In the distance he spotted one of the two Lumáles quartered here in the capital city.

The flighted animal was distant, but he could still make out the long neck, wide wings, and the even longer tail of the creature that made it obvious to any studied person, that this was no bird. They were indeed regal animals of beauty.

Aynward noticed Dagmara's fixation on the Lumále and knew she was dreaming of a place closer to the line of succession. She had often spoken of her dream to ride the majestic flying creatures. However, only the coronated king and his heir were permitted to travel to the home of the nearly-extinct Lumáles, the home of the Tal-Don line. A Lumále could only be ridden with permission and training from the Tal-Don riders, an ancient family predating Grojen Dowe's Rebellion. It was part of the heir's duty to be trained in the ways of war upon a Lumále's back.

The entire arrangement placed too much trust in a distant, unrelated family for Aynward's comfort, but the Tal-Dons had proven themselves loyal time and again. As recently as eighty years ago, when the Kingdom of Kael had crossed the river to claim North Halesmer for their own, Aynward's great-grandfather rode into battle atop a Lumále, supported by Tal-Don riders to crush the attack.

Dagmara had joked about marrying a Tal-Don in hopes of eventually persuading him to let her ride just once. That had been before her engagement to the Scritlandian prince was announced. She'd never spoken of such things since. But while Dagmara's hope to ride a Lumále might have been a child's impossible dream, it was one she continued to silently covet. The unusual sighting served instead as a reminder of yet one more chasm she would never span. She turned to Aynward, blinking away the moisture in her eyes, and said, "Be careful tonight and while you're away."

"I always am." He grinned, the seriousness of the moment vanishing in an instant.

She did not return his gleeful smirk. "I'll miss you, brother."

"I'll miss you, too. Now stop getting all sappy on me."

They stepped apart and she nodded, wiping away the tear that had formed at the crease of her eye, embarrassed.

"Balance centered," he said, assuming a swordsman's stance. She mirrored his position. Their eyes met only briefly before she turned and left the room. Nothing more needed to be said.

## CHAPTER 4

# KIBURE

KIBURE WOKE TO A DULL ache throughout his entire body. He couldn't think about anything else for the first few moments, until his thoughts ventured back toward the day before: the feat of unexplainable power he had displayed. Could that have been a nightmare like the one the night before? Both were troubling in their own right, but the two combined? *Insane.* And yet, as he lifted a hand to rub his eyes, the shackles on his wrists were harsh evidence that he had not been dreaming after all.

Musco Zagreb's angry voice pierced Kibure's musings. "You idiots didn't gag him?"

A higher-pitched voice from behind him replied, "Gag? Were we supposed to?"

"Yes! He's a rippin' tazamine! Nearly killed me! You want him doing his—his *magic* on you?" He spat the word *magic* as if it was poison in his mouth.

"Oh. Guess I—uh—didn't think about that."

*He wants to gag me?*

"Well, stop standing there and do it!" shouted Zagreb. "And double-check that his wrists are locked tight. Can't be too careful with tazamines and the like."

Kibure could hardly believe the title given him. Tazamines were demons of the night that emerged from the Dark Lord's underworld to kidnap naughty children who opposed the will of the great god Klerós, or so the stories went. These children would be punished and turned into tazamines, twisted weapons of evil, forced to do the Dark Lord's bidding. *I'm no tazamine! I didn't mean—I didn't know what I was doing!*

Some of Kibure's fight returned as the man pulled a rag from a pocket, but Kibure was far too weak, especially with his wrists bound. He stammered, "I'm sorry, I didn't mean to—I swear I'm no tazam—" The rag stifled his plea as it was shoved into his mouth and a rope was tied around his head to secure it.

Zagreb instructed one of the overseers, Archben, to bring Kibure along as he stomped toward an equipment shed near the fence. "We're just gonna have to leave him caged 'til I figure what's to be done with him. I'll be leaving immediately for town. I've an acquaintance who may be able to help."

After being dragged by the chains that linked his wrists, Kibure was forced into a cage meant for some other purpose. It was tall enough for him to sit upright, but not wide enough to lie down. To his relief, he was able to fit his feet between the bars, allowing him to at least extend his legs instead of remaining indefinitely huddled.

"Don't you go anywhere near this *thing* 'til I get back," Zagreb ordered his men. "And don't you go thinkin' he needs water or food. Serves him right after what he just done. Should probably just lop his head off to be safe, only I hate throwin' away coin if there's some to be had." His voice trailed off into the growing evening gloom.

Alone and forced to remain with his shoulders up against two metal bars with a dirty rag stuffed into his mouth, Kibure yearned for his usual place on the hard floor between the wall and the older slave, Parvel. However, the physical discomforts were the least of his concerns. What had he done? Zagreb had refused to touch him and spoke as if he were some demon from a nighttime tale meant to scare children. Surely he was not, but how could he explain what he had done? What if this power *was* somehow linked to the Dark Lord? Perhaps he had been possessed. But the Dark Lord was said to be lured by evil deeds. Was this a punishment for his poor production in the drogal fields? Perhaps his thoughts of freedom had drawn the Dark Lord's attention. He wished he could talk to Gabriladen. She was the one who told stories before sleep. Surely she would know what this all meant. He certainly wished he had asked her about his dream before heading out to the fields yesterday. Everything had seemed too real, and his memory of it was still so vivid.

Then again, she would probably respond the same way Zagreb did should he ask such a question. His admission to unexplainable—and therefore sinister—dreams would have designated him a further outcast among outcasts. And his use of dark power—Kibure had never felt power like that before and still wondered how he had done it at all. Would he be capable of doing so again? Would he want to?

That night, Kibure hardly slept and his body continued to ache, as if from the inside out. This was not the ache of muscle, but a deeper ache. Not only did he battle physical pain, but also apprehension from the incomprehensibility of recent events.

The silence of the second day within the cage was finally broken by the familiar sound of a raaven's coo. To Kibure's astonishment, Rave landed next to his cage. The creature used his small hands to pass a piece of cactus through to him. At this point, Kibure would have eaten anything. He would also believe anything. *No, this isn't strange. It's just a raaven bringing a prisoner food. This is normal. Just like having magic explode out of my fist.* That last thought confirmed that this was most assuredly *not* normal. *But that doesn't mean I can't accept the gift.* He moved his mouth to thank Rave; the muffled sound was his reminder of the gag. *So much for that.* The raaven had placed a piece of paradise within sight, but out of reach. A well-intentioned, albeit painful, punishment.

Rave released his own sound of frustration. Yet, never without surprises, the nimble creature clambered up to the cage and squeezed between the bars. Once inside, Rave maneuvered behind Kibure to take hold of the rope holding Kibure's gag, and began nibbling. Within a few minutes, the rope fell uselessly to the ground. *Don't bother trying to understand this. Just be thankful.* The taste of cactus fruit filled Kibure's dry mouth and he smiled. "Thank you!" he whispered to the raaven as it took to the air.

The treat didn't stave off his discomfort for long, but it did remove the fear that he might starve to death. He frowned as he considered that he was undoubtedly slated to die by much more painful means when Zagreb returned.

Kibure started from his hazy, upright slumber as the cage shook. "Curse you to hell, boy! Wake when I tell you!" Then Zagreb's eyes went wide in fear as noticed the cut rope sitting on the cage floor.

Zagreb jerked his hand away from the bars and hunkered behind a woman of perhaps twenty summers. Kibure had never seen her before. The woman stood several paces away.

She stared at Kibure as she spoke, but her words were for Zagreb. "Calm yourself, my friend. He can do us no harm, not with me here."

The Lugienese woman was thin, though much of her shape was obscured by the unembroidered gray robe she wore. She had ear-length translucent hair and yellow eyes, the telltale marks of a true-blood. Next to Zagreb, her lighter skin tone marked the only noticeable difference, yet she still had the olive coloring of the true-blood race.

"But the gag!" blurted Zagreb. "What if he whispers some sort of demon spell?"

She chuckled. "You've heard one too many child's tales. Contrary to popular, if misinformed, belief, wielding magic has nothing to do with spoken words or hand gestures. Admittedly many Klerósi priests speak those words as a tool for concentration, but the words are not themselves used in the casting of spells. It's about having oneness with the source, which, in my case, would be Klerós. In the boy's case—well—Klerós only knows, but in any case, I suspect this boy had no idea what he was doing."

Zagreb blanched as he processed her words. "He can do magic even with chains and gag?" Zagreb took another step back.

The woman considered. "Technically speaking, yes, but I will use a castration spell to separate him from his source of magic and you will have no more to fear."

"Truly?"

"Truly."

Zagreb eyed her expectantly, but she did nothing. "Well?" he asked.

The woman raised her eyebrows and pursed her lips. "Well, I don't work for free." She held out a hand. "You pay, I do."

Zagreb glared at her as he dug into his pocket. "How much?"

The woman considered this for a time before replying, "Three gold tómans should do."

Zagreb froze, and Kibure thought he might refuse the price. Then his hand came back to life within his pocket as he retrieved a handful. "Thievery," he snarled.

"You're welcome to call an ordained member of the Kleról. Though I believe they would not simply castrate the boy. They would take him into custody and you would be buying a new slave, which if my estimates are off would run you somewhere closer to ten gold tómans?"

Zagreb counted out a mixture of copper, silver, and gold coins to reach the sum, then dropped the coins into her outstretched hand. "Let me know when the deed is done. I leave soon for the Eastern Markets and wish not to have a tazamine running around on my estate when I do."

The woman rolled her eyes. "True tazamines have been all but erased from these lands."

"Well, whatever he is, I want him dealt with. And you've been paid." He turned and stalked away, leaving Kibure alone with the priestess.

She regarded him with thoughtful eyes. "My name is Sindri. What I am about to do is going to hurt, though not so much as if you had been wielding magic for a longer time. I have seen this performed on priests, and they are almost never right afterward."

Kibure had no response. *Are these supposed to be comforting words?*

"It is best for you that your master called me. Otherwise you would be on your way to a much worse fate than this."

*Worse than Zagreb taking retribution once I'm no longer seen as a threat?*

The hair on the back of Kibure's neck rose and he felt a tingling sensation as Sindri extended her arm, palm out toward him. He waited expectantly, fearfully, for the wave of power that would cause him pain. Nothing happened.

Sindri eyed him curiously. "You must have quite the threshold for pain. Even pagan wielders new to their power, like yourself, nearly always show at least some sign of discomfort when their connection to their god is severed."

Kibure just lowered his eyes and waited for her to leave. Sindri shook her head, then apparently took his hint that he did not wish to speak and she left without another word. The castration being painless was a small victory indeed. Soon enough Zagreb would be back, and things would get considerably worse for Kibure now that his musco had no reason to fear him.

As the hours rolled on, Kibure began to hope for Zagreb to show up, if only to be done with the beating, or beatings. The anticipation was unbearable. He carried this fear all the way into the setting of the sun and the return of the moons before his mind finally gave in to sleep.

Kibure opened his eyes and took a moment to reacclimate himself to his new reality, confined to the too-small cage behind a shed on Zagreb's estate. He noticed the eerie silence, the lack of a breeze, and finally the muted colors, or, rather, the lack of them altogether. He breathed in deeply, nerves working him into a panic. Another nightmare? Yes—it must be. But why was he having it? It was unlike any nightmare he had experienced before. There was no villain, not that he had seen, anyway. Why then was he so afraid? Perhaps he shouldn't be.

Yet there was something strangely disturbing about the lack of color and sound that made him yearn for a scary monster and a quick death so he could just wake up. Everything about this experience was otherwise just too normal. He felt too lucid, and seemed to have all of his other faculties, including his sense of touch. He could feel the cold of the iron bars at his back leeching the warmth from his skin, and the stagnant, windless air in his mouth.

He looked around. Everything else appeared exactly as it had been while he was awake. The moons in the sky, the shadow cast by the equipment shed adjacent him. The drogal trees in the distant field remained inactive sentinels, mostly plucked of fruit in preparation for Zagreb's trip to the Eastern Markets.

Then something captured his attention. He stared hard in the direction he had been looking, toward Zagreb's estate. He blinked, trying to rule out what he saw: a ripple in the air. His eyes did not believe what they were seeing. The humanoid outline grew in size, distorting the background as it moved, while remaining simultaneously translucent. As the shape drew closer, he saw a slight wisp of something opaque, but he couldn't fully get a sense of what he was seeing. A spirit? He did know that this was not good. *Shouldn't have wished for a monster!*

The spirit-thing was almost upon him. It must be some sort of demon, come to steal his soul. He saw the outline of arms reaching for the cage.

"Noooo!" he cried, but the sound died in his mind, unable to manifest in this place. Even knowing the futility of doing so, Kibure pushed the cage with all his might. To his surprise, his body slid free of it. In an instant, he was upright looking down on the cage and the ripples of air that took on the form of a human. The human started to glow.

*What the—*

Kibure closed his eyes, and when he opened them again, he was back inside the cage, his back stinging, the sound of his panicked breathing loud in his ears. He was awake—really awake! He felt something else, too, the tingling he had felt when Sindri had been using—

Then he saw her, standing in front of the cage, staring at him, features obscured by shadow.

He felt her power envelop him, immobilizing his entire body.

Then she spoke. "Be calm. I'm not going to hurt you, but it does appear that my spell was not successful after all. You were just using magic. It seems I have finally found my tazamine."

## CHAPTER 5

# GROBENNAR

## [Twenty-Five Years Earlier]

GROBENNAR ENTERED THE HOT, STEAMY room with another priest
close behind. He wrinkled his nose at the acrid smell accompanying his first charge as a priest of Klerós: a whimpering woman on a bed
of sweat-soaked, twisted blankets.

Behind the woman loomed an imposing figure, Baelor. Grobennar
had been warned that his new employer would prove a difficult man
to work for; the description did not disappoint. Baelor spared a brief
glance at the newcomers, his excited expression melting into a scowl.
He turned back to the woman, squeezing water from a rag to cool her
forehead as he grumbled, "I asked for more priests, not more children.
The Kleról must be getting desperate."

Grobennar, a youth of just twelve summers, considered explaining
the sleepless nights he had invested into his studies to earn the cov-
eted red robes, then thought better of it. He'd been justifying himself
ever since his hard-fought acceptance into the Kleról six years earlier,
the youngest ever to receive such a distinction. If his experience during
those years had taught him anything, it was that actions spoke louder
than words.

*"Blessed cosmos, your new employer seems to have eaten something that does not agree with him."*

Jaween seemed also to speak louder than words, insofar as Grobennar could always hear whatever the spirit had to say, regardless of whether or not he wished to hear it.

*"Should have brought that swine-sausage soup I suggested. Bribery goes a long way, especially in the priesthood."*

Grobennar ignored the comments, as he often did.

Instead he adjusted his tight-fitting conical hat, something to which he'd still not grown accustomed, and lowered his head in deference. "How might we serve, Fatu Kazi?" He used the priest's formal title, hoping to play to the man's evident insecurities.

Fatu Kazi Baelor gave him a long, appraising look. Grobennar half thought the man would refuse him altogether. Then he scoffed, "I suspect that *you* will *serve* with great difficulty."

*"Hmmmm, perhaps more than a digestive issue. He seems to have taken a particular dislike to you. I can't imagine why. I could speak with him about this . . ."*

Grobennar coughed "No" into a hand.

Baelor continued, "What's your name, young tadi?"

"Tadi Grobennar, my dear Fatu Kazi."

The grizzled man glanced over to the other tadi-level priest who had arrived with Grobennar.

"And you?"

"Tadi Penden, my dear Fatu Kazi."

Penden was five years Grobennar's senior, but apparently still a babe by priestly standards.

Baelor frowned. Then his mouth shifted into a sly grin. "I have a message for you to carry back to the Kleról. Tell them that while I appreciate the—"

A gravelly scream punctured the stagnant air.

*"Oh dear, she seems ever so upset. I told you we should have picked up a treat along the way. Pregnant women adore treats."*

Grobennar had determined years ago that Jaween had a particularly annoying obsession with the human consumption of food and potions, both of which eluded his understanding. He winced as the woman continued to moan but forced himself to remain steady, outwardly unmoved by his terror. *Be strong. You've worked too hard to ruin it all with a weak stomach.*

The enormity of the woman's need redirected Baelor's attention. Taking hold of her head, he mouthed a prayer. She shouted again but this one seemed distant. Her expression softened with an exhale while her breathing remained ragged.

Baelor looked up accusingly, as if he'd just given a command and awaited its completion. "Well? You want to serve? We need fever leaves, at least four. Go, and quickly!"

Grobennar and Penden bowed then sprang into action.

*"I still think you should let me persuade him. He would become so much more enjoyable to spend time with. At least consider picking up that soup while we're out."*

## CHAPTER 6

# AYNWARD

TENDRILS OF WOOD AND PIPE smoke snaked through the heavy evening air of the Flowering Bell Tavern. Only the breath of its patrons and the occasional swing of the entrance door disturbed the uncomfortably stale air.

Despite the boys' best efforts to dress down, Aynward and his three well-to-do comrades did a poor job of looking like anything but what they were. The Flowering Bell was packed with the typical crowd of local merchants, sailors, and a scattering of other less-desirable folk drawn to the fairly priced, poorly lit tavern. Common clothes just didn't look all that common without the years of wear and grime earned by those who wore them not as disguises but as a matter of course. Nevertheless the tight-knit group of friends preferred the whispers and stares of strangers to the meddling, judgmental eyes of their households, teachers, and peers. Often those looks brought with them a good welting, something none of them wished to endure if they could avoid it, especially tonight, their last evening together as youths.

A waitress tipped a pitcher of ale into the upside-down Kingdom bells sitting in front of the young men. After draining his third draft, Aynward began to relax. He was in no way happy to be leaving his home in Salmune, so he'd vowed to at least enjoy his last night to the fullest. The King had eyed him coldly when Aynward explained his plan to board the ship tonight, but as was often the case, no words passed his father's lips to dissuade. He was the kind of man to wait until a crime was committed before passing judgment. His mother meekly followed along with whatever his father said or did.

Running his hand through his neatly cropped auburn hair, he recalled how Dagmara had done the same to him earlier that day, teasing about the sun's added touches of gold that he so abhorred. While his brothers wore their hair long, neatly brushed, and flowing with shiny highlights, he preferred his much shorter. It was easier to maintain, but, more important, it set him apart from the rest of the royals. At five foot eight he was considered of average height, with a fair amount of adolescent muscle put on through sword practice and other athletic endeavors encouraged by the allotted physical segments of his schooling. But there was nothing striking about his features. His face was well proportioned; the only notable aspect was the dimples in his cheeks, which were sharpening with maturity.

Beside the fifteen-year-old Prince of Dowe sat his long-standing friend, Fronklin. Across the stool-height table sat Stannerd and Troyston. Aynward reflected on the exaggerated enthusiasm in the greeting he had received from his friends nearly an hour earlier. He knew the others were already deep into the ale, with an exception for Stannerd who, for religious reasons, abstained entirely.

Aynward understood, sort of, but nevertheless harried his friend. "Come on, drink up, the morrow's ever coming, best enjoy today while we can." He took a swig then raised the bell again. "To the youth we'll always recall but never relive." Bells raised, they all clanged mugs and drained what remained, while Stannerd sipped his water, unperturbed.

Aynward ordered another round. He wanted to drown his discontent at being forced to leave everyone he'd ever known to go to school halfway around the world. So long as he could find his way to the departing ship before morning, he would forgo restraint tonight.

"I still can't believe my father is sending me to school in the Isles. I could easily learn all I need to know right here in Salmune, or south in Scritler, or even Rynder. There's no sense in it."

"He's afraid you'll mess up and embarrass the crown if you stay here," said Troyston.

"Surely he'll do the same in the Isles!" argued Stannerd.

Troyston smiled. "Quite right, but this way fewer Kingdom royals will hear of it." He chuckled at his own wit, while the others forced out awkward breaths in the attempt. The statement was too close to the truth. Aynward's father had never said as much, but Aynward suspected that it might have something to do with this. And while there was merit to this sentiment considering Aynward's youthful exploits, the lack of trust from his own father still stung.

Aynward smiled. "Might be you're right about that, Troy. I'd best be sure and live up to his expectations. I'd hate to disappoint." He upended his mug again, and the fermented beverage flowed down his open throat until nothing remained. Slamming down the bell, he raised a hand and yelled, "Another round over here. Another round for the King's untrusted son and his brazen accomplices!"

The others sat there with incredulous expressions, perhaps at the reckless mention of his identity while in this part of town, or perhaps at his acceptance of Troyston's playful quip, or perhaps both.

Stannerd leaned in and spoke softly with an intensity that indicated he was very serious. "Aynward, it is unwise to reveal yourself in such a place. There are many here who might simply see silver where others see a title. And Troyston was *clearly* joking about your father's reason for sending you away." He hit Troyston in the arm to force confirmation.

"Oh, yeah, right. Merely a jest. The King probably just wants you to receive the"—he searched his mind for the right way to phrase the lie—"experiential knowledge"—his lie gathered momentum—"and firsthand cultural immersion he can't afford to risk for your older brothers who are more likely to inherit the throne, what with the added inherent dangers of vast cities of trade like Brinkwell."

Stannerd hit Troyston even harder. "Shadowed menace, Troyston! Do you think at all before you speak? Don't listen to him, Aynward. He's a little too far in the ale to speak sense." Stannerd continued to glare at Troyston.

Aynward was not put off by the statement. "No-no-no. Troy may have had a few bells of ale, but he speaks truth. Father has all but worded such feelings. He's made no secret of the fact he's glad for my distance from the line of succession, and he wishes me away from the city. Remember last year? He banned me from leaving the palace altogether after that not-so-harmless crash at the docks when we commandeered the fishing sloop for the day."

Fronk choked on his beverage as he attempted to drink and laugh at the same time.

Troyston responded, "Yeah, we hardly saw you for nearly a full cycle of the moons."

Aynward allowed himself to laugh. "Convincing him to curtail that ban was no easy task. No, I think it true that he wants me out of sight until I can mature into something more *refined*. That's why he chose Brinkwell. He's slated me to stay with my Aunt Melanie. I met her five years ago, a spinster with nothing better to do than boss me around and keep me out of trouble. She supposedly fell in love with some low-born man unsuitable for her station and ran away to the Isles. He died a few years later, but she never returned. She's a bit of a black sheep of the family in her own right."

Troyston said, "Maybe you can use that to your advantage. Perhaps you'll have an ally instead of a second watch guard."

Aynward paused to consider. "Huh. That's not bad. You might just be right." Then he sighed heavily. "But Dolme will be more than enough bad company to make life miserable. Ugh, it's going to be absolutely dreadful." He combated the thought with a forced smile and added, "Nevertheless, I vow to come back all the worse, just for spite. Wouldn't that be some irony? Come back shoddier than I left?"

Stannerd shook his head.

"What?" asked Aynward, raising the pitch of his voice in innocence.

"Oh, nothing. Just thinking of how valuable to the crown you could be should you focus all your energy on something besides resisting the expectations set out by your father and station. I mean, Tecuix above knows you were the most gifted student at academy in spite of the fact that you gave the least effort of anyone there. You could likely maneuver yourself to run the entire kingdom someday in all but name should you put even half a mind to it."

Troyston smiled and nodded, throwing up his bell to clink the cup of water Stannerd held. "I'll drink to that. I can still hardly put together an intelligible sentence in Scritlandian, and you go and win the logic tournament, speaking it like you'd been born to it. Few in attendance, excepting the judges, could even understand your logic proofs, and even some of them were struggling. And all that just to piss off Counselor Marben for nearly failing you last year."

"What was it you did to earn her ire, anyway?" asked Fronk. "I don't remember."

"Nothing, really. I challenged the long-held interpretation of *Gabriel and the Lance of Fire*. Wasn't a big deal. I put forth the possibility that Gabriel didn't actually betray his family, as is commonly taught. I merely pointed out that the Scritlandian word *devlem* can, in some cases, mean desire out of duty, instead of desire out of lust; and that there were other, perhaps better, words that could have been used to communicate the currently held interpretation. That simple shift in the interpretation of the word changes the motive for several of the other events leading up to the murder of his half brother, Lemphere. And, of course, it shifts other roles in the story a bit, turning Gabriel's death into a tragedy, not an old children's tale with a happy ending. I simply named him the unsung hero. Counselor Marben, however, was in no mood for academic discourse that day . . ."

Stannerd shook his head. "See what I mean? A ripping genius, though I must admit that I, too, prefer the story with its happy ending. Nevertheless here you sit, drinking your genius away. Your father must know how gifted you are. I'd wager he's praying you'll go there, find yourself, and come back willing to finally utilize your wits, thereby becoming one of the most valuable men of the court instead of continuing to embarrass the court with your shenanigans."

This struck a nerve with Aynward and he felt his face flush and his body tense with anger. The feeling vanished an instant later as he considered the source. Aynward had always appreciated Stannerd's open honesty, and he couldn't fault him for being who he was, even if he was a little too altruistic. *Time to cool the moment with a jest.*

"Please remind me again: why are we friends?"

Stannerd mumbled, "Because every once in a while a word of sense from me keeps you from doing something so stupid that even your father won't be able to get you out of it."

The young men erupted in laughter, including Stannerd, who bowed his head in mock reverence. "Service to Tecuix, and all of his people."

Fronklin spoke once the raucous laughter died down. "Aynward, you're forgetting the other perks of Brinkwell's locale."

Troyston met Fronk's eyes and grinned. They said it together. "The ladies!"

Fronklin went on, "My family once dined with a count from one of those Isles cities. Can't think of which one, but gods, was his daughter beautiful. Couldn't keep myself from staring. My face was nearly bloody with all the times my mother smacked me afterward for forgetting my manners."

"Eh, the Kingdom has plenty enough girls right here," Aynward retorted.

Troyston dismissed Aynward's protest with a drunken wave. "Bah, enough complaints! You want me to remember you only for your whining?"

Aynward's eyes narrowed, then Fronk clapped Aynward on the shoulder. "Plus, I've heard the Isles have the most exciting cities in all Doréa, and Brinkwell is the biggest, so you won't be able to help but have a good time." He lifted his recently refilled bell. "To good times: both past and future." Three of the four young men took long pulls of the brew before setting their bells down again.

Aynward felt better, though the cynic in him knew it was nothing more than the drink. He leaned back in his seat and stared at Fronk. Besides Dagmara, Fronk was his best friend and had been since childhood. Aynward studied him, as if for the first time, noticing how muscular he was compared to the other fifteen-year-olds. In the darkness of the tavern, Fronk could easily pass for a full-grown man, which would benefit him in his upcoming training with the School of War and Knighthood.

Although Fronk had the light-amber hair of central Drogen descent, like most within the Kingdom of Dowe, he did not have the typical gray eyes. Instead they were yellow like those of the far south or the grassy north, which made him unique among nobles, since most were of strictly central lineage. His mixed heritage made no difference to Aynward or most others who met him, though. Fronk's incessant smile made sure of that. It was unceasingly wide, prim, and gleaming, accentuated by a comical gap between his two front teeth. When Fronk smiled, it was difficult not to follow suit. This trait lifted spirits but also influenced far more scandalous behavior from Aynward than would have otherwise occurred over the years.

Aynward drained yet another bell after a few more minutes of small talk and friendly banter between the four. Then Stannerd suggested that they try their hands at a game of Kelkin.

Troyston looked to the others through half-open eyes. "Refresh me on the rules again?" His words came out slurred.

His friends rolled their eyes in his direction, but they knew that when Troyston was drunk, the only way to appease him was to humor him.

As the soberest of the lot, Stannerd took the lead. "Troyston, you know the rules." He balled his hand into a slightly opened fist as if holding a small ball. "You take the ball of pine, the lob, and throw it underhand from the ten-foot marker on the floor, and land it in the opening of the angled board."

Aynward butted in with an intentional cough. "I think you mistake the goal with the reality. To be clear, Troyston *tries* to throw the lob into the opening. Rarely, if ever, does it go in."

Stannerd shot Aynward an icy glare, but Aynward held his ground, raising his hands in supplication. "What? It's an important if not accurate clarification. Wouldn't want to serve up false hope."

Troyston shook his head and moaned. "Ugh, I do truly hate that game." He ran his hands through his disorderly hair. "The hole in the board is little bigger than the ball. It's near impossible to make the shots."

"And that's precisely why they cover the lob with a layer of wool, Troyston," stated Fronk, his voice filled with mischief. "To keep your rotten aim from injuring innocent bystanders."

"I hate Kelkin," Troyston repeated, slamming his bell on the table, spraying everyone with ale. He continued to grumble to himself but stood up to follow.

They began with a game on the far lane. The Flowering Bell, following the example of other local taverns and inns, set up their Kelkin in an area toward the back, away from the dining tables. Dividers were placed between baskets to keep lobs separated, which served to minimize discrepancies and, therefore, violence between adjacent players.

Aynward, who was generally a fair player, led the first game. He had a smooth stroke, letting the lob roll gently off his fingers with a nice arc as it traveled toward the hole with favorable angle for entry. Fronklin was inconsistent but had his good nights, generally those when he drank much less than he had on this evening. Stannerd and Troyston were both very competitive, but neither had much skill for a game that required a gentle touch and soft hands.

Aynward scored four of the five baskets needed to win before any of the others had scored three. However, Fronklin insisted he was just getting warmed up. To prove his point, he sank three consecutive shots for the win. "Ohhhhh, and there it is, victory to Fronklin Lungeweg, great knight of Dowe, warrior of the Kingdom, victor of the stars."

Aynward laughed. "All right, very good. I think it a string of luck, but a nice win, nonetheless."

Troyston laughed. "Yeah, lucky for sure. Jus—just had one good turn. My next drink says you don't win again—rest of the night."

Fronklin turned to face Troyston. "All right, how's this? For every game I lose, I buy all you guys a drink, but for every game I win, you guys buy me two, each. What do you say to that?"

"You've got yourself a deal!" Troyston roared. Fronklin winked at Aynward.

"I'm in," echoed Aynward jovially, impressed with Fronklin's conniving.

Aynward won the next two games. The following game, however, was Fronklin's, which meant six more bells, an ego through the roof, and a lot of noise and excitement from all.

Stannerd pointed to the tavern's owner across the room speaking to a broad, muscular member of his staff while staring in their direction. From past experience, Aynward and the rest knew it would not be long before they were asked—or forcibly enticed—to leave. Stannerd said, "Guys, we'd best be going, we're getting pretty loud, and the keeper just pointed us out to Alton, the strong-hand."

Fronklin brayed between words, each syllable dragging with inebriation. "Oh, you're just scared I'll win another game."

That was enough to get Aynward and Troyston back into it, howling with laughter.

"Tecuix be with us," Stannerd whispered, pleading with the ruling god of the Chrologal faith.

Before his friends could rebuff his attempt to skip out on the remainder of the evening's festivities, a barrel-chested man in his late forties interrupted them. "Couldn't help but overhear you gentlemen beside us been playing for stakes." His voice boomed over the tavern's evening rumble. He swept an arm out to indicate three other men. "Me and my mates here were just wondering if any of you had the stones to raise those stakes a bit and play for some coin." He inclined his head toward a dark-haired stick of a man leaning against the wall and chuckled. "Sterly here says you're just a purebred rich lot, not worth your weight in silver without hiding behind your surnames."

Something about the man unnerved Aynward, but he was too compromised to give his instincts much consideration. The thin man took an agile step from the wall, and in a surprisingly deep, gravelly voice, sneered to his comrade, "I'd bet forty talents to the man that the four of us wipe this lot clean. All four of us done before any one of them sinks their five." His voice gathered an edge as he continued. "But I'd bet twice that on these little boys not taking the challenge up in the first place. Even spoiled little pups like them know us sailors own the Kelkin courts. They're not fool enough to squander this week's allowance all in one evening."

Stannerd opened his mouth, likely to deflect the obvious baiting, but Aynward loved a good gamble and lunged forward, nearly striking the side of the thin man's head with his finger. "Make it fifty."

Sterly turned to face Aynward, grinning broadly. "I'll be twirled. Fearless *and* stupid. Fifty it is."

Aynward staggered a bit then steadied himself to meet Sterly's smile with a scowl. "We're gonna teach you and your rope-pulling friends exactly why our names carry with them all the gold and silver they're worth and more. And while I hate to add your hard-earned money to my already healthy coffers, I fear you'd not learn the lesson should I not."

Fronklin, who seemed to have sobered, chimed in. "I'd like to see the silver before we start. They probably don't have fifty between the four of them."

"Whatever they have on them is fine with me," Aynward replied, "so long as they leave with empty pockets—and soured egos."

Sterly spun his belt and produced a healthy-looking purse from beneath his loose-fitting shirt. He jingled the purse loudly. "Just finished a big job. Looking forward to making good on another investment."

The barrel-chested man who had initiated the conversation spoke up. "'Nuff talk. Us four each scores five before any one of you has yours. Fifty talents each. Even turns. Challengers begin."

With that, he and his comrades lined up to begin their first turn. Each made their first shot. And second. And third. Aynward realized that these men were indeed frequenters of the game and prodigious players at that. He also realized that Stannerd and Troyston were becoming dangerously frustrated with the results of this high-stakes competition. Troyston had already bloodied his knuckles on the wall, and Stannerd's volume control was long gone.

He felt a slight tingle in his chest as he reveled in the absurdity of his predicament. The tingle came not from fear, but from an exhilaration he got when up against difficult odds. He preferred the more calculated games with cards, dice, or both, where his intellect would allow him to better select bets in his favor, but this would do. He was a fair Kelkin player, and though his nerves tickled at him, he had a drunken confidence that he could beat the odds. Well, maybe not beat them, but he'd have a fair shake at victory nonetheless.

Aynward missed his first, smiled as he waited for his next, then made the following four. Stannerd had three, and the two others were still at one. Aynward's opportunity to save the evening came when one of Sterly's men missed again, still stuck at four. The young prince guessed that he would not miss again. Confirming his thoughts, the man's next shot floated into the basket to give him his five points. Aynward chided himself for missing his first—so close, but a loss. But why wasn't the man celebrating his victory?

*Idiot. Even turns*, recalled Aynward. His four opponents stood waiting for him to shoot. If he made his next shot, he and his friends would win the bet. Troyston smacked Aynward on the back for good luck, an unnecessarily heavy hand wrought by too much drink, but in his current state Aynward hardly cared.

Aynward looked away from the smug expressions of his opponents, took a deep breath, and released his grip on the lob. It sailed almost perfectly through the air toward its target, only to strike the bottom lip of the angled opening. His heart sank. Remarkably, the lob deflected up instead of down, struck the side of the hole, and bounced in for the point.

Both Fronklin and Troyston's celebratory actions ventured beyond obnoxious. They danced and hollered, and even Stannerd put forward a few modest boasts, something about the gods' favor.

Fronklin puffed up his chest and shouted a mere handsbreadth from the closest opponent's face, sloppily formed words accompanied by a spray of saliva. "Guess this means you'll be headed back to the seas a little lighter than you thought now, doesn't it? Pay up! Bahaha!" He turned and did a little jig.

Initially Aynward also shouted in excitement at his surprise victory; the thrill of tempting fate and winning warmed his whole body. But the reactions of the four challengers finally gave him pause while the rest of his friends continued their unruly taunts. The smallest of the four men smiled in a way that made Aynward's stomach turn. The triumphant sensation of the high-stakes victory seemed to race from the sky to sink deep into the bellows of the underworld.

The mangy, hollow-eyed man named Sterly pointed to Aynward's feet. "Foot fault."

His words didn't initially register with the prince, and certainly not with his friends, but Sterly said it again, with an eerie, collected calm in his voice. "Foot fault."

Aynward stared at him blankly, confused.

The man who'd initiated the challenge spoke up. "You stepped over the line, *boy*. Foot fault. That counts for a miss and loss of turn."

Sterly nodded. "You lose."

The other man held out a hand and yelled. "And now *you* pay!"

Fronklin stepped forward. "To hell with that. He made the shot!"

Sterly smiled flatly, his cavernous voice still somehow rough and smooth at the same time. "Your comrade cheated to make the shot. His foot was over the line. Nobles been cheating their way to riches for generations, but not here. No, in here we play by the people's rules. You pay up and leave or things gonna get real ugly, real fast."

Fronklin pushed the smaller man. "We're not paying a thing."

Sterly hardly moved, but his smile disappeared, replaced by a wicked snarl.

Stannerd grabbed hold of Fronklin and pulled him back while Aynward stepped forward to take his place, separating them. He may have been deep in the drink, but he was no fool; he and his friends would not win, not in here. They'd been played for dupes and there was nothing for it but to pay up and leave before things got out of hand. "My apologies. He's tipped his mug a few too many times this evening."

His mind raced. These ruffians didn't appear to be in the mood for persuasion. Aynward and his friends needed to pay quickly and be gone before they made good on their threat. Just as he reached into his purse, movement in the corner of his eye caused him to stop and hold his breath.

A lob zipped past his head and slammed into the skull of the big man. He staggered back, wobbled as if he might collapse, then shook it off, and instead lunged forward.

Aynward stood frozen in place as he watched events unravel in slow motion. The big man threw a haymaker at Troyston. Aynward tried to grab his other arm to prevent him from connecting another blow, but Sterly punched Aynward in his slack stomach. Aynward doubled over in pain, before a glancing uppercut sent him upright. Sterly grabbed him around the chest and pinned his arms to his side in a bear hug. Face to face, the man snickered, his liquor-laced breath assaulting Aynward's nostrils. "Oh, we're gonna get our money, good sir. You can be sure of that."

Serly's other two companions engaged Fronklin and Stannerd, who had leaped to Troyston's defense. Mustering his courage, Aynward stretched his head back and snapped it forward into his captor's face. He'd seen the move demonstrated before but had always wondered about its value. Now he knew: Serly's hold released instantly as he reached for his bleeding, broken nose. This catapulted Aynward into the action.

He landed a powerful blow to the temple of the barrel-chested man, who was still pummeling Troyston. The man stumbled then dropped limp but was replaced immediately by another. Aynward's eyes grew wide as he became conscious of his surroundings. All the Flowering Bell's patrons had snatched up the excuse for a brawl.

Aynward found that the hand-to-hand combat he'd learned on the school field held little value in the cramped tavern battleground. He couldn't identify who was on whose side as men of various shapes and sizes swung fists and slammed into one another from every direction.

He caught glimpses of his friends as they struggled to hold their ground, but he was too engaged in his own skirmishes to come to their aid. He could barely tell where the exit was or from whom he was trying to defend himself. He pulled back to punch a burly, bearded man who was running toward him, but someone caught his arm from behind so the bearded man crashed into his stomach. As he stumbled backward, gasping, whoever had grabbed his arm from behind fell on top of him. After a few shots to the face, he regained his ability to breathe. Thrusting his hips while pulling the man's elbow, he rolled on top of his attacker. Several well-placed jabs and a right elbow to the side of the head rendered the man unconscious.

Aynward remained crouched for a moment, trying to locate his friends, but he couldn't pick out anyone in the chaos. He was about to give up when he spied Fronklin being held from behind along the wall while a tall, curly-haired man used his stomach, chest, and face as a punching bag. Without thinking, Aynward took off through the maze of falling, flying men.

Slamming into the curly-haired man from the side, he took both of them to the ground. Aynward sprang to his feet and kicked him a few times before turning to free Fronklin from the stocky, toothless man who still held him.

Just as he reached the man, his vision went black, and must and mold filled his nostrils. Nimble fingers cinched a cloth bag tightly around his neck and two sets of strong arms dragged his flailing body away.

As the sounds of battle became a muddled, distant buzz, the realization that he was no longer in the Flowering Bell struck Aynward harder than any blow he'd received during the brawl.

He stopped struggling for a moment to encourage the men to loosen their grip. When they maintained their strong hold, a second realization hit him: these men knew what they were doing. Changing tactics, he began screaming. He wasn't hopeful it would work, especially given the seedy locale, but maybe someone would intervene if they knew who he was. He bellowed about five words before a hand cupped his mouth, turning his screams to a muffled whimper.

To his surprise the hand fell away. Aynward filled his lungs with air to shout once more as the bag was lifted. Had they decided to let him go? He couldn't take the risk. As he parted his lips to yell for help, a damp rag was jammed into his mouth, stifling both his words and his hopes for rescue. Once more the cloth bag was yanked down and cinched tight around his neck. Nearly suffocating, he swallowed hard, his tongue trying to free the cloth. A bittersweet liquid trickled down his throat, making him lightheaded. His eyes closed, his body shut down, and his thoughts became tangled. No longer afraid, he let himself enter the abyss, his body floating as his thoughts descended into darkness . . .

## CHAPTER 7

# KIBURE

SPEARS OF LIGHT STRUCK KIBURE'S eyes. The morning sun seemed to have decided to rise more swiftly than normal. Kibure squinted as two silhouettes approached, obscured by the painful light. It was the priestess for hire, Sindri, and Musco Zagreb.

According to Sindri, Kibure had somehow used magic last night even after she enacted a castration spell that should have prevented this from being possible. What disturbed Kibure most was Sindri calling him a tazamine before leaving him alone to worry himself to sleep. He found it odd that she had sounded excited.

Kibure had no more time to collect his thoughts. As Zagreb drew close, Kibure could tell his master was feeling particularly prickly this day.

Zagreb stopped walking, still a dozen paces away. "What do you mean the spell failed?"

"I mean to say, he is immune to the spell. It is statistically rare, but it seems you were correct after all in calling the boy a tazamine."

Zagreb shifted his position so Sindri was between himself and Kibure. "Tazamine? Blast my soul! So what now? You kill him with your powers, right?"

Sindri glanced back in Kibure's direction. "Hmm—that is *an* option. A safe option to be certain. It's just—well, he could fetch ten times the price of an ordinary slave if you were to find the right buyer in the Eastern Markets of Sire Trinkanen. I've heard tales of tazamines inviting far more. The Isles, for all their profane tendencies, do have a few things in abundance—coin of course, but also an affinity for the unusual, as I'm sure you've seen in your travels to the markets."

Kibure could see Zagreb weighing his options, as if concern for his own safety waged war with his appetite for wealth. Kibure was terrified at the prospect of being sold to foreigners as some sort of amusement, especially knowing so little about this magic he was supposedly able to wield. Yet the alternative was . . . death?

He held his breath as Zagreb decided his fate.

"How would I transport him there safely? If he's still using magic, couldn't he just decide he wishes to be free and do so? I can't risk my entire cargo, let alone my life!"

Sindri replied, "A fair point. You would need someone with the skills of magic to keep his powers at bay, though he is an infant with the use of such. He is not able to call upon them on demand as of yet. But yes, you would need someone with abilities; no ordained Klerósi priest would ignore the standing order to deliver all tazamines directly to the God-king."

Zagreb glared at Kibure, then back at Sindri. He spoke through gritted teeth. "How convenient that I have someone like you in this moment of need. You will accompany me on this journey?" Kibure wasn't sure if this was a question or a statement.

Sindri looked up, surprised. "Oh. I hadn't considered that." Then she placed a finger to her chin, considering with some measure of skepticism. "I suppose I could. I certainly couldn't work for free, however. But for, say—forty percent of his sale price I *could* take a bit of time away from my business here."

"Forty percent?" huffed Zagreb. "That's criminal!"

Sindri placed hands on her hips. "I would be risking much by performing magic as we pass through the Empire's greatest cities, magic that undermines the laws of the Kleról itself. If a seeker sensed that an unordained priestess was performing magic—" She shook her head. "Forty percent is generous."

Zagreb turned his head and spat. "All you priestly folk are the same, ordained or not. Draining the lifeblood of the working folk. Forty percent," he grumbled.

"Very well. I will speak with the boy for a bit, then pack my things."

Zagreb glared at Kibure. "Yes, well, I will leave you to your business. Just make sure you leave the little monster in his cage."

"Have no fear. He will remain where he is, unable to do you or anyone else harm."

Zagreb nodded uncertainly then stalked away.

Sindri directed her attention toward Kibure. "So, Kibure, it seems we will be spending some time together over the course of the next few weeks."

Kibure did not respond. He didn't know what to say. She had, in essence, extended his life. But he had no idea to what end. Or what it would mean to be sold to a new master interested in purchasing a tazamine. The idea that this derogatory term now applied to him was still too frightening a concept to embrace. In the span of just a few days, he had become a monster of children's tales, or at least that's how it felt. It didn't fit. He was no wielder. At least, he didn't feel like he was one.

She spoke again. "Kibure, I know you don't trust me. And I don't blame you for that. You don't know me, and in truth, I don't know or trust you, either. But right now I am the closest thing you have to a friend in this world; and without my help, you will *not* survive this journey."

Kibure glared at her, but said nothing.

"I will leave you alone for now if you like, but you're going to have to eventually speak with me, one way or another."

Kibure nearly opened his mouth to respond, but caught himself. He couldn't identify just what stopped him. He simply could not muster the words. He hung his head, and Sindri sighed.

"I really don't want to have to coerce—"

She pivoted as Zagreb returned, two slaves shadowing close behind, Yeshire and Holden. Kibure knew them, though not well. They did not typically work in the fields and they slept somewhere in the estate, away from the others. They walked over to the cage and didn't strain at all as they hoisted the steel enclosure into the air, waiting for further instruction.

"Follow me," Zagreb told them.

Zagreb led Sindri and the slaves around the equipment shed to the other side of the estate, revealing a bustling caravan of wagons. The overseer, Archben, stood shouting orders to slaves who loaded crated goods upon carts, most of it drogal fruit.

Zagreb snarled to Sindri, "We leave on the morn. I can't stomach the thought of having a tazamine within the walls of my estate any longer than necessary." Glaring at Kibure, Zagreb said, "And don't even *think* about so much as *dreaming* a dream in which you even *think* about trying something like you did before. You do and I'll go straight to the Kleról! They'll dispose of you before you even know what you planned to do."

Kibure stared back up at Zagreb, trying to make sense of the jumble, finally settling on a simpler translation: *Don't use magic.*

Without another word, Zagreb departed.

Sindri glanced over at Kibure, winked, then said in a low voice, "I haven't been to the Eastern Markets of Sire Trinkanen since just after my expulsion from the Kleról. This should be a very *interesting* journey."

Kibure did not like the way the former priestess looked at him. Not one bit.

The following morning, Kibure's cage lay squeezed between two crates upon a large wagon, rolling along a dry gravel road spanning the Angolian southwest. He peered between the bars of his cage into the distant desert horizon. Having never been beyond the walls of Zagreb's estate, much of what he saw in the distance was completely alien. But he found its beauty remarkable.

All Kibure knew of their destination, the Eastern Markets, was that Zagreb traveled there each year with the season's surplus drogal and the occasional slave, who often did not return. The journey usually lasted several weeks, during which time his overseers took full advantage of their newfound autonomy to beat slaves to within a few strokes of death. But in spite of the woes of slavery, Kibure reflected upon the fact that he knew nothing else, and dreaded the possibility of befalling an even worse fate elsewhere.

The caravan moved south out of the village of Jarquin before turning east toward the River Lesante, named for the original prophetess. To Kibure's surprise, his sense of foreboding was balanced by his curiosity about what he might see along the way to the unknown, enigmatic Sire Trinkanen. He stared out in wonder.

Kibure's reprieve was extinguished by the sight of a crow flying high overhead. His heart fluttered at the black shape, hoping it might be Rave. It wasn't. He realized then that he had not had the opportunity to say good-bye to the little guy. Kibure had often spoken to the animal as it perched atop his shoulder while he worked. Rave had never responded of course, but Kibure had thought it nice to feel like *someone* was listening. He wondered if Rave would miss him too.

The day wore on and his fear of the unknown weighed upon him like the crates of drogal that strained the donkeys as they pulled the wagons down the road. Sleep did not come easy, but it did finally come.

Kibure jerked awake. The sun was just cresting the horizon as the sudden movement of his wagon roused him. He had found relative comfort by positioning himself in the corner of the cage with his head supported by three bars instead of two. He had banged his head on the bars to either side a few times as he drifted off before mastering the technique.

He closed his eyes again but a cough nearby caused them to snap back open. Then he saw her. Sindri. The sorceress was perched upon a crate looking down on him in his cage. "Ah, you're awake." She wore a pensive expression though there was a sparkle in her eyes. "I've been watching you sleep for quite some time."

The thought made Kibure's skin crawl, but he decided it best to keep that opinion to himself.

"You're a remarkable specimen." She brought a hand to her chin in thought. "While awake, you put out no magical aura whatsoever, at least so far as I can detect." She shook her head. "When you sleep, though, there is an occasional trace of *something*. It's much different than the, for lack of a better word, scent, of a Klerósi priest at work, or even of the rare tazamines we keep alive for the training of seekers within the Kleról before turning them over to the God-king. But even Klerósi priests put out no aura unless actually drawing or wielding the power of Klerós. You, on the other hand, you actually release small puffs every so often, thin wisps small enough that only a seeker in extremely close proximity would likely ever notice."

When Kibure did not respond, she continued, "I have done considerable research on the subject in recent years; however, foreign literature is difficult to come by, especially translated. From what I've gathered, few races have large numbers of innate magic wielders, what we would classify as tazamines, while nearly all people have the capacity to learn to one degree or another. You, however, seem a different stock altogether."

Kibure recalled several years earlier when Klerósi priests visited the farm to do testing on all of the slaves, though the purpose was not revealed until afterward. But they had left. He had passed scrutiny. They had found no tazamines. The encounter had simply ended, followed by a short sermon reminding the slaves that if they remained loyal to their masters and to Klerós, they would be allowed to enter the lower levels of eternal paradise as free men, forgiven for the sins of their ancestors.

Sindri brought Kibure back to the present. "While you were sleeping, I asked your musco a few things about your past. I will ask you the same questions in an effort to establish a baseline of trust between us."

Kibure didn't look up.

Undiscouraged, Sindri continued, "So, your name is Kibure. Is this your birth name?"

Kibure remained silent. If she knew all the answers, why bother asking? He had no idea what she meant by *baseline of trust*.

She sighed. "You're not much for talking, are you? I normally prefer folks like that, but in this case, it will go much better for you if you simply answer my questions."

He stared at her blankly.

She sighed heavily, then extended a hand in his direction. A tingling sensation ran up Kibure's body and he grew warm. The woman's eyes became vast cauldrons, boiling at their center. The heat increased and sweat beaded on Kibure's forehead far too quickly to be natural.

He panicked. "I'll talk! I'll talk! Please—please make it stop!"

The heat vanished in an instant.

"Excellent!"

Sindri folded her hands in her lap. "Kibure, I want us to be comfortable with each other, to be able to trust one other. I don't want to have to do things like that to you. But you must understand that this is my life's work and I *will* do as I must."

His reluctance was outweighed by his fear. He finally mumbled, "Yes, my birth name is Kibure."

He was certain that he should *not* trust her.

The woman stared at him through placid eyes. "So, you were not born to the Lugienese slave or free race. Have you any knowledge of your birth mother?"

"No."

His true lineage was indeed unknown. His skin tone was not like that of anyone he had ever seen. His extended days in the sun had done nothing to darken his skin, which remained sickly pale. He lacked the blond hair of most Lugienese slaves, or the translucent locks of Lugienese free-folk. His hair was, instead, inky black, darker than the longest Angolian night. But, according to others, his most distinct features were his eyes. His irises were said to be white like clouds, the only pigment being a bluish outer ring. Even fellow slaves rarely maintained eye contact and most avoided him altogether.

Kibure had asked about his mother several times but had been told little more than that she had shown up at the estate gates one morning, alone, speaking an unknown language, near to giving birth. Zagreb had eagerly taken her and her child as slaves. According to the woman who had served as his wet nurse, his mother had perished shortly after giving birth.

Sindri said, "Well, I can't say I've ever seen anyone of your complexion before, but let's move on to the reason I was called in from the town to visit. I would like for you to tell me about the magical attack on your master, Zagreb. I would like to hear *your* side of what transpired."

"I—I don't want to talk about *that*."

The woman leaned in closer, touching the bars of the cage. "Listen, I may be able to help you understand what you did, what you *can* do. But I have to be able to make sense of it myself."

*What I can do? What does that even mean?* Hadn't she said she could keep him from wielding his powers? Either way, he did not want to discuss this foul thing, this magic. He remained silent.

"Kibure. I mean you no harm, *but* I have been searching for someone like you for years. I intend on capitalizing on this opportunity." Her expression darkened and she gripped the bars to his cage so hard the olive skin of her knuckles turned white. "Do not mistake my kindness for weakness. I intend on discovering what I must from you, one way or another."

The tingling sensation returned and so did Kibure's shaky voice. "Where should I begin?"

Sindri became just as relaxed as she had been the moment she arrived, her intensity vanishing as quickly as the heat she'd fused into Kibure moments earlier. "Tell me of this little friend of yours. When did he first start visiting?"

Kibure froze. How could he explain Rave? He understood the raaven about as well as he understood the power he had used the other day. What could he say? What *should* he say? Would she try to capture and hurt Rave?

"I—don't know anything about—"

Another wave of heat enveloped him, this time stronger. It hurt.

"Okay!" Words flowed from him then, and he hated himself for it. He recounted the events of his magical *episode*, as he now considered it, as well as his limited interactions with Rave. He regained enough of his composure toward the end to leave out his dreams. Something about her was just plain *wrong*. And yet here he was, telling her everything she wished to know.

"That's all I know, honestly."

Sindri nodded, apparently satisfied, but made no move to leave. "When you attacked that man with magic, did you call upon a god, Klerós or other?"

Kibure stared up silently once again, defiance returning in full. Sindri repeated the question. This time her tone indicated that there would be a consequence should he ignore her.

Kibure hesitated. The incident had been the catalyst for his new uncertain fate. Observing the intensity of her stare finally convinced him to say, "No."

Sindri stared in anticipation of an explanation that did not come. Her eyes narrowed. "Well, what happened then?" Her scowl sharpened when his response was not forthcoming. Then he felt the heat of her magic.

"I—I already explained this! I don't know how it happened! He just kept beating me and I felt this power come upon me. But I don't know where it came from or how I used it. The whole thing just happened too quickly." *And slowly,* thought Kibure as he recalled the warped sense of time and the out-of-body-experience of the event.

Sindri smiled and nodded, her eyebrow arching upward. "It is as I suspected, then." She waited for Kibure to inquire about this, but when he didn't, she went on as if he had.

"The Kleról holds to the belief that all users of magic outside of the Kleról channel power granted by the Dark Lord of the underworld, just as we pray to Klerós to help us channel *his* power. And while this may be true in some cases, I believe there to be a more innocent culprit, at least in exceptional cases like yours."

Her expression grew distant, and dark. "I was forced from the Kleról over this very disagreement and have been searching for a tazamine like yourself ever since."

Kibure knew near to nothing about the Kleról, but had assumed she had simply been rejected for not being powerful enough or something. Even still, her explanation seemed lacking.

He said, "You left the Kleról over a disagreement about tazamines? Seems like—" He stopped himself short of insulting her. That would be very unwise.

She narrowed her eyes and said, "Seems like—a stupid reason to give up a lofty position within the most powerful organization within the Lugienese Empire?"

Kibure did not dare agree. He opened his mouth, then closed it. Silence was the safest answer. He had said too much already.

She nodded. "The truth is much more complicated than this, but *that* is a story for another time."

Kibure was just glad to have escaped his own stupidity. He finally replied, "So—you're going to—what—study me throughout the journey to the markets?"

Sindri sighed. "Well, sort of. Zagreb would surely turn us both over to the Kleról should I succeed in coaxing you to use your magic again. He does not understand it, and therefore, like most, is frightened by it. When I was in Sire Trinkanen, I heard tales of powerful wizards from the lands to the east. They can't all be followers of the darkness, can they?"

When Kibure did not answer immediately, Sindri answered herself. "No, I think not. So I will be observing you along the way. For now you can rest assured that you are safe, so long as you are truthful with me, and don't draw the attention of the Kleról by using your magic as we pass through cities with seekers along the way."

Sindri waited again for his response but he gave none. "I almost traveled east of the Empire to the Isles in search of answers," she said, "just after fleeing the Kleról. But I couldn't summon the courage at the time. What would I do for a living? It's bad enough having to work in the shadows to avoid the Kleról here. But would Klerós's magic be so strong beyond our borders? I just don't know. I should like to think it is so. He's Lord of the world, or will be someday, so it shouldn't matter where I am." Her expression hardened, as did her next words. "I intend to go this time." Again, more speaking to herself than Kibure, she said, "Of course, I still have to work out how I'm going to procure you once in the markets. Zagreb's going to want the coin I promised from your sale."

She slid over to the edge of the crate she sat upon, feet dangling over the slowly moving ground below. "Well, I've plenty of time to reason out a plan now, don't I?" She nodded her head as if convinced, then hopped off the wagon, landing gracefully with a smooth, reptilian gait that went so well with her sardonic smile.

Kibure sat in his cage, mouth agape. The thought of becoming the property of this woman terrified him perhaps more than being sold to a stranger. Yet what choice did he have? What would happen if he told Zagreb? Zagreb would surely call *real* Klerósi priests. They would *both* be killed.

Kibure needed to focus his attention elsewhere before he lost his mind. He peered out of his cage at the waking desert landscape, determined to cherish the small gift, ignoring the circumstances in which he experienced it. He doubted he would ever see such wondrous sights again.

The landscape slowly shifted from desolate Angolian desert to grassland. Zagreb had always decorated his vast living quarters with a variety of plant life in order to distinguish it from the others within the estate, but Kibure had never seen such a tableau of beauty as this. Diverse shades of green grass converged with the orange soil at the boundaries of the two landscapes in a display that made Kibure shudder with frustration that he had been deprived of such splendor. While the grass and other shrubs within the estate walls were well tended, these grasses were completely free of man's touch; he envied them.

Kibure heard Zagreb's voice up ahead. "There it is. The River Lesante! Keep to the banks and head north." Then he saw the massive, dark, slithering object. Rivers were made of water, so he had heard, but the thought had been difficult to comprehend. It rained only a few times per year and only ever for a few hours. Slaves hardly saw more than a small skin of water at any given time. The river snaked along the flat landscape in long, gently curving arcs as far as his eyes could see. The sight of that much water took Kibure's breath away.

As they reached the shore, Kibure was finally able to appreciate the sheer volume of water. The river was vast beyond his wildest dreams. He wondered how there could be so much water in one place with so little elsewhere. Why would Klerós bless one place with such abundance while cursing the rest? It was as fickle as the blessings and curses of the races.

## CHAPTER 8

# GROBENNAR

## [Twenty-Five Years Earlier]

GROBENNAR RETURNED WITH THE REQUESTED fever leaves within the hour. He now stood by, his face placid as the woman's eyes rolled back into her head. The child's father watched helplessly as Grobennar and the others labored to keep the woman nourished. The pain appeared to cut right through the numbing effects of the Lion's Blood.

Grobennar observed the father who wore no bracelet of marriage, along with the woman's lack of facial jewelry, which spoke of poverty, and yet they were both clearly of unbroken Lugienese ancestry. No true-blooded Lugienese would be denied birthing assistance by the Kleról. The woman's characteristic light-brown skin glistened, while her yellow, rounded eyes seemed to glow as beams of light sneaked in through a small window in the wall. She cried out once more, her voice growing hoarse.

"Should we call for a tazabi?" Grobennar asked, referring to the priests who specialized solely in the healing arts. Penden shot Grobennar a frightened glance at the suggestion.

Fatu Kazi Baelor looked up and scowled. "Listen here, boy, I've been delivering babes since before your own godforsaken parents suckled at—"

Baelor's face blanched as he glanced back to the woman. "The Child is crowning!" He laid hands upon her, lending strength from the Creator. The woman flexed her abdomen once more, using every part of her essence for another desperate push.

"It's here!" the young Penden shouted.

"What the—"

The woman's lover shrank back in horror at the abomination that emerged from her womb. "Klerós! How cursed am I! What dark sin escapes my recall that I might be punished so?"

Eyes glistening with tears, the father turned his head to retch.

Penden looked to Grobennar with a troubled expression.

The woman stretched a hand toward the father. "I'm sorry. So sorry . . ." The whisper stole her final breath, but the man was too caught up in despair to acknowledge her words.

Fatu Kazi Baelor stepped back, swirling his fingers up, a plea for protection against the frightful scene before him.

*"Ooooh what a treat! I can feel Klerós's touch on this child. How marvelous!"*

Grobennar's revulsion was replaced with awe as he recalled every word of the prophecy foretelling such an unusual birth. It was his unequaled knack for scholarship, after all, that had earned him entry into the Kleról. The priests couldn't deny a young boy's gifts after listening to him recite the seven major scrolls of Klerós from memory, a feat unmatched by even the most devout of working priests.

Grobennar's heart raced as he realized he was witnessing an event of unthinkably grand proportions.

Baelor was the first to move, lifting the red, egg-shaped object the size of a newborn baby. It sparkled in the light. He set the precious object down beside the corpse of the woman and opened his robes. Grobennar assumed he would pull out a small blanket. Instead the Fatu Kazi drew a dagger.

Fatu Kazi Baelor muttered, "Darkness descends, the Dark One approaches. Darkness descends, the Dark One approaches." Grobennar looked on in horror as the man raised the weapon with both hands, his crazed eyes narrowed with determination.

*"Perhaps you should let me speak with him now. He seems like he may need a bit of persua—"*

"Please do!" Grobennar ripped off his pendant and hurled it at Baelor. Jaween's ordinarily jovial tone became a gleeful hiss as he attacked the man's mind. The pendant struck Baelor in the chest, then clinked to the ground. That was more than close enough.

Baelor's eyes went wide, darting around the room in search of the source of the voice that assailed his mind. *"Release the blade. Your hand is too weak. Indeed, your fingers are already slipping. Give in to the weakness. Release the blade . . ."*

Grobennar could see Baelor's closed fingers trembling around the raised knife, his will struggling against the persuasive powers of the spirit, Jaween.

Baelor's expression hardened.

*"Oh. Oh! Impressive! His will is so strong! This will be more fun than I have had in ages!"*

Without time to consider the consequences, Grobennar's hand slid to the belt beneath his robes, unsheathing his own dagger.

Baelor let out a bestial scream, then raised the knife as high as it would reach. *Klerós forgive me.* Grobennar drew back and threw just as Baelor's weapon raced to split the red chrysalis.

The High Priest's knife glanced harmlessly off the hardening object, the strength of his blow weakened by the shock of Grobennar's well-aimed dagger, which slammed deep into his chest. The Fatu Kazi braced himself against the edge of the table, his face a mix of pain and confusion as he stared into the eyes of his executioner. Grobennar recovered from his own shock, then strode toward the man.

*"Ohhhh, nice shot, Grobes! Though I wish you had given me more time. I nearly had him."*

"What have you done?" shouted a lesser tadi priest in the room named Taldic.

Grobennar's eyes didn't leave the chrysalis. "Rescued the Savior of our people."

By the time Grobennar reached the table, Baelor's protests came out as mere gurgles, followed by rivulets of blood, which flowed from his gaping mouth. Grobennar thought he made out the word, "heretic." *No*, he decided, "hero."

Ignoring the dying man's pleading hands as they grasped at his robe, Grobennar yanked his dagger free, then shoved the soon-to-be corpse to the floor, where it collapsed like a hunk of meat for sale at the market.

Taldic sprinted for the exit.

*"Such a shame. I think you frightened that one. Should I convince him to stay? He really should stay to help."*

"No," muttered Grobennar. "Let him go."

Jori and Penden remained, staring on in disbelief. Meanwhile, the would-be father had shrunk down, shaking in the corner of the room.

Grobennar retrieved the pendant containing Jaween, then scooped up his prize. Within minutes of exposure to air, the outer tissues had hardened into a smooth, rounded shell. And as he suspected, its temperature was dropping rapidly. Wrapping the chrysalis in the folds of his robes, he raced out of the room. "Jori! Make sure the father comes with us. He must come!"

Upon his arrival at the nearby Klerósi temple, Grobennar handed the precious object to Penden. "Place this against your skin and keep it warm! Prophecy unfolds."

Penden's expression was one of confoundment, but he did as commanded. That would have to be enough.

Grobennar ran inside and headed toward the great furnace, which was generally reserved for ritual sacrifice. Three Klerósi priests lounged about, lazily seated, unmoving.

Grobennar shouted at them, "Light the fire!"

They didn't. The men looked more annoyed than anything. Grobennar recited the well-known lines of prophecy:

*The shell of Klerós's faith shall wrap the Savior in red.*
*The Child of Hope will emerge,*
*and with him the life of our Deliverer.*

They looked at him like he had just told them how many moons were in the sky. One of the priests, a slender man, replied, "Every man in the Empire knows the lines, what of it?" Arching an eyebrow and smiling, he asked, "Has another woman died delivering a child?" His voice was so condescending that Grobennar wondered how it even reached his ears from such a height.

The priest stood and took several steps toward Grobennar, then stopped and brought a cupped hand to his mouth as if to whisper. "A secret for you, since you appear to be new to your robes. Over one hundred true-bloods die giving birth to sons every year in this city alone. The hour is late and I don't feel much like burning a child's wrist this evening. Bring him in tomorrow and I'll have the holy flame burning bright to test the skin of your little *savior*." The intractable priest turned his back and started for his seat beside the others.

"*Shall we?*" came the voice in Grobennar's head.

Desperation flooded him. The ritual *must* be completed, and he couldn't do it alone. He let out a deep breath. *I'm going to hang for this.* "Try to be subtle," he whispered to Jaween.

"*Of course! Subtlety is one of my best assets!*"

Grobennar rolled his eyes. He was close enough to the other priest that he didn't need to remove the pendant.

"*Servant of Klerós.*" The man stiffened. "*The Savior has been born. Do as the young priest asks or burn in the eternal flames of damnation.*"

"So much for being subtle," mumbled Grobennar.

The priest looked around in confusion, then turned to regard Grobennar and frowned as Jaween continued his tirade.

"*To ignore this holy task is to bring about great suffering. Turn away from this sin and do as the priest asks.*" Taking a step closer the man growled, "So you learned the spell for mind speech and think we're all just going to follow your orders? I said, come back tomorrow!"

Grobennar felt the man gathering Klerós's power. Grobennar was a mere novice in the art of battle magic; he would be no match for a well-trained priest, even with the extra summoning power of Jaween.

"*Time for plan B,*" said Jaween to Grobennar's mind.

"And just what is that?"

"*Kill him, of course.*"

The man suddenly braced himself as if someone had just handed him a very heavy object. He covered his ears with both hands and let out a shout of pain.

Grobennar understood. He now had a very narrow window of opportunity within which to act. Jaween would be screaming at a painfully high frequency inside the priest's mind, temporarily immobilizing him. The others in the room rose to their feet, believing Grobennar responsible for the attack.

"*Time to kill.*"

Drawing his dagger once more, Grobennar took a quick step and lunged forward, but instead of driving his blade into the man's exposed abdomen, he sidestepped and slid behind.

"Plan C," he said to Jaween.

He drew a gash across the man's back, just deep enough to wound, then kicked the stunned priest behind the knee. The man buckled. Grobennar was no blade master, but all priests trained in the martial arts and this man was also contending with Jaween's mental assault. Before the priest could recover and defend, Grobennar had the steel pressed against his neck, feigning an eagerness to deliver the killing blow.

"Move and I slit your throat," he said in an even voice he didn't inwardly feel.

Then, looking at the other stunned priests, he spoke louder, more firmly. "I *will* kill him unless you do *exactly* as I command."

They didn't move, unsure whether or not he was sincere in his boast. They had all filled themselves with Klerós's power, he could feel each of them now, ready to strike. He drew a thin line of blood and the trembling priest whimpered.

"I've killed once tonight to see this prophecy fulfilled. I will *not* hesitate to do so again."

## CHAPTER 9

# AYNWARD

AYNWARD'S VISION BEGAN TO CLEAR, then faded again as dizziness overtook him. He thought this had occurred several times before but couldn't be certain as he descended back into the void.

He opened his eyes later and, for the first time in what felt like days, he was able to keep them open. Before he could concern himself too much with his environment, he realized something far more distressing: he could hardly move his neck—or the rest of his body, for that matter. He was on his back and wrapped so tightly he could barely breathe. He strained and struggled as claustrophobia set in. After a few moments, the initial shock of his confinement wore off, and he was able to calm himself enough to focus on his surroundings.

He had to strain his eyes to make out anything in the gloom. More challenging than the darkness was the dim crease of light that seeped beneath what must have been a door. It swayed and danced before his eyes. Slowly it dawned on him that it was not just the light swaying but his body, as well. Though he lay perfectly still, he felt as if he was slowly spinning.

A few minutes later, he thought he heard footsteps by the door, but this was also an untrustworthy perception. The sounds reverberated within his mind, yet he was certain that only the first sounds were truly real, unaffected by whatever had given him over to these hallucinations.

Even so, he was able to discern at least the basic dimensions of the room, about three paces long and similarly wide. The walls, ceiling, and floor were made of wood. Thanks be to Tecuix. Despite the strange sensory deceptions—by-products, he assumed, of whatever chemical his kidnappers had used to subdue him—his mind had been left unmolested.

As he scanned the cell, he spotted a strange arrangement of ropes stretching across the room. He wondered at their purpose, but he was more curious about why he was there in the first place. Memories of the previous evening flooded his mind. Then again, he couldn't truly be certain how much time had passed. Perhaps he had been unconscious for longer than a day.

Fear snapped at him as he remembered the fight and the sudden end to his consciousness as he was seized and drugged. He feared the worst for his friends, who could easily be dead now if things had continued to escalate after he was taken. Foreboding gripped him. Even if the least of his fears had come to fruition and his friends had escaped unharmed, there was always the possibility of getting dragged into Salmune's crooked courtrooms on bogus charges, although the judges often gave nobles an easier time of it.

Aynward's thoughts were interrupted intermittently by what he assumed were footsteps passing by the cell door again. He also heard faint voices. He couldn't make out what was being said, the sounds twisting into deep, hollow echoes.

He called out, thinking perhaps that the others had been taken captive, too. He shouted at the top of his lungs, calling out to Fronklin, Stannerd, and Troyston, or anyone else within earshot. No one answered, and the sound of his own voice was so loud and warped to his ears that he could hardly endure it.

Time dragged on for what may have been days. His frustration continued a cycle of climactic unbearability followed by sorrow as he tried to understand why he was being confined within this strange place. The effects of whatever was plaguing his senses wore off slowly then relapsed after his first meal, which was some sort of smooth, barely edible porridge, followed by a dark beverage, both of which were poured down his throat. The person who brought him this meal remained concealed beneath a dark hood and a scarf that covered all but the eyes.

Within a few minutes of ingesting the food, he experienced sensory-altering distortions. He wished his thoughts were also affected, because perhaps a bent mind would better cope with what he endured. Instead of a vague rotational sensation, Aynward felt as if a hole had just appeared in the floor and he was sinking through. He closed his eyes, but that merely compounded the sensation of accelerating motion and he was compelled to open them again.

There was just enough light to alter the shapes before his eyes, making the falling and spinning all the more vivid. It was accompanied by loud warbled noises that seemed to never end. Time was impossible to measure. Eventually the stimulation became too much for his mind to process, and he fell back into a comparably lucid sleep. His dreams were not much better than his waking visions, but at least they were set within the reality of what life should look, feel, and sound like.

When Aynward woke again, the effects were dulled enough for him to tolerate. He attempted to refuse the food and drink. Going hungry was preferable to what the drug would inevitably induce. But his captor was prepared to do battle. Aynward's nose was plugged, causing him to eventually open his mouth to breathe, and there was a metal tool awaiting him. The tool forced his mouth open. In the end, his resistance earned him cut lips and a bit of the drugged food smeared in his eye when he shook his head. Then the hell began all over again.

As time passed, he began to cherish those few hours within which he was not bombarded with the exaggerated, sometimes completely unreal sensations that gripped so much of his mind it had to shut itself down. During this time of seemingly gentle weightlessness his thoughts were able to stabilize and return to that which he knew.

His thoughts ventured home to his family, namely his sister Dagmara, who, to his dismay, had warned him of going out. Warned him that his rowdy behavior would eventually catch up to him. Aynward was the youngest of six children, and his parents were always busy with public affairs and court business. His next-closest brother in age had left the courts four years prior for a school in Scritler, where he would train and likely become Dowe's next general, despite there having not been a noteworthy uprising or military campaign in eighty years. Aynward missed his sister dearly now, and his heart ached at the continual reminder that his friends might no longer be alive . . .

After an undeterminable period, Aynward awoke to a sensation he thought he might never feel again: normality. At least his sight had steadied, and sounds didn't shift with echoes in his mind. There was still a motion about his body, but it felt more natural, almost real. He wondered how long it would take before his captors realized they had forgotten to drug him. The moment the thought crossed his mind, the door opened, and light shot in—real light that didn't bend or pulsate.

As Aynward's eyes adjusted to the brightness, he saw what he assumed was the same person who had been feeding him throughout his captivity. He was dressed in colors that were dark but not quite black. He was also tall with broad shoulders and an air detectable by the slight arch of the back that forced the chest forward. There was something almost familiar about his posture and size, but nothing Aynward could piece together in the few seconds he had before the person knelt before him, his face still hooded and wrapped, the shadows concealing his eyes.

As always, the person did not speak, but this time he set a canteen and a bowl on the floor a few paces away from Aynward. In it was something different from the porridge they had served him thus far.

Aynward's initial excitement disappeared as he considered the notion that different didn't necessitate better.

The man rolled Aynward's cocooned body over, forcing his face against the floor, and then pulled him to his feet by grabbing the wraps between his shoulder blades. A wave of nausea swam through Aynward's body then retreated a few seconds later. The man held him upright with one arm as he pulled out a knife from his dark tunic.

When Aynward saw the knife, he flinched and struggled, nearly falling to the floor. His captor gave him a swift elbow to the chest with his knife arm while struggling to hold him up with the other. Once Aynward was stable again, the man cut the cloth that had bound him like an ancient Scritlandian mummy of the stories. This allowed Aynward to separate his feet and stand on his own, though his legs were much weaker than he expected.

Once Aynward could stand, the man unwrapped the rest of the cloth that restrained his torso. Another individual—dressed in the same fashion, his face concealed—entered. However, this person was much smaller and far less intimidating. In his hands were a mop and bucket.

Aynward stood completely naked but for the rope that restrained his wrists. Neither of his captors spoke a word as they forced him to lie down on his stomach and spread his legs. A heavy boot kept him in place as a sudden rush of steaming water flowed over his backside, stinging his skin. This was followed by the mop. After a minute of scrubbing and a rinse with the now tepid water, the first man hoisted Aynward to his feet while the other used the mop to soak up the remaining moisture from the floor.

Throughout this process, no one spoke. Aynward had given up trying to speak to his captors after the first few times they had fed him. His protests had been met with silence. Yet perhaps this time would be different. His question came in a weak voice, since he hadn't spoken at all for a few days. His throat felt dry, the sound coarse. "Why are you doing this? Why am I here?"

No answer.

"Why have I been locked up here? What crime have I committed to deserve this?"

Neither of his captors responded. Aynward tried again, his voice halfway between a shout and a crackled whimper, this time directing his question at the larger one, whose covered face was at last turned toward him.

"What have I done to deserve this? Why have I been locked up in this hell? And what of my friends? Please tell me, do they at least live?" When no answer came, he took another step forward and shouted. "Answer me! Why don't you answer me?"

The ominous person drew a sword from beneath his robe and held it at Aynward's throat. It remained pointed at Aynward's neck while his other hand shot up in front of Aynward's face, his index finger moving back and forth, indicating that Aynward discontinue his approach.

Aynward was desperate to know what was going on, but he knew enough to stand down. He calmed his breathing, stepped back toward the wall, and crouched, his hands still behind his back, his jaw resting on his knees.

As the two turned to leave, the larger man stopped in the doorway and turned back. Aynward looked up. For the first time, he got a good look at the man's eyes, illuminated by the outside light. They were piercing and powerful, but there was also something familiar about them. The look lasted but a second, and then the man and his companion were gone again. However, they left behind the empty water bucket, along with the food bowl and the canteen, and Aynward was no longer confined to complete stillness.

It didn't take him long to figure out how to get his hands out from behind him in order to eat and drink what they had left for him. He simply lay down on his back, brought his legs up to his chest, and wiggled his wrists up in front. He felt far more comfortable and comparably free as he gulped down the chunky slop that, he noted later to himself, tasted like a harvest feast compared to the mind-altering porridge they had force-fed him until now.

The room was almost completely dark again, but once his eyes adjusted, he was able to locate the canteen. As he drank the first few sips, he felt every drop coat his mouth, travel down his throat, and into his empty stomach. His innards had never felt so dry or empty as to delight in something so trivial as a few drops of water. He scarfed down the remainder of the canteen and the bowl, but it felt as if his body consumed the food and water instantly, like desert sands sucking up what moisture they could before the sun summoned the rest back into the sky. It was not enough. However, in a few hours he felt relatively restored, although his muscles were stiff and atrophied from disuse.

## CHAPTER 10

# KIBURE

KIBURE'S HEAD BANGED AGAINST THE cage as a pair of strong deck-hands hoisted it into the air. Zagreb directed the two slaves toward a vast floating structure. They maneuvered tirelessly around a bustle of activity to keep up with Musco Zagreb as he debated where to stow his human cargo amid the chaos. The immensity of goods stacked upon the flat deck astonished Kibure as he considered the fact it was all floating atop an unknowable volume of water.

"That'll do fine right there." Zagreb pointed to a place alongside several crates filled with harvested drogal from the estate.

"Anything else, musco?" asked the shorter of the two true-blood workers.

"Yes, my personal belongings are to be stowed in the second room, starboard side." Zagreb tossed the young man a coin. "Be careful with it."

The deckhand smiled wide at the payment. "Of course."

The taller of the two workers looked at Zagreb expectantly. The tightfisted musco didn't flinch. "Well? Stop standing there and get back to work!"

The smile faded from the deckhand who realized the single coin was to be split between them. They disappeared around a tall pile of crates, both shaking their heads in frustration.

With the two workers no longer obstructing his view of the river, Kibure finally had a chance to survey what little he could see of it. The sun was not yet visible, but the eastern sky stirred with a hazy orange glow. He could see little else through the thick, frothy fog. This white mist hovered over the river, illuminated by the last of the night's moons. Arms of glowing moisture seemed to reach out to the world beyond the water like hungry hands in search of food, only to be absorbed by the thirsty reeds lining the shore.

Kibure had never seen fog like this. A plume of white mist swirled toward him, a hand reaching out to steal away with his soul. Kibure cowered in his cage, covering his face in futile defense against the unknown entity. He had heard tales of unbound ancestral spirits angrily awaiting passage into the afterlife. Had the river become a conduit for their vengeance against the world of the living? Kibure shook helplessly as the cold essence washed over him. He breathed a sigh of relief minutes later when nothing happened; the trembling in his hands remained long after.

More than an hour later, the activity onboard the barge had slowed only slightly. Zagreb reappeared from behind a stack of cargo alongside Sindri and a man dressed in a bright-colored jacket and trousers. Around them, men continued to work busily to secure the cargo with ropes.

Zagreb was saying, "Excellent news, Captain. We'll be off before the sun breaks the fog."

"Indeed," replied the captain, who smiled and nodded toward Kibure. "I must tell you, Musco Zagreb. I don't see many slaves chained *and* caged, especially not ones so"—he frowned—"sickly in appearance. He's not diseased, is he?" The captain's eyes narrowed. "Or is he one of those—tazamines?" Taking a step back, he growled, "I won't abide that onboard my ship. No sir. I won't test Klerós's patience upon the seas."

Zagreb forced an awkward chuckle. "No, no. Of course not. I just—well—you can't be too careful these days. He might not look like much, but he's quite the escapist and a runner. Too much work trying to chase him around is all."

A cluster of newcomers approached, stopping a few paces away. To Kibure's astonishment, three of them were tied together, more slaves. They were led by the taller of the two deckhands from earlier, who found a nearby post. "Here?"

A portly man squeezed between the slaves and the balcony to get a better look. He pointed to a tall post a few paces from Kibure's cage, one of the few remaining spaces available. "Right there will do nicely."

Zagreb greeted the newcomer while the slaves were being secured. "Ah, Bragden, it's been too long, brother." The two embraced in a firm hug and slapped each other's backs hard before separating. The similarity between them was striking; they could have been twins.

Stepping back, Zagreb said, "I was beginning to worry that you'd hold up our departure. Captain Tigue here says we're almost ready to lift anchor."

"Bah, you always were the early riser. Should have gone into town last evening. You'd understand my reason for keeping in bed a bit longer. *She* had a good-lookin' friend, *if you catch my meaning.*" He wiggled his eyebrows. "A man forgets the lively nature of these river towns after too long away. The women here are unrivaled!"

Zagreb shook his head. "I see you're still keeping to your marriage vows." Zagreb's retort appeared lost on his brother.

Noticing Kibure, Bragden remarked, "Whoa! I like the cage! This little mongrel must be quite the handful. Wish I'd thought to bring something like that. I'd sleep easier knowing mine were so secure!" Turning to Captain Tigue he continued, "You got any more cages?"

Captain Tigue seemed to awaken from a standing slumber at the mention of his name. "I—uh—no." Shaking his head, he mumbled, "You muscos are a paranoid lot. Perhaps I *should* invest in a few cages, could charge for rent." He excused himself by saying, "Best see to a few things before setting off, lest I make a liar of myself." He exchanged a quick handshake with the muscos before escaping from sight.

Zagreb nervously whispered to Sindri, who had been examining one of the nearby crates. "The boy *is* fully secured, right?"

Sindri smiled and answered loud enough for all to hear, "He is; though, if you're still frightened, I'd suggest maintaining a healthy distance. He's liable to"—she paused, then suddenly brought her hands up—"rattle the bars!"

Zagreb jumped.

Sindri grinned. "I've seen him do it. It's *terrifying*." She winked and let out a slight chuckle.

Zagreb glared at her. He opened his mouth, but Bragden interrupted their exchange.

"Here, here." Bragden's eyes swept appreciatively over Sindri. "Now I see why you remained with the cargo last evening." Licking his lips, he continued, "How much would it cost for an evening with *her*?"

Kibure cringed in revulsion. He had witnessed this sort of sexual bravado imposed on female slaves.

Sindri radiated menace. Zagreb put up a hand to silence his brother. "As aggravating as the lady Sindri's tongue may be, I would suggest restraint while in her presence. She is, after all, my hired *priestess*."

Bragden narrowed his eyes. "Priestess? She doesn't wear the red silks. What is she, a slag?"

Zagreb winced, eyeing Sindri for signs of reprisal at the use of the slanderous word, true as it might be.

Sindri surprised them with a broad smile, but Kibure noticed her hands slowly forming fists. "Why yes—Bragden, is it? I am indeed that which many call a slag. Not to worry, I am not ashamed. Having already forsaken the Kleról, I'm free to forgo restraint, especially with regards to those who offer offense. These last few years have been . . ."

The hair on Kibure's neck rose. *She's using magic!*

". . . quite liberating."

The man squeaked and took a step back. "Wh-wh—" He bowed deeply, then in a shaky voice pleaded, "My most sincere apologies. It's just, well, you—you seemed too young and—uh—beautiful for the robes. I—uh—I should be going to settle into my room now. Again—deepest regrets." He bowed once more and departed.

Zagreb lowered his voice. "Apologies indeed, Sindri. My brother has never been one for manners."

"I suspect he'll guard his tongue for the duration of our journey. If not, I'll be certain to further *educate* him in proper etiquette." She nodded in parting.

Zagreb shuddered then followed, leaving Kibure alone with his own thoughts, and the three newly arrived slaves.

Kibure spared a few glances in their direction, trying to remain inconspicuous. The two slave-born brothers had the typical reddish-brown skin, blond hair, and pale green eyes of the Lugienese slave race like his companions back on the drogal farm. The youngest was not yet very muscular, but he was still relatively stocky and square—at least compared to Kibure's slender frame. The older of the slave-breeds was full grown and well muscled with broad, rounded shoulders and a thick chest to match. His face was sharp and angular as if chiseled by a sculptor then left unsmoothed. He had wide cheekbones and a large jaw that protruded outward. His hair was probably due for a cut before arriving at auction, but even at this length, it sprouted from his head like the branches of a tree.

The other was of a different seed, and well into his adult years. He had bronze skin and long, shimmering, translucent hair. What stood out most about him was the ridged scar upon his face, which stretched from one ear across the center of his nose all the way to the other ear. Kibure could think of no reason for such a scar to have been created by design, but couldn't imagine how something like that could happen by chance.

The young slave-breed looked out at the morning fog and whimpered, "Are those w-w-water demons?"

Kibure realized he had not been the only one harboring fears of the fog. He glanced back in the direction of the three slaves who had been tied to a post a few paces away.

A deeper, empathetic voice responded to the pleading question. "No, those are no demons and they can't hurt you. Just clouds that didn't make it to the sky in time for the coming day."

"But how'da know?" replied the sheepish voice of the first slave.

"'Cause demons have been locked up for thousands of years. Klerós bound all the old spirits to the water, never to return. Try as they might, they've no power in this part of the world. This fog will be cast away as soon as the sun comes out. You'll see."

Kibure was careful to be discreet as he eavesdropped. His previous experience with the slaves from Zagreb's drogal farm had left little desire for further attempts at friendship. But as the conversation dwindled to whispers, he finally ventured another peek in their direction, only to see three pairs of eyes staring back at him. He averted his eyes in an instant, but couldn't stop the gasp from escaping his lips. He glanced up again and stammered, "Wh—what?"

The oldest of the group, the true-blood, spoke. "Where're you from?"

It took a second for Kibure to register the question amid his surprise. Finally he said, "Jar-Jarquin."

The man nodded. "What's your name?"

"Kibure." His mind raced as he attempted to speak and study the three all at once.

The true-blood looked up again and exclaimed, "Demons below! This whole slavery thing has really taken a toll on my manners. Folks call me Grenn and this older-lookin' fella here is Jengal. And if what they say is true, this younger one here is Tenkoran."

Kibure nodded.

The man continued, "So what of those who bore you?"

"Huh?" responded Kibure, confused by the question.

"Ya know, where'd your ma and pa come from?"

Kibure flushed. "Oh, I—well—I don't know. My mother passed when I was born, and I know nothing of my father. I've always been here—I mean—there in Jarquin, the drogal farm."

Grenn looked him up and down. "Well, you're not of the slave-breed, that's for sure. Or even a half-blood, like me. I've seen many outsiders, but none looked like you."

*There's one constant: no one knows where I'm from or why I look so different.*

Grenn continued, "But the world is vast, and I've not seen the half of it. Must be from somewhere beyond the Glass Sea, somewhere in Drogen. It's a much bigger place even than Angolia, so they say."

He seemed content with this conclusion. "Your name again—Kibber, was it?"

"Kib-*ure*," Kibure corrected.

The youngest of the slaves, Tenk—something turned his attention to Grenn. "Say, you never said you was only a half-blood."

Grenn smiled. "Well, you never asked."

"You let us go on thinking you was a full-on true-blooded Lugienese."

Grenn laughed. "I can't be expected to correct all of your assumptions there, Tenk."

"But you look—"

"I had the fortune of having a true-blooded father."

Tenk cocked his head to the side. "What's that got to do with anything?"

"Well, the looks of children with true-blooded fathers runs strong. That's why so many of 'em get away with having mistresses, slave or not, and the kids are usually passed off as legitimate. Meanwhile if a true-blood woman does the same—well, it's very obvious in their children's appearance." Grenn shook his head. "Women got the short on that one, to be certain."

Tenk's older brother spoke for the first time. "Learn somethin' new each day." Shaking his head, he added, "You even have their magic-lookin' hair. Can't believe I never made the connection. Not like my master never took a slave in that way. The child was always taken away . . ." He trailed off, then understanding dawned on him. "Then grew up beatin' us like they wasn't soiled with our blood."

Grenn cringed. "Well, it's not exactly something the Klerós advertises. And the true-bloods like my father do a fine job of hiding it." Noticing the glare from Jengal and Tenk, Grenn said, "No need to bore daggers into me with your eyes. My father wasn't rich, and didn't own no slaves. Nope, I never once whipped one of your kind."

Kibure grew curious. "So how did you find out you're not a true-blood? Your pa tell you?"

Grenn's expression grew distant. "Eventually, yes. Just before he passed. But I had guessed it long before that. If you know what to look for, there are *some* ways to know a half-blood."

His audience looked on expectantly. He brought a hand to his mouth and whispered, "Skin tone." Speaking more loudly, he continued, "Mine is slightly off when you compare it with my pa's."

Tenk and Jengal studied Grenn.

"Quit it, you two. You can't tell unless you have us both in the room to compare, and he's long passed from this world. Anyway, it seems children get at least some of their coloring from their mothers, and most everything else from their fathers. That's why my skin has a slight bronze to it, as opposed to the olive of my father. But because there are some differences even between western and eastern true-blood Lugienese, it's not enough to just go by skin tone. You need to compare with the father *and* mother if possible."

Tenk asked, "So you met your birth mother, then?"

Grenn shook his head. "No. Only the woman who raised me as her own. A true saint she was. No, my father found a slave woman and did the deed to make me, hoping for the son his wife couldn't give him. Took me away at birth and paid my birth mother to stay away and keep quiet, I guess."

The conversation continued, but Kibure grew tired of the topic and his mind wandered. His thoughts returned to Sindri and her plan to somehow abscond with him when they reached the markets. Steal him away so she could study the source of his unexplained sorcery. That plan held little appeal; however, if she attempted and failed, they'd likely both be killed.

He slouched back against the metal bars of his cage, pondering once more the unfathomable thought that he had used some sort of magic just days before. He tried again to make sense of that, along with everything else—he couldn't. Each piece was puzzling enough by itself. When combined it all made less and less sense. Where was he from? Why was his mother, a woman from some unknown distant land, traveling through southern Angolia? How had he been able to do—whatever it was he had done? What of the strange nightmares that started afterward? What did all of this mean? Could it be that Zagreb was right, and he really was possessed by one of the Dark Lord's minions? Would he know if he were? He shook his head in frustration.

Looking down at his shackles, he growled in protest and willed himself free of them. Forming fists with his hands, he tensed his arms, flexed his back, and strained with all his might. When they didn't budge, he dug deeper into his inner reservoir of strength and strained once more, but this time he felt—*something*. But that something was the nauseating pain of metal as it cut deep into his pale, weak wrists. He let out a loud, exacerbated breath in defeat. He was no sorcerer.

Shouts from beyond his sight resulted in the beginnings of a rhythmic splashing in the water and the feeling of movement. A faint sense of relief washed over him. Regardless of how things played out in the markets of Sire Trinkanen, at least he was on his way to meet that end.

## CHAPTER 11

# GROBENNAR

## [Twenty-Five Years Earlier]

GROBENNAR COULDN'T SEE HIS CAPTIVE'S eyes but he imagined them bulging with fear as his voice squeaked. "Do as he says. Klerós save us, just do it!"

The truth was, Grobennar hadn't had time to digest the fact that he'd already taken a life. Speaking the words aloud caused his resolve to waver. The admission began circulating through his limbs, weakening his grip on the knife. *No. I must be strong.*

Grobennar growled his next statement to mask his fear. "Where is that priest with the child?" Frustrated that no response was forthcoming, Grobennar shouted at the nearest person, a short, pudgy, middle-aged man. "Retrieve the priest at the door. His name is Penden, he has the child."

They entered the room less than a minute later, with the object visible between the folds of Penden's robes. The others in the room straightened as their eyes switched between Grobennar and the object.

The priest held by Grobennar exclaimed, "How can this be? Wha-what is it?"

"It is as the prophecy proclaims," Grobennar replied coldly. "'The shell of Klerós's faith shall wrap the Savior in red.' Few believe it a literal description, yet here it lies before us." Shifting back to the task at hand, he shouted, "Quickly, prepare the furnace!"

He knew the pathway to greatness and the return of their god lay in the hands of these few men. The Lugienese triumph over the world had been entrusted to them—and to himself.

Speaking to his captive, he asked, "Will you cause me further trouble if I release you?"

"No-no, none at all. Klerós's will."

"Good." He pushed the man away. The pathetic priest sprawled forward onto his face.

"Apologies; this is too important," said Grobennar.

The priest was busy pleading forgiveness from Klerós for his lack of faith. He didn't seem to hear.

*That was quite diplomatic. Not how I would have done it, but it appears to have worked.*

Grobennar waved Penden over and he felt the shell of the chrysalis. "Hurry, it's getting cold!" As he watched, an eerie, metallic blue enveloped the fading speckles of red; a sign perhaps that signified the life within was fleeting.

For minutes that felt like hours, the priests pumped the bellows. Grobennar stood still, gazing with wonder at the beauty of the object, like the mother might have done if the birth had gone as planned.

Grobennar released the breath he had been holding. It was time.

One of the others asked, "Are you certain we should place the"—he struggled with the word—"child in the oven? What if the heat destroys it?"

Grobennar simply replied with the verse: "A birth unlike all others, unmarred by the inferno, the cries of our Savior will ring."

Grobennar opened the door to the furnace and a wave of heat swept over his face as the hot, dry air rushed into the room. Despite the momentary discomfort, he was glad to feel the extreme temperature. He pulled the handle of the heavy slab, which rolled easily on a system of oiled stones that allowed for human offerings. Without hesitation, he pushed the nearly blue chrysalis into the oven.

The agonizing minutes of silence that followed were punctuated by the occasional lament. "O Klerós, forgive us. We of little faith did not act with haste . . ."

Then a cracking sound shot out from the within the furnace, and they knew something momentous had occurred.

*"Ooooh, I think something happened."*

"I think everyone thinks that," whispered Grobennar as he reached for the handle, his hands quivering with anticipation. A bright red light grew stronger as the object emerged. It was nearly blinding once the chrysalis was fully exposed.

The outer casing had cracked, and thick, sizzling, red fluids oozed out. Grobennar's hands steadied as his confidence grew, as did his voice. "Today we witness beauty beyond all that precedes us!"

The shell melted away, and a living child lay unscathed within the molten fluids, peering up at those around—him—the child was a male. Grobennar recalled the ancient writings of the faith and shouted, "The prophesied bringer of salvation! *He* whose name alone provokes the shining light of Klerós! The Child of Light and Fire lies before us today!"

*"A little on the dramatic side, don't you think?"*

The child began to cry and wail. Grobennar was no nurse, and the sound grated his ears. He needed to find a wet nurse for the child. But first—

Grobennar scooped up the child and cradled his tiny body as best he could, then he motioned for the oven to be closed. The child's father had entered at the behest of Tadi Jori, and stood motionless in a shadowed corner of the holy temple. Grobennar called him forth and he lifted his head, still appearing dazed by the entire experience. Grobennar regarded him with an expression of gratitude. "Yes, come forward, ye who sired the Savior of our people."

The man staggered toward him, still unable to comprehend the magnitude of such a birth or the devastating loss of his beloved.

Grobennar spoke in a low voice, coaxing the man closer. "Yes, that's it. It's all right. You, of all people, deserve to bear witness."

The child's cries were nearly unbearable. *This had better work.* Grobennar beckoned the man closer. "Look into the eyes of our Creator incarnate."

As the man looked on uncertainly, the child's eyes met his. The crying suddenly stopped. Grobennar was unsure how this next step would play out, but he left it to his god. The child's helpless, innocent demeanor changed the moment his gaze locked on that of his father. An unnatural heat swept over the room, like that which might have emanated from the now-closed oven. In an instant, Grobennar sensed the magic and knew.

The child's father fell to his knees, but his eyes remained fixed upon those of the child even as his own steamed and smoked. The man released an inhuman bellow before slumping to the floor. Grobennar stepped closer the father who now lay lifeless, his eyes charred to a crisp. A horrific smell lingered.

*"Quite the temper on this one. You had best stay on his good side."*

There was an awkward silence among the priests who had watched the infant slay a grown man in such grotesque fashion. Grobennar broke the silence with a cheer of triumph. The rest of the priests followed suit, like that of a mindless mob. Jubilation poured from the temple priests as they acknowledged that they would live in the foretold days of great change. The Lugienese Empire's Klerósi prophecy was coming to fruition, and they held the key. The red light from the oven porthole grew brighter as the priests repeated the name they had all been afraid to voice before the ritual was complete. "Magog . . . Magog . . . Magog! On this day, the Child of Light and Fire has been born." The chant morphed slowly into a prayer of thanksgiving, and the furnace became so hot that those standing closest were forced to retreat as their clothes smoked and their sweaty skin sizzled.

The infant let out a gentle giggle as Grobennar wrapped him carefully in red cloth, readying him for the royal palace, the senior high priest, and the second test of fires that he knew this child must face.

## CHAPTER 12

# AYNWARD

THE DOOR CREAKED OPEN. LIGHT blinded Aynward as his eyes struggled to adjust to the change. As the color bled back into his vision, he noted that unlike before, this person wore no disguise. Aynward was still so disoriented that it took him a moment to recognize the familiar face, and when he did, he could hardly believe it: Minster Dolmuevo Humiliab, his life-guide, his savior. Aynward was overwhelmed with joy.

"Dolme! Bless the gods you're here. I feared I would die here."

Dolme peered at him with that familiar look of disappointment, his fading hairline accentuating the creases in his forehead. It was the same look he gave Aynward when he completed a mathematical equation incorrectly because he had rushed through it or answered an oral question without thinking. The half smile shadowed by stern, slanted eyebrows and creased forehead told Aynward that Dolme was not pleased and expected some sort of reply.

Aynward's thoughts shifted to his father, who must have caught wind of the brawl and his disappearance. Aynward had missed his ship and would surely miss the beginning of this year's classes. It would likely be a month or so until another ship suitable for royalty would be leaving Salmune for the Isles.

"Aynward, you've much to learn about responsibility, duty, and even more to learn about the survival of a young man of royal blood. Your father would be very disappointed to know how you placed yourself in such an irresponsible position among a bunch of lowlifes in a meaningless dockside brawl, especially the night before you were to leave for your schooling. No doubt he'd see this as a direct challenge to his authority. Would you not agree?"

Aynward noted Dolme's diction carefully. "You ask this question in such a way that it implies that he does not already know. Wasn't he who sent you to free me from this place?"

Dolme's smile widened to a sinister grin. "Your father has awarded me certain *liberties* to do with you as I see fit, as long as you're prepared to service this great kingdom when your schooling is complete." He extended his arms to indicate the room. "With this flexibility in mind, I have taken the opportunity you provided me. So far as your father is concerned, you boarded your ship and embarked as planned, which is not entirely untrue."

He leaned on the doorframe and examined his fingernails. "To be honest, I don't know if he'll ever hear of it. I brought enough help with me to make sure your friends escaped safely, paid them kindly, and threatened them with their own parental disclosure should anyone hear of it otherwise. However, if King Lupren does catch wind of it, he'll have plenty of time to cool off before he sees you next."

Aynward was now truly confused. "What are you talking about?" A potential understanding of what this all meant was starting to form in his mind, but it couldn't be right. Dolme had always been a stern man, but surely this was just a joke or—

"Wait, are you saying—" Even as words formed, he felt a pit in his stomach. "*You* created this cell? I've been held captive here for two or three or however many weeks, tortured, tormented, and drugged—by *you?*"

A rare, wide smile crossed Dolme's face. "Aynward, Aynward, Aynward. You've so much to learn about responsibility." He shook his head. "I fear there was just no other way to teach this lesson quickly enough before arriving in such a dangerous city as Brinkwell. Fear not. We are indeed on board the *Royal Viscery* en route to the Isles, and this is your cabin. Being the concerned counselor that I am, I planned to follow you on your last evening in Salmune to ensure your timely arrival to the ship. I saw you and your pals indulge so heavily in the brew, staggering around the Flowering Bell like fools, which confirmed my fears about how unprepared you were to survive the dangers abroad. Prepared for this eventuality, I quickly went about finalizing one of a dozen potential measures. Couldn't have staged it more perfectly if I'd wanted. You did most of it all on your own."

Aynward lay naked as the day he was born in what he now realized was not a cell but his cabin on board the *Royal Viscery*. His anger at his counselor's words boiled. He would hear no more. He lunged forward with every ounce of strength he could muster.

Dolme, a seasoned swordsman, sidestepped the attack, swept Aynward's feet out from under him, then struck him from behind. Aynward landed facedown, Dolme's knee digging into his back. But this didn't stop the stream of insults and curses issuing from Aynward's lips. After a minute of struggle, his energy faded, and his cries of anger turned to sobs of frustration as he struggled to comprehend his shifting circumstances.

When Aynward calmed down, Dolme released his weight from the boy's back. "A simple thank-you for saving you from your father's wrath would have sufficed. Stay put and I'll send some servants to get you cleaned up. Perhaps someday you'll realize the value of this lesson." He grabbed hold of Aynward's wrists and sliced the rope that bound them.

Aynward emerged on the ship's deck—sponged down and dressed up. The *Royal Viscery* was impressive as far as river-going cargo ships go. The stern deck concealed three levels below, which consisted of the crew's quarters as well as a mess hall and some cargo space. The hold was filled with freight and food stores. The ship was unique to Dowe not only in that it had three masts but it also retained oarsmen for travel up and down rivers when the wind or current wasn't right. The oarsmen had it easy going downriver. However, the way back to Salmune would be a strenuous trek.

Aynward found Dolme gazing off into the distance on the starboard side, where a vast emptiness existed between Kingdom cities. Aynward guessed they had been traveling for more than three weeks and were approaching the merchant city of Mouthportu. All he could see to the north were the vast, light-green grasslands, marked by hints of pink and purple where flowers bloomed. As they neared Mouthportu, they would begin to see great green forests speckled with black where the Bracken trees grew. Aynward had never seen them firsthand, but had read a great deal about them.

He had come to the deck prepared to confront Dolme once more about the ill treatment he had received. However, the breathtaking landscape rendered him silent. He had hunted a few times with his father and brothers in the mountain forests that lay just east of Salmune, but it was one thing to be within the forest and quite another to see leagues of it from such a great distance.

He was still entranced by the scenery when Dolme spoke. "You've got a good head on your shoulders, you know. But you've much to learn about survival and the real consequences of adulthood in the world. Someday you will have to make important decisions that may affect a great number of people. Getting yourself mixed up with a bunch of brigands and drunkards at that inn was more than foolish. You could have been captured, tortured, ransomed, or killed had I not sent those agents to take you into custody."

Aynward began a defense. "Yes, but—"

"This does not require a response," Dolme interjected. "How far would that explanation get you had you actually been taken hostage by someone who recognized you?" He continued without waiting for an answer. "Like I said, you've a good head, you really do, but you've much to learn. Sure, you need the histories and war tactics and philosophies, but most important is simply learning to understand how far your actions stretch beyond your immediate circumstances. For one of royal blood, it is especially crucial that you learn to weigh every decision in light of potential negative outcomes—not only for yourself but for everyone else it may affect. Simply living for the moment and having a good time is not an option for you. There may come times when you have to make split-second decisions without a chance to consider options, and when those times come, you need be in a place where you know you will make the right choice without hesitation."

A small part of Aynward knew that what Dolme said was true, and shame trickled in. Not liking the way that felt, he clenched his fists and fought against it. No, Dolme had no right to punish him as he did, regardless of his intentions. And so what if he wanted to have a good time with his friends before shipping off to some alien world against his own wishes?

This was quickly becoming another one of Dolme's trademark lectures. "That is why I did what I did. I wanted to give you time to consider how your poor choices failed you. I hope you will not forget the glimpse of discomfort you felt during this time, not because I wish suffering upon you, but so you will know of suffering and that things could be much worse if you are taken by someone who truly wishes suffering upon you."

Dolme put a reassuring hand on Aynward's shoulder but he twisted away. Aynward had nothing to say in response, nothing that wouldn't result in him being thrown to the deck for another lesson in *respect*. He was livid inside. It was insulting to think that Dolme could think him so dim-witted that he required the experience of suffering in order to understand it. More frustrating was the lack of any ability to enact retribution on the man. Doing so would reveal his own folly, even if Dolme were the main culprit behind it. *He thinks he's so righteous.*

Aynward went belowdeck to his recently furnished cabin to brood. He lay on his back, swinging slowly in a hammock visualizing his revenge. This was not the first time, but it was the most vivid yet. He saw it clear as day: Dolme tied up and stripped down. He would be tied to a chair and dragged out into a public square where people would throw rotten food at him. After hours of humiliation, Aynward would walk by and say casually, "Consider how your poor choices have failed you. All actions have consequences."

Aynward would smile and walk away without releasing him. Dolme would plead with him as he turned his back, but his pleas would go unheard. He would remain publicly shamed for the night, knowing Aynward had given him what he deserved, knowing he was not so righteous after all.

Aynward didn't like to let such things fester, but could not let go of this offense. He would not forget it. He continued to dream of revenge until sleep overtook him. He woke up with a headache, and the bitterness turned over in his stomach.

## CHAPTER 13

# KIBURE

THE SOUND OF RENEWED CONVERSATION from the three slaves drew Kibure from his thoughtless stare at the water rippling by the side of the ship.

It turned out that Grenn was quite the teller of tales. Kibure had no reason to disbelieve any of them, but he thought Grenn sure had a lot of stories for one person.

Grenn was boasting of a time he claimed to have met the famed Emperor himself, Magog, a story to steal the attention of anyone in the Lugienese Empire with ears, slave or free man alike.

"I'd been working on the new palace, you see. His Holiness came to inspect the work personally. By mere happenstance I found myself in the very same room." His eyes went skyward, as if seeing it again for the first time. "He actually spoke to me, you know!"

Jengal let out a light chuckle. "Your stories just keep getting better."

"Klerós's truth he did!" insisted Grenn. "I was up on the scaffolding laying brick atop one of the ballroom pillars prior to the priests solidifying it with their magic. All of a sudden, the Exalted One walks in, trailed by several priests and a few architects. I was frozen silly, paralyzed with fear. I mean, what if I dropped something, or made too much noise, or he didn't like the way the pillar looked before magic polished it? Everyone's heard the rumors. He does not take kindly to flaws or failure."

Kibure wasn't looking in their direction but his peripheral vision picked up two heads nodding agreement.

"But he looked up to where I was and said—and I'll never forget it." He paused for effect. "He said, 'Looks good up there.'"

A sharp intake from Tenk was immediately followed by, "No way!"

When Grenn didn't immediately continue, Tenk asked excitedly, "And then what?"

Grenn seemed surprised by the question. "Oh—well—" He looked from side to side, then said, "He moved on to the other room."

"Oh," said Tenk, enthusiasm draining from his voice.

A bowl of stew surprised Kibure as it banged at the metal bars on its way between them. He had not seen the servant approach from the side. The food was no longer hot, but it was still better fare than the slave slop he had been served at the estate or the dried perversions of it that had been given during the trek to the ship.

Kibure spotted Grenn watching him with curiosity as he struggled with his shackled hands to awkwardly spoon the slop into his mouth. "Kibure. I've been thinking. You must be quite the feisty one. Chains while inside a metal cage!" He giggled. "Smallest of all the slaves here, yet you're strapped in steel twice over!"

Kibure just shrugged and forced a smile. "My musco is a cautious man."

"Cautious is an understatement! I'd say paranoid!"

Kibure commented no further, and Grenn left the topic alone.

As the day dragged by, Kibure warmed to the nearby slaves. Listening to Grenn's stories helped pass the time.

Kibure finally asked, "Grenn, how is it that you have visited so many places within the Empire?"

Grenn took on a faraway look before replying. "Well, when I was a free man, a laborer, I learned several skills in my travels to find whatever work I could. Sad to say, I never settled. I guess I was always looking for something new, something different." He sighed. "Never found what I was looking for, but I sure did see a lot of the world along the way."

"But how then are you now a slave? Someone find out you were a half-blood?"

If Grenn had a faraway look before, this question sent him to another world entirely. "No, nothin' like that. But I did work alongside many slaves over the years. And guessing my own heritage, I came to believe that these slaves were not the ferocious, beastly fools they were said to be. They're just a conquered people like any other. On my last job, up in the mountains of Surin, where I met these two louts"—he jerked his thumbs at Jengal and Tenk—"I witnessed a musco beating his slave. After a while, I couldn't take it any longer. The slave was nearly dead. I told the musco that the poor soul had had enough." Grenn shook his head. "I wasn't looking for a fight, but this savage was already in a rage. He rounded on me and swung the whip."

Kibure's eyes went wide with disbelief as Grenn continued.

"And he didn't stop at one swing. He kept swinging. He left me no choice but to fight back. I finally caught the thing in my hand." He displayed a white scar across the palm where the corrugated whip's rough, studded surface had opened his skin. "I yanked it from his grasp, and I guess I lost my wits in the heat of it and struck him one time too many. He never woke up. Worse yet, Bragden—Tenk and Jengal's musco—arrived on the scene just in time to see the fatal blow. He had me marked, bound, and crated until such time as he could sell me off into slavery, where I'll remain for the rest of my days."

He stared at his hands as he spoke, then looked up and pointed to the ridged mark on his face that Kibure had noticed earlier. "That's why I bear this scar. If ever I were to escape, and be free of a master, I'd be seen for what I am and put to death as a runaway."

The pain in Grenn's eyes was clear as he told the story, but his expression was hard, having accepted the finality of it.

The next morning, as the barge pushed upstream toward the city of Sire Haas, the slaves continued to pass the time with light chatter. This time it was Tenkoran who spoke. "I remember playing a game of finders with a friend, Dex. Not only did I go the ninety breaths without being found, but while in hiding I uncovered a stash of dried fruit our musco had set aside. I managed several mouthfuls before Musco Bragden barged in to catch me red-handed."

Tenk smiled wide. "It was well worth the treat." He turned his wrists up in front of him to reveal the price: several raised scars. "Have you ever had dried fruit, Kibure?"

"No."

"Well, it's marvelous. If heaven really exists, I'll bet it has plenty. And if not, it should!"

The day disappeared amid a steady flow of stories and chatter. Before Kibure knew it, two meals had passed and it was dark again, and his eyes were fluttering in their attempt to remain open. And then he was asleep.

When Kibure opened his eyes, he was quick to recognize that he was not truly awake. The familiar eerie silence gave it away now that he knew what to look for, or, rather, listen for. He had returned to that same nightmare. His nerves quivered as he struggled to orient himself within the unnatural place between true sleep and wakefulness.

Like before, his surroundings mirrored that of the waking world— minus color and sound. He looked over to where the others *should* have been but saw nothing. Except—no—it wasn't entirely nothing. As he regarded this area more closely, he realized he could see translucent outlines similar to what he had observed when Sindri had been standing in front of him in the real world before he woke. There was also the faintest speck within each distortion, a faint wisp of something opaque, a gray sliver. *I don't like this.*

That thought reminded him, however, that he had managed to escape from his confines on that night before waking. But how had he done so? He could feel the metal bars, not exactly cold upon his skin, but his mind registered their lifeless presence holding him upright. Had it been fear that drove him last time? Determination? If this were truly a dream, maybe he could do things that he would ordinarily be unable to do in the real world. *Worth a try.* Bracing himself, he pushed against the bars.

Nothing happened.

Kibure frowned. *This makes no sense.* He supposed that was sort of a rule for dreams, but it was still frustrating. Most things in the real world made little sense so he should have expected little better here in his dreams.

Nevertheless he tried again, this time straining even harder than before.

Nothing.

What was it that had allowed him to escape before? An idea formed in his mind, and while it seemed rather foolish, he decided what better place to rely on such things than a dream? He concentrated on simply *willing* himself free of the bars. He stared at the wood planks just beyond the bars, closed his eyes, and imagined himself there. He opened his eyes slowly, hoping to find himself standing beyond his bars.

He wasn't.

He tried again, focusing everything he could muster. Then he heard a voice, or, rather, sensed the words of a voice in his mind. "*You should keep from the world of dream while so close to the darkness.*"

His eyes snapped open, and he looked from side to side but he saw no one there. He tried to say something back, but like before, no sound was forthcoming.

"*Ah, you do not yet know how to will your words to life from within this place. This is just as well, for now. Your soul is not safe, here or in the waking world. Should you ignore this warning, know that you need only will yourself somewhere, visualize, and believe, and it will be so. It is much the same to speak into the mind of another while here.*"

A thousand questions sprang into Kibure's mind and he continued to look about for the source of the voice. "Who are you? Where are you? What is this place?" He willed those questions to go forth from his mind, but he was certain none did so. He was completely impotent here.

*I must go. I risk much in coming to these dark lands, even in dream. You too must keep from this place if you hope to survive. We will wait for your foretold arrival to the east in the—"*

The voice was cut off by the sudden sensation of—

His eyes snapped open and he shouted into the waking world. His body tingled with a thousand pinpricks—magic. Thick beads of sweat rolled down his face.

Turning his head to the left, he saw the outline of a woman—Sindri. It was too dark to see her features clearly, but her posture suggested a scowl.

Sindri tsked, then whispered, "You were using magic again, little tazamine."

She turned her head and the moon's faint light exposed a slight smile, but like a stone thrown into the air, it was quickly pulled down. Then she frowned as she turned back to face him, her expression disappearing into the shadows once more. "The aura you put out during your sleep tonight was strong enough to wake me from my own slumber. Alas Kibure, you can no longer deny me the *full* truth. This places both of us at risk."

Kibure sat stunned and silent. Sindri continued. "Come morning, we *will* discuss this, one way or another. Mind you, one way will involve far less pain than the other, but the choice remains yours."

Kibure remained speechless, due to the undeniability of his nightmares as well as Sindri's threat.

She turned to leave, then stopped to face him once again.

"And Kibure, please choose the former. I'd really like for us to be frie—well, perhaps that's not the right term. I'd like us to be cooperative affiliates, both sides benefiting to some degree or another. I worry that torture may strain what could otherwise be a very healthy relationship."

She tilted her head to one side for an instant. "I promise you that in spite of your fear of me, life with me will be better than what you had with Zagreb. Hell, when I've learned what I can from you, I may even set you—" She looked over and saw the three other slaves, awake and all staring in their direction, well lit by the light of the moons. "We'll discuss this further once I've made the necessary arrangements. You just think upon what you're going to say when next we speak."

She had turned enough that her face was again visible in the light of the moons. Her mouth curved up at the edges, forming a perverted smile. "You help me, and I'll help you." Then Sindri slinked her way around the corner, leaving a trembling Kibure alone with his thoughts.

## CHAPTER 14

# GROBENNAR

MAGOG'S VOICE WAS A DEEP growl, yet it remained smooth to the ear, a more imposing sound after Grobennar's last encounter with the volatile God-king.

Grobennar remained where he was, kneeling, awaiting the God-king's instruction. He could feel himself scowling. Rajuban's attendance at this meeting was yet another affront to Grobennar's station, and a clear threat to his position of favor with the God-king. Grobennar did not like it one bit.

"Fatu Mazi." Grobennar was surprised to hear his own formal title from the God-king. "We must act before the agent of the Dark Lord is upon us. It is evident that this evil approaches our doorstep. I felt his presence once again, stronger still than before. We must do everything within our power to extinguish this threat to Klerós's plan and the prophesied redemption of his creation, Doréa. I would trust none other than you, Fatu Mazi, with this task."

*Why the sudden reverence?* wondered Grobennar.

"This task is, of course, not without its risks."

*Of course.* Grobennar cringed. This was not good, especially if the plan truly originated with Mazi Rajuban.

Grobennar and Rajuban had been at odds since their time together decades earlier in the priesthood. The man had always been jealous of Grobennar's favor with Magog. It seemed to Grobennar that Raj had finally gained an advantage in their game of intrigue, a game Grobennar was not accustomed to losing.

Rajuban's serpentine voice goaded him. "Brother, you look tense. Fear not. The God-king has asked me to be in attendance for today's meeting merely to lend my expert skill in aiding his spell casting." He stepped forward and opened his arms before the both of them, a mockingly holy gesture considering the man Grobennar knew him to be. He continued, "After all, we wouldn't wish to see anything go wrong with the casting. One stray thought during the process could leave you dead or, worse yet, impotent. I don't think anyone would wish to see that. This great empire needs you."

*"Can't just bludgeon him to death? No one would suspect someone of your magical ability to resort to such mundane methods."*

*If only*, wished Grobennar.

"Truer words were never spoken," replied Grobennar wryly. "Your willingness to advise and aid the God-king is commendable. Though I can't help but wonder if this decision might be rash. I have long held that any verdict of importance not come without adequate consultation with Klerós, and those closest to Klerós's will."

Rajuban smiled. "I could not agree more. The God-king and I have been working over the particulars of this spell, and praying for the signs to use it for a number of months. Klerós has delivered both to us."

*"He's really outdone you this time, Grobes."*

"Of course you have. This is well. Klerós guides both of you."

That venomous snake had been working from within the shadows for months before striking. What could he say that would not cause himself further harm in the face of the God-king? Nothing. He could only pray this spell didn't actually kill or maim him.

"So what is this spell intended to do, exactly?" asked Grobennar, hoping it wasn't as dangerous as they were making it out to be.

Rajuban answered again for Magog. "This spell will replicate the God-king's blessed ability to sense magic more acutely, if only temporarily. We could not grant any mortal man the ability to wield as he does, but a temporary expansion of the ability to sense magic is possible. Based on our experiments, this ability will come close to that of the God-king himself!"

"Tried this on yourself, have you?"

Rajuban chuckled. "Demons no! We took on a crop of young, willing priests with the talent to seek, though none with a strong talent. These were all—expendable. Rest assured, our last two attempts succeeded without complication."

*Comforting.*

Magog spoke, "Let us be on with it. We have other matters to attend to this day."

Rajuban nodded and allowed his triumph to leak through his expression.

Grobennar considered Jaween's last suggestion for a moment. He knew things were dire when he actually considered one of Jaween's deranged plans. *If only.*

Magog placed his hands upon Grobennar's shoulders and began to hum.

*"Oooh no. This seems like such a bad idea. And yet to ignore your Lord after what happened last time would be far perilous—er? A grand predicament, indeed."*

Grobennar ignored Jaween as a swirl of energies shot through him. It was pain beyond anything he had ever felt, a deep, inexplicable jolt within his mind and chest, a burning so hot he wondered if he might combust from within. He tried to wriggle free, but he could not. Dark images, swirls of black and red light, did battle before his closed eyes. None of his priestly training prepared him for the pain that coursed through his body, growing steadily more intense until his mind could no longer bear it, and his ability to stand failed. He slumped forward, awareness fading as he fell headlong into an abyss of nothingness.

## CHAPTER 15

# AYNWARD

A YNWARD AWKWARDLY EXTRICATED HIMSELF FROM the hammock of his cell-turned-cabin and cursed the pain in his back.

*Gods! How can anyone get used to sleeping in one of these things?*

The sleep-deprived Aynward longed for nothing more than to collapse into the soft, pillowy comfort he knew remained back in Salmune, years now from his grasp.

Thoughts of his increasingly distant home brought back a shower of memories. Aynward had never been close to his family, with the exception of his sister, Dagmara, but he still ached at the thought of being so far from them. He cringed at his weakness, and attempted to brush those thoughts aside, recalling that his brothers were now occupied with the responsibilities of adulthood and his sister prepared for marriage. In fact, her wedding would likely be the next time he saw her.

Even he and his sister had begun the slow departure from childhood friendship as she entered into her training for womanhood. Yet he still counted her one of his closest friends. Often he had sneaked off to go riding with her in the royal pastures, and he had secretly taught her the basics of the sword, because women were prohibited from such activity. Yet she desired deeply to learn. He could see her light-auburn hair flow as she twirled about with the wooden sparring weapon. He nearly laughed as he recalled how angry she became when she didn't score so much as a hit on her younger brother. A foolish frustration considering he'd been forced to practice nearly every day while at school, while she had barely practiced more than a dozen times, in secret. Aynward's smile faded as he reflected on the loneliness he would endure for the next several years while away from everyone he'd ever known.

Then a voice from above caught Aynward's attention. "Land ahoy!"

*Gods be blessed! No more hammock!*

Aynward watched in awe as the *Royal Viscera* sailed into Brinkwell's expansive bay. The late midday sun gave the city, beautiful on its own, an almost mystical appearance.

Brinkwell was arguably one of the most important cities of trade in all of Doréa. This was one of the few places where direct exchanges between Angolian and Drogenese merchants existed on friendly terms, as enforced by the presence of Kingdom patrols.

Brinkwell's size was impressive in and of itself, but what made it more remarkable was the way the ground gently sloped upward from the bay, creating an appearance similar to the amphitheaters common in Scritler. Leagues of city rose up from the bay in all directions from the hub of trade that began at the docks. Aynward was amazed by the sight, in spite of his recollection that Salmune was actually a more populous city. However, the intensity of activity here was like nothing he'd ever before seen.

The *Royal Viscera* slowed to a near halt at the major dock in Brinkwell and ropes were thrown to the waiting dock crew, who pulled them into position so they could unload.

Aynward finally snapped out of his trance when Dolme slapped him on the back. "Ready to begin your true education?"

"Ready as I can be." His voice was intentionally devoid of mirth. He was unwilling to indulge his captor any more than necessary.

He looked around at the bustle of the city and tried not to allow it to overwhelm him. While he was unwilling to demonstrate any eagerness in front of Dolme, he had decided that he'd try to make the most of the situation. But Dolme would not be proven right by seeing Aynward enjoy his experience here. Not after what he'd done to him.

The docks were not much different from those back in Salmune, save for the fact that they extended for leagues around a significantly larger bay.

Dolme sent a messenger to alert the man who had agreed to show them to their residence upon arrival. The messenger returned minutes later with Kuerton, who greeted them at the dock with a few servants to handle their baggage. Kuerton walked with his entire upper body leaning back awkwardly, which Aynward assumed must have been necessary to support his robust belly. More than his odd posture, though, it was his eyes that gave the man a comedic appearance. The way they rested in his eye sockets gave him a beady, nervous appearance.

"Your things will be transported to your residence. I've arranged for us to walk so as to better familiarize the two of you with the city. I hope this will not be taken in offense by his majesty." Kuerton said all of this with unusual emphasis on certain syllables, lowering and elevating the pitch of his voice to accompany his words. His mode of speech alongside his appearance made him seem to Aynward a caricature from some roving street show act. Had Aynward been in better spirits, he'd have started laughing right then and there.

"That will be acceptable," said Dolme. "But I would ask that you not refer to this young man as 'majesty' but simply 'Annard.' While he's here, he is merely a student of little significance and we would prefer his identity remain unknown."

Kuerton raised an eyebrow. "Very well, then, Annard, and . . ." He paused, scanning his memory. "Ah yes, Dolme." He leaned in and spoke more quietly. "Apologies, I took special note of the informal offshoot of Dolmuevo, then went and nearly forgot it when I needed it."

Dolme appeared neither amused nor angry, just nodded for the man to continue with their introduction to the city.

Kuerton cleared his throat, visibly uncomfortable now. "So . . . Annard and Dolme, if you would please follow me, we should be on our way. I have arranged for us to have a hot meal at a place only slightly off the way to your residence. It will be a thirty-minute walk."

Dolme gestured with his head for the man to lead on.

Kuerton nodded, giving both of them a wry, quirky smile. "All right, then, let's be off." He turned and started down the dock toward the city.

As he followed, Aynward noticed the unusually thin robe the man wore. It was nearly transparent. He wore dark trousers and no shirt beneath the see-through robe. Aynward gathered it was the pride of people to flaunt their rotund bellies for all to see. *What a strange place.*

As they began their ascent into the city, Aynward expected strange looks from people noting him a foreigner, but no one took notice. He observed no homogenous look to the people. They seemed to come from all over Doréa.

Aynward also noticed that the docks were much less inviting when up close. He could see all of the clutter and imperfections of busy storerooms and lower-class housing. The first few blocks were warehouses with a smattering of inns, brothels, taverns, or combinations of all three. Despite its clutter and busyness, it was not completely repulsive. He found it interesting how different it looked up close compared with the glistening midday panorama from the deck of the *Royal Viscera*. Yet the breeze coming in from the Glass Sea removed much of the expected stench. Aynward recalled the stagnant, stinking air around the docks back home and shook his head. *Brinkwell has at least something going for it.*

After a few minutes of walking on small, hard-packed side streets, they reached a wide, busy avenue that made a straight line into the heart of the city. They turned right and walked up this street for another ten minutes. Aynward was surprised at the quick pace set by their plump guide. He and Dolme struggled to match his speed.

The street reminded Aynward a little of home, though it was busier and much more diverse. Several large, cow-like animals pulled wagons and carts full of food and trade items.

"Be sure to stay to one side or the other," Kuerton shouted over the bustling sounds of the awakening city. "Many have lost limbs and lives to the wagon drivers. They've places to go, and they will not stop or slow down for the meandering pedestrian."

"That's a comforting thought," Aynward mumbled as he merged further to the left. Kuerton maintained a reserved equanimity about him as they walked, speaking only when pointing out hazards or landmarks. He indicated several temples of varying religions, which was another oddity, because there was only one faith in the Kingdom. All others were deemed heretical, though devout faith was by no means a driving force within Dowe society, not like in Scritland to the south where the government and religious leaders were as one. Therefore, Aynward thought it odd to find so many faiths in one place.

He pondered this notion as they walked, and settled on a theory. In a place with refugees and travelers from all over the world, many different religious establishments were required to accommodate them. He'd heard of other religions to the far south, as well as many more in the Isles and west in Angolia, all with their own unique gods and cultic beliefs. He'd just never considered them all existing peacefully within the same city. He was struck again by the alien nature of this place.

They passed several bustling marketplaces filled with the shouts of merchants and buyers alike. Kuerton spoke as they passed one of them. "These central markets sell everyday supplies and food for the people living within a short walk. The Grand Market lies ten minutes east of here—about ten minutes south of where you'll be staying, if you'd like to see it. It is without question the most spectacular place to visit if you've got the coin and you're into rare items, luxury, relics, exotic pets, food . . . the list goes on and on, my friends. If there is something you want, or need, I assure you it is there." He smiled at them with his beady little black eyes. "However, you may want to have someone who knows their way around if you hope to find what you're looking for. The market is quite large, crowded, and confusing to the foreigner. You could spend an entire week going to every stand or merchant and not see the same one twice. I would be glad to escort you sometime. You have but to call on me." When neither Aynward nor Dolme responded, he shrugged. "Of course, you'll have plenty of time to explore at your leisure."

They continued their ascent, and Aynward's legs began to ache. They'd been walking a steady incline for what had seemed like the entirety of their journey through the city. He tried to distract himself from the pain by paying closer attention to what he saw as they walked. The buildings within this sector of the city looked older but better maintained, and the architecture was almost completely alien to him. Where the buildings around the docks fit right into his architectural schema, these were like a brand-new language.

He looked up ahead and saw a great stone serpent whose body below the neck looked like that of the wolves that often fed on sheep back home. It extended from the stone wall that served as the entrance. The pillars and sacrificial stone tablets out front made it obvious that this was another religious temple. Aynward had no idea what religion it represented, but felt certain he should keep his distance. He was glad when Kuerton turned east down another side street just before the temple.

Dolme turned and whispered to Aynward, "Quite a strange specimen, ah?"

Before Aynward had time to decide to ignore Dolme's attempt at conversation out of spite, Kuerton wheeled around and placed a hand on both Dolme's and Aynward's shoulders. His pudgy face hardened as he whispered to them. "Careful what you say about the temples here. Although the religions appear to live harmoniously within this city, evil lurks in the shadows. It's best not to voice such thoughts about the temples or the people while here."

Aynward noted a hint of fear in his eyes as they darted about. Then Kuerton smiled his strange smile again. "Not to worry, though. These things happen only on occasion. Just a minor precaution, but I'd be a poor guide if I didn't at least mention it."

As Kuerton turned, Aynward felt a strange tingling chill throughout his body. Yet he had no goose bumps; in fact, he felt like he was about to break a sweat. He was overcome by the uncomfortable sense that he was being watched. But when he turned, he saw only the bustle of people along the main corridor continuing along their paths. He shook off the jitters and tried to stop thinking about what Kuerton had just said.

## CHAPTER 16

# KIBURE

KIBURE HUDDLED IN HIS CAGE, petrified, not only by the frightful nature of his last vision, but also by the complication that now involved Sindri. How had she known? Did she truly sense that something was happening within him? Something related to magic, or had she simply been nearby, heard his scream, and assumed as much?

He looked over at the three slaves, embarrassed. Tenk finally whispered, "What the blazes was all that stuff with that witch about? You all right?"

Kibure felt no more like explaining himself to the slaves than he did explaining to Sindri, though for different reasons. He had come to really enjoy their company. He did not wish to lose their friendship by exposing his *demon dreams* or whatever they were, or the true reason he was caged. Yet surely they would hear his conversations with Sindri, or worse yet, witness her torturing him when he denied knowledge of his magic.

He relaxed his posture as best he could. "Yeah, I'm—I'm fine. Just had a bad dream." He tried to laugh to add a sense of credibility to his feigned lack of concern—his lie. "I have nightmares often these days. My musco thinks my nightmares are sent from the Dark Lord. It's ridiculous, really. It's just . . . being the coward that I am causes me to cry out when they get bad. That's—that's the whole reason my musco wants rid of me. He's so superstitious that he actually believes me a tazamine, and hired Sindri to keep watch over me. Worse yet, she believes him!" He laughed awkwardly—and unconvincingly, he thought. "I mean, a tazamine! I'm no more a tazamine than I am a free man."

The three slaves sat unmoving and silent for a time before Grenn finally put in, "Indeed, though having nightmares does not make you a coward. I won't inquire after the nature of your—dreams, but if they are indeed frightful enough, and seem real enough, perhaps the fear is warranted. Can't say it happens so often to me, but I've certainly woken with a fright a time or two in my day. Glad to know it was just a dream."

Kibure stumbled over a few responses in his head, but settled on, "Thanks," appreciative of the comforting words, regardless of whether Grenn truly believed him.

The conversation ended. Kibure leaned back against the bars of his cage, afraid to return to sleep and the possibility of another nightmare. In the end, he was too tired to resist sleep's beckoning arms. A dreamless slumber overtook him, and the barge continued upriver into the heart of the dry desert wilderness that was the Angolian southwest.

Kibure wished to tether his mind to the world of sleep, but a sense of momentary weightlessness as his cage swayed from one side to the other caused him to stir. He slowly opened his eyes. When he focused he saw Sindri, but she was below him.

"What in the—"

Kibure oriented himself and noticed the shoulders of men beneath both sides of his cage.

"Good news!" said Sindri excitedly. "I've convinced Zagreb to have you relocated." She smiled wide. "We'll be seeing much more of each other, and I'll not have to guard my tongue about your—disposition." She glanced in the direction of the three other slaves just as the cage disappeared beyond their sight.

"Your musco is ever the paranoid one and insisted I not discuss your"—she paused a moment, her lips fumbling with the beginnings of several sounds before settling on—"your unusual nature in the presence of others, slaves or not. Not that you couldn't just as easily freely discuss your—*talents* with them, anyhow."

She clapped her hands. "Now I'll be able to visit you without guarding my tongue. Isn't that great?"

Kibure had come fully out of his stupor. "No."

Sindri tilted her head in question, but her smile could not be dissuaded.

Kibure continued, "I like the company of the other slaves." Then in a more pleading tone, he added, "Please don't do this."

Sindri smiled coolly. "It's for your own safety, Kibure. And we'll make far more progress this way."

Kibure felt panic rising at the thought of spending the coming weeks all alone but for Sindri's company, especially after finally beginning to enjoy the company of the other slaves. He almost considered them friends, the first human friends he'd ever had. "No! I don't want to go. Please let me stay!" He knew it was foolish, futile even, but he ignored reality. He threw his body against the bars to one side of the cage. The man on that side lost his grip, causing the entire cage to topple over. A shout of pain resulted, and Kibure grunted as his head bounced off the bars. He tried to right himself just as the cage was tipped back up, causing him to fall to the other side.

Then it struck him. Not a physical blow—he would have preferred that. Instead his entire upper body careened into the back of the cage. He attempted another plea, but found that he could not move his lips. He was completely and utterly paralyzed, rigid up against the metal bars. Sindri was using her magic against him! Anger replaced fear. Kibure strained against her power with all of his might. *Come on!* He tried to find that same supernatural ability he had used before. *Come on! Where is my blasted power now? Come on!* It was like trying to swat a fly that he couldn't see. He remained motionless and silent as his cage was carried to the second level of the vessel, just outside of Sindri's quarters.

Sindri sent the two men away, then bent down and grabbed the bars opposite Kibure's helpless form, still held by her mystic power. Her face contorted into a rictus smile as she spoke. "In spite of my fall from the Kleról, I've more than mastered what power I *can* summon. I could best nearly any Klerósi priest should the need arise, let alone a tazamine who doesn't even know how to summon his power. Do not test me further."

Then, as if days had passed and tempers cooled, her voice took on a light, melodious tone. "Oh my, but I've digressed. What was I going to say before your foolishness took us off course? Ah yes, I'd like for our relationship to be one of mutual benefit. However, if this is to work, it is imperative that *you* do *your* part."

She shook her head gently as if remembering some great tragedy. "You know, I really don't like causing you discomfort, but if you leave me no other choice, I will do as I must."

Sindri released whatever magic had been holding him. Kibure sagged forward before his muscles realized they could again be used to hold him upright.

"I hope our next conversation is much more pleasant. You've much to tell me of your dream."

Kibure swallowed hard, still astonished at what the woman had been able to do on a whim. He'd seen the seekers of the Kleról work some magic when they came to test each of the slaves, but they had strained in their work, focusing all their attention on what they did. This woman, in contrast, had performed the magic as if she were deciding to turn her gaze from one item to another in the midst of a boring conversation. Her stare reminded him that she had asked a question. *I should answer before she pins me back against the cage.* "Yes—yes, of course. I will tell you anything you ask." He tried to sound convincing.

*Can I, though?* He would certainly have to tell her more than he had thus far; but what could he afford to disclose? He wasn't exactly sure what he knew in the first place. He did not understand his recurring nightmares, of that he was certain. He was also certain that he did not trust this woman with his secrets. They were simply too intimate, too personal for someone like Sindri to have her nose in. But he had to tell her *something*. Would she know if he held back? There was another possibility worth considering. What if Sindri could shed new light on the meaning of the dreams? She did seem to have a great deal of knowledge and was surely versed in the use of magic. He shuddered at the thought of telling her. *No. No way. She cannot be trusted.*

He argued with himself for the rest of the day. Finally, as dusk settled on the land, Kibure was distracted by the sight of a growing number of huts and shacks. Despite losing its vivid color to the disappearing sun, the developing scenery was much more than Kibure could have imagined. Huts became buildings, and buildings became a village. And the village did not appear to end; the buildings continued to grow in size. The rooftops divided the last beams of light as they streamed through to Kibure's eyes. Shadows grew deeper and darker by the minute, further defined by their contrast with the glowing western sky. This had to be one of those megacities, called sires. Grenn had said there were only five such cities in all of the Lugienese Empire, including their destination, Sire Trinkanen.

As the sunlight faded, the city took on a texture like that of the sponges they occasionally used for cleaning, though the color was different; an array of oranges, yellows, and reds punctuated by deep pockets of shadowed darkness. His eyes were overwhelmed by the beauty he beheld. *At least I'll die having seen something beyond the inside of Zagreb's estate.*

To Kibure, the city looked like the cooling embers of a fire. Grenn's sad eyes had spoken volumes when asked to describe these cities. Kibure wondered how much it had hurt the man to be condemned after a life of freedom. He pitied Grenn's lifetime of experiences, for he realized that Grenn knew just what he'd given up, while Kibure and the others could only wonder at the feeling of true freedom.

Kibure finally faded into sleep just as the glow of the city faded in the distance, the faint sound of the barge cutting through the water and the cool night breeze setting his mind at ease.

## CHAPTER 17

# GROBENNAR

JAWEEN'S VOICE TRICKLED INTO GROBENNAR'S mind. *"Oh, good. You're not dead. I grew worried I would have to find a new companion. You are by far my favorite in at least a millennium."*

Grobennar groaned. His—everything hurt.

Rajuban's voice intruded. "I'm told that the pain fades within a few days. I brought you some tea, though I'm afraid it has cooled."

Rajuban had some nerve, Grobennar thought. Gloating after his recent victory should have been beyond one of the priesthood, but then again, this was Rajuban. He continued, "The God-king and I thought it best to give you a few days to heal before being plunged into the task of vanquishing this agent of the Dark One."

Grobennar's vision cleared just in time to catch the man's sinister smile, the corners of his cheeks extending toward his ears. He peered down, an intense loathing evident in the inferno that lay behind his eyes.

"You have crossed a line this time, Raj. I will not forget this."

The man placed a hand upon his chest. "You wound me, old friend. I have given you a great gift! Much glory will become of your ability to locate and dispose of the enemy of evil."

Grobennar swung his legs to the side of the bed and winced as he tried to stand. Nausea floated through him like a door left open to the cold of winter. He staggered then sat back down.

"I would remain here in the infirmary for at least another day, *Fatu Kazi*."

Grobennar tried a basic spell of healing, but this only served to increase the pain. He cringed.

"Oh, you didn't try to heal yourself, did you? Yeah, the thing about the spell we cast is, it affects the part of the mind where magic is channeled. Until that heals, you'll be unable to use the powers of Klerós. No need to worry; I have Magog's ear. I'll ensure that he continues to receive sound counsel in your absence."

Rajuban rose to his feet and left the room, his lithe swagger providing just one more reason for Grobennar to hate the man.

"I am beginning to consider your suggestion that we kill that man, Jaween."

*"I have long held that you should follow every suggestion of mine."*

"Well, for the time being, how about you go ahead and heal me through the link so I can get on with planning this quest to find and destroy the enemy."

Jaween communicated something akin to a sigh, then said, *"Very well."*

## CHAPTER 18

# AYNWARD

KUERTON STOPPED. "AH YES, HERE we are, the best place to meal on this side of the city." He tilted his head slightly and raised the pitch of his voice. "Though some would argue for the Cladgrab just north of here. You'll have to decide for yourselves. For now, take my word that this is the best place to ease your belly and mind while in Brinkwell."

Dolme pulled at Aynward's shirt. "Mark this place in your mind."

The seriousness in this tone startled Aynward.

"Few things are more important than knowing the location of a good meal."

Aynward rolled his eyes and let out a sigh. *I need to find a good tavern.*

The prince nodded his understanding, and Dolme removed his stern gaze. He had a well-known love for food despite his fit frame. Aynward reluctantly followed Dolme toward a large building adorned with a brightly painted sign featuring two foaming mugs laid upon a shield of green and two hammers painted on opposite corners. The sign read "Hammerale's." The building was well kept with a wooden porch and second- and third-floor balconies, which were commonplace in the city. The paint on the rest of the building was light brown with a shine that indicated it had been recently refinished.

Kuerton took them to a side door of an old shabby-looking building with no windows or signs. They took a flight of stairs down to a belowground walkway made of stone, turned down two hallways, and returned to the surface via a winding staircase. They ascended to a room outfitted with twenty booths capable of seating up to six people each. The room was completely open, with a raised platform at its center. Aynward's gaze drifted up to see second- and third-story seating along the perimeter. He scanned the room in its entirety, then did so again when he noted that there was no visible kitchen.

He turned to Kuerton. "Um . . . this is great, but where's the kitchen?"

Kuerten nodded to a woman who emerged from a different descending stairwell he'd not noticed. "This room is strictly for dining and the enjoyment of performances. Hammerale owns the adjacent building, as well. Those stairs lead down a corridor that tunnels across the alley to the kitchen." He made an exaggerated gesture of sniffing the air, which was surprisingly rich with the scent of cooking food. "They piped in vents so the aromas still make their way in here. True genius, I tell you."

They were escorted to a booth on the first floor near the stage. Aynward didn't know what to order, and reluctantly took Kuerten's advice of eggs over bread. He'd only had egg once before and couldn't remember if he'd liked it. Poultry was regarded as a poor man's food in the Kingdom, but Kuerton assured him that it was all the rave here in the Isles.

Movement to his right caught Aynward's eye and he glanced over to see a woman in a gray cloak standing on the stage. She was ghostly white, with dark silky hair and small delicate features. Although she didn't speak loudly, her voice carried well, and at a smooth, constant level.

"Blessed are you this evening to see the *Fall of the Dordron*. Prepare your hearts for a story of love, betrayal, and redemption. We will begin shortly." She spun and the cloak billowed as she escaped down yet another previously unnoticed stairwell hidden next to the platform.

Kuerton rolled his eyes and let out a low-pitched sigh that seemed contrary to his upbeat nature.

"Something the matter?" asked Dolme.

He shook his head. "Well, it's just the troupe performing tonight. They're relatively new to the city and not exactly Brinkwell's finest. No idea how they managed to get themselves booked here. Quite regrettable. In fact, if you'd like, I can find us another place to dine for the evening." Kuerton looked at Aynward questioningly.

Aynward didn't care either way about the performance. The rumble in his stomach reminded him of how much he craved something, anything besides the salted fish and porridge from the ship, and he was not about to postpone that again for something as trivial as a performance troupe.

"This place is fine. The show can't possibly be bad enough to warrant any further delay. I'm famished!" Then in an attempt to remove any argument, he added, "Plus, I'm curious about the dordron. Is this story about the species of giant bird or some lesser-known nation of people of the same name?"

His friends had been correct in their statements about his lack of effort in school, but they had also been correct in stating that he made a habit of *knowing things,* and the title of the story puzzled him, and therefore intrigued him.

Kuerton looked up uninterestedly and replied, "Who can say?"

His disappointment at the decision to remain was evident in his response, along with the newly acquired sag to his shoulders. He had gone from a vibrant grape to a dried-up raisin in a matter of seconds.

Drinks arrived, and this reduced the severity of the plump man's frown. Kuerton was still solemn but he did engage in further conversation, if light and meaningless in nature. After a few minutes, he said to Aynward, "If you'd like, I could tell you a bit more of these creatures before the show begins."

Aynward nodded eagerly, since his knowledge of dordrons was limited to the most rudimentary of facts.

Kuerton smiled, reinvigorated at having a task again. "The dordron is a bird similar in nature to the eagle, which I'm sure you're familiar with, but at equal size to your Lumáles, and just as smart, according to some sources. They're just more stubborn."

Aynward's eyes widened, then narrowed in suspicion at that statement, for Lumáles were known to garner intelligence dwarfing even that of horses.

He continued, "Unlike your Kingdom Lumáles, who willingly associate with humans, dordrons want as little to do with humans as possible."

Aynward knew the falsehood in that statement. Lumáles were not willing servants of the Kingdom, but had been bound to service through centuries-old magic, or so the legends went, and were still used almost exclusively for war of the gravest nature. He remained silent, and nodded for Kuerton to continue.

"They feed almost entirely on fish taken from the sea, and are very rarely seen by humans in spite of their size."

Aynward was about to interrupt with a question about that when a voice cut through all the sounds. Its clarity and volume were curiously loud as it flowed from the center of the room. Aynward's gaze shifted to the woman, who was now center stage, arms outstretched. She wore a gray cloak despite the evening's warmth. The cloak was plain, excepting the symbol stitched onto the left chest. Aynward guessed it was the mark of her guild or troupe. He squinted as he tried to make it out. It appeared to be an open scroll with a symbol in the middle. He was too far away to make out anything more.

In a deep and heavily accented voice, she began, "Long, long ago, in the once fertile lands of southern Drogen"—she swept a hand through the air, spinning a full circle to include all the patrons in her story—"begins a story lost to most." She nodded confidently. "Lost even to many of the most well-read scholars of the modern world. But I come here tonight to shed light on the truth about the fall of the dordron."

She paused just long enough for people to recall what it was that had been described earlier in the day. "We begin with the tale of two children and two tribes. The first is that of the tribe Luguinden, one of the few remaining of the once strong confederation of Luguinden people. Most people know of this tribe, victor of the centuries-long Warring Tribes Period of southern Drogen. Yes?"

A rhetorical question, but many in the room nodded. Aynward was familiar with this history and followed along intently, curious about the deviation the story would likely take.

"Most know of the Lugien flight east, later to form the Lugienese Empire; the Lothlem flight north, leading to a series of wars between the Scritlandians; and eventually the birth of the Dowen kingdom." She took the listeners through the migrations of the five tribes until only one remained in southern Drogen, the Luguinden, whose ancestors still resided there, a splinter of what they once were.

She crouched, and her voice dropped to a soft yet audible whisper. "The story of the Qassem tribe and the fall of the dordron is known only to a scarce number. So erased from history was their demise that few have even heard the name."

This grabbed Aynward's attention. The know-it-all in him hated to be ignorant of anything, regardless of its triviality. Truth be told, he enjoyed knowing odd, frivolous details that others didn't. This allegedly "useless" knowledge came in handy more often than anyone besides his own pride would ever openly recognize.

"The Qassem tribe dates back to the third millennium of the chaos years, a golden age in Luguinden history nearly eight thousand years in antiquity. A tale so painful and cruel it's been spoken of only in whispers since.

"It centers on the birth of two children born to Calnaki, the king of the Qassem, a tribe of greater might at the time than even the Luguinden. These children were born of the same womb, twins as some call it, but male and female. This blessing called for great celebration, and the entire tribe came together in prayer and thanksgiving.

"At the height of this celebration, their mother prayed publicly to Tequen, the maker of life, requesting gifts worthy of both children. Tequen responded by blessing each child with a gift of their own.

"To the male heir named Dardrin came the gift of one hundred dordron, a new species made to obey him. The dordron would be creatures of great might and aid him in conquering all enemies. Conquest became Dardrin's goal.

"His sister Lumalia's gift was that of the like-named Lumáles. They were magical creatures of beauty and elegance, but were also meant to protect her from harm.

"As the siblings grew into adulthood, Dardrin nurtured goals of conquest and the destruction of enemy clans. With the power the dordron lent him, none dared stand against him and the Qassem tribe grew even stronger.

"Lumalia, conversely, sought out friendship and affection otherwise unknown to her. While it was expected that she and Dardrin would marry, Lumalia desired nothing more than someone with whom she could speak and who would enjoy her company, as her brother never did.

"So while her brother flew about consolidating power for himself, Lumalia searched for companionship. She was rewarded with a Luguinden boy named Stennen. For more than a year, she frequented their lands. Meanwhile, Dardrin demanded that she remain at his side for the conception of their own heir, an act that would officially legitimize their marriage. While she was willing to be Dardrin's wife and bear his children, her heart continued to reach back to Stennen.

"One day she left Dardrin to seek Stennen's company. When Dardrin discovered what she had done, his rage could not be quelled. In his anger, he brought with him the armies of the Qassem and his fleet of dordron, which he unleashed upon the Luguinden.

"Lumalia pleaded with Dardrin to forgive her and spare the Luguinden people, but this only fueled his lust for destruction. When she discovered his plan to kill every Luguinden man and enslave the rest, she raced to protect them, employing her Lumáles. When she arrived, she found Dardrin standing over the slain body of Stennen, a spear piercing his neck."

The storyteller was either moved by the tale or else good at faking it, because when she turned to face Aynward's table, tears streaked her cheeks. Then her expression shifted into a demonic scowl, and her voice turned gravelly. "Lumalia shouted to her brother from atop her most cherished Lumále named Strayben. 'My wrath will swallow all that you've achieved. I will strike down all that you've made of our people, and vanquish it from memory. I will not rest until your very name is but a forgotten whisper.'

"And so began a campaign marked by the utter destruction of people like nothing known to the world before. Strayben and the other Lumáles turned from beasts of beauty to bringers of death. Magic formerly used to create awe and pleasure was used to stun and confuse their enemies before the killing blows.

"For the next seven years, a brutal battle raged, and one by one, the other tribes who had been brought under Qassem control rebelled, putting Dardrin and a handful of Qassem survivors on the run. Their final battle became a rout while Dardrin attempted to escape north. He was surrounded and captured. It was there that Lumalia could have ended him—and the dordron—for good, but in that moment, she felt a pang of compassion for the beasts, which had only acted in accordance with their master's will.

"And so the fall of her brother Dardrin led to the exile of his beasts. All surviving dordrons were cast out from the lands of Drogen, a ward placed upon all those remaining and their descendants, while Dardrin and his surviving human followers were put to the sword. From that day forth, the dordron have been forbidden to fly the skies above Drogen, and the leash Dardrin held over their kind was severed, never again to be remade."

She stopped speaking, and bowed. A gentle applause followed, and a few patrons threw coins to the stage, but the woman fled the room, her face downcast in apparent regret.

Aynward wasn't sure if this was just part of the act or true feelings of remorse for the outcast dordron. The two seemed to bleed together. This gave the skeptic in him pause. Could this be more than just a story? It had seemed very real as she spoke it, yet some part of his mind urged caution and whispered words like "folktale." Then again, his teachers, Dolme among them, had always stressed the notion that every story has roots in the truth. He wondered just how much of the story was only that—a story—and how much was truth.

He had been told as a child that the Lumáles employed magic, and were obedient to his family by means of a magical bond made thousands of years ago, but he didn't exactly understand how that worked, if it was true at all. He'd never even seen one of these Lumáles up close. "You'll never have need of them, as you'll never be king," his father had argued. In any event, if this Lumalia woman had been Luguinden, how did the line of Dowe come to control the only remaining Lumáles left in the known world?

The story said that Grojen Dowe, the founder of the royal line of Dowe, had prayed to the Creator Tecuix for help in his rebellion against the Lothlem. Aided by Scritlandian forces, and the gift of the Lumáles from Tecuix himself, he'd been able to defeat the overlords, scattering them to the four winds.

Aynward decided that perhaps both stories were fraudulent.

His thoughts were cut short by the arrival of their meal. A look over at Dolme shoveling meat into his mouth reminded Aynward of a much more pressing concern: revenge. And while he didn't have a plan, exactly, he imagined various end points to these unthought-of schemes. He pictured himself towering over a duped, defeated, and tied-up Dolme. In this vision, Aynward cackled as he dished out sarcastic regurgitations of speeches Dolme had given about the consequences of his actions, and Dolme's face was finally one of remorse.

One of these speeches in his mind was cut short by Kuerten.

"You look to be rather enjoying the local cuisine, Annard, this is so?"

Aynward took a second to play back the question in his mind before answering, so far was he into his own imaginings. He glanced over at Dolme and couldn't help but smile the widest, most sinister smile he'd felt cross his face in months.

"Oh yes, quite so. Quite so, indeed. Savoring every bite."

## CHAPTER 19

# KIBURE

KIBURE ROSE FROM HIS SLUMBER to the first rays of sun. As his eyes adjusted, he gasped. He had spotted—or thought he had spotted—a familiar shape amid the shadows of the cargo. When he glanced back a moment later, he saw nothing. *So I'm losing my sanity now, too.*

Then came Sindri's voice. "It's time to talk, my friend."

The sunlight cast shadows on the woman's deep-set eyes and curved nose. This only accentuated the baleful grin of a woman ready to acquire information, one way or another.

Kibure sat cross-legged in the early light of morning. Directly opposite the bars sat Sindri, her position mirroring that of the young slave. "So what have you to say of your demon dreams?"

Kibure had to decide that moment how much to reveal of his nightmare.

*I need more time to think.* "I'm sorry for not mentioning my nightmares before. I didn't think they were important. They are new to me, and I remember very little of them afterward, anyway. It's nothing to do with magic—I don't think."

"The magic radiating from you during such events suggests otherwise. Why don't you let me be the judge of things related to magic? You just tell me everything you can about these nightmares." There was no mirth in her voice, just determination.

"As you command," replied Kibure, a habit of subservience.

*All right. I have to tell her something.* Hesitantly, he began, "Well, I have had these—these dreams. Three times. Only they aren't like other dreams . . ."

Kibure divulged everything of his nightmare except the voice. He still needed to digest the words of that voice himself.

He silently recalled, *"I risk much in coming to these dark lands, even in dream. You too must keep from this place if you hope to survive. We will wait for your foretold arrival to the east in the—"*

Sindri had stolen him away from the dream before the message had been completed. Either way, there was someone, or something, that apparently believed his nightmares somehow placed him in danger, and also expected him to arrive *somewhere*—that is, if he survived whatever danger lurked in these lands.

Sindri sprinkled questions where Kibure's telling was too vague.

"How often do these dreams occur? Tell me more of what you saw while there . . ."

Kibure answered them as best he could.

When he had finished, Sindri's attentive smile became an angry frown. "So that's it? This meaningless dream was the cause of the magic I felt radiating from you while you slept? There is nothing further you would like to add?"

Kibure's body tensed at the change in Sindri's ordinarily calm voice. Then pain shot through his body, pain comparable to that of the whip but worse, for it bore much deeper than the surface of his skin. The intensity of the woman's penetrating eyes told a story of rage, perhaps even murder. Sindri made Zagreb's anger at Rave appear a mere annoyance. And still the pain increased. The air around Kibure squeezed his chest until he could no longer take in air. *I'm going to suffocate. I'm going to die!*

## CHAPTER 20

# GROBENNAR

GROBENNAR WALKED THE LONG HALLWAY leading into the Grand Palace Kleról, where he would be most likely to find who he was looking for.

*"So, what's the plan? Are we going to whack Rajuban once and for all?"*

Grobennar stopped, hoping to put the issue to rest before he entered a place filled with *real* people. He turned to make sure no one was behind before he said, "You do recall that even with the healing, I can't yet wield Klerós's power without feeling like I've been poisoned. That notwithstanding, I still can't just kill the man. He's a member of the High Council! How about I focus my attention on somehow finding and slaying this agent of the Dark Lord?"

*"Yes, yes. You humans and your love affair with the sanctity of true-blood life. It's exhausting. I don't know how you endure such a restrictive existence."*

"Such a mystery, that millennia-old ban on the possession of spirit-charms. I just can't imagine what could possibly have been so dangerous about having powerfully persuasive companions with no scruples about indiscriminate killing."

*"I know, right—wait, you're doing that sarcasm thing again, aren't you? I'll have you know, the Karth-Kleról War was all a big misunderstanding. We just wound up stuck with the blame. Easy targets we were. Truth of it is—"*

"Yes, yes. You've explained this all before. I'm not sending you into the vault any time soon. But you need to let me get on with finding someone capable of assembling a team skillful enough to help me succeed in my task!"

Grobennar resumed his walk, attention back on his newest assignment.

Finding and slaying this being would be no easy feat. Grobennar wasn't even certain that the spell Magog had performed had actually succeeded. Thus far, whatever *sensitivities* Magog had given Grobennar had been either nonexistent or masked by the initial pain of the spell itself. But Grobennar wondered if his whole thing may have been no more than a ploy to temporarily incapacitate Rajuban's biggest rival, while simultaneously providing an impossible task for Grobennar to fail, thereby losing favor with the God-king.

To make matters worse, Jaween's healing had, for some reason, had no impact on the part of the mind used to channel Klerós's power. Whatever Rajuban's spell had done to his mind would have to heal naturally. Being unable to wield that which had been so integral to him since a young age left him feeling sightless and hollow. He imagined that must be what it was like to lose one's eyes, or become paralyzed. *This is only temporary,* he reminded himself.

He entered the vast chambers of the Klerós, an enclosed amphitheater built to hold up to five hundred mazis, the High Council. There was not currently a session in progress, but Grobennar had called for an emergency meeting, where he would announce the preparations for the mobilization of their armies. It would take weeks to gather the troops before launching their first attacks.

Grobennar scanned the faces in the room. He was more than an hour early, but if he knew Paranja, she would be—*there!*

He wound his way between clusters of red-robed figures until coming to a stop a few paces shy of the woman. He took a moment to appraise what he could of the middle-aged woman's figure while he considered what to say. The fit of the priestly robes was modest, but she was curvaceous, and the robes could only hide so much. Grobennar shook his head and cursed himself—that was not why he sought her out. He stepped into her line of sight.

"Paranja, might I have a word?"

Her eyes lit up as she recognized him. She allowed a smile, then bowed. "Why of course, Fatu Kazi."

"What I am about to say is of a sensitive nature. Please follow me." Grobennar gestured toward the door behind the podium, the focal point of the amphitheater, center stage. He directed her into a series of chambers until they were far from any who might search for gossip or scheme. He closed the door.

Paranja let out a breath, then exclaimed, "Roaming evil! You look like you just broke out of prison. Whatever this is about, it must not be good."

Grobennar decided to get right to the point. "I've been assigned to seek out *the* agent of the Dark Lord." Paranja's eyes went wide, but Grobennar held up a hand to stave off her response. "Rajuban, curse him, convinced our God-king to cast a spell on me that will allow me a heightened sense of the use of dark magic. As this agent of the Dark Lord gets closer, Magog believes I'll be capable of discerning his general direction. I am to track him down and destroy him."

Paranja's expression turned contemplative. "You're putting together a team."

Grobennar nodded. "Actually, I was hoping that perhaps you would."

She shook her head, then laughed. "Never a conversation with you that doesn't involve some sort of business favor, is there?"

"I—"

"It's fine. You are what you are, and you're probably right to ask me. You spend more time talking to yourself than others, and while you could order a team, you'll be better off with capable volunteers."

*Talking to myself?* Grobennar cringed.

"How many?" Paranja asked. "And when do we depart?"

"I—not sure. I haven't yet sensed anything. I'm still recovering from the spell, but they should be ready to move on a moment's notice should the opportunity arise. Ten should suffice. Too many would just create chaos."

"Will there be anything else?" Paranja gave him a look, but he had never been particularly good at interpreting social cues. He knew there was some deeper meaning hidden within her expression, but it was as much a mystery to him as Rajuban's spell.

"Uh—no. I—need to prepare to speak to the Council. Thank you, Fatu Mazi, Paranja. I—uh—appreciate you."

She put a hand on his shoulder, then rolled her eyes and turned. As she opened the door, she said, "I'll have a list of names sent to you by the end of the day, Fatu Kazi." She smiled, shook her head, and departed.

Such a strange woman; they all were, Grobennar reflected.

*"I'm no human, but if I didn't know better, I'd say that Paranja has designs to—"*

"You don't know better. Now hush so I can think! I do actually need to prepare a speech!"

## CHAPTER 21

# KIBURE

KIBURE WOKE SLOWLY. HIS BODY ached and his mind felt like someone had dropped a crate of drogal upon it, then repeated the process a dozen times over. He stretched, or tried to. His head hit the metal bars and the horror of his circumstances returned.

"Welcome back, my little tazamine. Are you feeling more—cooperative after the induced nap?"

The last thing he remembered was overwhelming pain. He must have passed out under the pressure of her magical torture. Kibure gripped the metal that restricted his coming and going. What could he say? He had told her . . . *almost* everything.

Sindri let out an exaggerated breath of disappointment, then spoke with disturbing calm. "I told you before, I do not wish to cause you harm, but you *have* to tell me the truth, and I do not believe that you have done so—not *all* of it, anyhow. You will tell me the rest, or what you've felt thus far will seem like a mere prick of a needle."

Kibure quivered. But if he revealed that he had indeed held something back, there was no telling how much the woman would expect him to reveal in the end. His trust would be shattered and Sindri would likely continue to demand more, constantly believing more existed even when it finally did run out. And yet: *I have to give her something. She'll kill me if I don't give her something more.*

He considered the words in the nightmare once again. *"You should keep from the world of dream while so close to the darkness . . . Your soul is not safe, here or in the waking world."*

He wondered: *What is this darkness the voice spoke of . . . or, rather, who?* He looked up and met Sindri's glare. Any thoughts of revealing these words to her died right then and there. He couldn't. She could be the very darkness described in the nightmare, for all he knew.

His head sagged in anticipation of the torment to come. This was not unlike his experience as a slave. He whispered, "I have nothing further to reveal. Do with me as you wish." Then he closed his eyes and waited for the barrage of mystic needles; his shaky voice having betrayed the calm he attempted to communicate.

He felt her gathering magical strength, the tingling sensation rising in the air like a cool wind. *Here it comes . . .*

"Very well." The magic disappeared in an instant, unused. "But if I find that you have lied to me about his, the cost will be great."

Kibure finally dared glance up, to see Sindri inspecting him closely. She appeared both furious and content at the same time. But her stare finally relented. She stood and stalked away. Then Kibure released the breath he hadn't realized he had been holding.

His thoughts ran wild as Sindri retreated beyond sight. His emotions became converging winds. His initial relief at appeasing Sindri's interrogation was replaced by the need to look inward once more. Why had he suddenly been able to wield magic? Why did he have these nightmares? What had the voice meant by *darkness*? What did the voice mean that they would await his arrival . . . somewhere? None of it fit together.

The message certainly suggested that he was in grave danger. But danger from whom, or what? A small part of him wished to reenter the dream, and scream at the source of the voice for answers; but by the sounds of it, the voice would not risk coming there again, if indeed it was a place. Yet even the ability to choose when he had one of these nightmares seemed subject to chance. Kibure could no more force himself to have one of those dreams than he could force his way out of his metal cage.

With tears rolling down his cheeks, Kibure allowed his exhaustion to take over and his worries melted into sleep. They would still be there when he woke, but until then, the nothingness of a dreamless sleep would be a welcome reprieve. But sleep defied him, so Kibure stared out at the passing scenery.

The landscape rippled with small huts as the ship approached the outskirts of what Sindri had said would be the capital city, Sire Karth. This placed them just short of the halfway mark on their journey to the markets if what Grenn had told him was true. The immensity of the city grew with every passing minute. Kibure observed several structures rising into the sky like tall, branchless trees, reaching for the clouds. He studied the closest such building. The base twisted upward like the vines Zagreb grew in one corner of his estate, but these grew in perfect unison, and at the top, barely visible, was the shape of a four-sided star. These were Kleróls. There were none made of this design in Jarquin, but Grenn had described their like, and the sigil of the four-sided star was found on the robes of every priest he had met. Kibure shivered as he considered the countless spires shooting up from the vast city, and the multitude of dangerous cleric wizards inside.

## CHAPTER 22

# GROBENNAR

"QUITE A MOVING SPEECH."

"Really? I thought it went rather poorly."

"Well, yes." Paranja allowed a warm smile to sweep across her face before it returned to its ordinarily smug position. "But it went well, for you. Perhaps one of your best."

"Ah," replied Grobennar. "Speaking of, have you given any moving oratory performances of your own regarding our team?"

Paranja looked up to the flora growing around the bench, upon which they sat in the palace gardens. "As a matter of fact, yes."

When it became apparent that she was not going to elaborate, he said, "And?"

She gave him a look that rested somewhere safely between angry and confused. Then she said, "What do you think? You have a team of the best clerics suited to the task, ten of them as requested."

"I suppose I should have expected nothing less from you."

"And that might be one of the most intelligent things you have ever said. My, my, you're on quite the roll here lately. Pray your success doesn't wane before we complete the task at hand."

"Your humility is commendable, Paranja."

She sighed. "And yet I rarely receive commends."

"Perhaps that has something to do with your incorrigibility."

"Hmm—perhaps."

Grobennar's stomach growled, reminding him that he had been many hours without food. He stood. "I need a hot meal. Care to join me in the dining hall?"

Paranja fluttered her eyelashes, then rose to join him. "I would be delighted."

The two wound their way silently through the maze of well-kept trees, shrubs, and flowers that comprised the palace gardens, located within the central courtyard. Small buildings appeared every fifty paces along the central walk, mini Kleróls for prayers of a more personal nature.

Grobennar opened his mouth to comment on the ivy that had consumed the better part of the mini Kleról up ahead, a peeve of his. He had only the first syllable formed in his mouth when pain stifled the rest. A wave of powerful energy struck as suddenly as an assassin from hiding. Grobennar's knees buckled and his hands went to his temples as he fell to the floor. He could hear Paranja's voice but she seemed leagues away, her shouts like cold winds hiding behind a well-caulked window.

Grobennar reverted back to one of the first breathing exercises he had learned in the Kleról, allowing the volume and timing of each inhalation to return to normal. As his world righted, he realized that it wasn't so much the pain that was responsible for his disorientation; it was the sensation of powerful, alien magic. Realizing he had assumed the fetal position upon the floor, he worked his muscles to regain a position of dignity, and made it to his knees. At that point he began to make sense of what he felt.

He isolated the alien sensation to one part of his awareness, while the rest of his mind was restored to use. This done, the memory of his principal objective returned: track and kill this agent of the Dark Lord.

Paranja's voice continued to persist, but she may as well have been in another city. He had a job to do. Nothing—no one else mattered right now. With his mind focused on the magical sensation, he grabbed hold of it. He felt a throbbing in his head, not dissimilar to when he had been trained to seek out the magic of a tazamine, only this was a different magic altogether, and far stronger. To his dismay, he realized the source of this magic was still far away—across the city. The being must be powerful indeed to be felt at such a distance.

As he tightened his grip on the sensation of twisted magic, he allowed his mind to traverse the waves of energy. He felt a tug, a faint pressure in his forehead that pointed him in a general direction. He sent tendrils of his consciousness along the lines of power, and they went. Whether because of the volume of magic being used, or the sensitivity to magic granted by the spell casting, Grobennar was able to discern the shape of the world through a magical awareness. Never before had he experienced such a thing, at least not without taking over the mind of another living creature. This was—incredible! *And* unnerving all at once. He felt the impressions of buildings, and even people, yet he was unable to focus on any single object. It was like walking through a thick fog with only the slightest sense of what lay beyond. He followed the trail of power northwest toward the river until it suddenly winked out.

The real world blinked back into being and Grobennar gasped. He felt hands gripping his arm and he instinctively ripped free. A cry rang out as the attacker crashed to the ground. Only then did he recognize the voice—Paranja.

He shook himself free of the haze, and helped her up. She yanked herself free. "What the hell is wrong with you?"

"I—I'm sorry." He took a step backward as she found her own footing. "He's here in this city!"

Paranja narrowed her eyes. "What are you talking—"

Understanding formed in her expression.

"Gather the team," commanded Grobennar. "Meet in front of the palace gate within the hour."

"Yes, Fatu Kazi. It will be done."

Grobennar turned without another word, his destination now in the opposite direction.

*"This is beginning to get exciting."*

Grobennar scowled.

Hours later, and still not fully recovered, Grobennar cursed as nausea attempted to take him. Wielding Klerós's magic still caused Grobennar significant pain, but with his newfound sensitivity to magic, he easily detected the aura put forth by this agent of the Dark Lord with whom Magog was concerned. With his team of powerful clerics organized by Paranja, however, Grobennar had only needed to direct them toward the source of the magic; the rest took care of itself. He smiled in triumph. Capturing the boy had been refreshingly simpler than expected. Grobennar narrowed his eyes as he acknowledged the possibility that Rajuban had been right to encourage them to seek the enemy now, before his powers were fully realized.

The weak slave boy—tazamines were always of the slave race—was being held between two priests, his head slumped in defeat. He had denied any dark nature, any ill intent, but that was to be expected.

Grobennar stood regal, victorious, as Magog approached the enemy wielder. The God-king glanced at Grobennar. "I had expected a more powerful adversary. This one is hardly different from any other tazamine brought before me."

Grobennar frowned, then nodded toward Rajuban, offering a painful admission. "As Rajuban suspected, the Dark Lord's agent was but an infant in his strength." Shrugging, he added, "We could always set him free if you would prefer a greater challenge once he has grown more formidable."

Magog glared at him. For a moment, Grobennar feared he had overstepped once again. Magog's new sense of autonomy was difficult to navigate for one who had previously been in control. The God-king looked back to his quarry, the boy, and stepped forward.

"The Dark Lord was foolish to send you to my seat of power without preparing you for the strength of this great land. I will enjoy transferring your soul into the very strength I will use to conquer the rest of the fallen world. The perfect irony, don't you think?"

The boy pleaded for his life, it was pathetic.

Magog extended a hand, and Grobennar winced as a wave of power filled the room. No matter how many times he witnessed Magog consuming the soul of another, tazamine or not, it was still a disturbing thing to witness.

The boy released a guttural scream of agony. The depths of pain in his shouts caused Grobennar to cover his ears. The boy's skin lost color, and his eyes burned as if Magog had placed hot coals within them. The sound reminded Grobennar of eggs frying on a hot pan. Steam rose as the boy's soul was ripped from his body leaving behind a shell, eyes still smoking and charred. The boy was released by the two priests who had been holding him; he slumped to the ground and all was still.

Magog inhaled deeply, then reached up with a hand and felt above his right eye where a fresh red scale had formed to join the others, glistening with his own beading sweat. He released a loud sigh not unlike what one might expel while stepping into the soothing, warm water of a perfectly prepared bath.

Rajuban broke the silence. "Great days lie before us. Today was but another small taste."

## CHAPTER 23

# AYNWARD

AYNWARD'S FAMILIAL HOSTESS, YOUNGER SISTER to his mother, stood on the porch of a modest, upper-class city dwelling. Her hands were on her hips, and she looked a great deal older than she had five years ago when he'd last seen her. Side by side with her, his mother would look the younger now. Years outside of court must weigh heavier on a person, Aynward thought. He knew she'd run away from her family's ancestral home in Quinson to be with some low-born merchant years ago and rarely attended court as a result. Her scowl was a harsh contrast to her fine, silky black dress, and Aynward just couldn't resist.

He leaned over and whispered to Dolme and Kuerton, "Geeze, good ol' Aunt Melanie looks like a sunbaked turd, set inside of a polished shoe."

Kuerton was momentarily without words. Then he said, "I, uh, hope the tour was to your satisfaction. I should be on my way now. Much to do, much to do! But please call upon me should you have any further needs within the city."

Aynward flourished a hand and tossed a copper piece toward the guide.

He caught it and said, "Many thanks. Good day to you." The plump man smiled, bowed once more, and departed without further comment.

Dolme's jaw had tightened at Aynward's indecorous comment about Aunt Melanie. Sensing that Dolme was soon to begin a spout of scolding, Aynward decided to do his best to postpone. "My dear Aunt Melanie!" he yelled up in an overly friendly voice. "You look—you look resplendent. My, how the years have been kind to you. And the black dress, what is this, honeysilk? If darkness could be made to glow . . ."

Aunt Melanie had been a crass lady five years ago when she'd last visited Salmune, having made some crude if not true comment to one of his uncles; this had become a part of family lore ever since. The disapproval of her decision to run away in her youth had never been forgiven, and crassness was her way of fighting back; either that or she'd reached that ripe age of not caring what others thought. But she was still a woman at heart, and her posture shifted slightly at Aynward's compliment. Her glower became a flat, expressionless stare. It may as well have been a smile. She looked years younger, if only for a moment.

In her nasally voice, she said, "Your belongings arrived . . . hours ago." There was no satisfaction in that voice, and accusation was written on her pinched face.

Suspecting that Dolme would attempt to take hold of the conversation, Aynward quickened his next few steps, then halted to offer a slight bow, which, considering his station as a prince, would mean a lot to anyone familiar with court etiquette. This was no modest gesture of deference, and, therefore, one that Dolme wouldn't dare interrupt.

"My apologies," he said, head still inclined. "Dolme insisted that our guide give us the full tour of local cuisine. I hope you didn't have a warm meal brought up here to meet us." Guessing the answer, he gasped. It was a ridiculous sound coming from him, but she'd only met him once as a boy years earlier so she wouldn't know just how out of character this whole performance was.

"You did, didn't you? Well, if your taste in food is as refined as your taste for decor," he said, gesturing to the flowering planters lining the steps. They were looking a bit dilapidated, but a few were in bloom. "Then I'm sure we'll find our appetites soon enough."

He loped up the four steps to land before their hostess and wrapped his arms around her.

"So glad to see you again, and thank you so much for having us," he said in his best voice of exhausted sincerity.

He held on for a touch longer then released and stepped back. Aunt Melanie looked as if she might just call him out for the fraud that he was, but instead she nodded and said, "Of course, of course. It's a great honor to serve the family. Blah blah blah, nothing like giving an old spinster some purpose."

By then Dolme had ascended the steps to kneel before her. "Indeed, thank you, and our sincerest apologies for keeping you. We're truly grateful for your hospitality."

Her frown returned in full. "Oh, get up. You're the one who wrote me with the urgency of keeping your young prince's identity quiet. You're practically parading it around with all this kneeling crap."

She cleared her throat, and continued before he could respond, "Enough butt kissing. Let's get you two settled in. I'll fetch Gervais to show you to your rooms."

She glared at Dolme as he rose, but when her eyes settled back on Aynward, something close to a genuine smile touched the corners of her mouth. It was subtle, but Aynward knew he'd played a good first hand in a game that might last months, maybe years. He'd need an ally if he was to be afforded the freedom he wanted in order to enjoy himself in this city, and to plan his revenge on Dolme.

His aunt's home was like nothing he'd imagined for a woman of royal relation, even someone as distant as she. Not that he had put much thought into it, but the *humble* residence he'd pictured had included more opulence than this. There were no great pillars out front, no marbled floors, no pool-sized baths, and only one measly servant, a man named Gervais.

He was short and thin, and his youthful face suggested he was perhaps ten years older than Aynward. He escorted them through the foyer of the home and pointed in both directions, "There are stairs located on either side. Mr. Aynward, your room will be on the east side of the home, so you will likely wish to ascend the eastern stairway, while your servant will likely prefer to take the—"

"I'm *NOT* his servant," interrupted Dolme. "I'm his—"

"Of course, of course." Gervais smiled brightly and inclined his head. "You'll find that people here care far less for titles than those of the mainland. Moving on"—he turned on a heel—"we'll climb the east stairs and get Mr. Aynward into his room. He will wish to rest. He does, after all, have his testing tomorrow, and he'll want to be at his best."

Aynward looked at Gervais, then at Dolme, eyes wide in question. Gervais made eye contact but either did not understand the expression or decided to ignore it. He strode toward the stairs.

Aynward hurried to catch up. "What are you talking about—test? I have a test? I haven't even taken a class."

Gervais was halfway up the stairs when he answered, and did so without so much as glancing back. "That is precisely the point, my good sir."

"Huh?"

Gervais stopped and turned. "How is the university supposed to enroll you in classes without first learning what you truly know? My, what a disaster that would be!"

Aynward turned back to Dolme, who was close behind. "Didn't Brinkwell send transcripts of my coursework?"

Dolme started a reply but was cut short by Gervais, who had stopped at the top of the stairs. "Transcripts?" He chuckled. "Forgive me for speaking the simple truth, but transcripts are more often than not a bought and paid for commodity. Transcripts get you in the door, but no school with any integrity would enroll a student solely on some piece of paper, especially papers coming from the son of a royal who thinks his little princeling is a genius."

Aynward fired back, "And just how would you, a mere servant, possess any knowledge of this? Have you seen much of this in your extensive experience scrubbing my aunt's laundry and dishes?"

Gervais was unfazed. "I must confess, it has been a few years, but I spent some time at Brinkwell Commons. To be sure, this is an admittedly less prestigious school than the university to which you've been enrolled, yet even there I met several privileged sons of gentry blood who were without the prerequisite knowledge required for the courses. I put the pieces together after about the third time I was asked to tutor one of them."

Aynward shook his head; he did not like being made the fool, particularly by a servant, especially when his own ignorance was the cause. "But what would the point be in enrolling a student in coursework they're not prepared for?"

Gervais smiled. "The aristocracy here in the Isles is very *different* from that of the mainland. That being said, I suppose I can hardly fault your ignorance on the subject." He gestured with a hand. "Come, you have had a long day and a longer journey. The stairway is no place for even this briefest of explanations."

Aynward followed and rounded the corner at the top to see a hallway dimly lit by four candles set deep within brass sconces outside of each doorway. Natural light flowed into the hall as Gervais opened a door to what would be Aynward's room. *Thank the gods, a window*, said Aynward to himself.

Gervais waited at the door allowing Aynward and Dolme to enter then said from behind, "There are few frills, but we'll make sure you have what you need."

Aynward looked around and saw that the two chests with his belongings had been delivered to rest beside a simple wood-frame bed. There was a matching wooden chair and desk with several candles beside the large window, and two additional sitting chairs in the corners opposite the bed. Gervais motioned for them to sit. The room was a composite of shadows and weak illumination, as the faint beams of sunlight seemed to have responded to the evening's call for an orderly retreat.

Dolme and Aynward sat in the chairs located in the corners while Gervais seated himself in the wooden desk chair. Aynward melted into the comfort of the cushioned chair and sighed quietly in relief at being off his feet again.

Gervais sat upright and crossed his legs, showing no sign that he cared at all to be sitting but for the courtesy of company.

He gave a wry smile. "I'm going to assume a certain baseline understanding of trade and local culture here in an effort to avoid intellectual insult as well as unnecessary long-winded explanation, the hour of day considered. Do stop me if something escapes your comprehension."

Aynward held an eye roll in check. "Yes, of course. Go on."

Gervais folded his hands over his topmost crossed leg. "These pretests are actually a relatively recent development in the university enrollment process. I'm not sure how much you've been taught about the economy of the Isles cities, but this last half century has marked a significant growth in Isles trade as the middlemen between the Angolian and Drogen mainlands. This in turn has allowed for the rise of new merchant families, some of whom have come to rival the wealth of the older names that have ruled for centuries. This has caused a great deal of competition over business contracts here in the Isles.

"And while there might be financial similarities between these two groups of wealthy classes, the gentry have attempted to separate themselves from the others in hopes of a return to their former exclusive prestige. One such tactic involves formal schooling, something many of the newly risen families lack. The aristocracy has come to recognize and respect the reality that the newer merchant class holds an advantage in the invaluable job skills acquired while working alongside parents or relatives in the field. Anyone who themselves works in commerce knows that much of the theoretical knowledge obtained at university pales when compared with the total immersion experience on which many working low-bloods are raised."

Aynward did not care for the suggestion Gervais was making about people born to privileged lives, but there was hardly a break for him to interject.

"Therefore, the last half of this century has seen a pushback from many of the notable families to discredit the rising low-blood working families in another way. They've spent a great deal of money on printed ads to perpetuate the credibility of formal schooling. And they all, without exception, send their little princelings to university so they can have the distinguished graduate badge sewn into their fancy doublets. To a large extent, it has been a success and many believe this contrived fable, shying away from using any contractors who don't hold a *degree*, relevant to the service or not."

Aynward asked, "So why don't these low-bloods just go get the schooling they need in order to keep up?"

Gervais brought a hand to his chin in consideration. "Well, this has happened, *to some extent*, and the universities have expanded, but space is still limited. And if you're the dean of a university with limited seats for enrollment, who would you prefer to offend, a Duke's son or some merchant's child?"

Aynward assumed the question rhetorical and replied, "But if many of these royals are, as you say, so ill prepared for the schooling, but the universities take them anyhow, what's the point of the pretests?"

"Gold! Plain and simple, gold. The universities have become a mixture between a place of learning and a business operating on high profits. They're certainly making a fortune off of the growth in enrollment, but this is compounded by the fact that these students are not ready for the general coursework. The testing allows for the universities to make even more money off of these willing, heavily coined *customers*."

"I don't follow," Aynward said. "I understand that enrolling more students fills the coffers, but how does the testing add to this?"

Gervais put both feet on the ground and leaned forward. "Well, the change in clientele has definitely not changed the demands put forth by the professors. It was the guild of professors, after all, that demanded these tests in the first place. But instead of using the tests as acceptance exams as they wished, they're used to select the courses each student is qualified to take after acceptance."

Gervais must have seen the puzzlement written on Aynward's face, because he had stopped as if done then spoke again to answer the unasked question.

"If you score poorly, you simply must take extra courses before you're able to take the *real* courses. And the professors' guild doesn't mind because the universities now pay students in their later years to teach these prerequisite courses to students who aren't ready."

Aynward paused for a moment then said, "You seem to know quite a bit about the inner workings of the university system."

Gervais smiled and rose to his feet. "I know many things outside of my general realm of expertise, that of scrubbing your aunt's laundry and dishes." Then he winked and moved toward the door. Dolme rose to follow him.

Aynward stood as well and stopped Gervais with one last question. "So which one were you: a quickly risen family or an ancient name trying to justify your significance with a degree?"

Gervais responded with an odd mixture of nonchalance and pride. "My father was a fisherman who did well locally, enough so that he was able to pay my tuition at Brinkwell Commons, though he could only afford one course per semester; it would have taken me many years to graduate."

"So you quit and became my aunt's servant?"

"Not quite. I was determined to take as much time as was necessary to graduate. However, fate smiled on me during my second year when I crossed paths with your beloved aunt here at the bank of the Seducead. I was waiting in line when I recognized that the banker was taking advantage of a poor old lady. She wanted nothing more than to keep her remaining family wealth secure. The scam was well hidden to the untrained ear, but my coursework was primarily commerce based; it was clear to me that she was being cheated. I pulled her out of line amid the teller's protests and explained this to her, then brought her to a different bank to do business, where I negotiated fair terms on her behalf. She was so delighted that she offered me a position on her staff as both a servant and the financial manager of her estate. She also paid for the remainder of my degree and allowed my father, rest his soul, to obtain several loans against her own secured monies, which allowed him to purchase numerous more fishing boats at no interest. He passed a few years back, a proud man with no debt."

Gervais straightened. "Have you any other questions, or may I show your"—he paused, then said smugly—"traveling companion to his room?"

Aynward shook his head.

Gervais pointed to the bed. "You'll notice an extra trunk over there. I've taken the liberty of purchasing a few sets of clothing that may help you assimilate, though that mop of auburn hair still shouts of Kingdom blood."

Aynward hadn't noticed the third trunk sitting beside his own. "So people here will trust my measurements, but not my transcripts." He said it aloud, but it was a petty statement, considering that Gervais had nothing to do with the university's policy. Aynward was still upset at the notion of taking an insultingly unnecessary test the day after he arrived from the most miserable voyage he could have imagined en route to a place he did not wish to be. He forced himself to move his lips from a downward scowl to a position of detached neutrality.

Gervais said, "I'll leave you to your rest. Your testing is scheduled for midmorning, and I'm told that they do not respond well to those who arrive beyond the courtesy of strict punctuality. And I presume you'll wish to eat and"—he sniffed the air—"and wash before we depart. I'll wake you at first light."

## CHAPTER 24

# KIBURE

KIBURE OPENED HIS EYES AND recognized the pale, disquieting silence for what it was: another nightmare.

His heart raced, an instinctive reaction to the warning from the voice he had heard last time. Sindri had also warned about the use of magic. They were drifting through the most populous city in the Empire, one overrun with seekers highly sensitive to the use of magic. And here he was, trapped within a cage within a dream, within a cage. He could not be much more vulnerable than this.

He looked out at the colorless image of the city as it passed slowly, soundlessly by. The barge would continue to move at all hours so long as the moons provided enough light. Kibure hoped they would be out of the city before his nightmares drew the attention of—

A glowing figure appeared along the edge of the canal, too far away for Kibure to make out much detail. But there was no doubt in his mind that this figure stared directly at him. It was eerily silent as Kibure sucked in a breath.

*This is bad. This is very bad.*

*Come on, Sindri.* Kibure looked around for the approaching ripples in his sight that might be Sindri. *Where is she? She should be awake by now, dragging me out of here with her magic!*

He looked back in the direction of the city to see what had become of the glowing figure when it—*he*—materialized just a pace away. Kibure jumped back. To his further shock, he found that he was no longer bound to the cage but was instead standing beside it, facing down the glowing man. The masculinity was undeniable; he was broad of shoulder, thick of chest, and the cheekbones belied a physicality unto themselves. But the glow was by far the most striking feature. The figure almost pulsed with power. Kibure could feel its aura, an inferno of raw energy, of destruction. Kibure suddenly realized that he was in grave danger—this was the darkness he had been warned to avoid.

Then a booming voice spoke into his mind, leaving no room for doubt. "*The Dark Lord is bold to send you to my city.*"

Kibure's mind raced, as did his heart. *Dark Lord? Your city?*

"*He is also a fool to do so. I have power enough to sense your magic from leagues away, and you are not skilled enough to mask it. Did you truly think to catch me unawares as you stumbled through the dream realm to plan your attack?*"

Kibure looked around frantically. *What is this guy talking about? Come on, Sindri, where are you?*

"*Have you nothing to say? No message from the enemy before you are struck down?*" The figure took a step forward toward Kibure.

Not wishing to be any closer to this *being*, Kibure took a step backward. *I wouldn't know how to deliver it even if I had one! This is not good.*

"*Very well.*" The glowing energy inside of the figure coalesced, and Kibure felt a change in the pulsing energy of his adversary. Kibure wasn't certain he could die while within this dream realm, as the entity had called it, but the voice of the woman who had spoken to him previously had indicated significant danger in coming here, not that he had much choice in the matter. Yes, he decided, he was going to die.

Particles of light swirled around the man's hands, forming two long objects—swords, Kibure realized—made entirely of light.

Kibure turned and ran. "*Coward!*" shouted the voice in his head. Kibure did not mind the insult. It was absolutely true. He dashed around the corner and sprinted the length of the barge, only to stagger to a halt when the man popped into being just a few paces in front of him, weapons at the ready.

*How does he do that?*

The figure suddenly streaked toward him. Kibure closed his eyes and lifted his arms in defense. He couldn't watch. *I really am a coward.*

His end did not come. Instead a guttural growl echoed in his mind. "*Arghhhh! You snake! I should have guessed a trick such as this from the Dark One!*"

Kibure opened his eyes and saw the figure staring up. Kibure followed his gaze to see a small glowing object streak through the air. If he didn't know better, he would think it was—

A familiar coo sounded in his mind as the small creature, or at least a manifestation of a raaven, raced toward him. So too did the shape of the enemy.

Then his vision shifted and true sound emerged. It was quiet, but the sound of a gentle breeze, shadowed by his panicked breathing, then the coo of a raaven, though Rave was nowhere to be seen. Kibure was back in his cage, heart thumping, but at this point that meant he was not yet dead and he counted that a good thing, though his worries were far from gone at the memory of what had just occurred.

## CHAPTER 25

# GROBENNAR

GROBENNAR HAD NOT BEEN EXPECTING to sense dark magic so close at hand, not after having just witnessed Magog devour the soul of this Dark Lord's agent. If anything, he expected the Dark Lord to recoil from further such attempts within Magog's city. But there was no mistaking the taint in the magic he felt at the moment. *Either the Dark Lord is very foolish, or*—Grobennar felt concern rise within him. Could that first tazamine have been merely a probing mission? A ploy? A distraction?

Like before, Grobennar tentatively followed the tendrils of magic through the city to their source, a cargo ship in the northern reaches of the city. The flat-bottomed vessel was heading out of the city along the River Lesante. Then he saw his charge, a faint outline, a slight figure silhouetted in sparkling lines of gray, hunkered down; in hiding, perhaps? The figure was surrounded by—Grobennar didn't have time to take in more than a glimpse. The being vanished like a heavy iron door slammed shut; the magic disappeared, along with Grobennar's connection to it.

Grobennar sat up cursing, his body slick with sweat. *I need to gather the team. We sacrificed the wrong tazamine. Well—not exactly. But the Dark Lord sent more than one to the city!*

He cringed when he considered telling Magog that the boy captured earlier had been a tazamine of little importance. This one was far more powerful. He started directly for Magog's chambers then paused. *If I felt it so strongly, surely Magog did, as well.*

Then he heard a roar echoing from Magog's chambers, a primal shout of rage.

*"Dear me. The God-king does appear rather displeased at the arrival of another tazamine in the city. He won't think to blame you for snatching up the wrong one, will he? Perhaps you should arrange for one of those fruit muffins to be sent on your behalf while we seek after the enemy."*

The door to Magog's chambers burst open, the God-king's form silhouetted by the orange light of the furious torches lining his room. Recalling their last dispute, Grobennar quickly found his place kneeling where he had moments before stood. *I need to reassure him that this is under control.* With his head still bowed, Grobennar said loudly, "I have sent for my team. We will seek and destroy this second arm of the Dark Lord's plans, Your Holiness."

Grobennar dared not look up, but could see the shadow cast by his king, rising and falling with every breath, rage barely in check. He also felt the God-king gathering his power.

*Klerós protect me.*

*"Do try to keep him from turning you to ash. I don't believe I can heal you in such a state."* Grobennar ignored Jaween's comment.

Then the God-king spoke. "This tazamine will be the bane of everything we hold dear. He is the dream walker foretold by the prophetess, Lesante, herself. I faced this enemy from within the dream realm this evening. His powers are far from developed. But be warned, this boy is accompanied by—something else," he spat. "A thing of spirit. I believe they intend to flee the city. You will bring the both of them to me, or destroy them at all cost. Their very existence is an anathema to all that is good and holy."

Grobennar's mind swirled at the revelation, but he responded, "Your will be done, Your Holiness. We will give chase at once."

The shadow cast by Magog disappeared, as did the power he had summoned, likely in case Grobennar's response was not to his liking. Grobennar relaxed his tense body, if only slightly, as he waited for Magog to disappear behind his thick chamber door.

Once free to stand, Grobennar rose on shaky legs. The God-king's words about the enemy disturbed him. Dream walker? Thing of spirit?

He could feel the disquieted emotions through the red gem about his neck, as well. An uncharacteristic foreboding leaked through the emotional connection between himself and Jaween.

No time to worry over the details. Magog's wrath would be far worse than anything this boy and his helper could possibly muster against Grobennar and an entire team of competent priests. He rushed back to his rooms and shouted for a servant to attend him to pack the requisite items for the journey. He would then seek out Paranja to gather the team while he secured a ship. The God-king was right; the barge he had seen was indeed headed out of the city toward Lake Lagraas. It would then turn east. They would give chase upon a much swifter vessel.

## CHAPTER 26

# AYNWARD

THE UNIVERSITY WAS A QUICK ten-minute walk from Aynward's new residence. Gervais led him and Dolme to the gates of the university before bidding them farewell. "Here we are." Putting up a hand, he continued, "The instructions indicated that you are to enter the gate, then head straight down the walkway into the central building ahead. However, they also stated—"

Two armed guards emerged from either side of the tall gate, placing hands on the hilts of their swords. They did not draw, but their postures made it clear that they would do so if challenged.

Dolme shifted to his own defensive position. Aynward knew that he would have two sizable daggers at the ready in the blink of an eye if he chose it so. His primary obligation was to ensure Aynward's safety, after all.

"State your business," said the bronze-skinned guard to Aynward's right in a higher-pitched voice than he'd have expected from such a muscular man. He wore no armor, but his robe looked light and specifically cut to allow ease of movement. He was no infantryman. Bearing weapons without armor spoke volumes of confidence and skill.

Aynward shrugged to himself. Either that or the university needed little protection and chose not to equip their guards with additional steel because the most expensive items inside included some old scrolls. Aynward elected to not put these theories to the test.

Gervais replied on behalf of the shocked and silent Aynward and the ready-to-draw-weapons Dolme. "This here is Annard of Salmune. He is on the roster for the testing."

Aynward rolled his eyes at the name change. Anyone with half a brain would see through that disguise in seconds. Then again, how many Kingdom princes attended universities so far from home? No matter, he was here and people would glean what they would. He wasn't overly concerned about his identity leading him into harm's way.

The guard responded to Gervais with an extended hand. "Paper, please."

Gervais handed a single sheet of thick parchment to the guard, who scanned it quickly then signaled to his compatriot, who had not yet relaxed his combative posture. "Very well, Annard, you will be escorted by an apprentice guard to the correct location."

Dolme stepped forward, which caused the other guard to do the same, his hand still on his sword hilt. "None but students are allowed on the premises," this guard said curtly.

"I am his personal guard, I go with him," said Dolme, his gaze never leaving the guard.

The first guard retained a passive position, confident that his associate could handle Dolme if the need arose. He replied evenly, "No one but students are allowed on campus. This should have been made clear in the paperwork that was sent over in the application process." He opened his palms and smiled. "It is a rather lengthy document, so I suppose we won't begrudge you for missing some of the details. Nevertheless this policy is inflexible. He enters alone, or not at all."

Dolme looked over at Gervais, his ordinarily stonelike expression incredulous.

Gervais gave a curt nod. "Very well. Thank you, gentlemen, for your service to the city. Apologies for the misunderstanding, we'll be going now." He nodded again to Dolme and turned, a hand moving to Dolme's shoulder in an effort to turn him away, as well. Aynward didn't think Dolme would concede but he finally turned and left without another word. Aynward observed his retreat with satisfaction.

Aynward turned back to see the two guards back in their original positions on either side of the gate, only now a third now stood between them. Aynward didn't know where he'd come from; he'd only looked away for a moment. This young man couldn't have been much older than himself, a thick set of brown curls rested atop a soft face marked by a piggish nose and too-small eyes. He smiled uncertainly. "I'll be escorting you to the testing, Mr. Annard of Salmune. Please follow me."

He led Aynward along the central cobbled walkway while additional brick paths fanned out toward other buildings. Aynward turned his head from side to side taking in the scene, or as much of it as he could. The campus was a city within a city, fully cut off from the outside by a thick, fifteen-foot-wall on all sides. The buildings were all crafted of gray stone bricks marbled with thin streaks of blue; they glistened in the early light. Aynward and the young guard approached the building that lay straight ahead, dwarfed by the others around it. The circular building couldn't have been more than fifteen paces across.

The guard opened a thick wooden door that swung on silent hinges to reveal an empty room excepting a single bench, where sat a robed man of indeterminable age. His face was as pale as the white marble of Salmune's palace pillars. The bench was just large enough for two, but it would have been an uncomfortably tight fit. Aynward could see nowhere to write, but perhaps this would be an oral exam? He had no idea what to expect. *Idiot, I should have asked more questions of Gervais.*

The man didn't look up as they approached. They stopped a pace before him and he still didn't move. *Is he a statue?*

The apprentice broke the silence. "Annard of Salmune has arrived for the testing."

Then he bowed swiftly and scuttled out of the building. The man on the bench remained immobile. Aynward opened his mouth to ask what he was supposed to do but paused; maybe this was part of the test.

Could it be? Seemed pretty pointless, but so was this whole enrollment test in the first place.

Finally Aynward stepped to the right and crouched down, face to face with the man. Yet the immobile being didn't so much as blink, and his eyes still hadn't acknowledged that they saw anything. The man just stared, unseeing, into nothingness. He was either blind or he really was a statue. He was pale enough.

Aynward waved a hand in front of the man, then lost his patience and said in a loud voice to the entire empty room, "Hello. I'm here for the—"

The man sprang forward, his hands waving frantically. Aynward jumped back in shock, stumbling in the process. He was pretty sure that he yelped, too, but couldn't think about that as he scrambled backward and up onto his feet, a safe distance from the crazed person in front of him. The man's cackling relaxed Aynward for about as long as it took him to realize that this had been a sick joke. Blood ran to his face and anger replaced relief.

The man continued on with his grotesque laughter. "Ah ha-ha-ha-ha . . . I . . . love . . . ha-ha . . ." He hunched into a fit of coughing, his head almost to his feet. "I . . . love . . . ha-ha . . . testing duty . . ." He moved his hand to the side of the bench and a low rumbling noise started behind him.

Aynward jumped again; well, at least he didn't fall this time.

The man was still cackling but it had died down a bit. Aynward wasn't sure the man had even noticed his second reactionary cowardice. The laughing was on a slow but steady retreat.

Aynward gathered his pride and used what remained of his self-control to not begin cursing at the man. Then he stepped forward and moved around the bench. As he did so, he could see the opening that had emerged from behind it. The stone floor had rolled away to reveal a staircase with flickering red and yellow lights disappearing down a circular path that descended beyond sight.

The man was still chuckling. Aynward took a long hard look at him, vowing to make him pay before he was done here in Brinkwell. The man turned to fully face him, giving Aynward opportunity to capture the face in his memory for later use. Streaks of healthy colored skin marked lines where tears had wiped away the powder that had given him the deathly, elderly complexion. The powder was a complete farce designed specifically to mislead. This *man* did not appear to be much older than Aynward himself. He was just a student at the university who got a real good laugh at Aynward's expense. Aynward might not be the only victim, but that didn't matter. This *man* would be added to his list of others who would see a debt repaid in full if Aynward had anything to say about it. But he remained outwardly silent as the still chuckling student disappeared from view.

The circular stone steps seemed to lead to the very bowels of the university; Aynward descended slowly, careful not to miss one. The staircase was furnished with torches secured in sconces just close enough to give vague impressions of the steps. He ran his hands along the stone of the wall for added balance as a precaution.

He took two consecutive steps on the same plane and breathed a sigh of relief that he was again walking on level ground. A faint light shone straight ahead and he started toward it. A few strides before he reached the glowing outline of a door, a loud voice commanded, "Stop there."

Aynward stopped in his tracks. Light suddenly poured out of a small opening in the door, and an article of black cloth was held out for Aynward by a hand.

"Put on the blindfold," said the voice. "Once it has been secured over your eyes, you'll be escorted into the room."

Aynward did as he was told. Moments later he heard the soft sound of a door swinging open on well-oiled hinges. A strong hand gripped his arm, dragging him into the room to sit. The air was stuffy and the flat-backed chair uncomfortable, but at least they were finally getting on with the charade.

Then he heard the door shutting, thick metal striking thicker stone. He sat in silence again as time passed, trying desperately to ignore his annoyance. *So much for getting on with it.* He fumed. *If this test is one of patience, I'll be sent home in short order, a failure.* He slouched in his chair and crossed his arms, preparing a tirade for the next person who spoke to him.

A new voice from behind placed his scathing verbal attack on temporary hold.

"State your name."

*Thank the gods! It's actually starting!*

"Annard of Salmune."

"What is your purpose for wishing to study here at Brinkwell?"

He could think of several scripted answers: a desire to learn, serve the world, serve his kingdom, and blah, blah, blah. Alas, those answers were beyond his ability to use; his pride simply would not allow it.

"Well, if I'm to be honest, I've little desire to study here at all but my father doesn't trust that I'll be able to keep from embarrassing him if allowed to study anywhere near home so . . . here I am."

Aynward smiled as he listened to a slight shuffling from behind him. Then a different voice said in an angry, heavy Isles accent, "Then leave. We needn't waste your time or ours."

Then a different voice, similarly accented but feminine, said, "No, no, you stay right there." More rustling from behind gave the impression that there were several people behind him, a few rising to stand.

The woman spoke again. "Give us a minute. We'll be right with you." He heard the metal of a door connect again with the stone that made up everything else, followed by several hushed but agitated voices. *This is interesting.* Aynward smiled.

The unintelligible muffled speech stopped after a few moments and the heavy latch of a door was heard again.

A harsh-sounding male voice with an accent that he could not place said, "The dean made it very clear to us that you have sufficient previous schooling to be enrolled. However, *we* must determine where you should be placed by our own means. This test is the first step in the placement process. After the testing, you'll meet with an adviser to discuss specific courses of study. Please remove the covering."

The relatively bright light of several torches momentarily blinded him. As clarity returned, he craned his neck to catch the source of the voices from behind him, but as he suspected, they were hidden from view. A mesh screen covered the entire wall. Aynward had seen ones like it in the palace used for eavesdropping or confidential conversations. They could see him, but he could not see them. He turned back to what was in front of him, a table with scroll, parchment, feather, and ink.

A voice from behind said, "Go to the table. There you will find several documents. Each one tests a prerequisite skill necessary for enrollment in our jurisprudence degree track, as indicated in your enrollment request. You will either be asked to summarize, plan to solve, or explain the context surrounding a given written work." There was a slight pause, then the man added, "Keep in mind that failure to comply will result in automatic enrollment in the most elementary of coursework, regardless of any previous training. If you truly don't wish to be here any longer than is necessary to earn a degree, we encourage you to take this process seriously."

Aynward ground his teeth. He didn't like the condescending tone, or the monotony of testing before enrolling. Yet the man had struck a nerve of truth. He was at their mercy, and if he didn't play along, he'd be in Brinkwell far longer than he wished.

He unrolled the first scroll and began to read.

## CHAPTER 27

# KIBURE

KIBURE NARROWED HIS EYES, SEARCHING for the black creature who had somehow rescued him from the world of dream, from the God-king himself? The raaven must be there, somewhere, somehow. Kibure closed his eyes in thought. *This is insane. Was it all real? No. I'm losing my mind.* He shook his head. Then he felt a faint prick of magic and stiffened. They were found out: a seeker had felt his magic and located them. Unless—he jerked his head around to see the rogue priestess staring back at him. "What of your dream?" she asked coldly.

Kibure swallowed hard. "It was the same as the last." He still did not trust her with whatever it was that was happening in these dreams. "A soundless, colorless world, and me sitting here, stuck in this cage." That was mostly true. He simply neglected to mention the other *not* new things.

He felt the sensation of unnatural warmth; *she doesn't believe me.* He braced himself to go crashing into the metal bars at any moment. Then the sensation vanished without further incident.

Sindri glared at him. "Foul bricks for building!" She grabbed the metal bars of his cage and he instinctively jumped. "Klerós above, it doesn't take a mind delve to tell that you are lying. It's written all over your face." She stared at him expectantly, but he held firm, and silent.

She rolled her eyes angrily. "I *will* punish the truth out of you if you force my hand." She let go of the bars. "But we are still too close to the city of Sire Karth right now. Your use of forbidden magic while dreaming alone is enough to have interested any seekers in the immediate vicinity. I doubt very much any would have been able to pinpoint our exact location in that time, especially as a moving target on the water. But if they're searching, I do not wish to give them anything more to track." Frustration was evident in the woman's voice. She threw at him, "You *will* tell me the rest once we are safely away."

Kibure opened his mouth to repeat his denial, but the words never left his lips. She wouldn't believe him, anyhow.

Sindri stood, then left without another word.

Kibure stared off into the shrinking city as the vessel moved out of the bay and into the open waters of Lake Lagraas. An altogether different sort of helplessness developed then. He thought about some of the stories Grenn had told, tales of the great beasts coming out from the depths of the sea, wreaking havoc upon helpless seafaring vessels. Those stories had been frightening enough at the time but Grenn had confirmed that the river was too shallow for such monsters; it was the open seas one had to be afraid of. As the barge turned east, Kibure saw the water stretch all the way to the horizon. The previously unimaginable size of the river was but a grain of sand when compared.

Kibure's fear diminished as a thick fog took shape in the waning light. This served only to encourage his imagination. The inky unknown depths of the water became yet another ominous, unseen foe, something Kibure would be helpless to defend against. He finally closed his eyes and tried to imagine that they were still upon the river, that the oars he heard splashing below were still slicing through the shallow waters of the River Lesante. He cursed Grenn for filling his head with nightmares; he had enough as it was.

The thought of Grenn dragged Kibure's thoughts to the three slaves hunkering below. What would be their fate after all this was over? Kibure's hands formed fists. They would be sold off in Trinkanen. Grenn had answered Tenk's agitated question about why they were being shipped all the way across the continent just to be sold to new Lugienese masters. Why not sell them in their home city, or the next closest? They had probably passed dozens of slave auctions already on their journey. According to Grenn, the answer was simple. The east was not nearly as settled by the Lugienese and therefore the demand for slaves there was higher. He guessed their muscos would make thrice their value in Trinkanen than they would have in Sire Haas or Karth. And since their masters already planned to travel to the Eastern Markets to sell their drogal, fetching more profit from the slaves was a boon.

Guilt trickled up to the surface of Kibure's mind. If what Sindri had told him was true, that she would release him when she was finished with him, then he could eventually be a free man. Granted, he didn't entirely believe that she would keep her word, but the notion that freedom *could* happen gave him a sliver of hope, and that sliver of hope caused him a great sense of guilt as he thought about the futures of the three slaves below. All had treated him better than any people he'd ever met, and all would be returning to a life of labor, torture, and despair. Where was *their* chance at freedom? Why did he deserve a fate better than theirs?

The more he considered the plight of his friends, the more certain he was that he could not stand for that ending. He would do something even if the effort was futile. Exactly what that was he did not know, but he would have to figure something out, and soon.

## CHAPTER 28

# GROBENNAR

DARKNESS HAD FULLY WRESTLED THE light of day into submission by the time the ship's ropes were finally untied at the dock. Much to Grobennar's frustration, collecting the members of his team had been no easy task after their false victory, even with Paranja's assistance. They had gone their separate ways, celebrating the demise of the false agent of the Dark Lord. Not to say that this tazamine was innocent; they were, of course, all agents of the Darkness.

Grobennar's greater frustration came in waiting for the captain of the ship they had commandeered. The man was no doubt eager to serve his god, but most of the ship's crew had been enjoying themselves in nearby taverns, and rounding them up had been no small task, even for a shipmaster who was keen to please the highest-ranking priest in the empire, the Fatu Mazi.

Grobennar gathered the team on the main deck once they were under way.

"You have been selected because you are the best at what you do. Our work here is paramount to the continuation of Klerós's will within this realm and beyond. The Dark Lord is conniving, and relentless in his pursuit of our demise. We have been sent by none other than the

God-king himself to vanquish yet another of the Evil One's representatives on this world, one who had the audacity to enter into the heart of our kingdom. This cannot—will not—be abided."

The priests all nodded in affirmation. Grobennar closed his eyes. "I have not yet returned to full strength, which I must have before we wage war on this dark being. I do, however, need to ensure that we are still on the right trail." He looked up and scanned the group before continuing. "I will need three of you to lend their strength for a clasp."

He could have attempted to channel through the gemstones he wore on each ring, or through Jaween, but he did not wish to diminish a source of safer channeling that he might need again before these could be restored.

Every one of the priests stepped forward to offer their aid. Paranja had indeed selected a willing bunch. He pointed to the first three, then told the rest to find a place to sleep. They would need their strength shortly. He prayed that the rest of his mind would recover sooner rather than later. He also worried about attempting even this simple clasp in his current state. But he had to know for certain that they were closing on the enemy. The Dark Lord was ever the clever one, and Grobennar could not afford to have this agent lure them out of the city only to double back and attack while they were gone.

He removed the cloth from the top of a waist-high cage. A hawk perched on a wire suspended across the bottom of the enclosure. Grobennar had been wearing his rank on the walk to the docks and used this to appropriate the bird from a known vendor who was pleased enough to oblige the Fatu Mazi. Grobennar had no other options than this, for he was certain he did not have the strength to seek out and seize control of a host animal at a distance, not in his current state. He prayed that he had enough strength to do what he wished with the perching hawk in the cage before him.

*"I wish you had been more patient and sought out the other vendor. A falcon would have been a much stronger choice."*

Grobennar ignored the voice of his perpetual critic. "Let us begin."

The three priests were no strangers to what they were being asked to do. They gathered around the cage and took hold of one another's hands to form a circle, leaving space enough for Grobennar to join.

*Please Klerós, lend me strength*, prayed Grobennar.

Grobennar opened his mind to summon Klerós's power, but instead of summoning strength from his own direct connection with his god, he absorbed Klerós's power from those around him who summoned and channeled Klerós's power on his behalf. He felt the rush of energy enter his mind's reservoir, and to his delight it remained without the rush of nausea he had felt when he attempted on his own. He quickly stanched the flow for now, still uncertain how much he would be able to hold. Perhaps it was only the portion of his mind utilized for direct connection to Klerós that still needed to recover. Nevertheless he did not wish to overextend. The clasp he was performing on the hawk should not require any more than he had just taken.

He maintained his handholds with the priests in case he needed them, but focused his attention on the hawk. He sent a tendril of energy into the creature's mind, easily penetrating the mental wall that was its will, its innate sense of sovereignty. Grobennar sent his own will along the connection, then waited.

After a momentary pause, his vision shifted and saw himself through the eyes of the winged predator. Using the voice of his human body, he said, "Open the cage. The clasp is complete."

Paranja had remained close by and did his bidding. This done, Grobennar sent instructions to the hawk, and it hopped out of the cage, then took to the air. Grobennar could feel the sensation of pleasure through the connection; this bird had been a long time confined and enjoyed the freedom in spite of the alien presence within its mind.

*"This bird is almost as happy to have you as you were to have me. So nice to see other symbiotic relationships flourishing as ours has."*

Grobennar attempted to relay an emotional reaction of displeasure at the interruption without revealing his secret to the others by speaking this out loud. It was no use. Jaween was more often than not oblivious to boundaries of privacy, anyhow. Even if Grobennar did speak his displeasure, the debate to follow would take hours only to end in an agreement to politely disagree on the matter. Instead Grobennar returned as much of his attention as he could to the task at hand.

He sent the bird speeding to the east, allowing its instincts to determine how best to take that direction. The thick fog worried Grobennar, but as the bird flew higher, he saw that from above, it was only speckled clouds, and with the light of the emerging moons, he could easily make out his own vessel; the hawk's vision was far superior to that of a human's. He was certain he would recognize the enemy's barge when they neared. It shouldn't take more than a few hours to reach, so long as it had continued along the known coastal route to the east, likely heading toward the River Kleros. With the connection established, Grobennar would be able to easily maintain control across a vast distance without the need to summon more energy from his fellow priests.

Sure enough, by the time the moons crested high in the sky to indicate midnight, he spotted the shape of a large object disturbing the water's calm below. The fog had thinned farther away from the converging waters of the river and the lake so his view of the object below was crisp.

Having located the barge, he considered swooping lower to confirm that his quarry remained onboard. Yet he needed to be careful not to alert the enemy to his presence. He was not certain if the Dark Lord's agent had the same sensitivity to foreign magic as he now did, but he would be a fool to think otherwise. He prayed that the magical signature of this clasp was small enough, and distant enough, to go unnoticed. Instead of taking the risk of revealing himself to the enemy, he sent the bird instructions to follow the vessel, but to stay only close enough to see it, no more. This simple instruction would let him reduce the strength of their connection while the bird continued to do as commanded. He could then rest in preparation for the much larger clasp he had planned for the enemy. He would need to be fully recovered before that could take place. He suspected he would be ready in two days' time, and their vessel would be much closer by then, as it could harness the power of wind while the barge was limited to the paddles of slaves.

He released the hand to his right and left. "Go, rest. The enemy has been found. I'll continue to check on his location, but for now, we wait until the time is right to strike."

The priests did as instructed, disappearing belowdeck to find their quarters.

Paranja remained. "Do you believe you will be strong enough to battle this being by then?"

Grobennar allowed his confident facade to fade now that the others were gone. "I do not know. But whatever strength I have must be enough. We will have to strike while the waters are still deep. The closer they get to Trinkanen, the shallower the lake becomes."

Paranja eyed him thoughtfully. "I will pray for your recovery."

She bowed, then she too disappeared belowdeck.

*"I think I know what you're planning, and I think I like it! This is going to be so much fun!"*

"Fun will be the celebration that takes place after we succeed."

*"You miss the point completely, my dear Grobes. 'Tis the journey to victory, not the victory itself that brings about the ultimate pleasure. You're much too goal oriented. Someday you will possess the wisdom to understand this."*

"If I don't succeed, I fear the journey will be meaningless, and a new journey that includes demotion and embarrassment will follow. So I'm putting my hope in the outcome alone. We can talk about journey after we succeed."

*"Mmmhmmm."*

Grobennar started toward his own private topside quarters. "I need to sleep." And within minutes, he did just that.

## CHAPTER 29

# AYNWARD

THE FIRST SCROLL TESTED HIS familiarity with the abacist study in basic algebraic problem solving. While some of the more theoretical studies in this discipline had not been his strongest area, he could appreciate the practical side reflected in the question he was given. This was simple currency conversion. He was given a baseline value for three currencies and asked to determine an equal value of the other two if given a larger portion of the first. He was then given a different rate of exchange and had to duplicate the comparative values. He'd been drilled enough on this type of question that he could have completed it in his sleep.

He moved on to the second scroll, interrupted only briefly by a hooded being who materialized to collect the first; Aynward paid him no mind. The next scroll inquired after the rules, origin, and identification of the parts of the common tongue: prefixes, suffixes, subject pronouns, predicates, adverbial clauses, and so on. He then had to differentiate and interpret the nuances of a few short passages based on indicative versus subjunctive mood, diathesis, and the author's choice of verb tense. Nothing particularly enjoyable, but he made quick work of it. As with the last, it was collected and taken into the other room without a word.

The next scroll contained three obscure passages from the Scritlandian historical archives that had been translated into the common tongue. He was asked to translate them back into Old Scritlandian as best he could, taking care to replicate his best imitation of the ancient Scritlandian diction and sentence structure. *This is more like it.* He smiled and brought his hands up toward the ceiling, then extended them out in front of him before shaking them out. *Might as well have a little fun with this one.* Feeling revitalized, he set out to capture the full essence of the author, who was no doubt locked in the stereotypical Scritlandian endeavor for austere piety. He supplemented his translation with a liberal sprinkling of monkly self-loathing. He was confident that he had otherwise reproduced the pieces verbatim.

This parchment was followed by a series of questions regarding historic events, of which he knew nearly all. He'd always taken a special interest in the chronology of the major Drogen empires, battles, and wars, many being an integral part of his own Dowen heritage.

After perhaps an hour, he pushed away the last scroll. He leaned back, extended his arms toward the ceiling, and yawned in triumph. He wanted them to know that they'd truly wasted both his time and theirs by forcing him to legitimize his previous education. The smug smile that had taken hold of Aynward's face slowly withered as time dragged on without being dismissed after the last scroll was collected. Was it really necessary that he wait around while they read through his responses?

Fed up, he said, "So terribly sorry to have to scoot out so soon." He shrugged for the benefit of whoever might be watching. "But turns out that I made plans to eat dinner this evening. On behalf of my stomach, I really must be leaving."

He stood slowly, looking around. "Okay, so . . . I'll await notification to discuss my courses in the near future. You folks take—"

Strong hands clasped firmly upon the muscle between his shoulders and neck, resulting in the escape of a castrato-esque sound from his mouth. He tried to shrug the hands off but the grip held fast.

A deep voice spoke gently into his ear. "Please, do sit. You've only completed the first portion of the testing." The grip relaxed, a little. "Any literate child could have completed that first portion. Now that we know you are at the very least a literate child, we can move on to determine if you've the aptitude for university studies." The hands released his shoulders.

Aynward was too stunned to take offense at the slight. He reached a hand up to wipe the cold sweat gathering at his brow. The remnants of tingling fear made his legs as flimsy as an old scroll. They would not support him much longer on their own. He sat.

A robed figure entered and deposited another bundle of parchments. He sagged in his seat as he unraveled the first. Somehow he suspected he'd not be smiling again this day.

Aynward moved on to the last parchment in the second round of testing after what seemed an eternity. This portion of the testing was without a doubt more challenging, tasking him with questions of rhetoric and debate concerning the works of several well-known philosophers, Chrologal theologians, and historians of mixed backgrounds. Throughout the process, Aynward's confidence in his own intellect had returned, a steadily building crescendo of self-satisfaction that felt all the more painful as it struck an unseen solid wall of confusion. He had just finished reading the last parchment. His intellectual legs developed a limp that slowly turned into paralysis.

The last parchment contained a story of sorts—a story about stories—but it made little sense. And the question assigned to it was equally baffling, especially when considering the literature associated: *What are its sources and what ways exist to harness its power?*

According to this legend, whose origin Aynward couldn't begin to imagine, the world's first ant, Sihriy, sought stories to tell his young children. The selfish god of the sky had taken all of the world's stories and hidden them away within his home in a cloud that circled the world.

Sihriy roamed the entirety of the world in search of help, but no one was willing to take on the sky-god just for the sake of recovering stories. Finally, after years of searching, Sihriy found an unlikely ally in a black bat named Rihlah, who was willing to ferry him to the sky-god's realm in the clouds.

After a great struggle that seemed unlikely but—what the heck, a giant ant was already in the clouds battling the sky-god—so . . . the battle ensued and Sihriy was victorious, returning with a giant sack full of stories from throughout the world.

In his absence, Sihriy's children had grown old and cared nothing for these stories. He ended up selling them to a roaming shepherd for a few golden coppers.

*What are its sources and what ways exist to harness its power?* Outside of the seemingly pointless story, Aynward found the question a tad on the vague side. What exactly was the *it* being referred to? The story itself? Did it refer to the power of stories in general?

Aynward's renewed confidence sagged. He spun the wheels of his mind without any traction for minutes upon minutes debating possible ways to answer the question. Finally someone entered and Aynward snapped back to attention, realizing he'd drifted into a state of self-inflicted hypnosis.

The robed person approached to retrieve the parchment. Aynward fumbled for words, embarrassed and aggravated at his blank response. "I, uh, I didn't finish this last one." Irritation grew with every word. "The story was pointless and the question so vaguely worded it seemed senseless to even bother answering."

The hood of the robed man moved in a way that suggested understanding. Then the hand picked up the scroll.

The sound of laughter trickled in from the observatory room. It was muffled, but it was definitely laughter.

Aynward rose to his feet and raised a fist. "Are you all so lacking in true purpose that you must spend your days condemning everyone else to mirror your own worthlessness?"

The laughter was only that of one man, but it escalated from a light cackle to a bellowing chortle. Aynward opened his mouth to shout again, frustrated that he couldn't even see the person who mocked him from a hidden vantage. He took in a deep breath, ready to shout anew, but his roar was aborted by the sudden end to the laughter. This was followed immediately by a man's voice.

"You're just like the rest. Arrogant, privileged, and entitled, but in reality limited to glib comments aimed at convincing others that you're so much more intelligent than you really are. Most people at least make an attempt at the final question, though very few actually puzzle out the riddle, and fewer still satisfy my appetite for true scholarship once they do."

The voice was like nothing Aynward had ever heard. He couldn't place the accent, but even the enunciation of syllables was strikingly odd. Each sound was ejected from the mouth as if associated with spoiled food. This halting way of speaking seemed very much *not* academic. But the words themselves caused him to stumble forward and brace his hands on the desk.

No one besides his father and Dolme had ever dared take such a reproachful tone with *him*, a prince. His mouth hung open, but no sound came out.

The voice continued, "Good luck to you, Princeling Dowe. I'm sure you'll be enrolled in the university, and eventually mature enough to watch over some little duchy on behalf of the King, but nothing more."

Aynward stood there, mouth widening in surprise.

The man said, "You may go."

Aynward played through what had been said once more, concerning himself less with the strangeness of the man's speech and more with the meaning. It hit him like a sword tears flesh. He really *was* an imbecile. How had he missed it?

Panic welled up in him. He had no idea what courses the man taught, and didn't care. He hated being on the outside of anything, especially when it reflected poorly on his wits. He might be stubborn, he might be lazy, he might have the absolute worst attitude for someone in line to advise anyone about anything, but he was no fool. Hopefully he wasn't too late.

"Hey!"

No response.

"Hey! You with the scroll! Bring that back. I've got to finish my answer."

For a painful minute he thought he was too late. Just then, the other door opened and the robed man returned with the parchment. He silently dropped it back on the desk.

Aynward scampered back to his seat and scanned the passage again, this time looking not at the story itself but at the patterns within the writing. He'd spent hours with Dagmara working to break hidden meanings in the puzzles created for them as a pastime between academic cycles. They'd even created several of their own as a way of disguising their correspondences regarding swordplay.

Once he knew what to look for, he found the pattern within minutes. It was a simple anagram, using the first letter of the last word of each paragraph. It spelled out—*sorcery*? His renewed vigor was crushed as he read the word aloud. The *it* of the question was *sorcery*?

What were the sources of *sorcery* and what ways existed to harness its power?

What kind of question was that? Had he been duped? Then he realized the ploy; the reason so many failed this part of the test. It must be a decoy. He worked then for an immeasurable time. It passed differently when he was determined. He would find the *real* code. He tried another batch of more complex patterns, but nothing came together.

Finally his stamina swayed and he took his eyes from the scroll, massaging the fatigue from them. He'd exhausted every trick he'd ever seen or imagined, but nothing even hinted at a coherent message.

*Wait. What about Scritlandian?* He went back through all the possible groupings he'd found. He couldn't expect anything like this to work after a full translation of the message, there were too many variables. The slightest error in word choice could disturb even a simple message. But what if the message itself spelled out something that then needed to be translated? He went back through, forward and backward until—there it was.

He frowned. Spelled backward, the word was *sheudha*, the Scritlandian word for magic, or *sorcery*. He stared at it for several breaths, completely dumbfounded.

Frustrated at the pointlessness of this entire experience, Aynward stood up to leave, turned, then paused. He shook his head and sat back down to scribble out an answer to the question. *May as well prove that I cracked the code.*

He wrote: "The source of sorcery, or *sheudha*, is the affliction commonly known as idiocy. Its power is harnessed through a strict regimen of devotion and reverence to whatever gods happen to be the flavor of the land."

He exited the room without a word, his mind set on finding relief at the bottom of a barrel of ale.

## CHAPTER 30

# GROBENNAR

GROBENNAR STARED DOWN AT HIS hand as a ball of nimbus light formed to illuminate the darkness of his quarters. It was a simple enough spell, one that required minimal power; a safe test of his readiness. He needed to ensure that he could channel Klerós's power without the side effects wrought by Rajuban's *experiment*.

He felt nothing.

A twinge of excitement was quickly followed by a rare sensation: fear. Having worked so hard to get to where he was now, the thought of failure was unimaginable, and yet he thought it. There was nowhere for him to go from here but down. The fact that success would bring great glory to his nation, to Klerós himself, did nothing to assuage his desire that this task had been given to another. Acknowledging this fact was proof of yet another stone missing from the foundation of his faith.

Grobennar's blossoming self-loathing and fearful despair was interrupted by the voice in his head. *"Oooh, you've used magic without curling into a ball like a small child. Does this mean we are finally able to attack the enemy, or have you discovered further excuses for delay?"*

Grobennar rolled his eyes. "I only ever voiced a single reason for delay, and it was a darned good one."

*"Oooh yes. I can almost taste the carnage!"*

"You can't taste. You don't even eat."

Jaween might have rolled his eyes back at Grobennar if he could, but had to settle for a mental jab. *"Figurative language notwithstanding, I am quite excited to experience the carnage, if through my ever wise human companion!"*

"Do I sense sarcasm, Jaween?"

*"Who, me? No. Never would I resort to such a petty means of communication. Sarcasm is far beneath my kind! What could possibly give you cause to suggest such an affront? Does some aspect of my compliment not sit well within the reality of the almighty Fatu Mazi?"*

"Okay, now I know you're being sarcastic."

*"That obvious, was it?"*

"Yup."

Jaween exclaimed, *"Wonderful! Just wonderful! In spite of my many years, the subtleties of sarcasm always eluded me. This just goes to show, it's never too late to learn a new trick!"*

"Happy for you," replied Grobennar flatly.

He did not comment further. Instead he extinguished the orb of light and exited his room. "Gather the priests," he shouted to the captain when he reached the deck. "Time to vanquish evil."

Grobennar strengthened the connection between himself and the hawk he had told to follow the enemy's barge, then reestablished control to verify that it had maintained its course along the coast. It had.

Taking a deep breath, Grobennar severed the connection. He would need every ounce of strength he could muster for this next spell, so he could not risk maintaining the connection with the hawk.

Minutes later, a ring of priests stood upon the deck of the ship in the fading light of dusk, shadows hiding expressions of determination. "This will be no easy task," Grobennar said. "The strength of our enemy is not known to us, but we must assume that it is great. And yet, we have in our possession a weapon he will never wield, a weapon more potent than any steel, any spell, or any ideology. We have the favor of the great Lord Magog, and the God of All Creation, Klerós. I have no doubt that we will be victorious, whether he ordains it on this night or further down the road. So long as we act in accordance with his divine will, we cannot be denied, in this life or the next. Let us begin!"

A collective cheer punctured the air, curt but vibrant. The silence that followed seemed to ring louder. The priests clasped hands. Rough, callused fingers fondled Grobennar's hand until forming a cold, resolute grip; it was Froncerrer. Meanwhile, Paranja's gentle, somehow discerning hand made contact with his other. Inexplicably, she was able to communicate the confidence in Grobennar that he did not feel in himself with just a touch of her palms. Without further delay, he opened his mind to the combined powers of all those forming the circle, and drank of it.

It had been a long time since he had felt such a vast well of Klerós's wild, untamed energy. It was a dangerous sum, enough to turn his bones to cinders before he knew what was happening, if he was not careful. He could incinerate everything and everyone within a hundred paces should he will it. He could send a blast of energy so hot his quarry would dissolve without so much as a puff of smoke. He could—

*Focus.* This much power was dangerous, and he could drink and become drunk on it as quickly and perilously as a puff of the pipe of an addict. He needed to keep these powers at bay. He needed to stay the course.

He sent his mind into the depths of the sea in search of a creature capable of doing the work of Klerós. He reached the depths below, then extended his search for life along the floor until he sensed the mind of that which he sought. Only once before had he felt such a consciousness, only during the ultimate test of a priest's abilities would such a feat even be attempted. But Grobennar would not have been satisfied with anything short of cresting the summit, surpassing the ultimate pinnacle of power and skill in his field. He had claimed control of the king of the seas only that once, and it had been terrifying and exhilarating.

It was a creature of chaos, and strength, and hate, and he felt all of those again as he pushed against its will to take control. It was a stubborn, proud creature, more intelligent than most, yet still more bestial than sentient. But this time Grobennar had the combined power of ten additional priests. His mind formed a sledge, powered by boundless magic, and toppled the being's will in an instant. Its last scraps of autonomy scurried to the furthest recesses of its mind, fearful that this too would be vanquished.

Grobennar felt the mouth of his worldly body form a smile while the body of his creature began to respond to his will. The Dark Lord's servant would meet an end far worse than the will of this creature in the coming hours.

## CHAPTER 31

# KIBURE

THE RHYTHMIC SPLASHING OF THE oars, the creaking wooden planks, and the swooshing of the vessel cutting through the mild waters of the lake were a trio of singers, soothing his weary mind. And yet Kibure remained awake.

He peered across the water, still uneasy about the view; small bubbles of white dancing as the oars stirred the otherwise shiny flat surface illuminated by the arrival of the moons that had chased away the sun once more.

Kibure finally felt his eyelids flutter, releasing his troubled thoughts to sleep. His body relaxed and the tension of his circumstances melted.

Then he heard something *different* in the water. The music had changed. Like an off-key note or an out-of-time clap of hands, something was wrong. He stiffened, and his mind jumped back on the alert. He wasn't sure what he'd heard, not exactly, but something was amiss. He listened intently, pulse quickening.

Nothing. But there *had* been *something*; he wasn't crazy.

He paused and held his breath for a time, listening with keen ears. Still nothing. He shook his head and said to himself, "I'm just tired, imagining things."

Just as he shut his eyes again to try settling his mind for sleep, he heard something else. "Coo coo."

His heart fluttered. Now he was certain he was hearing things. That sounded like—"Coo coo." There it was again, but that was impossible. How could—

Then he saw a silhouette cut into the moon just above Sindri's door. *Rave!*

Excitement filled the young slave; excitement and confusion. Why was Rave on the ship? How had he found it? He couldn't have been there the entire time, could he? What did it mean?

"Coo coo coo coo."

The hair on the back of Kibure's neck rose and his heart beat out of control. Something was *wrong* about that coo. It sounded more urgent than mischievous. He had acquired an ear for Rave's noises. There were variations, minor alterations in pitch and tone. This sound was not the celebratory taunting coo made after having bested Zagreb, or the sorrowful one when recognizing Kibure's fresh gashes after a beating. This coo was an alert.

Kibure could still see the outline of Rave perched above Sindri's door, head darting about nervously. *What is wrong?*

"Coo coo coo coo."

Another noise sounded from beyond—water splashing hard on the deck. Seconds later, the barge let out a deep groan.

Zagreb's voice boomed, still groggy but perturbed. "What in the blazes is going on out here?"

He rounded the corner just as Sindri's door flew open. Her answer delivered deeper chills than those already wracking Kibure. "Something *very* bad."

"You!" Zagreb had spotted Rave. "I knew I heard that rippin' noise!" He turned and started back where he'd come from.

Sindri's voice shook. "Where are you going?" She was always cool and collected, almost completely devoid of emotion, but not now.

"Gettin' my bow!" He'd turned his head, eyes bulging with rage as his gaze met Kibure's.

"No, Zagreb!" yelled Sindri.

"No?" asked Zagreb, incredulous. "Last I checked I was still the one who pays—"

The wooden vessel groaned deeply, then cracked. "Deal with the raaven later!" Sindri turned to glare at Kibure, just as furious with him as Zagreb. She likely believed Rave had been there the entire time, Kibure figured, with him keeping the raaven a secret from her.

She turned back to the source of the splashing water and breaking wood. They heard several voices responding to the disturbance. Then shouts, but still nothing could be seen from where Kibure's cage sat on the vessel's port side. Kibure's blood thickened with fear as the noise continued beyond view.

The wood cracked again, this time louder, a chorus of snapping boards. The ship's captain sounded from beyond Kibure's sight. "Weapons! All hands on deck with weapons, now!"

Men poured out of the cabins below with spears and swords to ward off this still unknown enemy. Horrified cries rang out as men emerged to see what lay to the vessel's starboard side.

Kibure looked at Sindri, who now stood motionless, hands outstretched, grasping for an invisible force—her magic. Terrified shouts echoed to his ears, a single repeated word above the rest: *Kraken*.

"What is Kraken?" shouted Kibure.

Without turning, Sindri yelled back, "Sea beast." Her voice was cold again, but thick with an emotion falling somewhere between anger and confusion.

Zagreb emerged from around the corner and took hold of her sleeve, eyes wide with fear. "Do something! You're the witch here!"

She didn't move a muscle. Her hands were still outstretched. "Something is wrong."

Zagreb shook her arm again. "Darn strappin' right! That thing's gonna sink the ship and kill us all if you don't do something!"

"Something is *very* wrong," she said. Then she jerked her arm free and started for Kibure.

Kibure's fear rose to even further heights. *She must think I have something to do with this.*

Zagreb's voice sounded from behind her as he moved to follow. "You're going the wrong way! Curse us all, what are you doing?"

The air rippled around her hand, then something struck the lock of his cage.

Zagreb growled and reached for her arm again. She whirled and struck with invisible power, causing him to hurtle across the deck. "You want your precious cargo to drown if this thing goes under?"

Zagreb scrambled away on his hands and knees then gained his footing and ran, shouting back, "You're a dead woman!"

Kibure had little time to think more on the peculiarity of the threat upon the former priestess. Sindri yelled for him to get out of the cage. He did.

She grabbed his chained wrists and the locks fell to the ground. "Stay out of the way. I'm going to do my best to stop this thing."

With that she hiked up her robes and darted around the corner, toward the sounds of destruction.

Kibure followed and found the entire crew on deck trying to fend off the beast as it ravaged the vessel. Men's cries grew with every passing minute. Kibure looked to where Rave had been but there was no sign of him.

Kibure caught a quick look at a man flying over the cargo hold before crashing through the outer railing and into the lake below. The closeness of his agonized scream and the snapping of bone caused Kibure to clap his hands over his ears.

Then he remembered Tenk, Jengal, and Grenn. They were probably still tied to the post below. He had to free them before—

Another man landed just a few paces from Kibure. He must have been dead before he struck because he made no sound. His body, however, slapped loudly against the wood, his bones crunching like dry weeds underfoot on a hot summer day. Similar sounds filled the air as the ship's wood lost the battle against the beast.

He had to move *now* if he wanted to get to his friends in time. He ran to the edge of this level, grabbed the ledge, and leaped down, stumbling upon landing. He scrambled back to his feet then sprinted toward his friends.

Jengal was frantically tugging at his ropes, a useless effort. Tenk encouraged him with panicked screams while Grenn seemed to have lost hope altogether, content with his fate in the midst of the chaos.

Something touched his shoulder! Kibure jumped and spun to face—no one. But he recognized the dark shadow still in his periphery. Rave had landed on his shoulder, distraught as the rest. The wily creature shuffled around and cooed like a maniac.

Suddenly Kibure understood why. To his immediate left, a great wave rose up like a mountain. The water fell like a dumping bucket filled with rocks, revealing a thing unfit for nightmares. The Kraken roared.

Kibure closed his eyes, despair reaching up to swallow him whole, but he could not un-see the beast. He opened his eyes and faced the creature of death. He stared into a pair of sharp, narrow eyes with bottomless black pupils. Those two black chasms were surrounded by thick rings of red and yellow, creating a maze of color that flickered like flames of a great fire. The sight paralyzed him. The tangible gloom seemed to envelop him, pouring across the path of their gaze.

The probing stare was broken by a war cry from the highest level of the vessel. A man jumped, sword in hand, and swung at the neck of the great beast. Before the hero could strike the deadly blow, the Kraken snapped its head with shocking speed, sending the man careening through the main deck. He was dead upon impact, his body motionless upon the splintered wood.

This offensive alerted the men from the other side of the barge, and a great number of them appeared, weapons in hand, bravely and stupidly ready to attack. They were not soldiers, though, and none of them had likely ever fought anything like a Kraken.

The beast's reptilian head rested on a neck of equal girth that stretched as high as two men atop one another before connecting with the muscular upper body. The rest of the monster lay hidden below the water. Its forelimbs, however, were very much visible, and active. They were longer even than its neck, as tall as a drogal tree, each slithering like a serpent.

Kibure watched helplessly as one of those arms came down upon the enraged captain, who stood upon the deck, ax at the ready. He was too slow for the snappy reptilian movement of the Kraken; he died quickly. All the while, the beast's other arm disposed of numerous other foes.

At that moment Kibure finally acknowledged the need for action despite his fear. As if reading his mind, a shriek from Rave turned his attention to the deck. His furry friend fluttered away, but he had deposited a sword at Kibure's feet.

Kibure snatched it up and ran to free his friends. His initial downward chop on the rope proved ineffective, so he worked the sword from side to side to cut the fibers. He had just finished Tenk's when a vast darkness overtook them all.

Kibure turned his head just in time to see the snapping limb. He reacted with a swing of the sword. He had never before touched a metal weapon, but the sharpened wooden machetes used to harvest drogal had at least allowed him a practiced chopping form. His sword cut satisfyingly deep into the flesh of the tentacle, but its momentum was too great and he was still sent sprawling across the wooden surface of the ship.

The Kraken let out a bellow that captured pitches both high and low; but instead of retracting to lament its injury, it launched its entire body at the vessel, snapping its massive jaws in an effort to devour Kibure.

He managed to roll to the side as the creature's head crashed through the deck where he had just been. A moment later the Kraken's body slammed into the port side even harder than before, shaking the entire vessel, splinters flying in every direction. This action, however, worked against the creature, whose tentacles flailed in frustration. Kibure realized it had gotten itself stuck.

"Run, you fool!" came Sindri's voice from behind. He turned and spotted her a few paces away. "It's compelled by magic. *Run!*"

She was holding up her hands, using her own powers against the Kraken. Kibure felt the tingling of her magic so close to him.

A blast of energy shot out from her hands to strike the beast. The thing craned its head around and its gaze bore down on Sindri with an all-consuming revulsion. It had stopped trying to wriggle its body free. All of its attention was on the priestess. Then, if it was possible for this monster to smile, it did so, bearing its hideous teeth in an expression vile enough to make the Dark Lord himself cringe.

Sindri screamed. She looked down at her hands in shock and horror. She cried out again, then fell to the deck, attacked by some unseen force, writhing in pain. The priestess who had boasted great power cried out, "Nooooo! This cannot be!" It was a cry not of frustration or true physical pain, but the deep cry of great loss like Kibure had heard back at the estate when a fellow slave passed into the afterlife. "Klerós, why have you forsaken me?" she cried.

Kibure's sense of self-preservation returned then, reminding him to flee to safety. But the ship rocked as the beast finally twisted free of the jagged planks. Once loose, it moved to close the distance between itself, Sindri, and Kibure. Then, from one of the tentacles, shot a bolt of sizzling energy. It struck Sindri and she disappeared from view; a hole in the deck where she had been was all that remained.

Something pushed past Kibure's fear. A pathway opened to the part of him he hadn't known, but which last time had resulted in a powerful display of—*something*. It compelled him to turn and face the Kraken.

That same disturbing emotional imbalance leaked into his veins, that tingling sensation, similar yet discernibly different from the one he sensed when Sindri used magic. This was an awareness of power that grew from within. He felt his fists close tight. His eyes locked on those of the beast.

Kibure felt almost weightless as he drank in the power. Then the beast's tentacle snapped and a blast of energy zipped toward him. Kibure threw up his hands, a vain defense; but as he did, his feet sank into the wood below him and the rest of his body followed. The heat of the blast ripped past where his head had just been as he plummeted through a cloud of dust. Before he had time to finish coughing the dust from his lungs, a rush of chilly wetness consumed him. Disoriented, he attempted another intake of air—but this time he inhaled water.

## CHAPTER 32

# AYNWARD

AYNWARD KEPT HIS HEAD FORWARD and eyes focused on the main gates of the university as he emerged from underground. The light of day was mixing with the darkness of night. He wanted out of this place, striding toward the gates, stomping out his frustration.

The next thing he knew he was tumbling toward the ground. He managed to catch himself with an outstretched arm before plunging to his face. *What the—?*

Recognition registered: he'd bumped into something or had been bumped into, he wasn't sure which.

"Oh, I'm so sorry. Are you okay?" The voice was definitely male, and definitely *not* hailing from anywhere indigenous to the common tongue. Sounded almost like a Scritlandian accent, but somehow different. *Well, it's a big continent.*

Aynward looked up. "Yes. Yes. It's fine. I'm fine. Just trying to get the heck out of here."

"Oh, same, same. Well, then, apologies and acceptance in equal."

The man, or boy—he seemed somewhere along the transition between the two stages—was about the same height as Aynward. Skin dark like that of the Scritlandians, but eyes red like blood. Aynward had read about a group with those characteristics but couldn't budge it out from hiding within his thoughts.

The young man gestured with a hand for Aynward to go on ahead. "After you." He made a short bow and Aynward began walking toward the gate ahead of him.

Then an idea hit. "Hey, you." Aynward turned and shouted. He had only taken a few steps. "You wouldn't happen to know a good place nearby where I could grab an ale, would you?"

The young man brought a finger up to his cheek in consideration.

Aynward added to his request. "I'll buy—if you show me the way."

They met gazes. "Yeah, I know a place. But I'm late in delivering a package so I can't take you there right now. I can tell you how to get there, but we've got to keep walking. My name is Hirk, by the way. You are?"

"Annard." The name spilled out of his mouth before he considered whether or not he would actually use it once enrolled. *I'm guilty of aiding and abetting the genius of fools.* Apparently his name was now Annard.

Hirk's directions were simple enough, especially since the place was only one turn past where they had to part ways.

"Offer on those drinks still stands. Stop by after you've delivered whatever it is you need to deliver."

"I'll think about it," was all Hirk said before turning down the street in the opposite direction.

Aynward's dark mood returned as soon as he was alone again. It wasn't long before he'd crossed the street and had to start looking for the place Hirk had described. It was supposed to be a brown building with an unmarked red door. He was to knock five times in quick succession, pause, followed by another three.

The door opened. Aynward moved to step into the room, halfway surprised that the knock had actually worked, when a large figure took up residence within this newly vacant space. Aynward reconsidered trying to push past the structure built of hardened human flesh. He stepped back, hoping that perhaps the man had been leaving at the exact same time Aynward was entering. *Kitay owes me a bit of benevolent alms after today.*

"What do you want?" The voice matched the wide shoulders and nearly snowcapped height of the massive man perfectly.

"A tall mug of ale would be nice. But I'll settle for whatever mood-enhancing beverages you're willing to part with. In exchange for some of my hard-earned coin, of course."

"We only allow students. You're not dressed like a student and I've never seen you before. Good evening."

The man began closing the door.

Aynward muttered a curse. *I guess the goddess of luck has stored away my credits for a later time.* He slid his foot inside the door jamb just as it moved to shut him out. It struck his boot, which held in place.

"I'm sorry, Mr. Mountain-of-a-Man. I'm a new student at the university. I just had the testing today. I'd really appreciate some decency."

The man's cold eyes glared out at him through the foot-sized opening. Then the gap widened slightly. "Your testing was today, huh? Heard it's pretty brutal. I bet you really could use a good ale."

Relieved, Aynward replied, "Oh, thank the gods! It was absolutely dread—"

"Unfortunately, you will be having that ale somewhere else this evening. Not sure how you heard about this place, but you're not a student until you're enrolled and accepted into the university, and have undergone the *desposition.*"

The man's larger-by-twice boot pushed his own to a place that was assuredly not inside the doorway. "Good evening."

Aynward stood motionless for minutes facing the closed door before taking a short step forward to kick it. He turned and headed back toward the university gate. As much as he wanted to continue searching for a place to drown his frustrations in fermented goodness, he was not about the get himself lost in an unfamiliar city. Kisin, the trickster god of the underworld, had enjoyed a productive-enough day already.

He resigned himself to retracing his steps from the university to his new home, keeping an eye out for anything along the way that might quench his thirst. If he discovered such an establishment, he'd consider it providence; if not, he'd redouble his efforts when the sun shone bright again the next morning.

Luck was on the side of sobriety that evening, so Aynward arrived back home disappointedly coherent. He did manage to find a loaf of bread that had been sitting out all day at a bakery packing up for the day. It was hard and tasteless, but his empty stomach didn't complain. He'd eaten half the loaf upon reaching his aunt's home.

Dolme was sitting on the front porch, arms crossed, crossed leg in constant motion, awaiting his return.

Feeling a bit miffed by the evening's events, Aynward said, "Well, you look to be your ever-chummy self. I presume you're reflecting on the great joy you've had on your first full day in Brinkwell?"

As Aynward had intended, Dolme's scowl darkened, which of course had the opposite effect on Aynward's own mood. The counselor replied, "I was advised to return home on threat of arrest for loitering in the mere vicinity of the university gates. Me, a Kingdom knight, counselor, and protector of the prince, forced to leave the premises. It's unconscionable."

Aynward's pent-up aggravation continued to melt at Dolme's suffering. "Well, that makes one ungrateful visitor of us. I, on the other hand, had the great pleasure of spending the entirety of the day without so much as a meal in pursuit of proving the truthfulness of my transcripts."

Aynward had continued approaching the front door as he spoke. He paused, holding the door open before saying, "But I imagine the freedom to wander the city in search of its finest cuisine, shops, and womenfolk all day must have been agonizing. I'll leave you here to complete your sulking."

Being given the opportunity to make a hypocrite out of the man who had always reprimanded Aynward for any hint of complaint inspired such pleasure in Aynward that he figured he'd be up half the night savoring the sweet feeling of self-satisfaction. Dolme's silence seemed to boom like thunder. Aynward shot through the door and bounded up the stairs to his room, his exhaustion having temporarily evaporated.

A while later, after he'd blown out the lamp and lain down to sleep, his emotions finally normalized. Only then did his growing concerns about the university return. He couldn't identify exactly the cause of his growing discomfort, but it was certainly there, and the more he recognized it, the worse it became. These feelings were almost entirely alien to him, so he had difficulty understanding their source and how to confront them. He was more accustomed to anger, annoyance, and the opposing feelings of victory, pride, and joy. These new feelings challenged his confidence, a hallmark of who he was. He did not enjoy the uncertainty.

Tired of such negativity, he maneuvered his thoughts in a more pleasant direction: plans for revenge against his enemies. He thought of Dolme, and the prankster from the entrance to the testing, and his most recent, the behemoth who barred his entry to the *exclusive* university pub. He imagined himself making amends with the man in a few weeks' time, offering a drink to the petty misunderstanding. He could sense the enjoyment he'd feel from knowing that hours later the man would be sitting on the privy, painfully emptying his bowels for hours from the senna leaf oil he'd have slipped in before handing it off.

He didn't realize he'd been asleep until he opened his eyes to morning light at a sharp knocking on his door. Aynward tried to ignore it, but it was insistent, so he rose and threw on his robe.

"Yes, I'm coming." He opened the door to see Dolme, clothed for business.

"Get dressed. We need to leave now."

Aynward was still groggy at the interruption from a very deep sleep. "Wh—why? The sun's just crested the horizon. How about a meal and some time to wake up before I go gallivanting around the city with the likes of you?"

Dolme's expression looked as if it had been carved of stone shortly after hearing a comment of disrespect directed at his mother. "You've been summoned to the university."

## CHAPTER 33

# GROBENNAR

THE FATU MAZI PEERED THROUGH the eyes of the beast as most of the wreckage sank to the bottom of the lake. The Kraken still held firm to the innate bloodlust Grobennar had exploited so well, making it difficult to end the destruction of all things floating long after the job had been finished. The Kraken seemed to take offense to—well—everything that was not distinctly the Kraken itself.

Shrapnel still drifted about in the dark, but after allowing the creature to take control of the mayhem, Grobennar's concerns that anything had survived were satisfied.

*"Now, that was exhilarating! So much death! How do you feel?"*

Grobennar moaned. "I feel like I just channeled a great deal of magic and need to rest."

*"You really need to learn to enjoy life every now and again."*

"I will enjoy resting."

## CHAPTER 34

# LIANDRA

## [Five Years Earlier]

L IANDRA CLUTCHED THE LETTER SCRAWLED in a laborer's heavy hand as the barge approached the dock in Sire Krepe. There was no question as to the authenticity; this was her father. "*Liandra, please come home. It's about your brother. Make haste.*" It was not like him to worry. He, like his two children, had endured much with the loss of their mother at the birth of her brother.

Liandra had been only two years old then, and much as she tried, she could not remember anything of her mother. Her father had raised them alone, enduring an unceasing drudgery of manual labor to pay for the schooling that had afforded Liandra the chance to test for her robes, and for her younger brother Lyson to gain an apprenticeship with the baker's guild.

Liandra sat impatiently rubbing a section of her silk red robes between her fingers; this mark of the priesthood had afforded her free travel and the ability to move about as a single woman unmolested. As a pureblood in her early twenties, traveling alone without the robes would have been unwise. She finally stepped from the barge as it neared the dock and assumed a quick pace toward the outskirts of the city where her brother, Lyson, and father still lived. The hot summer sun and her hurried steps had sweat running down her face within minutes. By the time Liandra knocked on the door of her modest childhood home, she was filthy with the dust of travel caked to her skin.

"Hello? Father?"

She heard shuffling in the other room, then her father's voice. "Liandra! Thanks be to Klerós, you're here."

Liandra didn't bother taking off her sandals; the floor was the same packed dirt as the streets of this part of town. Her father took one step in her direction then Liandra rushed to greet him. He opened his burly bricklayer's arms and she allowed his chest to swallow her as she slammed into the embrace. "I missed you, Father."

"You too, Leelee."

Her father finally released her, and she took a step back, seeing the unusual growth of beard upon her father's face. He attempted a smile, still trying to protect his only daughter from the darkness in the world, but she could see the sadness *and* worry behind that smile.

"Where's Lyson?"

Her father gestured toward the only other room in the home. Liandra gave him a look, then walked slowly, afraid of what would greet her. She sighed in relief at the sight of Lyson, alive and well by the looks of it, sitting up on the bed. Her next words stuck in her throat as she saw that his eyes were red and puffy from crying.

Liandra turned back to see an uncharacteristically grim expression upon her father's face. "Liandra, your brother—he—he is in danger."

Lyson's voice squeaked from behind his hands. "I didn't mean to. It started happening again."

Liandra felt dread grow within but did her best to keep her voice calm. "Lyson, what did you do?"

He shook his head. "I can't help it. It just happens—"

That's when Liandra felt it—*magic*. Her brother, her innocent, soft-spoken brother, was an innate wielder of Klerós's power.

"Lyson, you've been using magic?"

He nodded but didn't speak.

"You haven't hurt anyone with it, have you?"

He shook his head and Liandra felt some of her fear drain away. This was not so bad, then.

Liandra sat next to her brother on the bed. She glanced back and gave her father a reassuring smile before turning to say to Lyson, "You needn't be afraid. You are blessed by Klerós. You could be admitted directly into the priesthood without the testing should you wish it, now that the talent has manifested."

He shook his head.

Liandra replied. "Very well. Then there is the castration spell. I know you're frightened, but it is nearly painless if you've only been using the power for a short time."

Her father spoke then, his voice pained. "Leelee, we had the castration performed three weeks ago."

Liandra looked from her father back to Lyson. Understanding dawned; the spell had not worked. Liandra considered, then said, "But we're true-bloods, so they must have made a mistake with the spell."

Lyson's face peered out from behind his hands. "Please, I don't want to have the nightmares anymore. I just want to go back to Master Gorton and finish my apprenticeship."

Liandra tried to console her brother. "You need not worry. I can't do anything about nightmares, but I can help with the magic. I'm sure the priest simply made a mistake. It happens from time to time."

*Best get it over with.* "I can do it myself, if you like."

Lyson looked up. "Truly?"

"Of course." She reached her hand out and put it on his shoulder. She drew in Klerós's power, and then—her concentration was shattered as the front door burst open.

Liandra looked up to see two red-robed clerics, one male and one female. The female cocked her head to the side, likely confused by the presence of the unknown priestess who had beaten them to their own sector of the city.

Lyson whimpered beside her.

Liandra stood and took a few steps to greet the newcomers.

The closest of them, a middle-aged priestess, regained her composure then paused as she recognized Liandra's tassels of rank. She bowed her head slightly. "My apologies, Razir Gazi. We have been tracking the use of magic in this quadrant for a few days and finally traced it to here."

They stared at Liandra expectantly, waiting for an explanation as to why Liandra, a seeker with both the seeker and battle sashes, was outside of her own quadrant of jurisdiction.

Having passed the battle and seeker proficiencies, Liandra outranked these two. They were merely a seeker and seeker-in-training—a razir and tadi razir, respectively.

"I was here on special business and sensed this magic all morning. Your inaction persuaded me to deal with this of my own accord."

The woman glared at her and opened her mouth to reply but Liandra cut her short. "Don't bother with excuses, I'm in no mood. I will castrate this one, *correctly* this time. If you can manage to stay out of my way, I will consider omitting this incompetence in my report to your Fatu Kazi."

The woman continued to glare, then said. "I castrated this one myself a few weeks back. I did not make a mistake." Looking over to Liandra's father, then back at Lyson, the woman said, "Boy's mother was probably slave-born. Hard to tell when it's the mother. Either way, bet my robes he's a half-blood and a tazamine."

Liandra would hear no more of this. She opened her mouth to silence the woman when Lyson's voice bellowed, "My mother was no such thing! Liandra, tell her!"

*Lyson, you idiot.*

The woman tilted her head as she looked back to Liandra. "Razir Gazi, how did this boy come to know your birth name?"

*No sense lying now.* "Because he is my brother. Care to offer any more insults about my deceased mother's heritage?"

The woman's face blanched and she knelt. "My sincerest apologies, Razir Gazi. I—perhaps I did make a mistake before."

That response satisfied Liandra. "I was just readying to perform the spell when you arrived. Perhaps the both of you could benefit from observing a castration performed *properly*."

The woman and her apprentice both nodded, but neither spoke.

"Very well." Liandra turned back to her brother. She extended her hand and sent the power of Klerós into him, severing the part of the spirit that would channel power into the mind and body, thereby breaking the connection to Klerós's power. "There," she said. "All done."

Her brother smiled. "I'm—I'm all better?"

"All better."

"I don't feel any different."

"That's because you're exactly as you were before. You just cannot touch Klerós power. You are otherwise unchanged, as I told you."

The priestess in the doorway spoke hesitantly. "Razir Gazi, I didn't catch the name of your Kleról."

Now it was Liandra's turn to glare. "That is because I did not offer such."

The woman replied sheepishly, "As you know, we are required to catalog all castrations by quadrant, and the resolution of each."

Liandra felt frustration overcoming her trembling fists. "You said that you performed such two weeks past, isn't that right? Save yourself the embarrassment and pretend your first castration was done right." *That should be enough to shut her up and get her out of the way.*

Liandra turned her back to the woman and her apprentice, hoping the issue to be resolved, but then she felt magic, the same magic as earlier. But this time she noticed the nuance that she had previously missed; this was not the magic of Klerós. Only a fully trained seeker like herself, and likely *the other woman*, would detect this subtle difference, but it was undeniable now that she felt it. She stared at her brother in disbelief, and confusion, then looked at her father, who sat quietly in his chair.

*My brother, a tazamine? Impossible!* If her brother was a tazamine, that meant, her mother was—and Liandra—

A chill spidered through her as she turned to face the clerics. The woman had returned to her feet, and her posture had become one of authority. The reverence was gone from her voice as she said, "Razir Gazi, your brother is a tazamine. You are aware of our protocols. He must be transported to the God-king, the father must be castrated for the crime of mixing blood, and you must submit yourself to a council for scrutiny."

Liandra felt everything closing in around her. The shock that her very own brother was a tazamine was enough of a blow, but this revelation slandered her mother, father, and herself, as well.

The priestess pointed to Lyson and said to her apprentice, "Take the boy to the Kleról for quarantine."

Liandra stepped to block the apprentice's approach. He was still several paces away, but he froze at her movement, looking to his master for guidance.

The woman stared at Liandra. "Don't make this difficult. Neither one of us wants to make a spectacle of this."

*And yet you force my hand.* Liandra felt the river of her fury flow beyond the break wall of her self-control—and she let it go, sending a narrow blast of raw power straight past the boy, aimed at the woman. To her credit, she reacted swiftly, dodging the brunt of the blow, but she was still taken from her feet, the power striking her unevenly, spinning her through the air. She landed hard, a cloud of dust rising from where her feet struck the floor.

"Liandra, what are you doing?" her father cried.

"Protecting my family."

Liandra sent out a tendril of energy, connected it to the door's mass, then pulled it shut just as the male seeker-in-training attempted to flee the scene. *Coward.* He turned, eyes wide, then glowered and pulled his knife.

Liandra was more concerned about the woman. Her training would be far greater than that of her apprentice. The woman had assumed a crouch and drew her own priestess's dagger. Liandra would not give her the chance to use it. She sent another wave of power directly for her, but the woman rolled to the side, precisely where Liandra had anticipated. The second blast, a narrow blade of energy, caught her square in the chest just as she rolled to one knee ready to throw her knife. Liandra did not hear the crack of her chest, but she was confident the woman would not rise again.

Her apprentice lunged forward to throw. All priests trained with the blade, as well as with their bodies, but a gazi priestess like Liandra had no need to worry over the elementary training this boy had received. He all but announced exactly where the knife would go. But as Liandra prepared to sidestep and throw her own dagger, the sound of footsteps from behind stole her attention.

"Liandra, look out!" her father called. Before she could respond, his body had slammed into her own, knocking her out of harm's way. She instinctively spun away before his momentum could take her with him to the ground. Liandra growled then ran for the boy. She would scold her father later.

The boy had assumed a warrior's stance and awaited her arrival. Liandra leaped toward him, leg extended in a kick. Based on the way his feet were staggered, the young seeker would dodge to the left; he did. Liandra abandoned the kick, instead bringing her other leg about as she landed on the first. Her leg swept her opponent from his feet. She plunged her knife into his neck before he could recover.

She rose then strode over to inspect the priestess's body to finish her if need be. Her chest did not appear to move. As Liandra bent over to check for a pulse, she heard her father moan.

Turning, Liandra saw the cause and abandoned the priestess. The apprentice's knife had taken her father in the ribs. His breathing was ragged, labored, and to Liandra's ear his lung sounded punctured. She had only rudimentary training in the healing arts, but she had to try. She bent down and cradled his head, then placed a hand on his chest. She needed to try to mend his lung before removing the knife, lest the bleeding fill the lung further.

Her father's voice interrupted her work, as did his hand, which pushed her own away. "Liandra, leave me. Save your brother. But before you go, you should know something of—"

A coughing fit overtook him, and she could hear the liquid in the sound before she saw the blood spill from his lips. He tried to swallow, but this only caused another fit of coughing. Finally he managed, "Your mother. She was no slave—"

More blood; too much blood. Indeed, her father convulsed, then was still.

*No. This cannot be. Not Father! He is too strong, too good.* She felt a tear run down her cheek even as she reached up to wipe the tears that formed in her father's now-closed eyes. Then Liandra felt a chill overtake her, a hardening of her heart against Klerós for allowing this to happen.

Her brother's voice pulled her gaze from her father's corpse. Looking up, she saw Lyson, still huddled on his bed, trembling, tears flowing freely.

She knew only one thing for certain: they needed to leave the city. Now.

## CHAPTER 35

# KIBURE

KIBURE AWOKE, SUDDENLY AWARE OF—MEMORIES flooded in and he gasped. He was drowning, he felt the cold water surrounding his skin. But he was breathing and he could see that he was no longer trapped within a sinking ship. It was still dark; only a single moon remained, low in the sky, its weak light sparkling off the choppy waters of Lake Lagraas. He was surrounded by water, and partially immersed within it. His body was held afloat by a large piece of wood, leftover from the carnage of the attack.

Then he felt the touch of a hand upon his back.

He heard Tenk's voice, just behind him, which explained the hand upon his back, but little else. "Kibure! You're awake."

Then Jengal's voice sounded to his right, "I was beginning to worry you had entered the eternal sleep."

Kibure shook his head, and forced a slight grunt in response as he took in his surroundings, looking out to the black silhouette of the coastline before he finally realized what was happening.

After a moment, Tenk prodded him again. "You all right?"

Kibure was slow to answer. Finally he nodded.

"Think you can kick your legs?"

He felt weak, but he nodded again. "Yeah, I think so. What happened?"

He moved his legs awkwardly, this being his first experience with more water than what he might drink. He tried to put all the pieces together, from the start of the evening with the Kraken, to the dream where he met Magog himself, or some dream version of the God-king. Then there was Rave, who had been absent for weeks, then had suddenly shown up in his nightmare to rescue him from danger. It was a lot to process, and he wondered how much of what he recalled was reality, and how much imagination.

"After you fell through the floor, the Kraken continued to wreak havoc upon the vessel. I guess it really didn't want our boat floating around in its water. It made certain that nothing but a few splinters of wood remained." Tenk took a few deep breaths. "I was finally able to get my hands on a sword and cut Jengal and"—he paused, then swallowed—"and Grenn free just in time."

His voice cracked at the mention of Grenn, which brought Kibure's head up to search the waters. He turned back to see a thick trail of floating debris behind them, but he didn't see any other people. The wind had picked up, causing the water to jump about, obstructing his view from much of the wreckage. He turned to the other side and saw someone about twenty paces away with one arm clinging to the remains of a cylindrical beam. He squinted. "Is that Jengal over there?"

"Yes." Jengal's voice cracked even worse than Tenk's.

Kibure knew the answer to his next question, but he had to hear it nonetheless. "Grenn?"

Tenk sniffled. "He was struck as I cut the last portions of his rope. I did not—see him after."

In the silence that followed, Kibure's memory returned to his confinement within the sinking vessel. "How'd you get me from below?"

Tenk tilted his head, confused. "I didn't. You were passed out upon this very crate. I might not have found you were it not for this strange flying animal."

That gained Kibure's full attention.

Tenk continued, "The thing started making all sorts of noise, then flew away once I found you. You must have crawled onto the crate then passed out."

"Rave," he said to himself.

"What?"

"Nothing."

Kibure didn't know how to respond to that news, so he didn't try. He had no idea how he might have escaped from the hold, no idea how much of anything he'd done was truly possible, but it was all somehow connected. Rave, his dreams, his feeling of power just before falling through the floor. He was glad for the silence that followed. He needed some quiet to rest his thoughts and mourn his friend Grenn. And he wondered about Sindri, too. After all, she had set him free. If she hadn't, he wasn't sure he would have survived. He looked about again but still saw no others.

She had gone to face the thing, yet it came for him minutes later seemingly unfazed. She had not survived, of that he was certain. He had known both of the deceased for only a short time, but it still felt like a piece of his heart had been ripped out. Kibure had come to respect Grenn and could hardly accept the news that he had not survived. He felt empty as he fluttered his tired legs and pushed toward shore.

His feelings about Sindri were more conflicted. After all, she had tortured him. Yet she had set him free before going to face the Kraken. No matter his dislike of her, he recognized that he was still saddened by news of her death. Surprising as it was, the feeling of loss in the pit of his stomach could not be denied.

Sorrow overpowered any joy he might have felt at the death of Zagreb, for that revelation should have outshone all others. Zagreb had been the source of a lifetime of suffering for the young slave. Yet he could barely find a ray of happiness beneath the cloud of sadness. Even the thought that Rave had returned, and evidently survived the torrent, did nothing to dampen his grief. It just added to the mess of confusion. What was Rave? Why had he returned? Where was he now? None of what had happened made any sense to Kibure.

They finally arrived at the shore after what felt like hours in the water.

Once in the shallows, Jengal suggested they stay in the water and follow the coast as far as they could unseen before stepping upon land to leave tracks. "If you're to escape, no one can see your footprints leading away. This way they'll assume you drowned with the rest."

Jengal looked to Tenk, his face twisted with pain. "Move along the coast in the water. Stay away from any towns or cities and you'll be okay."

He winced again.

"Why do you keep saying *you* instead of *we*?" asked Tenk.

Jengal stood up out of the water and turned to reveal a piece of wooden shrapnel lodged deep in his abdomen. His head hung low. "I'll never survive the journey. You've got to go without me."

"To hell with that!" yelled Tenk. "You'll die here if you stay. You've seen what they do to injured slaves!"

"My wounds are too grave. I'll only slow you down. Death has come for me. At least here it will be quick once I'm found." His voice was firm yet weak.

Tenk would not accept this and continued to plead with his brother.

Kibure remained where he was in the water, cold and afraid as he listened to the debate. Then he thought about capture should they not succeed in escaping. This fear turned his stomach, yet he was pulled also by the message he held in his mind from his vision the night before and the ones preceding that. There were too many coincidences and unexplainable events for him to ignore. Conflicting feelings tore at his innards like the great beast had torn through their vessel just hours before.

Kibure looked up to see Tenk give his brother a long, remorseful look, begging for a change of heart, but he was met with a mirrored expression of helpless anguish.

"Stay along the water for as long as you can so no one has cause to believe anyone but me survived. Head east through the mountains and don't stop until you reach the borders of the Palpanese Union. Good-bye, brother."

"Until the afterlife . . ." Tenk replied. There was regret but also grim acceptance in his voice. He turned without an embrace and began trudging through the waist-deep water.

Jengal attempted to say something more, but no sound came out. He sank down in the shallow water, floating toward the shore where he would surely die.

Kibure took a labored breath then looked across the water behind them before turning to follow Tenk. Tears ran down his cheeks. He turned back to say farewell to Jengal, but words would not come. Kibure was certain that the image of a broken man, crumbled in the cold, death-ridden waters of Lake Lagraas on that night, would never fully leave his mind as he fled east behind Tenkoran.

They worked their way quietly but quickly along the coast for another two hours before finally deciding it was safe to climb up onto shore. Kibure looked back a few times to see if anyone followed but saw none. This did little to put him at ease. He was cold and exhausted, yet he knew they needed to go farther inland to be safe for the day, which was approaching quickly. As he looked to the eastern sky, he could already see the beginnings of dawn.

Kibure had only a vague sense of where they needed to go. He knew only that they must head east, and avoid cities. That was the extent of his plans. The sun rose in the east so they'd travel toward that.

Tenk finally broke the silence. "We need to get inland, then travel east across the Drisko Mountains. From what"—an uncomfortable pause—"Grenn said there is a pass through those mountains. If we can make it there we'll be safe from the Empire, though I think he said there is a desert between that and the freedom of the Palpanese Union. But just imagine, there are no slaves there. We'll be safe!"

"How far do you think that is?"

Tenk shook his head and his posture sagged. "I have no idea."

Kibure realized the enormity of the task before them and his legs felt weak.

Soon, it was bright enough to notice their surroundings and decide upon a real direction for their course. The horizon was lined with ridges of low-lying hills. Tenk was excited, stating that these had to be the beginnings of the Drisko Mountains. "I think we should try to get to those hills before the bright light of day. We cannot stay here in the open; we need to get to the south of them."

Still not familiar with travel and the perception of distances over the vastness of flat terrain, Kibure was irritated by the slowness of their progress toward the hills. The sun continued to rise, yet they seemed to advance no closer. The beauty of their surroundings helped alleviate Kibure's frustration only slightly.

The sun had not yet emerged over the hills, but beams of light escaped to the open sky from behind the distant peaks. They shot up into the scattered clouds, which were deep blue and purple in color. A slight haze obscured the lower portion of the sky where the night's fog had not yet been vanquished. The highest mountain ridges cut a silhouette like the dark center of an eye surrounded by the whites beyond. Both boys stopped a moment to admire the scene before them.

Tenk finally broke the silence. "We'd best keep moving. It's not safe."

The sun finally broke free of the hills and forced them to keep their eyes slightly squinted and downturned. Kibure noticed that the soil began to change color and they had begun to ascend ever so slightly. The terrain changed, too. A few outcropped rocks could be seen within a hundred paces, but Tenk still appeared on edge. Sensing his discomfort, Kibure also remained quiet, realizing how fragile their freedom would be while within the borders of the Lugienese Empire.

They found shelter in a canyon that ran modestly up the Drisko foothills, which were beginning to look a lot more like mountains in the distance. A small creek meandered along the canyon floor, nearly dry in response to the summer heat. By the time they stopped moving, Kibure judged by the position of the sun that it was nearly midday.

Tenk pointed to a distant shape that had emerged along the canyon wall to the north. "We can rest and take shelter beneath that overhang."

Kibure nodded. "Rest . . . I like that idea." He was glad to have reached a place where they might finally repose after a sleepless night of battle, swimming, and hiking, and loss.

Tenk had mentioned that it would get colder as they ascended. His time mining in the mountains to the southwest had at least given him some knowledge of the terrain they would face. But they were still at an elevation low enough to survive without additional clothing to supplement their current attire, which consisted of a large, tough, rectangular piece of fabric folded in half, wrapped around the waist, and thrown down the front and out behind, where it was tied off at the side.

They lay down on their backs beneath the shade of a thick, overhanging outgrowth of smooth shale. This would not be a safe place during the spring melts, Tenk explained. But it was as safe a place as they would find within the valley on this day.

## CHAPTER 36

# AYNWARD

AYNWARD FOLLOWED THE PAGEBOY SENT from the university, a lad of no more than ten summers. He wore a long purple robe with high slits on both sides, exposing his white hose. So far, every student he had spotted, few as that may be, had been wearing this exact same garb. But this boy couldn't possibly be a student, could he?

He had a few minutes before they arrived, so he decided to ask.

"You seem a bit young to be a student. Are you one of the counselor's servants or something?"

The boy stopped in his tracks and whipped around to face Aynward. "I'm no servant. I'm in *the program*." He turned and walked, faster now.

"Oh, right, *the program*. How could I have missed that?"

That comment met no response, and Aynward started to wonder if the remainder of the trek was doomed to silence. But the boy finally turned his head back slightly and said, "I work for the college to pay for secondary school. I learn what I'll need to know in order to get in once I know it."

"Hmm, I see. They're pretty strict on who they let past the gates; you just seem a bit young to be a student."

The youth didn't turn around. "They allow a number of us poppers to earn a place at the university. The count holds a competition each year, and the top three finishers earn a scholarship. I will still have to go through the testing just like everybody else, but I'll be ready in short order."

Aynward couldn't imagine a program like that going over well in Salmune. He could hardly believe that Brinkwell would allow urchins and peasants to learn alongside the nobles, but decided he didn't need to comment on that. He said, "Oh," and left it at that.

A few uneventful minutes later, they were passing beautiful buildings, shimmering in their gray-blue stone, ivy growing up the sides. The university was stirring, people passing from building to building in small numbers, all wearing the same purple robes accented by a chain necklace with a circular amulet marked by a crest. He didn't get close enough to observe whether the crests were all the same.

The boy stopped at a door between several identical buildings.

"Open this door, take a right down the hallway, and knock on the third door on the left. Good day."

He scuttled away without another word.

Aynward stood there wondering what this meeting would bring. Nothing good, he presumed. But as his old friend Fronk would always say, "Nothing for it, but toward it." *Here we go.*

He followed the directions, found the door, and knocked. This was rewarded with the sound of rustling, then it opened. Aynward expected to meet the eyes of the person who had summoned him, but no one was there. He spotted a messy desk, scrolls strewn about, along with stacks of multi-size books, which lined the walls, as well. He had opened the door to the world's smallest, most compact library. Aynward's attention shot back to the door as it continued to move.

A child emerged from behind, turning away from him as he moved toward the messy desk. It wasn't until the child turned sideways that Aynward realized that this was no child after all. It was the tiniest man he'd ever seen!

The small person rounded the normal-size desk and ascended a little stool that led to the normal-size chair.

"You—you're not a child!" blurted Aynward. He was horrified the second the words left his mouth.

The little man didn't smile. "Well, you're a smart one, aren't you? What gave it away? Was it the beard? Must have been the beard."

"I'm sorry. I just—I've never seen a—I've never seen a person who looked like you."

The man couldn't have been more than half his own height. He had matted, ear-length hair, cropped by a long red beard. He wore a purple robe trimmed in yellow and two thickly chained amulets, one resembling those worn by the other students, the other housing a large blue gemstone.

"Never seen a Renzik in person, I take it. Aye, we don't make our way down to the lands of the big'ns all too often. We're a bit of a cliquey folk, to be sure. I'll try not to be offended by your ignorance."

Aynward had heard stories of the northern folk, mostly fables and nightmare-type stories told to children before bedtime. Most believed they weren't real; Aynward was no longer among them.

"You're likely wondering why you're here or assuming incorrectly why you're here, so let me clear that up before we go any further."

It struck Aynward then: the man's voice. He'd heard it yesterday during the testing. It was unmistakable, the halting sound to his speech, the odd way of cutting off sounds at the end of his words before they were finished, like he was in a hurry to spit each word out before he changed his mind. This man had insulted him. He played it back in his mind—*arrogant, privileged, and entitled*, to be specific. These insults had, however, motivated him to go back and figure out the riddle of the last scroll, but the audacity was still infuriating. He'd had no right. Aynward's face warmed as he remembered the insults.

His anger was interrupted by the half-man. "I am Counselor Dwapek. And you're here because I have convinced the testing council to allow me to take you on as my pupil."

## CHAPTER 37

# GROBENNAR

GROBENNAR SHOUTED TO THE CAPTAIN, "Turn this ship around. Return to Karth at once!"

Jaween scoffed. *"You're not going to bring back a body for the God-king as proof of your success?"*

"Why in the lower hells would I bother to do that? Magog said to capture *or* destroy the enemy. He's destroyed. Mission accomplished!"

*"Mind you, I've only been around a few millennia, but in my experience, even with assassination, nine times out of eleven, the sort who order these things done wish to see evidence of the deed. The lake is not likely to bring word of its victims, so . . ."*

"Nine out of eleven? At least get the phraseology right when attempting to prove a point."

Jaween made his tsking sound of disapproval. *"You misunderstand. I do not refer to an arbitrary number set for the sake of hyperbole. I refer to the fractional percentage of assassinations for which I have been involved—the actual number being far greater, of course. As I said, people who want other people dead have a tendency to wish to see the corpse. I believe it provides a sense of closure within the skeptical human mind. The God-king is at least a little bit human."*

Grobennar replied with a harrumph, but otherwise ignored the spirit as he made haste toward his quarters. He needed rest.

An hour later, Grobennar sat up, stomped over to the nearest wall, and punched it as hard as he could. Then he cursed as he repeated the process. He could not expel the certainty that Jaween was right. He would return home having completed the mission, only to have Rajuban spell doubt in the God-king's mind that he had failed. If the enemy were to have continued along his eastern route to Trinkanen, or beyond, the lack of magic on his behalf could be explained in this way! Rajuban would be certain to sell this story to the God-king.

"Curse that man!" He punched the wall for a third time and winced as his knuckle crunched.

Grobennar swallowed a mouthful of pride and pain as he headed to the captain's quarters to give the order that they turn around. Grobennar exhaled loudly; he would need to find a creature of the seas capable of searching and retrieving a body from within the wreckage. The Kraken had been the weapon of choice for destruction, but was not the best option for locating and recovering a body. Perhaps Klerós would bless him and he would find the corpse floating along the surface.

He shook his head, knowing full well that he would receive no such blessing. This would be a long day ahead.

Grobennar ground his teeth. Jaween had the good sense to not gloat, proof that the generally imperceptive spirit recognized Grobennar's acute frustration and chose not to exacerbate it.

However, the problem with having a direct mental connection to a spirit was that oftentimes thoughts and feelings bled through even in the absence of intentional communication. Therefore, Grobennar felt the echoes of Jaween's triumphant laughter. That was infinitely worse. *A long day, indeed.*

## CHAPTER 38

# LIANDRA

## [Five Years Earlier]

"STAY HERE. I WILL BE back in a few minutes. I need some coin so we can get you set up outside the city, away from other seekers while I can figure out how to help you with your—problem."

After days of travel, and good reason to fear the priesthood, Lyson nodded and sat, hesitant, but appearing pleased to go no closer to the vast Kleról in the heart of Sire Karth.

Liandra had not the slightest idea about how she might help him. Everything she had learned insisted that he was evil, touched by the Dark Lord. The only solution she knew was to turn him over to the God-king, never to be seen again. Rumors about what happened after that were as numerous as they were diverse—none of them good where her brother's fate was concerned. But she knew her brother, and knew that turning him over was wrong. There had to be another way. Perhaps there was a way to remove the taint of the Dark Lord, if indeed that was the cause of this ailment. The east was rumored to have all manner of sorcerers and wizards. According to everything she had learned in the Kleról, they were all heathens and doers of evil, but perhaps a small few were not.

Liandra left Lyson sitting at the fountain square built as a tribute to the mighty Kleról before which it was built. This Kleról was also the location of her rooms, and her stash of coin. She also needed inhibitor tea leaves to keep her brother from using his magic by chance, exposing the both of them. She wasn't sure how much the Kleról had on hand, but she would try to requisition as much as she could carry. This tea was the only means known to the Kleról that was capable of preventing tazamines from touching their dark magic. She would otherwise have to find an apothecary with these leaves, which would likely not prove easy as they weren't used for any other purpose for which Liandra was aware.

She approached the tall doors then pushed her way through. She was greeted by Steffen, a seeker new to his robes serving door duty for the morning. Perhaps it was just her imagination, but he seemed taken aback upon seeing her. She smiled anyway and said, "Greetings, Tadi Razir Steffen."

He paused awkwardly, then nodded and bowed. "Praise be to Klerós."

"Blessed are we." Liandra supplied the rote response to the greeting, then hurried through the foyer past the sanctuary toward the adjoining building and her rooms. She glanced back as she opened the door then paused; Steffen was no longer guarding the door. *Something is off.* Liandra took a deep breath and shook off her paranoia, then continued toward her rooms.

She slowed as she neared the hallway where her rooms were situated, a sudden instinct. Peeking around the corner, she spotted a priest just standing there, attempting rather poorly to act casual. She did not recognize him, and she knew all of the priests of this Kleról by name. She ducked back around the corner. What did this mean? There was no way they could know what she had done in Sire Krepe, was there? She had most certainly stabbed the apprentice in the throat, a fatal blow to be sure, and the priestess had been—oh no. She had fled before verifying her death. *Fool!* If she had somehow survived, she would have told her superiors, those with the ability to send a mental message to the Kleról here in Karth before Liandra's arrival.

The Kleról was expecting her, and her welcome would not be warm. Her coin and the tea leaves would have to wait. She needed to leave.

Liandra turned back the way she had come. As she approached the door to the sanctuary, she heard the patter of footsteps; two, three, perhaps more by the sounds of it. Not good. Praying the sanctuary would be open, she gripped the handle to the closest side door and pushed. It didn't budge. Panicking, she sprinted back to the next door and pushed.

She crashed across the threshold just as a contingent of priests stepped through the sanctuary door.

This room was a small library with nowhere to hide. If they had spotted her, she would be found and would have nowhere to run. This room's entrance was also the only exit; so perhaps not the best hiding place.

*Klerós, please!* She could only lean against the near wall and pray as she listened to the sound of feet pounding the floor. The priests drew close, moving swiftly, the sounds of their footfalls coming to her from underneath the recently closed door. Then the sound waned as they continued down the hallway. *Phew.*

*I need to go.* Liandra slid past the door, then closed it quietly before darting back into the hall, through the sanctuary, and out the—

The young priest, Steffen, stepped back into view. He had returned to his post and now barred her way. "Excuse me, Razir Gazi. The leadership would like to speak with you."

Liandra had already killed at least once to save her brother. She did not wish to do so again. She knew this boy, he was a good lad.

"If you would follow me, I can take you to them."

This would be so much easier if she could use her magic to bind him, but she did not wish to risk drawing attention to her location by doing so. She nodded. "Very well."

Steffen released a breath full of tension; he did not wish to fight a gazi priestess. He gestured with a hand. "Right this way."

Liandra, now beside him, took hold of his outstretched arm at the wrist, then struck with her other fist as hard as she could just below the armpit, cracking a rib. While Steffen staggered in shock and pain,

Liandra pulled her knife. She sidestepped behind him and lowered her level to slice just behind the heel. She managed to sever the tendon before he could react. He buckled, and Liandra stood and kicked his back. He collapsed to the floor.

"I'm sorry," she called back at Steffen as she pulled open the main door to the Kleról. And she was sorry. Steffen would likely make a full recovery, but she had to move quickly if she hoped to do the same. She sprinted toward the fountain where she had left Lyson.

Liandra slowed as she realized—*He isn't here.* She looked around as the streets of the morning filled with pedestrians. Maybe he had just grown curious about a passing merchant and wandered from the fountain. *We don't have time for this! Come on, Lyson, where are you?* He was nowhere to be seen. Then she felt the power of Klerós directly behind her. *Stupid!* Steffen was no gazi priest, but he was smart enough to know that using his own magic, even if mundane, would draw the attention of others. *No time!* Then she felt a much stronger force, though more distant. This too was the power of Klerós. It was followed by the sensation of foreign magic, Lyson's tazamine magic. She traced both forces to the same location. Liandra turned to face the main thoroughfare as it extended from the fountain east—toward the God-king's palace.

*No! This can't be.* Liandra ran—toward the sensations of magic.

## CHAPTER 39

# KIBURE

KIBURE WOKE FROM A RESTLESS sleep to a growling stomach and ferocious thirst. He walked out from beneath the shadow of the rock overhang and into the light of the cloudless night sky. The moons provided ample light for his purpose in finding a place to drink from the stream.

Kibure bent down into a crawl, sticking his entire face in the water to drink. He felt the coolness of the water as it traveled down his throat to coat the lining of his empty stomach. It felt wonderful, and he gulped it down.

Refreshed, he sat up and surveyed the surrounding area. He could determine little, because the canyon walls cast so many shadows to keep the moon's light from revealing their secrets. From what he could see, the only vegetation here was that of brittle shrubs and an occasional patch of grass.

Kibure sat and enjoyed the glimmering stream as one of the moons reflected off the water. It looked almost as clear in the water as it would have appeared if he were staring right at it. He considered the value of such properties and moved toward the water in the hope of catching a glimpse of his own reflection, something he had rarely seen.

He slid his face out over the flattened area where the water pooled. Staring back at him were smoothly accented contours of a young face that still looked foreign to him. He wondered how many others would not recognize their own image were it presented to them at such an age. He peered with wonderment. The bluish light of the moons created pockets of darkness upon his downturned face while the water acted in accordance with the laws of the world. Slow as it was, it still created a shifting image before the intrigued boy.

His eyes and slightly opened mouth were dark craters in an otherwise pale-skinned backdrop. He couldn't quite see the details of his eyes, which he had been told were sorcerous for their general lack of pigment, but he was able to catch the shimmer from their moist glassy surfaces, and that was enough of a gift for someone who had gone his entire life with only a few momentary glimpses and limited verbal descriptions of his appearance—most in the form of ridicule.

Movement to his right caused him to look up. His entire body stiffened as he turned his head to focus on the moving shadow. He slid back from the water then crouched down. The dark shape was not moving toward him, at least not directly. It moved methodically but with an air of grace. It was about twenty paces from where he crouched and stayed along the edge of the canyon wall, pausing periodically. Every few moments, a rounded shape emerged from the shadow cast by the natural walls surrounding them, then disappeared back into the gloom. Kibure realized the creature's destination was the overhang where Tenk lay sleeping. Kibure felt the hair on his neck rise. His stomach coiled as fear set in with earnest.

He had experienced this same feeling on the boat the night before, but as he thought back to the blur of events that had transpired, his mind went back to his nightmares. And the thought that Magog had wanted to strike him down. The water beast, too, had been sentient, as if sent by some dark power. The voice in his nightmare had spoken of a darkness in these lands.

Part of him still wondered if he had merely gone mad and would soon awake inside the slave shack of Zagreb's estate, exhausted from dreams but ready for another long day's work.

And yet, as the shadow neared the place where Tenk lay, Kibure's resolution affirmed itself. He would do whatever he could to defend Tenk.

Beads of sweat formed beneath his nose and on his forehead, accompanied by contradictory goose bumps. The hair on his arms rose like blades of grass erected by the wind. He was not ready for this, but he knew he needed to act.

His mind churned through ideas and scenarios. The most appealing, of course, was for him to shout out to alert Tenk of the intrusion. The thought of losing the element of surprise dissuaded him from that course. So he remained crouched, trying frantically to think up a plan that might work—time was running out.

When he spotted movement only a few paces from the overhang, he knew he had to do *something*. He looked about desperately for a rock—anything. It was no use. The largest stones were nothing but pebbles.

Then, about five paces to his left, concealed by the shadow of a small, leafless shrub, he spotted a fist-sized stone. He crept toward it and picked it up.

Without further thought or pause, he shouted to Tenkoran and hurled the rock toward the menacing creature. Then he sprinted toward the darkness, fear gripping his every bone, but driven forward by adrenaline and the desire to help his only remaining human friend. He heard stone striking stone and cursed to himself for missing, then redoubled his pace. But when he was just a few steps outside of the shadow, Kibure saw something that caused him to jump to the side in order to avoid his intended collision. This sudden change of course landed him awkwardly on the ground.

He looked up to see Tenkoran and breathed a sigh of relief. Tenk stood over him with arms crossed, his face full of confusion.

"What're you doing?"

"I—I thought you were—I don't know." He laughed. "I thought you were still asleep so when I saw movement along the edge of the rock wall, I thought something or someone else had come to attack us." Kibure was confused and still trying to register his relief after having triggered such a rush of now useless adrenaline.

As he dragged himself into a sitting position, another burst of movement caught both of their attentions. A dark shape moved swiftly to Kibure's left, causing him to gasp and push off with his heels, out of the way of the approaching shape. Tenk also jumped back.

The black movement ended abruptly, right between the two fugitives. Kibure suddenly recognized the shape and size of the shadowy creature—Rave.

His initial relief disappeared when he saw yet another shape emerge from the shadows behind Tenkoran. He recognized this one as well, and this time his fear returned.

## CHAPTER 40

# AYNWARD

"**P**UPIL?" RESPONDED AYNWARD DUMBLY, STILL reeling from his recognition of the voice.

"Yes, you will be my pupil, I your adviser," responded Dwapek.

Aynward was thoroughly confounded. This man, or half-man, or Renzik, or whatever he was, had insulted him more harshly than anyone in his entire life, save Dolme himself, but then turned around and volunteered to take him on as his pupil? *Perhaps pupil is something different here in the Isles.*

"So what does this mean, exactly?"

The man folded his miniature hands in front of him and rested them on the desk.

"It means I was *told* by the simpletons on the council that it is part of my *duty* to work with and advise at least one pupil. With much reluctance, I have selected *you.* You've been enrolled in the courses I saw fit and I shall ensure that you satisfy all academic requirements while under my tutelage."

"But why? It was you yesterday who berated me at the end of the testing, was it not? Why choose me after all that?"

He chuckled. "Oh, that? I suppose my northern accent gave it away. Can't seem to shed it. Guess I'm just not made for subtlety."

Aynward bristled, but Dwapek didn't give time to interrupt. "In spite of what I said yesterday, I did see a sliver of potential beneath that thick layer of egotism you wear like second skin. You're smart. Though that doesn't take much. Being smart is merely the act of appearing less stupid than everyone else around you, which, considering the other enrollees—*still*." He paused and smiled wide. "The way the other counselors drooled over your quick work of the test, I couldn't help but stake my claim, in my fashion. And none of the other big'ns wanted you after what I'd said. They're all too fickle and driven by impulse and emotion. I changed the entire room's mind about you in seconds. I don't care for wasting time arguing over pupils when there's so much else that needs doing."

He held up his finger for effect. "But to be clear, this doesn't mean I truly think you hold much promise. I'm quite confident in my initial assessment of you."

Aynward opened his mouth to set the man straight but was interrupted.

"Yes, yes, you have a million and two insults for me. I'm going to firmly decline to be an audience for that. As I said, I've more important business. Such as getting you set for tonight's festivities. Classes start tomorrow, and you can't be walking around the university looking like some foreign noble idiot. Better get you the robes and crest. This'll get you into the exclusive university pub down the street, as well." He winked and pulled out a small scroll.

*How did he—*

"Your father, and by proxy, the dean, has made it very clear that you're to study jurisprudence, the science of the elite, as they say. You're quite capable of doing so. I see no need for academic remediation: yesterday's testing revealed full mastery of the trivium's grammar, rhetoric, and logic. You'll start immediately with the following courses: Foundations of Thomist Law, Althusian Ethics, and Apotheca."

Aynward was confused by the last one. "Apotheca? Why would I be taking a course in potion making? What does that have to do with law?"

Dwapek smiled, and the blue gemstone that hung around his neck caught a glimmer of light, appearing to almost glow with excitement. "Why, nothing at all. But trees don't always grow in the forest." Aynward waited for further explanation, but the little man seemed content with the vague non-answer. He continued, "You'll also be taking—"

Aynward cut him short, frustrated that his question had been ignored. "None of what you said makes any sense. If this course has nothing to do with law, why am I taking it?"

Dwapek's expression switched back and forth between smug satisfaction and annoyance. Aynward wasn't sure the man had the ability to express any other mood. His face settled on smug; Aynward decided that he hated him already.

"Apothecarian knowledge will not help you rule or advise others, but it may one day keep you alive when cowardly enemies attempt to kill you or those in your care. Therefore, it is standard university practice to require those students we think capable to take this course. It seems that when people are alive, they do more things worth being proud of. It's good advertisement for us when our graduates go on to live long enough to utilize the knowledge and skills they acquire while here. After all, the wind swirls something nasty to the west."

Aynward rolled his eyes at the furtive insult wrapped with another nonsensical proverb.

"Point taken," he said in defeat. *Is apothecarian even a real word?*

"Good, good! You're getting the picture." He pointed somewhere to Aynward's right and said, "Now be a good little big'n and get yourself some proper garb. The council simply won't abide our students walking around looking like regular folk, or, in your case, spoiled foreign gentry." He chuckled to himself, or maybe for Aynward's benefit, he couldn't be sure. "Don't get blue on me, laddie. I'm merely cleansing you of your former lack of humility. I'll ease up once you've accepted an appropriate reduction in self-worth."

Aynward was furious, confused, and speechless. He stood there dumbly, trying to process everything the man had said, along with what the man had actually meant, or what Aynward thought he might have intended to mean.

"Run along. I've work to do. Get yourself dressed and fed before tonight's festivities. The desposition is mandatory before enrollment becomes official."

"So I've heard," he said, thinking back to the university pub.

"Good. Two doors down on the right. Tell the man that Dwapek sent you. See you tonight."

Aynward finally found his tongue again. "Where do I go for this *desposition*?"

"University square. That's right; need your schedule, too. Classes begin tomorrow. Here, here. You take this. I've got it written here." He pointed to his temple.

He rolled the tiny parchment back up and tossed it Aynward's way.

Aynward caught the mini scroll in his left hand and vacated the room as quickly as possible. Never before had he been forced to back-pedal his emotions like this. The smaller-than-life man had put him on the defensive the moment he'd entered, and he still wasn't sure where he'd landed by the end. It was like being in a room with his father, but without the throne and all the yelling. He was pretty certain he hated the little man, but couldn't put his finger on why. Was it the way Dwapek pattered him with insults like a steady rain? That was likely part of it. Then why was he struggling to identify how he felt about the whole exchange? It should have been cut and dry.

Then it dawned on him. He hated Dwapek, but there was more to it than that. He also felt some measure of respect for the little man who was willing to insult someone whose kingdom would likely not even give him an audience because of his stature alone, not to mention that he was likely of ignoble birth. Yet the man treated him much the same as Dolme did, but without all the self-righteousness. Aynward hated Dwapek to be sure, but he also felt a desire to prove the man's assessment of him wrong, something he couldn't say about his relationship with Dolme.

All this took place in the time it took him to pick up his student uniform, all three sets, as well as a thick-chained amulet with the university crest. He donned the first robe and tights, placed the amulet around his neck, then headed back to his aunt's house. He dropped off the extra sets of uniforms then went in search of a good meal. Dolme insisted on escorting him while the city was still new to him.

He frowned when Aynward showed him the parchment with his schedule but said nothing more than, "Good. You're enrolled now."

They ate in silence, which Aynward appreciated. He had a lot to think about.

Hours later, he ventured back to the university for the mandatory induction ceremony. He was wearing his purple robes, which were surprisingly light, as well as the crested amulet around his neck; an image of a scroll with a sword protruding from its spine to symbolize the power of knowledge, the hallmark of the university.

He was holding it in his hand as he passed the gates and crossed the campus to the university square. He stopped in his tracks when he saw the crowd of hooded figures that formed a circle in the middle. It must have been the entire student population. A few of the nearest hoods turned to face him. Their faces were obscured by shadow, but he could feel their sinister smiles.

Three moved toward him. He stood motionless as they approached. As they guided him toward the center, his heart began pounding. The men at the center were wearing the robes lined by yellow, the counselors. They were wearing masks.

## CHAPTER 41

# GROBENNAR

GROBENNAR ESTABLISHED A MENTAL CONNECTION with the other priests in his party: *"Gather all bodies for inspection."* He had only seen his enemy's face through the colorless sight of the Kraken, but he was certain he would recognize the boy in the flesh.

Within a few minutes, the first body was dropped at his feet, a mangled but surely Lugienese man. The dark skin and translucent hair indicated that this was not the one he sought, but he rolled it over with his foot to inspect the face, if only for the sake of the priest who had transported the pungent corpse.

Hours later, more than a dozen bloated bodies lay in a heap along the sandy shore of Lake Lagraas. Grobennar had already scanned the lake bottom through the eyes of a smaller fish, failing to locate his prize. As the day wore on, his confidence that they might find the body at all waivered. Once Jaween had spoken the words, Grobennar knew, if begrudgingly, that they were true; without proof of his success, he would not receive the credit he deserved for doing Klerós's will here.

Paranja's voice sounded from behind Grobennar, interrupting his thoughts. "How goes the search, my Fatu Mazi?"

Without turning, he replied, "The enemy has yet to be discovered."

She came around to stand before him, and dropped another body off, remaining quiet as he inspected the cadaver. He shook his head disappointedly and she nodded her understanding.

Grobennar felt a growing sense of despair at the sight of each new body that was not that which he sought. He had sent a priest along the coast in both directions with instructions to seek out any human tracks. Had anyone managed to somehow survive his attack, they would need to verify that the survivor was not the Dark Lord's agent. The fact that neither priest had contacted him with news of any such evidence after a full day of searching was at least some consolation. There was certainly a difference between a successful mission that lacked proof and an unsuccessful mission altogether. Even if Rajuban convinced Magog that these two were one and the same, Grobennar would know the truth of it, and that would be enough to lay his head down to rest at night. *Perhaps if I tell myself that lie enough times, it will eventually come true.*

Grobennar's thoughts continued to meander. He recalled one of the crew members who had fought against him during the attack, a woman; she had wielded the power of Klerós against the Kraken. This had failed the woman, of course; whoever she was. But what gave him pause was the question of whether or not she had known whom she opposed, whom she defended. The thought of a priestess of Klerós defending the Evil One's chosen vessel was reprehensible. And yet the Dark Lord was aptly named the Great Deceiver. The mere notion that the Dark Lord might corrupt the Kleról itself galled Grobennar.

Still, the priestess's body had not been among the corpses. Coincidence? He shuddered.

A voice splintered the silence that wrapped his contemplations. "Fatu Mazi, we've found a survivor."

Grobennar's heart leaped, but he knew he needed to swallow the mixture of excitement and trepidation. This could be nothing, and it probably was.

Grobennar asked Tomenar, "What is the condition of this survivor?"

The young but adept priest was speaking too quickly. Grobennar held up his hand to silence him. "Speak slowly, embrace the precision of language you've been taught."

The excited Tomenar took a few deep breaths and then proceeded. "It is a man, slave bred. His breathing is shallow. I initially believed him dead. When I went to pick him up to bring him to you, he coughed and I realized he yet lived. He has been wounded, perhaps fatally. I am not skilled in the healing arts, so I thought it better that you came to see him, lest I deliver the lethal blow while carrying him."

Grobennar was glad once more to have brought with him one of the best tazabis, or healers, in the Empire. He didn't have to say a word. Paranja followed close behind, eager to do her part.

Minutes later, Grobennar knelt beside a male slave in his younger adult years. This was not the boy he sought, but anything the slave had seen could be useful. Grobennar needed to ensure that he lived long enough to be questioned. As he looked at the grievous festering wounds, he prayed Paranja was indeed as talented as he believed her to be; the man appeared ready to pass on to the afterlife at any moment.

Once more, Paranja did not wait for instructions, taking Grobennar's uneasy stance beside the body as a sign that the work was urgent. Grobennar was glad for her intuition in the matter. After a few minutes, she let out a breath of frustration. "I'm going to need help if you want this man to survive." Without looking up, she continued, "I can't remove this plank from his abdomen and safely mend the wound fast enough with my strength alone, and it can't be left as it is much longer."

Grobennar weighed the options. He needed his own still recovering strength if the enemy had indeed survived. Seizing control over the Kraken had required a vast amount of his own energy, even with the strength he had borrowed from the others. He had also channeled Klerós's power in order to search the lake bottom for the body. If he expended much more magic before resting, he would run the risk of shattered bones. He could not afford such a setback.

Grobennar sent out a quick message with his mind, taking a few other priests away from the search to assist Paranja. Minutes later, several priests formed a ring around her, each lending their strength. Paranja called upon the powers of Klerós while the rest murmured prayers of their own. Grobennar stood apart, admiring the beauty of Klerós at work in his people. Paranja caressed the crusted areas surrounding the wooden fragment until it slid free of the laboriously breathing slave. That done, she continued to mend the wound itself.

Finally Paranja stood, leaving the rest of the group on their knees. Her face took on the mixed expression common among the Kleról's elite warriors; the look of extreme fatigue after a grueling workout, combined with the proud look of accomplishment at having managed a great feat. She was sweating heavily. "He will live, but he needs water, and he'll likely not wake for days. If you wish to extract any information from him before then, you will need to delve his mind."

"Thank you, Paranja. You've done Klerós a great honor today."

She nodded.

Grobennar turned to address the others. "Set up camp. We must all rest. We'll resume the search tomorrow."

The second Grobennar spoke the words, the fatigue he'd been ignoring for hours struck him like a giant fist. As much as he hated the idea of resting while a task of great importance remained unresolved, he knew his team, himself included, could do little more until they had recovered their strength. They would rise early to begin anew.

## CHAPTER 42

# LIANDRA

## [Five Years Earlier]

THE GOD-KING'S PALACE LOOMED ABOVE the rest of the city like the soul-catchers of legend, come to collect the day's quota of naughty children. The tall spire of the Kleról cast a knifelike shadow that sliced the city in half as the sun rose in the sky. Lyson stumbled forward as he was forced toward the source of this very darkness, and no doubt his untimely death.

As Liandra drew closer, she realized the futility of rescue; Lyson was accompanied by six gazi priests, and she recognized a seventh man, his vile nature perceptible even in the way he walked. This was Fatu Ma-razir, the high seeker of the realm, a man named Rajuban. With two additional sashes of mastery, he was one of the most dangerous men alive. The only sash he had not earned was that of the scrolls, though he was no doubt as well versed as any scroll priest. But it was the rumors of his cruel nature that had earned him notoriety within the Kleról; whispers of betrayal, deceit, and other dark sins were always close to the man. The thought that he would be a part of her brother's demise brought the taste of bile to Liandra's mouth.

She gazed up at the vast walls of the palace as they came into view, then to her brother, Lyson. The difficult truth of this moment struck her like a tempest wind from both directions; this would be the last she ever saw of him. A part of her itched to launch an assault upon his captors, knowing full well that she would perish in the effort, but she lacked the courage. *I'm so sorry, Lyson. I should have never brought you to this place. And I can't help you now. I—I—don't want to die.*

Liandra couldn't be certain Lyson had spotted her, but she imagined his pleading eyes all the same, and felt the full weight of her shame as she abandoned him to his fate. Shame for allowing her father to be killed, and now her brother. She had lost her robes, for she knew she could never don them again, and for what? For nothing. Everything she had worked for, and everyone she loved—all gone in the span of a few days.

Liandra turned away from the sight of her brother, pulled along in chains—she had to. She had felt her heart rip at her father's passing, but now—her heart ceased to exist altogether. Her brother was worse than dead, or soon to be. And her fate would be no different if she didn't shed her robes and flee the city.

Teary-eyed, Liandra ducked down a side street and confronted the first common woman she saw, forcing her to strip on the spot. No one would refuse her while she wore the red of the Kleról. Now in the clothes of a peasant, she began to walk. She had no destination in mind other than away from the palace, and her brother. She needed to be far enough away to not feel the magic used to torture and kill him. That much she knew would break her beyond repair—that is if she were not already too far gone.

Liandra's numb feet took her among the shanties that lined the outskirts of Sire Karth, a place any child of pure birth, poor or not, was warned never to go. But she did not fear anything or anyone but her own foolishness, her own cowardice. She walked as tears of shame streaked her dust-covered face.

Liandra's feet ached, but she paid them no mind. No physical pain could compare to what she felt inside. Her imagination was relentless; she saw her brother tortured as the priests attempted to learn where his sister had gone. Liandra could only pray they would tire of the questions and end him quickly. No amount of walking would allow her escape from such demons as these.

Her thoughts were shoved aside by a man's voice. "What's a lass like you doing alone on the road?"

Liandra looked up to see a middle-aged, pock-faced man.

"Leaving." Liandra tried to walk past the man.

He stepped in front of her, barring her way in the narrow street, a sinister grin spreading across his face. "Why the rush? I could use the company. What's your name, lass?"

*Liandra died with Lyson.* She had not considered what she would call herself now that she was a slag on the run. Liandra reached into her traveling cloak and found her knife, but decided against pulling it; she preferred not to leave a longer trail of blood in her wake. The man's breath reeked of spirits. Disgusted, she struck his mouth first, a quick jab, followed by an open hand to the left side of his head. She continued without pause, immediately kicking the right knee. The brute did not fall. *Change of plans.* Capturing his outstretched wrist, she spun beneath, coming out behind, his wrist, elbow, and shoulder all exceeding their normal range of motion.

Liandra wrenched the man's arm toward his shoulder blade, earning a yelp. Now fully in control, Liandra considered what she might call herself. Much to her surprise, the name came to her without much thought.

She jerked the man's wrist upward, feeling the snap of bone and ligament, followed by a cry of agony from the man. Still holding his wrist with one hand, she kicked out his knees, and pulled her dagger. She placed it at his throat and said, "You will never approach a woman the way you approached me again. Ever. Do you understand?"

The man nodded.

She twisted his wrist ever so slightly; the man shrieked.

"Do you understand?"

"Yes, yes. I will never! Please."

"Good. Let this small injury serve as your reminder." She drew a shallow cut across the man's throat, careful not to cut any deeper than needed to draw blood. "My name is," she snarled, "Sindri."

She let go of the loathsome man, then kicked him in the center of the back. He collapsed, holding his arm.

Then a hollow, male voice drifted to her ears from the shadows of the adjacent alley, startling her.

"Sindri. A good name for a rogue priestess. But perhaps someday you will not fail to keep the one's you love from harm. Perhaps someday this name too will be laid to rest."

Still driven by emotion, knife in hand, Sindri rushed to meet the source of the intruder. But when she reached the alley, it was empty. She scanned the entire area for life but found nothing but the whimpering fool behind her. *I'm losing my mind.*

She shuddered, then balled her fists and continued out of the city, away from pursuit, away from her failure.

*Sindri. I am called Sindri.* It was ancient Luguinden for *shame.*

## CHAPTER 43

# KIBURE

THE TWO SLAVES STOOD FACING a woman garbed in tattered robes. Tenk had his arms crossed as he addressed her. "Tell me again, why we should trust *you*? Last I knew, you were one of *them*," he said disgustedly, referring to the Lugienese true-bloods.

"Look, I did not follow you all this way just to pretend to be your friend for a few days before capturing and killing you. Had I wished it so, it would be. But I am in as much danger as the both of you, and have been for a number of years."

Tenk shook his head. "Don't believe you. Lugienese true-bloods simply do not help slaves. Why would you, a priestess, do so?"

Sindri maintained her composure in spite of obvious frustration. "I have discussed my intentions with Kibure already, as well as the fact that I am *not* a priestess, not anymore. I had planned to leave the Empire from the start, long before this attack. Ask him yourself."

Kibure had been deep within his own thoughts about Sindri and barely heard the question. Tenk eyed Kibure. "Well?"

"Huh?"

Tenk repeated the question.

Kibure responded, "Oh—well—yes. She's telling the truth about that. Though she left out the part where I was still to be her slave until after she—has used me for a time." He caught himself before revealing his *condition* with Tenk. He didn't wish to spoil this friendship.

"Then that settles it. She can't come." He balled his fists and assumed a wrestler's stance, ready to fight.

Kibure turned to face his friend. "Tenk! She's a priestess—or used to be. She could have us hanging upside down by our feet right now if she wished."

Kibure had made his decision. He was surprised by how easily he had decided. Then something crossed his mind and he paused. "Sindri, how is it that you arrived here, *with* Rave?" His excitement at seeing Rave again had blinded him to the implications of their arrival *together*. She had said she wished to study the creature. Had she found and captured him? The thought made his skin crawl.

Her reply came without any hint of consideration. "After washing up onshore, I searched for survivors and saw none. After nearly an hour of searching, this furry little creature flew over and started making all sorts of noises, cooing and cawing until I realized that it wanted me to follow. The knowledge of your *unusual* relationship with the creature convinced me. And he led me straight to you."

Kibure eyed her closely. He decided he had to *try* to believe her. His decision upheld, he said to Tenk, "She comes."

Tenk was taken aback. "Dark One below, are you mad?"

"Probably, but since she could easily make prisoners out of both of us anyway, and we have no idea where we are going, how to get there, or what to do even if we do reach this Palpan—whatever place, it seems like Sindri is our best option."

Tenk opened his mouth to protest but Kibure cut him short.

"*East* isn't exactly specific. Across the mountains; again—not specific. We have no idea where to go even if we make it across. Those things Grenn spoke of called maps? I bet Sindri has seen many. How about you?" He gave only a slight pause in wait. "Didn't think so. We might not like her company, but I think we'd enjoy being captured and enslaved again a lot less, or dying halfway up a mountain from starvation after getting lost a dozen times. Tenk, she's our best hope of escape."

Tenk relented, taking a seat right where he was. "I don't like it. I really don't like it." He glared at her. "Don't like it one bit." Then his gaze moved back to Kibure. "And I expect you to explain this woman's interest in you. And this—this creature? It's the same one that alerted me to your body in the water before flying away. A raaven you called it? You have a lot of explaining to do. While we're at it, I saw you do some things on the ship that—well—I thought I'd imagined them, only now I'm not so sure."

Kibure just nodded, dread building like a coming storm. "I'll tell you in the morning. As much as I know, anyway, but I warn you: I don't know much, and you may not like that which I do know."

Kibure's nerves now tingled with nausea. *Well, the sun's up on my secrets. And likely another friend lost.*

Sindri spoke again in a mockingly cheerful tone. "Well, now that that's all settled, I'm exhausted. I'm going to go lie down over there." She pointed to another place beneath the overhang. Looking at Tenk she teased, "Please don't try to smash rocks on my face while I sleep. I really don't feel like punishing either of you so soon into our journey."

She spoke to them as if they were children, but Kibure figured she couldn't be more than ten years older than he. Of course, her experience and power as a priestess certainly granted her a position of superiority, so perhaps she was not wrong to speak down to them.

Then, in a more serious tone, she said, "And I'll remind the two of you once more, I mean you no harm, truly. I wish only to escape alongside you." With that, she strode to a place in the dark and made no more sound.

Kibure lay down and tried also to sleep. So many things ran through his head that he could hardly focus on any one of them. None of his previous questions had been answered; in fact, Sindri had added a few more to his existing list. He wondered how many more questions he could have running through his head at one time before he started forgetting some of the first. He and Tenk lay down a safe distance from Sindri.

"Kibure?"

"Yeah?"

"It's time for you to start explaining."

Kibure sighed. "Tomorrow."

Tenk growled, "Now. I won't sleep until I know."

Kibure considered, swallowed hard, and said, "Promise you won't think me some sort of evil, sorcerous creature. I swear the truth of everything I'm about to say, and that none of it has been my own doing. I swear it on my life."

Tenk did not have much patience for Kibure's theatrics. "Yes, of course, just tell me what in the blazes is going on with all this."

"All right. Well, to begin"—he sighed again—"I've been having . . ." He didn't know just how to describe them, his dreams, and decided he should start with Rave and work his way from there. "For starters, this little creature, Rave, has been around for as long as I can remember." He indicated Rave with a nod of his head. The creature darted about overhead from ledge to ledge. "He's just always been with me. Well, not always. He sometimes disappears for days, even weeks, but he seems to be around more often than not. The more I think about it, the more he seems to have been looking out for me, though I don't understand why. He certainly hasn't done much to prevent anything but the worst from befalling me. But he does seem to have an odd way of showing up—"

"With a sword to help you defend yourself against an attacking sea beast?" interrupted Tenk, with no attempt to mask his sarcasm.

Kibure coughed in surprise. "You make it sound more heroic, but yeah. I think that was probably one of the most extreme cases. He usually just brought me extra food when rations were cut. Stuff like that. And much good that sword did me, anyway."

"Much good? Without that sword to cut us free, I'd be dead right now."

Kibure placed a finger on his chin. "Hmm, it's a stretch, but I suppose we could count that as a positive." He was getting the knack of this sarcasm thing.

Tenk was in no mood for merriment. He just nodded and continued to stare Kibure down.

Then Kibure spoke of his nightmares, careful not to include anything about the voice; he wasn't ready to talk about that yet, if ever.

But he decided the part about Magog was too important to keep to himself. He wanted Sindri's opinion about what it could mean. He had better wake her.

"Sindri?"

She gave a deep, annoyed-sounding, *"Yes?"*

"You may want to listen in on this. There's a few things I haven't had the chance to tell you, and I thought you might be able to make more sense of it than I."

Sindri sat up. "You have determined that this can't wait until morning?"

Tenk answered for him with a firm, "No!"

"Very well," she grumbled as she sat up and scooted closer.

"During my last nightmare, I saw someone else in it. I think it was Magog."

There was a silence, and he could not see her expression in the darkness. She finally said, "What do you mean, you think?"

Kibure hesitated. "Well, he spoke to me. And he seemed to think I had been sent by the Dark Lord and was wandering around the realm of dreams to plan an attack upon *his* city. Then I think he tried to kill me."

There was an even longer pause than the last time. Kibure half expected Sindri to call him a liar and string him up with her magic. But it was Tenk who spoke next. His breathing became heavy and stilted; angry breaths.

*Uh-oh*, thought Kibure.

His voice came as a rasp, "You-you-you killed my brother! You killed my brother, and Grenn, and nearly killed me, too!"

Tenk was on his feet in an instant, diving straight for Kibure. Kibure barely rolled out of the way, and not before one of Tenk's fists struck him in the face. It was little more than a glancing blow, but the shock of it was enough that he still shouted in pain. Kibure scrabbled away, but Tenk was already back on his feet, barreling after him.

"Stop this right now!" yelled Sindri.

Tenk continued straight for Kibure.

"Stop right this instant!" shouted Sindri again.

Collision. Rolling. Punching. Chaos. Then finally it stopped. Tenk had rolled off of him. Sindri must have finally wrapped him up with her magic. *About time.* His body, especially his face, throbbed with pain.

He turned his head and heard Tenk's labored breaths of anger turn to sobs. Sindri released her grip around his body. She had physically taken hold of him from on top of Kibure. Why had she not simply used her magic? She'd been more than willing to throw him around like a sack of drogal when he was in his cage.

Then he remembered her saying that other priests could feel the use of magic. That made sense. If they were being searched for, any priests would feel her magic.

"*You* killed them, you monster!" Tenk let out between his sobs.

Kibure sat up, then took Sindri's outstretched hand and stood. Kibure took a step and offered a hand to Tenk, but Sindri pulled him back. "He needs to mourn. Give him space."

She stepped forward and spoke to Tenk softly. "We need to rest or you also will meet the fate of your brother and friend."

He remained seated. "If the God-king himself seeks Kibure, we'll be found, it is our fate."

Her voice had regained that cold strength about it. "He has wanted my head for years. I'm still here."

Tenk continued, "I want nothing to do with the likes of him. If Magog wants him so bad that he sends Kraken, then I want to be days away when next he is found."

"That might be wise," she said. "But for right now, I am the only one who knows how to find our way through the mountains to safety, and I plan to keep Kibure with me."

In an even more serious tone, she said, "You are not the only one who lost something dear to you back there. Life must go on. Use the quiet of the night to mourn."

She turned and started back to her spot to lie down, grabbing Kibure's arm as she went. "Give him space."

Kibure had sunk deep inside his own mind once more. He felt as if he were carrying a pack of sorrow heavier than his own weight. Tenk, one of the first and only human friends he had ever had, now loathed and blamed him, perhaps rightfully so. Had Tenk's brother and another close friend not been near Kibure, their deaths would never have happened.

Sindri only tolerated his curse because she viewed him as a specimen to be examined then discarded. She didn't care for him; she just wasn't frightened enough to flee. He felt a pit in his stomach expanding to take up the entirety of his innards. Fatigue conquered him before he could puzzle out anything more.

## CHAPTER 44

# GROBENNAR

THE SOUND OF WAVES CRASHING upon the shore of Lake Lagraas focused the efforts of the Fatu Mazi as he channeled the power of Klerós. The unconscious slave's memories could no longer remain hidden, not while his mind remained intact within. Grobennar pushed past the man's will as easily as a stone might punch through water.

Grobennar sensed the slave's panic at the touch of another mind within his own. The slave, having no training in the magical arts, could do nothing to stop or steer the priest's mental advances, though he did emit surprisingly powerful emotional bubbles of fear and anger, which slowed Grobennar, if only slightly.

In spite of his ease of entry, every mind was different, and Grobennar would still need to take some time to understand the mind, and its system of organization. Without a general sense of the way memories were stored, one could remain in another's mind for hours without ever getting close to the memories they sought. Grobennar was no novice. Within a few minutes, he knew this slave's name, Jengal, and more important, he knew that this man had seen the face of the Evil One. They had spent days together. This Jengal had remained ignorant of the Evil One's plans, unaware even that he was capable of the dark arts. The

Dark Lord had remained humble, quietly lurking among these common slaves. He must have entered Sire Karth to gather information, then jumped ship to escape quietly without a trace, wishing to remain undiscovered by all. He had *almost* succeeded.

Grobennar continued along the slave's trail of memories leading up to the attack, and smiled as he witnessed the attack on the ship through the terrified eyes of this witness. The Kraken was a chilling sight to behold. In fact, this slave's mind *could* be used as evidence of Grobennar's success if the Evil One's body could not be found. He watched as the repulsive conduit for evil was struck down—wait—something was off. He watched again. The bolt of energy he had believed to have struck the boy had missed! He watched again. The Dark One had—the wooden planks dissolved beneath him. Then again, the ship had sunk soon after, and the Kraken had continued to strike down any bodies he'd seen moving or not in the water for a long while after.

*"Perhaps Magog will not notice that you missed. You yourself had to watch several times. This man's mind could serve as proof enough."* Jaween's hopeful tone reeked of pity. That from a spirit-being who never pitied anyone or anything.

This was an all-time low for Grobennar. He did not respond; others were too near. He continued to follow the slave's consciousness forward in time. He saw the lifeless water after the ship had sunk, and then—

Grobennar's remaining hope withered when he saw the Dark Lord's agent floating on a plank of wood in the water in the aftermath, alive. He followed that memory all the way to the shore. Then watched helplessly as the Dark Lord's agent departed with another slave, virtually unharmed. Grobennar played back the slave's last conversation with the *enemy*, but there was little more to be taken from it. Delving into a mind had its limitations. One could not see a person's thoughts, they could only *see* their memories or what the person in question remembered seeing with their own eyes. There was no sound to accompany these memories, either. His captive had pointed east, and the Evil One had started off in that direction with another slave. Nothing further could be gleaned from the interaction. Grobennar released a string of curses as he watched his target disappear back into the water. All he had was the knowledge that his mark was alive, and the general direction he had taken.

He wished he could go through more of the man's interactions with the boy, if any existed, but he had lost precious time already. He released the slave's mind, and his own vision returned. He growled to himself.

Grobennar chose one of his priests to stay behind to nurse the slave to health as well as to ensure his confinement once conscious. Perhaps he could be of further use at a later time. For now, Grobennar needed to find and capture or kill the Dark Lord's avatar, the abomination. Grobennar spat. The attack should have killed the boy.

He sent out a mental message to his team: *"Return to the ship. We're bound for Korinth."*

*"Am I missing something, or are you assuming the boy plans to not go through the mountains?"* asked Jaween.

Grobennar stormed toward the vessel, far enough away from others to not be overheard as he said, "Our target will need to be tracked. You have any tracking skills that I don't know about?"

*"I have a great many skills that have yet to be revealed due to their lack of applicability thus far in our relationship. But alas, tracking is not among them."*

"Very well, then. I need to find someone who has those skills, or we'll be wandering through the mountains blind."

*"Ah."*

This was as much of a verbal victory over Jaween as Grobennar had experienced in years, yet the circumstances prevented him from enjoying such. Grobennar's glower was beginning to feel as natural upon his face as the glib smile nearly always worn by Rajuban.

## CHAPTER 45

# AYNWARD

THREE STUDENTS SEPARATED THEMSELVES FROM the horde that made up the disturbingly cultish-looking desposition ceremony. Aynward stood motionless as these students approached then flinched when they took hold of him.

They guided him toward the mob that filled the square; each step increased the speed and ferocity of his pounding heart. Aynward was *almost* too surprised to register his terror once he reached the crowd, where more hands found his body, adding to the current that pushed him to the center of the throng. Unfortunately, the word *almost* applied only to idealists, and Aynward was anything but that. Terror struck him like a barrel of wine tumbling clumsily down a set of stairs. And he was not alone in the frenzy; he could see others being similarly herded to the middle. His apprehension cemented as he noted the tightening enclosure made up of upperclassmen. The word *civilize* was being whispered by all in attendance, the hiss becoming a chant from within their ranks.

As he was shoved into the small opening at the center, an arm caught hold of his, clamping down hard. He turned around to see a face that confounded him. It seemed strangely familiar. Aynward's consideration of this riddle was interrupted by the demand, "Lower your head, you ignorant beast."

Aynward looked around and noticed that many others were wearing strange contraptions on their heads: varying-sized horns, to be specific. He complied with the demand, but looked up in the process. He scrunched his eyebrows as he wracked his brain for where he had seen this individual who was tying horns to his head. He became more and more certain that he *knew* this person, which was puzzling because he'd met virtually no one from the university, aside from—the boy at the entrance to the testing!

He owed *this* lad some payback and it seemed the sum would be increasing. The fabric that tied the horns to his head pinched the skin on his neck.

"Ow!" yelped Aynward. "Easy on the—yeow! Gods!"

The boy pulled hard on the horns, testing the skin-pinching tightness, then turned Aynward around and tied his hands behind his back before pushing him away, apparently satisfied with his work. Yes, Aynward promised himself: that one's debt would be extensive, indeed.

Just then, the masked men in the center each raised a hand and the hissing chant came to an abrupt halt. One of them spoke in a booming voice. Aynward assumed he was the university's dean. The man had a distinct hunch to his posture, a frailty to his physique, but the strength resonating from his voice neutralized all considerations of weakness.

"Mankind in all its glory has shaped this world, and all its inhabitants to their will. Yet the struggle to domesticate ourselves has been a long and tumultuous story of blood and suffering. Our history is stained with tribal conflicts, civil wars, betrayal, and conquest. And while you now live in a time when man has some claim to civility, you remain apart from society's highest echelon. You may yet be above the fish of the sea, or the sheep of the fields, but until you are stripped of the ignorance of your inner beast, you will never ascend the summit of civilization that awaits only those worthy and willing to climb its difficult reaches.

"This desposition is a tradition handed down to us from the first scholars to recognize the importance of passing on and further growing the knowledge of the elite. The knocking of the horns symbolizes the transition from beast to civilized man. And while the actual process is a gradual erosion of the ignorance celebrated by the masses, we replicate the destruction of the old self tonight as a reflection of what your education here will have on all who embrace it to the end."

The orator lifted both hands and the other masked figures—counselors, Aynward was sure—all followed suit. Aynward suddenly understood what was to take place as he stared at more than a dozen wooden clubs, raised in the air by the counselors. They were going to literally knock off the students' horns with clubs. *What happened to all that talk about being civilized?* Did his father know that he'd entrusted his son to a bunch of lunatics? *Probably.*

These thoughts came to a sudden halt when pain erupted from the left side of his head. He turned just in time to see one of the masked men taking his second swing. Aynward's natural reaction was to move out of the way of perceived danger, but his natural reaction was too slow and the blow struck the horn tied to the right side of his head, slid off, and collided with the top of his skull. It did not feel good.

Before he could think to complain, he was struck from behind, on the rear. This was followed by laughter from the upperclassmen surrounding him. *They're making fools of us.* He'd turned to face the source of his embarrassment only to expose his flank to the initial perpetrator. He tried to avoid the next swing that came for his head but his movement was interrupted by the surprise from behind, and the laughter thereafter. This swipe at his head struck only the horn, but the horn stayed true while the strong fabric holding it shot pain across his chin where it slid and pulled.

He turned once more, away from the last club at the same time the counselor behind him knocked him in the side of the head, and he saw stars as he toppled to the ground in pain. He lay there with his head spinning for a moment before things straightened out. Someone knelt over him and put a hand to the ties on his chin. *Bless the gods, it's over.*

The hand gave a slight tug on the ties. Satisfied that they were still tight, the male said, "Get up. The horns of ignorance *must* be eradicated."

Aynward didn't move.

"Get up!" the voice shouted as a boot made heavy contact with his stomach.

Aynward lay still, boiling with a mix of fear and anger. This was insanity. What did it have to do with—"Ohh!"—another boot to the stomach.

*That's it.* He rolled away from the next kick. He then arched his muscular back enough to slip his still-tied hands down underneath his bottom, around his feet, and to the front of his body. He stood and turned his back to the crowd where he could face the counselor who'd been kicking him. The mask of some unknown beast faced him; then its wearer swung.

Aynward had been training with swords since he was a child. Once he had his balance, the right movement was second nature. The club missed his head and horns completely, putting the overextended counselor off balance. With his hands now in front of him, he could catch the club between the tied fabric of his wrists and twist. The club wrenched free and Aynward stooped to pick it up.

"Hey, what are you—you can't do that!"

Aynward held up the club then struck at the masked portion of his former attacker. He heard the rewarding shout of pain as the counselor dropped to the ground. The students around him exhaled in unison. It wasn't cheers of joy or anger, just the high-pitched sounds of surprise. Aynward turned and smiled. "Watch me."

Without any thought about potential consequences, Aynward intervened in the struggle of the closest horned student he saw. His club thudded against the counselor's downward strike, preventing the desired contact.

The man attempted to face Aynward, but Aynward timed the man's step and used his own leg to sweep out the counselor's opposite heel. The masked figure toppled to the ground, accompanied by a satisfying scream. This time there was a mixture of laughs and shouts from the crowd. The student he'd saved, a boy with curly red hair, stared back at him as if he'd just committed murder, eyes wide in terror. Aynward winked at him, then ran to intercept another blow for someone else.

This time he met the swing and returned one of his own, and again he attacked the back of a leg. These men were no fighters, that much was certain. They clunked around like fools. *Where I come from, civilized men learn their way around a sword.* It was *his* chance to bring about civilization.

"Stop him!" rang the dean's voice from somewhere to his left.

He easily toppled two more before enough shouts echoed to create concern in the others. When that flurry ended, he faced down a counselor wearing the mask of a giant rat. But this one was cautious. He backpedaled slowly, unwilling to engage. *Well, this is boring.* He was ready to turn and find someone else when the man froze in place. Aynward could see his eyes looking—behind him.

He ducked just as a body careened over him, upturning the counselor instead. Aynward looked back to where the poorly aimed human arrow had come from and saw that the ceremonial circle was losing its shape. A few of the students who made up the circle had entered, and the ones behind seemed unsure of what was happening but moved backward, creating space between them.

Aynward pivoted as the crowd behind made sounds of excitement. This saved him, as the person who had just flown over him had recovered and ran toward him once more. "These people really aren't as smart as I'd have expected," he said under his breath.

This student had a club now. *Must have taken it from the counselor. Smart. Running forward—not smart.* Aynward froze then, barely avoiding the blow as he recognized the same face that had tied his horns, the same face that had pranked him upon arrival. He recovered his wits and reacted to the missed strike. He turned and stepped closer to the boy, too close for either to swing, and brought up his knee. It struck a hard stomach that was flexed because of his movement, and yet the boy still grunted in pain.

Had it been some unknown, Aynward would have just knocked him from his feet, but this was too perfect an opportunity. He used the close proximity to his advantage, and while the boy was still hunched from the hit to the stomach, Aynward elbowed him in the back of the ribs. He did so just hard enough to ensure that the boy would remain hunched over as he stepped past him, turning quickly to face his back and clubbing him straight between the legs. The resulting squeal was just the reward he had hoped for. The boy toppled.

Aynward made sure to look him in the eye before continuing. The expected look of contrition, or embarrassment, was nowhere to be found. The boy's eyes had tears in them, but behind the tears was a look that made Aynward wonder if he'd just made a mistake. There was malevolence in those blue, crystal eyes that frightened him. The expression said, *This isn't over.*

Motion to his right forced Aynward to abandon the disconcerting stare. He was being encircled, and five non-masked upperclassmen surrounded him, armed with counselors' clubs. After a few feints to test their reactions, Aynward knew that at least two were no novices. He would put his skills up against most, but with both hands still tied together, his balance wasn't perfect, and he was one against five.

He considered just setting down the club and letting them whack away until his horns were off. He'd proven his point, though he wasn't sure exactly what that point was. He was certain he had proven it, nonetheless.

But his pride refused to stand down, and they all attacked at once.

He felt the pang of wood hitting his body in several places but he was moving and only one connected with real force. His knee burned, but he used the chaos of movement between them to his advantage and broke free of the circle, turned, and put two on the ground before they'd landed another blow.

The crowd had remained intact and he found himself enjoying the audience's hoots and hollers. Only a few curses seemed directed at him. Plus, they'd alerted him to danger twice now.

Then pain shot up his back. *Where were you on that one, people?* He didn't fall, but he knew his body would be cursing him the moment the bloodlust left him.

Before he could turn to face the new foe, another club connected with his back, though not as hard. Whoever it was hadn't wound up quite as far. If they hoped to beat him to the ground before he could defend himself, it was working.

He collapsed after the fourth or fifth hit, a few hitting his spine. Then the battering stopped and the crowd shouted in surprise. He used his elbow to protect his face as he turned to see what had happened.

He could hardly believe his eyes. Another boy with horns on his head had negotiated his hands so they were in front of him, and he was holding a club. The upperclassman responsible for the pain in Aynward's back had dropped his club, hands covering a nose that was oozing blood all over his face and down his neck.

Aynward stood up and stared at a curly-haired lad who stood with a sense of confidence that didn't quite align with his physique. He was half a head shorter than Aynward, and parchment thin. He did have an inviting smile, which was being employed at this moment.

"You're welcome," he said.

Aynward noticed a red welt with a swollen lump on the lad's forehead, and understood.

"Let's embarrass a few more of these blokes before we're expelled."

Aynward hadn't considered what might happen to them as a result of their defiance during the ceremony, but expulsion did seem fitting. He shuddered when he pictured the look on his father's face when he returned, disgraced, before classes had even started.

The fear that gripped him in that moment slipped away the instant he saw an attack coming from behind his partner in crime.

Aynward yelled, "Duck!"

A club came with force enough to knock his head from his shoulders. But the boy not only ducked, he spiraled down into a crouch. This let him strike out at his assailant's midsection. As the body fell, the boy pivoted off of his left foot back onto both feet.

Aynward, too, had to sidestep the momentum of the felled mass of the upperclassman. The pair was quickly encircled by more than a dozen, but only a few seemed to have much skill and fewer still seemed willing to risk being embarrassed as others had. Aynward was impressed with the grace of this other student and wondered if he might be better than himself.

"What's your name?" asked Aynward as he connected with the ribs of another brave fool.

"Kyllean, if you please. You?"

"Annard."

"Pleased"—swing—"to"—kick—"meet you."

He was good, very good. While Aynward was taking hits every here and there and knew he would be laid up with bruises the next few days, he wondered if this lad had taken any injuries after deciding to join the fray.

Then the shouts of the frenzied students changed to quiet murmurs, and Aynward got the feeling that the fun was coming to a close.

The dean's voice boomed. "Put down your weapons—*now!*"

The crowd parted and Aynward saw a score of soldiers wearing armor, carrying swords. He looked over at Kyllean, eyebrows up.

They both dropped their clubs in unison.

The orator stepped toward the two boys after they were surrounded by the armored guards. His face was stormy red with anger. "You, insolent, little . . ." He spoke between clenched teeth, loud enough for only those nearby to hear.

In a louder voice, he said, "These two cling to their ignorance like newborns do their mother's teat. So it falls on us to break down these walls of defiance for them. In this extraordinary case, symbolic action seems to have been insufficient. We must find the literal walls and break them."

He stepped forward between the guards and kicked the clubs they had stolen out of reach. With his expression still smoldering, he said, "Break them!"

Several of the masked counselors had retaken their clubs and moved toward them, shuffling past the soldiers who were apparently only there to ensure that no further resistance took place. A pit in Aynward's stomach formed, but there was no more fight in him.

He brought his hands up in front of his face before the first blow. It was not gentle, nor was the next. He did not stay on his feet long and caught a glimpse of Kyllean, also curled up on the ground as he was beaten by a rotating group of counselors and their helpers. Aynward closed his eyes for most of it.

There was a pause and Aynward thought maybe they were finished, but then he saw the smiling face with crystal blue eyes just before a foot struck him in the ribs. A loud popping sound resulted as fire sprouted from that location. He'd cracked a rib as a child, but the experience didn't make this second time any less painful. More blows came as the rotation continued.

## CHAPTER 46

# KIBURE

MIST ROSE, ONLY TO BE struck down by the early light of dawn as the trio ascended the canyon slope farther. The fluffy light cousin of clouds whooshed along as the wind guided it through the corridor. They walked in relative silence that day. Tenk seemed content to never speak to either of them again, and Kibure was afraid to try, for the sound of silence was better than the sound of condemnation.

As dusk approached, they sought another suitable place to rest for the night; it would do no good to twist an ankle or break a leg while sneaking around in the dark. The canyon had diminished slowly as they continued up in elevation, and the stream that accompanied it had disappeared into a cave a short while back.

The climbing had intensified as the angle increased. There were now little more than a few boulders and smaller crevasses within the barren landscape in which to shelter for the night. Rave had stayed with them throughout the previous night and had even taken a position upon Kibure's shoulder for a time before flying off.

Just as the fugitives considered sleeping out in the open, the raaven's coo sounded behind them. They turned to see him resting above a small ridge. They looked at one another then turned back to investigate.

The ridge gave way to a small, otherwise hidden cave. The entrance was narrow, so they had to crouch down to get in. There was little light inside, but enough of the fading light bounced in to at least outline the cave's largest features. After about five minutes of hugging the walls, they found that it opened up considerably. The opening could not have come at a better time, because they were about to turn around for lack of light and hope. Around a corner, a small fissure in the ceiling allowed in several thin beams of moonlight, revealing an oval cavern, stone arms reaching down from the ceiling and an equal number reaching up, some even joined in the middle to form columns. They cast eerie shadows across the ceiling and floor. The cave had an unpleasant, almost fecal, smell to it, but it was tolerable for the sake of safety. After surveying the area to make sure they were alone, they settled down to rest.

Kibure felt his fatigue, but found that sleep was not forthcoming this night. The silence between him and Tenk was palpable, and it stung his heart.

There was also the frustration of not understanding the interconnected events leading up to this point. He lay for hours playing over how it would sound should he try to put words and a chronology to these events. It was maddening to know that it might be months, or even years, before he and Sindri found someone who could help him puzzle out some of the strange things that had been happening to him; that is, if they survived that long.

The fugitives awoke indignantly to Rave's high-pitched cries echoing through the cave. They determined to seek out the cause of such ruckus, though Sindri articulated several punishments for the creature should the noise prove to be without just cause. Rave must have heard their footsteps, for his noises stopped once they began moving.

They proceeded with supreme caution as they approached the cave entrance, for they had no idea what ill fate might await them outside. Kibure emerged first, apprehensive, but after a moment, he motioned for the others to come forth. He was surprised to see that the sky was already waking with color. They had slept through the entire night.

The black creature shouted again then dropped a freshly killed rodent, nearly his equal in size. Sindri looked to Kibure, eyebrows flat above her eyes, and then picked up the dead animal. "I think someone thinks we might need a meal before we continue." She pointed to the rising sun. "Darn good timing, too." She added, "Seems Kibure's friends aren't all so terrible, eh?"

Tenk merely grunted, then said, "We should cook this meat over a fire."

The thought of meat cooked over a fire caused Kibure's mouth to water.

Sindri cut that dream into pieces. "No time to start a fire."

Tenk rounded on her. "Couldn't you just conjure up a fire with your magic stuff?"

"Sure. But if the Kleról is looking for Kibure, they will sense the use of magic and find us all the sooner."

Tenk grunted again and ripped off a rodent leg with his mouth and began to chew.

Kibure said nothing; just shrugged his shoulders. All three ate what meat they could scrounge from the large, rabbitlike creature. It may have been raw, but they had been days without any sustenance. No complaints were forthcoming.

They continued to ascend the foothills of the Drisko Mountains. None of them were full from the meal, but it provided enough energy to fuel them for many hours. Rave took a place upon Kibure's shoulder once more as they continued their ascent.

They climbed for half the day before stopping for a break within the cover of a few man-sized shrubs. They rested on a small rise along the side of a taller ridge of mountains to the north. They had begun moving eastward along the northwest side of the Drisko Mountains.

Sindri noted that they needed to continue moving east, parallel with the mountains, before turning south, at which point they would need to find the pass to cross over into the freedom of the Palpanese Desert.

As they hiked, hunger and fatigue began to tug at Kibure. Rave flew ahead a few times, finding the few patches of berries to be found in such a sparse environment, but it was not enough to sustain them for an arduous journey through the imposing peaks of the Drisko Mountains. Just before dusk, they crossed another small stream of fresh, cold water, which rejuvenated them before they stopped for the night.

For the next two days, they climbed upward before descending into a high valley. By the time they reached the other side, they were within one of the last remaining groves of pine, one of the few places left in all of Angolia where a vast number of trees still grew south of the northern forests.

Sindri stopped suddenly.

"What? What is it?" asked Kibure.

"Logging."

Kibure looked at her with an expression that he hoped communicated his bewilderment.

Tenk answered Kibure's confusion. "We're near a village?"

Sindri nodded. "I didn't realize just how far we'd traveled. We need to get a closer look. If possible, we need to steal some supplies."

They followed the logging trail at a distance, paralleling it through the woods just in case anyone was about.

They stopped atop a hill marked by several boulders. They jutted upward like scars on a slave's back. The group looked out over a more gently sloping portion of the valley within which rested the village they sought.

It was small, smaller even than Jarquin. There was only one little Kleról, built from wood, and poorly crafted compared to those in Sire Karth. There were perhaps fifty homes scattered throughout the valley.

As they circled the village, Kibure saw a drogal farm much smaller than the one where Kibure had worked. An eerie dread filled him, who feared returning to a life of servitude, especially harvesting drogal.

The three retreated back up the valley as the late afternoon light streamed through the trees. They would rest until nightfall, before conducting their raid. However, Kibure's jangling nerves allowed only a light sleep.

Just before dusk, Sindri stirred them from their slumber. Still groggy, they began their descent into the village. Despite Rave's efforts to supplement their diets, they were starving. As they reached the fringes, Kibure, Sindri, and Tenk split up, each with precise objectives in mind.

Kibure was to obtain as much drogal as he could carry, Tenk needed to abscond with weapons for hunting, and defense, while Sindri would steal clothes for the cold climate of the higher elevations, and packs to carry their supplies. She also stated a desire to find one of those map things that would tell them where to go. They were to meet back near the trail, where they originally began that evening.

Kibure's nerves were nearly unbearable as he approached the drogal farm. He was not used to sneaking around, and the ground was littered with twigs too numerous to avoid. The crackle of each step echoed like a choir of shouting voices, and he was certain someone would wake at any moment to discover him. Thankfully, he was surrounded by trees, which cast long shadows, making him feel less visible under the partially clouded night sky.

After taking a few minutes to collect his courage, he made his way into the farm. He walked along a line of drogal stalks until coming to the edge, where he stopped to survey the area. The cloud cover had thickened, offering less light than he would have preferred, but at least he would be more difficult to spot should he happen across any villagers.

Kibure identified the entrance to the slave quarters roughly twenty paces from the outhouse but could see nothing else of interest in that direction. The thought of slaves locked away in that small stone dungeon made his heart ache, but he knew he could do nothing to help. Even if he were able to free those slaves, he knew that many would refuse to risk fleeing. Additionally, larger numbers would make their group easier to track. He shook his head, no; he had only one objective while on the farm: gather food for their journey.

He looked to the right and saw the large stone barn. It was not at all like the barn that held drogal at his former estate, but he attributed this to the fact this estate had no walls or guards, while his estate had both. He examined it quickly from where he was then moved in to finish his work. He was beginning to feel more and more uncomfortable with surroundings that resembled the life of slavery he was trying so desperately to escape.

When he reached the barn door, he found that it was locked, another thing that was different from his own where tall walls, strict penalties, and guards prevented all fears of theft from within.

The door was thick and sturdy, and did not budge from Kibure's frustrated attempts to open it. After a few moments, he conceded that the effort was of no use. He had hoped he would be able to at least force open a window, but those too were barred.

"*No—no—no!*" He slumped to the ground, moisture forming in his eyes as he realized he would have to return to the others without one of the most important items for their journey across the mountains.

He sat there for several minutes, lost in despair until startled by a shadow emerging to his left. The shadow became a man, not a big man, but big enough, and armed. Kibure's heart nearly stopped. There was nowhere to run, and he was completely exposed where he sat. The man would have to be blind to miss him. The guard swiveled his head to face Kibure, now only ten paces away, and Kibure turned to make a run for it.

An odd sound stopped him and he turned back. The man had decided to lie down on the ground, which Kibure determined made no sense at all. He looked around cautiously, but saw no others. He approached slowly. When he was only a few paces away, he identified the reason for the man's condition. A stone the size of two fists lay on the ground, and the back of the man's head leaked blood. Kibure didn't have to look to the night sky to know what had happened. Instead he rummaged through the man's belongings. To his relief, he found what he needed: a set of keys. Kibure had never used keys himself, but he had seen the overseers on the estate use them plenty enough times to understand the basic concept.

Before moving to the door, Kibure glanced up to see Rave's crisp silhouette as he glided through the air before an opening in the clouds. Kibure couldn't help but smile at the helpful little enigma that was the raaven.

He gathered what he could, a half-full crate, then exited through the field and into the woods. Half an hour later, he reached the rendezvous point to find Sindri waiting with a bundle filled with clothes and another pack with which to stuff the drogal. Kibure's excitement melted when dawn became midday, and Tenk had not yet returned. That could mean only one thing.

## CHAPTER 47

# GROBENNAR

GROBENNAR AND HIS PRIESTS SAILED onward to Korinth. They needed to hire a woodsman to track their prey. Their guide, a short, gruff-looking man no younger than fifty, named Sija, led them directly into the Drisko foothills.

They rode swiftly atop horses; animals brought in from the east hundreds of years back for their speed, strength, and endurance. They avoided the open rocks of the valley where horses were known to stumble and slip. Sija was confident that they would recover the fugitives, whom they knew were headed toward freedom in the east. The grizzled man boasted that there had not yet been a fugitive he couldn't find. At this time of year, there were only two passes through the mountains that the boys could hope to survive. And it would be clear which one they would be headed for once they caught their trail.

After an arduous day of travel, they arrived at a forest village where they would leave their mounts until the return trip. Sija spoke with a contact he had in the village then returned minutes later with a swagger and a crooked smile. "Looks like some minor thievery was had here last evening, probably enough to get two lads through the mountains should that be their goal. However, they did leave us a little treat." He waved a hand. "Come along."

Grobennar and his contingent of priests followed the tracker to a small building at the village's center. It was guarded by two men and the village priest. The elderly priest stood with his head downcast, his robes looking very ordinary even when compared with the travel-weary crimson worn by Grobennar's entourage.

Sija hopped off his horse and waited by the door for Grobennar to follow. The priest inhaled loudly and knelt at the sight of Grobennar's gold-laced trim, which signified his esteemed position within the Kleról.

"It is a great honor, Fatu Mazi."

Grobennar had no time to exchange pleasantries. "Yes, yes, of course. You may stand. My tracker says you've found something that may be of aid to our mission. Please show me." Manners were an unnecessary courtesy, given the discrepancy in station, but Grobennar had vowed never to behave like those he had hated so much during his own rise to prominence; those who had exuded such egotism and arrogance. To be blessed by Klerós was no excuse for becoming supercilious; he believed himself better than that.

Grobennar stepped into the building and gasped. Before him sat the familiar face of an adolescent slave boy.

"*Oh Klerós, bless us—what a joyous day for celebration!*" cackled Jaween.

Having entered the mind of the slave, Jengal, Grobennar knew this boy had survived the wreckage, and, furthermore, had fled alongside the Dark Lord's agent. "Klerós shine upon us," he said. Indeed the Great God did, to have brought the boy into their custody. Some quick mental probing and he should be able to track down the other with ease.

Wasting no time, he moved to sit beside the bound child. "We need to find your friend. And while I'm sure you would be willing to tell me everything, and truthfully, I'm going to ensure that nothing is lost in translation. This will not hurt, but it may be—uncomfortable." The boy glared at him. Grobennar grabbed hold of the boy's head. The slave attempted to wriggle free, but it was of no use; his hands were bound behind his back and his ankles tied. Once inside the boy's mind, Grobennar would be able to control all motor function and stop any remaining struggle from within.

Grobennar felt near to full strength, having rested the night in Korinth before departing. A small mental probe would put little strain on his restored bones. So he dove headlong into the slave's mind. Sinking in quickly, he struck a thick jellylike wall of resistance, stronger than the one found in his brother, and different. This boy was full of contempt, a palpable anger. Grobennar could hardly blame a slave for holding such emotions, for Klerós had surely forsaken his people. The resistance was futile, however, as the boy was ignorant of the discipline necessary to protect his mind. Within minutes, the Fatu Mazi had shattered this mind just like the last, just like every mind he had ever entered.

Images bombarded Grobennar until he slowed and sorted them, deciphering the order within the chaos. *There! The enemy.* Grobennar furrowed his brow; an unusual creature appeared to accompany this boy he sought. Grobennar had seen a raaven once before, on display; smart creatures. But as he sifted through the slave's memories, he realized this was no ordinary raaven. It was some sort of meddling agent of the Evil One. This must be the spirit of which Magog had spoken.

*"Spirit of the Dark One,"* sneered Jaween.

Grobennar would have to ask Jaween about more on that when he was alone, but he did not like the sound of this one bit.

Then another image chilled his blood further. The woman. The one who had attacked the Kraken with Klerós's power. She too had somehow eluded death. Grobennar had stripped her of her ability to summon his god, but as he studied her face through the boy's memories, Grobennar realized something more disturbing: he knew her, though she had been much younger when last he had seen her. His recollection returned with the name, Liandra, though she likely went by another by now. They had trained within the same Kleról in Sire Karth for a short while. She had become a powerful seeker. He had heard word that she had been deposed, stripped of her robes, though for what reason he could not recall. How she had originally been expelled from the Kleról without a castration spell was a mystery to be solved at another time, but he had successfully castrated her while clasping the Kraken. Of this he was certain. *Slag*. He smiled as he recounted her slumped posture and the sound of her cries.

And yet she had survived, and worse—she aided the Dark Lord's agent. No matter, they had only recently left, and he now had collateral if he was able to get close enough to speak. Plus, without her powers she would be helpless against his contingent of clerics. She would be yet another minor problem for him; *minor* problem, he reassured himself.

Jaween was not so certain. *"He has a spirit guide and a sorceress. It will be no easy task to capture or kill them."*

"She is a sorceress no longer. Klerós has guided us this far. He will provide a way."

"*Perhaps*," responded the red-jeweled amulet.

Grobennar exited the building and spoke to the guards. "Please bring the prisoner back to the capital to be held with the other one. They may yet be of use to us."

The men bowed deeply and quickly complied.

Speaking only to Sija, he said, "Our target departed recently, he goes east."

"Then we should be off. I can track as quickly as your fastest men travel. We should be upon your prize in less than two days. It will take five, perhaps six, to reach the pass." He smiled. "You will have your slave soon."

Grobennar returned Sija's smile. "The Holy Emperor will reward you well when we succeed. This capture is of no small importance to his Holiness, Magog himself."

"Well, then, we've half a day's travel left in the sun, let's be on our way."

Grobennar smiled again and shouted to his team of priests and priestesses. "We go. Klerós sets glory before us; let us take hold."

## CHAPTER 48

# AYNWARD

AYNWARD LAY ON HIS BACK staring up at a blue-stone ceiling. He was certain he had never before slept in such a place. He was therefore curious about how he had managed to arrive. The last thing he remembered was the crowd of people as he approached the desposition ceremony. The excruciating pain as he attempted a deep breath brought with it a barrage of memories.

*I'm an idiot.*

He craned a stiff neck to both sides and saw the boy, Kyllean, lying in the bed to his right. The boy's face was blotchy with cuts and bruises. His brown curly hair was the only feature that identified him as the same boy from the fight. His left eye was swollen shut and his other cheekbone was misshapen. Aynward assumed that his own self didn't look much better.

Kyllean glanced his way. "Guess they've decided to let us heal up before sending us home. By the way, our previous meeting did not allow for proper introductions. My name is Kyllean Don Votro; I hail from East End or thereabouts."

Aynward had been forced to memorize all of the families of influence within the Kingdom of Dowe, and several from neighboring kingdoms as well; Votro was not among them.

East End was a midsized city located in the eastern most portion of the Kingdom, originally founded as a military outpost. It now enjoyed the wealth that came with connecting trade to the rest of the east. Aynward figured that Kyllean must be the son of a well-to-do knight; that would certainly explain his talent with a sword.

"I don't recognize the surname. Where in all of Doréa did you learn to fight like that?"

Kyllean smiled. "My father is a Tal-Don rider. Don Votro is the surname given to bastards of that line."

Aynward gaped. Tal-Don. East End. *If Dagmara knew I've met a Tal-Don, she'd lose her mind!* "You're serious? A Tal-Don?"

"Well, no. I am a Don Votro, but I share the blood. I haven't been trained to ride the Lumáles, if that's what you're wondering. We don't learn any of that until we return home from our schooling, and that's only if we swear an oath to join the others within the fortress where we will serve until we die. Most of us do, though I'm not certain it's the right line of work for me." Then he winked. "They teach us to fight either way, though."

"I'm grateful for the latter. And pleased to formally make your acquaintance, though I wish the circumstances were a bit less"—he tried sitting up and winced—"painful." He attempted another uncomfortably deep breath before continuing. "My name is—"

Aynward paused as he considered the asinine name given to him as a cover: Annard.

"My name is Aynward of Dowe."

The boy stared at him as if waiting for him to say more, and then laughed, though it became more of a cough. "Aynward of Dowe? Not *the* Aynward of the *royal line of* Dowe." Kyllean made a similar attempt to sit up, and found it an equally difficult feat. But he managed, and eyed Aynward suspiciously. Aynward wondered if he'd made a mistake in telling the boy. Aynward would be made to feel the fool if Kyllean didn't believe him. Should he bother taking the time to prove it? What would be the point?

"Well, you certainly have the auburn hair and gray eyes. Then again, so does eighty percent of the population. Of course, it does seem a lousy sort of lie to come up with. I hear *that* particular son of the King is a bit of a good-for-nothing. Hmm. Sort of fits—I suppose I'll take your word on it for now."

Aynward responded with a glare, but inwardly sighed in relief. He could work to prove a rumor false.

Kyllean continued making conversation as if they were old pals, not caring that he was speaking with his liege lord, or that they were both seriously injured and likely to be sent home shortly in disgrace. "So how are you enjoying Brinkwell so far? Haven't seen you in the dormitories. Must have arrived just in time for the fun."

The jovial tone in his voice clashed violently with the situation. The part of Aynward's mouth that wasn't quite as swollen as the rest moved to form a smile. Kyllean was clearly insane.

## CHAPTER 49

# SINDRI

"WE'VE GOT TO GO BACK for Tenk!" cried Kibure.

"Absolutely not," replied Sindri.

"We have to!"

Sindri grabbed Kibure by the shirt with both hands and pulled him close, saying through clenched teeth, "Do you wish to die?"

"No, but—"

"Then shut up and get moving! You saw how many priests they have. All rescuing him will do is get the both of us killed. You think that's what Tenk would want?"

Kibure shook his head. "I—I don't care. I won't leave him behind like this. How could I live with myself if I knew I hadn't at least tried?"

Sindri's grip on Kibure loosened at those words. Her hands suddenly weakened and her throat tightened as the memory of her brother's pleading eyes returned in full.

She turned away and said, "You would be surprised the kinds of things one can live with. All you need is a shovel and a willingness to bury the self-loathing deep enough that you cover the stench."

"How can you talk about someone's life like that?" Then Kibure's eyes narrowed. "I should have known. Slaves mean nothing to your race, and the only reason you're helping me is because of your obsession with my magic." His voice was ripe with disgust.

Sindri did the only thing she could do to overcome the converging rush of emotion she felt; she patched it with anger and denial. "I care not if someone is slave or free. I can talk about someone's life like that because I know that life is already doomed, and trying to help them will only do the same to my own. And I would like very much to survive. He knew the risks of fleeing; Klerós above, he left his own brother to die. He could have waited with Jengal and the wreckage to be taken up by a new master. He chose this path, and the risks that came with it. His capture is not your fault, it's not my fault, and there is no—dishonor in continuing toward freedom."

Kibure shook his head in frustration. "I'm going to try to rescue him."

*I'm going to lose him. I can't lose this chance to understand.* She was trapped. She couldn't very well knock him unconscious and carry him, yet she knew with every ounce of her being that they could not hope to overpower a dozen priests and priestesses, especially now that she was without her own magic.

Kibure turned and stomped back in the direction of the village. Then Sindri saw them. *Oh no.*

She raced to catch up, grabbing his arm and pulling him behind a thick maple just in time. Kibure turned and jumped in the same motion. "Wh—"

"Shh." Sindri looked him in the eyes, then glanced to the right.

Kibure followed her gaze. There must have been ten, maybe twenty men and women, all dressed in deep red.

She felt faint. "Search party. And they're looking for you. I can explain later, but right now *we need to go.*"

"What?"

"Listen, someone is using magic in the village. Tenk is dead, and we will be too if we don't move now." Shaking her head, she said, "It may already be too late."

The two fugitives remained where they were until the contingent of priests passed beyond sight. Kibure was visibly shaken by the reality that he must leave his friend behind to endure whatever fate awaited him at the hands of the Kleról. He took one longing look back toward the village before turning to run in the opposite direction.

Sindri felt the nearly crippling burden of shame at lying to Kibure about Tenk. She did not know for certain that he lived, but neither did she know that he had perished. Knowing that the Fatu Mazi was not among the priests in the party, she guessed that the magic she felt was him delving into the mind of Tenk to learn what he could of his companions. She tucked her lie deep beneath a blanket of pragmatism, survival, and her heaviest quilt, shame. *I am shame*, she reminded herself.

CHAPTER 50

# KIBURE

A<small>S THEY CLIMBED, THE TERRAIN</small> changed again and they came across a growing number of massive, sheer rock surfaces. When Sindri started leading them higher above one of those ridges, Rave began cooing frantically. He pointed toward the opposite side of the mountain. Both Kibure and Sindri came to the same conclusion about Rave's guidance: they should follow it.

She grumbled, "He is certainly no ordinary creature."

"Agreed," said Kibure.

Sindri followed, shaking her head. "Never thought I'd put my life in the hands of a flying lemur. Oh, how the mighty have fallen." The last bit came out as a sigh.

Pulling out that piece of parchment that supposedly told people where things were, she continued, "This lists major landmarks, and a few trails, mostly traveled by smugglers taking the pass toward the Palpanese Union. But there's nothing on here to really help us cut the most direct path. Whatever village that was back there, it was not important enough to include on this. I can only gather our general direction. We are truly at the mercy of your little, furry friend."

Apart from that, they spoke very little as they negotiated the difficult footing. As Kibure fatigued, he resorted to an old habit; he began singing:

> *Move, move, up the hill,*
> *Running for our lives,*
> *Left—STEP—*
> *Right—STEP—*
> *Don't trip on the loose stones,*
> *Left—STEP—*
> *Right—STEP—*
> *Don't trip on the loose stones,*
> *Run, run, run away,*
> *Run away or die,*
> *Left—STEP—*
> *Right—STEP—*
> *Don't trip on the loose stones,*
> *Left—STEP—*
> *Right—STEP—*
> *Don't trip on the loose—*

"Are you sure it wasn't your singing that caused the other slaves to dislike you?" interrupted Sindri.

"Well—wait! What do you mean by that?"

"It's quite terrible. I'm ready to throw a rock at you, and you've only been at it for a minute. I can only imagine what it would be like to work all day listening to that."

Kibure scowled. "It helps me focus. You should try it:

> *Move, move, up the hill,*
> *Running for our lives,*
> *Left—STEP—*
> *Right—STEP—*
> *Don't trip on the—*

"Ow! What was—"

"You'll never make it to freedom if I let you keep that up. I'll wind up killing you myself."

Kibure harrumphed, but continued on without another word of song. He thought he detected a bit of play in Sindri's tone, but he didn't know her well enough to test her word. They trudged on in silence.

They found another place to rest once it became apparent that the clouds would not relent and the gloom of the night would render travel in darkness dangerously impossible.

They rose early the next day, still fatigued, but motivated by the fear of capture. They traversed several smaller mountains and continued to gain altitude. As they rounded another peak, they saw an opportunity to catch a glimpse of their surroundings on an exposed rock cliff near the summit. The peak was mostly tree-covered, but it had openings from which they could gauge their progress toward the eastern peaks.

Kibure was overwhelmed by what he saw. To the south lay leagues of beautiful dark-green hills spiked with tall pines, and speckled with their shadows. This landscape went on until it met the orange soil of the desert below, in a gradual grade from desert to hills coming from the south.

What truly took Kibure's breath away, though, was the view as he turned his eyes to the southeast. They had finally come within sight of the high peaks of the Driskos, which extended south, and he could see a profile as the land transitioned from flat desert to snowcapped peaks. As he looked upon the wall of mountains to the southeast, he understood why they stood as an undisputed eastern boundary to the Lugienese Empire.

He also realized the peril that awaited them as he considered climbing over such an immense physical structure. He remained speechless for many minutes while his emotions swirled, a mix of adoration and fear.

The pair took one last look at the path they would take, then began anew. They counted two massive ridges before they would finally meet the menace of the high peaks. This meant perhaps two more days of travel until they reached the pass. They might just survive this journey after all.

They had crossed the first ridge and were on their way down when they decided to stop for the night. Rave had found them a shallow cave along the hillside. It would provide them with cover from the weather, which had become a concern as the day wore on. The clouds moving in from the north had begun to grumble with distant thunder and flashes of lightning. They didn't wish to be caught outside when it struck in full.

Kibure was in good spirits as they lay down on their blankets. "If we get rain, it'll wash away most traces of our movement, right?"

"Yes. This rain and wind could be good for us."

Coming from Sindri, that may as well have been a statement of celebration.

They rested just inside the cave, eating drogal and freshly killed squirrel, supplied yet again by their winged companion. Kibure thought deeply about what he might do with his freedom once they reached the nation Sindri called the Palpanese Union, and, eventually, the Isles farther east. Surely she would retain him for some time to study, but he did believe her when she said she would set him free afterward. The uncertainty of it all frightened him, for he knew so little of the world he would enter. For that matter, he knew very little of his own world within the Lugienese Empire. He thought about their journey thus far, about everything he had seen since leaving Jarquin, and determined that this change was good.

Reminiscing also brought with it the sting of confusion. He still had so many unanswered questions about his nightmares, his abilities, Rave, and more. Kibure looked over to ask Sindri about the people of the Palpanese Union, but she had already fallen asleep. This brought about the realization that his eyelids were feeling heavy, as well, and it was not long before his thoughts drifted out of reach and scattered to make way for slumber.

Kibure awoke to thunder and rain driven by strong winds. He lay listening to the wind and rain as they ravaged the forest. The strange whistling of the pines as they braced against the wind became increasingly enjoyable as he considered the damage this would do to any sign of their passing. Surely no one could track them after what the storm was doing to the forest.

To Kibure's surprise, Rave had remained outside, perched on a ledge within the elements rather than coming in to enjoy the safety of cover. Kibure had given up trying to understand the enigmatic little creature long ago, so he let the curious behavior go without much thought.

As he lay on his back appreciating his freedom, a different sound caught his attention. He sat up. This sound was far more distressing than the distant crashes of lightning and thunder. It was men's voices. He also felt—*something*.

He woke Sindri and they crept to the mouth of the cave, but it was too dark to see much of anything. Only periodic flashes of lightning hinted at what lay beyond.

Sindri finally said, "It's them. I can feel the use of Klerós's power, probably for light. Let us pray they pass us by." Doubt soaked her every word like the heavy rain outside.

Kibure was too frightened to focus on anything but the voices. He felt an ache in his gut; the ache of despair as his hopes of freedom disappeared.

A flash of lightning lit the sky and everything beyond the cave mouth. In that instant, they saw the outlines of several men, perhaps only forty paces distant. The image was brief, but it told them everything they needed to know. Their momentary freedom was over. Kibure longed to go back to the drogal farm in Jarquin, to know nothing about what lay beyond. He struggled to breathe as the weight of terror consumed him.

Sindri gasped. "*Gods*—they're coming right for us!"

## CHAPTER 51

# GROBENNAR

THE DARKNESS OF NIGHT CLOSELY trailed the approaching storm, seemingly eager to put an early end to the day. Darkness was accompanied by the heavy pounding of rain.

"We need to take cover, Your Holiness," shouted Sija over the storm. "I might be able to safely navigate the terrain in this weather, but your team will not. I know of a safe place near to here where we could wait out the storm."

Grobennar shot him a glare then realized that the gloom surely concealed it.

He replied sharply, "No. We will continue. I have two tazabi priests here to heal wounds. I intend to catch this vermin. Lead on!"

Sija seemed to consider the risks of defying the order for only a moment, then nodded and continued trudging forward.

*"Not that I have a physical body to worry over, but this seems a bit on the desperate side, don't you think?"*

"I think that's exactly what this is. These are desperate times . . ." Grobennar found that every so often, arguments with Jaween became slightly shorter when Grobennar simply agreed with his machinations. It was as if the spirit didn't know how to carry a conversation that wasn't

276

of a discordant nature. Grobennar counted his last response a major success; Jaween remained silent in the minutes that followed.

As the evening wore on, the storm intensified, and Grobennar finally gave in to reason. When Sija returned from scouting ahead, Grobennar said, "Sija, we've traveled far enough this evening, find us shelter."

The man nodded, then said, "There appeared to be a place above this ridge, but let me verify before risking the entire group. I will be back shortly."

He disappeared into the gloom.

Minutes later, a shout from the darkness called for the procession to follow. Lightning flickered and the outline of Sija appeared briefly before the darkness swallowed him again.

Sija shouted down, "It's slippery, and steep. I'm bringing a rope down to guide you."

He skittered and slithered back to Grobennar's position and forced a rope into Grobennar's hands. Then Sija issued another warning. "Move slowly. A fall from the top could kill one of you before Klerós's power has time to heal."

Fatu Mazi Grobennar did not enjoy zigzagging his way up and across the narrow, high ledges before reconnecting with the rest of the more predictable mountain slope, where the shelter Sija sought was located. He and several other priests created localized orbs of light just bright enough to illuminate their next step, but small enough that their magical signature would be nearly indiscernible unless the enemy were close at hand. They did not wish their presence on the enemy's trail to be known until it was too late.

Twenty paces away, lightning revealed the outline of a cave mouth sure to allow a dry and restful reprieve from the punishing rains of the bellowing sky.

As they neared the entrance, another quick illumination revealed a small, dark shape; Grobennar's heart skipped and without further thought, he drew in Klerós's power.

That same instant, his keen sense of magic detected a faint, alien scent. The strands of energy were unusual; slippery, even. He reached out with his mind but couldn't identify the magic or its intended use. He stood at the ready, his magical reservoir full.

Sija stopped suddenly up ahead, arms held out to the sides to prevent anyone from venturing farther. "Step back . . . slowly." The uneasy sound in his voice told Grobennar to take heed, though he wondered how Sija recognized the danger without his own sense of magic.

He didn't see Sija's motive for retreating until a crack of lightning lit up the area before the cave mouth again, revealing several large, dark shapes with glowing eyes. Forgetting his fear of Klerós's power being detected, Grobennar created a bright red nimbus of light with his hand, illuminating the approaching beasts.

Several lurched forward, then slowed again, stalking their prey. More followed from around the corner beyond the cave. They walked on four legs, the front two connected to muscular shoulders. Thick fur covered their bodies, which included long tails that curved slightly upward. They were higher up the slope, so it was difficult to gauge their exact size, but Grobennar guessed their shoulders would meet his lower chest, putting their jaws level with an average man's throat. Not a pleasant thought. The low, red mystic light revealed a few light speckles of color on the beasts' otherwise black coats.

Red eyes glistened in response to the faint light that lay between the approaching beasts and the slowly retreating men. Some of Grobennar's strength had been renewed through his limited rest, but he had hoped to save it for the destruction of the one he knew would surely push him to the limits of his power even if he were fully rested.

"Wolves," cursed Sija. "I know you're powerful practitioners or whatever, but I suggest we not engage them. Could be as many as forty of the cursed things, all familiar with this area, and they are savage predators."

Grobennar doubted Sija's estimate, but more and more gleaming eyes seemed to reflect the dim red light that served to measure the distance between them and the approaching enemy. And there was still that faint sense of magic floating around in the air. Could that be a coincidence? Likely not, but controlling multiple animals simultaneously? That would require vast amounts of power as well as unthinkable mystic precision. Was this the enemy priestess? She couldn't have possibly already found a team of priests to restore her connection to Klerós. It must be the *other* one, then, or perhaps the spirit-being. Could the spirit of the Dark Lord touch this world so directly? Jaween certainly could not. Either way, the amount of magic necessary to control a large pack of animals should also create swells of energy, detectable from a great distance, not the mere whisper of magic he now sensed. None of it made sense.

"*The evil spirit. Dark magic!*" Jaween's voice dripped with disgust, and even—fear?

No time to consider. Sija spoke in a steady, nonthreatening tone, loud enough for all to hear, "If we can get back into the valley, we might be able to avoid a very costly confrontation."

They moved slowly, step by careful step, back toward the ridge they'd climbed from the mountain valley below. The wolves continued their approach but seemed content with their current distance, moving slowly to match the speed of the retreating priests.

After a few tense minutes, Grobennar looked back to see that a few of the priests' lights had disappeared from sight. The first of his party had reached the relative safety of the narrow ridge where they could descend to safety.

A terror-filled shout to his left shredded that hope and replaced it with panic, especially as similar sounds echoed throughout the group. His world became a blur. The wolves he had been watching in front of him lunged forward, and he realized his men had been flanked and were being attacked on three sides. The rain let up slightly, but the darkness of the cloud-covered sky still oppressed their vision, broken only by jolts of energy that his fellow priests sent forth to scathe the horrid beasts.

All at once, three sets of teeth hurled themselves at the Fatu Mazi. Only his quick reaction saved him as he fell to his back on the muddy ground sending forth a seething burst of energy shrouded in flames to blow apart two beasts whose path had stayed true. He rolled over and sent out bolt after bolt of destruction, decimating several more snarling wolves before they had the chance to attack.

A similar battle ensued on all sides until Grobennar had the time to chant a more complex, more energy-consuming spell that created a protective barrier around the entire party. Finally, the barrier shut out any new beasts from entering, and the beasts still within were handled, but not without further injury. His men halted their attacks to begin helping the injured to the safety of the ridge below. The barrier he had composed would hold for a few minutes while they made their way down.

He stopped at the unmoving body of a man dressed fully in animal skins. Horror filled the priest as he came to terms with the reality that it was Sija, lying face up, his throat and chest mangled beyond repair. Two of his priests had met a similar fate, unable to defend themselves in time.

Once within the meager safety of the valley, the High Priest was thoroughly sickened by his foolhardiness. He had wanted so badly to conserve his powers and avoid detection that he had failed to set up adequate defenses, especially once they met the wolves. It would have taken thrice and more of his energies, but he could have at least summoned a mobile sphere of protection for their retreat or blown the beasts apart before they'd had the chance to attack on their own terms. Now he had lost his guide and two other valued members of the imperial assembly of the Klerósi faith, men who had entrusted their lives to Klerós, this mission, and him, the Fatu Mazi.

An older priest named Vlanhir put his hand upon Grobennar's shoulder, seemingly reading his mind. "You mustn't blame yourself. They died worthy deaths in the name of the Holy God. Their names will be written forever on the walls of the eternal pure. None could ask for better."

"Klerós . . ." Grobennar said in a quiet, ritualistic manner. Then he turned to address the remaining men. "We've lost our guide, and we have been shaken by misfortune. This means only that we need press harder to do what must be done in the name of our holy king and our god. Rest now. Tomorrow we finish this business."

For safety, he had one of his men erect a protective barrier through the collective powers of the priests and priestesses so as to not weigh too heavily on the strength of any one individual. The rain finally relented, but he slept sitting upright against the valley wall to keep his face free of the wet ground on which he sat.

As he tried to clear his mind for rest, he couldn't help but return to his questions about the magic he had detected during the attack. It had completely dissipated and he could once again sense nothing of the adversary that he knew had been mere paces away. He searched his subconscious memory for clues. His hands made fists without conscious thought. He would not be taken unawares again.

## CHAPTER 52

# AYNWARD

AYNWARD STIRRED AS SUNLIGHT STREAKED into the room. It was the morning of the third day since his attempted overthrow of the desposition ceremony. The serenity of a restful sleep was shattered by someone shouting. The tone in the demand suggested that this argument had been escalating for some time.

"Get up. Get up! You lazy, spoiled twerp, get up! And you too, idiot friend of his."

Aynward recognized the voice, and then realized how close it was. The sleeping fog slowly departed, replaced by the image of a shorter-than-normal, bearded eight-year-old-child. It was Dwapek, and he appeared beyond the expected level of anger that came with his irritable disposition.

"Get up. Don't care how much it hurts. Wait, yes, I do. You both deserve every bit of it after that spectacle you created, you prattling little wussies."

Aynward groaned as he sat up. Unlike the day before, he was able to do so without a splitting pain in his rib. *Definitely not cracked, then. Well, that's something.* He reached down to touch the place on his left side and winced. It was still tender.

The two boys followed Dwapek from the infirmary all the way across campus to his office. By the time they arrived, Aynward had grown numb to Dwapek's incessant yelling. It was like the half-man had survived some accident but lost his ability to hear how loud he was. He was at least creative with his expletives, Aynward acknowledged; very creative.

Both boys entered, then Dwapek slammed the door shut and shuffled to his desk, took the step stool stairs to his chair, and remained standing as he turned to face them.

"You two really were cut from the same Kingdom cloth, weren't you? A tightly stitched fabric embroidered with foolishness."

Aynward and Kyllean looked at each other but neither responded; seemed like it might have been one of those rhetorical questions that people asked when they were angry. People usually became *more* angry when you attempted to answer those questions, Aynward knew, so he decided it best to stay silent this time.

"Kyllean, your counselor has refused to continue as your sponsor and the council has recommended that you be dismissed from the university. Not to worry, you're not alone—your bedfellow here was elected for dismissal, as well."

Aynward was ready for this reality, and after a few days to ponder his actions, he wondered if maybe he'd made a mistake after all. He certainly feared his father's response when he returned home early under such conditions.

"The two of you have only two things going for you." The little man was standing on his chair, two fingers extending from a raised hand. "One, I despise the desposition ceremony: a foolish waste of time giving undue credence to the idea that a degree from this university will grant all who carry it some sort of magical relevancy within the world."

He shook his head and spoke more softly. "As if the big'ns here need any further justification for believing themselves above the rest of society."

Dwapek looked up and met Aynward's gaze.

"Haven't attended in thirty-plus years, but I sure had a good laugh when I first heard what happened. Stopped laughing when I realized it was done by the one idiot student I'd been coerced into sponsoring. Told you before, I've important things to attend to, and arguing about why my pupil shouldn't be expelled for whacking the university counselors with clubs is not one of them!"

Aynward's mind did a flip. The little man had defended him?

Dwapek continued, "I am not well liked here, you know. A bit of an outsider, if you hadn't noticed; it makes for crooked stares. Being a different race of man tends to result in an assumption of inferiority from others. But what they hate most about me is my total immunity from their politics."

He smiled. "Little-known fact: I have the full support of the university's largest subsidizer, which grants me virtual impunity while within these walls. Unlike the rest, I'm generally able to escape the fickle whims of an organization guided by the whispers of self-important, robed men and women. They've been able to secure separate jurisdiction for this little pretend city they call 'The University,' and have even managed to fortify exclusionary laws for university students who venture out into the city. Yet they are unable to control *me*, and it vexes them."

He bent over and placed closed fists on the desk. "So when they have a chance to take a stab at me because the one student I've chosen to sponsor causes anarchy during their precious ceremony, they gladly do so. And there is a process and precedent for dismissal that may supersede the ordinary first rights of the counselor to issue his own justice for a first infraction. I have no doubt that even *you*, Annard—it is Annard, right?"

Aynward figured if he were getting kicked out, he may as well be right about his true name, more as a matter of pride than anything else. Plus, he'd already told Kyllean.

"Yeah, I've decided to drop the whole Annard ruse. That was my counselor Dolmuevo's doing. Call me Aynward, if it please you."

Instead of the expected retort for interrupting him, Dwapek let out a haughty laugh. "Well, that's the smartest thing you've said yet, *Your*

*Grace.*" The little man gave a shallow, mocking bow, then straightened. "Now, shut up before I rescind this undeserved act of mercy. Where was I? Ah yes, *Aynward*, your dismissal. I'm certain you will be expelled from this school the second a council vote is taken. And you, Kyllean, well, you've already been dropped, as was the right of your assigned counselor to do."

Kyllean nodded, having accepted his fate already.

"I would have allowed both of these eventualities to take place were it not for the precious thought of that nincompoop, Dean Remson, lying on his back, red-faced in front of the entire university. And you both no doubt deserve to be expelled after such shenanigans, regardless of how much I dislike some of the staff here.

"But instead I have taken you, Kyllean, on as my own pupil. In exchange for allowing the both of you *idiots* to remain, I have agreed to join a committee, an act which I abhor. As additional atonement, I've agreed to forfeit your traditional service duties to me. Instead your duties have been transferred to Dean Remson, who promised that by the time you're done serving your penance, you'll both wish you *had* been expelled."

Aynward saw Kyllean's eyes light up with a mixture of confusion, joy, and uncertainty. Aynward had seldom seen someone's expression teeter between so many emotions in such a short period.

He, too, was uncertain how he felt. There was always a price to pay when the old witch granted wishes in the stories. Of course, Dwapek was male. *What was a male witch called?* Either way, he had to assume that this price would be high.

Kyllean brought him out of his reverie. "What exactly will this penance involve?"

Dwapek paused for a moment, probably deciding upon some clever yet demoralizing way to announce their punishment. "You will clean the university sewers every third day."

Aynward glanced over at Kyllean, who stared back with an expression of incredulity. "You can't be serious."

Dwapek smiled. "Tut-tut. Quite serious, indeed."

He waved his hands in an arc as if telling a grand tale before a crowd of thousands. "This university dates back half a millennium, built upon the oldest sections of the city, which began as a small Kingdom outpost connecting trade with the Angolian continent. It was not built to support the numerous occupants now present in the city. The sewer flow slows quite frequently without preventative maintenance. No one is happy when that happens."

Aynward could hardly believe his ears. To expect nobles to clean sewers was unthinkable. "Surely the city has enough little orphaned urchins willing to take on this job for a few coppers and a meal."

"This is undeniably so. However, the university maintains its own sewer line, literally and figuratively barred from the rest of the city line in order to *protect* us from those we don't wish sneaking in. However, those bars are part of the reason our lines get backed up. Objects catch between them, creating nasty problems from time to time. Not a well-designed system."

Aynward wrinkled his nose and said, "You seem to know a great deal about the sewers."

Dwapek smiled. "You two will be the real experts in a few weeks, but I've been down there once or twice."

Aynward raised his eyebrows at the admission.

Dwapek explained, "That was my first assigned duty as a new counselor some forty years ago: I oversaw the cleaning of the sewers. They meant to humiliate me into submission. That is, until I then exercised my right to select the location for our monthly special committee meeting. One meeting down in the main sewer line was enough for the lot of them."

He finally took a seat in the chair at his desk.

"I had it cleaned up real nice, but you can only get a turd so clean. They never forced me into another committee position again. Not until now."

He seemed to have cheered up at the memory. "That reminds me. As an added boon for your courageous behavior during the ceremony, I've assigned you both to an additional course."

The boys exchanged another concerned look.

"An elective course, elected by me, titled 'Properties.' It's a theoretical course. It's new."

Aynward scowled. He felt like they'd been bamboozled. "Dare I ask what this course is even about, or should I just assume that, like Apotheca, it will one day save my life from improbable danger?"

Dwapek's smile was sinister. "You could say that."

Aynward rolled his eyes.

Suddenly the half-man was standing on the chair again before hopping his way down the makeshift stairs to the floor. Aynward thought it was a shockingly graceful maneuver for a person of—how old was the half-man? He started a quick estimation of likely preparatory education in addition to his forty-some years as a counselor here. His thoughts were cut short.

"Time to go, time to go! I've many things to attend. Here are your new schedules; you begin tomorrow."

Dwapek tossed both boys their own hand-sized parchments, rolled up and tied with a yellow ribbon. "Aynward, I'm told your tutor caused quite a scene at the gates the other day when you did not arrive home before sundown. I suggest you attend him as soon as possible. Be certain to pick up a full serving of finely seasoned atonement soup for him, and be sure to limit the malarkey. The flavor is very distinct, and is sure to ruin anything it touches."

Aynward finished processing the odd remark too slowly.

The half-man sighed and mumbled to himself, "Should have considered the potential damage done to the boy's skull before I agreed to his vindication. Now I'm stuck with a witless fool. Yet another lesson learned."

Dwapek shooed them out of the room. "Get some rest. You've a full schedule, after all."

Aynward began exiting the room. "Yeah, thanks for that." He made no attempt to guard his annoyance as he said it.

The door closed behind them, and Dwapek started off in the opposite direction, but he shouted out for them to hear, "Water isn't always as wet as it may seem. Make some friends. You've certainly made enough enemies." He disappeared around the corner, leaving Aynward and Kyllean to ponder his last words by themselves.

Kyllean tilted his head and said, "What in all of Doréa was that about? Water? Wet?"

Aynward laughed nervously. "He seems to have quite the proclivity for sayings that mean less than nothing."

"Uh-huh. He's a bit *different*," said Kyllean.

Aynward chuckled. "Yeah, I had a few *other* epithets in mind."

"Well, I guess at this point he's our only supporter, so he'll have to do."

"A sad truth indeed," Aynward said with a snort.

They walked on in silence to where the row of buildings ended. "Well, this is me. This leads to the forest dorms. I suppose I should take Dwapek's advice and spend some time resting up before the big day tomorrow."

Aynward nodded and replied, "Yeah, I'd best check in with my beloved counselor, though at this point it's likely hopeless. The scowl on his face will surely have dried solid by now. I can only hope that means he can no longer open his mouth to speak."

Kyllean let out a laugh. "Enjoy the verbal lashings, *Your Grace*." Kyllean bowed ever so slightly, then waved good-bye.

Counselor Dwapek had all but confirmed Aynward's true identity. That must have been all the proof Kyllean needed. While Dwapek's lack of reverence for the title was disconcerting to Aynward, Kyllean's casual bow was a relief. Aynward was happy that his new friend wasn't going to start acting weird now that he knew who Aynward actually was.

Dolme was pacing up and down the narrow porch at the entrance to Aunt Melanie's home. She sat silently on the porch, sewing a quilt. A pleasant surprise, as Aynward had found she'd been surprisingly absent since he arrived. Perhaps her presence would curb Dolme's reaction.

Dolme spotted him and stopped at the top of the stairs. When Aynward was close enough to begin his ascent, Dolme began his inquisition. "Have you learned nothing? Have you respect for nothing? Have all my lessons been in vain?" Dolme was nearly shouting. Aunt Melanie stayed silent in her chair. She didn't even look up. *So much for having an ally.*

Aynward continued up the steps to the porch. He was in no mood for deference, especially not to someone like Counselor Dolme. "Were those—what are they called—rhetorical questions? I get so confused about whether or not to answer." He brought a finger to his chin in thought. "Guess I'll answer. Yes, I suppose I do respect *some* things. Brewmasters, for start—"

The porch went sideways. *Wait—no, it's me.* Aynward went sideways, slamming hard into the floor. *Gods, that hurt!* The side of his head felt like it had landed in a furnace.

"Minster Dolmuevo! Is that necessary?" shouted his aunt. Aynward couldn't see her; the blow to the side of his head had landed him facing the other direction.

"Yes," replied Dolme as he placed a foot on the exposed side of Aynward's face. "You little brat. After all my sacrifices, all of my patience. You respond with blatant contempt. Do you think I wanted this job? Do you believe I enjoy wiping up the messes that spew from your mouth and bottom alike?" He increased the pressure of his foot on Aynward's face before the prince could grunt out a reply. "Now *that*, Aynward, was a rhetorical question."

Dolme finally removed the boot that had been pinning Aynward's head to the wooden floor of the porch. "I do it because I'm a loyal subject to your father, and no one else was willing to take on the challenge of civilizing the most egotistical, insolent, good-for-nothing child the line of Dowe could possibly beget. I was stupid enough to believe that I *could*, and felt therefore that I *must*, undertake it, for the good of the realm. *That* is the only reason I'm still here."

Aynward groaned as he rolled to his stomach. His body was not ready for any more of Dolme's *lessons*. Intermittent pain persisted as he slowly crawled to his feet.

Dolme spoke again. "I've nothing else to say to you. Go."

Aynward nodded, but didn't otherwise respond. He couldn't trust himself not to say something that might get him whacked again, and wasn't sure he'd be able to get back up if that happened. He started for the stairs. Dolme stopped him with the tone of his voice. "Don't bother asking if I've written your father about this *incident*. The answer is no. I don't have the heart to confirm his suspicions about your chances of success here. The fact that you're still wearing the university garb confirms that you've not been expelled. I plan to wait until after your next reckless gambit. They'll see the light then, ignore your title, and expel you."

"Good night, Dolme." Aynward trudged up the stairs.

In spite of the early hour, he was ready for sleep. His body was hardly healed after the damage it had undergone. The thought of sleeping in a bed that was not in the infirmary was something he'd been looking forward to for the entire walk back. He rounded the corner at the top of the stairs.

"Aynward, you're back."

The sound startled him. Then he saw the manservant-accountant. "Gervais, yes I am." Aynward's tone held only the hint of *I don't want to talk* in it. In an effort to reinforce this agenda, he continued walking down the hallway without looking. Gervais seemed to miss the message. His aunt's helper extraordinaire walked directly toward him to stop in front of the doorway to Aynward's room.

"So glad to see you back. You're looking remarkably well, all things considered. May I have a quick word?"

Was the *all things considered* used intentionally to indicate his knowledge of what had transpired at the university? Of course it was. *Hopefully his version of "quick" reconciles with mine.* No longer making an effort to hide his annoyance, Aynward grumbled, "Well, you're already standing in the doorway to my room in a completely not-presumptuous manner, so why not? Let's go inside so we can sit. As you well know, the last few days have been full of excitement." *May as well not grant him any satisfaction by acting embarrassed about it.*

Gervais took a seat in one of the chairs and crossed his legs. *One can never trust a man who sits like that comfortably.* Aynward seated himself in the adjacent chair, trying not to show the physical discomfort he was experiencing as he lowered himself down. He waited for Gervais to speak.

"I'll not waste your time with frivolous small talk. Here it is. I have a favor to ask of you."

Aynward was opening his mouth to respond with a commanding *not interested* when Gervais held up a hand to stop him.

"As a man of business, I recognize that you owe me nothing, and that my request comes with no apparent leverage, and therefore no incentive for you to so much as hear my request. However, I suspect that a worldly lad such as you has heard the phrase, 'It's not what you know, but who you know,' am I right?" He waited for Aynward to nod before continuing. "Well, Your Grace, you are quite a distance from home, and that means your former network of friends and favors is effectively inaccessible. Sure, you have a meager allowance, but that's guarded by Minster Dolmuevo, and we both know he's going to be tighter than ever with that. This current limitation of yours is where having someone like me, someone with connections and means, would be advantageous to your Brinkwell experience. Having someone like me, owing you a favor? Well, need I explain further?"

Aynward's mind did a somersault. He had never cared for making deals when he wasn't the one coming up with them. There seemed to be something in human nature where people always tried to give themselves the upper hand when forging agreements. He had no aspirations of getting the lower hand. But—the man made a strong case. His list of persons against whom he sought revenge seemed to be growing, and he did have limited means of exacting it. Not that he wasn't resourceful, it was just—it could pose a considerable challenge.

"I'll hear the details of the favor." He needed to turn the angle of negotiations, and for that he needed to know what he was up against.

Gervais smiled. "Of course."

He folded his hands atop his left knee, which was still slung across his right leg. "A client of mine has been searching for a certain book. He has sent merchants to several major cities around the civilized world, but remains empty-handed. We have reason to believe that this book can be found in the archives of the university library. As you might guess, we have no way of pirating it from the archives."

Aynward laughed, rejecting the idea of getting involved in a fool's errand such as this. "You want me to steal a book from the archives of the university? No, thank you. I'm new to the university, but I'm thinking they don't treat kindly with students who steal valuable, one-of-a-kind items from them. Doesn't seem like a great idea to abscond with highly guarded university property, that is, unless my goal really is to be expelled in record time."

Gervais took it in stride, sitting back comfortably as if expecting this response. Once it was evident that Aynward had completed his rejection of the favor, Gervais replied, "I understand your hesitation; however, this favor is much simpler than you presume. You see, I have good information that leads me to believe that there already exists a book smuggling network within the university. All you have to do is tap into it, pay the fee, and deliver the book to me. You will return the book shortly thereafter. This is a completely harmless exchange."

It didn't sound quite as impossible when he put it like that. But Aynward had learned how to negotiate, and he'd get more out of this before agreeing to anything.

"That's still far too dangerous. I can't risk my university status, especially for a simple favor in return." He had learned something else about negotiation: always let the other side begin the bidding. Gervais knew the game, as well; he didn't take the bait. He smiled and said, "Is there anything in addition to me owing you a favor of your choosing?"

*Well played.*

By the time they completed the exchange, Aynward felt like he had fared well. They were both coming away with something they needed. Aynward would still be owed his one favor, so long as it fit within the confines of the law, but would also be paid a generous weekly stipend for the first six cycles of the moon.

As he reflected, the amount Gervais was willing to pay per week gave Aynward pause. The book he wanted, or the knowledge contained within, must be astronomical if it was worth so much. Yet he couldn't turn down the opportunity. After all, what fun would he ever have if he was limited to the meager rations Dolme was willing to shell out on his behalf?

There was still the whole problem of uncovering a secret black-market thieves network within the university, getting them to agree to work with him, and not getting caught in the process. But at least he finally had something to strive toward. Life just wasn't interesting enough without taking chances.

The pain throughout his body seemed to melt away with thoughts of the days to come. Hope had a way of doing that. He slept soundly straight through to the next morning.

## CHAPTER 53

# GROBENNAR

"WE'RE GETTING CLOSE." GROBENNAR FURROWED his eyebrows and dipped his head forward with added determination to forge on ahead, leading the remainder of his contingent up the steep, snowy path. They'd reached the snow-covered ground of higher elevations, snow that showed two sets of fresh human tracks.

One didn't have to be a renowned tracker to make out the boot prints of a woman and young adolescent headed east along the ascending path en route to the only accessible pass through the mountains this time of year.

Grobennar's focus was so keen at that moment, so intent on the impending battle with this demigod of the dark, that it took him a few minutes to sense the taint in the air as snowflakes began to fall. It wasn't until he looked back on his trail of companions that he realized he could only see the closest three for the thickness of precipitation. He opened up his mind to sense the glimmer of magic in the air. *They're making it snow!* He knew of no priests capable of weather magic, but the scent of magical disturbance and the severity of the untimely arrival of snow could be no coincidence.

The High Priest glared into the snowy wall of flakes and saw nothing but white. Then a sound to his left turned his eyes in that direction. A small black shape cut through the white, no more than a few paces away, then disappeared again into the thick powdered air. An odd, almost chirpy noise floated to his ears as the shape melted away. Without further thought, he released a burst of searing energy in that direction, followed by several others. He had no idea if he hit his target, but his frustration had gotten the better of him. *Blast it! That's probably exactly what the enemy wants! He's trying to frustrate me into wasting energy before the inevitable battle. I'm better than this!*

Tired as he was from his travel up the mountain slope, the middle-aged priest redoubled his efforts and quickened his pace.

"Hurry, we're close! Make haste!"

## CHAPTER 54

# KIBURE

"**I CAN'T SEE A THING!**" **SAID** Kibure as he and Sindri stumbled their way up the slope.

"Well, I can feel the magic, it's your little friend's doing, so complain to him. At least it conceals our tracks."

"Much good that'll do when we stumble right into the people who are chasing us because Rave keeps leaving us behind!"

Sindri grabbed Kibure's long sleeve and yanked him forward. "Just keep moving. We've just got to trust your little friend. We have no other choice."

"We're not even going uphill anymore. It didn't look like this pass had a lot of downhill from below," complained Kibure.

"Shut up and keep moving. This snow is miserable enough without your whining."

They marched on in silence other than a few minor spats of bickering. This continued for half the day, long enough to test Kibure's physical and mental resolve and Sindri's patience with his complaints that they were still lost. They traveled uphill first, then neither up or down but certainly on a slant, then finally made a steady pace downhill for the last three or so hours. And then the wall of snow simply stopped. One minute, Kibure could hardly see his hands before his face, and the next, he was staring into clear skies. He turned back to make sure he wasn't going mad or having some sort of new vision. Sure enough, the storm of snow was still assaulting everything behind. Rave cooed up ahead for them to follow, then flew over and used one of his small arms to point in that direction downhill. He pointed once again, then flew back into the storm.

"What is he doing?" asked Kibure, frustrated.

"He's up to something. Come on. Looks like we've given them the slip for now. We'd best make use of it," replied Sindri.

"But—"

"Come on," she said.

Then it all started to make sense.

## CHAPTER 55

# GROBENNAR

"Fatu Mazi, I think these people we're chasing are no longer ahead of us, at least not along this pass."

This same doubt had been festering like a dirty wound within Grobennar's mind, but he had refused to acknowledge it. Hearing it from someone else forced him to reconsider, though not without a fight. They had been moving hard for days in the mountains in hopes of overtaking their adversary. Grobennar stopped walking and looked at the snow-packed path ahead. The others stopped behind him, and Vlanhir crouched down with him to examine the ground.

"I am no tracker, but I believe this snow has been here for many weeks," Vlanhir said.

Grobennar agreed. There had been not so much as a print anywhere along the path since the storm had ended that day before. Grobennar walked over to one of the canyon walls and rested his hands up along its surface, allowing his head to sag forward. How could he have let this boy escape his grasp when he had been so very close?

He knew the answer to that question, and his open hands formed fists upon the wall.

"That cursed little creature! Frazzling demon-spawn!"

That wretched thing had continued to appear ahead of them periodically, just beyond reach. This had persisted for two days as the conjured blizzard harassed their pursuit. Each sighting had inspired greater haste, and fed the hope that they were just on the heels of their quarry.

Grobennar had rationalized the lack of tracks afterward by acknowledging the amount of fresh snow, and the winds whipping through the valley, both of which could have worked together to cover evidence of their enemies' passing. The deeper reality, though, was that there had not been any tracks, at least not in the direction they had continued.

Worse yet, Jaween had been all but shouting in his head that they were being tricked from the very beginning of the snow. Grobennar had determined that Jaween was wrong, and had from that point forward determined to prove this to be so. He ground his teeth. There were few feelings worse than being wrong, and few beings who would enjoy reminding him as often about it as Jaween.

He turned to face the rest of his contingent, who had all formed up with concern over the uncharacteristic display of emotion. "They're days gone. Likely headed south to round the mountains altogether, else one of the other passes is still open and navigable."

Paranja had moved to stand next to Grobennar and said, "Shame that our tracker died. What're we going to—"

The back of Grobennar's hand halted her words as it connected solidly with her face. The blow sent the priestess to the ground in a heap. He ignored the stinging pain of his own flesh and looked down at the woman lying there.

The other priests and priestesses all stood motionless, on edge. A few looked as if they wished to help Paranja, but must have seen Grobennar's enraged expression and thought better of that. "Curse you, woman! Don't you think I know that? Darkness below! This whole mission has been botched attempt after botched attempt. I'll be lucky to keep from becoming another red scale upon the body of the God-king, let alone retain my station. Klerós above knows the Great Lord has killed others for less." The last of his words came out in choking sobs.

*Am I really crying? In front of all of these people?* He shook his head and tried to cut off the tears.

Paranja crawled over to where he had slid to the ground, back against the wall. Droplets of blood fell from her lip to strike the unblemished snow below, the deep red soaking the flawless white canvas. It was beautiful, and terrible.

She moved in closer and whispered so only he could hear, "I'm so sorry. I didn't mean to—I-I-I-just—everything will be fine. There's nothing more you could have done. The Great Lord knows this. You're too valuable to him to be punished for what is beyond your control. There's no way you could have anticipated such evil and power from the enemy, especially one as dark as he." Her tone became more menacing. "That little snake and his dark helpers."

She caressed Grobennar's neck. "We may have lost ground, but let's not forget that you have other means of tracking. The enemy no longer has the cover of trees."

She looked up to the open sky above, where three eagles floated in the air. "Let's go kill this vermin, his traitorous witch friend, and that furry little demon spirit!"

Grobennar pulled her in close for an embrace, then rose to his feet. He cleared his throat and shrugged off the embarrassment of his child-like sobbing. He spoke as if he'd been standing there scowling the whole time. "Let's move, we've ground to cover. Rest your minds; I will borrow some of your strength for another clasp. We'll see if a set of eyes from above can't help us find what has been lost."

## CHAPTER 56

# AYNWARD

AYNWARD DAWDLED AROUND CAMPUS THAT morning before finally asking a student for directions to his first class. He did the same for the next class before his midday meal. He made a mental note to stop into the library to view a campus map so he could memorize it before heading home that day.

The campus was only a ten-minute walk across at its widest point, with the library directly at the center. However, it was still large enough to bring about frustration after walking in circles, since he didn't know exactly where he was headed. He was just glad that his wanderings were limited by the massive wall securing the entire perimeter of the campus.

He was moving in the direction he'd been hesitantly given by a student at the mess hall when he spotted Kyllean. They met gazes as Kyllean yelled out, "Greetings, comrade!"

"Well met, fellow miscreant."

Kyllean extended his left arm, and Aynward reciprocated, left hands clasping the opposite forearms in greeting. This was a long-standing salutation among soldiers, but had been growing in popularity among Kingdom-born males as a whole. The habit had been commonplace for Aynward, who'd grown accustomed to such greetings from his knight-in-training friend, Fronk. It felt just as natural with Kyllean in spite of their short tenure as . . . *friends?* He'd heard his father's soldiers speak of the bond forged by battle, and while his foolish coup hadn't been a full-on battle, it qualified in its own. *Perhaps friends, then.*

"You know where we're going? I was headed to check the university statue—"

"Nope, just came from there. I've asked three students since my midday meal and not a one had a clue. And it's not on the campus map, I checked at the library."

Aynward pulled out his schedule and unrolled it to confirm the exact wording.

"Course: Properties."

Kyllean completed it for him. "Location: beneath the trees. Yeah, he could have been *slightly* more specific."

Aynward laughed. "Do you think this is his way of punishing us?"

Kyllean nodded. "Well, yeah. I think he made that pretty clear."

"No, not the added class, I mean the whole thing. What if there's not even a course at all? What if he just put this on there so we'd end up searching around all night in vain?"

Kyllean stopped in his tracks. "He does appear to be just the right sort of crazy for a thing like that, doesn't he?" He brought his hand up to his chin. "And it's a good scheme, because I know I'm definitely going to continue looking so long as the possibility exists that this course is real. Sure not going to knowingly skip the first class with the man— Renzik—whatever he is, who saved us from expulsion."

"Fair point. Well, we'd best keep asking around."

Kyllean said, "The last person I asked was the kid who pointed me toward the statue. Just a bunch of stone tables with some trees sprinkled throughout."

Aynward had spotted the statue from a distance, during the deposition ceremony. It was hard to miss. It stood at a height of at least five men stacked atop one another; easily visible from the open square.

Aynward shifted course toward where Kyllean had been headed, away from the statue area, since there was nothing past it but the northern section of the wall. They rounded a large, egg-shaped building containing two major lecture halls. Aynward was assigned to one of them the following day for his Althusian Ethics class. Then the library came into full view. It was the centerpiece of the university, a circular tower constructed of the same blue stone as the rest, with three distinct levels, each a smaller cylinder atop the one below.

Then Aynward remembered something. "Hey, I walked past an outdoor stone amphitheater earlier today with some trees near it. That could be what it's referring to."

"Is that over by the dean's house?" asked Kyllean.

"Um . . . probably. Would that have its own smaller wall with a locked gate in front of it?"

"Sounds about right. Yeah, I do remember seeing that on the map. It's probably not at the amphitheater itself, since that was labeled, though I don't recall the name. But we could be meeting in the stand of trees near there."

Less than ten minutes later, they stood in the shade of a beautiful grouping of tall elm trees. They stood alone.

Kyllean's expression of disappointment lifted. "Why don't we ask one of the guards? They've got to know the campus better than any people here. Except maybe the dean."

Aynward followed Kyllean's gaze to the walled-in, two-story building where the dean resided.

"Too soon?" asked Aynward.

They both laughed.

"There are always several guards at the university gate. Let's see if one of them has any insight."

The gate was nearby so within a few minutes they were approaching two men standing at attention.

Aynward raised a hand. "Greetings to thee, most highly esteemed guardians of the gate."

He was trying to be formal, and polite, but wasn't sure that he sounded anything less than patronizing. He'd have to get better at this.

His suspicion was validated when the men resumed positions looking straight ahead, neither returning the greeting.

The boys continued their approach until they stood directly in the guards' line of sight, making it more difficult to be ignored. This time Kyllean addressed them.

"Apologies, my friend here has read a few too many adventure stories and doesn't know how to speak to real soldiers."

Aynward started to raise a hand of dissent, but Kyllean casually blocked this with his own hand and continued to speak.

"We came over here in hopes that we might benefit from your expertise in university geography."

He paused to let the compliment register.

"See, one of our counselors has listed the location of our meeting place in such a way that we first-years are unable to find it. We assumed that if anyone on campus would be able to solve this riddle, it would be the people who protect these walls and everything inside them day in and day out."

The two men slowly looked at each other, then came to a silent consensus. The man on the left spoke. "What is the description given?"

Aynward decided that Kyllean had proven himself the better communicator for this and remained silent.

"The course location is listed as, 'beneath the trees,'" Kyllean replied.

The same man considered for a moment. "There are five locations, possibly a sixth."

He described all the places on campus that could fit this description. They had already checked two of them, and had unknowingly walked by a third, leaving only the courtyard hidden within a building near the square, and two locations hidden within the forest that surrounded the dormitories.

They thanked the guards and headed for the courtyard, agreeing that it seemed more academic than the forest.

They entered the building and walked around until they located the entrance to the courtyard. There were two sizable trees on either side of the rectangular space, and a few others with much less foliage toward the center.

"This looks promising," said Kyllean, glancing at a small group of students sitting on the grass beneath the tree at the far end of the area. They heard someone speaking but were too far away to discern words. The source of the voice was blocked from sight by the tree trunk.

By the time they were close enough to hear the voice more clearly, Aynward became certain it didn't sound right. "That's not Dwapek," he whispered.

Kyllean whispered back, "Maybe he has a graduate student running the class. That's pretty common for first-year courses, even if the lead counselor's name is on the schedule."

That seemed plausible to Aynward, especially since Dwapek had made it clear that he had more important things to do.

Aynward's next step brought the speaker into view, and the blood in his veins curdled. That face again. He stopped and tried to turn away before he was recognized; too late.

"Well, well, if it isn't the boy who couldn't handle a little paddling. Oh, and isn't this sweet, he brought a Kingdom-born cousin. Or is it a lover? Both?"

The eyes of the seven others seated on the grass turned to look at them. Aynward felt his shock turning into anger.

The boy continued his mockery. "How sweet of you to join us, but unfortunately only legitimate students are allowed to attend these meetings. You know, students who've successfully endured the desposition, and, of course, whose fathers didn't bribe their children's way through the admissions process in the first place."

*Does he know who my father is?*

Kyllean grabbed Aynward's arm and whispered, "This is not the class, let's go."

Aynward didn't break eye contact with the student who'd insulted and embarrassed him twice now. He responded, "Yeah, I guess it must seem odd that we didn't like being paddled by a bunch of saggy-skinned counselors." He assessed the boy's appearance, similar enough to his own to be Kingdom-born, but he seemed to hold it in contempt. That would suggest he was from Kael, Dowe's centuries-old enemy to the southwest.

"I guess the boys and girls of Kael are a little more into the whole pedophilia thing," Aynward sneered.

If the comment angered the boy, he controlled it well. "Enjoy the rest of your walk. I'm sure we'll be seeing each other again soon. I look forward to that." Then he blew a kiss at them.

Kyllean grabbed Aynward's arm and pulled. "Let's go." He said it quietly, but his sense of urgency convinced Aynward to abandon his standoff with the enemy whose name he didn't even know.

They exited the building and Kyllean turned him about and pushed him. Aynward yelped at the pain in his still-healing ribs.

"Ow! What was that for?"

"Are you a total moron or just socially incapable?"

"What do you mean?"

"Let's walk, we're already late. The dorms are up here and to the right. The soldier said the one possible location in the forest was along the back wall near the dean's house, so we'll start at the wall and go until we find what he described."

They assumed a quickened pace along the path to the opening in the forest that led to the dormitories.

"So what is it that has your thighs chafing, Kyllean?"

Kyllean ignored the slight. "Well, for starters, this boy, who seems to already know a bit about us, is a graduate student. He's got the gold graduate backing on his amulet. This means he likely has friends and resources that would make it easy for him to make both of our lives miserable if we give him good cause. Remind me, how many friends do you have here?"

He held up a hand to forestall the answer and continued. "Don't count me on that list just yet. I'm not sure I wish to be counted among this short or nonexistent list if you're going to be so good at making enemies."

Aynward interjected, "I didn't choose him!" Aynward didn't want to get into the embarrassing prank before the testing, so he went straight to the desposition. "We were bound to be enemies from the start! He was one of the students who jumped in to defend Dean Remson during the ceremony. He remembered me. You were just as much a part of that as I. The only difference is that I'm not coward enough to stand by in silence while he mocks and belittles me!"

Kyllean matched Aynward's rising volume. "And you're just *so brave*, aye? Does bravery require stepping into the line of an enemy swing without a weapon of your own? That sounds more like stupidity to me."

"I didn't seek this out!"

They stopped walking and turned to face each other. Kyllean lowered his voice. "Listen, I'm glad I joined you at the desposition. That was a worthwhile, yet still *very stupid*, fight. But this other nonsense isn't. Maybe this kid does have it in for you, or both of us, especially after embarrassing him during that fight. We may have to defend ourselves, but right now we don't even know where our next class is. We're not equipped to handle any more conflict. Think Dwapek will be able to keep us from being expelled if we get into another violent confrontation? We've been given a gift by being allowed to stay. I just don't think playing into this kid's hands is wise."

Aynward hated being wrong, but he knew that he was. His anger floated away, replaced by shame. "All right, let's just try to find this place and worry about this other rubbish later."

Kyllean let out a loud breath and started walking toward the path into the forest. Aynward caught up to him but they walked in silence. Within a minute, the path opened up to reveal several long, blue-stone buildings: dormitories. This was where all underclassmen lived for their first few years if they were unable to secure housing within the city itself. They passed five such buildings, situated close together, separated from the rest of the campus by dense woods.

They reached the line of trees that abutted the eastern side of the university wall.

"Well, I don't see a path, but it's this way," said Kyllean, as he stepped into the wooded area.

Aynward didn't object, but he soon wished he had.

The foliage wasn't exactly sparse. He earned numerous scratches on his still tender, healing skin, but Kyllean continued without complaint and Aynward wasn't going to be the one to start. He trudged on.

They were making so much noise as they crunched twigs and kicked up leaves that Aynward almost missed the sound of a voice. Almost. He stopped and listened. He heard it again.

"Hey—I think I hear someone talking."

Kyllean stopped moving, and then the voice came clear. It was unmistakably Dwapek.

They followed the sound, abandoning the wall that had been their marker, and finally emerged into a small clearing, kept free from trees by large slabs of stone. It looked something like the other amphitheater, but much smaller, and significantly dilapidated.

Sitting on the second row of stone were three other students. Dwapek turned to face Aynward and Kyllean. He pulled out a small golden object and clicked a button, causing the top to snap open. "The bell chimed more than a quarter hour ago. This class begins precisely at the hour."

Aynward raised an eyebrow. *A pocket watch?* There were only a handful of them in the world, and they were immensely expensive. His own father had only just received one the year before. It had come as a deposit toward the dowry for Dagmara's hand in marriage as she waited for the boy to come of age.

Dwapek's scowl became a smile. "However, there's a way for you to make it up to mine self and your more responsible classmates."

"How is that?" asked Aynward through clenched teeth.

"Why, you two will go to the library to obtain all of the titles required for next class. I was planning to ask for volunteers, but you've simplified things. Of course you'll want to take a more conventional path to get here next time. Can't have you trouncing through the forest with parchments and books: you'll ruin them."

Aynward looked around and saw the small opening in the forest opposite from where they had come. "Would have been nice if the guard had mentioned a path," he said under his breath.

Dwapek waved them to sit. "So, where was I? We can do introductions again later."

The student directly to Aynward's right raised his hand.

Dwapek rolled his eyes. "Stephonous, there are only five students here, you needn't raise your hand to speak when I ask a question. This isn't primary school."

The skinny boy shrank. "Sorry."

"Go on, then."

The boy straightened a little. "You were explaining the, as you called it, 'capricious' interactions between various priestly mages of religions around the world. Or, rather, our complete and utter lack of understanding on the subject."

Dwapek nodded. "Seems you were paying attention after all. Sometimes the droplet actually lands in the pond. Thank you for the summary."

Aynward looked over to Kyllean, who glanced his way for only an instant to register his chagrin at the odd metaphor, and the course topic. Priestly magic? *What kind of spurious course is this?* He was already three days behind on his other class readings, and now he had this? He nearly stood up to leave, but recalled how dependent he was on Dwapek now that he'd made enemies of nearly every other counselor, and apparently several students, too.

Dwapek continued, "History has seen myriad clashes between religious wielders of magic, many claiming power from deities of opposing religions. Are all of them real? Are none of them real? If not, where does this power originate? Did different gods create different races of man? If so, how can it be that migrant people are able to wield the power of foreign gods? Do these gods extend power to any who ask with a sincere heart? Is it all the same god? If so, how does he or she decide who gets which power?"

He paused to let the questions linger in the air. No one spoke. Aynward was impressed. The little man had raised questions that would have gotten him flogged or burned in nearly every kingdom in the world, civilized or not. No religion Aynward knew of was compatible with the validity of any other gods. Almost all of Dwapek's questions undermined every religious institution Aynward knew about.

Aynward was no saint, and certainly not a devout follower of the Chrologal faith, but even he felt uncomfortable with the questions.

Dwapek said, "These are the questions I intend to answer during our time together. Though it is not I who will answer these questions, but we. I will be facilitating your exploration of the histories to see if we can glean some clarity on this subject."

Aynward noticed motion to his right. He cringed for the sake of the boy next to him. Stephonous had raised his hand again.

Dwapek stopped his pacing when he saw the hand, and sighed. "Yes, Stephonous?"

"Well, I'm honored to have been chosen to investigate these questions, but it's just, well, I don't understand why we're doing all this. I mean, are we going to publish our findings to try to set straight the fragmented world of competing religions? I figure we'll more likely wind up burned as heretics just for asking the questions, no matter our findings."

Dwapek frowned, but remained quiet and pensive as he considered an answer. He finally settled on, "Things may be occurring across all of Doréa, things that could bring a certain sense of importance to these questions. I believe our research could play an important role in the security of this region and others in the future."

He turned away from the class and said almost whimsically, "Leaks don't always spring from the same place." This time the entire class exchanged similarly confused looks. Then Dwapek added, "That is all for today. Thank you for coming. I'll see you in two days' time."

Everyone stood up, slowly, not sure how to react to the shock of the day's lecture. Aynward thought the whole thing insane. But it was coming from a man who intentionally avoided anything that was an actual waste of time, including conversation. So why would he create a course whose entire premise fit the description of *waste of time*? It didn't make sense. The dwarf of a man must be deranged.

As if hearing the insult from within Aynward's head, Dwapek turned to face him.

"Here's the list of titles for next class. I expect you to have them all with you. And show a little vim and vigor and be to class on time."

Aynward took the list started to turn away but Dwapek stopped him with a raised finger to the sky. "Oh, you'll need something else." He dug into his robes and his hand returned with a yellow card lined with intricate glyphs. He handed it to Aynward. "This will get you into the special collections department of the library. Don't lose it. These are very difficult to come by, and expensive to replace."

Aynward took the card with trepidation as his recent conversation with Gervais came back to mind. He'd been too busy shuffling around from class to class to even think about how he was going to infiltrate the secret underground book smuggling ring, and use that network to steal—borrow—a book for Gervais. He wasn't sure, but he figured that the yellow card would at least get him a little further toward that end.

## CHAPTER 57

# SINDRI

SINDRI COULDN'T BELIEVE THAT DARNED creature had somehow led them through a snowstorm to a secondary mountain pass just a few days' hike south of their original path.

She removed the scarf from her mouth, inhaled, and coughed. How could any place be so deathly cold? Her lungs burned as she sucked in the icy air. Filtered through a cloth scarf, each breath was stuffy, but at least it hurt less.

Kibure took out the waterskin he had stowed between his body and his cloak to prevent it from freezing, then took a few pulls. He handed it to Sindri, who exchanged a piece of dried meat she had kept similarly against her body. She took a drink then shook her head, saying through labored breaths, "I can't keep this up much longer."

They sat with their backs to the wind, facing downhill the way they had come. The unnatural snow had let up for the first time in days and they could see for leagues as the trail snaked about below. Kibure opened his mouth to reply, but his response was silent. He squinted as if trying to see something below. Sindri tried to follow his gaze, but saw nothing—

Kibure stumbled to his feet. "Oh gods. We need to go—now."

Sindri tilted her head in question. Kibure responded with an outstretched finger. "Look!"

She squinted. "What—I don't—wait—is that—"

"They've caught our trail."

The group of travelers was a great distance below, an entire day's hike, perhaps two; it was difficult to gauge distance in a place like this. Sindri could see the dark shapes against the otherwise white background, down where the trail snaked back into view from where they were currently situated. But there was little doubt about who these people were, or why they traversed the pass so dangerously late in the season.

Sindri was beginning to doubt her own ability to survive the trek by simple virtue of the elements. The thought of increasing their pace was unimaginable, but they had no choice but to try.

## CHAPTER 58

# KIBURE

KIBURE TURNED AND CAUGHT ANOTHER glimpse of his pursuers along the snowy ravine; they had reduced the distance between them significantly. The sight of the group having gained so much ground so quickly was just as discouraging as the knowledge that they had discovered their trail in the first place.

Since he and Sindri had last seen the small shapes below, they had rested only half as often and for half as long. The word *exhaustion* could not capture their utter fatigue. The fugitives hardly spoke a word now, even during their brief stops. It seemed the slightest exertion might make the difference between continued flight and the end.

The fact that their pursuers were quickly gaining ground was so discouraging that Kibure feared to verbally acknowledge it, lest the inevitable came true all the sooner. Thick snow began to fall and Kibure knew Rave was trying to slow down their enemies, but it was too late. He knew that.

Kibure looked back to Sindri and realized she was no longer walking. She had fallen again. Kibure caught up and reached down to help her, but she pulled her arm free.

"The sins of my past are too great. Klerós was never going to allow me to esca—"

She closed her eyes.

Kibure had seen that look of complete brokenness in fellow slaves, and knew with near certainty that she was finished. Kibure gripped the sleeve of her woolen cloak, and yanked with all his might. No response. In spite of the futility, he couldn't stop himself from trying.

"Sindri." Shake, shake. "Sindri, come on, get up." Shake, shake. "Sindri, we've gotta keep moving. We can't stay here. Sindri, come on!"

Kibure's own legs buckled and he crumbled beside her. Just then she opened her eyes, but there was little life left in the glazed expression that stared back at him. She appeared to hardly recognize him or his words. "Sindri," he pleaded in a weak, cracking voice.

It was no use; her strength, her fight, was finished. Tears formed in his eyes as he started back to his feet. He didn't make it three strides before his own leg cramped, landing him right back on the ground. He fervently struggled to rise, but his strength was sapped and his will to survive had come to an end.

Defeated, he crawled back over and cuddled in close to Sindri's shallow breaths. She was a near corpse. Rave flew in and landed on his shoulder, but he hardly noticed. The cooing sound only helped woo him to sleep. He just hoped the weather took his body before the enemy. His mind was at peace as he closed his eyes and allowed the cold to consume him.

## CHAPTER 59

# AYNWARD

AYNWARD'S MOUTH WENT SLACK, SLIDING open like a glutton in the presence of a smorgasbord. He was standing in the foyer of the university library. It was easily ten times larger than the grandest library he'd ever seen; in fact, he decided his working definition of library needed to change. The Kingdom palace had a *book collection*, not a library.

Kyllean had already been inside. "Pretty incredible, isn't it?" he said, trailing off as he stared.

"They must have every word ever written in the history of mankind," whispered Aynward as the book list fell from his hand.

The vastness of the collection was enhanced by the open ceiling, which exposed the walls lined with books on all three levels. Aynward had assumed, when seeing it from the outside, that most of the space was for reading and studying; however, there weren't many tables at all. The few tables that could be found were separated by rows of shelves, also filled.

Kyllean interrupted Aynward's trance. "Well, we'll have plenty to gawk over for the next few years; let's get the books. We still have to report to the sewers before lunch."

Aynward looked down at his hand where Dwapek's extensive list had been and realized he'd dropped it. He bent down and picked it up, then said, "Fair point, though our time here could be considerably shorter: we're probably only one mistake away from never being able to see this place again."

Kyllean started walking to the main desk. The librarian on shift was a portly, dark-skinned Scritlandian who seemed more interested in reading than in attending to those in need of assistance.

"Excuse me, good sir," said Aynward.

The librarian held up an index finger while his other hand continued its path along the writing in the tome. Aynward was about to say something when the book slammed shut and the librarian looked up.

"How may I be of assistance?"

Aynward held up the list. "We've been commissioned by our counselor to obtain all the titles on this list. We were hoping you might be able to help us out."

The Scritlandian extended a hand, flapping it impatiently until Aynward handed the list to him.

Looking at Kyllean he said, "Say, I recognize you. You were here yesterday asking about a campus map. You ever find that class?"

Aynward and Kyllean exchanged an exasperated look as they recalled their trip through the forest, then Kyllean answered, "Yeah. Had to ask around a bit, but we found it. That's actually why we're here."

"Mmhmm, I see your counselor didn't bother indicating which titles are located here versus Special Collections. Who's your counselor?"

"You haven't even looked at the list yet. How could you know that?" asked Kyllean.

"The yellow pass in your friend's hand is a pretty clear indicator."

"Oh," said Kyllean, turning pink.

"So, your counselor?"

Aynward answered, "Counselor Dwapek. The short—"

"No need, everyone knows *that* one. He's an *odd* one, odd indeed." The librarian frowned. "And *lazy*, too. This will take me a while, since there are a few even I don't recognize. I'll have to look them up."

He took out a quill and dipped it in ink, then looked up. "Mind if I write on this?"

"Uh, no, as long as it's still legible, I guess."

"Of course. I'm just going to check off the titles I recognize. The rest I'll have to locate by way of the catalog."

There were fifteen titles altogether. He checked off four of them, then got up and walked over to the wall behind him. He turned his head and said, "You fellows may want to take a seat or explore the place. I'm going to be a while. Just be sure not to touch anything."

Kyllean led the way, directly toward a staircase. Aynward followed him up to the second floor, which they circled until they found the staircase to the third. The walkways were all open, overlooking the main floor. The second and third floors were nothing more than platforms outlining the perimeter of the room, giving access to the books lining the walls.

When they reached the third floor, Aynward decided not to follow Kyllean to the right. He wanted to enjoy the view on his own terms. He stopped at one of the tall, narrow windows located between each bookshelf and gazed out at the beautifully landscaped campus. With his higher vantage, he could see past the university walls to the city beyond and the deep blue water behind that. The view was breathtaking, even for a cynic like Aynward. He finally pulled his gaze away and saw Kyllean standing in front of the next window, moved by what he saw, as well. Neither one said a word. A few more minutes passed in silence, both boys quietly circulating the space, taking it all in.

Like cold water on a sleeping drunkard, the loud voice of the librarian echoed, snapping Aynward out of his reverie. "Your books are ready."

When he reached the main floor, he heard Kyllean exclaim, "Gods above!"

Aynward couldn't see his friend over the mountain of books piled on the desk.

The librarian said, "These are the requested titles available up here. There are six more located in Special Collections. Do you gentlemen have a plan for moving all of these books?"

Aynward paused. "I was thinking we'd just carry them, but—"

"Can we leave these here for a few hours?" interrupted Kyllean.

The librarian glared at him but nodded. "A few hours. But if you don't come back before my shift is up, I'm putting them all back and you can find them again on your own."

"Fair enough. Thank you," Kyllean said.

Kyllean brought Aynward away from the desk. "We're going to have to split up. I'll head into the city to see if I can find some mode of transportation for all these books. Can you get the rest of the titles from Special Collections?"

"Yes. You have enough coin?" Aynward hadn't received much from Dolme, but he could probably request more if he explained the need.

"It's no problem." Kyllean smiled. "I've been given a very sound stipend to ensure that my needs here are met. I'll meet you back here in, say, two hours?"

"Okay."

They went their separate ways.

There was no sign indicating the entrance to the Special Collections portion of the library, but there was a door, guarded by a soldier. That seemed like evidence enough for Aynward.

He walked up to the soldier and held out his pass.

The man took the pass and inspected it closely before handing it back. He stepped forward and opened the door for Aynward.

"Thank you."

The man nodded him past. The door opened to a spiral staircase. Aynward followed it down until the floor leveled out. He found himself standing in a dark, poorly lit room. It was vast, at least the same size as the main floor above, lined wholly with shelf after shelf of books and scrolls.

"Can I help you?"

Aynward jumped at the voice then spun to face the direction of the sound. He saw only darkness at first, but the shadowy outline of a thin man eventually materialized from within the gloom. The figure stepped into the light cast by the nearby glass lantern, but it was positioned behind him, allowing little more than a silhouette to be seen. However, he did notice the light glint off of the gold chain of a university amulet, as well as the embroidered insignia that marked him a student.

Aynward sucked in a few measured breaths before answering, "Uh, yes, well, I hope so."

He extended his hand with the list. The student took the parchment and held it up away from his own shadow. The main-level librarian had crossed off each title as he collected it, so it was easy to see the remaining six. That reminded him: he needed to get better at asking about names. He had few enough friends here; he should at least be making some acquaintances.

"Yes, this will be no problem," the student said.

"Thank you. My name is Aynward."

"Greetings once again, my name remains to be Hirk. If I'm not mistaken, yours has changed."

Aynward was taken aback. "I—yeah." He had met several students in his first two days, not to mention the number of others he'd simply seen, but the name Hirk did not stand out.

*Stupid, you need to say something.* "I was trying that other one out. Didn't stick."

"Huh."

He continued to stare at the dark-skinned boy, his face still obscured by shadow, and then the memory hit him. *Oh yes.* This name had been stored away on a different list, the list of those who needed to be repaid with vengeance. Probably not the best timing. He'd have to wait until he'd gotten his books—and hope he didn't need any more in the future. *God's above! I'm beginning to think like a real statesman. To hell with that.*

"Thanks, by the way. Your directions the other day were fantastic, brought me right to the pub. I had a wonderful time being denied entry. Really good stuff, well played. Is that a common welcome for new students?"

The boy's head shot up to face him. "Beg your pardon?"

*Going to make me spell it out?* "Your little prank the other day. Well done. That's all I was saying."

The boy stepped around the desk swiftly enough to make Aynward jump back, not sure what the student would do. His expression of confusion was almost believable. "I'm not sure that I understand. You say you found the pub, correct?"

*Now he's just gloating.* Hirk grabbed a lantern and turned into a deeply shadowed row of shelves, list in hand. Aynward followed behind and said, "Oh yeah, took me right to it. I'll say, I'm a little disappointed that there wasn't some sort of mixed concoction ready for me to vomit back up or something. Solid prank in terms of roping me in, but the finale was a little anticlimactic. I was disappointed, if we're being honest."

The student was suddenly coming back up the row, right toward him. Aynward stepped aside once again. Hirk walked past him toward the desk, set down a scroll, then headed down a different row.

He responded to what Aynward had said in a loud voice as he moved farther into the depths of the room. "I remain ignorant of the ascribed scheme. If you are glad for the directions, you are welcome. If you are wounded by the service you received once there, perhaps I should have disclosed that I have never been inside. I am merely aware that it is the preferred watering hole of many students because it is outside the walls, and cheaper by half than the monopolized prices of the on-campus pub. You seemed intent on vacating the campus grounds, so I directed you to the closest place beyond the walls that was known to me."

The orb of soft yellow light grew once more as Hirk returned, this time carrying a thin book as well as a thick tome. He placed both next to the scroll, then immediately headed down a different aisle. The shifty light brought back memories of the nights when Aynward and his sister had lain on the palace roof to watch the evening sky, the moons playing hide-and-seek with the broken clouds, moving swiftly in the strong wind. The partial lantern light here was just as unpredictable and infrequent while Hirk moved about the dimly lit room.

What Aynward found most surprising was how quickly Hirk navigated the myriad books to find the requested titles. The room was enormous; there had to be thousands of bound books and scrolls, with no obvious system of organization, yet this kid was able to pick through the chaos while maintaining a conversation.

More important than the mystery of how he did it was the lack of emotion at Aynward's prodding. Hirk was either very good at disguising his inner smugness at the small victory, or he was telling the truth. If it was the former, Aynward would do well not to admit any further injury; if it was the latter, the boy didn't seem to understand the humiliation of such an experience, and groveling for sympathy would be an act far too desperate for Aynward's taste. In either case, displaying his anger about it would only embarrass him; he'd been a fool to bring it up.

*Okay, change the subject. You do not need any enemies in the library.*

The light had nearly disappeared altogether. Aynward could see the slight illumination at each corner of the room, and then—yes, there it was. He must have set down the lantern to pick up one of the tomes, which placed Hirk at the far wall.

Aynward nearly shouted, "So is there some sort of organizational system that allows you to find these titles so quickly?"

"Yes," came the reply from afar.

Aynward waited for further clarification; it never came. Hirk reappeared with the fourth and fifth titles, set them down on the desk without a word, and slithered back into the nest of rows once more. *Well, that conversation withered quite nicely, didn't it?*

A few moments later, Aynward was standing in front of a pile of old tomes, scrolls, and parchments and Hirk was seated at the desk scribing the titles in his ledger with Aynward's name next to each.

"Will there be anything else for you today?"

He was about to reply no, he certainly couldn't wait to get back out of this mole's lair, but a glint in the distance captured his eye. He squinted, but couldn't make out anything further. It was faint, located halfway between two of the lanterns.

"I'm not sure, I'll be . . ." Aynward trailed off as he walked over to get a closer look.

As he neared, he noticed a shape taking form, several shapes, all having a similar glossy look, muted by the available light. He stopped about two paces away when it all came together to form the armor of one soldier on either side of a blacker-than-everything-else hole in the wall.

The armor was completely still. *I wonder if—*

"Don't."

Aynward stumbled back, crashing into a shelf of books. Fortunately the shelf won the bout and Aynward ended up spilling onto the floor.

The voice was deep, raspy, and, most important, unexpected. He would have been no less surprised than if a complaint had echoed up from the privy during a hearty deposit.

Aynward groaned as he rolled onto his stomach. "How about a lantern, maybe a sign reading 'Creepy, motionless guards prohibiting entry into the forbidden?' Would that be too much trouble?" His voice came out in labored breaths as he pushed himself back to his feet.

Neither guard moved or spoke.

Aynward started back toward Hirk's desk. *Well, found the entrance to the archives.* This didn't bring him any closer to infiltrating the rogue network of book thieves, but he only needed to do that if he wanted to make strides toward fiscal security and vengeance upon his enemies.

Aynward reached the desk and picked up the stack of mismatched literature.

"Uh-uh," clucked Hirk. "You must sign for these in the ledger."

Aynward set down the stack and stepped to the large book to sign and date his name six times.

Without looking up, Hirk said, "I see you stumbled into the entrance to the archives."

Aynward was in good spirits about the whole thing so he laughed it off. "Sure did. Gave those guards a good scare, too. Almost walked right in unseen."

"Yes, that's exactly what it sounded like," said Hirk, a hint of mirth in his voice.

Not thinking, Aynward said, "Say, you wouldn't happen to know how many people have access to the archives would you?"

"Huh, what? No. I mean, very few. All counselors are granted access and a choice few others who must follow strict procedures. That number is fixed by the quantity of entry bracelets in circulation." The mirth in his voice had vanished like a thief disappears into a thick crowd.

"So, do some students have access?"

"In rare instances, yes. I believe counselors have to go to the dean to get approval before assigning an entry bracelet, and even then it's usually for a limited time. Why are you so interested? There's nothing but dust and some original writings too fragile to be touched."

"So you've been inside?" asked Aynward, curiosity piqued.

Hirk didn't answer right away, fingers tapping on the desk. "Only once, during my training last year. It's really nothing special."

Aynward returned to his stack of books. "Oh, okay. I was just curious since it's kind of hidden away, and heavily guarded. What could be more interesting than the forbidden, am I right?"

"Sorry I didn't have a more exciting story of its grandeur to tell. Enjoy your studies."

"Thank you for your assistance. Good day."

Aynward made his way back up to the main floor of the library to wait for Kyllean. All the while, his thoughts were pounding at a door that simply wouldn't budge.

How was he going to discover who was stealing the books from the archives? He couldn't just walk around asking. Unless, of course, he set up camp in the archives near the entrance, just out of sight, all day for a few weeks to see who went in and out. That should be no problem at all. He could easily devote multiple days in their entirety, ignoring his classes. And surely Hirk or whoever else wouldn't mind him just hanging out like that. And once he'd discovered the culprit, it would be no problem at all to convince them to steal books on his behalf instead of just killing him for finding out such a dangerous secret.

This entire quest was preposterous.

Maybe that was Gervais's angle all along: he was no friend, after all.

## CHAPTER 60

# KIBURE

IBURE WOKE UP TO A violent shaking, and the touch of strong hands upon his body. His mind was slow and his body stiff, and he had no ability to resist. He identified the shadowed shapes of several cloaked figures lurking about while a pair of hands continued to shake his body.

His throat was dry and his mind so weak that he hardly felt fear. His life was at its end and he knew it. He prayed Rave would just stay out of it at this point. He had accepted the beckoning of the cold as it fed on his fatigue.

"Hey, he wake!" shouted a coarse, high-pitched voice.

A deeper tone responded, "Good, good. Many question."

Kibure's eyes cleared, and he saw the shape of a man cloaked in shadow, looming ominously above him. His only discernible feature was red eyes, with a sparkle of light illuminating them without touching the rest of the features. The snow had followed them and puffy white flakes assaulted Kibure's upturned face as he looked to the dark space behind the hood. A deep voice in strongly accented Lugienese asked, "Who are you? Why you travel in such company toward freelands?"

*You are the one who chased me through the mountains . . .* He wanted to speak it but instead remained silent, unsure of how best to respond. Why did this man even ask the questions? Did he just need assurance that he had captured the right person? Was he looking for some sort of confession? *Well, I am a tazamine and I serve the Dark One. You're welcome to execute me now.* The man's features seemed unnaturally obscured by darkness, more so than warranted by the drawn cowl of his thick fur-lined cloak. Perhaps it was just Kibure's imagination, or his fatigue, or maybe the contrast with the thick powdery snow that continued to fall between them.

"Answer question!"

A voice from another dark shape to the side shouted, "Just kill. Be done."

A hand slammed down upon Kibure's head, jarring him, causing his already delicate stream of consciousness to flicker.

"Who are you? Speak!" came the voice again.

Kibure started to open his mouth in response, still not exactly sure what he might say, but all his strength had departed and the edges of his vision faded. He heard Rave's cooing and saw the raaven's blurred image as he took a place on Kibure's shoulder. To his surprise, he also saw the light of the sun as the mystic snow fizzled out around them. He wanted to shout out for Rave to flee, that it was too late to help him, but his mouth and body failed. A tear ran down his cheek as everything disappeared before his eyes, sleep overtaking him once more.

The next time Kibure was conscious enough to hold a thought without losing it seconds later, he recognized a vaguely familiar sensation. Was it his stomach? Was his stomach full? But that made little—

It came back to him in a rush of fragmented memories. A hazy vision of his hands holding a canteen filled with a bitter-tasting beverage that the hooded man said came from a distant fruit. He had tried to describe it, but Kibure hardly recalled. This was accompanied by mouthfuls of dried fish and nuts. He must have been too tired to even bother asking himself why the Klerósi priests had changed tactics so swiftly, or why they would want to keep him alive instead of simply killing him.

This registered in his mind now, and panic welled up again. If they thought he was some sort of demon, and he had not responded to questions earlier, perhaps they had decided to bring him back and torture the silence out of him. It was the only rational explanation. His stomach did a somersault and he nearly vomited its contents.

He sat up and felt a dizzying haze, but it cleared and his vision returned. He counted eight forms. All but one moved about like ants throughout the campsite, collapsing tents; they were preparing to move again.

One hooded figure sat beside him, arms crossed upon his bent knees. "Ah, blessed one, he wake. You are well, yes?"

The demeanor of the speech befuddled Kibure. He was almost certain that it was the same man who had been interrogating him earlier.

"My speech too strong? Or you no speak Lugienese?"

He tried again with a few garbled sentences in another language Kibure did not understand. This gave Kibure time to at least recover his wits as he answered.

"No, no, Lugienese, I speak Lugienese."

The man's emphasis on certain sounds while neglecting others did make him difficult to follow, not to mention the lack of certain words, but he got the gist of what was said.

Looking around Kibure thought of Sindri, and his heart sank. Had they also fed her? Had she been awake earlier? He couldn't remember. She had been in worse shape than he before they were captured. Then he spotted her motionless body a few paces away. His emotions reeled. He couldn't tell if she was breathing.

"Is she? Is she . . . ?" He tried but couldn't finish the question. There was a palpable fear in his voice that he could not control. He supposed it mattered very little now, and was perhaps better if she were dead. A dead person couldn't be tortured.

The hood moved, perhaps as a nod. "Your friend alive."

*So much for that.*

The man continued, "Yes, very weak. She no walk for many day, but live, yes. Need much rest. Why does you and she travel this place alone and no prepared? You be corpse if we no come."

The malice in the man's voice from his first bout of questioning was completely gone, replaced with curiosity and perhaps a sense of awe? Was this some sort of trick? What was his angle? The man knew he was running from him and his priests, or at least, trying to escape slavery. As much as Kibure appreciated not having questions shouted at him, he equally despised the notion that this man would belittle him with questions he already knew the answers to. Well, if he wanted a confession, Kibure would give him one.

Kibure snarled, "After being told I would be sold to a new slaver in the Isles, the ship we traveled on was attacked by Kraken conjured by Klerósi priests, so I decided my best chance for survival was to get as far away from the Lugienese Empire as possible. I fled to the mountains. Sindri here has her own reasons for leaving, but we've been headed east ever since, still unsure exactly why we're being chased in the first place."

He paused, took a deep breath, and continued, this time with venom oozing from his tone. "Why don't you tell me why you've bothered to pursue someone so insignificant? Don't you and your priests have more important people to worry about than an escaped slave and an exiled *priestess?*" He nearly spat the last word.

The man stood and took a step toward Kibure, who stiffened, ready for an attack, all the while knowing he would be helpless to stop it. His anger did little to quell the fear that sprang up in him at that moment. The man stopped right in front of Kibure, whose heart raced.

Kibure nearly fell backward in defense when the man moved his arms, but the hands moved slowly, harmlessly, toward his own face. He pulled back his hood completely, exposing his naked face for Kibure to see. "No Klerósi priest," he said in a stern, deep voice.

Kibure gasped in surprise. The man's skin was completely black, his eyes red. The shocking strangeness of his appearance was nearly as frightening as the anticipated attack itself. He had never seen such a man, and while Grenn had mentioned the dark-skinned people of the east, he had never expected such a literal blackness.

"My name Jonglin, I am merchant." His lips cracked a smile. "Sell of illegal."

Then his eyes became large and darted from side to side. "What of priests, they follow?"

It took Kibure a few seconds to respond, so relieved was he by the revelation that this man was not one who had been chasing him.

"I—I don't really know. They were close behind a few days back, we thought we lost them in a storm, then saw you and thought you were them. They may still be behind us."

The man nodded to himself. "I send Janx back, he see for priests. We move. If followed, we have more speed. I think priests are not best at travel, yes?" He held up his hands.

Kibure protested. "I'll never be able to keep up. And Sindri . . ."

Jonglin smiled then laughed out loud, a deep bellowing laugh. "No walk for you." He pointed back at the contraption. "Jonglin carries you."

He gestured to one of several angled wooden contraptions. Kibure saw that others were also loaded, men picking up the narrow ends with ropes that they'd hooked around their shoulders and chests. They would be pulled by the men as they traversed the pass, allowing them to carry a great deal more weight than normal. "Travois carry many weight. You ride, keep strength."

Kibure fretted. If these men weren't the priests who had been chasing them . . . well, that didn't explain why they would suddenly begin helping them. Carrying them up the mountain. It still made no sense. He had to know.

"Why help me? Why help Sindri? You could just as easily leave us here and continue the rest of the way without these priests having any care at all of your passing. They'll kill or enslave you for helping if we're captured."

The man was unperturbed by the dose of reality that should have had him rethinking his decision.

"Good reason." He turned but continued to speak. "We talk later. Now we go."

He moved to another individual, speaking quickly in another language. The man looked over to Kibure, nodded, and immediately disappeared downhill the way they had come.

Within minutes Kibure was gently tied at the waist to the travois and moving up the slope at a greater pace than he could have hoped to match on his own. The rhythm of Jonglin's steps coaxed Kibure's nerves as he fell into a deep sleep.

A shrill cry from above shook Kibure from his stupor. The familiar timbre of the scream, and the pain it implied, caused Kibure's eyes to open wide as his blood curdled. His gaze immediately shot up and locked on a dark shape overhead. Large wings extended out like the shady branches of a tree, easily carrying the large body of the predatory bird. But the sound had not been that of a bird, it had come from the much smaller, struggling black shape painfully secured within the bird's talons.

"Rave!" shouted Kibure in horror.

Kibure sensed the use of magic as the two creatures did battle in the air, though battle was not true to what occurred above him; this was a slaughter.

Another cry echoed into the valley, and this time the travelers all stopped. Kibure's gaze had already locked on the events of the sky, but he could hear quiet murmurs around him. He started working the knot that secured him to the travois as he watched one of the bird's monstrous talons claw at Rave's body above. Then it latched around his throat and Rave's cries became a gurgle.

The little creature had overcome great odds indeed, but this looked grim, and luck could only be so abundant. Kibure's entire body went stiff with fear, but the worst part was his inability to intervene. The struggle took place far above so he could do little more than watch in horror as his beloved guardian, his friend, was choked to death by the much larger adversary. The anticipated loss hit him like a sandstorm armed with grains of nausea and his stomach pitched what little remained inside.

Kibure looked down for a moment to finish undoing the rope then let it fall to the snowy ground. By the time he looked back up, Rave dangled there completely limp, the large bird continuing to close around his throat. The mystic creature's arms and legs swayed lifelessly above.

Then the commotion he had been ignoring around him finally registered. Several of the men had taken out stringed weapons. "Bows ready," came a deep voice, and they took aim. Kibure had seen weapons of this like used a few times back at the estate, used exclusively for *target practice* on condemned slaves. They could be lethal, but they weren't generally very accurate. He was no expert, but the struggle above looked too high and far to grant a good shot.

The first shaft flew harmlessly past the above commotion—but it flew past, not short of it! Hope rebounded within Kibure just as a shot from another bow pierced the wing of the large bird. The trajectory of the two changed instantly, a downward spiral—yes! Another arrow buzzed by, missing by a handsbreadth. A third was so close it must have brushed feathers, but then the creature suddenly leveled out and spread its wings again and the next arrow whizzed by to hit the nothingness where the bird should have been. Its open wings displayed nothing where the arrow had been lodged, and the quarrel fell harmlessly from the sky.

*Magic*, he cursed.

Again that feeling of helplessness punished Kibure as the bird, which was now much closer, surged forward. It finally released the lifeless black corpse from its talons up ahead. At this point, Kibure wished nothing more than to let his anger overtake him so he might tap into his own magic. As evil as the stuff might be, it could have possibly protected Rave, and could at least now serve to offer revenge. But that option seemed beyond his ability to control.

Kibure darted ahead of the others to retrieve Rave's body, a sliver of hope remaining. He glanced up to see that the giant bird had turned back toward him and the others but was gaining altitude. The fugitive slave redoubled his efforts to reach Rave.

Shouts of warning resounded as he slid to a stop before the motionless Rave. He glanced up in horror as the vastness of the winged predator closed on him with lightning speed.

Kibure barely had time to shield himself with his hands before the bird struck with the full force of its weight, knifelike talons leading the way, driving Kibure from his feet. Warm tendrils seemed to spread from where the talons hit, and a jolt of pain shot down from his shoulder from the impact with the hard ground. He tumbled forward and rolled to the right in a tangle of fear, pain, and confusion. His arms attacked the body of the bird, clawing in a frenzy as he rolled about the ground. Something sharp pierced the skin on his palm and he recoiled.

In spite of the dizzying pain, he used his bloodied hand to scoot backward from the attack and was quick to get to his feet in readied defense. Only then did he realize his enemy lay in a heap, completely still. He wondered if it was a cautionary measure, awaiting Kibure's next move. But on closer inspection, he noticed the unnatural angle of the beast's neck, and the way its wings had sprawled along the ground.

That's when he saw the arrow. It had entered where the left eye should have been and exited through the upper neck. A red stain blossomed along the packed snow below. He stared at it in near disbelief until a deep voice from behind him interrupted his reverie.

"Kibure."

He turned to see Jonglin, a motionless black object cradled in his arms. It seemed much like the dead assailant.

Kibure's heart tore.

## CHAPTER 61

# GROBENNAR

PAIN EXPLODED THROUGH THE LINK as it was severed. Grobennar's eyes shot open and he let out a throaty bellow. He lay on his back as he oriented himself, staring up at the sky, cold fluffy snow melting into the hair on the back of his head where the hood had shifted to the side.

The concerned voice of Vlanhir to his left asked, "Fatu Mazi, are you well?"

He grunted and nodded in affirmation.

The recollection of his minor success entwined with the larger plate of yet unfinished work made his temples throb. He had managed to slay one object of great personal ire, but the true abomination still ran free, and he and the other priests were now days behind.

Dizzying pain accompanied his movement toward an upright position, but he was prepared for it. He had done a great deal of training in the art of clasping, and all priests were forced to experience multiple deaths during such preparation. This was one of the unfortunate side effects of the clasping process, but in order to have the necessary dexterity while within the mind of an animal, one had to allow those parts of the mind to be relayed through the link. Skilled users such as Grobennar were capable of partial clasps to allow muted sensation to flow from the animal, but unfortunately flying required a completely unfettered link. And so a significant surge of energy had been released, and he would feel the pain and weakness for days, even with a healing.

His mind replayed the image of his adversary's body going limp, and an upright shift at the edges of his lips appeared.

"What happened? Were you able to find the boy?" inquired Vlanhir.

"Yes," replied Grobennar.

The plump priest hovering over him opened and closed his mouth without a sound, unsure if he should ask anything further after the High Priest's one-word response. He finally gathered his courage.

"Wh-wh-what are we to do now?"

"We pursue. The Evil One has acquired allies and they move with haste. *Smugglers* by the looks of them."

Smugglers, especially foreigners, were regarded as less than slaves by the priesthood. Merchants and smugglers alike always brought more with them than just goods. Avoiding their poisonous ideas and customs was a main reason why trade within the Lugienese Empire was so tightly controlled.

"We need to get moving. Pack up the camp!" Grobennar shouted as he struggled to his feet. Two others helped him as he wobbled on unsteady legs.

"You're injured. The severed connection has weakened you!"

"I'm fine," he growled. He would have Jaween heal what could be healed through their connection once they were moving. "The link was severed, true, but I'm fit to continue as planned. I know where he is, *and* where he is going."

Paranja trotted over to him, concern written on her features. "The God-king contacted me while you were . . . busy." Her index finger habitually spiraled upward at the mention of Magog. "He bid me tell you to contact him as soon as the clasp was ended. Didn't say anything else, but I'd guess he wants an update on our progress."

A spike of fear struck Grobennar's spine. "Of course." He inclined his head to send her away. He had been hoping for more time, and better news than what he currently had. But he knew he could not refuse or delay such a request.

*"I have a bad feeling about this, Grobes."*

"So do I."

A wave of weakness moved through his body, a reminder of just how fatigued he was. He gritted his teeth and tried to shake off the light-headedness that came with his condition. Then he shouted to the retreating Paranja.

"Hey!"

She turned swiftly, her expression impassive as she awaited instructions.

"I will need at least three of you to lend me your strength for the connection with the God-king. I have not the strength for it at such a distance, not in my current state."

He snapped his fingers then hung his head, feeling the need to sit once more. He knew Paranja would comply.

Within five minutes a link with the Blessed One had been firmly established. The God-king's voice boomed in his head like a Palpanese gong, but, unlike a face-to-face conversation, Grobennar could not cover his ears in protection and he dared not sever the connection.

"I was recently updated on the progress of your mission, which has failed. I am recalling all priests and priestesses to Sire Karth in preparation for the first stage of the Purge."

Grobennar considered the phrasing of his next question carefully so as to not offend, deciding that a direct question was too risky.

"Your Excellency, I recently killed the body of the spirit, and rediscovered the location of the Evil One's agent. I should be able to perform another clasp once my strength returns. They are moving quickly, but if we were to—"

"No. You will do as I command."

The heavy response nearly stole Grobennar's breath away. "As you say, Your Greatness. I—I did not intend to question your superiority." Grobennar reflexively found his knees and bowed in supplication. "I have failed you, Your Excellency. Your will is iron. We will return to the capital with all haste."

"No."

*No?* "Your Grace?"

"*You* will not be returning to Sire Karth with the rest. Every city with agents has been given a description of this agent of the Dark One. If this pestilence turns up, he will be dealt with accordingly. *You* will be traveling to the Isles city of Brinkwell to ensure preparations are made for the invasion there. The agents have their instructions. You will oversee their work."

Grobennar's dread expanded at these words. "But Your Greatness, as Fatu Mazi I should be by your side for the invasion."

"Indeed. The Fatu Mazi *will* be with me. *Your* failure has cost you this honored title. Your early work for the Empire will never be forgotten, and you will retain your seat on the Council for now, but you can no longer remain atop the pedestal we've placed you. The station of Fatu Mazi cannot afford to be tainted by failure of such magnitude. The position has been filled by another. It is done. See to your new orders. And do not fail me again."

Grobennar choked on the cold air around him. *This cannot be. It simply cannot be. The prophecy; the right seat of Magog, his sword—I was supposed to vanquish the Dark Lord's agent. That was to be me!* But he had to get out of his own mind and respond. He pulled himself out of the chains of anguish just long enough to say, "I will not fail you again, Your Excellency."

He felt the link end, and the agony of his new reality struck like a dozen arrows. Fear of Magog's response to the delays in their mission had become a lurking shadow, present among his every decision, but he had not anticipated this end, not really.

How could Magog have known what had happened? Had Paranja betrayed him? Had it been another?

Grobennar shook his head. He should have expected Rajuban to have compromised at least one member of his team. Grobennar would know the truth of it at the next session of the Council when he saw who had risen in rank without due merit. But with his recent failure and demotion, what did any of that matter, anyway? Betrayal or not, he *had* failed his king.

Paranja interrupted Grobennar's thoughts. "What message does the God-king send?"

Grobennar replied through the fast-growing lump in his throat. "Our mission here is finished."

Paranja was smart enough not to question this further, for sorrow could quickly become rage.

Grobennar turned away, feeling the dam of his emotions about to break. He could hardly wrap his mind around his new reality. He was being relegated to a task previously assigned to those deemed unfit for the mainland Kleról. And yet Grobennar had given his entire life in service to the Kleról. Without his service, their God-king would not be, the Purge would not be, this very mission would not be.

How could Klerós allow such a vital servant to be disgraced, and by one so obviously interested in only self-elevation, not the greater good of Klerós? Grobennar felt the pendant around his neck and anger flared within him. Without another thought, he ripped the pendant from his neck and hurled it against the wall.

"Hypocrite!" he shouted to himself, not caring who heard. He had risen to the highest position within the Kleról, expecting others to follow the commands, while he had violated them all along by retrieving that which had been forbidden for centuries: a spirit. His decision to forsake the law after finding Jaween had benefited him countless times, but maybe Klerós only tolerated this sin so that his fall from grace would be that much further when it came. Perhaps his punishment for a life of hidden sin had now arrived. How could he have expected anything different? And yet—

The small voice in the back of his mind reminded him that he had not violated the laws of Klerós; he had violated the laws of men.

The esteemed Lesante had been the one to unlock the secret to summoning the spirits of Klerós, his agents within the world. It was only their own weakness that caused men of the Kleról to ban the use of the spirits. Grobennar walked over and stooped down to pick up Jaween. Grobennar's duty to his faith and to Klerós was clearer than ever. He needed to succeed in his new task, then regain his position of favor. He needed to rescue his king from the clutches of that parasite, Rajuban. This setback, a grand setback indeed, was but a test.

Jaween remained silent, but Grobennar could feel a quiet brooding through the connection, though not directed at him. The spirit had never taken well to being slighted. An insult to his host was an insult to him. Jaween had long encouraged Grobennar to kill Rajuban. Perhaps he had been right all along. The passionate anger leaked through the connection and Grobennar felt his own emotions shifting from sorrow to rage. But this was not the fast-burning rage of tantrums; this was the deep-seated inferno that burned eternally. Grobennar would do as he was commanded, but he would find a way to get his revenge, and next time it would be the sort that could not be returned in kind.

## CHAPTER 62

# AYNWARD

AYNWARD HAD TO SQUINT AT the bright light striking his eyes for the first time in two hours as he pushed the heavy door up from the vertical ladder to exit the sewers. He breathed deeply of the fresh air as his eyes adjusted.

Kyllean climbed out and exclaimed, "Thank the gods, I can breathe again! How often are we down there?"

"Every other day," grumbled Aynward.

"I'm definitely starting to regret my decision to join you at the desposition." Kyllean looked down at the smears of wet filth covering his robes. "Correction: I definitely regret joining you at the desposition."

"I'm starting to feel similarly," said Aynward.

Kyllean replied, "Well, let's get a move on. Wouldn't want to be late for Dwapek's class again."

They headed toward Kyllean's dormitory to retrieve the books they'd gathered from the library.

Ten minutes later, Aynward slammed the sack full of books down on the stone slab where class would be meeting shortly. Letting out a loud sigh of relief, Kyllean did the same. Aynward flexed his hand to alleviate the cramping, but it did little to help. There was just no easy way to carry such an awkward grouping of heavy items.

"Ah, glad to see you were able to make it on time today," greeted Dwapek. "And what's this? You've brought something for me?"

Aynward responded, "Why, yes, of course. It was our great pleasure. I'm just thankful we were given the opportunity. Thank the gods you decided to have us meet in a secret, unmapped, and poorly described location, thereby forcing our maiden late arrival, and the subsequent reward for that. I couldn't have wished for a more enjoyable start to my Brinkwell experience."

Dwapek opened one of sacks and started sifting through the items. "Your humility blooms like a flower. I suspect you'll outgrow the victim's role in no time."

Kyllean was the only person there to laugh at the jape, on account of their effort to be extra punctual. However, Kyllean's laugh was uproarious enough to make up for the lack of others.

"Hilarious," mumbled Aynward. A gust of wind disturbed his robes, filling his nostrils with the rank scent of the sewers, reminding him of yet another of his *misfortunes*. He was going to have to increase the frequency of laundering, and make sure to always carry a spare. And he would need a satchel. He did not wish to make a habit of lounging in a soiled uniform.

Over the next thirty minutes, the other three students trickled in and introductions were officially given. Stephonous had already made an impression as a quirky, self-conscious, young lad from Hexlore's Tears, a small trading post on the other side of this same island.

There was another Kingdom-born student in their group, named Minathi Van Odla. She hailed from Quinson, one of the southernmost cities bordering Scritland. Her dark hair and caramel skin were proof that she was a product of Scritlandian *and* Kingdom heritage. Aynward immediately thought of his betrothed sister, Dagmara, whose pairing with the Scritlandian prince would produce offspring to match Minathi's coloring. If this girl was any indicator, the union of these two bloodlines would make for some very good-looking children.

Thato was the last student to arrive. He was a near twin to the Special Collections librarian, the Palpanese named Hirk. He seemed a good-spirited lad with a healthy, innocent bounce in his step as he approached. He had the dark skin tone of a Scritlandian, but the blood-red eyes of the Palpanese. Aynward hadn't been able to place Hirk or this boy until his heritage was announced, and then he felt the fool. He had heard the stories to go with the red eyes. They were descendants of a Scritlandian tribe that had fled the Lothlem occupation of central Drogen a millennium ago. It was said that the red eyes were a sign that the gods had left them because of their cowardice.

Aynward's musings were cut short by Dwapek. "Now that all you big'ns know each other, let's get to it."

He walked over to the source of Aynward's cramped hand, and picked up a small leather-bound book. "Each of you will be assigned three titles. If you don't think you can remember the specifics of what you're to do with them, I suggest you take out your notebooks and write this down." He paused; then, when no one moved, he sighed and said forcefully, "Take out your notebooks and write this down."

Aynward had always prided himself on his memory, but Dwapek's *suggestion* seemed a little more on the *mandatory* side.

"You will read, reread, then read again each of these titles, writing down every detail in connection to magic. I want to know who used it, how they used it, whom they used it with or against, when they used it, and finally the locations where each instance occurred." He paced back and forth in front of the books. "You will begin with the oldest of your three assigned texts, and on from there. And you *will* arrive next class with a full report on your first text."

He distributed three volumes to each student then announced, "Butterflies flutter. Birds flap. They both tend to fly." He coughed, then added loudly, "Dismissed."

Kyllean leaned over and said to Aynward, "That man should really publish a volume of his own. I can see it now"—he flourished a hand—"*Musings of an Insane Person*. Wait—no." Bringing both hands into the fray, Kyllean continued, "Now I've got it—yes. *Musings of an Insane Person Who Walks Beneath Tables Without Hitting His Head.*"

Aynward tried to stop himself from bursting into laughter, but that only forced his amusement to escape from his nose in a horrific snort that hurt his throat. This was only momentarily interrupted when Minathi leaned in and said to both of them, "That's a fantastic idea!" She tapped her notebook with the quill. "I just made a note. I'll bring it up next class." She grinned. "And no need to worry. I wouldn't dare steal credit for the *creative* title." Before either could respond, she turned to leave.

Kyllean blanched, and Aynward's chortle found renewed strength. As she departed, Kyllean yelled after her, "It's a working title!" Then to Aynward, Kyllean said, "She wasn't serious. She couldn't have been serious about that. Could she?"

Aynward smiled. "I couldn't say. Perhaps you should catch her and ask."

Kyllean hopped to his feet. "Great idea! See you tomorrow."

Kyllean darted out of sight, leaving Aynward to return his thoughts to the more serious happenings of the day, which now included an assignment to read a significant volume of nonsense for a class that he would not have been enrolled in were the person in charge of it not his personal sponsor. *I really do need to start thinking before I act—or speak, for that matter.*

The next evening, Aynward stood alongside Kyllean at the pub door where he had previously been denied entry. In answer to how Kyllean's questioning went with the girl, there stood Minathi, her dark hair glistening in the available light. This time Aynward wore his university attire. He executed the same sequence of knocks as he had on testing day. The giant of a man opened it and stared out at them, expressionless, without a word.

As the moment approached awkward, Aynward said, "So, can we come in?"

The big oaf eyed him, carefully, then reached out and clasped his amulet. He brought it close to his face to determine if it was counterfeit, then scanned his friends in like fashion before finally stepping aside to allow entry.

"Many thanks, oh holy gatekeeper," said Aynward as he stepped past. He didn't look back to check on the response. He had plans to offer conciliatory flattery to him later, anyhow.

The room was long and narrow, and heavily populated. Aynward led the way directly to the bar. He had been extra obsequious all week, returning home well before dark to complete his assigned readings, attempting to demonstrate his dedication to school and success for Dolme. He had made sure to speak with Dolme for long enough in each passing to establish that he retained full sobriety. So when he finally petitioned for some additional coin to allow him a nice dinner out after classes, Dolme had acquiesced.

But now, after two trips into the sewers and hours of drab class readings, coupled with coin enough to splurge, he needed a break from being entirely "good." He wasn't looking for a wild night of debauchery, but it had been weeks since he'd had good ale, or any ale, for that matter. A sickly thin man filled three large mugs and rasped, "That'll be six coppers." Aynward hadn't yet been to the on-campus pub, but Kyllean's expression of excitement at the price of one round suggested that this was a bargain. Considering what he had in his purse at the moment, Aynward realized that he probably had enough for a few evenings out, if he paced himself.

They found one of the few empty tables and sat. Aynward took a large mouthful and gulped it down, feeling the stress of his exertion melt away like cold morning fog, fleeing from the heat of day.

"So what is your first book about?" Kyllean asked Minathi.

She took a dainty sip of her ale and smiled. Then she lowered her head without breaking eye contact, creating an expression of deviance.

"The journal of a Scritlandian's journey into the Swordlore forests. It's dated year 147."

Kyllean offered a look of incredulity to match Aynward's own.

Aynward replied, "No one has ever returned from the Swordlore forests. They're cursed. Everyone knows that. You'd be better off trying your luck returning with your sanity from the Hand of the Gods," he continued, referring to the cursed peninsula in the southeast of the Drogen continent, a desolate place home to ruins from a long-forgotten age. Those few who did return either couldn't recall what they saw or returned stripped of their sanity, gibbering nonsense for the remainder of their days. Yet the Swordlore forests were even more a mystery, for according to legend, no one had ever returned.

Kyllean said, "That's nearly five thousand years ago. Maybe it was before the curse? I mean, we don't exactly know what caused it, or when, do we?"

"There are theories," Aynward said, "but I'm not sure. Never had reason to care." With nothing more to add, he finally asked, "Well? What did it say?"

She leaned forward and folded her arms on the table. "Funny you should have mentioned the Hand of the Gods, Aynward. This Scritlandian monk named Tezra believed there was a connection between the Swordlore forests and the Hand of the Gods. Apparently a few oral legends had survived, tracing the same evils of the forests to the people of the Hand."

She took another light sip of her drink, and Aynward did likewise, though his came from the bottom of an empty mug. He raised his container to the server and requested another.

"Without any substantial written proof, Tezra took it upon himself to dare entering the Swordlore forests. He packed a few weeks' worth of provisions, and went. The forests turned on him almost immediately, but—and he doesn't explain exactly how he was able to do this—he managed to hold off their wielders long enough to speak with them, after which they sent him home, unharmed."

"So this mysterious people just happened to speak Scritlandian?" said Aynward doubtfully.

"Well, no. They spoke a Luguinden dialect. However, according to Tezra, he *was* able to communicate, at least insomuch as they were willing. They rebuffed all his questions but one: the reason why they didn't admit foreigners. 'We await the wars of the enemy, the battles led by the Almam,' they replied. According to Tezra's best guess, it referred to some prophesied messianic figure who was yet to come. Apparently all outsiders threatened to corrupt his goal and must be pushed back until the appointed time."

Kyllean butted in, "So they gave him this information then just let him leave?"

She shrugged. "Apparently. He doesn't explain that part."

Kyllean asked, "Did he say anything about the magic they used? They must be powerful to be able to keep themselves protected from outsiders for over five thousand years."

She nodded. "And if his tale is true, he must have been powerful in his own right to have rebuffed their attempts to dispatch him the first time. However, he's conveniently vague on just about everything we'd wish him to be more detailed about."

"The first time?" asked Kyllean.

"He ran out of room in this journal, but he was planning another trip. I checked the library for a second volume, but none exists. Seems he was not so fortunate the second time he entered."

Aynward chimed in, "Sounds like a total loon."

Minathi smiled. "Probably. The scholars of Scritland seemed to think so."

"Wonder how Counselor Dwapek even found these titles. Think he's read them all?"

Kyllean belched loudly, then said, "Wouldn't make much sense to have us all assigned to gather information on stuff he'd already read, would it?"

"True," said Aynward. "And I supposed if he'd read them all himself, he'd realize that he's created an entire course on the best works of fiction, authored by insane people."

"Hah!" shouted Kyllean, beginning to slur his words. "The class should be titled, *Tall Tales Well Worth Forgetting Forever.*"

That got a laugh out of Minathi, causing ale to leak out of her nose, which consequently resulted in all of them laughing.

Finally she said, "Well, what of your story, Aynward? I'm guessing yours was just as *historically sound* as mine."

He ordered two more drinks, both for himself, then responded, "That depends. If *historically sound* means more farfetched and ridiculous, then yes."

His drinks arrived, and he took a long drag on one, then pulled out a small sack he'd purchased from the university apothecary earlier that day. His two companions stared at him, confusion written on their faces.

"What? This? It's nothing. Just a bit of tea leaves. I've got an old friend here who seemed to be exhibiting some of the symptoms associated with digestive difficulty, so I took it upon myself to read ahead in one of the texts for my Apothecary course, *Natural Herbs and Remedies.*" He plunged several leaves into the glass and stirred. "Don't mind me, I'm just going to let this steep for a bit."

Kyllean's expression contorted into one of confusion.

Minathi replied, "Is that really wise?"

Aynward chuckled. "You were at the desposition, were you not?"

"Oh yes, I saw your *genius* there. I just assumed you'd learned a valuable lesson."

"Ah, well, I did. I learned to go about revenge in a slightly less straightforward, public way. Let's consider this an experiment. I'm attempting to discover the line between blind foolishness and strategically planned foolishness."

"Gods, you're daft," she exclaimed.

Aynward looked around in jest. "Dad? Daddy? Is that you? Why is your voice so, so, so feminine?"

"Unbelievable." She sighed. "How about your story?"

Aynward looked around a few more times before retiring his joke, causing the other two to roll their eyes.

"All right, all right." He gave the tea leaves another stir then started. "You're both familiar with the Lugienese prophet, Lesante, right?" Without giving time for either to respond he said, "Good. Well, my text is basically the forgotten chapter of the Luguinden histories, probably because it never happened, but hey, maybe the most learned people throughout the civilized world were mistaken when canonizing Drogen history."

Aynward patted his pocket for effect. "I have in my possession a chronicle written by an eyewitness to an epic magic dual that was somehow recorded by no one else. The author, identified only as Voros, describes the well-known clash between the Lugiens and the Lothlem regarding disputed lands in the northwest portions of the territory. This is where the prophetess Lesante receives her first visions from Klerós, beats the Lothlem back, steals their ships, and flees to Angolia, and so on.

"But according to this account, there was yet another confrontation, this one between Lesante and a group of seven women who were, without a doubt, not ethnically affiliated with any of the Luguinden tribes. The women are described as having milky-white skin, and the ability to wield powerful magic.

"No explanation is definitively given for where these female wizards came from or why, but apparently they showed up as the Lugienese were boarding their ships and attacked Lesante and her contingent of new Klerósi clergy.

"This alleged witness says that these women moved large objects with gestures from their hands, and even opened a chasm in the earth beneath the feet of their adversaries. If Voros is to be believed, the prominent scar on her face was not a marking from her time with Klerós, but a wound earned during this battle."

He stopped there to allow the audacity of the story to sink in.

Minathi took his cue and commented, "Yeah, I think yours might top mine. Does this person happen to mention where these sorceresses came from, who they were, or where they went?"

Aynward nodded. "Well, first, this Voros claims to have been a Lothlem ship captain, who stuck around to watch his stolen ship sail out to sea. He describes his perplexity as to who these people were, but was certainly rooting for them. He initially stated that they must be avatars of the Luguinden pantheon, Tequen, Dred, Pyrea, Trarken—you get the picture. But with their failure, he held to his faith and decided they could not have been such, for surely a heretic like Lesante, whom they believed had been lured in by the blood-god Ramn, would have been overrun should the other gods truly wish it. Voros's chronicle says that Lesante and her Klerósi priests seemed equals in battle, though Lesante was able to escape with the scar, and her adversaries unharmed. The women who attacked Lesante then disappeared, never to be seen or heard from again."

Kyllean said, "Well, isn't that convenient."

Aynward responded, "Very."

"But what is the motivation for conjuring up this unusual tale?" asked Minathi.

"No idea. It doesn't exactly fit any scheme I could conceive, considering who the man claims to be. The only credibility he has going for him is the fact that there seems little to be gained from it in the first place. In the absence of some profit, I don't see why someone would develop such a lie. Though I'll admit that just because we don't know the motivation of a Lothlem ship captain from five thousand years ago doesn't mean the motivation didn't exist."

Feeling that the momentum of his synopsis had run its full course, Aynward stirred the three shriveled tea leaves once more, then reached into the mug to pull them out. He gave them a final squeeze, then shoved them into his pocket.

"Please excuse me for a moment. I can deny my benevolent calling no longer. I sense the pain of digestive inactivity." He formed an expression of mock determination.

The place was getting more crowded, and Aynward spilled bits of the mug twice in his trek through the tight spaces between patrons. He was beginning to feel the effects of the ale. But he finally arrived at his target, with a mostly full mug. His quarry was leaning with his back against the door in order to feel the sequenced knock of those hoping to enter. Aynward had second thoughts as he recalled just how big the man was, filling the doorway with his broad frame. But Aynward had spent perfectly good booze money to acquire these leaves, and this behemoth had wronged him.

*Here we go.*

## CHAPTER 63

# KIBURE

KIBURE PANICKED WHEN HE SAW the emptiness in his hands where his dead friend, Rave, had last been. He must have released his grip when his exhausted body pulled him into sleep.

As he turned about to look behind him, he felt a furlike texture on his neck. He reached up to take hold of—

"Ah!" yelled Kibure when the furry corpse took flight. The surprise in Kibure's heart was both painful and jubilant as a new reality collided with his former belief of Rave's fate. This mystical guardian, or whatever Rave was, never ceased to surprise him with his adeptness at survival.

A rumbling laugh sounded from behind Kibure. Jonglin said, "You think him dead, but he no dead. The raaven of story always with the Changer. We know he live. Stories show Changer and raaven together."

Kibure craned his neck around to see the back of Jonglin's head. The merchant continued trudging forward, pulling the wooden contraption that carried the former slave. "Stories? What stories?"

Jonglin laughed again in his low, gravelly chuckle. "You are Changer, this known by all people." He laughed again, this time lighter. "Foreign man, followed by raaven. All know this is Changer. Changer comes, then death, fire, war, and maybe happy day, maybe no. End is clear like

350

snowstorm. All say Changer battle gods, world destroy world. Many prophet write different thing so no one know end. I prays you win. This why we bring you to safe. Too young for face gods. Changer is man, not boy, yes? All know this."

Kibure had so many questions he didn't even know where to begin. He needed to ask Sindri about this. She would know more. What wasn't she telling him? He asked Jonglin a few clarifying questions, but his answers were curt and vague, his breathing becoming labored from talking while carrying such a load up the steep slope. Yes, perhaps he would ask Sindri about this when they stopped for the night.

Kibure leaned back to rest against the wood of the travois and his heavy-laden thoughts were lightened by the return of Rave, who landed on his chest to nestle in. The crushing weight of uncertainty fizzled with the soft cooing sounds of Rave. His troubles weren't any less real, but the thought that he had at least one ally, and maybe more, made the situation bearable for the time being.

## CHAPTER 64

# AYNWARD

AYNWARD STOOD BEFORE THE DOORMAN of the pub with a mostly full mug of ale, a peace offering to bury the acrimony between them. At least, that was the message he hoped to send.

"Greetings, Mr. Human Doorman who could crush me with one hand." He bowed ever so slightly in deference. "I feel like we got off on the wrong foot last week, and I wanted to make it up to you."

The statue carved of muscle didn't move, except his eyebrows. His arms remained as they were, crossed in front of his sizable chest.

"So, I see you're not much for small talk, that's okay. I, uh, I bought you a drink." Aynward extended the beverage in his direction.

The man didn't move a single muscle, and Aynward thought he may have wasted his money on the ale, and especially the tea leaves. Just as he started to lower the gift, the man nodded his head, reached out, and took the mug. It was like a grown-up clasping a child's play cup. Aynward didn't have to worry about waiting to see if he drank it. The doorman tipped the mug back and poured the amber liquid down his throat.

*I guess that's that.*

He belched and extended the mug back toward Aynward. "I accept your apology."

Aynward took the mug and smiled. "I'm glad that you do." The man patted him on the back to solidify the peace, and Aynward almost felt bad about the trick. *Almost.*

He quickly made his way back to the table and found Kyllean in the middle of an animated conversation; the ale clearly taking a toll.

"Yeah, claims the plague had been sent by their enemies during the last battle with a vanquished empire whose name was not to be spoken. He was very disturbed, but who was he to say anything? So he swung the ax and had done with it."

Aynward interrupted, "Did you start telling your story without me? Seriously?"

Kyllean shrugged. "I figured there was a good chance that your big friend over there might taste the poison in his drink and beat you over the head with the mug until you stopped laughing."

Aynward held up his index finger. "For one thing, it's not poison: it's an effective digestive remedy that may or may not have been necessary."

"Definitely *not* necessary," interrupted Kyllean.

Ignoring him, Aynward raised a second finger. "For two, even were he some sort of ale connoisseur, I think he missed the refined fertile flavor of the tea leaf as he poured the drink down his throat in one gulp. Third, he thanked me. So come on, what did I miss?"

Kyllean drummed his fingers on the table. "All right. Mine was written by one of Hakbar the Uniter's executioners. It was a letter written to his family begging they ask forgiveness of the gods for exterminating the Empire whose name was not to be spoken. He believed his sins too great for redemption, but prayed his family might be spared from eternal damnation."

Aynward interrupted, "This is the plague that killed seventy-five percent of southwest Drogen's population, right? The end of unity between the five tribes?"

Kyllean nodded. "That same plague, yes." He chuckled. "Everyone knows this plague was contracted as a result of trade with the now-lost

Denclaws, east of the Hand, but this claims that the last of the prisoners of the Great War promised a great plague, weeks before it swept across the continent. He described their hysterical laughter, even as he swung the ax of judgment."

Minathi chimed in, "Sounds like this guy felt guilty for executing disarmed prisoners of war and made up an alternative story about the origins of the plague." She shrugged. "I feel bad for him. I could certainly sympathize with losing one's sense of reality after exterminating the last remnants of an entire race of people."

Aynward was starting to feel the effects of the drink in earnest, but this story temporarily sobered him. "This one might actually be true."

His two companions looked up at him, questions written on their faces. "Well, I don't know, this one *could* be true. Did he benefit by making this claim in a personal letter to his family? It would be quite another thing if he were a Luguinden priest trying to affect the morality of the people after wiping out an entire race, but he's just writing to his family in a panic after what sounds like a disturbing execution."

Kyllean responded, "I see your point, but this man could have written the letter after the plague broke out. I mean, it happened so long ago, who's to say when exactly it started? Or it could even be that everything in his letter was true to his knowledge, but the timing is off. What if the plague had already started working its way through the land and the prisoners caught wind of it? Well, why not take credit for it? Maybe they even claimed to be able to stop it, should they be released."

Aynward's excitement drained like ale spilling from an upturned mug. He'd always been intrigued by the myths associated with the mysterious Hand of the Gods, home to inaccessible ruins and a throng of legends. Everyone knew that there was some sort of magic protecting this land, or cursing it. But no two sources agreed about its origins, or about the people who had built the great abandoned cities. The Luguinden claimed to have defeated this people under the leadership of Hakbar the Uniter, but all remnants of who these people were had fallen into legend. Kyllean wasn't wrong in his assessment, but he wasn't necessarily right, either.

Aynward said, "You're right, he could have made up the entire thing. But isn't it also possible that the curse of the Hand was actually a curse left behind by the defeated? A last-ditch effort to thwart the Luguinden once they knew they'd been defeated? Maybe a few of their wizards survived and this was their way of keeping the Luguinden out of their lands indefinitely. They cursed their own land and sent a plague to punish Hakbar and the Luguinden who had destroyed their entire people."

"The ale has finally reached his brain," said Minathi, shaking her head. Kyllean released a hearty chuckle.

The blood rushed to Aynward's face at her remark and he raised a hand to respond, "It's not the ale, I'm perfectly fine." But his own mouth betrayed him, words bleeding together like spices in a warm soup. He shook his head, tried again, and failed as he slurred, "I'm perfectly sober, and I'm right about the story. You got a true one, I think."

Kyllean stood up, perhaps too quickly for his own good, and stumbled to the side, tried to catch his balance on a man at the next table, failed, and landed on the wooden floor.

"I'm fine, I'm fine. There's a divot in the floor there."

"Of course there is," she said. "But I think it's time to go, anyhow."

Aynward stood up, carefully, feeling the room sway beneath his feet, but steadied himself on the back of his chair. "See? Totally fine." He took a few steps on his own, then smiled and said, "Lightweight," nodding toward Kyllean, who was again balancing with an arm around Minathi. Then Aynward too gripped a nearby chair for balance.

They made for the door, Aynward earning more than a few grudging stares as he stumbled into people along the way. As he neared the exit, he realized he'd not seen his adversarial gatekeeper. He hadn't expected the tea to work *that* quickly.

He opened the door, then turned back for a quick scan of the room. *There.* He locked gazes with his victim and smiled at his handiwork. The man was leaning against the adjacent wall, sweat glistening on his brow, face contorted in a grimace. He must have recognized the satisfaction in Aynward's expression. His eyes became a pair of burning coals. Aynward realized belatedly that looking back to admire his triumph was not the best way to ensure anonymity.

The gatekeeper straightened and started toward him. Aynward turned to flee, but before he was out the door, the ogre-like man stopped in his tracks, eyes wide in shock, then fear, and then—*yes*—embarrassment. The tea leaf was definitely working. The oaf's expression flickered between concern and outrage.

*Yeah, time to go.*

Aynward was out the door seconds later, nearly losing his footing in the process. Minathi was right behind him, with Kyllean propped up next to her.

She said, "Are you going to be okay to get home? I don't think I can carry both of you."

"Of course," scoffed Aynward. "I'm perfectly capable of making my own way. The *real* question is whether I should swing back to the university for overpriced pub fare and a few more drinks, or if I should get adventurous and find somewhere within the city?"

Minathi's head sagged in exasperation. "You can't be serious."

"Quite the contrary," Aynward slurred. "The night is young. And thank you. I really appreciate your chivalrous help with our friend. Just try not to take advantage of his weakened state." He winked. "As for me, there is much yet on this evening's horizon." He held up a finger. "That's basically a metaphor."

Minathi rolled her eyes, turned with Kyllean, and started in the direction of the university. She shouted behind her, "You're even more pretentious than normal when you drink." She followed that up with, "That's *not* a compliment."

Aynward sauntered off in the opposite direction, toward home. He wasn't sure exactly where he was headed. But he knew he didn't feel much like turning in just yet. The city was still unknown to him so he figured he shouldn't venture too far away from the familiar areas, but a little investigation would be all right. He could take care of himself.

The crisp night air felt nice in his lungs, and he breathed it in deeply. Besides his difficulty walking in a straight line, the drinks had melted away his worries, if only for a while. He decided to just walk straight down this street until he found something interesting.

Within five minutes he started seeing more activity in the distance. The street had started up a long incline toward the home of the city's de facto king, Count Gornstein. Aynward didn't know much about him, and didn't much care. He saw some streetlamps up ahead to indicate possible nighttime activity, and maybe he'd check out the palace while he was at it. This evening was turning out to be an enjoyable one.

A sound from behind caused Aynward to turn, but when he did, he saw nothing. He could have sworn he'd heard footsteps. Up ahead, a sign attached to the front of a building stretched out into the street, beckoning him with the picture of a barrel of ale. *Yes, this is a great stopping point.*

Then he heard the sound again, and turned just in time to see several moving shapes, the closest of which was swinging a club. In his current drunken state, responding with automatic athletic precision was not a feasible option. The club struck him solidly in the side of the head. His vision went temporarily black and his thoughts were scrambled.

He tried to rise as his eyes righted the world, but this merely allowed him to watch as a helpless witness to the second blow. A quick thought of Dolme flashed into his mind. This had his stink all over it. He was likely trying to teach him yet another lesson in responsibility, and Aynward was enraged to have allowed himself to be so vulnerable to it. This thought was fleeting as the cobbled street became his pillow. All thoughts but one vanished when the club made contact for the second time: *darkness.*

## CHAPTER 65

# KIBURE

"KEEP YOUR HOOD PULLED FORWARD. We can't risk being seen by
one of Magog's minions," Sindri said. Kibure sagged his shoulders, tipped back his head, and rolled his eyes.

Sindri took his hood in both hands and adjusted it once again. "I've
told you, they have eyes in every city, and can communicate with each
other at great distances. They will have deduced our destination, as well
as how long it would take to get there." She adjusted the cowl of her
own hood. "Can't risk it."

Jonglin led the way through the tight winding streets of the Palpanese
merchant city. Even from behind the narrowed view shaped by the
drawn hood, Kibure struggled to keep from drowning in the cacophony
of sights and sounds. He had never been in a city. The buildings were
mostly stone or adobe, and myriad colored banners adorned the doors
or hung from balconies. The streets were alive with activity, though
Kibure could only guess at the nature. People shouted and pushed past
one another, carrying more than seemed possible in some cases, while
others dragged carts. The more fortunate rode in carts dragged by people or animals.

The language too was different. Jonglin and his companions had used it among themselves on occasion, but the intensity of it here amid rushing urban chaos was unlike anything he had ever heard. It was harsh and guttural; everyone seemed to be upset about one thing or another. There was also a variation in pitch between words that seemed more emphasized than in Lugienese.

They emerged from a narrow side street to find a wide-open area where two streets converged. There were many carts and stands in the center area surrounded by people waving their arms and shouting what Kibure guessed must be obscenities, based on the ferocity in their voices. Kibure bumped into the man in front of him and was apologizing when he felt Sindri run into him from behind.

"Wh—"

Kibure saw ahead that Jonglin had stopped. Then he turned and pointed back in the direction they had come. "Move!" He yelled something else in the incomprehensible Palpanic language, and the others turned, hastening their pace. Those in front disappeared back down the narrow street at a near run. Sindri and Kibure struggled to keep up with the man in front of them who weaved in and out of the bustling crowd as if they weren't there.

When they arrived at the next street, Jonglin's men remained, waiting for him to catch up. Quick words were exchanged and the group split. Jonglin and two others led Kibure and Sindri, while the rest took off in the other direction; a diversion, Kibure guessed.

The next ten minutes were a blur of quick turns around people, carts, and tight alleys. Kibure glanced to his right after hearing a high-pitched yelp from a muscular animal tugging a colossal cart in the opposite direction. When he looked back, Jonglin was nowhere to be seen. He was just—gone. A few quick steps brought Kibure to where he had last seen the man, but there was not one there. He started forward again, a panicked sprint to catch up, but an arm shot out from the side and yanked him down a set of steep stairs. He was dragged through an entrance low enough that he had to duck to avoid knocking his head.

He squirmed and thrashed to no avail. Whoever had taken hold was far too strong for him. Sindri was also pulled down, and similarly constrained. The door behind them shut and the room went black. After a few agonizing seconds without sight, Kibure's eyes adjusted to take in the light of a few small flickering candles. Whoever had taken hold released their grip on him, and he whirled around to see a dark figure whose face was hidden behind a cloak. Then a voice to his left sounded and he breathed a sigh of relief . . . Jonglin.

"We be safe here for some time. Priests did not chase, but fools me not. They watch and wait. Always they watch, always they scheme."

Kibure was just relieved that he was safe for the time being. The thought of making it so far only to be captured again chilled him. Sindri, however, had other concerns.

"Where do we go from here? Are we to slip out in the night and head north to the Handelik River toward Trinkanen?"

Jonglin lit a torch and removed it from a sconce on the wall. The light cast dancing shadows upon his face. Kibure could see a smile forming on it.

"We make safe for you. For something so important as Changer, we spare nothing. You escape Angolia so Changer fulfill prophecy."

Kibure had felt chills the first time he had heard Jonglin use the term for him. In spite of everything that had happened, it was easy to focus simply on the task at hand and forget. It was also preferred. His mind reeled every time he attempted to understand, or to accept the thought of wielding magic, Rave, the voice in his nightmare, or, worse, Magog's apparent interest in him. He forced himself to dismiss these thoughts again, and concentrate on escaping to safety. These men would help, and he was grateful. He did not have to be whatever these people had mistaken him for; he needed only accept their help and survive.

He took a sip of a pungent beverage handed to him by one of Jonglin's men and let his face relax into a smile, the first he had allowed himself in weeks.

✻ ✻ ✻

Kibure opened his eyes in the hazy candlelit cellar. Had he heard something? He glanced over to see Sindri sitting up from the makeshift bed their smuggling deliverers had put together for them.

"Ow," sounded the voice of Sindri followed by a curse. Kibure saw her feminine shape turning its head this way and that, her other features lost to the shadows. He too sat up and stretched his arms.

She noticed him. "Not a whole lot of consideration for the comfort of someone they believe to be so important. Unless you've got something different than scratchy wool atop prickly straw?"

Kibure had not given it a thought. He had been so utterly exhausted after weeks of sleeping on the rough ground, he was just thankful to be beneath something more substantial than a propped-up blanket, out in the open, ready to die in his sleep.

He felt straw with his right hand. "It feels like paradise to me."

Sindri harrumphed. "Remind me to find a prophesied Savior more worthy of extravagance the next time I accept the hospitality of his rescuers."

A deep, rumbling voice startled both of them. Sindri's sharp intake of breath was her only giveaway, but Kibure heard it, right after his loud yelp.

The man-shaped shadow nodded his understanding. "I risk much. Not complaint. This just true. To me, this risk good thing, because it help Changer. I die maybe. But risk more than need? No. Who want this? Only fool. I do not like to be killed by them. I bring you here, I pay good merchant, you go on ship. No one see this thing, you and I live long."

## CHAPTER 66

# SINDRI

SINDRI SAT IN THE CRAMPED cabin of a trade vessel bound for the Isles. It would be a long voyage, but she would finally be free to discover the truth about tazamines, Kibure, and her brother. She could never bring him back, she knew, but perhaps she could prove to herself that he had not been the monster believed by the Kleról. She could prove that she had not defied the leaders of her own faith for nothing, that she was no heretic, not in truth.

And there was this other business with Kibure, and this prophecy believed by Jonglin and his cultish following. Jonglin had been tight-lipped about the specifics of what they believed, but there was no doubt that Kibure and his raaven were vitally important. Sindri didn't know what to make of all that, but perhaps something more might be learned about this, too.

Last, there was the matter of her separation from Klerós's power. She needed to find a way to reestablish this connection. There was an emptiness within her that needed to be refilled. Could the priest of another faith restore such a connection? Sindri prayed this were so. She felt empty without it and knew she would never be satisfied to live out her days as a mere ordinary person. She felt like a bird whose wings had been clipped. And yet, even without Klerós's power, she and Kibure continued to survive terrible odds mounted by the forces that sought to capture and destroy them.

As Sindri lay in the dark cabin, the creaking of the floor brought back the nightmares of the attack on their last vessel. She smiled at the thought of Grobennar explaining failure after failure to the God-king, especially now that they failed against such adversaries as a castrated slag, and an untrained tazamine. They made a unique team, the two of them. And she was beginning to suspect that their journey was far from over.

## CHAPTER 67

# AYNWARD

I T WAS DARK WHEN AYNWARD stirred, head throbbing. He heard voices nearby, but couldn't make out what was being said. His bound hands and gagged mouth reminded him that he had been ambushed, and taken captive, as well.

He ignored the fear he knew he should have been feeling. This wasn't altogether unfamiliar, and it reeked of Dolme. He decided to skip straight to anger. He was done with pretenses of civility. To hell with responsibility to his elders, his kingdom, to his father's trust. Dolmuevo had no right to treat Aynward like—like a common criminal. How much was he paying these thugs? That was *his* money. Dolme was wasting *his* money, on *real* criminals, to punish him. And for what? For having a few drinks with friends?

He breathed deeply through his nose, calming himself. He needed to focus, endure, and then he was going to redouble his effort to make good on his vow to punish this man. He worked his hands against the ropes, but they didn't give. Instead he rolled over to his stomach so he could tuck his legs underneath him. Then he pivoted to sit. No sense trying to stand. The cloth sack over his head prevented him seeing anything, anyhow.

"He's awake."

"So," another drolled, "our little prince stirs."

*That voice.* Aynward winced.

He heard boots approaching.

"Wonderful, wonderful. I was almost afraid that I'd hit him too hard. Would've ruined all the fun," said the same, chilling voice.

Another thug chuckled.

This was not the work of Dolmuevo, Aynward realized, not unless the counselor had somehow allied with—he didn't even know his biggest adversary's name. Poor form, indeed. He had heard this voice just a few days ago in the courtyard while in search of Dwapek's class. That boy had promised they'd be seeing more of each other. And Aynward had let down his guard only days later.

His anger at Dolme withered, replaced by a pit in his stomach that he recognized as fear. He didn't want to believe this kid would inflict any *permanent* harm, but how could he be sure? The law was thinner the farther away one went from the heart of the Kingdom of Dowe, and they were more than a thousand leagues from the shores of those borders.

A voice interrupted Aynward's thoughts. "Hey there, *friend.* Sorry about the whole blindfold thing. I've no qualms about you knowing my identity, but I prefer to keep my affiliations a little more on the mysterious side. You understand."

Aynward grunted. He had a few choice comments in mind, but the gag forced him to put them on the agenda for a later date, if he lived to see one. However, if this weasel was concerned about Aynward being able to see his associates, then perhaps he wasn't planning to kill him.

"Let's start with formal introductions, since I've not yet had the honor, 'Your Highness.'"

Aynward wasn't surprised this time by the title being used, especially in such a mocking tone. The boy continued, "My name is Theo. Unlike you, I have no family holdings, but perhaps someday I hope to follow the example of the count, earning my way to the top. But other than the whole noble-blooded, privileged brat thing that you have going for you, we aren't so different, you and me. A real shame we got off on the wrong foot; I think we could have been friends. As I understand it, you're quite the easy study, good with a sword, and have a tendency to hold a grudge. That sound about right?" He chuckled, "Oh, right, the gag. Well, I'll just assume you agree with me. That was a compliment, so I'm sure there's no discrepancy there. Well, I, too, am an easy study, skilled with sharp objects, and I never forget a slight."

The voice grew closer, circling like a hawk preparing to dive after its prey.

"That's where our similarities end, however. See, unlike you, I grew up on the streets, learned to read in the city orphanage, and trained with knives as a means of survival, not with swords as a pastime for royals. I'm here now because *I* earned it. The count's annual scholarship has given me the opportunity to prove that I and others like me are just as capable as *the rest* if given the chance. And then there's you: a pompous tyke who believes he and his *superior* blood to be special; incapable of accepting subservience, even for the brief time required of a centuries-old ceremony. You just can't seem to shed the thick skin worn by all high-borns. Fortunately for you, I'm going to help with this problem. I'm going to shed at least one layer of that skin for you today."

Aynward could hear the smile on the boy's face. He just prayed that he was still speaking metaphorically. Without further warning, hands on either side yanked him to his feet, then something hard struck him between the legs and he gasped. The fingers holding him relaxed and he fell to the unforgiving ground, curled up in a defensive position as he roiled in pain, waves of nausea pulsing through his body.

"That's for the other day," said Theo. "All right. Time to move."

Aynward was hoisted into the air by two strong sets of hands. He resisted as best he could, but a few blows to the stomach convinced him to hold still. Minutes later, he was thrown to the ground along with the next command from Theo. "Strip him."

Aynward could hardly believe it. He went back to full resistance, but the feeling of cold steel on his throat gave him reason to stop moving.

"That's a good boy."

Next thing he knew, he was aware of the cold dew of the grass as it wetted his bare skin. Only the cover on his head and his smallclothes remained. Then a series of ropes were placed around his body. Aynward was concerned, but they weren't painfully tight. Yet.

Finally his blindfold was removed.

"We want people to see your face, don't we?" He laughed again.

It was still dark, but Aynward could see a hint of morning's approach. He looked about trying to catch a glimpse of who was helping Theo, but they had donned hoods. Only Theo was identifiable. He approached and tied a set of animal horns from the desposition ceremony to the top of Aynward's head. Before he had any more time to think, the ropes around his body pulled taught. His feet left the ground and he was suddenly sitting upright in midair, a fair distance above those below.

"I know this isn't the kind of throne your lineage is accustomed to, but rope was the best we could do on such short notice. You understand, right?" Theo's goons got a good laugh at that.

Aynward looked up to see his rope basket was connected to a thick, master hoist, which looped around the branch overhead. The hooded figures had raised the contraption by pulling on the other end of the rope and were in the process of tying it off around the trunk of the tree to ensure that he remained suspended for all to see when the sun came up.

He had been beaten, stripped, dressed in horns, and put on display for the ultimate humiliation. He was hanging from the tree, at the center of the university, next to the library. It was the highest-traffic area on campus. Theo had won this duel.

"Well, I think that about wraps up our time together for now. If you're good, and you don't piss me off again, I might count us almost even, considering how easy you made this for me. But I'd watch your back for a while, anyhow, just to be certain."

He nodded and his hooded minions broke away in various directions. There were four in total. Theo turned and said, "Enjoy the fresh air, your high-ness." He started laughing hysterically. "Your *high*-ness. Get it?"

Theo disappeared around the circular library, his snicker bringing bile to the back of Aynward's mouth.

*Well, this is just great,* thought Aynward as the sun slowly worked its way toward his debut as the campus laughingstock.

## CHAPTER 68

# KIBURE

KIBURE STOOD AT THE SHIP'S bow, gaping at the city before him. It seemed to have grown as naturally as the harbor itself, buildings nestled into every natural feature of the land as it sprawled along the bowl-shaped rise. This became less the case as they neared, but his awe of the city did not end.

"So what's the plan now?" asked Kibure.

Sindri didn't answer right away. She seemed caught up in a trance of her own, her expression reverent. Kibure wasn't sure if it was a reaction to seeing the city itself, or the implied sanctuary that the city represented to them. He opened his mouth to repeat his question, but her movement cut him short.

Sindri flinched, and her fixed stare broke as she turned to regard him. This lasted only a moment, then her eyes returned to the city.

"We'll have to find ourselves suitable clothes. I can't go around asking questions while looking the part of a desert vagabond. From there, we'll seek an inn until I can secure us more-permanent residence. Then I suppose I'll start seeing if there's anyone in this city who can help me find the answers I seek. If not, we move on. East."

Kibure frowned. "And what am I to do while you're out searching the city for answers? Sit in our room? Or are you planning to cage me once again as you resume your study of me?"

She turned with an incredulous expression, but he could see that she was just stalling. Her eyes belied her; she was searching for an answer she didn't have, or for a false truth to mask an answer that she did have. *She hasn't yet decided if she trusts me, but is bound and determined to study my magic, no matter the cost.* Her hesitation was answer enough. She really had considered caging him, hadn't she? His initial statement had been more a product of frustration at not knowing what came next than out of true suspicion, but now he saw that he had slid a knife right into the heart of Sindri's scheme.

Her expression held firm for a few more long seconds, then, like a wave crashing against the side of their ship, it fell away. As if her lungs had been holding several breaths worth of air, her body seemed to shrivel as she let out a long sigh. With her ordinarily hard posture softened, she seemed a completely different person. The defeated look that replaced the confident facade took away any desire for Kibure to pursue the attack.

He saw that moisture had gathered in the creases of her eyes, yet she hardened the skin around them, as if trying to will the tears away. To escape direct eye contact, she turned and faced the approaching city. He heard her swallow hard and clear her throat before speaking again.

"Listen. I know we started off on the wrong foot. I know you may not trust me, but I tell you the truth. I want answers. I want more than anything to know the source of your magic. It's something I've sought for many years, a question that cost me my station, and nearly my life. I've wanted to understand it from the moment I realized there was difference. I still seek these answers more than ever, now that Klerós's magic fails me. But I won't force you to help. Not after what you've been through. However, I would think that you would wish to try to understand your magic as much as I do, if for different reasons. Wouldn't you like to have control of it? To master it? I can help you with that, so long as I understand what it is, and from where it comes."

She turned her head to look him in the eyes. "Kibure, like it or not, we're in this together."

She seemed to almost plead. "We *can* help each other, much as we have since our escape began. But you *have* to trust me."

Kibure didn't know what to say. He wanted to trust her, but couldn't shake his memory of her using magic to pin him up against the bars of his cage back in Angolia. He held her eye a moment longer, then inclined his head. *I'll trust you, for now*, he thought as he disappeared into the organized chaos of ship-hands as they scurried about collapsing sails, and throwing ropes to men along the docks.

Kibure smiled, recognizing that for the first time in his life he was truly free.

## CHAPTER 69

# SINDRI

DETERMINED TO REMAIN TRUE TO her plans, as soon as they were able to leave the ship, Sindri started searching for the first signs of a thoroughfare, and the commerce toward which it might lead. Within a few city blocks, they had their pick of cart vendors.

Finding exactly what she was looking for in clothes proved more a challenge, but with the abundance of selection, it was just a matter of patience and persistence. Finally she spotted a cloth merchant.

"We're looking for four sets of clothes, two for him, and two for me." She inclined her head in acknowledgment of Kibure.

The woman gave her a suspicious look, tilted her head to the side, then narrowed her eyes further. "You're one of them—them Luggers, ain't ya?"

Sindri paused a moment as recognition blossomed. Luggers was an abbreviation for Lugienese; it was meant to be insulting. Sindri had heard the term before from an angry fur trader in Sire Trinkanen a few years back.

The woman started to turn away. *I'd better answer.* "Yes, though I've come here in hopes of starting a new life away from all the *Luggers.*"

The woman spat. "Dear cousin o' mine was strung up and burned by them folk, least that's what his crewmates say. He was s'posed to be makin' a big sale there. Now his poor kids barely get themselves one decent meal a day. No. Don't fancy doin' business with them kind." She spat again, her wad of saliva nearly striking Sindri's dirt-caked sandals. "Be gone."

Sindri stepped forward and jingled her heavy purse, one of several gifted them by Jonglin and his people. "Listen, I didn't kill your beloved cousin, and you just lost yourself some *very* profitable business." *Fool.* Sindri turned and stalked off.

From behind her the woman's voice sounded. "Whoa, wait just a minute! Think I might be able to help you out after all. Hell, I didn't even like little Jared, that—"

The rest was lost as Sindri continued in the opposite direction.

Kibure caught up to her. "Hey, I think she changed her mind if you—"

"Not interested."

The next cloth merchant they found had only male garments, but the prices were low and the clothes satisfied their needs. Sindri eventually found what she needed for herself, and within another hour, they were both dressed in the local garb, with an extra change of clothes each. Their acquired attire was purposefully insignificant, and unmemorable. They would appear common to this Isles city's working-class folk. For Sindri, this meant a simple white shift, covered by a loose-fitting tan dress, cinched at the waist by a thick, Isles-made belt. *Back home I'd be mistaken for a common servant.* But for their purposes, that was the intention. Ask questions, get answers, and be forgotten.

Kibure's attire was similarly unremarkable as far as the Isles were concerned, though he was reluctant to believe it did any good. His leggings were white, complemented by a brown tunic and trousers. There was little to be done about his conspicuous complexion, unusual eyes, and contrarily ebony hair, but dressing the part socially would do wonders to mute the racial disparity.

Sindri then secured them a room at an inn called The Roving Sail, a short distance from the docks. It was moderately priced and close enough to commerce for such an odd set of travelers to not attract too much attention.

The following morning, Sindri took to the streets in hopes of learning the name and location of a few local temples. In her time living in Sire Trinkanen, she had learned that trade cities in the Isles housed a multitude of religious institutions. Within the Lugienese Empire, the mere stirring of a deviant faction, even within the Klerósi faith itself, was eradicated immediately. The idea of entirely different belief systems coexisting within the same city without perpetual civil unrest seemed fantastic. In fact, the idea of different beliefs existing in the world at all was blasphemous to the Lugienese. Yet this city all but defied this. Beyond the multitude of citywide activities, most of which related to trade, she had seen little hostility, and learned the locations of three different temples, with several others yet to be tracked down.

The first had been nothing more than a shrine with no one around. The second allowed them entrance, but the priests were either unable to answer her questions or did a good job pretending to be completely aloof.

Kibure followed along as they investigated the third. In spite of Sindri's preference to go at it alone, she had decided to include Kibure in her plans. His questions about her intentions had forced her to demonstrate a few acts of goodwill, and bringing him along seemed like a good start. It was imperative that she earn his trust, and if that meant sacrificing some of her efficiency, it would serve her goals more effectively than simply trying to impose her will upon him. At this point, without her magic, she wasn't sure how successful she would be at controlling him, anyhow.

As they approached the third place described by the innkeeper, Kibure sighed loudly and asked, "What makes you think these people will know anything more about magic than you do?"

She cloaked her annoyance with a jovial smile. "I don't. But it's a starting point. I expect we'll have to visit several, and as I've said before, we may not even find our answers here. But we have to start somewhere. The answers certainly aren't in Angolia, or if they are, they're tightly guarded by powerful priests like those who chased us halfway across the continent."

That thought brought her back to the moment she had been severed from her powers. She was still deeply disturbed by her confrontation with the Kraken. Whoever controlled the monster had been extremely powerful, and the team of priests who had pursued them into the mountains had to have been commissioned by a very high authority. She shook off the implications as Kibure blabbered on.

"Well, I don't know why I'm here with you. I don't understand a word any of these people speak."

If Sindri's mind had its own inner set of eyes, they would have rolled heavily at the irony of Kibure's complaint after being included on the plans for which she originally planned to leave him out. But she smiled outwardly and forced her face to take on a thoughtful expression.

"You'll learn the tongue quick enough. It took me only two years, and I only got bits and pieces of practice while visiting the merchants of Sire Trinkanen. You're now in a city filled with the common tongue, as they call it. You'll absorb it like the desert does rain. Plus, I trust you. You might notice something I miss during one of these meetings."

They rounded a corner, taking the small side street that the innkeeper had said would save them ten minutes in their walk. "Like I said, we're in this together. We both have a stake in learning the source of your magic. There may even be someone here who can teach you to wield it at will."

Kibure appeared to teeter between suspicion and acceptance. It would take time, she knew, but Sindri hoped this act would help earn some of his trust. And there was certainly some truth in her rationale to take him along, though she would have preferred to work alone.

The building they approached stood out in the midst of all of the two- and three-story buildings around it. The roof began at Sindri's eye level, with no door visible at first glance, only a sign out front, painted all black but for two differently sized white circles overlapping each other. Written above the image was "House of Stone." Sindri saw an opening in the iron front gate with a walkway that led to a set of stairs. She approached with trepidation. She had been told that these people were unlikely to speak with an outsider, that they rarely spoke with anyone who was not indigenous to the Isles. This belied the appearance of citywide harmony, but fit more into her original expectations for a city with multiple religions, all of which were likely to have conflicting beliefs. She paused at the top of the stairs, exhaled, then began her descent; Kibure was close behind, and silent.

They snaked their way down, with natural light fading at each step. The stairs stopped abruptly at the end of what might have been their third full loop around. The door at the landing was crafted of solid stone, and only discernible from its rectangular shape, which was framed by a raised outline of beveled stone. The other noticeable feature was the thick piece of metal that curved outward from the center of the stone door. She reached up to pull the handle, wondering whether the door was made to swing left or right. As she pulled, the bottom of the metal pulled away from the door, attached by a hinge at the top. She tried to pull as the bottom of the handle was extended out toward her at a right angle, but the door didn't budge.

Then it dawned on her. This was a knocker. Of course! This group of isolationist monks would not simply allow public entry; the door would be locked, and guarded. She let the heavy metal knocker drop. The sound took her by surprise. It was high pitched yet relatively quiet, considering how hard it had struck. The sound did not at all match the action. After a brief pause, she lifted the handle once more.

Then she jumped back, colliding with Kibure, who had been silently observing from behind. Two sets of eyes had appeared in the door; one above the knocker and one below. The surface of the stone could still be seen, even where the eyes were, but these two areas had become instantly translucent.

She huffed, then sighed quickly. "Sorry. I didn't expect—"

Kibure removed her hands from his hips and stepped to the side, still behind her.

Before she had time to gather herself to speak to the eyes in the door, two voices spoke in unison. "Who dares disturb the House of Stone?" The voices were surprisingly clear, as if there was no barrier between them and the visitors. Sindri glanced to either side of the door to check for a different origin for the sound, but found nothing but shadow.

"Who dares disturb the House of Stone?" the voices repeated.

Sindri spoke in the common tongue as best she could. "I am called Sindri, I was of the faith of Klerósi priestess. I have want to learn of the some answers—"

"You will want nothing here, outlander." The initial cadence was neither malignant nor warm, simply devoid of emotion. But these last words were unfriendly, with notes of hostility as the pitch curled at the end of each word. "The Lugienese have no business here with the people of the Stone faith. Your race is viler than even the invasive merchant folk of the Isles. You will leave now."

"Please, I have departed of the faith. Please, I only have want of the answers. I will leave of this place—"

Her plea was cut short again by the same venomous duo of voices. "You will leave us, now."

The translucent slits in the stone faded, leaving behind the original stone. Sindri reached for the knocker to try to get their attention again, to plead her case, but as her arm extended, her hand disappeared into a cloud of unnatural darkness. It seemed to almost swirl as it swallowed her hand. The hairs on the back of her neck lifted and tingled at the expenditure of magic being used.

She may not have been able to use her Lugienese priestly magic anymore, but she was still sensitive to the use of any magic around her, and this was without a doubt magic. Fear coursed through her veins as she considered that this magic might become less benign should she refuse to leave as requested. Kibure had no way of understanding what had been said, but before she had even started to move, he grabbed her wrist and said, "We need to leave."

Fronds of darkness grew rapidly from the walls and enclosed the small space. The light from above disappeared completely, and so did Kibure. Except for his hold on her wrist, he no longer existed. A faint, high-pitched sound started in her ear, too.

"Come on!" He yanked again. His grip started to hurt her wrist, and her feet finally broke their paralyzed state. Her foot caught on the first step but Kibure kept her balanced as her entire body weight fell upon that one supporting hand. She recovered and continued to follow Kibure's surprisingly strong arm, pulling her around the steps leading up to the daylight that could no longer be seen. The high-pitched sound grew louder, penetrating her mind beyond what her ears took in.

The sound became so intense that her legs weakened in spite of the strength afforded her by fear. Sindri missed a step and stumbled forward. Kibure lifted his arm, the one holding hers, and she regained her footing. Her eyes hurt momentarily as light rushed in to meet them. She turned back, ready to resume the retreat from the pursuing darkness, but there was nothing there. The outside of the temple looked exactly as it had before they had entered.

Sindri just stood there, allowing her proud posture to melt away, replaced by fear and relief that she had survived. She wasn't sure what the monks of this temple were capable of, but she had no desire to find out in that manner, not without magic of her own.

"That seemed to not go so well," said Kibure.

Sindri was still too flustered to think clearly. "We . . . we should head back to the inn and see about getting a lead on another, perhaps more accommodating, priesthood."

Kibure didn't say anything more for the rest of the walk back. He didn't seem angry, but there was a sense of disenfranchisement in his body language. Sindri then realized that as resistant and distrustful as he was, he too was hopeful about learning to understand and perhaps even to fully wield his magic. He wanted it much more than he let on. She tucked this thought away, knowing she'd have to feed that fire gradually, but consistently, especially if they were going to continue to meet resistance along the way.

Once back at the inn, Sindri sat down at the bar and started up a conversation with a grizzled man to her right. He wasn't able to tell her anything she didn't already know, but she did get the name of a place where she might find the sort of people who might. She slept well that night, still hopeful for tomorrow.

## CHAPTER 70

# AYNWARD

AYNWARD'S EYES HAD GONE WIDE with concern, but his mouth failed again to make much of a sound. With gag firmly in place, it was useless.

"I think he's trying to express a desire to be taken down. It's just that, well, I can't quite hear what he's saying," said Kyllean, followed by a few more laughs.

Kyllean had found him earlier than Aynward would have anticipated, considering the condition his friend had been in the last time he'd seen him. However, it had still been much later than he would have liked. He was certain that every single student on campus had walked past him at least once. Apparently none had believed him in enough danger to help of their own volition.

But Kyllean had been quick to fetch a few guards. Aynward was surprised that he hadn't seen one before this, since the library employed several, but the main entrance was around the bend so it was possible that they came and went from the other direction.

"Mrrrrrrmm!" Aynward tried to shout as he plummeted toward the ground. To his relief, Kyllean and the guard caught him before he hit.

Kyllean untied the gag first.

Aynward half-coughed and licked his lips, then finally looked toward the tree and said, "Thanks for the warning."

A guard was still standing next to the tree with his sword unsheathed. He placed it back in its scabbard and nodded his acceptance, ignoring Aynward's sarcastic tone. The other guard had pulled a knife and worked to cut the ropes binding his hands.

Aynward rolled and massaged his wrists once they were free.

"Thank you," he said, this time with sincerity.

Aynward stepped out of the mess of ropes that had been his make-shift mock throne, and the awkwardness of his near nudity returned.

Kyllean tossed him a spare robe. "Put this on, for all our sakes."

"Thanks."

His friend looked him over and said, "Man, I thought I was in rough shape when I woke this morning, but in seeing this, I'm feeling pretty good by comparison."

Aynward replied, "Yeah, well this damsel is more on the male side, and has an affinity for abuse."

"So what exactly happened? That big fella catch up to you before you made it home?"

Aynward reached up and felt the goose egg protruding from his skull from where he had been struck. "Not exactly." He pursed his lips then said, "Theo."

Kyllean's expression said *I have no idea what you're talking about.*

"I'll stop by your dorm on the way to our Properties class and tell you about it on the walk there." Aynward turned toward the university gate. "I need go home and grab a few things before my first class. I think I can still make it on time. I just hope I can stay awake."

Kyllean nodded. "Okay. Well, take care of yourself."

Aynward was already distracted by another realization. He cursed under his breath. "They took the scroll from our Properties class." Then he felt around more. "And my purse!" He'd been so overwhelmed by the whole experience that it had not registered that they were taking his money along with his other belongings. He was suddenly glad that he had opted not to carry his sword. It wouldn't have helped him defend against the attack from behind, anyhow; he would just have one less irreplaceable sword to his name.

He let out a muffled scream of frustration and kicked at the ground. "I need to go."

Kyllean looked at him sympathetically. "See you later."

As Aynward shuffled home, he prayed to Kitay that he might have the good fortune to slip quietly into his room to pick up his other book and be gone again without having to face Dolme, but he supposed his chances of this were limited, especially the way his luck had been behaving as of late. He shook his head. He needed to be ready to answer for not returning home last night.

So Aynward imagined what he might say:

"I'm running late, we can discuss your disapproval of my every decision tonight after my last class."

Dolme would surely not accept this, responding in kind with something to the effect of, "No, I think we'll talk about it *now.*"

The conversation would only escalate from there.

Aynward dismissed this approach out of hand. He also considered that while Dolme was overbearing in his management of Aynward's life, it was possible that Dolme was wiser than Aynward gave him credit for, and that Aynward was less wise than he pretended himself to be. What was it Dwapek called him? *Arrogant, privileged, and entitled.* Perhaps there was a sliver of truth to that.

As much as Aynward hated to admit it, he had to acknowledge that he had perhaps, on occasion, held a slightly higher than healthy opinion of himself, often to a fault. The situation that had resulted in his overnight stay in a tree was just the most recent example. His actions had often relied upon an infallibility that simply did not exist.

Aynward could feel what little swagger his still muscles allowed waver as he traveled down this dark road of self-doubt. *No, I can't doubt myself.* Something Dolme had once said to him resurfaced in that moment. *Humility is the honest measure of oneself that fosters growth.*

Aynward decided that perhaps it was time he took the road of humility. He would apologize for not returning, and admit that his arrogance had placed him in unnecessary danger.

Aynward cringed as Aunt Melanie's home came into view. Dolme was sitting on the front porch, hands overlapping on his lap, waiting. The false sense of patience radiated from him like hot coals felt from afar. This was going to be one of those times when Dolme followed the old proverb of leadership that stated, "Hit first, question later."

Aynward attempted to remain optimistic. *You can do this. Just sound sincere, be truthful, and be humble.*

Aynward could feel Dolme's sharp arrows of disapproval burrowing into him as he took the steps onto the porch. Yet he remained silent. Aynward stepped toward the door. *Maybe he'll let me pass without having to explain.* Aynward was preparing to say a word of praise to Kitay as he reached for the handle unopposed.

Then Dolme froze him with one word. "Wait."

The aged counselor rose to his feet slowly but purposefully.

Aynward bowed his head, and spoke in a passive voice. "Listen, I know I messed up. I should have returned home last night. I let down my guard and was ambushed by a few unsavory fellows from the university."

Aynward glanced up to gauge Dolme's reaction just as a heavy open hand smacked him upside the head. As his poor run of luck would have it, Dolme struck the exact place on Aynward's head that he had been struck the day before. "Ohh," groaned Aynward. "Come on!"

"That goose egg on your head a part of this ambush, or does it grow with each lie like that fabled wooden boy's nose?"

"Part of the ambush," said Aynward, still reeling from the redoubled pain.

"And what part of this *ambush* prevented your legs from returning you home?"

*Be truthful.* "I was tied up and hung from a tree in the middle of the university."

Dolme's eyes went wide, then narrowed. "An ambush, you say?"

*Does he not believe me?* "Yes, a boy named Theo, I offended him a few weeks ago and he gathered some friends and took me unawares." Aynward didn't need to be any more truthful than that; mentioning the heavy drinking that had made him so much more vulnerable would be just plain foolish.

Dolme pulled back a fist, and Aynward readied himself for the blow. It never came. Dolme exhaled heavily and relented, "Go. Go to your class. Gods help us if you don't grow up soon." He shook his head in defeat. "Don't expect any more of your allowance. Any necessities that must be purchased outside the university will be purchased by me personally. Anything else will require a purchase order from the university itself."

The disappointment in Dolme's expression almost made Aynward feel bad about the way he treated the man. Aynward opened his mouth to give a sincere apology, but the words wouldn't come. What had his humility just earned him: a smack to the head and a lost allowance?

Instead he recalled being kidnapped, drugged, and essentially tortured by Dolme. That memory brought him right back into his true comfort zone, doing everything counter to the man's wishes, guilt free. And he still owed the man a debt, though Theo had quickly topped the list. Without his allowance, however . . . he really needed to figure out how to make good on his deal with Gervais.

Before he stepped through the door, he said, "You can expect a bill for a very old scroll from the university Special Collections. It seems to have gone missing in recent hours." He scowled as he passed through the door, wondering if his humility had failed because of his long history of arrogance. That he would need to demonstrate wisdom and maturity for a considerable length of time to truly earn Dolme's trust. Then he dismissed the thought. Vengeance was so much easier, and it felt much better, anyhow.

✵ ✵ ✵

"Gods above, you look worse than you did this morning!" exclaimed
Kyllean.

"Thanks again for the rescue," responded Aynward, ignoring the
comment.

"You finally going to tell me what happened to you?"

Aynward thought about where to begin. "Remember the graduate
student we saw running that rather dubious meeting in the courtyard
the other day on our way to class?"

"The one who threatened you?"

"The same, yes."

Kyllean nodded, waiting for Aynward to continue.

"Well, I should probably mention that I also faced him down during
the chaos of the desposition fiasco, and I *may* have landed a solid blow
to the baby-maker in the process. That, along with his professed hatred
of all those born to noble station . . ." He recapped the entire event as
best he could.

"So this Theo, he took your scroll, too?"

"Yep," said Aynward darkly, but he smiled as he added, "Dolme is
going to probably give me a matching goose egg when he gets the bill. I
checked with the library today to see if it had been turned in, and if not,
the cost to replace it." He paused for effect and they rounded the last
bend in the trail leading to the meeting place for class. "Let's just say, I
could probably have purchased drinks for our entire class for an entire
year for what it is going to cost the crown to pay for that scroll. Dolme
will have to request funds from the treasury."

Kyllean shook his head. "Your poor parents." He looked pensive as
they sat, then he started to laugh. "No pun intended, but it is fitting."

Aynward sat next to Minathi, who glared at him. "You're in rather
good spirits, considering what happened to you last night—yes, I heard
about it, along with every other student on campus." She examined his
face for injury. "If the desposition didn't grant you notoriety, this did,
though probably not exactly the kind you were hoping for."

"Yeah, tell you about it later," he said as the last student arrived. Dwapek was tapping his foot impatiently.

"Everyone read their stories, aye?" he said dryly.

All five students looked around, all five nodded in answer.

"Good, good. So who wishes to report first?"

Eyebrows went up around the room. No one moved. Dwapek had that blunt way about him that made for easy humiliation. Aynward knew for certain that he wasn't looking forward to hearing all of the important points he'd missed while reading.

Aynward was also wondering if Dwapek had learned of the chastening he'd earned that morning. If so, he knew the blame would be placed on him for allowing himself to be exploited. But perhaps Dwapek's detached connection to university politics would work in Aynward's favor. He might not be up on all of the gossip. The fact that Dwapek hadn't said something immediately was promising. He didn't give the impression of someone who would, or even *could*, hold back if he knew. That gave Aynward the courage to volunteer to report first.

"I'll go." He couldn't quite muster up a voice of enthusiasm, but he managed to speak first. Like a boy being asked if he was stealing a honey biscuit while his hand was in the jar, there was nothing to do but hang his head and embrace it.

He told his story from his reading, attempting to be as concise as possible without cutting away any of what he perceived to be the main points. He was careful not to imply too strongly his belief that the story was a complete fabrication, along with the rest. He'd not read the second and third texts yet, but after hearing the remaining stories from his classmates, he was all the more confident that none were rooted in truth.

Aynward was half expecting Dwapek to begin a tirade, scolding them all for not thinking for themselves and realizing the farce sooner. Instead the little man sat behind the group, writing furiously as they spoke, only occasionally clarifying this detail or that, with the questions often having little or no decipherable relevance. *Quite a ruse, if this really is just a cosmic lesson in gullibility.* Then again, if anyone was stubborn enough to keep up the pretenses for as long as it took for someone to point it out, it would be Dwapek. Aynward determined to risk Dwapek's ire by the end of next class if no one said anything before then. *If nothing else, maybe he'll tell us what in all of Doréa this has to do with anything.* The class still seemed like a complete waste of time, especially considering how much of his time it demanded. His next text was much longer than the first.

Dwapek closed his leather notebook as the last student finished their recounting. He stood up as the other student sat. "Thank you. You will all present your second texts in two days. Dismissed."

Once everyone registered that class was over, they rose immediately to their feet in an effort to escape any further assignments.

Aynward turned to leave, trailing Kyllean closely, but was cut short by Dwapek's voice. "Not you."

Aynward stopped. Dwapek hadn't used his name, but somehow—well—he just knew.

The half-man approached, keeping his voice uncharacteristically low as he growled, "Stay away from Theo."

If Aynward had been walking, he would have lost his footing. He turned to respond with one of the hundred questions that came to mind, but Dwapek was already headed in the opposite direction, toward the forest, which ordinarily would have warranted further consideration in and of itself. He shouted after him, "What do you mean? What do you know about him?" Frustrated that Dwapek didn't so much as turn to acknowledge him, he shouted louder. "Hey, answer me!"

This last demand earned a response. Dwapek spun to face him. "I don't take orders from big'ns like you. However, you've caught me in a good mood today, so I'll offer you this." He paused only briefly before admonishing, "Sometimes others know more than you, and listening to them keeps you safe." He turned and continued toward the forest and shouted behind him, "Get some rest—you look like you were tied up and rolled down a mountainside."

Aynward didn't have any witty comebacks to combat that. He left without another word, jogging to catch up with Kyllean. "The old coot is somehow connected to Theo, and I think he's protecting him!"

Kyllean stopped. "And how could you possibly know that?"

"Because he just explicitly warned me to stay away from him."

Aynward's friend looked to the overcast sky in thought. "Okay, well, that doesn't necessarily mean he's protecting him. He could be protecting you. Especially if he learned what happened to you, which he must have; else he'd not have warned you in the first place."

"Maybe. But when I asked him about it, he blew me off and just told me to trust that others know more than I do. Why wouldn't he just tell me that Theo is dangerous, or, better yet, if he knows so much about him, why wouldn't he just do something about it?"

Kyllean considered this. "I still think you're making too much of it. Dwapek doesn't seem the meddling type. Maybe he's just trying to make sure you don't do something stupid to get yourself kicked out."

"All right. Well, I've gotta get home," grumbled Aynward. "Dwapek was right about one thing. I need to get some rest."

"Good idea. And try not to do anything too stupid before the next time I see you."

"That seems to be beyond the scope of my ability as of late."

Kyllean just shook his head and started toward his dormitory. Aynward let out a large breath of air, and took off toward his own residence. His thoughts whirled as he weighed his suspicions about Dwapek against what Kyllean had said to debunk them.

His spirits lifted when he arrived at his residence to smell home-cooked food.

"Aynward, is that you?" came his aunt's voice from the cook fire.

"Yes."

"I just finished up a batch of sugar biscuits if you want a few to take to your room."

He walked over and took a wooden plate from her. "Oh, these smell delicious." Not willing to wait to get upstairs, he bit into one. The stress of his restless mind melted, if only for a moment. "Thank you, I really needed this."

She gave a concerned expression. "Long day?"

"More like long week."

"Well, just remember, no matter how big your problems may seem, there are always others who'd willingly trade places in an instant."

*Not helpful. But the sugar biscuits easily make up the difference.*

"Thanks. I'm going to get to my readings, and get some rest. Good night, Aunt Melanie."

Aynward rushed up the stairs, hoping to avoid any further advice from his older-than-dirt aunt, or his cantankerous counselor, who had silently eyed him down from the porch as he walked up the steps. He untied his sandals, lit a candle, and grabbed the second text he was to read for Properties. He leaped into bed and sank into its soft padding like a foot slides into a well-worn shoe. He sighed in relief and opened the ancient text to the first page. The handwriting was smooth, and he felt his mind melting into the pages the way his body had melted into the covers. He didn't perceive sleep's entrance into the room, but it came, bringing with it the best rest he'd had in months.

## CHAPTER 71

# KIBURE

TWO DAYS PASSED BEFORE SINDRI returned with any new leads worth investigating. After the second fruitless day of following her around as she attempted to ask inconspicuous questions about a *very* conspicuous topic, Kibure chose to remain at The Roving Sail. She promised not to act on any tips without him; therefore, he wasn't missing anything.

By midday Kibure regretted this decision. The simple task of ordering a meal at the inn was a challenge almost worth going hungry for. He ended up miming the act of eating, and then nodded his head and shrugged his shoulders enough times to communicate that he didn't understand, but would take whatever food could be had. By the end, the innkeeper appeared just as exasperated as Kibure felt. But he was given his food, and had picked up on the words for eat and drink. He thought Sindri's timeline for him learning this language was a bit ambitious, if not unattainable.

Sindri returned a few hours before sundown with a rare smile upon her face.

"Did you eat?"

"Yeah, took me half the afternoon to order, but I managed."

"Good. Let's go. We've got a lead. If we hurry, we can get there and back before sundown."

"Okay," answered Kibure as she tugged on his sleeve, turning him in the direction of the door. "Why are we in such a hurry?"

"There's an apothecary. The woman I spoke with said she heard from a reliable source that the owners are witches, or wargs, or something. They sell potions and charms, many of which are acclaimed to have magical powers."

She picked up the pace and shouted behind her, "Place closes at dusk so we need to move if we want to catch them before then."

"Are they closing up forever, or just for the evening?"

Sindri did not respond. Instead her pace quickened and Kibure knew she would entertain no further complaints. She was focused on a task, and no amount of whining would convince her to postpone until the morning.

They walked for nearly an hour, Sindri cursing as she struggled through missed turns, blaming them on poorly given directions. In the meantime, Kibure began his own struggle; to focus his attention on only small sections at a time wherever they traveled. Sindri had suggested this as a coping strategy for him after growing tired of listening to his complaints about the nauseating effects of the city's chaotic activity. Kibure initially dismissed the suggestion, but his head was spinning minutes after leaving the inn, and he found himself narrowing his field of vision as recommended. To his surprise, it actually did minimize the overwhelming effects of the bustling city. He silently acknowledged that this was not a long-term solution, and it left him vulnerable to any potential lurking enemies, especially once he started traveling alone. Soon enough, he would need to acclimate and be able to widen his focus to take in all of his surroundings without feeling nauseated. Kibure shook his head, hoping this would indeed prove true.

They emerged from a narrow street onto the larger thoroughfare, and Kibure's eyes did as Sindri had said, focusing on the first image that took his attention. His gaze was immediately drawn to an enormous bronze sculpture of a bird, silhouetted by the afternoon sky. He flinched at first glance, believing it real. Only after a few long moments did he realize a bird would not remain in a pose of outstretched wings for such a long time without actually flying. The poised position was one of imminent flight, as if ready to launch into the sky with the next flap of its mighty wings. He prayed that there was no such bird living, for if sculpted to scale, it was large enough to take a man in its beak, or crush one in its mighty talons. No, it had to be the imaginary deity of some sort of bird-worshiping cult. He shuddered again at the thought of a giant man-eating bird of prey.

His neck was craned halfway around before he was able to wrest his gaze away from the disturbing bronze statue. He turned just in time to catch himself from running into Sindri. She had frozen in place, and her body had gone rigid. She slowly lowered herself into a crouch, hands extended from her sides in a defensive position. She felt around behind her until she found Kibure, then backed them both slowly to the wall between a cart and an adjacent building. Her face had gone pale, and her vision remained fixed ahead. Kibure followed her gaze to the building across the way. The cart now blocked most of their bodies but she peered over the top, eyes still wide.

It was a small shop with vials, dried hanging plants, and jars lining the visible areas of the interior. Kibure was puzzled by Sindri's reaction but knew enough to trust her instincts. Based on her description of the place they were seeking, this was it, but something was amiss.

"What is it?" Kibure whispered.

"The shopkeeper," she whispered with a ghost of a voice. "The shopkeeper is . . ." She trailed off without finishing the statement, but Kibure saw it now.

There was no mistaking it, even with the shaved head to conceal the translucent hair of the chameleon. To someone who knew what to look for, this man, with his light-brown skin, bulbous eyes, and rounded features, was, without a doubt, Lugienese.

## CHAPTER 72

# SINDRI

SINDRI STARED IN DISBELIEF. A Lugienese man? Here? But why? Lugienese despised all other cultures and emigration was strictly prohibited. Sure, they had emissaries who negotiated trade agreements, but even they loathed the experience. It was a necessary evil to achieve a greater good. But this man was seemingly—

"Are we going to stay here crouched behind a cart until we're noticed," said Kibure, "or are we going to get the heck away from here so we can figure out why there's a Lugienese man selling potions in this city?"

Sindri returned from her state of perplexed immobility with a strong desire to smack Kibure in the mouth. He had become increasingly aggravating since their journey began. He had no idea how utterly *wrong* this situation was. She wanted to throttle his arrogant little—she stopped the thought short. No, he wasn't arrogant, he was ignorant. And she shouldn't fault him for that. She could still find it irritating, but he was right, after all: they needed to get out of there *now*.

"Come on," she said as she straightened and turned her back to the shop. If this man's Lugienese features were so easily recognized, so would hers be. And she needed to know whether this man was a secreted priest or just a civilian who had broken Lugienese law and escaped to some-where new. She hadn't sensed the use of magic, but if he wasn't using it, or merely sold magically enhanced trinkets, she probably wouldn't. Plus, there could be more of them than just the man at the counter.

They broke into a run as they left the bazaar. Just as Sindri reached full speed, a cart emerged from a side street. She pivoted to avoid the fruit-laden obstacle, only to crash headlong into hard flesh. A flash of shining red enveloped her sight.

## CHAPTER 73

# GROBENNAR

GROBENNAR STEPPED ONTO THE DOCK in the Isles city of Brinkwell, revulsion already weighing heavily upon him. His unassuming brown cloak seemed to drag as if made of iron, his burden a powerful wind blowing hard against his every determined step. It had taken all the willpower he could muster to avoid striking down the Lugienese merchants who ferried him from Sire Trinkanen to Brinkwell: heretics, the whole lot of them. How could these men have strayed so far from the ways of Klerós? Then again, it was proof that this world could no longer remain free to *choose* the ways of evil; the choice was too appealing, the lure of sin too strong for the feeble of mind. The choice *had* to be removed.

He reached into his cloak and pulled out the directions to the rendezvous he had been given to make contact with his fellow priests. Grobennar looked forward to fellowshipping with like-minded brethren as he took over the operations here. This would be the first city outside of Angolia to fall to the Lugienese. Success here would set the stage for control of the Glass Sea, and the eventual conquest of the eastern kingdoms of the Drogen continent, and then the rest of the known world.

He clenched his teeth as he walked. *This is but a test. Brinkwell is merely the beginning. I will regain my honor and rightful title.*

Grobennar reached beneath his cloak and clutched the jeweled medallion he wore at his neck. As if on cue, Jaween spoke into Grobennar's mind. *"So much weakness here. Their minds are like ants beneath our feet; numerous, fleeting, and oblivious to the danger we pose. This is going to be so much fun! I haven't been outside of Angolia since— before being summoned to this stone."*

Grobennar paused, thoughts muddled by the statement. How could Jaween have been previously summoned outside of the Angolian continent, and in a different form? Lesante, the founder of the faith, was the first to bring Klerós's helpers to the surface. Grobennar sighed, thinking once again that the spirit he had found was at least partially defective. He also considered that there were perhaps *very* legitimate reasons why these summoned spirits had been banned by the Kleról. Jaween, of course, had convinced the young Grobennar otherwise when he discovered the medallion years earlier. If Jaween was any indicator, the whole lot of spirits had indeed gone mad. But Jaween was not without his uses, not while in the hands of one so holy as Grobennar.

What the priest witnessed in his first few minutes in Brinkwell returned his thoughts to the present task. His disgust with the Lugienese who had transported him to Brinkwell did nothing to prepare him for what he saw as he stalked his way to his contact point. He counted four different temples to four different deities. But the worst part was not the existence of the temples themselves; it was the seemingly blissful state of oblivion with which the people of the city carried themselves. Within the Lugienese Empire, priests could part a crowded street with their mere presence. But here, Grobennar, a *former* Fatu Mazi, found himself fighting for space with each step. Though how could they know who he was? He was wearing his mundane traveling clothes. How dare he hide the light of his god? At least some of the fault lay within himself. *No more.*

Without another thought, Grobennar pulled off his cloak, his red silks catching the light to reveal the almighty Klerós's power over humanity. He felt his confidence magnify with the pride of Klerós and the knowledge that others would now see this and tremble.

As he reached into his pack to stuff his cloak inside, a powerful force struck him hard in the chest. He tumbled over in a heap, gasping for breath.

Jaween hissed in Grobennar's mind.

## CHAPTER 74

# KIBURE

KIBURE COULD HARDLY BELIEVE HIS own strength. Without thinking, he grabbed hold of the tough fabric at the back of Sindri's tan dress and yanked; her fallen body rose easily and he didn't let go until he had dragged her around the corner of another street.

"Hold on," advised Kibure as he stopped to peer back around the corner. "He's not coming. Not yet, anyhow. We'd better keep going."

Sindri's eyes focused as she regained some understanding of what was going on. Still sounding woozy, she asked, "Was that a—"

"A Klerósi priest," interrupted Kibure as he continued walking quickly. "C'mon."

"I just—this makes no sense."

They arrived back at The Roving Sail unharmed and proceeded to order a hot meal. They consumed their respective bowls of warm stew and accompanying mugs of ale. It did not take long to find the bottoms of each. They were exhausted both physically and mentally, and they spoke few words over dinner.

"We need to get some shut-eye. We'll get to work at sunrise learning all we can about that shop and its *owners*," said Sindri, standing.

Kibure followed her to the room. As they approached the door, he asked, "What are we going to do if there's a team of priests here in the city? This city is big, real big, I guess, but if they're here, and know to look for us, they'll find us sooner or later."

Sindri pushed open the door and took a few steps in before turning to respond. But something caught her eye and her reply became a muffled gasp.

## CHAPTER 75

# SINDRI

SINDRI STARED WITH A MIX of disbelief and fear. In the back of
their small room was a man wearing a dark robe, seated comfortably at the wooden chair between the two beds. She was close enough to
the door to escape, *maybe*. She took a slow step back, keeping her gaze
firmly fixed on the intruder.

Lifting two empty hands, he said, "As you can see, I possess no
weapon, and while you cannot know for certain the full truth of my
words, I would like to express with sincerity that I do not mean you or
your companion any harm." He tilted his head slightly and spoke from
the side of his mouth quietly, almost to himself, "Pending your cooper-
ation and the outcome of our findings, of course."

He was thin to the point of frailty, but had a rigid poise about
him that suggested an out-of-place strength. The opening in his robe
revealed a large gemstone necklace that seemed to catch the light in
ways inconsistent with the poor lighting of the room. He continued,
"Truly, you have little to fear"—he coughed—"for the time being." He
coughed again. "I am merely here on a friendly visit, as a messenger on
behalf of my employ—no, no, that's not quite right. My partner?" His
hand moved to his leathery face, where it stroked a long beardless chin.

"He does supply me with a healthy wage, protection, living quarters, and tasks to complete, so perhaps that does make him at least some form of employer. Hmmm. Then again, I'm not subject to his will." He tilted his head to the other side. "But he could probably impose it should he choose."

He shook his head then his sunken eyes snapped forward to meet Sindri's. "My apologies for the digression." He coughed again, a nervous tic, perhaps. "A close acquaintance of mine, with whom I am in league, has an interest in meeting the both of you, tomorrow at midday."

Sindri stood still, not daring to look away in spite of the man's assurance of passivity. She felt a twinge of anger well up in her. This man had broken into her room, and now made threats and demands dressed up as a friendly invitation. What right did he have?

"Why do we wish to meet of your—your—person who tell of you to do things? He sends of you to break of our room, and tell us that we need to visit for tea?" Her struggle to communicate in the Kingdom tongue only elevated her feelings of frustration. The more she spoke, the crosser she felt. As if speaking had provided the fuel and air to grow a flame into an inferno.

She felt herself digging for the well of magic no longer at her disposal, causing even more rage. All fear of the mysterious man was gone. Before she knew what she was doing, she had taken two steps forward and thrust her finger toward his face.

"I will not be told of what to do. I do not meet of this person. I lose of much to be here, and do not follow of orders. Your boss will meet of us in hell."

Her other hand had reached down to the outside of her thigh, where a slit in her tan dress allowed her to grab another one of Jonglin's gifts to them, a dagger. She had lost her ability to draw on Klerós's power, but her priestly combat training was something that could not be taken away from her. The knife was out and her arm raced forward with a quickness that surprised even her.

Kibure's voice rang out. "Sindri!"

Her knife sped toward the neck of the intruder, who was too slow to even raise a hand.

The blade struck something hard and her body went completely still. She stared in disbelief at her knife hand, frozen in place before the man's neck. He had not moved a finger, but the hair on the back of her neck and her inability to move told her that he had employed a powerful spell of immobility. How had he done so without even a word? This was the same way that Kibure—no, she couldn't worry about any of that now. *I just tried to kill this man, he knows it, and he stopped it. We're in trouble.*

The man stared at her without the slightest shift in his expressionless face. Then his lips slowly morphed into a smile. It was not a warm smile, but it wasn't wholly cold, either. It was the kind of smile people gave when they were about to apologize for something beyond their control. It was a smile of pity, which fell right in line with the movement of the stranger's hands as they interlocked upon his already crossed legs.

"I understand your frustration. Yet there is little to be done but comply. My compatriot has a certain way of always getting what he wishes. It's quite remarkable, come to think of it."

Sindri couldn't see what Kibure was doing behind her, but he must have moved to act once he realized the man had used magic on her. A simple "Nuh-ah" and the shake of his head was all the man gave away before continuing. She sensed another rush of magic and knew that Kibure was now also unmoving in accordance with this man's will.

"I'd like to save you both the time and effort, as an act of good faith."

He moved his other foot to the ground and placed each hand upon a knee as if readying to stand, then paused and lifted a finger.

"You may think to leave this inn to take up residence elsewhere, hoping to avoid myself and my compatriot, or to even flee the city altogether, but I can assure you that we will know precisely where you are at all times until the meeting has taken place to his satisfaction, and perhaps longer. This meeting is *not* optional; however, the means and conditions under which it occurs? Well, you still have *some* control there, though I fear your choices are contrarious."

He gestured with his upraised hand as he spoke. "As I've said, he is requesting that this meeting begin at midday tomorrow. The place is called The Feather. If you choose to run, the meeting will take place a few hours later at a different locale, after capturing and transporting you under far less comfortable conditions. For now, he plans only to ask you some questions. The nature of your inquiries around the city has *captured* his attention."

He stroked his chin in thought then added, "You may bring your dagger, for this city does have its share of dangers, but I'd recommend keeping it sheathed during your meeting. I do not think it would be repaid with as painless a defense as I have employed here this evening."

He stood but had to duck beneath Sindri's still outstretched, frozen arm. He sidestepped awkwardly and took a few steps before speaking again. Sindri tried to get in a question but her lips would not move. Her attempted words were reduced to grunts and gurgles.

"The Feather is well known to most in the city so you will have no trouble finding someone to describe its location. And fear not, this spell will wear off within the next five or so minutes. Good evening."

And just like that, the man was gone.

## CHAPTER 76

# GROBENNAR

GROBENNAR STOOD SLOWLY, DISORIENTED AFTER being knocked off his feet. He thought he caught sight of the familiar translucent hair of a Lugienese woman fleeing the scene, but he couldn't be certain by the time he finally righted himself. Plus, any Lugienese citizen would be begging for the gift of penance after so much as brushing against a Klerósi priest in the Empire. This cretin didn't even have the goodwill to apologize. *Vile city.*

Jaween snarled, *"We should give chase. There was something—that woman was Lugienese. And there was something else—"*

"Every heretic here will burn in the end. That is, if I can refrain from reciprocating every single minor offense. We have to remain focused on the big picture." Jaween whined in the back of Grobennar's mind, but he ignored the excitable spirit. Jaween had his uses, but he could not be allowed to drive this ship.

Brushing off the dirt from the street, Grobennar started again toward his contact: a drogal merchant whom Grobennar hoped was not too much farther away. The former Fatu Mazi was in an even darker mood by the time he finally found the man, a painstaking twenty minutes later. "You are Baghel?"

The man's eyes went wide at the sight of him. *Finally! Someone who respects the priesthood.* Fear was one of the greatest forms of flattery, and respect, after all.

"Yes. I—I am he. You—you are wearing the robes of the Kleról." He said this as if he had never expected to see a priest, ever. Yet there were several here in the city already. *He must know of them. Strange. Perhaps he recognizes me from before coming here.*

"Is my attire a problem, servant?"

The man looked down at his feet. "No, Your Excellency, of course not. I—it's just—the others here. Well—they don't show themselves so *openly.*"

*Strange, indeed. Are they ashamed? Why would they hide themselves, thus shaming Klerós?*

"Klerós abounds in all things. Klerós rules all things. Klerós's will be done in all things." He spoke the phrase he had been given to indicate he had been sent here by the Kleról.

"Klerós's will be done in all things," the man responded. Baghel then pulled out a small, sealed parchment and handed it to Grobennar, who said upon taking it, "Klerós bless you and the Empire."

Grobennar broke the seal and began reading. He turned without another word, restlessness to begin his work driving him forward.

A delightfully brief walk ended with yet another gawking Lugienese merchant, this one as hairless as a babe. His confused expression turned to one of accusation. "What are you doing flaunting around in your robes? You're going to ruin everything! Get over here!"

The man grabbed Grobennar as if he was an insolent child, dragging him into the shop, which resembled the sort one might find in a child's tale. All manner of dried plants, vials, and glass containers covered shelves upon shelves in the cramped space. Grobennar was pulled through a door in the back.

By this point, his surprise at the disrespect had worn off and he was certain that his glare dwarfed that of the man who now stared him down. Grobennar spoke first as he yanked his arm free. "What is the meaning of this? How dare you disrespect a priest of Klerós!"

Grobennar felt the tingling of magic and realized that the man was drawing on Klerós's power. This man too was a priest. *Could have fooled me. He hides himself like a roach beneath the dung of this city.* He drew his own power from Klerós, no fear that this man could match his volume or control of the holy gift. "I recommend *not* using Klerós's power on your new *master.* I know of only one other whose power surpasses my own, and he is no mortal man. I"—he hesitated as he remembered to remove the Fatu from his title—"am Mazi Grobennar. I do not wish to debilitate an underling as the first action as head of this operation, but if you force my hand, I'll harbor no regrets."

The priest's glare held firm, but Grobennar felt him release his hold on the magic. *Bold of him.* Most priests back home withered at the mention of a mazi. He was either powerful in his own right, had been too long away, or was simply *very* stupid. But he did stand down; Grobennar just expected a greater show of respect at the mention of his title, not the begrudging acquiescence this man demonstrated.

Grobennar allowed himself an audible exhale to release the tension of the moment. He was not lying about wishing to avoid conflict as his first act in Brinkwell. *Now to find out what in the lower hells this man was thinking.* "You will explain yourself. What is the meaning of this shameful disrespect you show me? And why do you hide the glory of Klerós from these people?"

The man had the gall to ignore the question. "I assume you have papers from the Kleról to corroborate your alleged status here?"

*This man is insufferable. Pray the rest aren't so or I will have to put a few in their place after all.*

Jaween imparted his own thoughts on the matter. "*I could persuade him to take a different tone with you.*" Grobennar ignored Jaween, though there was certainly an appeal to the offer. Grobennar responded with a simple, "Of course," albeit through clenched teeth. He reached into his pouch to retrieve the parchment with Magog's unbroken wax seal and personal signature. The man had likely never seen such. He handed it over. The man's eyebrows rose as he studied the seal, then the document, but the rest of his expression remained unchanged.

Finally he said, "I would have thought they'd have briefed you on what we're doing here before sending you to take over. Very well, *master*. Change your clothes, then follow me. I'll have to close up shop for the day."

*I have more work ahead of me than I thought. Perhaps these men have been too long away from home. I'll see that they remember where they come from and the hierarchy of respect therein.*

## CHAPTER 77

# AYNWARD

AYNWARD EASILY FINISHED THE SMALL tome before Dwapek's class; the not-so-subtle stares and quiet laughter from other students who recognized him as the boy who'd been tied up in his small-clothes made certain of that. Reading became a means of escape. And while the Properties class was, without a doubt, lower priority than the others, this particular text piqued his interest.

The story itself was no less befuddling than the others, yet he found himself visualizing the events in his mind's eye as he read. The author was so passionate, vivid, and sincere in his diction that Aynward believed the *author* believed his own words. It took a few minutes after each reading for reality to overrule it, as the events described in the tome forced him into the realm of fairies and dragons.

He stood up to summarize the text before the class.

"This text pairs quite well with the former: another perspective on the Lugienese flight from Drogen. However, this was penned by a Luguinden priest. According to this man, Rajul Daye, this final battle, where Lesante and her new order absconded with the entire Luguinden fleet, was a bit more one-sided than other sources would have us believe. He claims that a slaughter ensued from the onset as he and his fellow priests and priestesses were rendered powerless, forsaken by their own gods.

"According to him, it was as if their gods had fallen asleep as soon as the battle began. Many of them were never able to wield their magic again, while others found it possible, but without the same ease and strength. This, of course, runs counter to the great volume of well-known canonized historical accounts of this same battle, but I have to admit that Rajul Daye's skills as an author of fiction are commendable."

Aynward was the third to present during this class and no one had been so bold as to question the validity of what they were reading. He paused long enough for Dwapek to interject, but the moment came and went without so much as a flinch, so Aynward continued.

"According to Rajul, his ability to wield his god's power waned until he could no more cast a spell than a priest can hold his liquor. Though, if I had to guess, I'd say he used up the rest of his magic in story crafting—a taxing magic if the legends are true."

That got a laugh out of Thato, and smirk from the rest, but Dwapek's expression had slipped from his ordinary look of general disapproval to a full-fledged scowl. One glance in Dwapek's direction from Thato turned his chuckle into a choked cough.

Dwapek stood up tall, which placed him at eye level with the rest of the class in their seated positions. "So, according to this account, no priestly magic could be wielded against this new order of Lugienese wizards. Is that correct?"

"Yes, that's correct. However, in my previous text that order of female sorceresses did just that and are alleged to have nearly killed the prophetess with magic. These are direct contradictions."

Dwapek glowered for a moment, then his eyes lit up and a sinister smile formed. "True. That is, unless they aren't contradictions. The sun can exist both to the east and the west."

Aynward furrowed his brows and threw up his hands. What in this godforsaken world was that supposed to mean? *The charade ends here.* "I mean no disrespect, but what is the point of all of this? We're spending all our time reading the warped stories of long-dead liars, or, at best, insane people. And for what? What point are you trying to prove?"

Dwapek bellowed, "Be seated, you little twit. All you're proving with this whiny demonstration is that your counselors did their job in convincing you to be a masterful, parroting fool. All you big'ns' histories are jesters' truths, spun to warm the sheets. And the second your little blankies go missing, you cry like babes, because the truth isn't so soft." He looked each one in the eye before continuing. "What you know of the histories are but children's tales crafted to help you sleep at night. I assure you, the truth is a nightmare, and the tale isn't yet complete. The wolf has left his den in search of new prey."

No one dared speak. Aynward might have allowed one or two choice retorts to slip out if not for the conviction in Dwapek's voice. He appeared to believe what he was saying, which deflated Aynward's resolve to argue. It was like picking a fight with a cripple; it would serve no honorable purpose. At the least, Dwapek did not seem to be doing this as a means of penal retribution.

Minathi spoke. "Might I ask, who or what is this wolf of which you speak?"

Dwapek glared, but not at her. He eyed down some unseen force, something only his mind's eye could see. "I fear we'll all find out soon enough."

He came out of his trance. "Thato and Kyllean, you present next class. Everyone else, you have a two-day extension for your last text. Then we can start putting the pieces together and see what the picture really looks like." No one moved. He spoke once more, this time louder. "Dismissed."

None of the students spoke until they were beyond earshot of the old, eccentric fool. Aynward breathed a heavy sigh of relief when he rounded the first bend in the trail leading out of the secret forest meeting place.

"It's official: he's lost his wits."

Kyllean looked over at him. "Well, he's grabbed hold of my fear strings, even if I don't know what it is I'm supposed to fear."

Aynward waved a hand in dismissal. "If there was really something going on, don't you think other people *might* be talking about it? The gods know Dolmuevo would have shipped me home weeks ago with even the slightest sniff of danger on the horizon."

"Fair point," conceded Kyllean. "But something sure has the little man riled up, and it makes me nervous. Like seeing tears in a grown man's eyes; they're rare and never without sincerity."

Aynward laughed. "Now *that* is a fantastic analogy, but I'm still not convinced he's anything more than a frightened, three-foot-tall loon." Without leaving a long enough pause for a reply, he continued, "Not to steer this conversation in a different direction, but my aunt said she was making some sort of stew today if you want something besides poorly seasoned meat and overcooked potatoes."

Kyllean brightened. "I can get behind that segue." He rubbed his belly. "I'm starving. Tell me more."

The boys strode down the main thoroughfare toward Aynward's residence. As they walked, Kyllean pointed to a sign. It was staged in front of one of the local temples of the Stone faith, a building shorter than all the others around it.

"Have you heard of this dual-moon eclipse thing?"

"Huh?" Aynward shook his head free of other thoughts, then replayed the question in his mind. He had walked by the granite sign dozens of times without noticing the carving in it of two interwoven circles. "Oh, um, no. But I'm assuming that's like a regular eclipse, except with moons?"

"You guessed it. But did you know that the moons are supposed to cross paths tonight? The very focal point of their entire faith occurs this evening! It can only be seen clearly here in Brinkwell and a few other nearby Isles cities. And it happens only once every five thousand years." Kyllean was bubbling with an excitement Aynward found obnoxious. "They believe the moons crossing paths is a coupling of the mother and father stone, and the resulting birth will manifest itself in the form of one lucky soul's wish. According to the Stoneys, that's how the sun came into being in the first place. Oh, and I think some sort of catastrophic event is supposed to coincide with that, too, but I didn't catch that part."

Aynward glanced back at the sign. "How do you know all this?"

"One of the kids in my dorm is a Stoney. He claims the moon god, Ursual or something, will grant one of the faithful whatever is their heart's desire, so long as it is pure."

Aynward said, "Why are you telling me this?"

Kyllean patted Aynward on the shoulder. "Because, my friend, according to my sources, every tavern in town will be serving drinks at half price tonight!"

Aynward felt his mood lift slightly but then sag. "I'm too far behind in my readings, plus, discount or not, I've precious few coins right now. Dolme has cut my allowance down to a steady flow of distrust."

Kyllean let the conversation go as they stepped into Aunt Melanie's home and the strong smell of food greeted their nostrils.

"Mmm, home-cooked meals. There's simply no substitute," said Kyllean through a mouthful of steaming, half-chewed stew. "Aunt Melanie, if you ever get sick of Aynward's unappreciative, whiny nature, I'd be more than willing to swap places." Then he added, "With him, not you."

Chuckling, she replied, "Oh, you're much too kind. Had I another room available, I'd be glad to have you. Alas, I am but a sister to the King, on his wife's side, a title that pays disappointingly little."

Kyllean replied once again through a mouthful of food, "A pity indeed."

Aunt Melanie raised a finger. "But I may have something else to offer both of you." Looking at Aynward, she said, "Gervais mentioned that he has a few tickets for a performance tonight, in honor of the dual-moon eclipse, if you'd like to go." Smiling, she added, "Sounded like he's got enough for a few friends."

Aynward had more reading to do, and little desire to see a performance. *No thank you.* Before he had even opened his mouth to decline, Kyllean nearly shouted, "We'd love to go!"

Aynward was in the middle of swallowing and nearly choked. Clearing his throat he turned to Aunt Melanie and said, "Apologies. My *friend* here left out a very important word. He meant to say was we'd love *not* to go."

"Oh, come on," pleaded Kyllean. "You're hardly allowed out as it is. You can't possibly expect me to believe that you'd rather sit around here by yourself and, what—read?"

"As a matter of fact, that is exactly what I plan on doing. And I'm not one for breaking plans."

Aunt Melanie jumped into the fray as if she were a schoolgirl all over again. "Well, then. Suit yourself, Aynward. Kyllean, this invitation does not hinge upon Aynward's attendance. I intend to go, and I am also not one for breaking plans. You've time yet if you'd like to invite another friend."

Kyllean's eyes lit up. "Really?"

"Of course!" she said, with an expression of satisfaction on her face.

"Oh, thank you! You're the best aunt a friend could hope a friend to have."

Aynward rolled his eyes. Kyllean was as easy to please as a five-year-old at the winter solstice gifting. He'd be happy with a box of air so long as he was allowed to unwrap it.

Kyllean wolfed down the rest of his food then excused himself. "Thank you so very much, Miss Aunt Melanie, ma'am. I'll be back like a fat man barreling toward dessert."

He patted Aynward on the back. "Have a really good read"—then scooted out of the room.

Aynward sighed as Kyllean disappeared. "Well, I *suppose* I should go get myself freshened up before we leave."

"Change of heart, hmm?" asked his aunt, knowingly.

"My heart remains unchanged, it's just a little more on the annoyed side now."

"Glad you've decided to come. You won't be disappointed."

Aynward grudgingly left the room without another word. He could feel his aunt's clever smile the entire way.

Perturbed as Aynward was that Kyllean had volunteered them to go to the show, it was nothing compared with his irritation at Dolme imposing his own attendance. *This could hardly get worse.*

Aynward, Kyllean, and, no surprise, Minathi walked about twenty paces ahead of Aunt Melanie and Dolme. Aynward glanced behind once more, hoping in vain that Dolme would have changed his mind and headed back home. He hadn't. Speaking just loud enough for Dolme to hear, Aynward remarked, "Should have just taken him up on his offer to stay home if I didn't want him there. Not like *I'm* the one who wanted to come in the first place."

Kyllean laughed. "Can hardly blame the man for wishing to supervise you. Look what happened the last time you went out without a chaperone."

"I was ambushed, *by five people.* At least I walked out of the pub on my own two feet," argued Aynward as he gave Kyllean a shove. Kyllean shrieked as he stumbled directly into the path of a man walking in the other direction with an arm full of animal skins. Kyllean managed to dive to the ground just out of harm's way at the last second, still earning a number of imaginative curses from the angry merchant.

Kyllean groaned as he started to his feet a few paces back.

Minathi commented, "Perhaps it's the combination of the two of you that has the man tagging along to babysit." Flourishing her hands, she continued, "Can't even walk a few blocks without causing a stir."

Kyllean held up a hand to disagree but Minathi cut his words off before they left his mouth. "How many of Aynward's recent mishaps occurred absent of your involvement, Kyllean?" she teased.

Kyllean had caught up to them and held up a finger as he retorted. "I wasn't there when Aynward was ambushed, elsewise it would have been they who were strung from the tree."

Minathi tsked. "As Aynward said, you were unable to walk, my good sir. No, you would have done nothing but joined him in the tree."

Kyllean allowed a harrumph to escape him.

Aynward smiled. "I think I like her, Kyl."

Minathi skipped ahead. "Me too."

The walk to the inn was otherwise uneventful with the exception of being pulled aside by Dolme, aghast that everyone was calling him Aynward. Aynward had forgotten to inform his counselor that he had given up on the Annard alias weeks earlier. His admission had transformed Dolme from a mere irritation to a nearly insufferable burden, like the difference between a buzzing fly and a swarm of hungry mosquitoes.

Thank the gods, Kyllean drew Dolme's attention away as he pointed to the sky and hollered, "Look at that!" The sun had disappeared behind the buildings, replaced by the two moons as they melting into each other high above. Aynward had never heard of a dual-moon eclipse before that afternoon, but he had to admit it was a stunning sight to behold. The entire party stopped to admire the awe-inspiring scene, a cloudless sky illuminated by the haunting, bluish glow as the two moons appeared to collide above.

It was breathtaking.

"Just like that temple's sign," remarked Kyllean.

"Pagans," cursed Dolme, ruining the moment in his usual fashion.

The inn was located on the other side of the city, just over a thirty-minute walk from Aunt Melanie's place. The building itself wasn't much to look at from the outside, but the facade fell away when they stepped through the door. The beams were inlaid with exquisite scrollwork, the walls covered with mural after mural, and the ceiling was white with dark arching beams, forming the semblance of a great nautical skeleton. Aynward stared, mesmerized by the craftsmanship.

They followed a serving woman around the stage and finally settled at a table large enough to accommodate their group of five. "My name is Jessa, I'll be keeping you all comfortable this evening. Master Geddrick has made it especially clear that you are not to go without this evening, and he will accept no coinage from the Lady Melanie, or her companions."

Aynward's eyes widened. He leaned in and whispered to Kyllean, "Wish I had known—"

Kyllean jumped to his feet. "Two ales for myself and—let's see, one for Aynward? Minathi? Aunt Melanie? My good man Counselor Dolme, he could certainly benefit from a few bubbly—"

Dolme interrupted loudly enough that Jessa jumped. "We'll take water only. Thank you." His tone left no question about whether this change was going to be contested, and Jessa promptly went to fetch the water.

"Oh, come now," said Kyllean. "What's the harm in a few drinks? After all, we've got the great Counselor Dolmuevo in our company to ensure moral conduct. More important, the brew is free!"

"Not on my watch. Aynward has proven himself unable on *numerous* occasions to comport himself in permissible *adult* fashion. It is therefore suitable that he be prohibited from enjoying *adult* privileges."

"He's got you there," said Kyllean.

"Oh yes, and you're a regular gentleman, refined in your drunken stumblings, aren't you?" returned Aynward to his friend.

Kyllean straightened, chest out and rigid. "I most certainly am. No one drinks to excess with more grace than I."

"Yeah, mature like moldy cheese."

Minathi laughed at that, and Kyllean reddened.

Jessa interrupted the banter with their waters. Aynward shook off his frustration and grabbed his mug. He raised it high and said, "To finding merriment in spite of the oppressive regime that is Counselor

Dolme." The three students clanged mugs and Aynward took a large gulp.

He half choked as a burning sensation ran down his throat. Kyllean's reaction was similar. "What the—"

He caught his aunt's eye and she winked. Understanding dawned on him. She must have somehow signaled Jessa to switch his water for a sort of clear spirit. It was bitter and harsh and he had never developed an affinity for the stuff, but he could appreciate his aunt's attempt to circumvent Dolme's strangulating grip over all things fun.

He knew he needed to say something quick, before Dolme suspected anything was amiss.

"Well. I guess it's not so bad," he coughed. "Suppose I should have expected the water to be warm. Yet another reminder that we're not in the Kingdom." Chilled beverages were rare even among Kingdom royalty, and Dolme would know that, but it was the only thing he could think of in the moment.

Dolme's face remained impassive, which was generally the best one could hope for. Aynward took another swig of the clear beverage, working hard against his natural reaction to cringe at the awful taste. Were it not for the psychological pleasure he felt at defying Dolme, he would have called Jessa over to replace it with real water. This stuff tasted like poison, or what he imagined poison might taste like.

Minathi set her mug down and flared her eyes at him. She then looked to her "water" and back to him, attempting to communicate that her water was *not* water. Aynward tilted his head in the direction of his aunt then shrugged.

Aunt Melanie sat innocently holding her own cup, absently swirling the liquid as if nothing were amiss.

Minathi shook her head and rolled her eyes. Kyllean, conversely, was savoring the flavor with each sip. Aynward leaned over and whispered, "You're deranged, you do know that, right?"

Kyllean just smiled back at him and laughed. "I simply appreciate the finer things in life."

The conversation ended with the arrival of Gervais, who had managed to commandeer an empty chair in the overcrowded room. He pulled it up to their table, right between Aynward and Dolme.

"Greetings." He patted Aynward's shoulder. "Glad you decided to attend. I don't think you'll be disappointed. This troupe has been causing a lot of buzz around the city, but this is the first time they've advertised where they would be ahead of time."

Aynward was confused. "What's the point in doing a show if no one knows about it?"

"I've wondered the same thing and don't quite understand it, myself. Maybe that's part of what creates the draw. Like a woman playing hard to get?"

Gervais inclined his head toward Kyllean, who attempted to clasp Minathi's hand, only see her move it beyond his reach. Gervais appeared not to notice, saying, "It only increases the allure. Well, that and the fact this troupe's stories are tremendously unique. As far as I've been able to puzzle out, they've not repeated one show."

Aynward felt an eerie sensation develop in his stomach.

The boom of a gong reverberated through the room, causing several patrons to jump in their seats.

Aynward knew what he would see before he turned his head to the stage, yet he still felt the hair on his arms rise as his eyes registered the performer.

## CHAPTER 78

# KIBURE

AFTER SINDRI HAD FINISHED INTERPRETING for Kibure the essentials of what their uninvited guest had said, he quickly concluded that they had little choice but to do as requested. Not that he had much say in the matter once Sindri had made up her mind. It just so happened that they both came to the same conclusion on this one.

He did have one burning question that could no longer be ignored. "Sindri?"

"Yes," she said, already sounding annoyed that the conversation wasn't quite finished.

"I remember you saying that you could best almost any Klerósi priest. So was that man really so powerful that you were able to do nothing against him?"

He watched her reaction closely, and saw something unexpected. Instead of anger, he saw sorrow. Was she really that ashamed?

She finally answered, "I—I haven't been able to—" She shook her head, and tried to wipe away a tear discreetly. "I haven't been able to wield Klerós's power since the Kraken."

Kibure's eyes went wide. So that was why she'd refused to help him rescue Tenk! She couldn't. That also explained why she was so motivated to learn what she could of his magic. She wanted to get her own power back—or something to replace it.

"But how? Why?"

She sniffled, all attempts at hiding her despair gone. "When someone is cast out of the Kleról, whether it's because they could not summon enough power to be accepted, they are deemed heretical, or any number of other reasons, their connection to Klerós is revoked through the same spell I cast on you, the one to which you were immune. This castration spell severs the connection between the wielder and their source of power. I was fortunate to have escaped this during my flight from the Kleról, but a castration spell was used on me by whoever controlled that Kraken. I have not been able to wield my power since."

Kibure didn't know what to say. "I'm—sorry."

She didn't respond.

That night was one of the longest nights Kibure could remember in a long time. Lying in bed staring at the ceiling unable to sleep, he was eventually able to make out the various patterns in the wood as the sun crept over the horizon. He enjoyed trying to make sense out of the chaos. Each piece told a different story, and even if he didn't understand it, he liked the idea that each had its own unique path, each had a story that ended the same way, cut down and set into this ceiling. And not one of them likely had any choice in the matter. Much like his life. How much choice had he had in any one of the events that had transpired thus far? *Very little.*

He shook his head. No, that wasn't entirely true. He could have turned himself back over to the Lugienese. He could have stopped running. Sure, he couldn't control everything, but he did have *some* choice. He focused back in on the wood of the ceiling and felt pity for each and every board.

The intruder had not been lying about the local notoriety of The Feather. Their innkeeper was able to easily describe a route there. According to him, The Feather was just a short walk from where they stayed. This knowledge did little to ease the suffering of anticipation that had plagued Kibure throughout his sleepless night. Sindri had paced back and forth in their room all morning, unwilling to even humor any of his questions. It was nerve-racking, especially to see this reaction from the ordinarily unshakable Sindri. Kibure was surprised to note his own relief when she finally said it was time to leave. If they were going to die, he figured, best just be done with it.

Myriad sights and sounds attacked Kibure as he and Sindri walked the busy streets of Brinkwell. Sindri had asked for the most direct route to The Feather; their *visitor* having made it clear that they would be watched at all times, and things would become far less pleasant for them should they appear to do anything but attend this meeting. Walking in fear of the easily distinguishable Lugienese was something Kibure was growing accustomed to, but he now saw a potential enemy in every breathing soul in sight and imagined more in hiding just waiting for permission to strike. These suspicions turned his breakfast into poison.

Consequently, the short walk to The Feather seemed to last forever. Sindri finally stopped abruptly in the street, her head turned to the left. Kibure didn't have to frustrate himself with being unable to read the sign this time. The otherwise plain building consisted of two windows and a double door, above which rested a large framed carving of a silver feather.

"We're here. We're likely going to be asked questions. Don't say anything about your *magic*. As far as we know, you don't have any, at least not for now."

Kibure grunted his assent.

Without another word, Sindri started toward the door. Kibure took in a deep, shaky breath and followed.

A portly, brown-haired woman stood in argument with two men, gesturing to the room of fully occupied tables. The men were not pleased at being told to wait. Then she spotted Kibure and Sindri and snapped her fingers; a man materialized from around the corner and strode toward them. He wore the same plain black garb as the woman and spoke in the same unknown language as most of the people in the city. The message to follow him was understood by Kibure before Sindri even said, "Let's go."

The man brought them past tables bustling with activity, the two upset men at the door shouting curses from behind. Their escort brought them toward the back and Kibure swallowed hard as he spotted the man who had entered their room the night before. The mage lifted his chin and smiled. His countenance was as it had been the first time: a clouded riddle of expressions that left Kibure wondering if he were new to mankind, attempting to mock the mannerisms without mastering any.

The man sat with his back to the wall, holding Kibure's gaze as his hand moved to the seamless wall where a door materialized and opened. Then the mage's eyes returned to the beverage in front of him, while Kibure and Sindri followed their escort out of the room. An ominous click from behind caused Kibure to turn. To his dismay, the doorway dissolved once more into a seamless wall.

The room was bereft of furniture but for two tables at its center. One of them sat inside a canopy of nearly transparent fabric. Kibure noted that there were no visible exits to the room, or none that might be accessible by mundane means. Their escort approached the canopy and pulled a flap allowing them to enter and then urged them to sit. Once inside, Kibure realized that it was no longer transparent. Some sort of magic trick, he guessed. The escort said something he didn't understand then departed.

Kibure looked to Sindri. "What now?"

"We are to stay here. He's going to bring us some refreshment and notify our host of our arrival."

"Sindri, I don't like this. I don't like this at all. The door we entered— it vanished behind us. There's no way out of this room."

"We've no choice in the matter," she declared.

Kibure wanted to scream, wanted to run, wanted to fight, but refrained from each. Sindri was right. They had no choice in coming and he shouldn't expect their options to have increased upon entering the restaurant. They were at the mercy of whoever had summoned them; that was that. Kibure did notice that in his frustration he had at least managed to stop shaking.

The servant reentered the opaque screen and served them both a steaming beverage and biscuit along with a cut of glazed meat. Kibure salivated at the smell, but the taste of bile in the back of his mouth reminded him that keeping food down would be no small difficulty, that is if they survived long enough for it to matter.

After a few nibbles, he was surprised to find that his stomach felt a bit more settled. They picked at their food in silence until Kibure saw Sindri go rigid. He opened his mouth to ask her what was wrong but held his tongue because he felt the same thing. An odd calming sensation had trickled into his consciousness. His alarm at the change was short-lived, for the release of tension was so powerful that he couldn't help but embrace it, even knowing its source might have malicious intent. He hadn't felt this sort of peace since before leaving the drogal farm weeks earlier. Ever since, he had experienced varying levels of uncertainty, fear, dread, remorse, sorrow, and a storm of other emotions all lurking in the background even when not attacking him directly. The sudden freedom from that was euphoric.

Then he heard soft footsteps approaching and knew that this was the person who had called the meeting. The sound stopped at the other table, the one outside of the sheets obscuring the person's identity. A man's voice sounded, and even the magic could not fight Kibure's horror. The man spoke Lugienese.

## CHAPTER 79

# SINDRI

SINDRI RECOILED AT THE SOUND of the Lugienese language. Her thoughts clashed against one another like leaves in a storm. It didn't make sense. How could Klerósi priests have established such a strong network within a foreign land? And working with priests of another faith was blasphemous, yet the man who had entered their room the night before was no Lugienese. Had they truly sacrificed such highly valued tenants of the faith to achieve their goals? It seemed impossible.

*Stop this. He's talking.*

"Sindri, or so we've heard you called. You are Lugienese, yes?"

"Yes, well, I was." She was muttering like an idiot. "I am from the Empire, yes." *No sense lying about it.* "I was of the priesthood, but left in disgrace."

"And now you have come here, with someone who is *not* Lugienese."

"Yes." *And I am sitting in a chair and I cannot see you because you're hiding behind a screen. Does this man just like stating the obvious or is he going to actually ask a real question?*

The man was silent for an uncomfortable length of time, which gave her time to determine something of significance. His voice was familiar, recently familiar. The hollow sound to it was harder to make out because of the harsh accent he had while speaking Lugienese; he was not a native speaker. He had used the Kingdom tongue yesterday, but this *was* the man from last night. The man they had walked past minutes ago. Why would he need to obscure his identity behind the sheet when they already knew what he looked like? Something was definitely off here.

The fact that he spoke Lugienese gave her further reason to fear. He could be working with the Lugienese to recapture them. Perhaps he was going to ransom them.

And even if he was unaffiliated with the Lugienese, she was still in a room against her will, held by a man who could use magic to do with her and Kibure whatever he pleased.

"You are wondering why you've been brought here. Curious about my interest in you, and the reason for the current anonymity." Another pause. "I grant you those answers." He gave her a moment to digest that then continued.

"Your Lugienese origin combined with the nature of your inquiries around the city. That covers all three questions. And your answers to my questions now will determine our level of continued interest in you and your companion, and the extent of that future you will be allowed to have in this city."

*Okay, right to it then. Vague answers and threats.* This meeting was not off to a good start.

"Tell me, why have you come to this city?"

Sindri paused, considering exactly how to phrase her lie, especially considering the possibility that he was working with the priesthood.

A tingle ran down her spine; *magic.* She understood the purpose; this man wanted her to answer swiftly without time to craft each lie. She needed to stop analyzing everything or she'd really not have a future to worry about. Her eyes widened and darted about at the touch of magic, fearing what he might do with it. It wasn't being employed, *yet.*

"I—I—"

"Ah, so you do sense it then. We can get back to that first question in a bit. I'm inclined to believe that you may be telling the truth about having been a part of the priesthood. Yet you did not use magic when threatened yesterday. Were you expelled before learning to wield the power of the gods?"

How much could she tell without endangering herself and Kibure? She scowled in frustration. They were already in danger.

"I was removed from the priesthood for heresy. But I did learn a few spells before this time." No need to tell him more than necessary. And it was partly true.

"Yet you use none of your magic now. Why is this?"

Sindri ground her teeth. "They performed a castration spell, separating me from my former source of power."

"So you can no longer wield magic?"

"No." *Otherwise this situation would be quite the opposite right now.* "The Kleról does this to all dissident members."

The man was silent for a time, then replied. "So you're unable to touch his magic, yet you are able to sense the touch of mine. Interesting . . . let's get back to my earlier question. Why have you come to this city?"

She had rehearsed the lie in her head on the walk over, expecting this question. But now that she was here, she was no longer confident that it would serve. Moreover, she was no longer confident that it would benefit her cause. Instead she would answer the question truthfully, the consequences be what they may. She didn't know what faith this man professed, but whatever her answer, it was likely to be blasphemy anyhow, so what difference did it make? She had sought an audience with magic users in the city since her arrival and she had certainly found one. With death on the table, she had nothing else to lose.

"I seek to learn magic. The *other* magic. This is the short reason of why I was expelled from the Kleról, and I will not abandon it. The loss of Klerós's touch has only served to fuel my desire to learn this thing." This was also partially true, though she had never been formally expelled; she had run before that was possible. And with her crimes against the Kleról, she knew her penalty would be far worse than a mere castration and expulsion. She would be sent directly to the God-king himself were she captured.

"I see." This was followed by a dramatic pause. "And what of your silent friend? He is not Lugienese. He does not seem to be from anywhere known to—Drogen or Angolia. Yet he speaks only the Lugienese tongue."

She made to answer but he silenced her with his voice. "This question is for him. I have chosen to speak the Lugienese tongue for his benefit, after all."

If her fear had been a flower, it was now in full bloom.

"Kibure. Where are you from, originally? I have never seen your like."

She had not expected this, and she had found Kibure to be particularly bad at lying. This did not promise to go well.

Kibure seemed unfazed by the shift in the interrogation. He answered without a pause. "I was born on a Lugienese drogal farm. I only know what my musco told me of my heritage. My mother was found in the water, brought to the estate, and died while giving birth to me. I know nothing else."

"Your musco. You were a slave, then?"

"Yes."

"So how does a slave come to the Isles in tow with a disgraced Klerósi priestess?"

Sindri swallowed hard in fear of what he might reveal about himself, or about her former abilities.

"I was being brought to market for sale, for I am not a very good slave. But our vessel met dangerous waters and was destroyed. I fled the wreckage and crossed paths with Sindri. The gods smiled on me again, for she was on her way out of the country, as well. She allowed me to follow along and I have since pledged myself to helping her complete her quest. I am certain that I would not have escaped without her help. I owe her my life."

Sindri breathed a sigh of relief. Had she underestimated Kibure? He had responded with precisely enough detail for plausibility without compromising them further. Hope returned, if only a wisp. That tuft of hope, however, was smothered by the stifling doubt that came in the silence to follow. She couldn't be sure but she thought she heard whispering, but it was too faint and her current state of trepidation made her senses unreliable.

Then the silence was shattered by a different voice.

"They may live."

This was still in the Lugienese tongue, but the voice was not the same. *Well, that explains the veil.* It was this man's *employer.*

The familiar voice returned. "Very well."

A moment later, the sheets parted and the tall, spindly man stepped inside and opened his arms in the same passive gesture of peace he had used the night before. "You may return to your rooms. My compatriot wishes you to live. You will be contacted shortly with further instruction. Rest assured, your safety is secure so long as you don't try to leave the city. You will continue to be monitored for your own safety." He bowed and started to leave but turned. "My name is Draílock." And then he disappeared.

Sindri sat there speechless, emotionally drained. Kibure looked back at her, expression flat, eyes determined. Perhaps she needed to rethink her opinion of him. But she would have plenty of time to replay the interaction in her head later. For now, she just wished to get away from there. "Let's go."

They exited the room from a door that materialized from within the solid wall, its location different from the one they had entered through. It opened into an alley catercorner to the main entrance. They walked in silence, and Sindri bounced from thought to thought unable to focus on any one for long. She was too rattled to dissect the exchange just yet. Perhaps a few hours and a good meal would dismantle the confusion that afflicted her.

## CHAPTER 80

# GROBENNAR

ROBENNAR WINCED AS THE BLADE slid across his scalp. His translucent hair, the mark of his people, the chosen people, fell in a wet heap to the stone floor of the underground lair these men used as their headquarters. *Lord Klerós, forgive me.*

"There. Now, so long as you leave your silk reds here, you're welcome to go out and see the city before its great demise." The man who had just been demoted by virtue of Grobennar's arrival had convinced Grobennar of the purpose in remaining secreted here in Brinkwell, though not without great effort. Grobennar ground his teeth, frustrated partially by the lack of respect they offered their new leader and partly by his own lack of preparedness. He should have been sent to Brinkwell with a full briefing and objective instead of going in blind.

*This isn't Magog's doing. He's not the conniving type.* He narrowed his eyes as he imagined Rajuban's lies to Magog about his trust that Grobennar would be the perfect man for the job, all the while sabotaging his chances of success. He could see the new Fatu Mazi back at court laughing as he imagined Grobennar stomping around, botching their plans, while Rajuban secured his place of power alongside the Great Lord.

Grobennar shook off his frustration. *One thing at a time. First I need to foil that plan by ensuring Brinkwell is as ripe for the taking as the drogal of late fall. There won't be a sorcerer in all of Brinkwell left to resist the fleet when it arrives.*

"You—Baghel. You will give me a detailed tour of the city, *now*." Turning to another of the four priests in the room, the one who seemed to be in charge, he said, "You there, Hamid, I expect a full report on current Brinkwell leadership, political factions, guilds, militia, allies, religious groups, rebels, and anything else you think could possibly qualify as relevant to our goals. I want to know every single thing you know of this city, down to the most *infinitesimal* flakes. Anything you've reported back to Sire Karth—everything. *You* will pay for any future ignorance of mine in this regard. And I promise, should you fail me, you will learn exactly why I was once called Fatu Mazi, and why I will again hold that title."

As he and Baghel started up the stairs to the trap door, Grobennar overheard Hamid's distant voice say to the others still in the room, "Where the hell do you think you're going? This is on you as much as it is me. You're going to help!"

Grobennar smiled to himself. *Now, that's more like it.*

Jaween commented, *"I would be lying if I said I'm glad that these men have at last determined to follow your command. I grow bored of this place already. What good is a sword left always in its sheath?"*

Grobennar answered, "A sword is not used to cut steak, or to harvest wheat, it is used to strike down enemy combatants. We're in a city full of the latter. You'll get plenty of use in good time here, I'm sure of it."

*"If you say so,"* sighed Jaween.

## CHAPTER 81

# AYNWARD

A WOMAN STOOD ALONE ON THE stage. She was not the same woman he remembered, but he could make out the stitching on the left side of her gray cloak, an image of a circle resting on an open scroll. It was the same he'd seen on the performer on his first day in the city.

Her voice reached out and took hold of everyone in the audience. "Tonight I share a story from the past, as well as the future. This connection to the past runs further than any of this fallen world can remember."

The accent, too, was a near match to the one he recalled.

"Long, long ago, in a land forgotten to time, lost from reach, there was a great garden in the palace of a mighty king. Within this garden was a flower, the mere scent of which was said to bring about happiness and the blessings of eternal life. This king loved his people, and wished the fruits of his garden to be shared and cherished by all. No one who asked was refused entrance to enjoy them and breathe in their many gifts. People came from the furthest edges of the land to visit the garden, but it was forbidden to take from the garden."

Aynward rolled his eyes and leaned toward Kyllean to whisper something clever regarding the triviality of parables, but something about the conviction in the woman's voice caused him to forgo the comment.

"In time, the most powerful of the king's spirit-helpers grew envious of the love given to his master by his subjects. He whispered deception into the hearts of these men. One such man, a prince named Betrog, grew so jealous of the beauty and gifts of the king's garden that he attempted to create one of his own, one of equal splendor. But he found that even with the help of the Evil Spirit, he was unable to replicate the majesty and power of the eternal flowers. His heart hardened, and once again he gave in to the whispers of the Evil Spirit; he broke the sacred law. Taking seeds from the garden, he and the Evil Spirit fled the borders of their homeland in search of a new flower, one more beautiful and grand, filled with gifts greater even than the king's. They would create a new garden.

"Many people followed Betrog on his quest, craving the new gifts promised them. They traveled many years in search of fertile land where these seeds might grow, but they found none. The seeds they had stolen were sterile without the blessing given to their homeland by the one true god. Finally they discovered a land of rich soil, with flowers to rival what they had stolen. Betrog and his followers worked for many years cultivating what they'd found to exploit this beauty until they had achieved perfection. The Evil Spirit had grown more powerful as his following increased and granted greater and greater gifts to those who worshiped in the new garden.

"But not all were deceived. A small few wished to return to their home and the purity of the blessings therein. When they tried, however, they found that they no longer knew the way. They were forced to seek newer lands still, apart from Betrog.

"These people tried as best they could to return to the life they'd left behind. They used only the flowers of the king's garden they'd taken with them and followed the old laws. They called themselves Mezgaaval, and their new kingdom flourished, becoming a mighty nation. But the sins of their past were not forgotten, and they were not protected in the same way their ancestors had been.

"As the years turned into centuries, Betrog's people grew jealous of the might and splendor of the Mezgaaval. Centuries of warfare ensued, and in the end, the Mezgaaval were defeated. Before their defeat was final, however, they prayed for redemption. Their prayers were answered through the prophecy of a child who would bridge the old and the new. Many distrusted the fulfillment of this prophecy and joined the ranks of Betrog, while others grew tired of waiting and fled.

"A smaller few remained, clinging to the old ways, clinging to the truth in the fulfillment of the prophecy. Meanwhile, Betrog's new world has survived and prospered. The Evil Spirit has chosen his people carefully, and cast his own prophecies of inspiration. He has powered their magic more strongly than all of the other deceived ones. He and his host of followers move east, leaving only destruction in their wake. The promised Savior has been born, and Betrog's people must work to fulfill their own prophecies, that they might rule the world once and for all. A sign was given to us as a warning. The wolf will howl for all to hear when the moons join as one. The rest of his pack will come to join in the feast."

Her voice amplified in volume, echoing through the room. "The wolves come to feast on the flesh of the lamb." Aynward felt the words begin to echo in his skull. "The slaughter has already begun, and carnage will follow all the way to the last battle in the east. Death to all who remain."

The crowd was silent and unmoving, hanging on a thread. The actress remained still for several breaths before finally letting an inhuman screech escape her voice. It was both high pitched and deep, and reverberated in Aynward's head, but the word was unmistakable. *"Run!"*

Aynward closed his eyes as the sound in his skull reached its apex. When he finally opened them, the woman was gone.

## CHAPTER 82

# GROBENNAR

**M**AZI GROBENNAR'S FEET ACHED FROM the day's excursions. And he was certain he had seen less than half of the city. Yet he was hopeful about his prospects. According to Baghel, the Lugienese here had already eliminated one of the most obvious threats to a smooth Lugienese conquest. The Stone faith was purported to be the most powerful, and, as an indigenous faith, the largest of the blasphemous faiths in Brinkwell. Most of their clergymen had already been captured, castrated, and then eliminated.

"We left only the least powerful of their underlings alive to continue with the faith. We don't want the people here to understand what is coming."

"Yes, of course," Grobennar said absent-mindedly. He was tiring of the self-praise Baghel seemed intent on repeating. "What of—"

His question cut off as his focus shifted to the dark shape he saw fly from one rooftop to the next—a raaven. *But that can't be! I killed that little menace!*

His mind fought to deny what his eyes had just seen, but he replayed it in his head. The slender yet lengthy arms, the dexterous hands, and the beady eyes filled with ill intent; there could be no doubt, it was the raaven. His shock turned into anger at the resilience of the thing. But this also meant—*The Dark Lord's accomplice is here in the city. Perhaps Klerós smiles upon me after all. Redemption is truly close at hand.*

*"Ooh, the dark spirit is here in the city? Perhaps we'll have a chance to meet in a more intimate setting before this is through,"* cackled Jaween.

Baghel finally asked, "You were asking a question, Mazi?"

Grobennar looked to the place where the raaven had been, then shook off his stupor. "Ah, yes. So I was . . ."

They walked the darkened streets back to their headquarters as Baghel continued to educate Grobennar on their progress. "We have, unfortunately, in recent weeks, found that the number of other users currently willing to practice their respective witchcrafts seems to have dwindled well below our initial estimates of those in the city. It appears that many of the remaining heretics in this city have wizened to the disappearance of so many of their brethren, even if the public hasn't caught on. So, naturally, sniffing them out has become more trying as of late. And there is one particular group of witches we'll have to discuss at a later time. They seem intent on—"

Grobennar silenced the rambling fool with a hand. He sensed *something*; faint, but close. He could feel Jaween's consciousness wake at the touch of magic, his sensitivity often more adroit than Grobennar's own. "Someone is using magic."

He stopped in the middle of the narrow street and closed his eyes. Thin wisps of a foreign energy floated through the air like pollen. Baghel probably wouldn't have noticed.

Jaween whispered in his mind, *"It's coming from the northwest."* Grobennar opened his eyes to see a ramshackle building directly aligned with the power he sensed.

"In there," he said as he pointed. "Come." This would be his first in-person confrontation with a trained priest or priestess outside of the Klerósi faith. He had put down his fair share of tazamines, but they were unskilled, wild, untrained. His skin prickled with excitement at the prospect of a worthy opponent. What a strange sensation; he should have been more nervous.

The spirit's excitement was bubbling over, affecting Grobennar's feelings in turn. Better to go into the fight without apprehension, he supposed.

Baghel interrupted his musing. "Mazi Grobennar, Your Grace, this appears to be an inn. There will likely be many people inside."

"And?"

"Well, it's just—that means many witnesses."

Grobennar rounded on his servant. "Do you think me a fool?"

Baghel winced. "Of course not, it's just that—"

"Good." Grobennar lowered his tone to a deep rumble. "Follow me."

They entered a surprisingly spacious room, considering the outward appearance of the place. Grobennar was equally surprised to see the place filled to capacity. It looked like a service at the Kleról. *Just what poison are these heathens worshiping tonight?*

Grobennar could feel the magic more strongly once inside. Stepping past a thick man near the entrance, he began to see a pattern to the array of tables and chairs. They were positioned to view an elevated stage where stood a woman dressed in a thin gray cloak. She too was thin, and deathly pale, with dark hair like night.

Just then, he heard her voice reverberate unnaturally within his mind from across the room. She was more than thirty paces away, but he felt her gaze lock on his as she said, "The wolves come to feast on the flesh of the lamb."

*What is this heretic doing?*

Grobennar whispered to Baghel, "The woman on the platform. We mustn't let her escape."

Baghel didn't respond. Grobennar looked at his servant. Baghel stared at the woman with an expression of awe, and *fear?*

The weak-minded servant finally muttered, "It's one of *them*."

"What in the dark is that supposed to mean? Speak sense, man," growled Grobennar. But he sensed something from his connection with Jaween, as well. It wasn't fear. It was more a sense of strain, as if Jaween had eyes and was squinting hard to focus on a distant image.

Baghel finally opened his mouth to respond to Grobennar's command, but no words materialized from his mouth. Instead Grobennar's mind was bombarded by a powerful mental intrusion, a single message thrown forth like a hammer. "*Run!*"

Grobennar stumbled back, shocked at the strength of the mental intrusion. He blinked then surveyed the room. The mental push appeared to have affected everyone there equally. Jaween was no exception, releasing a high-pitched shriek of his own in response. *To project her voice into so many minds, and with such force, was no small feat of magic.*

When Grobennar looked back to the raised platform, it was bare. He scanned the room frantically. "Where'd she go?" said Grobennar, gripping Baghel's sleeve.

"I—I don't know. I took my eyes off of her and she was just—gone. Mazi Grobennar, we've met these wo—"

"Let's go," interrupted Grobennar. "She must have slipped out the back."

Grobennar didn't bother to see that he was followed. He would do this by himself if needed. There was something strange about this magic, and he was not going to let her get away.

Once outside, he ran. His legs felt weak after the long journey confined to the small spaces of a ship, but he ignored the aching burn. This was important. He rounded the corner to the back of the building just as the trail of a thin cloak disappeared around a corner. "There!"

By the time he turned the corner once more, he had closed the gap considerably. She wasn't running. He would catch her. She was walking blithely down the narrow, dimly lit street, completely alone. *Klerós, don't let me lose this prize. For your glory.*

He was only ten paces away when she rounded on him. Startled, Grobennar stopped where he was and drew Klerós's power through the stones in his rings, keeping the integrity of his bones intact. There was no telling what evil the woman might attempt to unleash.

"Do not bother," she warned in the language called the common tongue by those in this part of the world. "Your *god* has no power over me, servant of the Dark." She raised a straightened arm, palm extended toward him. A familiar pose.

*The witch is going to use her magic!*

Grobennar whispered a phrase of concentration before unleashing the spell that would cut her off from her false gods, indefinitely. The magic of this spell flowed with ease; he had stripped many apostates of their power. The witch's hand remained open while his spell consumed her. He lowered his own hand, satisfied.

Jaween bellowed a warning just as the thunderclap struck Grobennar, knocking him from his feet with the snap of breaking bones. The wind was stolen from his lungs as he landed, forcing him into a fit of painful gasps, followed by a string of coughs. He sucked in a breath full of air and released it in relief as Jaween healed what probably would have been several cracked ribs.

Grobennar stood in time to see the woman walking quickly away. *Her magic should be unreachable! She shouldn't have been able to strike me!*

Baghel reached him then, taking hold of his arm to help him up. "Mazi, are you injured?"

Grobennar yanked his arm free. "I'm fine."

He wasn't fine.

His body rebelled as he struggled to his knees, but he managed. *Can't let her get away!* He was just in time to unleash a bolt of searing energy toward the fleeing sorceress. But without so much as turning, she batted his magic away as if it was a stray leaf blown into her path.

*Impossible.*

Then she turned to regard the two priests, now some fifty paces away. She seemed to contemplate something, then, with only a distant flicker of magical warning, she snapped her wrist and something hard slammed into the former Fatu Mazi's face.

Grobennar saw stars as he rolled back to his stomach. *Wait.* When had he fallen? He pulled himself up to his knees and saw a single brick, drops of his blood coloring the otherwise gray material. By the time Grobennar recovered his wits and looked to where the sorceress had been, she was nowhere to be seen. He worked his aching jaw, then glanced over to the far wall where the brick had originated. The mortar had been completely dissolved surrounding a brick-shaped hole.

"What was that?" asked Grobennar as much to himself as to Jaween, and Baghel.

Baghel just whispered, "Witch."

Jaween remained uncharacteristically silent on the matter, before finally responding, "*Old magic.*"

## CHAPTER 83

# AYNWARD

AYNWARD LOOKED AROUND THE VAST room of the inn following the unsettling performance. He stared out at a room of dazed expressions. A few blinked away their confusion and chuckled; others wore looks of puzzlement, but most looked as if they'd just seen a long-dead enemy come to steal away with their children.

Kyllean, of course, joined those few who chuckled, but it was awkward, a defensive response to mask his own fear. "Well, that was uplifting, don't you think?"

Minathi responded, "More like off-putting."

Aynward opened his mouth to add to the conversation, if for no other reason than to combat the feeling of foreboding that developed in his chest. However, something captured his attention and only air escaped. He saw the back of a man no more than half his height. *Dwapek?* Why would he be here? He felt an involuntary shudder. That last part about wolves. Isn't that the way Dwapek had described the coming danger? He felt queasy, and the lasting flavor of the liquor did nothing to help the situation. His mouth hung open and he lifted his arm to point, but the small form had been swallowed by the crowd.

Gervais spoke up. "Is everything all right, my good sir?"

"I—"

He swallowed the bile in his throat. "Yes. I—I just need some water." He grabbed for his own, remembered that it wasn't actually water, then felt the tightness in his throat move to his mouth. The contents of his supper would be making an appearance any second. He grabbed Dolme's recently refilled mug. Without concern for how he would react, Aynward took several large swallows of the water. He wiped his mouth and breathed a sigh of relief. With the fear that he would retch right there at the table abated, he decided he was safe to move.

Dolme stood abruptly, his chair tipping over behind him in the process. "How dare you! Where are your manners? I wasn't finished with that."

Aynward had too many thoughts running rampant in his head. He needed to get away from the noise to sort them out. "Sorry. Yell at me tomorrow if you're still thirsty, would you? I think I'm coming down with something."

"You're going to come down with a smack to the back of the head if you don't show some respect." *Well, Dolme seems his normal, irritable self again.*

Aunt Melanie chimed in, "Easy on the boy, Dolmuevo. Didn't you see his face? Would you rather know how well he chewed his supper, or have your mug of water?"

That deflated Dolme's ire. He grunted in reply.

"Aynward, let's get you home so you can sleep off whatever it is that's at your stomach." She stepped around Aynward to rub his back like his mother used to when he was a child. He was too flummoxed and nauseated to shoo her away.

She whispered to him, "Not one for the liquor, aye?"

She wasn't wrong, though in truth, he was certain that the cause of his discomfort went far beyond the half-finished drink he'd left on the table.

He just nodded and turned toward the door. "I'm okay. Thanks, Aunt Mel."

Kyllean and Minathi came up alongside as the group moved toward the door. He looked about and saw that the buzz of the room had resumed its pace, as if nothing had happened. He had seen expressions of concern from many in the audience when the story had finished, but it had apparently not left a lasting impression. People were back to laughing, drinking, and playing cards.

Kyllean spoke softly enough for Dolme not to hear. "That drink not sitting well with you, I take it?"

Aynward shook his head. "Not sure. Something about—"

He didn't know how to explain it, and wasn't certain why he was bothered by the performance, not exactly. He did know one thing that held his attention: "Dwapek was here."

"Wait—what? He never leaves the university proper, like, *ever*. At least that's what I've heard," said Kyllean.

"Well, unless there is another three-foot-tall, robe-wearing Renzik in the city, he was here."

"Huh," was all Kyllean managed.

Minathi must have overheard. "That's strange, especially considering the woman's story. Almost like she read from one of the texts we've been reading, then added her own twist at the end."

Aynward's eyes widened. "Think they're connected? Could Dwapek somehow be involved with this troupe?"

They stepped out into the crisp night air, which helped Aynward's queasy stomach.

Kyllean said, "It seems like too strong a coincidence for them to not be."

Aynward felt self-conscious about continuing their conversation once out in the open where their voices would carry to all nearby ears. Gervais made him especially uneasy, silently walking alongside, his indifference seeming almost contrived. Aynward wasn't comfortable pursuing the conversation any further with such an audience.

He said, "Let's get some rest and talk about this tomorrow."

Minathi had looked over at him and noticed Dolme and Gervais, and nodded her understanding. "Good idea," she said.

Kyllean looked at the both of them, eyes squinting in confusion at the sudden end to the conversation. He finally caught Minathi's *just trust me* expression and kept quiet.

The conversation drifted toward lighter fare, and shortly they were parting ways by the university gate. Once Kyllean and Minathi had split off, Gervais put a hand out to separate Aynward from Dolme and his aunt. "Go on ahead; we'll catch up in a few."

Aynward had a strong suspicion about the topic of this conversation.

"So, Aynward. How goes your progress toward fulfilling your end of our little deal?"

*Right to it, then.* "So far I've—not very well. I've been down there, to the Special Collections, but the archives are under constant surveillance by a guard. Plus, there's the guard above there just to get into the Special Collections area. I can't imagine how anyone would break in to steal so much as a glance in the room, let alone an actual tome. It has to be an inside job. But finding a way to uncover the culprit behind it is no small task."

Gervais seemed unperturbed. "Perhaps a list of those employed by the library would be a good starting point."

Aynward looked over at him, considering the suggestion. "Hadn't thought of that. I mean, that information would certainly make it easier to narrow down. But that's kind of an odd thing to inquire about, don't you think?"

Gervais smiled. "Well, there we have it. Let's make things easier to narrow down, then."

He produced a piece of parchment from within his cloak and extended it toward Aynward, who stood dumbfounded. He had to see it for himself before commenting. He unfurled a detailed list containing not only employees of the archives, but also the entire library staff, approved guards included.

"How did you—"

The servant held up a hand. "I am not without resources. Even still, resources alone are not enough."

Aynward's heartbeat ramped up. He considered how he might use the list to achieve his end, and was again frustrated by his limitations. Even with the list, he couldn't follow each person around all day waiting for them to come out of work, then pat them down to see if they might have snagged a book on that particular day.

Gervais sensed Aynward's doubts. "I find that when one wants something badly enough, one finds ways to achieve it."

*How badly do I want Gervais's money?*

Aynward shook his head and extended the parchment back toward Gervais, who made no move to take it. "As much as I would love to reap the rewards of fulfilling my end of our exchange, I'm just not desperate enough to exhaust all my time on something I'm not even sure *can* be done. I'll keep my eyes and ears open, but don't count on me. I'm sorry."

"Very well. The choice is yours. I will begin working other angles. But the deal stands until such time as I procure the text by another means."

He waved his hand at the list. "Keep it. It may prove valuable yet."

They had reached the final stretch of the walk home from the university, and Dolme and Aunt Melanie could again be seen up ahead of them. Gervais slowed. "I have other things to attend to tonight. You are a safe distance from your residence. Get some rest, you look to be in desperate need of it. Good evening."

The servant, who seemed much more than a servant, turned down a side street and disappeared into the lengthening shadows, leaving Aynward alone with his many thoughts.

He stared off into the night sky. He could only see one moon, but it glowed brighter than any moon he'd ever seen. This *was* the dual-moon eclipse. Yet for such a beautiful sight, it brought with it ominous tidings.

## CHAPTER 84

# KIBURE

A HEAVY KNOCK ON THE DOOR the next morning dragged Kibure's unwilling mind from slumber. To his surprise, Sindri did not yet appear to be awake as he walked toward the door. She let out a sound somewhere between a moan and a yawn and rolled over to face his direction, but her eyes remained closed.

"Psst, Sindri."

Nothing. Kibure didn't think it wise to open the door without her conscious.

"Sindri."

Her eyes flew open and she sat up looking like she was ready to kill the next thing to move. Kibure remained still. "Sindri, someone's at the door," he whispered.

As if on cue, the knock repeated.

She swung her legs around to sit at the edge, then nodded toward the door. "Open it."

Kibure unhitched the lock and pulled. He was surprised to see the old, bony wizard again; it brought him no joy.

Speaking in accented Lugienese, the wizard began, "My apologies for the early hour, but my days have become quite busy as of late." He made a gesture with his head and arms that Kibure didn't understand, then continued, "Nevertheless your reason for coming to this city begins its fulfillment today. But we must first travel to a safe location."

Sindri spoke before he had turned. "The boy comes, too."

"We expected as much. I'll be downstairs when you're ready."

Kibure and Sindri shared a look. Sindri slipped into her traveling clothes while Kibure made no effort to hurry. Then he reminded himself that this was why Sindri had come here. She had been searching for this opportunity for half a decade, if she was to be believed. Kibure knew that he too needed to be able to control his magic, though he had not had an episode or dream in a few weeks.

Now that the opportunity was actually here, he wasn't sure how ready he was. To pursue his magic was to pursue the most powerful wizards in the world, who had chased him halfway across Angolia, and still likely had agents looking for him. It also brought up the nightmares that had plagued him, and the unanswerable mystery of Rave, who had saved his life on several occasions. Since he had escaped the Lugienese, spent weeks without a nightmare, and his magic seemed to have gone missing, he felt little compulsion to dig back into any of it. He was happy to leave it all behind, continue east, and perhaps someday wonder about the strange things that had happened to him as a child.

One look at Sindri's face told him his procrastination was over. He finished putting on the uncomfortable articles of clothing worn by the people of this peculiar land and followed her down the stairs to meet Draílock.

They zigzagged along numerous side streets before stopping in front of a row of small buildings, behind which was tall stone wall. Curious as always about city structures, Kibure asked, "Why the wall in the middle of a city?"

"Keeps the goings-on of the university separate from the rest of the city." Draílock gestured toward the closest of the buildings. "Let's go in and I'll answer your question."

Once inside, Draílock flourished his hands. "This is my home. But we're going somewhere more secure for your training."

He led them to a small room and opened a smaller door in the corner. Sindri finally spoke up. "What are you doing in the closet?"

Without turning to acknowledge her, he said in muffled speech, "You'll see."

They waited patiently for an uncomfortable period before they heard a click and Draílock disappeared from view. His voice echoed up to them, "Come on down."

Sindri led the way without a word, but Kibure could tell she was growing uncomfortable. They descended a ladder. Kibure's own apprehension intensified when the opening above clicked shut, cutting off all natural lighting.

"Come," Draílock said before Kibure had any more time to consider. The glowing orbs that lined the underground corridor put Kibure slightly more at ease as they followed, but it was still darker and less aboveground than he would have liked.

The tunnel dead-ended ahead, but Draílock felt the wall and depressed a point that resulted in an additional opening. They followed him into a room.

## CHAPTER 85

# SINDRI

THE ENTIRE ROOM WAS LINED with a narrow channel within which burned an unnatural fire. The flicker of flames that encircled them cast a red hue on Draílock's face, making an already ominous situation seem perilous. But Sindri hung to the promise of training, perhaps to her own detriment.

"Please, have a seat," said Draílock, motioning to one of the two couches in the room. He took the lead in doing so, facing them as they positioned themselves across from a low, stone table. Sindri was surprised at the comfort of the spotless, white cushions; especially as she recognized that the couch itself was hewn from the very stone they walked upon.

As excited as she was to begin her training, she felt compelled to ask, "Is this training so dangerous that we must hide beneath the ground?"

"The training itself? No. However, the detection of magic is something we are becoming more cognizant of. As you must already know, the use of magic is detectable by anyone sensitive to it. There are rumors of priests and even herb gatherers disappearing inconspicuously over the last few weeks."

"You mean, someone is capturing wielders in this city?" Sindri asked in concern.

"We've no concrete leads yet, but my compatriot has his suspicions. We're simply taking precautions against unnecessary uses of magic, and doing our best to hide everything else. This room, for instance, has been enchanted to mask the use of magic."

Sindri didn't like the sound of that at all, especially after having seen those Lugienese in the city just days earlier. Then again, this could also be a ruse to keep her from practicing magic outside the confines of this room. If so, it was the kind of ruse that would work.

"Do you wish to begin your training?" Draílock looked from Sindri to Kibure and back again.

"Yes," Sindri finally said.

"Very well. Before we begin trying to tap into the source, you need to understand some of the principles of magic you were likely never taught. My compatriot discovered these truths for himself not more than thirty years ago, yet he still works to understand them more fully. Suffice it to say, ateré magic is the single most complicated study known to man, yet it's also the simplest." Putting up a hand, he added, "No, that's not supposed to make sense. Not yet, anyhow."

He brought his hand to his chin and turned his eyes to the ceiling. "Where to begin? Hmm. Well, for starters, it has been discovered that there are two basic streams of magic, if you will. The first is certainly the most common, that which you've always attributed to your god Klerós. I will refer to this as priestly magic, while you may also hear it called *diomancy*, as the power is summoned from a dios, or god. This priestly magic is similar from one religion to the next. One learns to hone in on the magical energy from their god or gods through focused prayer. One must learn the discipline of compartmentalizing the mind to channel it, funnel the appropriate amount of magic for a given task, control it, et cetera. You, Sindri, likely have all of those skills, which will in some ways make learning to control the other form of magic easier for you, so long as you can learn to tap into it and learn the limitations of your surroundings. It can otherwise be more dangerous than priestly magic.

You also have to consider the same bone mass limitations. The learning curve for your friend here will likely be steeper, as the skills of control, compartmentalization, and channeling, along with bone mass degradation, will be longer in the learning."

Draílock leaned forward, placing his elbows on his knees. "The origin of the magic harnessed from the gods is still something we don't exactly understand because of the many contradictions we've seen, historically speaking. But the other form of lesser-known magic is quite a bit simpler, though perhaps more challenging to discover and use. Ateré magic exists—well—everywhere. The world is filled with its energy."

"Meaning?" interrupted Sindri.

"*Meaning*, everything, dead or alive, has magical potential within it, and we can borrow portions of that power for our use. I'll get into more detail about how this works later. First we need to discuss the dangers that lie within. Sindri, you know the risk of deteriorating bone mass. This same danger exists for ateré magic, and at a similar rate. Would you like to explain this aspect to Kibure yourself?"

"I—sure." *Where to begin?* Turning to Kibure, she said, "Well, in essence, channeling magic weakens your bones." She considered for a moment that perhaps what she had been told by the Kleról was not accurate, but decided that didn't much matter. "The way it was explained to me was that Klerós created mankind without the need to use magic. It's said that it wasn't until the Great Corruption that we humans had a need to channel his power and only as a way of combating the Dark Lord. But Klerós did not want anyone to become too powerful, lest they too become corrupted, so he placed upon us limitations on how much we could safely channel at a given time. So when you channel magic, it draws strength from your bones. If you were to continue using magic without giving your bones time to repair themselves, you could fall apart. I've only seen it once, in training. Two young lads trying to settle the score on who was more powerful; by the time they were finished, both had broken legs, and one fell forward, shattering several other bones in the fall. He was lucky to have survived."

Kibure's eyes were wide with fear.

Draílock smiled. "You needn't worry, Kibure. You'll have time to practice in small doses to master your limitations."

Then speaking to both, he added, "That said, the strain that channeling magic places on one's bones is real. We believe that even priestly users are utilizing a sliver of their own internal ateré magic, even when they channel magic from their gods, and that this is what weakens their bones."

He held up a finger to stop Sindri's forthcoming question. "The density of organic material within an object determines how much energy may be drawn from it. When channeling, your body defaults to the hardest object connected to your body, your bones. This is why many priests wear gems to protect themselves from bone loss, am I right?"

Sindri nodded. This was something she was aware of, but had never understood the rationale behind the function. In light of what Draílock said, it made perfect sense. When wearing gemstones, the channeling process drew power from the object touching one's skin, instead of from the bones themselves.

"Metals and precious stones tend to maintain their density, meaning, they allow you to channel their excess energy to a certain point, but retain enough at all times to prevent themselves from losing form. Therefore, one can draw upon their power without ruining them. They will recharge automatically, just like our bones do. Once that energy has been used, it will slowly leak its way back into the original object. That's the simple explanation. What's important for you to understand is that if you decide to start channeling magic somewhere that has no metal or precious stones, you may wind up drawing on softer objects around you. You may do this anyhow if you're not careful, as softer objects tend to have a weaker hold on their energy. This is where things can become dangerous. For instance, you could draw on the wooden support beams within a room to the point where they lose their stability, or dissolve altogether. Next thing you know, the roof comes crashing down on you."

Sindri looked at Kibure and recalled him suddenly falling through a hole in the deck of the ship during the Kraken attack. Is that what had happened—he had used ateré magic?

Draílock continued, "So it is very important to make sure you're not walking around the city experimenting with these powers. They can be very dangerous if not managed properly. You need to develop the dexterity to draw on specific objects of your choosing, and be aware of which ones will hold their form in addition to knowing how much you can draw without destroying your internal composition. But, before any of that becomes much of a concern, one must first be able to sense *that* magic and draw upon it."

He walked over to the side of the room to fetch a small container. Placing it on the table, he pulled a cloth from the top to reveal a box filled with small black objects. Sindri blinked to be certain; *Dark Lord below, they're moving!*

Sindri looked to Kibure to measure his reaction. He merely frowned. "Crickets?"

Draílock leaned back in the sofa and brought his hands back behind his long head. "Crickets, indeed. We've found them most conducive to first leaners of ateré magic. See, the magic in living objects tends to be easier to detect. They all give off small bits of energy since the matter in them isn't quite so static, like it would be in, say, a stone or a gem. However, it's also not as strong, since the density is far less than that of a stone or a gem. But crickets, having the hard exoskeletons, while also being alive and numerous, make suitable candidates for training. They're also safer than most objects, since living organisms are more difficult to draw from. You may feel their magic, but harnessing it is more difficult because living beings tend to have an affinity for staying alive, and hold tightly to their own energy. Dead things, on the other hand . . ."

Sindri thought of something just then and blurted, "Does this mean an ateré wielder could sap energy from another human's bones? Could you kill someone in this fashion?"

Draílock smiled. "Theoretically—perhaps. But the larger the object, the stronger its hold to its energy, especially when it comes to living organisms. The amount of your own bone mass needed to draw from someone else's bones would make the process inversely efficient."

Sindri said, "Meaning?"

"Meaning it would take more of one's own bone mass to tug on the energy of the other person's bone mass, so you would shatter your own bones first. In fact, I'm not certain that it would be possible to draw from another's bones at all." Then his finger went to his chin in thought. "Although . . . if the other person had weakened themselves to the point of critical bone loss, their body would be more vulnerable in that state. Hmmm. So possibly, given the right conditions. I have never heard of such an occurrence. I will have to ask my compatriot. He has had more dealings in such matters."

Looking back to the box of creepy critters, an uncomfortable Sindri asked, "So what are we to do with these crickets?"

Draílock reached into the box and removed a small black cricket, held upside down by the leg. "Hold out your hand."

Sindri stared at him, incredulous. "You want me to hold on to that wretched bug?"

Kibure surprised her by reaching out and taking the critter in his own hand. Crickets were almost as bad as spiders in her opinion. But as revolting as the prospect was, with Kibure so eagerly participating, she could hardly refuse.

She reached into the box herself, ignoring the involuntary scrunching of her nose and tightening of her lips, and took hold of one. Cupping it between both hands to keep it from escaping, she said, "Okay, now what?"

Draílock remained calm as he said, "You must clear your mind and focus on the cricket. Well, not the cricket itself, but on the energy within. It will be a very small amount, much less than what you were likely accustomed to funneling from Klerós, but it *is* there. You, Sindri, already have the ability to sense the use of expended ateré magic; you have proven as much already. This energy is similar, but in its natural form will feel *different*. The untrained mind will naturally be blind to it. It will feel like a tiny ripple in the air, a wisp, gone again in a blink. You must then progress toward holding on to that ripple, that sense of the magic. Once you can feel it, and hold it in your mind, you may begin the process of borrowing portions of its energy. The density of the object will determine how much you can draw. It will also determine whether the object will retain its form, or if the object is likely to dissolve when too much is drawn. You needn't worry about this with regard to the crickets. Living objects are almost impossible to overdraw."

Draílock smiled and said, "Begin."

Sindri looked over to Kibure, his eyes already closed in concentration. *Guess I'd better get started.* She closed her own eyes and reached her consciousness out to feel for the magic in the cricket. She cleared her mind of all thought, much as she had been trained to do in the Kleról, then focused all of her attention on the dreadful insect cupped in her hands. She could feel the tiny legs touching the delicate skin of her palm, and pushed beyond revulsion to empty her mind to work deeper toward the energy of the cricket itself. Moments turned into minutes. *Nothing.*

Recognition that time had passed in this state without so much as a tickle of sensation akin to magic returned her to the present. A rush of emotions flooded in: fear, doubt, and frustration all fought for control. She blocked them out, replacing them by sheer determination before plunging her attention back into the cricket. Time stretched on without any notice of its passing until the silence was shattered by a distant voice. *Is this the cricket speaking? Does it have consciousness?* Louder now, Sindri recognized the sound, and the world came rushing back toward her, her disappointment boundless. *Draílock.* The name was a curse in the current circumstance.

"Our time is up for today."

Sindri shook off the trancelike effects of deep concentration and said, "But I felt nothing! How can we end without any progress?" Then another thought occurred to her, one that made her feel foolish for not yet considering. "There is a spell to reverse the castration spell that severed my link to diomancy, as you called it. Can you perform such a spell on me?"

He shrugged. "Perhaps. My compatriot would be more qualified to perform such a trick, though this is not to say he would be willing to do so just yet. I will speak with him about such. Anyhow, I wouldn't say that there was no progress." He looked to where Kibure sat, but Kibure returned an expression of frustration, remaining silent. "We will meet again in two days' time."

Rising to his feet, Draílock said, "Do not worry yourself over failure on your first attempt. I too came from a clergyman's background, and while I was unable to sense ateré power for weeks, it did eventually reveal itself to me. Once you find it, you will progress quickly. It wasn't until I stopped trying that I felt my first touch of the ateré, and it wasn't during a session. I would caution against this if possible. The temptation to use the magic once you feel it will be strong. We don't want to add you and your friend here to the list of missing people within the city."

Kibure stood and started toward the door, and Sindri reluctantly followed. Draílock said from behind them, "I will open the latch to my home, then a servant will escort you the rest of the way."

Moments later the corridor lit up as the ceiling to the closet above them illuminated the ladder. Draílock warned again, "Be sure and avoid the temptation to seek after ateré until our next session." He started back in the direction of the enchanted room but stopped and turned. "Ah yes, I nearly forgot. Sindri, you have been enrolled in a course at the university. You will attend this class tomorrow, under escort. I will see the both of you here in two days' time for your next session. You will meet me upstairs at my home."

Back at the inn, darkness had won the battle with the light of a weakening day. Sindri and Kibure sat at the end of their small beds, consumed by thought. Sindri wondered, what was this university course? Why had she been enrolled in it? What did Draílock mean when he replied to her with the implication that there had been at least *some* progress in their training? He had looked at Kibure when he said it, but Kibure hadn't spoken since to confirm. She could resist that particular question no longer.

"You have been very quiet since our training. Draílock implied that you felt the ateré. Is this true?"

Kibure's shadowed face remained downcast, peering into the very soul of the floorboards. "Perhaps Draílock hoped to inspire you through jealousy. He seems to have picked up on that particular weakness of yours."

"And you're deflecting the question. Seems you're always clinging to one secret or another."

Kibure looked up, jaw set, face still shrouded in darkness. "Believe whatever you want. Nothing happened." He crawled under the covers without another word.

## CHAPTER 86

# GROBENNAR

GROBENNAR BRISTLED AS HE PREPARED to berate his four under-lings. Baghel especially should have warned him about a cult of users able to defend against Klerós's power. These four were lucky he hadn't perished in the fight. He vowed that if ghosts were real, he would remain as such before heading to the eternal bliss just so he could seek revenge if he perished on account of their ineptitude.

The most infuriating predicament he faced at the moment was that he couldn't unleash the firestorm he wished upon them because it would notify any other magic users of their location within the city, undermining the entire operation!

He had them assembled in the largest room of their underground lair. "I don't know what's worse, the incompetence or the disrespect! What am I to do with the lot of you?" He paused in honest consideration. The threat of magical punishment held no weight. *But maybe—*

"Perhaps I should simply contact Magog directly to inform him that I'll be needing new assistance here in Brinkwell." *No matter that I would need all of their powers combined to be able to communicate at such a distance, and even so, I don't have enough jewelry to protect myself from the bone-burn from channeling the requisite power. A letter, perhaps.* "Inform him that you fools have botched the preparation so badly that he'll have to postpone the invasion until I receive reasonably competent help just to clean up your mess!"

Grobennar smiled to himself as they squirmed beneath his false threat. Fear of Magog's wrath was something people simply didn't speak of, not as he did. But he was no ordinary man. He would be the Fatu Mazi as he once had been, the most powerful mortal man in the world. He also knew that in order to regain his rightful seat, he would need to succeed where he was expected to fail.

"So, any takers? Shall I prepare my mind for contact?"

There was a mishmash of what sounded to be sincere apologies. They may not have been sorry for the reasons he wished, but it was a start. "Well—now that I have your attention, perhaps one of you would like to explain just how in the lower hells that witch was able to shield herself from a castration spell, and defend my attacks as if I were no more a threat than the moon is warm."

No one spoke. Grobennar began to shake. He opened and closed his fists, then took hold of the closest object he could lift, a chair. The former Fatu Mazi threw the chair into the stone wall as hard he could manage. The cursed thing didn't even have the courtesy to break! Instead it bounced back to land on his foot. He ignored the pain.

*"I know you told me to remain silent, but I can't help wondering what might happen if you allowed me to persuade one of them. Use me . . ."* Jaween let the idea linger in Grobennar's mind. It was an enticing offer, but Grobennar did not bite.

He took in a deep breath, then released it. *Focus. You can't reveal your secret to them, for to do so would mean you would have to kill them. And you can't just kill them. You need them, at least for now.* He had to remind himself of this unfortunate truth more than he liked. He let out another breath. *Okay. Let's get some answers.*

"I'm going to pretend this is review for you, that you're all familiar with the history of our people's flight to Angolia. Lesante—"

He twirled his finger to the sky in acknowledgment of the first seer of the faith. "Lesante battled and defeated a superior force only after

Klerós proved himself to be the one true god, rendering the power of their enemies' false gods flaccid when in direct conflict with his own power. So unless something has changed, *these* heretics should *not* be able to wield their power against us, not after we use Klerós's power to castrate them!"

Baghel finally responded. "If I may . . ." He spoke in a calm, respectful tone. Grobennar detected none of the condescension from the day prior. "What transpired yesterday was a repeat of our only other direct encounter with one of these—*women*. Three weeks past, I cornered one and cast a spell of castration, followed by immobilization, and, as with this evening, both were equally ineffective. The enemy then somehow dissolved the wooden floor I'd been standing on, causing me to land unceremoniously into a storage cellar. I was fortunate to live to tell the tale. We've been working to catch one of them unawares, or, better yet, discover the whereabouts of their nest. It is my belief that direct confrontation is too dangerous until we know more. And I do apologize for not getting into this from the beginning. I didn't trust that you would believe us about these witches. I would have had difficulty with the concept myself had I not seen it with my own eyes. Yet you are correct, Mazi, it should not have been withheld from you at our discretion.

"I've been asking around about these women, but no one seems to know much more than we do. We do know that these witches aren't native to the city and haven't been here for more than a year. It seems they arrived about the same time we did. But I've been gathering texts in the hope that one may clue us in on who they might be. Did you notice the symbol on her cloak?"

Grobennar thought back and recalled seeing some sort of image, but nothing specific. He shook his head.

Baghel continued, "It's an image of a circle overlaying an open scroll. Unfortunately, our knowledge of the goings-on of the Drogen continent since our people's departure more than two thousand years ago is nearly nonexistent. But we've begun asking questions of the locals, and reading, and we're learning quite a bit. We're working to uncover anything we can. I have a contact with indirect access to the university library.

After exhausting the cataloged texts there, we've begun obtaining some of the rarer, older texts that are no longer in circulation. We have them in the next room. This appears to be our best source of information in the city. I'm hoping to find a reference to this symbol or a group that fits their description; nothing yet."

Baghel hung his head in submission, but Grobennar saw the remaining flare of defiance. Yet the man was right. Could he blame Baghel? Would he have acted differently had he been warned of these witches? Perhaps he would have attempted more stealth, but he would hardly have believed that he could be bested by some foreign witch in direct magical combat. Grobennar ground his teeth.

Nevertheless he needed to send a message to these men. Allowing another deep breath to exit his lungs, Grobennar settled on recourse. Without any warning, he leaped into the air in a spinning motion, extending his right leg as he spun. Then, with a satisfying crunch, the hard bone of his ankle slammed into the side of the unexpecting Baghel's face, toppling him. Grobennar landed gracefully on his feet.

*"Splendid! Just marvelous! Now we're getting somewhere!"* cheered Jaween.

Grobennar masked his own pleasure with an icy calm. "You are correct, servant. You should not have withheld vital information from your mazi. And you will *not* do so again. That was your last warning, one more than should have been granted. Next time, I'll be sending for aid directly from Magog himself"—he twirled his finger to the heavens—"along with the sad news of a priest who lost his life to the evil we face here."

The response was the most sincere he had seen from Baghel yet. The rebellion went from his eyes. Grobennar had broken him. *Good.* "Now, let us begin the work we were sent here to complete. Let's get our hands on more of these texts. And this time, tell me *everything*. I don't wish to have to hurt any of you again."

Grobennar shot Baghel one last icy stare. The man was standing back up and wiping his bloody lip, but his expression was one of resigned acceptance.

Jaween giggled in Grobennar's head. *"Oh yes. That one will trouble you no further. Well done, indeed!"*

Baghel said in the most respectful of tones, "Please follow me. We've much to discuss."

Grobennar shook his head. He had something else that needed to be done at the moment. "Your willingness to do the Lord's will is noted. We will resume in earnest tomorrow. There is something I wish to do, and do alone. Be prepared to assist me should I call."

*The Evil One's servant is here somewhere. Jaween and I must find and capture him if possible, kill him if not. Either way, this takes precedence. Then I can deal with the witches.*

## CHAPTER 87

# AYNWARD

A YNWARD LENGTHENED HIS STRIDE, TRYING to overcome the tingling in his stomach, his nerves. He knew that as soon as he stopped moving, his body would begin to shake. He had picked up some cheap, common clothes earlier that day, but he still felt the stares of people who seemed to intuit that he didn't belong among them. *It's just your imagination. Keep moving.*

After his conversation with Gervais, he had enjoyed a lunch sprinkled with fruitless discussion between Minathi and Kyllean about having seen Dwapek at the show. He had then taken his leave to do some asking around at the university about where one might find expensive, hard to come by, and possibly illegally obtained items. This eventually brought him to a place near the harbor. It had taken some convincing, but Gervais had finally parted with several coins as a means of loosening lips. It had seemed like a good idea at the time, but he now questioned his judgment as he navigated one of the most poorly patrolled parts of the city at dusk.

He was looking for a shop sign with three interlocking circles, called a pingus. This was apparently the mark of such an establishment. He had been told that this was a pawn market for lending to those who hadn't the reputation or sturdy enough collateral to receive traditional bank loans. It was also a place where one might rid oneself of expensive items obtained by unscrupulous means. Aynward figured stolen, expensive books might qualify.

He spotted what he was looking for up ahead and his heart felt like it was going to bounce out of his chest. *Am I really going to do this?*

The sign was crooked and nearly falling off its hinges. The shop itself didn't look much better. The wooden siding was warped and rickety, but as he walked up to the open door, he could see that the frame was thick, and the oak door was solid. He hesitated in front of the door, trying to decide if he wouldn't be better off just turning around.

"Need something?" The voice came from the right and he reflexively jumped to the left, dropping the coin purse he'd been nervously gripping.

*At least I didn't squeal this time.*

Bending over to pick up his dropped purse, he replied shakily, "I—yeah. I was just going to see if the owner was around. I'm looking for something."

A figure stepped out from the cover of the shadows into the fading rays of sunlight. His entire outfit was a hodgepodge of eccentricity. His long sable hair was decorated with colorful beads, his nose and ears filled with gold piercings, and his shirt looked like a poorly decorated cake, ruffles going in every direction, almost enough to distract from the multitude of colored necklaces exposed by the plunging neckline. Aynward figured the rules of fashion did not apply to this man; either that or he obeyed an entirely different, unknown set of foreign ones.

"Well, you may just be in luck, I happen to be in the business of reuniting people with lost or missing somethings, though I rarely open my doors after my evening meal. But, for you, I think fifteen coppers would help me locate the keys to the door."

Aynward had been told to expect as much even during the daylight hours if he wanted to get any real information. But fifteen coppers was more than half of what he'd been able to get from Gervais, and this was just to get the man to speak with him. He hoped the price for information was not so steep.

He reached into his purse and counted out the fee.

The man smiled, then reached for the door. It moved without a fuss. "Mm, seems I forgot to lock it. Come inside."

The quality of the establishment improved dramatically as they crossed through the threshold, the shabby outside evidently a facade. The man's appearance made much more sense as Aynward gazed at the similarly eclectic mix of expensive, unrelated accoutrements. There were four long aisles filled with jewels, clothing, flatware, and any number of odds and ends. The decor along the walls exuded wealth. He stepped onto a plush Scritlandian-made carpet ordinarily found only in the homes of noble families.

"My name is Vasbar; I own this place. Would you care for a drink?"

Aynward's impulse was to say yes, but he managed to resist the urge. *I need to be clear headed, plus he'll surely charge for the "complimentary" drink one way or another.* "Thank you, but no."

"Suit yourself. If thirst strikes you, merely say the word." The man seemed disappointed at the rejection. Perhaps his hospitality was also a method for loosening purses for sales. "So what does a young Kingdom-born noble such as you hope to find in a place like this? Mm?"

*Much good these clothes did me.* "I'm looking for a book. Well, two books, actually."

"Mm, I see." He lifted his chin up in thought before continuing, "I have a few here, mostly family anthologies and lineages that I'm holding as collateral against loans. I assume you seek particular titles and you have their names?"

"Yes. They are both from the university library. The first, titled *The Chronicle of Voros*, is actually a thin, leather-bound journal. I believe it is an original, written in old Luguinden. It went missing about a week ago, and the other, well, I'm hoping you might have some means of obtaining it from the archives. I've heard this can be done?"

Vasbar's eyebrows rose, but the rest of his face remained unshaken. "The university library, aye? Missing books do sometimes find their way into my shop, but I've not seen the title of which you speak. However, seeking after something that is rightfully secured in an establishment like the university library, that is well above the threshold of stomachable activities for this establishment. Do you think me a thief?"

The man seemed sincere to Aynward, yet there was no sense of anger about him. Was this an unwritten formality?

"I—no. Of course not. It's just, I wouldn't guess you'd do such a thing yourself. No. But maybe you know of someone who has the means of uncovering such an item. I'm growing desperate, is all."

Vasbar remained calm but stern. "You juggle semantics. I have no team of thieves to fill this room with items of sale. I give loans to people who cannot obtain loans elsewhere. It's little different than what the banks do; I would never knowingly deal in theft."

Vasbar stared at him for an uncomfortably long time. Aynward grew uneasy as he reevaluated his surroundings. The only remaining light came from the two lamps in the room, all natural light from the outside having been extinguished by the coming of night. He had been warned that the authorities kept their distance from this part of the city. Perhaps this was not the wisest way to go about finding the books.

"I cannot help you," Vasbar finally said, gesturing toward the exit.

Aynward had expected as much, but breathed a sigh of relief when the man was willing to let him go. Aynward didn't know if Vasbar had any sort of security hiding out, but with so many items of value, he must. Aynward would be glad to be out of the shop and back to safety as soon as possible, book or no book. *Apologize, and be gone.*

"Thank you for your time. And I apologize for the offensive implication that stemmed from the ignorance that informed my question. I meant no disrespect to you or your line of work. My desperation to find these items caused me to err, listening to the words of fools. You were merely a last hope. Good evening, sir."

The man nodded as he walked him to the door. "Apology *accepted.*" His last word dragged out, as if a thought had just occurred to him. "*Perhaps* I do know of someone who *may* be of some help to you."

Aynward's anxious retreat ended midstride.

Vasbar said, "There is a man whose associates brought me items of worth a few times. But after having my shop turned upside down by the authorities in search of one such item, I cut ties with him. This was nearly two decades back. I hear he has lavish holdings in the city these days; he does quite well for himself. I suspect that he may still be involved with folks who could do this thing you wish."

Aynward's heart fluttered with hope. He waited for Vasbar to continue with more details, but he said nothing more. Time stretched as Aynward's patience shrank. Exasperated, he said, "So who is this man?"

Vasbar's smile glowed in spite of the darkness. It reflected in his voice as he said, "Huh, I seem to have forgotten his name. Not to worry, this happens frequently. I'm very confident that the sound of, say, another ten coppers dropping into my purse would remind me in short order."

Aynward felt his temper rise. He gritted his teeth but ultimately succumbed to necessity.

After the exchange had taken place, Vasbar let out a sigh. "Well, my memory has been fully restored. Let's see, you were asking about an unscrupulous man with the means to seek out a missing book, as well as add another book to the library's missing book list. Ah, yes. I suddenly recall his name. He called himself Latru then, but I believe he now goes by the name Alti-jara Sultan Kubal."

Aynward recognized that as a Scritlandian name meaning *trade king*. *That's a little pretentious!*

"He runs a very successful enterprise in the sale of imported carpets and porcelain, if I'm not mistaken. But I believe his ships may also carry other, *less legitimate* cargo from time to time. I warn you, his price will be steep and the danger great. This kind of man will attempt to ensnare you in his perilous world if you're not careful."

Aynward's curiosity was piqued. "How, then, have you escaped this danger unscathed?"

Vasbar chuckled. "Let's just say, I could have turned his world upside down when he was first getting started into this sort of business here, but chose not to. I reminded him of my benevolence once."

Wanting to be away from this part of the city as quickly as possible, Aynward asked for the last piece of critical information. "So where do I find this man?"

Vasbar was quiet for a moment, then said, "I would ordinarily charge more for that kind of specificity, but"—his shadowed form shrugged— "it seems I like you, a rarity." After another moment of hesitation, he said, "Wait until daylight; follow the water around the harbor to the grand bazaar. Ask around about the sultan's carpets and they'll send you to his shop. Finding Alti-jara Sultan Kubal in the flesh may be a more trying task, but I suspect he'll be made available if you tell an employee that Vasbar sent you with a message."

"A message?"

"Yes, when you find him, tell him Vasbar is pleased that he found his prosperity."

Aynward waited for him to say more, but he retreated into the shadows of his store without another word.

"Thank you," said Aynward as he slipped through the door into the night air.

Reminded of his vulnerability by the sudden darkness, Aynward started for home. His eyes darted about at any hint of movement along the way. Every figure he passed was an assassin in waiting. But he wound up ascending the front porch steps without a scratch. Unfortunately, he was not as lucky as to sneak past Dolme without a lecture about being out past dark again. He was too mentally exhausted to put up a fight, which must have been interpreted as subordination. It was one of Dolme's briefest sermons. Aynward's mind still strayed: how was he going to convince Gervais to refill his purse without having earned more than a name?

He'd sleep on it and maybe something would come to him once his energy was restored. He opened his door and walked straight to the bed. *Praise the gods, I'm finally—*

A voice caused him to gasp and jump to the side. "How went your field trip to the docks?"

Aynward took in several deep breaths before feeling recovered enough to use his lungs again. "It—it went." *Keep talking.* "It went well. I mean, I was able to get a name and location of someone who should be able to help."

"I see." If Gervais had not responded to acknowledge that he'd heard, Aynward might have thought otherwise. His expression hadn't changed at all. The silence was too uncomfortable for Aynward to bear.

"There is a wealthy merchant named Alti-jara Sultan Kubal, who this man believes to launder stolen items under the protection of his legitimate carpet importation business. He has a personal connection that should get me an audience with this man."

Gervais nodded his approval. "I have heard that name before. He is well known within the city. Quite powerful." Gervais drummed his fingers silently on his leg in thought. "He may prove difficult to sway. I will refill your empty purse, but a petty bribe will likely not suffice."

*How does he know I spent my entire purse?*

"You will need to be very careful about what you agree to do in exchange for this man's help. He may wish something you can't, or shouldn't, deliver in return for what you ask. Men like Kubal do not give away favors without getting something . . . something more than what they offer."

Aynward shuddered.

"Sleep on it. This is important to me, but I wish you no harm."

He rose from the chair. "One more thing," and Aynward saw that he was holding something in his hand. "This arrived today from the university."

He tossed the small missive to Aynward, seal unbroken. "There's a package right there by the bed, as well. Good day."

"Good day." Aynward repeated the valediction just before the door closed.

Aynward's curiosity was greater than his fatigue, and he cracked the seal of the message. He looked first to see who it was from: *Dwapek!* Then he read the detailed note, confusion and annoyance souring his mood. He didn't need to open the package; the note explained that, too.

*I really need to find a way out from under the debt I owe him.*

## CHAPTER 88

# SINDRI

THE KNOCK AT THE DOOR startled Sindri, not sure exactly when her *escort* would arrive. She opened the door to see a young man who looked a few years older than Kibure. He took an assuming step into the room, looked from Sindri to Kibure, then said, "Which one of you is Sindri?"

Sindri raised her eyebrows at the contempt coating the lad's voice, but replied, "I am she."

He stared at her, narrowing his eyes, then said, "You're . . . you're Lugienese?"

*No sense denying it.* "I am." She let the tone of her answer come out with an accusatory flavor, implying her own question about why he cared to know.

He didn't pick up on it. "Hmh. I always imagined a Lugienese would be taller, gender aside."

*The world is full of disappointments, boy, get used to it.*

With the conversational momentum halted, the silence matched the awkward shuffling of the boy's feet in the doorway. Sindri finally said, "You bring me to this place, this university, yes?"

That revived the adolescent's condescension, his expression returning to one of mild irritation. "Yeah, and here"—he pulled something
from a satchel and tossed it at her—"put this on. Be quick about it, we're
already going to be late."

She unfurled the purple fabric to find a robe to match the one the
boy wore. There was also an amulet attached to a gold chain. She threw
the chain around her neck then pulled the robe over her tan dress and
said, "We go."

Without another word, he started down the hall. Sindri fell in
behind him until they were out in the street where they could walk side
by side. "So," she said, "what do you call yourself, and of what part have
you to the university? I did not believe this to be a place of . . . servants?"

He turned and gave her a look of incredulity. "Gods no. I'm not a
servant. I'm bringing you to *my* class."

"Oh. You are"—she wasn't sure of the right word in the eastern
common tongue—"a person to give to students of the knowledge?" He
looked barely old enough to enroll in the Lugienese equivalent to a
university, the state-run Klerósi Kleról, but perhaps she knew less about
this place than she thought.

He seemed to consider for longer than necessary before answering.
"I like to think that I do give knowledge to some of the students, but my
title does not go beyond that of student, at least not here in Brinkwell.
You're thinking of the word *counselor*. And my name is Aynward." He
continued walking, but inclined his head perceptibly enough to indicate
that he was officially acknowledging her in greeting.

*About time.*

Then he asked, "So—is Sindri a common name among your people?"

Sindri was surprised by such a forward question. It was considered
taboo among the Lugienese to inquire after the meaning of one's name
unless formally courting. But she decided to give Aynward the benefit
of the doubt, assuming him to be of a less refined stock. She responded
without reprimand, "No. Sindri is not of the common."

She noticed the boy's expression flicker between perplexity and
uncertainty. Finally he said, "Family name, then?"

"No. I am only Sindri."

"Huh. So your parents . . ."

She waited for him to complete his question, but when nothing was forthcoming, she asked, "What of my parents?"

"Oh—um—were they scholars of the ancient Luguinden language, by chance?"

*He knows the language and wonders why they would have chosen that word as my name; a scholar, indeed. But is he also a fool?* Sindri decided to see how this played out.

"They had not of this knowledge of the language, I think. Why?"

More hesitation, then he shook his head and replied, "No reason. Just making conversation."

*Not a total fool, then.*

Not much else was said until they arrived at the university gate, but Aynward did manage to steal a few glances. She wondered if she were *that* strange-looking as a foreigner, or if he were just being a typical adolescent boy.

He was a good-enough-looking lad; wide shoulders, strong jaw, confident gait, but he was also probably ten years her junior and she was here for a purpose. No distractions. She'd have to nip this in the bud if it turned out to be anything more than a little ogling.

Once past the guards, the splendor of the university served as a welcome distraction. The blue-stone masonry mixed with the green grass and flowing walkways. They passed a maze of hedges, and there were even several copses of trees. Their mighty branches spiraled toward the sun in innocent majesty, dwarfing anything she'd ever seen in sparsely forested Angolia.

"The trees have beauty." The words escaped her lips before she realized she was speaking them out loud.

He looked to the nearest tree, three men thick, with a vast canopy, resting right next to a cylindrical tower, and said, "Yeah, I could live without them. Dangerous things, those."

*He is a strange one.*

The size and scope of the buildings were nothing impressive for Sindri after having lived in Sire Karth for years, but that didn't diminish her appreciation of the beauty of the craftsmanship, or the artistic design of the place.

The boy startled her when he finally spoke again. "I don't know what you've been told about this class, but I feel an obligation to tell you that it's a little bit . . . *different.*"

She gave him a curt, "Hmh." She would see for herself soon enough.

He led her toward a grove of trees that grew into a small forest. They wound their way down a narrow dirt path that eventually opened up into a small amphitheater, though it was dilapidated. It existed in sharp contrast to the rest of the well-maintained buildings and grounds of the place. Had there not already been three other students, one being female, she might have grown nervous that she had indeed been led into a *different* sort of gathering.

The female student stood to greet Aynward. She placed an arm around the boy next to her and said, "So, who is your new *lady friend*, Aynward?" The flirtation in her voice was overtly suggestive. The boy next to her seemed surprised by the show of affection, and disappointed when it suddenly ended. More to Sindri's surprise was Aynward's reaction; he shied away. "Ugh, it's not like that. I was ordered to bring her here." He shook his head. "Dwapek!"

Sindri was not familiar with this *Dwapek* curse word, but she understood the general disgust in the accusation. *Well, that clears that up.* Aside from the personal insult, it was relieving all the same. That was the last thing she needed right now, a juvenile chasing her around, or anyone chasing her, for that matter.

The female extended a hand to Sindri. "My name is Minathi, and this is Kyllean."

"I am called Sindri. I greet you with pleasure."

"And you," replied Kyllean and Minathi in unison.

Another pair of students entered the clearing through the forest, made her acquaintance, and took a seat just as the smallest adult humanoid Sindri had ever seen appeared before them all. The effect was almost immediate: conversations quieted and the students sat.

The heavily bearded man cleared his throat to extinguish the remaining fragments of chatter then said, "Welcome, welcome everyone. I see our newest addition to the class has arrived." He looked directly at her. "My name is Counselor Dwapek, and this class is called Properties of Magic, which in essence is the study of magic across distances and time and its interactions between various groups of people. We'll review some of the specifics in a moment. Sindri, why don't you stand up and introduce yourself to everyone before we begin?"

She stood shakily, self-conscious in front of a group of total strangers. "I am called Sindri. I do not speak so well of this language. I look different to the eyes. You see this. I travel here for to learn these things in my home, Empire Lugienese, these things are not allowed." She tried to be as vague about that last part as possible.

Counselor Dwapek smiled. "Thank you, Sindri. For class today I would like to briefly recap everything we've learned thus far, then add Sindri's personal experience to the puzzle to see if we might glean anything more."

The students exchanged curious glances. Who was she to show up on her first day with anything of value to offer? But at one stern look from the counselor, even the silent communication ceased. Each student stood and summarized the texts they had read, along with any analysis of it that had been discussed in class. This took the larger part of an hour. Sindri found it difficult to keep it all straight in her head. Aynward seemed disdainful, as if the whole thing was a waste of time. Knowing what little she did about the existence of ateré magic, she had a few theories.

Dwapek thanked them all, then startled Sindri by saying, "Sindri, an acquaintance of mine who is familiar with the research conducted for this class recommended your enrollment because of your interests, as well as your personal experience. I hope I'm not revealing too much by telling the class that you were once a Klerósi priestess." He paused for her to confirm.

*Your hope is irrelevant since you revealed it, anyway.* "This is truth," she said, unable to mask the agitation in her voice.

Unfazed, Dwapek turned his attention to the whole class. "I pray this revelation adds some value to her testimony and insight into matters of magic. Sindri, you were once a wielder of Klerós's power, is that right?"

She wanted to turn and run, but her desire to learn more nullified this. She had to unclench her teeth to answer. "Yes. I was before—proficient to channel of the power of the Klerós. I have not now this ability. I am useless like a person of the regular."

Dwapek gave a wry smile. "I think you may be of more value than you think. Have you any insight into the magic described in the story summarized by Aynward? Likely you detected his questioning tone regarding the veracity of the source describing the mages who were able to strike Lesante even while the Luguinden wielders were without their power."

Sindri had been so overwhelmed with the amount of information she had not had time to process much of it. She had a thought but wasn't certain it was valid. She was also wondering what she was going to get out of a class like this, but ventured, "The evidence of the words of these stories say magic of the gods not of the Klerós cannot fight the power of the Klerós. This is the truth we teach in the Kleról. All know of this thing in my land. This truth happened to me when I use the power the Klerós against the priest of the Klerós. The Kleról have of"—*is there a Kingdom word for castration spell? Likely not*—"a spell to steal of a sorcerer power, for permanent." Sindri was intrigued by the mystery of the contradictory evidence presented in Aynward's story, but there was a simple explanation. "But I think explanations better can be possible for to explain this story. Maybe this man speaks not of the truth, like Aynward say. Or maybe these wielders to hurt Lesante use of the magic of the ateré. We have in my land some user of the magic who this spell has of no effect. We name of these people tazamines. We say they use of the power of the Dark Lord. But it may be that they use of the magic of the ateré."

Judging by the looks on the faces in the group, no one was familiar with this term. Chatter broke out among them. She looked to Dwapek, but saw no expression: only the growing creases at the edges of his eyes. He might have been resisting the urge to smile, but it was difficult to say for certain.

The counselor put up his hands for silence, then said to Sindri, "Please explain this ateré magic."

She eyed him, wondering what his game was. Was he truly ignorant, or was this just a terminology issue? Maybe she had said the wrong word by accident, or pronounced it wrong. The whole concept was new to her, after all. But this Dwapek seemed too emotionally controlled to be hearing of the existence of an entirely unknown strand of magic for the first time.

"I am not the expert on this ateré magic, but I learn magic of the different place can exist, magic does not always need to be of the gods. Power from the things living, but do not now live—dead things." She sighed in frustration with her limitations with the common tongue. "I do not well explain. Dead things have energy, and some people use this energy like power of the gods. But maybe people of the story is not Luguinden, and the power of a god different than of we know. But I think to not ignore this story because they have different knowledge. This is a flaw common of others who learn."

Dwapek clapped his miniature hands and smiled. Sindri sat; she was glad to be appreciated by someone, though she had just alienated every student in the class. Perhaps she should have chosen to remain silent.

The counselor spoke. "One more question for you, Sindri."

Her eyes narrowed. She wanted to be forgotten for a while. "Yes?"

"I have read some of the mainstream folklore surrounding this Lugienese Emperor, Magog, that his namesake is foretold to save his people and redeem the world. I haven't been able to get my hands on any of the actual prophecies. I'm told that these are strictly guarded, but I've heard rumors of large-scale mobilization on the Angolian mainland. Have you any knowledge of this from your own training at the Kleról? Or perhaps you saw preparations for war before you left your lands?"

Sindri felt her face go cold as the blood drained out of it. *Mobilization?* She knew of the recent increase in military conscription, and the prophecies, or at least most of them. She had never taken them seriously, at least not insomuch as Magog was concerned. It had all seemed like a propaganda stunt on behalf of Grobennar to help elevate himself. But if Fatu Mazi Grobennar was pushing it, and had convinced Magog that he was indeed Klerós's redeemer, then mobilization could mean that they meant to at least attempt to fulfill the prophecies.

*I'd better say something or my silence will be answer enough.* "I do not know of this mobilization when I flee. If this is truth, then . . ."

Her mouth went dry. She could feel her tongue sticking to the roof of her mouth, begging her to stop talking. "The prophecies tell of the story of the conquest total. Any who fight are destroyed. Prophecy of great battle of the east, where armies of the heretic mage of power fight the army of the Klerós. No one can survive this, only if they convert of the faith of the Klerós. They become servant to the Lugienese blood and faith."

No one said a word, no one moved. Even the breeze seemed to stop. Her mind was racing, and she considered the logistics as she continued. "But Lugienese have need of ships. Lugienese does not have ships of the many. To make the prophecy truth, they need of many ships."

Dwapek was no longer smiling. "So it seems the villain's soliloquy can earn an audience. Thank you, Sindri." He nodded for her to be seated. "That will be all for class today. Those of you who were supposed to present your last text will do so next class. Dismissed."

The little man started for the trail before any of the other students had moved.

Sindri looked over at Aynward. His expression was strained, but she couldn't identify a specific emotion. Then he stood and looked her way. "All right, let's go."

Her expression soured. She didn't care to be told what to do by some stranger ten years her junior. He gave her the impression that he believed himself more intelligent than everyone around him. Her direct challenge to his theory had demoted him to nothing more than a clever fool, at least for today. That likely explained his mental strain. He was trying to puzzle out where he had gone wrong, or how he could explain his way back to being right. He held no concern for military dangers that might present themselves years from now. He just wanted to be *right*. However, she didn't wish to further frustrate the lad. That would gain her nothing. She stood and followed.

Aynward's friend Ky-something tried to lighten the mood. "Say, Aynward, do you and Sindri wish to take the evening meal with Minathi and me? Just a quick nibble for both couples?"

Sindri thought to help Aynward by replying on his behalf. "I have need to return, but I give thanks for the invitation."

Aynward glared at her for interjecting, then answered for himself. "She's old enough to be my mother!"

Now it was Sindri's turn to be offended. She wasn't *that* old!

"Whatever you say," laughed the other boy, enjoying the entire exchange.

## CHAPTER 89

# KIBURE

KIBURE LOOKED ABOUT THE SOUNDLESS grayscale room and knew that his midday nap had brought him back to the world of dream, the world of nightmare. After his last time in this place, and the encounter with Magog, he was eager to return to the world of the waking where everything made sense, or at least more sense than in this place.

While sitting in his bed where he had awoken, if this nightmare could be considered a form of wakefulness, he decided to take a walk. He didn't exactly know how to wake himself up, anyhow. Last time it had been Rave who had somehow expelled him. But he had not seen much of Rave since arriving in Brinkwell, though he seemed to always be close by.

Kibure entered the common room of the inn downstairs and was not surprised to see no one there. He now recognized the slivers of light he saw around the room for what they were—people—though he had no idea what any of that meant or why they appeared as they did in this place. He continued to walk toward the door and pushed his way out into the street. He felt an odd desire to explore. The fear of being attacked by Magog for whatever reason became a distant concern.

He felt instead an odd sense of calm as he walked the empty streets of Brinkwell.

He couldn't say for how long he did so, but it was long enough that he had no idea where he was within the city in relation to where he had begun. This caused him little concern. He would eventually wake, and he was pretty sure that he would open his eyes to the room where he was staying at The Roving Sail.

Then a thought occurred to him, a thought that gave him pause: they had seen a Klerósi priest in the city. Could that man or his friends enter this realm of dream in the same way Magog had? No sooner had this thought occurred to him than he saw a distant glowing shape, much like Magog had appeared before him. He only caught a glimpse as it disappeared behind a building, but there was no mistaking the humanoid image, or the instant terror Kibure felt at seeing it.

Kibure turned and ran as fast as he could. When he looked behind him, he opened his mouth to cry out, but it made no sound. The glowing figure stood half the distance from him as it had been when he had started running, an impossible shift in position if not by some magical means. The silhouette of a cloak blew in the soundless breeze, masking the shape of the body that stalked him. Kibure returned his gaze to some path of escape, though he knew it would be no use.

Then he felt a grip on both of his arms. Again he tried to cry out but heard nothing.

## CHAPTER 90

# SINDRI

AYNWARD AND SINDRI WALKED IN silence for most of the way back to The Roving Sail. As they neared the inn, Sindri decided to make an attempt at friendship before Aynward permanently viewed her as an enemy. "Thank you for the escort of me, Aynward. I hope you do not see the interpretation of mine to be of a challenge to you. I mean not to offend. I have experience to cause different thoughts of the history."

Aynward's expression hardened and he let out a defensive huff. "I don't care about that. Maybe you're right, maybe you're wrong. That class is a waste of time, anyhow, just like my assignment to escort you to and from it."

Then he finally looked her in the eyes, and she saw the embarrassed, stubborn facade fall away, if only slightly. "But thank you. Your interpretation makes sense, considering your past. The truth of it all, well, hopefully it won't ever matter."

She sensed he didn't believe his own words, but she didn't need to call attention to that. "Yes, I also hope . . ." She trailed off as a familiar sensation gripped her: that tingling she had been trained to sense: *magic*.

*Kibure!* She needed to get back to their room immediately. "Thank you, I have need to go."

Aynward seemed surprised but not offended. She did not care either way, considering what the use of magic could mean for herself and Kibure.

Sindri heard Aynward's voice from behind her. "Good day, Sindri."

She ran the rest of the way to the inn, then burst through the front door. She resumed a quick walk until she hit the stairs; then she ran down the hall. The magic grew stronger as she neared the door to her room. Was Draílock there? No, it felt different from his ateré magic, yet it was familiar. Less precise. This was pure energy, though not the significant volume she had felt before. *Kibure!* He was using it *right here!* She swung the door open, ready to yell, but the sound caught in her throat.

He lay on his back, eyes closed, nothing else amiss. His breathing was too slow, too deep. He was asleep. One of his dreams. She needed to wake him.

"Kibure!"

He didn't move.

"Kibure!" She moved to his bed and shook him by both arms. Still he remained in his trance. Shaking him again, she repeated, "Kibure!" This time he woke with a yelp. His eyes opened wide and the magical sensation abruptly ended.

"I was there. The dream place," he gasped. "I was being chased!"

"Yes, you were radiating magic!" She relaxed as she looked about, realizing nothing else seemed wrong. "I felt your magic from the street."

Kibure appeared dumbfounded; he took a deep breath, but said nothing.

## CHAPTER 91

# KIBURE

SINDRI SCOWLED. "THIS IS YOUR fault! You felt the ateré magic during our last session. I saw the look on your face. And Draílock suggested as much, yet you hid it. Outright lied about it. And now this!"

Kibure stammered, "No! Well, um, not—exactly. I felt something, but I don't know what it was. It was different from the other times. Those were beyond my control. What I felt from that cricket was nothing in comparison. And I didn't use the power!"

It didn't matter. None of that mattered now. He had been chased within the dream, and something told him that whoever had been in the dream was also physically somewhere in this city. Even if not, he had no way to prevent himself from returning to that dream place where he was fairly certain he could be killed. He was in serious danger.

"We need to go see Draílock," he blurted. Draílock had said that the room below ground was somehow protected so magic use could not be felt from outside. Perhaps Draílock could similarly protect this room so others could not sense his magic if he had another dream. And maybe Draílock knew something about these dreams that could help him if he had another.

Sindri closed the door. "Agreed, we didn't come all this way just to be uncovered by a stray use of magic. You heard what he said about magic users in this city. They're *disappearing*."

Just as Kibure stood to leave, he sensed it.

"Sindri, is that—" He knew the answer, and he saw her stiffen.

They were too late. The door exploded behind her.

A brown-robed figured emerged from the space where the door had been seconds earlier, with two others following close behind. The man in front did not hesitate before extending his hand to send a streak of energy toward Kibure. It hit him square, but without any of the physical harm he expected, though he did feel *something*.

Then the man smiled and regarded Sindri. "Greetings, Liandra. Or do you prefer a different name these days?" He chuckled. "I suppose it won't matter soon either way. Heretics don't prefer much of anything in death besides escape from eternal torment, and I'm afraid it's too late for that."

Kibure could see the shock in her eyes, but he wasn't sure if it was in response to the threat or at hearing this other name. She answered coolly, "And what brings the great Fatu Mazi Grobennar so far from the safety of his cushy den? Did the line of credit on your childhood deed finally run dry?"

The man's arrogant expression became a venomous scowl. He turned to his men. "The woman is of no value. You may kill her on my order." Then his sinister grin returned. "She's already been castrated so you need not worry."

While the man's head was turned, Kibure caught a flash of movement from Sindri and a knife suddenly sped toward the Fatu Mazi. Hope flared for just a moment, but the man seemed to have expected the attack. Without looking, he lifted a hand and the knife flew harmlessly into the ceiling, where it stuck.

The man's deep, throaty laugh filled the room. "I see you're still excitable. Shame we can't play a bit longer, but we have a great deal more that needs to be done here in the city." He eyed Kibure then, and without looking away, he commanded, "Take this one alive, he too has been castrated, though he's likely immune. We'll need to get inhibitor tea running through his veins. Go!"

The lackeys sprang into a run toward their prey.

Kibure had no time to think. He ducked below a punch then lunged forward, rewarded with a grunt as his shoulder smashed into the man's stomach. Wrapping his arms around the man's waist, he drove forward with all of his strength. To his surprise, he landed atop the intruder, but surprise didn't stop him from hitting the man's face.

Before he could manage a second blow, a hand caught his arm and rolled him onto his back. His adversary pinned him to the floor with his weight while doing all he could to inflict damage with his hands. But his strikes had no effect. With Kibure's resolve to fight back came the touch of a familiar tingling within himself, and his hope flared again—but it was only a wisp, slipping from his grasp like an oily noodle. A fist to the face caused his vision to flounder and he felt a rope around his wrist cinch tight.

Sindri's screams told a story of a similar struggle across the room. He knew she was a fierce fighter, and certainly carried extra knives, but she seemed to be—

*Crash!* Glass and wood sprayed Kibure's face as Sindri's body whirled through the second-story window out onto the street below. Someone then tied his hands and hoisted him to his feet, dragging him over to the Fatu Mazi. Rank breath stung Kibure's nostrils as Grobennar whispered to him, "I've been searching for you a very long time, old friend. So glad we could finally meet face to face." Then the man turned him to face outward. "Unfortunately, we're going to have to finish this conversation later."

Then Kibure heard something he had not heard in weeks: a raaven's angry shriek. But a moment later something struck him in the back of the head and he saw only blackness.

## CHAPTER 92

# AYNWARD

SURROUNDED BY AN ARRAY OF exquisite Scritlandian carpets, Aynward said to one of the shopkeepers, "I'm looking for a man by the name of Alti-jara Sultan Kubal."

The pudgy islander frowned. "Yes, well, a great many people seek an audience with my employer. Alas, he is an important man and cannot attend every request. Perhaps *I* can assist in this matter."

"Unfortunately, I have a message for his ears alone. It is from Vasbar, an old acquaintance, or so I'm told."

"Vasbar, you say?"

Aynward crossed his arms. "Yes, Vasbar."

The man radiated arrogance. "I have no guarantee of when next I'll see him, but I'll make sure he is made aware that a boy stopped by with a message from this *Vasbar*. Stop in, say, tomorrow or the next day, and if he wishes to see you, he'll leave me with instructions."

Aynward wished to protest, but this was too important for him to botch by upsetting the staff. His bargaining chip, an insignificant message, might get him an audience if he were lucky, but if he puffed up the significance of that message any more than he already had, the reception would not be pretty once the frivolity of it was realized.

"Very well, thank you for your assistance."

"Yes, yes. What is your name, that I might leave this with him, as well?"

"Kyllean." The name slipped out without much thought as he left the building. *He won't mind.*

All in all, he reasoned, this outcome wasn't bad. He would know in a day or two whether this angle would play out. His thoughts wandered back to the newest addition to his Properties class: Sindri. Something about her intrigued him, though he wasn't sure exactly what. She was attractive in an exotic sort of way, but that wasn't it. She was too old for him, and he was certain he'd never act on it, anyhow, but it bothered him that she kept returning to his thoughts, unbidden. She'd aggravated him more than anything else. Perhaps it was that. Maybe he wasn't attracted to her, he was just annoyed with her. She had shown up to a class after he and everyone else did all the readings and interpretations and presumed to just flatten all their theories without a thought. Who was she to do that? That must be it.

His musings were cut short when a man stepped into the middle of the street in front of him and held up a hand for him to stop. "You are Kyllean?"

The man wore a bright-yellow silk robe with a purple, ruffled scarf and a multicolored hat that looked like it belonged on a court jester. He had a well-groomed pointed goatee. This was *him*. This was Kubal.

The man didn't smile. "This way, please."

Kubal led him through the bazaar to the docks and onto a ship that put the Kingdom vessel he had ridden to Brinkwell to shame. This one was truly majestic. A massive brown flag stitched to look like a Scritlandian carpet, with the same swirling designs but covered in gold coins, waved in the wind. He was so entranced by the sight that he didn't realize just how dangerous the situation was until it was too late.

He sat on a plush pillow belowdeck, on a ship owned by a very rich, very dangerous man. If this conversation went south and the man wished to have him killed, no one would ever know. The only person who even knew he was going to see Kubal was Gervais, and by the time someone found his body, *if* someone found his body, there would be nothing to connect the wealthy merchant, nothing beyond speculation.

Kubal smiled coolly. "I'm told that you carry a message from an old acquaintance of mine, a man named Vasbar."

Aynward swallowed hard, lacking the confidence that had brought him this far. "Well, yes, in a manner of speaking. He sent me to you after I asked him for help in uncovering a few items of value. He did send me with a message. He assured me that a message from him would get me an audience with you."

"I see. Well, here we are. He was right on that count. Did he also tell you that we parted ways on rather strained terms?"

Aynward was dismayed to find himself shaking. He tried to keep his voice steady as he said, "He did. It was a risk I was willing to take in order to have a chance at uncovering these items."

Kubal studied him for a moment. Then he smiled, and this time it seemed almost genuine. "Well, let's have it. What did the old square have to say?"

Aynward exhaled slowly. "He said he was pleased that you found prosperity."

Kubal barked a laugh. "Is he, now? Pleased at *my* prosperity? That's a good lie."

He was silent for a number of breaths, and Aynward figured he had about a fifty percent chance of surviving this exchange. The man seemed just as liable to slit his throat as to throw him a gold chalice as a reward for bringing the meaningless message.

The goddess of luck decided to blow him a kiss, praise be to Kitay. Kubal said, "Well, the trick has gotten you all the way here, but it will work only once. What is it you seek?"

Aynward's voice was still shaky, but now more from excitement than fear. "I am seeking a lost book as well as someone able to acquire another more heavily guarded book."

"Books, you say? What makes you think I have any dealings with lost or stolen books?"

His tone warned of danger. Perhaps Aynward *was* still on the edge of peril. *Choose your words carefully.*

"Only the hint from Vasbar. He suggested you might have some associations with people capable of doing such things. I suggest nothing more."

Kubal chuckled. "I amassed this wealth of mine by never missing an opportunity to expand my ventures. I may be able to help you, but stolen items tend to be *quite* expensive. So the real question will be, have you the means to finance this venture?"

"How about I give you the details of what I need, and you name your price. I don't have bottomless coffers, but perhaps we can agree to a price."

Aynward described the lost journal as well as the title of the book he needed from the archives. The latter resulted in a robust laugh, but Kubal did not shrink from the task. When Aynward was done, Kubal eyed him for a time, likely deciding just how much he could charge. He seemed unperturbed by the enormity of the task. Vasbar had been right on that count.

"I suspect I could have this done for no less than ten gold pieces."

The number was astronomically laughable. Aynward had thought it preposterous when he was given the bill for the book he had lost, two gold pieces. Few even carried gold currency, ever. He now carried fifty coppers, the value of one gold piece.

Perhaps he could negotiate. He'd be a fool not to try. "I can do no more than five."

Kubal shrugged. "Then you will have no books. I don't haggle with endeavors of theft."

Aynward felt himself redden. "Ten it is," he said through gritted teeth, though he was certain that even Gervais couldn't put that kind of money together.

Kubal reached out an arm to secure the deal and they shook in the Kingdom soldier's fashion, an act that surprised him. "I'll expect half beforehand. Bring it here tomorrow and the deed will be done." Kubal gestured toward the door. "I have more business to attend to in the city so we must be going."

Aynward reached the deck and started toward the gangplank. Before he was halfway there, two sets of strong arms seized him on both sides. Having trained with the sword and in weaponless combat, Aynward fancied himself an excellent fighter, but these men had muscles sculpted by years of pulling ropes and carrying heavy cargo on and off ships. Once established, their grip on either side of him was unbreakable.

Aynward squirmed with all of his strength, but gained nothing for his panicked effort. These men would do with him as they were commanded, and he would have no say in the matter whatsoever.

"Help! Help! I'm being—" A handkerchief was stuffed into his mouth, silencing his cries.

Kubal now stood in front of him, knife in hand. Aynward couldn't believe that this was how his life was going to end. Dolme had been right all along. He was a fool! What was a Kingdom-born noble doing trying to navigate the world of piracy? And for what? So he could get a little payback on a few people who had slighted him? *Fool!*

The knife raced for his midsection and sliced.

The jangle of coins striking the deck mixed with his muffled cry. But there was no pain.

Kubal bent over and picked up the purse, tossing it into the air and catching it once again. Satisfied with its contents, he said, "This will suffice as payment for my time today. I expect to see you here tomorrow before dusk with the five gold pieces, or our deal is off."

He nodded to his men and they released Aynward with a slight push in the direction of the dock.

"A pleasure doing business with you, Kyllean, truly."

Aynward stumbled forward, then turned to eye the scoundrel. Myriad insults raced to his tongue, but he held them in check. Taking a deep breath, he turned and headed back into the city, toward the university, and his evening class.

He was so flustered by the experience that he almost didn't notice the familiar face he saw walking up the dock toward Kubal's ship. *Almost.*

The dark-skinned boy seemed dead-set on his objective, and Aynward averted his face the second he was certain of who he'd seen. Wearing the clothes of a commoner, he thought he might have gone unseen but he couldn't be certain.

Questions spun through his head as he disappeared into the city. Why was Hirk, the librarian, on his way to visit Kubal's ship? What did it mean? Several possibilities floated to the top of the list and Aynward knew then that he had just gained something more valuable than even the fifty coppers he'd just lost on the ship.

He smiled. as he thought, *I'm either very lucky, or very deranged; perhaps both.*

## CHAPTER 93

# KIBURE

EXCRUCIATING PAIN PULSED THROUGH KIBURE'S body. The torture was unbearable, and his muscles spasmed uncontrollably like the legs of an ant after its head had been removed from its body. He was unable to study his surroundings, the pain dimming his other senses. Within seconds of waking, he was attacked again, sending new waves of pain until his mind retreated once more into the realm of unconsciousness.

This cycle repeated for an unknowable time, but each awakening was weaker than the last. Kibure knew that one of these times would likely be his last. But then he opened his eyes, and his vision focused, and nothing struck him. The pain was still there, but it wasn't acute. He almost didn't recognize the world without the perpetual bombardment. Looking around, he observed two men towering above him on either side, both looking off to a third, who stood at Kibure's feet.

Kibure tried to move, but he was bound to a hard elevated surface. He struggled again, but the ropes held firm. He conceded the physical struggle while his mind continued to scream. *Breathe. Deep Breaths. Panicking won't help. You're not dead yet. Breathe.* He felt his body relax, if slightly. *Take in your surroundings.*

The shadows on the downcast faces before him made it difficult for Kibure to see much detail, but he did take note of their clothing. Crimson collars opened wide above the chest and stretched over their shoulders. Their silken robes were embroidered with black stitching at the seams and bore a crest upon the upper left chest. Kibure could not make out the details in the dim light, but he knew what would be there: the four-pointed star of Klerós surrounded by a crescent on either side.

These men were those same who had attacked the ship with the Kraken and chased him through the mountains. But why they had tortured him near to death instead of simply killing him was yet unknown, and perhaps more disturbing than anything else.

As he lay there, he heard the men speaking among themselves.

"Mazi Grobennar, he wakes."

"Yes, I can see that. Prepare a batch of healing tea, and another inhibitor. I have some questions for this one," replied the man at Kibure's feet.

"Yes, of course, I'll bring it in."

"Good. We cannot afford to make any mistakes with these *tazamines*," Grobennar cursed. "After those witches, we can't be too careful. Best to keep him drugged at all times."

There was something about the name, Grobennar, that touched on Kibure's memory, something Grenn had said, but Kibure couldn't place it. Sindri had called him Fatu Mazi. Kibure thought he should know what that meant, but he was too disoriented to think straight. Knowing that his captors were indeed priests of the Kleról was enough reason for his panic to return.

One of the other priests spoke. "I don't see why we don't just—" His eyes went wide, and Kibure sensed the use of magic. This man realized he had said something wrong. "I'm sorry, Mazi, it was not my place. Please—"

A choking sound followed. Kibure could feel the magic, faint, but apparently being put to great effect. The man fell to the ground, gasping and gurgling. After a few more seconds of writhing on the floor, he finally sucked in a deep breath followed by a fit of coughing. This mazi, the man who seemed in charge, spoke again. "This impulsive tongue of yours is going to get you killed someday. I pray that today is not that day. Unless, of course, you have any other misgivings you would like to make known."

"I am a fool, Mazi Grobennar. Please forgive my ignorance though I know I do not deserve such."

Kibure could hear the man shuffling about the floor, probably coming to his knees. The man at Kibure's feet, this Mazi Grobennar, took a step toward the one on the floor. He reached over and patted him on the shoulder like a child. "There, there. You have simply been too long away from home. You will remember your place"—his tone shifted back to one of warning—"or you will perish."

"Yes. Yes, of course, Mazi."

Then Grobennar focused his attention back on Kibure. He walked around the table toward Kibure's head.

"Where is that ripping tea?"

A voice from another room echoed in, "Coming."

The door opened a moment later, and the other priest arrived holding a tray with two small steaming cups. He set the tray down on a chair, then brought one of the cups around to the other side of the table. Kibure did not recall drinking any before, but everything during and between beatings had been a haze.

The man tipped a cup up against Kibure's lips, but Kibure turned his head away. He felt drips of the warm liquid run down his neck. Then a pair of hands gripped either side of his head, holding it firmly in place. A voice from behind him said, "Plug his nose. Even tazamines need air."

Kibure struggled against the hands, against the ropes, against the tea; it was useless. Finally his mouth opened, gasping for air. Warm liquid found its way down his throat. He tried to spit as much out as possible but he choked and swallowed several mouthfuls between coughs and breaths. The hands gripping his head lifted it slightly, then slammed the back of his head onto the table.

"Would you like our help in serving your second cup of tea, or do you think you'd like to help yourself?" The imposing man loomed above him, prepared to repeat the forced pour. "Your resistance is not worth the effort. We are going to get what we want from you, one way or another. Your level of comfort is the only choice you have."

Kibure sniffled and coughed again. His hoarse voice replied, "I will drink."

The second cup went down much easier.

Within minutes, Kibure felt his strength return; at least enough that he was able to remain awake. Kibure used this moment of clarity to absorb as many details as possible to determine where he might be and how he might escape. The room was small and unfurnished with the exception of a single chair, and the wooden table upon which Kibure was bound. The walls were made of stone, and the floor looked to be either hardened dirt or rock. Between the stone walls, the rocky floor, and the low ceiling spaced with wooden supports, he deduced he was somewhere beneath the city. The foul scent of sewage reinforced this observation. Sindri had explained that the filth of the city ran through enormous tunnels beneath it. They must have been close to one such tunnel; the air was pungent. These realizations did little to help his hope of escape. There was only one door, no windows, and he was bound to a table guarded by three men. Not even Rave would be able to get him out of this one.

He prayed Sindri was all right. He imagined even if she survived the blast, her injuries must be grievous. And Rave. Had the creature also attempted to protect him? If so, did its failure mean that it too had been killed?

Kibure saw motion and shifted his attention to Grobennar as he removed his hood. His head was shaven, but his skin was the typical Lugienese brown. He looked to be in his middle years based on the well-defined forehead creases, which were accentuated further by his current state of concentration as he studied Kibure.

After a few minutes of unceasing observation, Grobennar evidently decided that Kibure was ready for questions.

"So, who trained you to use the Evil One's power? Why did you enter the Empire, and what was your purpose for doing so?"

Kibure met the inquiry with silence.

Grobennar glared back at him, then glanced at one of the others and shook his head. "This one wishes to do everything the hard way, doesn't he? Should have kept the woman alive. Perhaps she would have been more willing to speak."

Sindri: dead. He had assumed as much, but to hear it confirmed so matter-of-factly caused the wall of grief he had been holding in check to break. Kibure rebelled against his restraints, anger and sorrow boiling. He wanted nothing more in this moment than to bring the ceiling down on all of them, his own life less important than the destruction of theirs. He dug deep, trying to sense the energy in his surroundings, the innate power that existed in all things, as Draílock had described it. Nothing happened.

Grobennar smiled as he stepped to the side of the table and reached for Kibure's neck. His icy hand gripped his throat and squeezed. "I will ask you again, one question at a time. Who trained you to use the Evil One's power?"

Kibure remained silent and the pressure on his neck intensified until darkness swallowed his vision and unconsciousness beckoned him back. Then the man released his grip and the room returned to focus. A barrage of other questions followed, but Kibure resolved to remain silent. He dared not speak of his escape from slavery, had no knowledge of his ancestral lineage, and the questions regarding his training in the magical arts were too ridiculous to even consider. He had only attended one session of *training* and had never intentionally used his magic; not even his dreams made any sense. He couldn't rationalize any of his magic to himself, let alone a stranger. He put his confidence in the fact that, given his brutal background as a slave, there was little punishment he could not withstand.

After enough physical and verbal torment, Kibure figured that Grobennar had been forced to choose between Kibure's silence and his death. The strength of the healing tea had worn off, and the strikes to his body had weakened him further. Kibure's inability to keep his head up or his eyes open finally brought a shout of frustration from the stocky man in charge. The two others stiffened and backed away, awaiting further instruction.

"Get him more tea. We will begin another round of questions as soon as he recovers."

## CHAPTER 94

# AYNWARD

AYNWARD FOLDED UP THE PARCHMENT Gervais had handed him days earlier, stuffing it back into the pocket of his robe. *And to think I tried to refuse this.* Planning this little interview would have required a lot more reconnaissance without it. According to the document, Hirk *should* be on his way to his shift in Special Collections anytime—*there!* Hirk rounded the walkway between the library entrance and the catacombs. He wasn't far enough along the cylindrical building to see the entrance, but Aynward glanced around once more to be sure there weren't any other people around, just in case Hirk needed more *convincing*.

He positioned himself with his back against the wall as he waited for Hirk to get close enough. *Not yet. Not yet. Now!* He stepped into the walkway and grabbed the librarian by the back of his collar, pulling it taught.

Hirk attempted to wriggle free, but it was no use. Aynward had him firmly in his grasp. Leaning in close, he gritted his teeth, and said, "Let's talk."

The librarian released a quiet whimper, but fought no further.

Aynward led him toward the entrance to the catacombs, and, as Aynward had hoped, Hirk was not equipped to resist. The university catacombs were a partially open area. The small foyer required no key, and housed the statues of prominent founding members of the university, each guarding a locked door to their crypts. Aynward had no intention of taking Hirk any farther. This place was rumored to be a popular location for the occasional coupling, but he had inspected it for residents before beginning his stakeout of the library. They were very much alone.

Positioning Hirk in the corner so he wouldn't be tempted to run, Aynward finally released his hold, giving him a good shove into the stone.

Hirk asked frantically, "What do you want? I've done nothing."

"What's your relationship with Alti-jara Sultan Kubal?"

Hirk's eyes bugged. "Alti-who?"

The fear in his voice encouraged Aynward to press his advantage. He punched Hirk in the stomach. "Don't lie to me. You were on his ship yesterday. What were you doing there?"

Hirk's eyes darted from side to side like a cornered animal.

"Don't even think about running. Just answer my question!"

Aynward brought his fist back, preparing to strike another blow.

The librarian cringed like a frightened pup then blurted, "He'll have me killed if he finds out I talked."

Aynward had never interrogated someone, but he guessed at the kinds of threatening statements one might make in his position. "There are worse things than death. Would you care to learn what they are?"

Hirk shrank to the floor and started rambling in what Aynward could only assume was his native tongue, Palpanese. *He's going to soil himself! Perhaps that last bit was a little too strong. A softer approach might have greater effect, now that he thinks I'm actually going to torture him.*

"Listen, if you just tell me what you were doing there, the truth of it, I'll leave you be. But I *have* to know. I don't want to have to pluck your fingernails from your body one by one." The last bit was more of a joke, but Hirk whimpered in response.

*Whoops.*

Hirk finally answered between sobs, "It was Theo—he forced me into it. He'll expose me if I stop. I'll be expelled from the university and the city. My family will disown me. I'll be ruined." His sobs intensified.

Aynward was thankful that Hirk couldn't see his shock at the name. *Theo?* He needed to know more.

"Hirk, I'm going to help you, but I need to know what it is Theo has you doing. I can't help if you don't tell me everything."

He sobbed louder. "You can't help me. They're too powerful."

Aynward furrowed his brow. "Try me. *I owe Theo a favor.*"

It took some time for Hirk to finally calm down enough to talk details, but by the time they parted ways, Aynward had learned what he needed to know. He just had to decide what to do with the information. One thing he knew for certain: he couldn't do it alone.

Gervais drummed his fingers on the arm of the chair in Aynward's room as he processed the enormous fee Kubal had placed on the retrieval of the books. The silence dragged on until Aynward's thoughts ranged from crawling into bed for sleep to killing the man out of frustration. Either one would be a welcome replacement for the silence.

"I believe that my employer will pay this fee. No monetary value is above the information they'll obtain from having this book."

"Must be *some* book."

Gervais cast a look of condescension, but otherwise ignored Aynward's transparent attempt at earning an explanation for why the book was so important. Gervais excused himself so he could obtain the funds for Aynward's deposit. "I'll have the money to you shortly. Wait here and I'll be back in time for you to make the drop."

Aynward stood and followed Gervais out the door. "I have to make a stop at the university before I go. Don't worry, I'll be quick."

Gervais shrugged. "Very well."

Aynward walked quickly; he needed to see Kyllean. He would also have to meet with Hirk before the final exchange was made. For now, Aynward would make arrangements to take full advantage of the situation.

He couldn't shake the smile that formed on his face as he strode toward the university to finalize his plans.

## CHAPTER 95

# SINDRI

SINDRI WOKE WITH A POUNDING headache; she sat up quickly. Too quickly. Nausea washed over her, retreating only as she lay back down. Her thoughts were slow, memories foggy. *Where am I? What happened?*

Coherent thought slid from her like feet on the slimy rocks in stagnant water. She stared at the ceiling, allowing some time for her mental feet to gain traction. Things started to come back into focus. As she took in her surroundings, she confirmed that she had no idea where she was. This allowed her to track her thoughts back to her last memory. Kibure. Lugienese men. Klerósi priests. The attack on their room. *Fatu Mazi Grobennar.* She panicked.

Ignoring her previous attempt to rise, she bolted to her feet. The room was small. She saw a bed, dresser, chair, a table with candles, and an armoire. None of that mattered. She needed to find Kibure. She staggered to the door, a stabbing pain in her skull. She managed to fight her way to the handle and push before her will was overpowered by the reality of her wounds. She pushed open the door, collapsing on the floor of a hallway, noting as the light faded from her sight that she still had no idea where she was.

## CHAPTER 96

# KIBURE

SHADOWS OF FLICKERING CANDLELIGHT DANCED upon the rafters above the small dungeon that was now Kibure's home, that is, until they tired of his refusal to answer their questions. Then he would die. The fugitive slave groaned as he tried in vain to adjust his position, strapped in place as he was upon the table that doubled as a bed and cell. The ache in his back from days of inactivity was exacerbated by the agonizing urge to pick and scratch at the many healing wounds from his initial interrogation.

Fatu Mazi Grobennar entered the room and sat in his customary seat to the left of Kibure. The priest told one of his henchmen to retrieve more of the healing tea.

"Today our session is going to be a bit different. Your refusal to cooperate has forced me to use more—intrusive methods."

Kibure didn't bother trying to comprehend the evil behind the man's words. His will to survive was at its end. There was nothing this man could to do him to change his course.

And yet, perhaps these priests could discover some of the very answers he had sought. Perhaps they were right and he really was possessed by some demon spirit. How would he know? Then again, they would surely kill him if he told them everything about his escape. Of course, they would probably kill him no matter what, wouldn't they?

Kibure's musings were shattered by the touch of the man's hand upon his head. "Let us see what your memories say to these unanswered questions."

Kibure's silent rebellion was met by a sudden physical sensation, like his head had been dunked in the cold water of Lake Lagraas, only far colder. This was like nothing he had ever before felt. It took him far away from the aches within his body and the inner debate of his predicament. Kibure felt his will weaken. Part of him wanted to just give in, but the thought of this man's smile, his holy facade—he could not surrender, not to this man. He could not relinquish control of his mind to this—this monster.

The man gave a feral growl, then climbed atop the table, the bulk of his weight settling upon Kibure's chest. He held both hands on Kibure's scalp, both slick with sweat while his silky red robes clung to his bronze skin. A pendant with a red ruby escaped the priest's collar and swung back and forth in front of Kibure's face, twinkling in the candlelight. To Kibure's utter horror, he realized that the yellow, hateful eyes of his captor no longer peered into his own, but much deeper, penetrating his soul.

Kibure recoiled. Then he heard a voice inside his head, and somehow he knew that it was not the voice of Grobennar.

*"Hello, servant of the dark. We're going to play a game."*

Kibure's weak body played out its resistance, but this had no effect on the mental intrusion. Kibure growled, "Get out of my head!"

*"This game is called 'I enter your mind and rummage through your thoughts until I've seen what I wish to see, and then we hand you over to the God-king to harvest your soul.'"* The presence giggled, then somehow yelled into his mind, *"Let's play!"*

Suddenly Kibure felt something far worse than the initial intrusion. If the first touch of his mind by Grobennar was a needle, this was a sword. The alien *consciousness* violated the deepest recesses of Kibure's soul. His personal thoughts, dreams, memories—they were all splayed out for this *being*. This was an obscene, impure, and altogether evil nudity. A desecration. It was *wrong*. And he was powerless against it.

## CHAPTER 97

# GROBENNAR

MAZI GROBENNAR BELLOWED, BUT HIS words weren't meant for the Dark Lord's servant, or the other priests in the room; his shout was for Jaween.

"What are you doing?"

Jaween answered, *"Why, I entered the prisoner's mind, of course. He is not skilled enough to withstand me."*

The priest named Jinnah answered Grobennar's question, alarm in his voice, "What's wrong, Mazi? I feel no foreign magic."

Grobennar ignored the priest. "Let me in!"

*"Oh, I am not stopping you—though you would likely not know how to make sense of what you saw even if you could gain entry. I have seen this mind's likeness before, it is like that of the ancients. Fear not, I will report to you what I discover."*

"No," snarled Grobennar. "If I can't see into his mind, then he is of no further use." Grobennar reached into his robes to grip his dagger.

"Master, he may yet hold valuable information. Much could be learned from such a one as he; this evil spirit that accompanies him. And the God-king, he will surely wish to take the power of this one's soul."

"No!" Grobennar drew his dagger. "Every breath he draws is an affront to Klerós." He lifted the dagger high in the air, poised to plunge it into the boy's chest. A rush of excitement filled Grobennar as he stared down on the vile abomination that lay before him staring back up at him in defiance. This *thing* was not worthy to set eyes upon him and live. And live he would not, for in his death lay Grobennar's rejuvenation, his redemption. This death was a fulfillment of the prophecies, with Grobennar earning an honored seat. *Yes. This is my destiny.* "For Klerós!" he shouted as he sent the knife speeding toward the Kibure's chest.

## CHAPTER 98

# KIBURE

KIBURE COULD SEE TINY RED lines crisscrossing the whites of the man's eyes, and the creases at the edges, likely born from lack of sleep, something Kibure was well accustomed to. He could see the droplets of sweat accumulating above the brow, ready to drip at any moment. Most powerful, however, was the hate he saw within those eyes. As the knife was hoisted into the air, Kibure saw that this man would enjoy every moment of his death, right up to the sound of metal cutting flesh.

He could look no more. Kibure closed his eyes. He would wait in darkness for the end to come. Yes, this was better.

Except—nothing happened. The initial pause became an unbearable delay. *Just do it, already!*

Kibure opened his eyes just in time to see the glint of light flash across the dagger as it fell from the hands of the priest to clang harmlessly to the table. The priest fell to the side and rolled off the table onto the ground.

A sliver of hope blossomed within Kibure's breast. Had someone come to his rescue? But the door remained closed and he felt no magic. Had one of the priests betrayed Grobennar? Kibure looked from side to side, but they seemed just as confused as he. Kibure wasn't dead, but—

Then that same voice spoke inside his mind. *"I'll be back for more. It seems I must first have words with my host. Don't go dying on me, not until I've finished enjoying your memories."* The presence imparted a mental cackle before exiting Kibure's head, a chilling reminder of the horrific violation.

As his mind was released from the *thing's* clutches, a rush of sensation returned; it was pure ecstasy.

Kibure had never appreciated the mundane, pain-filled world as much as he did in that moment it was returned to him. And yet the entity said it would resume its search within his mind. Somehow that was worse. Kibure wished the knife had just struck home.

## CHAPTER 99

# GROBENNAR

GROBENNAR SLAMMED THE SOLID OAK door behind him so hard he was certain the stone beneath his feet shook. Gripping the pendant that housed Jaween so tight his knuckles turned white, he yelled, "How dare you use your powers against me! Me! Your master. You don't control me, I control you!"

He glanced back at the door, a fleeting thought about what the other priests might think if they heard him yelling in a room by himself. He shook his head. At this point, he didn't care what the other priests thought of him so long as they remained unaware of what lay within the pendant. They would surely think him mad, but perhaps that was for the better.

Jaween finally responded. *"I was protecting you, dear master."*

"Protecting me from killing the boy?" sneered Grobennar. "What danger lay in killing the boy? He didn't draw any magic, I would have felt that. The only danger I *felt* was when you blasted my mind with—"

"*Oh—that.*" Jaween had the nerve to attempt his inhuman chuckle. *"That was me protecting you from wasting an irretrievable opportunity that could be used to further your chances of redemption before your Emperor. Unless you have learned how to bring the dead back to life?"*

Grobennar did not like having his hand forced, especially by one who wasn't even really alive. Well—he certainly didn't breathe. And yet, what Jaween had said did make sense. What better proof of his worth to Magog than to serve him one of the Empire's most prophesied enemies for his own inspection, in addition to having intimate knowledge of this enemy's plans while still serving a now helpless Brinkwell as an offering? Surely those acts combined would be enough to justify reinstating his position.

Grobennar allowed himself to relax. "The boy can live, for now."

*"Oh, that is a very good decision. You won't regret it one bit. And it's going to be so fun! I've only walked a mind of this likeness once before. You are wise, master Grobennar. So very wise."*

Grobennar ground his teeth. "*You* will *never, ever* do something like that to me again, or I swear to you, I will hurl you into the deepest, darkest part of the sea where no one will ever hear your pleas for another master. Do you hear me?"

*"Yes. Yes, of course. Your will is my command, after all, master."*

Grobennar then prayed to Klerós that none of his henchmen would test his patience in the coming hours, for he knew he was liable to kill the next person to cross him, breathing or not.

## CHAPTER 100

# AYNWARD

AYNWARD TOOK THE MAJORITY OF the gold pieces from Gervais and stowed them in his room. His new plans required a great deal less, but Gervais needn't know that. He took off toward the university to set the final pieces of his plan into motion.

It was dark when Aynward's plans began taking on shape. He tingled in excitement as he saw the pieces come together. *This is going to be wonderful.*

Hirk had told Aynward when and where to expect Theo, so it was not difficult to catch his trail. He wished dearly to be there to see the look on Theo's ordinarily smug face when everything came crashing down around him. The librarian's directions were impeccable, and Aynward caught sight of his sworn enemy striding along, confident as ever.

Aynward maintained a safe distance just in case he looked back. He didn't; not until eight university guards flanked by Kyllean and Hirk stepped out to bar his way at the gate.

It was then that Theo turned to see Aynward, who was striding down the middle of the walkway, arms out wide in satisfaction. Theo grimaced. "I should have known *you* would have something to do with this." Turning back to the guards, he shouted, "What is the meaning of all this?"

Aynward answered for them. "It seems someone caught wind of a book smuggling ring. Not sure how that could have happened."

Theo turned to Hirk. "You're a dead man. You know that, right? Dead. Man." Whirling back to face Aynward, he said, "And your fate will be worse, princeling, much worse."

Theo's tone was so heavy with hate, Aynward marveled that his legs were able to support the mouth that spoke the words.

He smiled. "I'm not sure exactly how you're going to see any threats to fruition from a university prison cell." When Theo didn't respond, Aynward continued, "See, I did some reading, and it seems the penalty for theft here at the university is based on the value of the items stolen. Funny thing that, considering the value of the item you have on your person, I figure by the time you're released, I'll be back serving the Kingdom on the mainland. And by then, I'm sure you'll be more concerned with things like remembering what the sun looks like, and how to earn money enough to feed yourself." Aynward had kept closing the gap as he spoke and stopped just a pace away. "No, I think we'll not see much of each other after tonight. That is, unless nostalgia strikes and I'm gracious enough to pay you a visit, though that will also depend in large part on your attitude in these next few moments. I especially appreciate compliments on my hair." He ran his hands through his shoulder-length hair to make his point.

Theo's eyes radiated hate, but he still appeared confident. More confident than he should have been, considering the circumstances.

Aynward shouted, "Guards! This man has stolen university property. Please search and detain him."

The men responded immediately, having already been briefed on the nature of the contraband carried by Theo. To the boy's credit, he didn't run or resist. He opened his arms and allowed the guard to inspect the contents of his satchel and robes. The man knelt down and started going through Theo's possessions, and even felt Theo up and down to make sure he didn't miss anything. "There's nothing here. Unless a copy of *Hobbes's Algebraic Theory* is being smuggled for the purpose of boring someone to death."

Aynward moved in closer to see for himself. "It has to be there."

Theo laughed and said, "That's enough fooling around for one night, boys."

The comment made no sense to Aynward until he heard the shout from Kyllean, followed by a similar, if more effeminate, one from Hirk. By the time he realized what was happening, the guard kneeling by Theo's satchel had swiveled and wrapped his arms around Aynward's legs. Theo sprang over the top to crash into Aynward's upper half; he toppled like a felled tree. Aynward could do little to maneuver his way out of the compromised position and Theo battered him with punches. Aynward blocked the worst of them, abandoning any offense after the first few hits struck; he covered his face with his arms as best he could. Nevertheless more than a few connected before Theo ceased the assault.

"Guards, please arrest these three for the crime of false testimony. I believe the penalty for such is punishable in equal proportion to the accused crime. Say, how much did you say this book was worth, *Prince* Aynward?"

Aynward opened his mouth, but no words came. He couldn't believe what was happening. Maybe Theo had left the book at his dormitory, but why? This was all wrong.

"Wait, no. He has the book! Detain him and check his room!" Aynward pleaded.

Theo found that amusing. "No. It is not in my room." He pulled out something from his satchel. Holding a thick tome, he said to the guards, "Gentlemen, I suspect you'll all be pleased to find out just how much this fetches. Your cut will be distributed by the end of the week. See that Aynward and his friends here find their way to the university dungeon to await sentencing. I assume you don't need me there just yet for testimony. The word of eight guards should suffice to keep these three out of my hair for a few—years?"

Aynward had been turned face down, iron manacles secured around his wrists. The man behind him answered, "These three will not be seeing the light of day for many seasons, and that's if the tribunal is feeling generous. After what the two Kingdom-born fools pulled earlier this year, I suspect it will be *much* longer."

Theo chuckled. "Please assure the dean that I'll be along to offer an official testimony as soon as the trauma of the incident has worn off. This has been a *very* stressful night. Oh, and Aynward, I may even pay you a visit. I especially appreciate compliments on my—intellect."

## CHAPTER 101

# SINDRI

SINDRI OPENED HER EYES. THE familiarity of her surroundings brought back the memory of the last time she had been awake. She was in the same unknown room. She had tried for the door and passed out. She had to keep her panic in check. *Relax. Your body is weak. Breathe. Slowly.* She looked around the room and froze, her calm shattered.

A man sat in the chair that had previously been empty. He smiled at her, his expression calm, almost sympathetic.

"Peace, Sindri. Peace."

The man spoke the common tongue, and didn't seem interested in harming her, but she remained unsettled. Was he associated with the men who had barged into their room and attacked? Where was she? More important, where was Kibure?

That last question was the first to cross her lips. "Where is he?"

The man was frustratingly slow to answer and devoid of emotion. "We are working on finding your friend. For now, he is *missing*. The eyes I had on your residence were unable to withstand all three mages. They were forced to choose between you and your friend."

Sindri sat up, a painful rush of pressure returning to her head, but not as strong as the last time. "Who are you?"

"I am the Count of Brinkwell, Count Gornstein. I am a friend of Draílock."

*The Count of Brinkwell? Draílock is connected to the Count of Brinkwell?*

None of that mattered. Not while Kibure was gone. "We have need to find him. These men, these men are Klerósi priests!"

"Yes. We're working to uncover his whereabouts," the man said, still too calm for Sindri's taste considering the grave danger Kibure faced. "Tell me, Sindri. Is your companion Kibure a wielder? Draílock mentioned that he was taking part in the training you were beginning to receive, but that neither one of you appeared to have made much progress. Is there more to him than you let on, or do you suppose your heritage drew the attention of these men?"

What could she say? The nightmares Kibure claimed to have had were inexplicable. His powers were likewise inconsistent—like her brother's had been. There was no doubt that he had been radiating magic right before the attack. She decided the more she told the count, the harder he might search for him. "He is one who wields of the power. You have need to find him! They will soon make him to not live!"

## CHAPTER 102

# AYNWARD

A YNWARD SANK BACK AGAINST THE wall, his voice hoarse from screaming.

Kyllean spoke up, "I'm sure they're sorting out the truth as we speak. We'll be out of here in no time. I hear the dean is a decent and fair fellow so long as you stay on his good—" Kyllean let his statement go unfinished, knowing he was the only one of the three captives to appreciate the warped humor, present conditions considered.

The prisoners were each chained to their own loop, which was anchored into the wall above. Thankfully the chain was long enough that Aynward could sit or lie on the stone comfortably—a very relative term, he realized. The jailer who brought them their second meal had said that the dean would be over shortly to discuss the criminal proceedings.

Aynward could still hardly believe what had happened. How had he been so stupid? Of course Theo had purchased the guards' loyalty. How else was he able to hang Aynward from a tree right out in the open with such impunity? Aynward's overconfidence had cost him dearly this time. And not only that, he had dragged others down with him. He was fairly certain that he would be released before a full term, as soon as

Dolmuevo sent word home to his father. The King would send a firm request with a sizable sum of gold, and Aynward would be released and sent home, though that prospect was not much better than the cell. He would be punished, probably for the rest of his life, but he supposed he *almost* deserved it at this point. Meanwhile, Hirk and Kyllean would receive no such leniency. Kyllean's family might be capable of persuading clemency, but he would still be expelled from the university upon release. And Hirk; he was a victim of circumstance, a pawn for both sides, yet he would suffer the most. Aynward had to do *something*. But what *could* he do?

The jangling of keys outside of the door announced the arrival of either more food or a visitor. Either would be a welcome change. A shadowy figure clad in robes entered. Aynward recognized the slouch in the man's stature and knew this was Dean Remson.

Aynward's excitement was crushed when Hirk was taken, followed by Kyllean. Each was returned before Aynward was called upon to attend the dean. Still shackled, he clanged his way across the dank, depressing floor.

He was brought into a different room and positioned across from Dean Remson at a stone table, the only illumination coming from oil lamps on either side. The dean was silent for an uncomfortably long time. Aynward decided he would be the one to break the silence.

"I know you won't believe my innocence in this. Theo made it very clear that he had paid the guards well enough that they'll all corroborate his lies. Not that it matters too much to you, considering your preexisting bias, but I have a bargain I'd like to offer in exchange for a full admission of guilt, untrue as it will be."

The dean barked a laugh. "*You* are in no position to bargain. You involved eight witnesses in your crime of false testimony. Your confession will be meaningless, especially when reviewing your *record* of mayhem throughout the university."

That wasn't exactly what Aynward had been hoping to hear. All the stories he had read that involved heroes who were temporarily imprisoned had involved some sort of bargain for favorable terms. He had been hoping to at least get Kyllean and Hirk exonerated. *Okay, desperate times call for desperate words.*

"You do know who I am?"

"I do." The dean appeared unimpressed, as if he had already weighed this fact.

"How do you think my father is going to treat this matter when he learns that you imprisoned me under false pretenses, along with another one of his subjects of the Kingdom gentry?"

The dean huffed, "Considering the falsehood of your claim, I don't think he'll feel any way about it besides disappointed, something I would think he should be used to at this point. There is nothing false about the pretenses in which you have been imprisoned. It is simple law."

Aynward gathered up as much confidence as he could for his bluff, then forced a smile. "Do you really think my own father is going to believe the word of your university guards and a former street urchin? I've already written him with the details of my injuries during your ridiculous welcoming ceremony, and he nearly sent a fleet here to retake my fees and bring me home. My own urging is the only thing that prevented that from happening. And I detailed my plans to reveal Theo's illegal activities to my personal counselor, Minster Dolmuevo Humiliab, before leaving to expose him. He's likely already written to petition my father on my behalf. So when *the King* hears of this clear violation of justice, I can't imagine he'll be pleased, or interested in whatever excuse you have brewing. I've heard him speak ill of the inherited burden of protecting all of the Isles cities; an antiquated arrangement, I believe he calls it."

Aynward paused, as if considering for the first time, which in truth, he was. "Wouldn't be too much to have our naval patrols sail right on past Brinkwell, would it? My father would be relieved to have the excuse." He gasped. "Oh my, how upset will the Count of Brinkwell be when he learns that the actions of the university dean caused the entire city to be left unprotected, especially with the Shep-Shin pirates so close by? That wouldn't be cause to, maybe, reevaluate the sovereign jurisdiction of this university within the city, would it?"

Aynward felt his confidence surge and his momentum accelerate as he went. He *almost* believed his own words. He leaned back and smiled, as if having just struck a debilitating blow in the game of kings. He loved watching opponents squirm as they realized their doom.

Before he earned a response, a loud knock sounded on the metal of the door. "Come in," said the dean.

A jailer entered and whispered something in the dean's ear. If the man had gone pale at Aynward's bluff, he had become snow at whatever news he'd been brought. "Very well. Please return the young Aynward to his cell." The dean stood and said, "Good evening."

Aynward had him right where he wanted him; he couldn't lose the hard-fought upper hand he'd gained when he was so close. He needed an answer. Now. "Wait. You didn't even hear my proposal. I'm willing to talk my father out of—"

"My sincerest apologies, but something requires my immediate attention. It cannot wait. We will resume this conversation on the morrow. Just"—he looked to the jailer—"don't allow him any parchment or ink. We need to finish this discussion before allowing any further communications with his home."

## CHAPTER 103

# SINDRI

SINDRI SAT UP IN HER bed, feeling better than she had in many hours. The more restored she felt, the more she wanted to be out in the city searching for Kibure. Count Gornstein had, through much effort, convinced her to remain in his palace. The Lugienese captors had already seen what she looked like, and they were magic-wielding priests. He assured her that he was doing all he could to find the boy, and that he had people with the means of combating the priests' powers.

After what seemed a long time, she could no longer remain cooped up. Finding her legs sturdy once again, she decided to take a stroll. Perhaps moving about would help keep her mind away from the reality that Kibure was likely dying, or dead. She didn't wish to think on that. She felt a pang of guilt as she considered her prevailing view of him as a mere tool, a means to obtain the answers she had sought since her brother's death and her exile from the Kleról. What was worse, Sindri had grown fond of the innocent boy with innate powers; powers that could not be explained. Part of her frustration with him, she realized, was how similar he was to her own brother. The nightmares, the wild, untamed use of magic, and even the youthful naïveté, though Kibure had grown considerably in these last weeks. All of this made his capture more painful to accept. It was like she had failed her brother twice. Her chance to redeem him, lost.

Sindri shook off those thoughts and used the inspection of her surroundings to distract herself. The count's palace was magnificent; nothing compared with the scope of Magog's grand palace, which she recalled vividly from her single visit years ago. But after years staying in hovels, inns, and a few caves, she could appreciate the grandeur of this place. Much of the stone of the walls was the same speckled blue as the university, a smooth marble-like material. And there was an artistic element to this design that was missing from Magog's palace; the geometric carvings and paintings that occupied the empty spaces here spoke of an appreciation for beauty that was rare within the Empire.

The scent of food caught Sindri's nose and she realized she was hungry. She followed the aroma to a wide, domed dining hall beset with breathtaking murals of majestic ships conquering varying degrees of stormy seas. Sindri's eyes didn't linger on the decor for long. There were four stately tables, each capable of seating a dozen people and more than half of the seats were occupied. Sindri quickly scanned the room in search of the count, but he was not in attendance. What she did notice, however, was the spreading silence as heads turned to regard her. Sindri noted that several of them had tears in their eyes. *What, in all of Doréa, is going on here?*

Having once been privy to the navigation of political intrigue, Sindri knew how to target a talker in a crowd. She surveyed the people more closely before settling on a wide-eyed bald man at the end of the nearest table. Eyes remained fixed on her as she approached, but the reasons for their discomfort varied. Some wore expressions of fear, while others donned scowls, and a small few seemed ready to stand up and attack. She decided she would use this emotional volatility to her advantage. Mustering up as much courage as she could, she strode to the empty chair beside the cowering man.

He shrank further than his poor posture should allow, putting his head comedically close to the surface of the table. Before saying anything to him, Sindri waved to one of the two matching gentlemen she assumed were servants and requested a meal. She didn't care what she ate, and made that point clear when the servant had tried to present a menu. This exercise in command brought back the attitude of confidence she recalled from her days as an active priestess.

Once the servant had departed, Sindri focused on her prey. "Excuse of me, sir?"

The man avoided looking in her direction. He was shoveling food into his mouth, ignoring all forms of dining etiquette, apparently hoping to be gone from the table before she had a chance to converse with him.

"Excuse of me, sir." This time more firmly.

The man sank lower than she thought possible. "Yes?" he said with a mouth full of food.

"Can you tell me why these people have of the fear"—she looked around then added—"and have anger of me?"

The man looked about, seeking eye contact with anyone willing to offer assistance. He found none.

"Sir?"

With no one to help him, he finally opened his mouth to reply. "A sh-ship arrived this morning to port, a Pa-Pa-Palpanese sh-ship." The man looked around again, and again found no allies. "Word spread that there was a L-L-Lugienese woman h-he-here in the palace."

Frustrated with the man's inability to make any sense, she stood up and pounded a fist on the table. What did she care at this point?

"What is common with me to the Lugienese and a ship of the Palpanese? Your words have no sense."

A young girl several seats away squeaked a response. "Rumors from those onboard the ship have begun to circulate. The Lugienese have conquered the Palpanese Union. This ship that arrived is the only one to have escaped the Lugienese assault. Brinkwell is believed to be their next target. Your brethren bring war."

Sindri's contrived confidence was sliced open by the implication. The Lugienese now had a legitimate navy, and if this rumor was true,

Brinkwell would indeed be their next target. They had only weeks if they were lucky. Sindri suddenly wished she had remained in bed.

## CHAPTER 104

# AYNWARD

A FAINT SOUND CAUGHT AYNWARD'S ATTENTION. He listened more intently, which was difficult with Kyllean's constant chatter and Hirk's incessant crying. There it was again. It sounded almost like distant yelling. For some reason, he'd always assumed prisons had lots of that: chained figures shouting for their freedom. However, as of yet, the atmosphere was more on the stagnant, silent side, excepting Kyllean, but Aynward figured even he would lose steam eventually.

So when the shouting grew louder, Aynward shushed his friend, who was in the middle of some theory about the most effective compliments one could give to women, depending on the color of their hair. Kyllean listened, too, as the sounds grew closer, much closer. The creaking of an iron door brought new clarity to the previously muffled noise. A hoarse voice yelled, "You can't do this! I didn't do anything. It was all him! All him, I tell you!"

Aynward knew that voice. But his mind couldn't accept it. Then he heard the dean's similarly distressed voice. "This is highly irregular—in fact, it's illegal! City guards do *not* belong inside these sovereign walls!"

A new voice responded. "Then I guess it's a good thing these men are not with the city guard, they are *my personal* guard, with the jurisdiction to go wherever *I* go, and I am currently here. Perhaps if your own university guards weren't beholden to the highest bidder, I'd not have had to get my own men involved in the first place."

Aynward did not know the voice of this man, but it held authority, that much was certain. Who could be powerful *and bold* enough to speak to the dean in such a manner?

"Do you have proof of this allegation?" stammered Dean Remson.

"Would I be here if I did not? This will all be moot in days, anyhow. I just needed to get the vermin out of my way so I can focus on more important things like saving the city or at least the people in it."

"Oh? Wait—what? What in the Isles are you talking about?"

Ignoring the question, the man said, "Where are the three who were arrested? I will be taking them. I have important business with one of them."

Aynward's head snapped up at that. What was he talking about? Could it be . . . ?

Now it was the dean's turn to attempt a tone of authority. "Absolutely not! They are charged with—"

The other man's voice took on an air of power that slammed the dean's voice to the stone floor. "They are guilty of truthful allegations against the very guilty man I just brought in! He was found on his way to the docks with *this* book, a book that belongs in *your* university archives. You've arrested these three young men for false testimony, and this proves their accusations to be true. You *will* step aside and open the door, or I will be forced to deliver you to the gatekeeper of the underworld a bit earlier than he was expecting."

"I—I—yes—I—of course, Count Gornstein. I meant no disrespect." the dean squeaked.

The mention of the title confirmed Aynward's unlikely suspicions as the hinges on the door groaned. A thickly bearded man dressed in all black but for the crest of Brinkwell stepped through the doorway, the count himself. He spoke. "This is them?"

Dean Remson scampered past him into the cell. "Yes. I'll release them immediately."

The dean averted his eyes the entire time he worked his shaky fingers to release Aynward, Kyllean, and Hirk. "There they are. Free and clear. I apologize for the mis—"

The man's voice cut him short once more. "Make preparations to hold a university assembly on the morn. The city will be under attack in days. We must evacuate. No one is to remain behind."

Looking to the three newly freed students, he said, "Gentlemen, please, follow me."

The dean had frozen, but finally managed to say, "Wh-wh-what? Under attack? Who? How?"

The count had turned toward the exit and continued down the corridor without looking back as he answered, "I'll send a runner with details before night's end. I suggest you begin packing your things, and making friends with someone who owns a ship."

## CHAPTER 105

# SINDRI

N O ONE KNEW WHERE COUNT Gornstein was or when he planned to return. And no one seemed to even know who Draílock was. Therefore, Sindri remained in the palace in a state of frustration while questions about Kibure's safety along with that of her own fate soured within her mind.

She paced the hallways for hours before finally settling into a chair in a small alcove. She must have dozed off because she heard herself yelp as the sound of footsteps snapped her back into the conscious realm. Her eyes initially focused on Gornstein, but her questions for him slipped when she noticed the boy who had escorted her to the university—Aynward?—along with his friend, whose name she could not recall.

The count greeted her with, "Ah, Sindri, glad to see you're feeling better," but he continued walking past, apparently having other, more important business.

"Uh—yes." She tried to stand, but found her legs less supportive than she had hoped. The boy, Aynward, was just passing by and reached out an arm to steady her.

Once on her feet, she placed a hand on the wall, then shook off Aynward's steadying hand. "Thank you, I have health."

Gornstein had rounded the corner and was heading down another long corridor. Sindri followed the trio into a study, the walls of which were lined with books. The majority of the space was taken up by a long, wooden table with more than a dozen seats, one of which was occupied by a man who appeared to have been waiting with arms folded for quite some time.

Count Gornstein took a seat at the head of the table, then gestured for everyone else to sit. He made eye contact with Sindri, and appeared to consider sending her away before finally nodding to indicate that she could remain.

Aynward took hold of the chair next to her but then froze in place. He addressed the man who had been in the room when they arrived. "Gervais? What are you doing here?"

The thin man's eyes flicked to the count, then back to Aynward. He smiled warmly. "I have been on the count's payroll for quite some time."

"You work for—wait—all that money you were able to come up with to pay off—Count Gornstein was the *employer* of which you spoke? Why would the count wish to have books stolen from the university?"

Gervais nodded, as if expecting the question. "A mutual acquaintance of ours teaches at the university. This counselor grew concerned over the disappearance of some very old, very obscure, and *very* valuable works of literature. Count Gornstein found this most intriguing and asked if I knew anyone else with less notable access to the university. It just so happened that one of my dealings in the city included a woman with a nephew who was to be enrolled."

Sindri watched Aynward's face as he spoke with the man. She was having a difficult time following the story without any context. But Aynward's scowl projected his feelings about the situation. "So I was merely a convenient pawn in all of this? You risked my safety for the sake of a few missing books?"

The count interrupted the exchange to answer, "The disappearance of several precious books, specifically historical anthologies of the various kingdoms and families of Drogen, and even more-obscure journals, was more than a mere curiosity. Someone seemed intent on identifying the lines of power east of Angolia, and was willing to pay vast sums of money to have this information stolen. I now believe this to have been the work of Lugienese spies hiding in the city. It was a matter of security. Someone had been supplying these people from within the university walls, and our acquaintance in the university was not in a position favorable to uncovering such goings-on with any semblance of discretion."

"So you used *me* to ferret out the information," stated Aynward angrily.

Sindri watched Gervais reach up to straighten his robe. He took his time; the accusation hung heavy in the air. "No, no." He paused. "Huh." He shook his head. "Now that you mention it, I suppose we did."

"I was assaulted!"

Gervais remained impassive.

Aynward added, "On two separate occasions, then arrested!"

Sindri could see the boy's frustration increase at Gervais's lack of empathy. Indeed, Gervais appeared to find the entire exchange humorous. "Well, you made enemies of Theo before his involvement was even known. I guess you're just a good judge of character."

Aynward snorted. "Your *character* is ranking very low right now, Gervais. Very low. What if you'd not caught Theo? What then? Was I to rot in a cell until my father sent for me to be returned?"

Gervais pondered the question as if he had never considered the possibility. "Pfft, I'm sure it would have all worked itself out. We had other contingencies in place."

"And just how *did* you end up catching the thief, anyway?"

Gervais smiled. "I had my concerns about your safety during an exchange with Kubal. I contacted the count about having some of his guard in the neighborhood ready to intervene if the situation grew perilous. When Theo was spotted leaving the university and you were nowhere to be found, I knew something had gone awry. So I had them seize and search Theo. He had the book in a satchel, and here we are: a happy ending." He flourished his hands, but the heavy tension in the room smothered his attempt at comedic relief.

Aynward finally shouted, causing Sindri to jump in her seat. "I was chained to a wall all night and into the next day!"

Count Gornstein coughed, drawing everyone's attention. "What's done is done. You are no longer in a dungeon. Brood and blame all you wish once you're safely out of the city. The Lugienese army is on our doorstep. We don't know when they'll arrive, but it could be mere days from now. Brinkwell is not defensible, not on such short notice. Most of our residents will be evacuated to the Isles city of Tung. We will begin setting up our defenses there in hopes that the Kingdom of Dowe will be able to intercede on our behalf before it comes to a siege.

"In the meantime, we have to vacate the city. I have five merchant ships of my own, four of which are in the harbor, the fifth due to arrive shortly. I'll be waiting for the latter with my personal guard while I ensure the rest of the city is evacuated. Aynward, Kyllean, Sindri"—he pointed at each as he spoke—"you and most other notable residents will be leaving on one of the four ships I have in port." Sindri was taken aback that he had pointed at her. He hardly knew her, and she was Lugienese!

"Unfortunately, I don't have enough vessels to carry everyone from the city. I sent doves to all of the closest ports, pleading for assistance in the evacuation, but I fear few will risk their own ships. Many residents will be forced to flee along the mountain road toward the inner isle; however, escape to the other cities may very well be futile. The Lugienese are not likely to leave any untaken for long."

Aynward spoke up. "What if your ship doesn't arrive in time?"

The count replied, "It may not. But that is the risk I accepted when taking on the responsibility of this office."

*A man of honor*, thought Sindri. *A rare trait.*

The count stood abruptly. "Go pack your things and meet back here before night's end. The city will likely devolve into chaos as word spreads. I'm going to utilize my limited resources to keep some semblance of order to this evacuation, but once the word is out, it will be very difficult to get you onboard any ship without bloodshed. The sooner you are all out of the city, the better. Your ship leaves at dawn."

Sindri had gone stiff. *If he thinks I'm leaving this city without Kibure, he has lost his mind.* She stood. "What of Kibure? You have found him?"

The man remained irritatingly expressionless as he answered, "We have not. Unfortunately this new development has placed significant strain on my resources."

She felt her hands form tight fists as she said, "I do not leave of this place if Kibure can still have life!"

The count nodded, unsurprised by this reaction. "I understand. Perhaps, with your health restored, you could answer a few questions that may help in the search. Draílock and another local ateré mage are working to uncover his whereabouts."

Fuming that she'd not been told sooner, Sindri nearly shouted across the table, "Well, where are they?"

## CHAPTER 106

# AYNWARD

A YNWARD WAS OVERWHELMED WITH QUESTIONS, yet seeing the intensity of Sindri's anger, he felt it prudent to not speak. But still, *magic? Real* magic? It was one thing to read about it in stories long dead, or even rumors from distant lands, but this was right here in their midst.

*Is Sindri a magic user? I thought she could no longer wield Klerós's power. Is the missing Kibure the kid who was in Sindri's room when I stopped by to escort her to class? How exactly had he gone missing?* Those questions were replaced by even more questions from earlier revelations. *What does Gervais actually do for the count? Does Dolme know about this connection? Does my aunt know?* And more disconcerting to him than all the rest: *does the evacuation mean I'm to return home?*

As much as he had initially dreaded leaving home, the prospect of returning now seemed a veritable tragedy. Conflicting feelings along with more questions tumbled around his head, each vying for supremacy.

Aynward thought it best to wait until Sindri and the count left the room before asking Gervais about that last exchange. He glanced over at Kyllean in the interim. His friend had remained surprisingly silent throughout the entire ordeal. Did he have similar questions? The jokester had not gone this long without speaking the entire time Aynward had known him.

Once Sindri and Count Gornstein had passed through the doorway, Aynward turned to Gervais. "I think you have some explaining to do, *Mr. Servant.*"

Gervais slowly turned his gaze to meet Aynward's eye, then finally said, "You're going to have to be a bit more specific with your question."

"How about we start with you telling me how long you have been one of the count's spies?"

Gervais didn't flinch at the accusation, which meant either that it was true or so ridiculous a claim it didn't warrant a response. He responded levelly, "I am an adviser of finance to the count. I handle many of his investments, much like I do for your aunt. I'll grant you that I do occasionally hear whispers in the city and my allegiance to the count prevents me from withholding them. But a spy?" He laughed.

Aynward supposed that if he were a spy, he would likely not admit such. He decided to lay that thought aside for the time being, but he didn't disregard it completely. There was *something* there.

He glanced over at the still silent Kyllean. Gervais's denial had caught his friend's attention, but he had merely rolled his eyes. Aynward continued his questioning. "Okay, well—as an adviser of finance, you should be capable of explaining the whole *Count Gornstein has his mages working on finding a missing person* thing. Mages must cost money to employ, right?"

Gervais chuckled lightly then said, "Yes, you are correct that this falls within my realm of dealings. But I fear there is little to say on that topic, as little is known. The woman Sindri arrived in the city with a traveling companion named Kibure. We believe three men attacked their room two days past, all of them Lugienese wielders of the Kleról. Sindri was injured after being thrown out of their building by some form of magical propulsion, so it was said. Little else is known, as Kibure was then abducted and has not yet been recovered."

That was—alarming. Aynward hadn't realized—

Kyllean broke his silent streak to ask a question of his own. "Wait—there are Lugienese wizards in the city? Like—right now?"

Then it clicked in Aynward's mind: *are they the same people who've been purchasing stolen books from the archives?* That made a frightening amount of sense.

Gervais made eye contact with both boys before replying, "It would seem there are indeed Lugienese sorcerers in the city. They have been hiding right under our noses, preparing the way for their brethren to take the city."

Aynward went on to his next question. "But Count Gornstein has wielders at his disposal as well, right? How many?"

Gervais sighed. "The count has a firm working relationship with at least three users of ateré magic, and a number of other priestly wielders of various faiths throughout the city. However, more than a dozen priests have come up missing or dead over the course of the last month, along with one of his ateré wielders. And we have no idea how many of the enemy are already in the city."

Aynward realized it was all connected: the abductions, Dwapek's class, and the stolen books. *Have to be.* This caused the danger they faced at a Lugienese invasion to further resonate. The Lugienese had been planning this for a long time. As if Gervais were thinking the same thing, he stood. "Well, young sire, I think it prudent we make our way to your aunt's residence, that we might prepare for the evacuation. Your aunt will be among those on the first ship and will likely need some time to decide what few items she can afford to bring. This will not be easy for her. And Kyllean, an announcement is likely being made at the university as we speak. You, too, should pack your things and return here. It seems someone at the university likes you. Your name also appears on the list of those to board one of the count's ships." He started for the door and Aynward followed.

Kyllean's attempt at a jovial response was a poor mask for the concern in his voice. "Well, my stepmother always told me my smile could win anyone's favor."

Aynward and Gervais walked with Kyllean to the university entrance and paused where they would part ways. Then Aynward asked Gervais, "Am I going to be forced to return home after this?"

Gervais took a moment to answer. "If you were my child, I'd be calling for your immediate return in the face of the danger that approaches. I suspect that a Kingdom vessel will be waiting to intercept you by the time you arrive in Tung."

Kyllean tried to lighten the mood. "Don't feel so bad. If and when I get home, I have to decide whether to be exiled and live in ignorance, or swear the family oath and never leave. Of course, I'd get my own Lumále if I survived the training." He brought a finger to his chin in thought. "Tough choice, this."

Aynward scowled. "See you soon, Kyllean."

Gervais and Aynward continued toward their residence. Aynward had come to enjoy the place and the people he'd met. Most of them. More importantly, he didn't feel like someone was judging his every action anymore. Dolme of course did, but Dolme was more like a discomfort Aynward had grown accustomed to and therefore could easily ignore. While in Brinkwell he was his own man. Few knew who he was, and even those who did seemed to treat him, well, *normal.* Back home, he felt the weight of his disappointment to his father every time he saw the man. Since arriving in Brinkwell, the burden may have still been there somewhere, but it felt more like he'd jumped into water, the weight seeming to float rather than crush him. The notion of returning home turned his stomach into a tighter knot than the thought of the approaching Lugienese fleet.

## CHAPTER 107

# SINDRI

THE LIGHT FROM THE AFTERNOON sun slipped away as Count Gornstein led Sindri farther below the main floors of the palace. She was near to voicing a complaint about the dangers of walking in the dark when the count lit a torch and removed it from a sconce on the wall. They continued their descent until they could go no farther. The steep stairs had led to a disappointingly small, circular room without doors. Sindri was further confused when the count walked over to the wall and began feeling around as if to climb it. She was about to ask what in Klerós's name he was doing when a low rumble sounded. She jumped ready to bolt back up the stairs. Then she saw that the solid wall was moving, becoming an opening into which Gornstein immediately disappeared.

"Come now, we're short for time," his voice echoed.

They moved beneath the city for long minutes, occasionally descending small flights of stairs. The underground tunnel frequently split along the way, and in some cases there were four or more directions from which to choose, but the count moved through the maze of tunnels without hesitation.

He finally engaged another pattern of depressions in a place where no tunnel appeared to exist and was rewarded by another gentle rumble of moving stone. Sindri froze in place. She felt *magic*. She knew she was being brought to see two magicians, but the sudden sensation of magic put her on edge nonetheless.

Gornstein turned. "Don't be alarmed, you're not sensing an enemy. Draílock and Arella are just beyond this wall."

"How do you—"

Intuiting her question, the count pulled an amulet from beneath his cloak. The gemstone set inside it pulsed with faint blue light. She had seen its likeness before: Draílock wore its twin around his neck. "I am no wizard," he was quick to say. "This enchanted amulet amplifies the sensations felt by the use of magic, allowing even the likes of me to know when sorcerers are working close at hand."

*Neat trick.* She nodded her understanding before following him into the corridor. She almost tripped over her own feet as she realized that she recognized this place. She heard two voices as they approached the room where Draílock had first instructed Sindri and Kibure in ateré magic. One of them was unfamiliar, a female, but the other was the unmistakably deep, hollow resonance of Draílock's voice. Considering the immensely costly, magical amulet and the existence of a tunnel leading directly to Draílock's underground lair, Sindri decided that the count worked more closely with these mages than he had initially implied.

The layout of the room had not changed; two stone couches faced each other at its center, made comfortable by an array of plush cushions. Draílock and the other mage were positioned at the far couch, facing where Sindri and the count had just entered. As she moved closer, Sindri saw that Draílock's shoulders were hunched in exhaustion. She had not seen him so ragged before. He appeared to be deep in concentration.

Sindri glanced at the woman seated beside him. She looked young, very young, though part of that impression was given by thin, delicate features. She had blond shoulder-length hair, olive skin, and determined eyes. She, too, was focusing hard on something. Neither one acknowledged the arrival of the two guests.

Sindri attempted to follow the magicians' line of sight; however, the subject of their attention was obstructed by the back of the closest couch. Sindri continued toward them to get a better look and nearly lost her footing as the object of the wizards' attention came into full view.

There was a small cage set at their feet. Sindri gasped just as a familiar sound escaped the black creature; a black raaven stared directly at her.

## CHAPTER 108

# AYNWARD

GERVAIS OPENED AUNT MELANIE'S FRONT door to a fuming Dolme.

"Well? Where is he?"

Gervais placed a hand on Dolme's shoulder, a gesture Aynward thought a bit risky considering Dolme's mood. "Peace, brother. As I promised, he has been brought here safely. And the count has made arrangements for our travel out of the city."

Dolme was dressed like a caravan mercenary, his clothes loose and designed for fighting, and his sword visible at his waist. Gervais noticed and swiftly attempted a compliment. "Ah, I see my message arrived safely, you're ready to travel. Excellent!"

Dolme did not share in Gervais's excitement about his readiness to flee the city. Ignoring Gervais's attempts to pacify his anger, he shouted at Aynward, "We're going to have a nice, long conversation about what actually happened these last few days. I am so naïve to believe Gervais's poor attempts to cover up the trail of stupidity you leave in your wake."

Aynward didn't respond, unsure of what to say. *Better to remain silent and be thought the fool.* He was generally not composed enough to follow that old proverb.

Dolme waved a hand. "Go gather your things. I placed a pack in your room. Fill it with as much as you can fit. Everything else remains behind."

Aynward turned to escape up the stairs and heard Dolme yell behind him, "Strap on your sword, and pray you're not forced to use it."

Aynward was glad when they arrived back at the palace without having to draw their swords. He could feel the tension throughout the city, but it had not yet bubbled over into violence.

It was dinner time when they arrived, and Aynward was quick to claim starvation, hoping to forestall the lecture he knew approached from Dolme's darker-than-normal mood. He was pleased to see Kyllean, Minathi, and a few other students from the university, as well as a number of university staff.

The palace was bustling with the families of local nobility, all readying for the same desperate escape. The palace kitchen staff were hard at work preparing as much of the food as possible; they knew that the rest of their stores would have to be destroyed. The count passed through the dining hall and found Gervais, who was happily shoveling mouthfuls of onioned steak into his mouth. Aynward overheard portions of this conversation in spite of Kyllean's yammering.

"Have we persuaded any more ships to take on people instead of cargo?"

Gervais shook his head sadly. "I sent out a few missives while the boy packed, but we will likely not hear back until tomorrow."

The count's shoulders slumped as he leaned in to speak more softly. Aynward placed an elbow on the table and turned his back to the pair, getting his ear close enough to catch what was being said. He hoped he wasn't being too obvious.

"Rumors of my ships have spread too far. I don't have room for all the people who've weaseled their way into the palace in hopes of boarding one of my vessels. I'm going to have to use my own guard to close off the ships tomorrow morning." Aynward could see Gornstein shaking his head from the corner of his eye. He finished, "And can you blame them for trying?"

"These are desperate times," was all Gervais could say in response. Aynward stole a glance behind him and saw Gervais rising to his feet. The spy looked around the room suspiciously as he said, "Let us discuss the rest of the preparations in your study."

"Very well," agreed the count.

Aynward surveyed the bustling clusters of people filling the room. A chubby man nearby shouted, "I've brought a wagon of my wine stores. I'm told we can't carry it aboard the ship, so let us not leave any to the enemy! Follow me!"

That got a cheer from several within earshot, and Aynward saw Kyllean spring to his feet. Minathi sat close by, but remained seated. "Don't worry; I'll grab one for each of us."

Something about the prospect of thousands being left for dead or worse at the hands of the Lugienese soured the thought of wine for Aynward. When Kyllean returned with his promised prize, Aynward was able to take no more than a few sips before setting down the goblet for the night.

"Excuse me, Minathi, Kyllean. I think I'm going to retire for the evening. I'm feeling unwell."

He figured he would find one of the many vacant rooms in the palace in which to lie down. He didn't know if he would be able to fall asleep, but he needed to get away from this place. He needed peace and quiet. He had managed to wriggle himself away from the watchful eye of Minster Dolmuevo, but as he crossed the room to enter the hallway, he heard his name. He cringed and pretended not to hear, but Dolme had caught his trail.

"Aynward! Just where do you think you're headed?"

The prince turned to face Dolme. It was a testament to Aynward's fatigue that he refrained from the sarcastic tone he would have ordinarily taken with the man he despised so much. "I'm tired, Dolme. I just want to lie down and rest. I've no great scheme planned, if that's your concern."

Dolme gave a doubtful look.

"Stand guard at the door if you wish. Spin me around if I sleepwalk toward the exit."

Aynward turned to leave without waiting for a response. He made it into the hallway before Dolme retorted, but the man had kept pace with him. "Go rest for now. You and I *will* have a *lengthy* conversation about what has transpired over these last few weeks."

Dolme was speaking to a moving target.

"There will be nowhere for you to hide once we set sail."

Aynward rounded the corner, his anger mixing with growing despair at what was coming to the city. He passed several occupied rooms before backtracking to the library. There were several padded benches and he settled on the nearest one. He cuddled up and felt the exhaustion of the last few days radiate through his body. He'd not slept well while in the prison, and the tumult of new developments had plunged him into a state of weakness he could no longer withstand. As agitated as he was, he slipped into a deep sleep within seconds of sinking onto the bench.

Aynward shouted as he fell and struck the wooden floor. "Wh-where am—"

Everything came back to him in a flash, and he scrambled to his feet. Too fast. His vision went black, his legs collapsing from under him. A strong grip held him in place.

"Whoa, easy there," came Kyllean's voice. Aynward felt his body accept the fact that he was standing again and patted Kyllean as he opened his eyes.

"Thank you."

"Of course." Kyllean held his arm a moment longer before releasing it. "Although, that Dolmuevo guy of yours was going to cut me open if I'd not gone to find you, so I didn't have much choice in the matter."

"I appreciate the honesty," Aynward said as he started toward the door. The hall was still lit by torchlight and he felt as if he'd not slept at all. Shaking his head, he asked, "How early is it?"

"A few hours before sunrise is what I heard. Seems about right to me, I guess."

Now that Aynward was awake, he noticed the slur in Kyllean's speech and shook his head. "You didn't sleep at all, did you?"

"Noooooope."

"Where'd you leave Minathi?" Aynward was surprised he'd allowed her out of his sight.

"She's back in the ballroom watching her and my things while I find you."

"Ah," replied Aynward. "So it's time to leave then?"

"That it is. That it is."

## CHAPTER 109

# SINDRI

"RAVE?" SQUEALED SINDRI, DOING NOTHING to mask her surprise. She looked to Draílock for explanation. When nothing was forthcoming, she turned back to Count Gornstein, who hadn't moved any farther into the room.

"Why is raaven of the cage?" Her surprise was still there, but she took an accusatory tone, wondering why they would capture Kibure's—well, whatever Rave was to Kibure. She still didn't understand that connection, but she did know that Rave had helped both of them escape from the clutches of the Lugienese priests.

Draílock answered, "We believe the Lugienese were using this creature to spy on you and Kibure."

Sindri almost laughed, but the situation was too dire. She snorted instead. "This creature is no enemy. He is the friend of Kibure. You have need to release him, *now.*"

The two wizards returned hard, distrustful expressions. Neither moved to release the black animal. Sindri took the initiative and walked around the couch. She rushed to the cage and started searching for the mechanism to open it.

Draílock raised a hand. "Unless you've progressed more than I suspect, you're going to need to first explain why we should release this creature. Our own form of castration spells were ineffective, but the cage is enchanted; you'll not open it without our blessing."

Sindri glared up at him. "I *tell* of you this before. Rave is the friend of Kibure!"

Count Gornstein interrupted the exchange between Sindri and Draílock. "I hate to interrupt, but I have much business that needs attention. Arella, this is Sindri. Sindri—Arella. Arella is a mage on the side of Draílock and myself. Draílock, I trust you've made appropriate arrangements in preparation for the Lugienese arrival?"

Draílock nodded and responded in his typical emotionless voice, "We're as ready as we can be."

"Good." The count started for the door. "I pray you'll ensure Sindri remains *unharmed.*" It wasn't a question.

Draílock nodded once again. "Of course."

Then the count added, "Sindri, please trust these two. They're going to find Kibure if possible, but our time is running thin and we can't afford to lose them here in Brinkwell. Their skills are too valuable in a fight against such an enemy. Do as they say and good luck in your search. I hope you find your friend."

The count disappeared from view, and Sindri turned her attention back to the two mages. Arella looked to be in her twenties, heritage close in appearance to the Lugienese slave race by virtue of her blond hair, olive skin, and the green tints in her otherwise brown eyes. By now she knew Arella was merely native to the Isles.

She missed a quiet exchange between Arella and Draílock during her inspection, and now their gazes returned to her.

Draílock said, "Knowledge of this *ally* of Kibure's would have been very useful hours ago, *before* I used up so much of my power trying to contain this thing."

Sindri heard the rare frustration in his voice. She did not wish to anger him further, but she could think of no better reply than the truth. "I-I-I did not know to trust you. You are still same man who enters of my room with no invitation, puts the magic on me, and forces me to visit of your *associate*. You threaten us with the death."

Draílock considered this. "Hmm, I see your point."

Arella glanced at Draílock with a look that said, *Let's move on*, and then spoke for the first time. "What can you tell us about this creature?"

Sindri thought for a moment, trying to decide where to begin, or even what to say. "I have not the knowledge of what this creature is to Kibure. Rave is of more than ordinary raaven. Kibure has told this of me, Rave follows him for as long as he has of the memory. Before, we traveled of a ship. The ship was destroyed."

She paused. *Have they mentioned the Kraken and the hunt by the Lugienese?* Keeping all this straight in her head was exhausting. "This creature help lead of us through the Drisko Mountains, bring food, and find of shelter. I have not the truth to understand the connection of the two, but if raaven is made to be free I think it possible we find of Kibure. Maybe he follow of Kibure to the place he now is."

The two wizards exchanged a skeptical look. Draílock said, "This creature is quite the anomaly. It *has* magic, and no small amount. It is a thing of lore."

Arella said, "Lumáles are animals of intelligence and magical ability."

"This is different," he said. "Raavens are not innately magical creatures like Lumáles. Not that I have ever seen. No, something about this is more than just irregular." Looking to Sindri he asked, "You know nothing more of this creature?"

*Nothing that will help us right now.* "No."

Arella interrupted, "The raaven does not have the taint generally found when dealing with Klerósi priests, so perhaps we can rule out direct control at their hands. And I think this new development gives us reason to find this boy. There is perhaps more going on here than we originally suspected."

Draílock shook his head. "I concede your point, but I still don't like it." He extended a hesitant hand toward the cage; a clicking sound followed. Rave apparently understood what had happened and pushed on the bars. One side swung on unseen hinges and the creature scrambled out. He flew directly to Sindri's shoulder. Rave snuggled into her neck and made his cooing sound.

Not that she thought it would matter, but she asked Rave in Lugienese, just to be certain, "Do you know where Kibure is?"

Rave lifted his head, and flew to land on the floor of the still open doorway. He turned back to face the three humans in the room expectantly. The raaven gestured with his little black hands, and flapped his wings impatiently.

"Extraordinary," whispered Arella.

Draílock rose to follow, a new look of determination in his eyes.

## CHAPTER 110

# AYNWARD

COUNT GORNSTEIN HAD BEEN RIGHT about boarding the ship early, Aynward realized. The city was still silently asleep as they walked down to the pier where his ships were docked. Their passage through the city went without incident. However, by the time they reached the ships, there were already lines of people in front of each. The boarding area was anything but quiet. Dolme, of course, was with him since he would not have trusted Aynward to leave the palace on his own. Aynward followed his counselor to one of the lines.

"Which ship is this?" he asked. The man in front of him growled, "Raked if I know."

*That's a new one.* Then Aynward caught sight of a few men equipped with swords and the dress of palace guards. One was shouting something. As they approached, Aynward saw that one of the guards held out a long parchment, yelling, "Check here for your vessel! No name, no passage!"

A woman was being dragged away from him by a different guard. She screamed, "I was at the palace last night! I have to be on the list! This is a mistake!"

Another man was shouting from the plank where one of the ships was moored at the dock. Aynward saw him jab a finger into the chest of a guard whose job it was to enforce the count's boarding list. "I demand entry! Don't you know who I am? I don't give a god's darn if my name isn't—"

Aynward heard a loud splash followed by several choice curses.

"Next," shouted the guard who held the list for that particular vessel.

A mixture of nervous whispers and quiet grumblings ran through the crowd who had lined up believing they held favor with the count.

Dolme gave the man his name, Aunt Melanie's, and Aynward's. All three were told to board the galleon before them. Aynward saw the huge white letters on the ship's starboard side; they read *Salamas*. The name had ancient Luguinden roots derived from their word for safety. *Well, that's promising.*

Dolme prodded Aynward, but he resisted, waiting to see to which ship Minathi and Kyllean were assigned. "I'll be right there," said Aynward, annoyed. Dolme stopped walking, his glare implying that Aynward could not be trusted to board the ship without incident.

"Name?"

"Kyllean Don Votro."

The guard scanned the page but said nothing before flipping it over. His eyes returned to Kyllean. "Sorry, lad, your name's not here." He waved a hand. "Next!"

Kyllean waited for Minathi to speak, but when she didn't he did so on her behalf. "Minathi Van Odla."

"What are you doing?" she protested.

"Making sure you're safely onboard your ship," he responded curtly.

"But what about you?"

"I'll figure something out."

The guard finished his scan of both sides of the paper. "No Minathi Van anything on either. I'm sorry."

Minathi's head sank. "I guess that makes two of us."

Then Kyllean stepped forward, his face close enough for the guard to guess the vintage of his last drink. "Check it again." His voice had none of its ordinary merriment, only steel.

The soldier scowled but complied, scanning the document for a second time, but his response afterward rang with a tone of finality. "There is no such name on this list. If her name isn't on my list, she does not board. Those are my orders."

Kyllean looked ready to strike. "Well, there's *obviously* a *mistake* with *your* list!"

"That may be. But I have my orders. If you don't like them, take it up with the count himself. Please step aside, others need their assignments. Next!"

Aynward caught Kyllean's wrist, which was attached to a clenched fist that looked ready to pay a visit to someone's face. "Don't."

Kyllean rounded on Aynward, eyes ablaze. "I don't care about myself, but she's—"

"You heard what he said."

Kyllean finally relented, taking a few deep breaths before saying, "All right. We'll go talk to the count and see if we can get on his last ship. You said another one should be arriving any day, did you not?" It was clear to Aynward that he did not believe his own words.

Dolme decided that they could wait no longer. "Aynward, we need to board. *Now.*"

Aynward snapped, "Hang on a minute, please." *Think. Think!* Aynward acted on the only idea he had, hoping it would be enough. He reached down to where his purse was tied and undid the knot. Looking to Kyllean, then Minathi, Aynward said, "Here, take this. There's a healthy sum there. If you can't find Count Gornstein, you should have enough to pay your way onto one of the ships still in port. I imagine most will be setting sail today."

Minathi held out a shaky hand to accept the pouch of coins. "Thank you, Aynward."

"Aynward, we need to go." This time there was a strong grip on his arm and Aynward knew he could delay no longer. He gave his Aunt

Melanie a pleading look, but even she nodded. And they were both right. There was nothing else he could do to help Kyllean or Minathi. The sooner they left to find passage onboard another ship, the better.

"See you soon."

Minathi nodded and tried to smile, but didn't say anything. She just sniffled and waved. Kyllean had resumed a more jovial attitude.

"Go on, we'll see each other in a few days," Aynward encouraged his friend.

"See you in Tung," said Kyllean, nodding, but the mirth was gone, replaced by an ominous expression that revealed his doubt.

## CHAPTER 111

# SINDRI

THEY FOLLOWED RAVE TO THE surface and found that the streets were as Gornstein had suspected: utter chaos. The entire city had become the frantic center of a bazaar, everyone haggling for something or running to get somewhere more important than where they were.

Children who didn't understand why they needed to leave were crying, and mothers who didn't know how to get their children to safety were likewise crying. Men who didn't know what else to do drank and fought rather than face reality. Sindri was glad for her current company. Draílock unnerved her, but he didn't seem interested in killing her at the moment; meanwhile, she was not so confident about some of the others they passed in the street.

Sindri's two companions, in their billowing robes, were given a wide berth, but as the streets narrowed and the smell of filth intensified, the glares became comments. Snickers and curses came from the shadows. Sindri moved one of her hands to the dagger she kept strapped to her side. She could feel her palm slick with nervous sweat against the blade's wooden hilt. The hecklers in the street would be nothing compared to what awaited them if and when they located Kibure. They should have brought guards with them. But she had heard the count; he had no men to spare. She just prayed that these two magicians would be enough to take on the agents of Klerós.

They were getting close to the water. The morning breeze brought with it refreshing doses of salty air to supplement the otherwise rank stench of Brinkwell's lower district. Rave flew into an alleyway to their left. She could feel fear attempting to immobilize her so she concentrated on deep, steady breaths. The air was still cool, yet sweat pooled above her brows and upper lip. She resisted wiping it, as if doing so would be an acknowledgment of its grip on her. It was foolish, she knew that, but she wanted to feel control over *something*. This might be the last victory of her life.

## CHAPTER 112

# GROBENNAR

GROBENNAR SAT BEGRUDGINGLY IN THE chair next to the *still-living* agent of the Dark Lord. He drummed his fingers on the table as he waited for Jaween to finish his latest attempt to inspect *its* mind. Jaween would never admit as much, but Grobennar suspected that his spirit-friend was having a more difficult time than he let on. This was his fourth time delving into their captive's mind. It had certainly never taken Grobennar this many entries to gain what he had wanted from a prisoner.

An incredulous-sounding Jaween spoke into Grobennar's mind. *"Ah . . ."* Jaween chuckled. *"This one is different—not what I first assumed."* Sounding almost confused, Jaween added, *"He may also be more dangerous than I suspected."*

Grobennar frowned. "And yet, by your hand, he continues to draw breath."

*"And so does that spirit of his."* That last part came out as a snarl. Grobennar thought there was something odd about Jaween's disproportionate hatred of the raaven. And he grew more agitated that his statement went ignored. *If a spirit confined to a red ruby could have wax in its ears, Jaween would be a prime candidate for a cleaning.*

Then Grobennar froze. He felt a familiar sensation brush his senses. He felt—*magic*. *What in the seven hells?* He stood and opened the door, his own magic conjured and at the ready.

"*Witch!*" Jaween spat.

As Grobennar craned his neck to see down the hallway, a red shape flipped through the air to land with a thud; the body of a priest. Then Grobennar saw *her*. The woman from the performance, the one whose magic had defied Klerós's power. *No-no-no!*

A blast of power just missed his face, a spray of stones and dust assaulting his skin. He fell out of the doorway into the corridor, fully exposed.

Jaween shouted into Grobennar's mind, "*You must kill the prisoner before they take him!*"

The spirit was right. But two more of the women arrived in the hallway. The first sent a bolt of energy hurtling straight for Grobennar. Still disoriented from the first attack, he had no time to counter or even defend. He rolled backward, the heat of the blast just missing his face.

Jaween bellowed, "*I am persuasion, I am death!*"

The closest assailant stopped in place, her expression turning to horror. Grobennar stood, a smile forming. *Oh yes, this revenge will be sweet.*

The woman placed hands upon her ears, then fell to one knee. She extended an arm toward the wall to keep herself from falling. Grobennar savored her display of weakness as he prepared to release a magical retort of his own. But before he could, a blast of power materialized from behind the woman. It struck him hard in the shoulder. His torso twisted and his head struck the stone wall, vision flickering. Grobennar shook off the dizziness and reacted without thinking. His backward roll had taken him down the corridor outside of another room. The door was open and he dove through just as another blast sent stone spraying in all directions.

"*How did they survive all these years undetected?*" cried Jaween.

"How did who survive?" Grobennar rolled to a crouch inside the study. He could feel Jaween's confusion and anger leaking through their connection, but Jaween did not answer. Standing, Grobennar slammed the door shut behind him just as another blast splintered the door jamb.

Grobennar recognized the frightened voice of Baghel. "How did they find us?"

Then Jaween screamed, *"You have to go back, kill the prisoner!"*

Grobennar held the door firmly closed, breathing heavily, ignoring both voices. He cursed as realization set in. He could not fight these women and win, not until he knew what they were and how to defeat their magic. Jaween had affected one of them, the closest, but apparently not all. No, escaping with his life superseded all else.

Turning to the cowering form of Baghel, Grobennar yelled, "Open the tunnel, you fool!" As Baghel scrambled, Grobennar grabbed the desk and slid it over to the doorway. Once there, he lifted one side of the desk and pushed it up against the door. "This should buy us enough time"—*or, rather, buy me enough time.*

*"He cannot be allowed to live! You must kill him!"* Jaween shrieked. Grobennar pulled the pendant from around his neck and slid it into a pocket in his robe, weakening their connection. *Yes, I will kill him.*

With the exit tunnel open, Grobennar rushed toward his escape. Baghel was just stepping inside when Grobennar stabbed him square in the spine. Then he jerked free his dagger and pulled the dying form of Baghel out of his way to crumple to the floor behind him. Grobennar tried to ignore the gruesome sound of death as he activated the magical mechanism that would close the stone door. When he looked up, he expected to see accusation of betrayal in Baghel's eyes as he lay on the stone staring up at his departing assassin, but there was only great suffering. And then—nothing. The door closed.

*"You have to go back! I will persuade them all! Kill him!"*

Jaween's voice was powerful within his mind, but he did not use his persuasion. Jaween must have believed Grobennar's last threat. Grobennar responded, "I will not die for the sake of that *thing*."

*"This is very bad."*

"Yes. Yes it is. And whose fault is that? Who was it that prevented me from killing the prisoner days ago?" Grobennar's words escaped gritted teeth, afraid the shouting he wished to do would reveal his location. He felt his way blindly through the corridor. He had no doubt that these women might eventually find the hidden door if they searched hard enough; he didn't wish to give them any help.

Jaween didn't respond to his last question, but Grobennar could feel anger mixing with shame through the connection. *Good. He should be angry; and he should definitely be ashamed.*

As Grobennar reached the main sewer line, the smell nearly overwhelmed him. He pulled his robe over his head and folded it into his hands for the time being. He did not want to soil it, or draw attention to himself once on the surface, not yet.

At this time the enormity of what he had done to his fellow priest came to the forefront. His feet became stone, weighed down by contrition. His guilt thickened the air until it felt as if he were wading through a torrent of thick water. He had killed before, dozens of times; but never like that. Baghel was no tazamine, no heretic. And yet Grobennar had stabbed him in the back without a second thought; he had murdered. He felt an immense weight bear down upon his every muscle. *What have I done?*

Jaween broke his silence. *"Now that—that was one of the smartest things you've done in a very long time. And you did so of your own accord. Oh, how you've grown!"*

"I committed one of the cardinal sins against a fellow priest as he fled from true evil."

*"Rules, rules, rules. It was a necessary evil. Klerós will not smite you. After all, you have your destiny to fulfill!"*

Grobennar considered: Baghel would have been the only other living witness to Grobennar's failure.

*"Yes. He would have surely betrayed you in order to elevate himself."* Grobennar knew that this had been his own thinking at the time. He tried to imagine Magog's response if this second failure of his were to be discovered. He felt guilt evaporate as he considered. *I could never fulfill Klerós's will without this deed. I need to regain my seat at the right hand of Magog. This is his will. The prophecy must be fulfilled.*

He climbed out of the sewer, eyes nearly blinded by Klerós's brilliant light. *A little evil must sometimes be permitted to achieve a greater good.* Grobennar inhaled in a deep breath of fresh air and felt renewal as the final remnants of regret were lifted. *Praise be to Klerós.*

## CHAPTER 113

# SINDRI

Rave stopped in front of a wooden door in the narrow alley. Heaps of discarded items lay strewn about the gap between the buildings, but there was a clear path to the door. As much as the building had the outward appearance of a place long abandoned, Sindri knew that someone had been using this space. *Deep breaths.*

Draílock stepped forward and put a hand on the door handle. He paused in concentration, then looked to Arella. "Do you feel that?"

She stiffened slightly and nodded. Draílock's blue-stone amulet dangled in the air. She saw it glowing faintly from within the shadows. He met her eyes as she looked from the blue stone back up to him, her question unspoken. He nodded and said, "Someone has been using magic here."

"Recently," added Arella.

*Focus. Deep breaths.*

Draílock seemed to expect resistance from the door, but it pushed open without effort. He looked back, looking unsure of himself for the first time since Sindri had met him. Her clammy hands begin to shake. A line of sweat broke rank and slid down her nose and into her mouth. In that moment it tasted more like blood.

Sindri stepped inside and let out the breath she didn't know she had been holding. The first room was empty except a broken chair and a few discarded articles of clothing. The inside looked and felt unoccupied. But they had sensed magic. Kibure was here, *somewhere*. They stepped gently, attempting as much stealth as they could. They needed to get as close as possible to Kibure without alerting the priests of their presence. The building was small, and Arella held up a hand as they prepared to enter the second room. She pushed on the door handle and the door creaked open to reveal . . . *nothing*.

Arella and Draílock exchanged another nervous look, then backed out of the second room and moved to the only remaining door where Rave waited. This was it, then. Kibure was on the other side. Sindri pulled two of her daggers out from hiding, gripping them harder than was necessary. Maybe she could squeeze out the excess sweat.

Arella stepped up to this last door and quietly checked to see if it was barred from the other side. It was. She stepped back, looked to Sindri and Draílock, nodded once, then leaped into the air. Her foot struck out with the force of a trained martial artist, and the door to the remaining room in the dilapidated Lugienese hideout crashed inward along the entire frame. The three rushed forward to attack.

## CHAPTER 114

# AYNWARD

AYNWARD DROPPED HIS ONE BAG down in the cabin he would share with Dolme. Everyone had a roommate on this ship. The large merchant vessel had been depleted of all but the barest supplies in order to accommodate the refugees. Some would have to squeeze into the cargo hold. Thus far, no one complained, seeming content with the prospect of setting sail ahead of an enemy assault.

"I'm going back up on deck."

Dolme eyed him suspiciously.

"What?" Aynward said. "I want to see the city one the last time as we depart. I'll likely never see this place again, at least not in its present condition." Everything he said was true; he'd simply failed to mention the other, more significant reason he wished to be up top. The sky had just started showing signs of dawn's approach when he'd gone below, and he knew it wouldn't be long before they set out for sea.

Dolme grumbled to himself, but nodded for Aynward to go ahead.

Aynward scurried above and found himself on the starboard deck looking up at the sprawling city of Brinkwell, a city that would be overrun with enemy wizards and soldiers in just days. The thought caused him to wince, especially as he considered the count's statement that those left behind would likely not be safe.

He stared out at the city, appreciating it more than ever, because he now knew and understood it. He could see the wall surrounding the count's palace, which nestled below the rocks of the small mountain. He could also see the university walls halfway up that same rise, and the blurry shape of the library extending above that.

His thoughts were cast into the water like the excess supplies when he heard the shout of the ship's captain. A bell rang out afterward and the crew responded by scurrying to and fro untying the ropes that held the ship in place. Aynward had not yet spotted Kyllean or Minathi.

He walked over to a man hauling in a massive rope and asked, "How long will it take to clear the dock?"

The man, who Aynward noticed had few teeth and reeked of fish and sweat, replied, "Worry you not. We'll be out of here in no time." He gave a few more hard pulls, took a deep breath, and continued, "Depends on the wind, though."

Aynward gave him a questioning look but he continued to work. When Aynward didn't move, the man sighed. "Unless it blows in the right direction, we'll have to warp until we're into deep enough water. That takes a bit of time." Then he added, "But I expect we'll be able to unfurl the sails and set course within a few hours."

Aynward didn't comprehend all of what the man said, but he understood that Kyllean and Minathi still had *some* time *if* they had managed to find the count.

Aynward paced the deck impatiently as he waited. The sun had not moved more than a hand's width when he heard a voice say, "Your Majesty!" Aynward turned to the right to see the familiar, rounded form of . . . Kuerton? The rotund man opened his arms wide in greeting. "So very happy to see you on your way to safety! Very happy indeed. I was worried about the Prince of Dowe, yes I was. It wouldn't do to have you snatched up by those blasted Lugienese. No sir. Not at all." He lowered his voice to a whisper. "Oh dear me! You're not still trying to keep your identity hidden in the midst of all this are you?"

Aynward shook his head no.

"Ah, good, good." Then Kuerton's face formed a comedic sight as his eyes sunk into his skull in anger. "Terrible business what those *Luggers* are doing. It'll take me years to learn a new city the way I knew Brinkwell. I mean, how's a man supposed to get hired to show folks around if he doesn't even know the place?"

"Yes. Terrible business," Aynward replied absent mindedly. Motion by the pier had stolen the bulk of his attention away from Kuerton's rambling. The gangplank was being pulled and he heard a shout as two sails were quickly unfurled.

Aynward felt himself begin to panic. "Wait, what's happening?" he asked.

Kuerton glanced around, licked the tip of his finger and held it up before his face then nodded. "It seems the gods favor us. The wind appears right for us to set off." He pointed astern and said, "See? They're pulling up the kedge they were planning to use to pull us into deeper water. The gods have decided to blow us right out to sea."

Kyllean had not returned, and the other ships in Count Gornstein's fleet, all smaller, were already gone. Aynward felt fear rising but throttled it. Maybe his friends had indeed managed to get onboard one of those ships. Kyllean would surely have taken that option if the opportunity presented itself. And he'd laugh about how worried Aynward had been when he saw him in Tung. But something in Aynward's gut told him that this was not so.

He stared out into the city praying Kyllean and Minathi were similarly on their way to safety. Then something in the distance caught his eye. A flag. A flag designed to look like a Scritlandian carpet. He hadn't noticed it earlier, but it was unmistakable. He could see Kubal's cargo being loaded, while other members of his crew fought back a crowd hoping to buy passage. But Kubal would not leave his precious cargo behind in lieu of saving others. Would this have been the same for other merchant vessels in port?

The possibility seemed too real. Kyllean and Minathi were going to be stranded in the city, and he decided they would not be there alone.

Just then, Dolme approached on his left. *Not now.* He blew out a breath.

"Say, Dolme, I'm going to walk over to port and grab Kyllean. He just boarded a few minutes ago with Minathi," he lied. "Apparently they worked out the mistake with the list. I figured I'd give them a few minutes to get situated."

"I didn't see them get on."

"Yeah, they're right over there, see?" He pointed to the biggest crowd of people on the other side of the ship. "Say, Kuerton, why don't you keep Dolme company while I see to my friends. He could really use the companionship."

To Aynward's relief, Dolme failed to follow. He merely stated, "You'd better not come back with any sort of *special* beverage in hand."

"The thought that you would even think such a thing within my character wounds me." Turning to Kuerton, Aynward said. "It was wonderful seeing you once again. I look forward to picking your brain later about the development of the Isles' Confederation of Counts."

Kuerton's eyes brightened at that as Aynward walked, as calmly as he could, away. He needed all the courage he could muster and needed to act before the sensible part of his mind convinced him to rethink his impulsive, potentially suicidal, plan.

The deck was still filled with onlookers hoping to catch their last view of Brinkwell, so it wasn't difficult to vanish among them. Aynward slipped behind the elevated captain's quarters, then broke into a run toward the ship's port side. He reached the railing and said a prayer to Kitay, then leaped from the deck.

The water below would be cold and unforgiving, but he couldn't turn back now.

*Splash!*

## CHAPTER 115

# SINDRI

THE THREE RUSHED INTO THE—*COMPLETELY empty* room. But how? Hadn't they sensed magic? What was going on?

They surveyed the room. It was like the other two; a few broken pieces of furniture, other discarded items, and now the decor included a splintered door accenting the wooden floor. There were no additional doorways and no stairs leading to a second story.

She cursed. They were too late. The Lugienese priests must have had sentries posted or somehow sensed their approach. Either way, they had fled the scene.

All the nervous energy that had fueled Sindri drained out of her and she felt a heaviness that would sink her all the way into the—

Rave made a cooing sound and flapped his wings just as the idea struck Sindri. She rushed to where the creature stood, fell to her knees, and began brushing aside wooden chips. She saw the faint outline where the wood of the floor didn't quite line up. She searched until—*yes!*

A small area of wood sank below the rest to reveal a handle. "Hey, I have found something here!"

Sindri pulled up and a square section of floor came with it to expose a stone stairwell. Sindri looked over at Draílock and noticed his amulet had begun to radiate a bright blue. He hastened to where she was and bounded down the stairs, Arella right behind him. Magic was being employed right then, enough so that Sindri didn't need to see the glow of the amulet, she could feel it.

The stairs led to a narrow corridor, wide enough only for one person at a time. Sindri couldn't see anything besides the two robed figures in front of her and barely that.

The two disappeared into a room to the left and Sindri followed. The door had been left ajar. It was a small room lit only by a single lamp on either side, furnished with a wooden table, two chairs, and a corpse. To her surprise, the body appeared to be a Klerósi priest, sprawled on the table. There was no blood, but the body lay at irregular angles unknown to the living.

Arella rushed out of the room and continued down the hall. Sindri stepped back, sensing another burst of magic. She would give the two magicians the lead. There was another room ahead and to the right, but it was identical to the last and likewise devoid of life, though not devoid of corpses: there was another, also Lugienese.

Hurrying to continue the search, Sindri saw the corridor bend to the left and heard the pounding of footsteps. *What—*

They raced forward and rounded the bend. Light exploded from an opening twenty paces away, another entrance, or in this case, an exit. Several shapes moved up a set of stairs through the opening. A small, pale body was being carried on the shoulders of one of the cloaked figures. *Kibure!* It had to be him. "Kibure!" she shouted.

He disappeared up the stairs. The last figure in line turned to face them, but the face was obscured by shadow. Sindri guessed from the thin stature that this was a woman, but she could make out nothing else besides the gray cloak. The woman stood atop the steps and seemed to consider what to do about the three who followed.

Sindri felt as much as saw Draílock send a burst of magic in the woman's direction, but she flicked it aside as if he had thrown a blade of grass. Then she stepped out of view and the door slammed shut behind her.

Arella and Draílock both cursed, though they selected different words. They continued forward and Sindri felt them both send a blast of energy at the door. It had no effect. The stairwell was dark, but she could hear expletives as both magicians tried to force their way through; the hard wood rebuffing each attempt like a stone wall.

Sindri heard Rave from the direction they had come and turned to follow. "Come! This way! Rave is to lead of us to him a different way!"

Sindri moved as quickly as her weakened state allowed, rounding the bend and continuing forward. The corridor was still dark; too dark. The only light she saw came from the two rooms on either side of this hall. This was wrong; they had left the trap door open. There should have been at least some light pouring in through it.

She slowed as she drew closer and heard Rave's mournful sound. The outline of the trap door above was visible, but, as she suspected, it didn't budge when she pushed up on it. "They have also sealed of this door!" she exclaimed. It must have been magically sealed like the other one.

She felt Arella climb the stairs next to her, no longer hurrying.

Arella said to Draílock, "Hey, why don't you go check that last room and see if there isn't another way out of here."

"Yes, yes. Good idea," he murmured, not sounding at all hopeful.

The sorceress placed her hands on the door and Sindri knew she wasn't trying to push up on it; she was examining the magic used to seal it. This would take longer, but brute force would not be effective against whatever held it shut.

Draílock returned. "Nothing. The last room was another study, and contained another corpse. Looks like he barricaded himself in, then died from a previously sustained wound. There is no apparent means of escape."

Arella tapped on the trap door. "And this is not the priestly magic of Klerós. I could sense the remains of that in those rooms. This is ateré magic, though I've never felt anything quite like it. There's not much of it here, but the complex design makes the spell stronger than it should be. We can't break through it, not yet. And I don't know how long it will hold. More than enough time for whoever it was to get away with the boy."

Sindri slumped to the floor, her back sliding carelessly against the wall. Kibure was lost, and so was her hope.

## CHAPTER 116

# AYNWARD

COLD, BRACKISH WATER JETTED UP Aynward's nose. He coughed as his head surfaced, blinking away the water so he could get his bearings. Moving his arms and legs through the water as he'd done a hundred times before, he found that swimming while fully clothed was much more difficult than he had hoped. Fortunately he was still close to the pier.

Minutes later, he was pulling his regretfully soggy self up out of the water. He took off his boots and poured out the water before sliding his still wet feet back inside. He looked out at the ship and saw it shrinking away, its grand square sails filled with the steady southeast wind.

He caught a few sidelong glances from people hurrying past, but none stopped to question why someone would be climbing out of the water on the now shipless berth; everyone else had their own lives to worry about. Looking around, he felt some semblance of security in knowing that he'd kept his sheathed sword strapped to his waist. Seeing the growing clusters of shouting people lining the docks, coupled with the decreasing number of ships, he knew things would only get worse. He needed to hurry.

He'd seen Kyllean and Minathi go to the right, so that's what he did. He moved through the mob as quickly as he could, but there were *so many* people, it was painstakingly slow. Over an hour later, he passed the last remaining vessel on that side of the harbor and had not caught sight of either of his friends. He breathed a sigh of relief. *They're both safe.* He couldn't be certain, of course, but *maybe.* He doubled back to be certain, this time wading more quickly through the crowd.

While keeping an eye out for his friends, he considered what *he* would need to do next in order to escape. He concluded that he would need to find Count Gornstein and pray that his last ship arrived before the Lugienese came to kill everyone. He soured as he reflected on the ridiculousness of what he'd done by jumping from the safety of the *Salamas*, especially considering that his friends appeared to be safe. He hadn't rescued anyone with his act of foolish heroics.

He passed the place where the *Salamas* had been and continued through the crowd to cover the last few piers, in the other direction. He walked up to where Kubal's ships were still docked. His men were still actively loading them, and still enthusiastically fending off people who desired safe passage, but the crowd around his ships had thinned. On catching sight of several bloody corpses, he understood why. He counted five ships, all flying the carpet flag that signified Kubal's business empire. Then an idea struck him. He didn't know if he would have enough time, but he could try.

Aynward turned toward the city and ran. He didn't stop until he reached the palace, wheezing in exhaustion. There was only one guard stationed at the gate, which suggested that all the others had been diverted elsewhere.

"Excuse me, would you kindly open the gate?" he said through labored breaths. "I'm on an important mission for the count."

"Sorry. Orders are to keep the gate closed. Might I recommend leaving the city?"

"Yeah, it's sort of about that," replied Aynward.

"Well there's nothing I can do," stated the guard.

"You *could* open the gate. That would be helpful."

"Orders," replied the guard again.

Aynward *needed* to get into the palace. Whether his plan worked or not, he needed to be with the count when his ship arrived. Aynward paused for a moment to think before saying something that might permanently collapse his chances. He sighed. It went beyond his ordinary tolerance for pomposity, but he decided this was an emergency.

"I'm the prince of Dowe. Prince Aynward Dowe."

"Oh yeah?" asked the guard, somewhere between annoyance and amusement.

Aynward reached down and gripped the hilt of his sword. "Would you like to inspect my sword?" He pulled the polished blade from its scabbard. It was still wet from his swim, and if not treated soon might not retain its sheen, but for now it still glinted in the morning light. The hilt was adorned with precious gems that likely amounted to more than this man would see in a lifetime.

The guard clearly did not expect Aynward's reaction. "I—uh, give it here." He extended a hand down from his perch on the wall beside the gate.

Aynward stretched the tip of the sword up and the man recoiled. "Hilt first. I'm not having my hand cut off!"

Aynward rolled his eyes and reversed his hold on the sword. It was difficult to balance it from the end of the blade, but he'd do whatever the guard wanted if it meant gaining access to the palace.

The guard looked it over closely, though Aynward guessed the man had no idea what he held in his hands. "See the crest on the pommel? That's the seal of Dowe. Only the royal family carries it."

The guard did his best to inspect it before conceding that Aynward must be who he said he was. Or, rather, he didn't know enough to *not* take his word for it.

The man looked both ways as if to verify there wasn't a horde of people hiding behind the nearest building just waiting for the opportunity to bombard the entrance. "Okay, I'm going to open the gate now, your—uh, Your Grace."

Aynward retrieved his weapon, accepted the guard's apology, and headed into the palace, praying he would be able to locate the count. The palace was a maze of hallways and rooms, but Aynward found his way to the room where he'd last seen the count; *of course* he wasn't there.

Aynward confirmed once more that he had made a huge mistake in returning to the city. He shouted into the empty hallway, hoping to catch the count's attention, but knew it would be fruitless. The count wasn't remaining in the city so he could idly wait for the Lugienese to arrive. He was helping orchestrate a mass evacuation.

Aynward yelled out nonetheless. It made him feel better. What else could he do? He couldn't very well go traipsing around the city hoping to just bump into the count. He had to pray that he returned soon enough for Aynward to share his plan to save a few more of the doomed souls of the city.

Unable to remain still, but knowing it would be foolish to leave, he wandered the halls. The palace was filled with the ghosts of the people who had stayed there the evening before, the servants not bothering to clean up. Most of the servants themselves had been offered passage out of the city onboard one of the four vessels that had departed that morning. He hadn't seen a soul since he arrived.

Then he heard a voice. It was so faint that he initially believed it to be his imagination. Then he heard it again.

Aynward said, "Hello? Count Gornstein? Is that you?"

He listened and heard footsteps to his left and started in that direction. He called out again. This time he was rewarded with a response. The voice was close, but it was not the voice he was expecting to hear.

## CHAPTER 117

# SINDRI

SINDRI COULDN'T TOLERATE WAITING IN place any longer and decided to look around the dwelling that had become their underground cell.

"Where are you going?" asked Draílock.

"I walk. Or do you discover how to break of us free?"

He nodded. "Very well." The insufferable confidence Sindri had come to dislike in him was gone.

She walked past the two rooms they had already investigated and rounded the corner to the third. It was larger than the others. She counted four small beds, and inhaled deeply as she nearly tripped over the body of the third corpse. *Draílock did warn me.* This one, too, was adorned in red silks, and was just as dead as the other three she had seen, though in contrast, this one looked to have perished through more-conventional means; a pool of blood surrounded the body. Curious, she grabbed the still-warm hand and pulled until the body rolled onto its stomach. The wound had been taken in the center of the back. *That's odd, but perhaps he was caught unawares before the others. At least we shouldn't expect any of their Lugienese friends to come visiting, not until the rest of them arrive by sea.* The thought gave her some semblance of security.

There was a desk in the middle of the room, but all the materials upon it had been scattered onto the floor. The floor was a mess of old tomes and scrolls. Some were open, some closed. Her memory of the conversation in the count's palace returned. These Lugienese *were* the buyers of all of the stolen books that had placed Aynward and his friend in so much danger. She wasn't sure it mattered at this point, but she tucked the thought away.

She sat down in one of the chairs, not trusting the beds. She looked at a stack of thick books piled high on the floor, and then up toward the ceiling. The ceiling was made of wood. An idea flashed across her mind. *It might just work!*

She called out, "Arella! Draílock! I think—I know how we escape!"

They came more quickly than she would have thought possible, trailed by Rave, who landed in her lap excitedly. Pointing up, she said, "The ceiling is of wood. This is true?"

"Yes," said Draílock slowly. "It appears to be."

"A ceiling can also be of the floor. This is true?"

"I—uh"—he frowned—"We don't have time for riddles, Sindri. What's your plan?"

"Answer of this question," she said more forcefully.

Draílock said, "Sure, a ceiling can also be a floor," still not grasping where she was going with the question.

Arella did. She brightened as she exclaimed, "There's no way those witches could have employed magic to protect the ceiling of this entire place! We can blast through it and climb right out. Providing something deathly heavy isn't resting above us on the floor."

A still brooding Draílock rapped a finger on the opposite arm and finally said, "Perhaps."

He took a few steps back and indicated that the other two should step away. "If someone is going to do it, it should be me."

He extended a hand and Sindri held her breath, waiting. Nothing happened. "Huh," he said.

Sindri and Arella stared at Draílock expectantly. Finally Sindri asked, "Huh, what?"

Draílock shook his head as if clearing it from a trance. "Oh—nothing. I just need to draw a little more energy from the wood. I didn't want to blow the whole room up without due cause, but these floorboards are being very stub—"

Wood splintered from the ceiling above the desk, creating a hole large enough to fit the entire desk and more. An object fell through the opening and landed square on the desk, spilling obtuse objects that rolled all over the desk and floor, and three wooden crates, no longer filled with fruit.

Sindri coughed as dust filled the air.

"This should do just fine," said Draílock as he picked up a red drogal fruit and tossed it at Sindri. "A treat for your troubles." He'd returned to his annoyingly smug self. He climbed out first and helped pull the two women out through the hole as they clambered from the desk to the pile of books and up to the floor of what appeared to be a small warehouse. They didn't see or sense anyone around. Sindri guessed it was one of the priests' fronts: merchants of the drogal trade.

Rave led the trio into the street and through the mayhem of people crowding the docks where they shouted and cursed the ships setting sail without them. Just like Count Gornstein said it would be.

A sense of urgency congealed in Sindri's gut as she realized that the people she sought must have a ship. She had a bad feeling.

Rave flew up over the crowd then darted right and out to the end of a short pier. He landed on the edge and stared after at a small, three-sail boat moving away fast. The black raaven cooed loudly. Sindri saw two women onboard wearing the same gray cloaks as the one who had prevented them from following, and knew for certain that she had found them too late. She saw a strange flag blowing in the wind; it too was gray, with an image of a gold circle resting on an open scroll. Rave looked over at her with his sad little eyes, and then took to the air, flying out over the water toward the ship.

The three watched in silence, knowing there was nothing they could do. Sindri saw the black shape of Rave disappear into the outline of the ship just as it sailed out of the bay, beyond sight.

Draílock spoke. "Those women seem intent on keeping the boy alive, and one can hope their intentions for him are better than those of the Klerist priests. We will resume the search anew if we survive this ordeal."

She nodded silently. *If we survive.*

Sindri prayed Rave would be able to protect Kibure until then.

She felt a delicate hand fall upon her shoulder. Arella seemed to know that words would not help, not yet. The hand was enough. Finally Sindri turned away and they began walking back toward the count's palace. "Perhaps it's time we find our own way out of this city," said Draílock. Sindri didn't disagree.

## CHAPTER 118

# AYNWARD

"Gods above, Aynward, is that you?"

Aynward recognized the voice before turning to see a swaggering Kyllean Don Votro emerging from the stairwell behind him, Minathi close behind.

"What are you still doing here?" asked Aynward, already knowing the answer.

"Same as you, I presume; seriously regretting the fact we weren't onboard the last ship out of this godforsaken city."

Giving Aynward a sidelong glance, he said, "Why in all the gods are *you* not on that ship? And why are you soaking wet? Don't tell me you fell over the railing."

Aynward looked down at his still soggy clothes and shrugged. "I decided to go for a quick swim. You know, to cool off. It just so happened that the ship was moving at the time and didn't see fit to retrieve me. I figured while I was at it, I'd check to see if my friends found a ship out of here."

"You're an idiot," remarked Kyllean.

"Yeah, I've been getting that a lot lately." Looking around, he said, "How did you get in here, anyway? The guard at the gate was about as eager to let me in as a farmer to invite drought."

Kyllean shrugged. "After failing to find a ship, I thought it would be nice to at least have my sword"—he patted the hilt fondly—"so I can kill a few Lugienese before I die. We headed back to the university and"—he pointed and looked to the sky—"someone was looking out for us. We happened upon Counselor Dwapek. That beautiful child-sized man escorted us back to the palace through this maze of underground tunnels that connect to his residence at the university." He leaned in as if to whisper but continued in his normal tone. "I get the impression that Dwapek is either a real creep, or he and the count are more familiar than appearances let on."

*So Dwapek is this "acquaintance" Gervais and the count have at the university.*

"He said the count should be along shortly. His last ship is supposed to be arriving today."

Aynward asked, "Where did Counselor Dwapek go? Shouldn't he be waiting with us to get out of here?"

Kyllean shrugged. "He didn't say. I assume he plans to leave on Gornstein's ship. He didn't seem particularly worried, though I suppose he's not the worrying sort. But he was perturbed that neither I nor Minathi were on the list to leave on the ship with you."

A number of footfalls sounded, and all three students saw the count along with several members of his guard approaching. Count Gornstein looked more imposing than usual, and he did not look happy to see them. "Why in all of Doréa are you all still here?"

Aynward explained the situation, leaving out the bit about leaping from the ship's deck. He figured that part would come out eventually, but he wasn't inclined to hurry that along. When he had finished recapping the events, Gornstein said, "A few priests of the Stone faith will be traveling on my last ship, but we'll make room for you. It's due in today. You *will* be onboard."

No one disagreed. Then the count turned and looked behind him. "Hey, where'd he go?" Several guards shrugged and looked behind, then two in the middle parted to reveal a waist-high bearded man. The count exclaimed, "There you are. What of you? Should I expect you on the ship, as well?"

Counselor Dwapek chuckled. "Oh, you needn't worry about me. My plans remain unchanged. I'll be leaving here by my own means, thank you. I wish to get an up-close look at the enemy before departing."

"Is that really necessary? We know—"

"Leaves don't always blow in the same direction," interrupted Dwapek.

Aynward couldn't help from chiming in. "Counselor Dwapek, I ask this with the utmost respect, but could you explain your penchant toward vexatiously vague phrases, you know, the kind that make about as much sense as a carnivorous herbivore? Are they actually supposed to mean something—to anyone?"

Dwapek offered a rare smile. "Well, aren't you the pithy one today!"

Aynward retorted, "I suppose I am, and yet, coins aren't always made from gold."

Dwapek chuckled. "Perhaps there is some hope for the princeling, after all."

The count interjected, "We really don't have time for this."

"Nonsense," replied Dwapek. "'Tis a fair question. One I am pleased to answer." He spread his arms wide like a street performer, then said, "Some of the things I say are a bit like—mmm—a dual-moon eclipse, often meaning absolutely nothing, while other times, well—they're filled with depth and wisdom worthy of decades of debate."

"Well, then. I'd say that clears things up like a smear of mud on a window," quipped Kyllean.

Dwapek winked. "One can never go wrong in sounding philosophical." Then he straightened and added, "But back to the danger at hand. Count Gornstein, be aware that if the Lugienese arrive early, you cannot rely on much help from the remaining priests in the city, Stone priests or not. Their magic will not be effective against the Lugienese."

"Then let us pray we are not too late," finished the count.

The three students looked at one another with eyebrows raised. Aynward's confusion was divided between the statement about the priests, and Dwapek's fittingly vague answer about his illogical proverbs.

The count said, "You three stay here until I return. I have to wrap up a few things before leaving." As Count Gornstein turned to depart, Aynward realized he was missing his chance to voice the plan to get more people out of the city. *This really can't wait.* "Count Gornstein?"

"Yes?" he said impatiently.

"I have an idea that may save the lives of a few more hundred people, that is, if there's still time. The merchant ships didn't look ready to set sail when I left the docks."

He had the count's attention, but he did not appear confident.

"Kubal still has five large vessels in port. He is refusing to allow passengers; he's loading every last item of value that he has in the city."

"That was to be expected from the likes of him," said the count impatiently.

"Well, you know for certain that he was behind the theft of those books from the university. You've enough witnesses to prove it"— Aynward gestured with his hands—"one of whom just happens to be a Prince of Dowe. You could offer amnesty for his crimes in return for transporting as many citizens as he can to Tung."

The count shook his head, and his voice was flat. "We have an arrangement, he and I. And that plan would fail even if we tried."

"But if you threaten to name him an enemy of the Isles and to offer a reward for his arrest, his business would—"

"No," boomed the count, the full weight of his authority echoing along the stone walls. "Threats mean nothing to the likes of Kubal, and I don't have the manpower to seize his ships or I'd have already done so." More gently, he continued, "My men and I will be transporting supplies to be loaded onto my ship. You remain here. You'll be able to see it enter the harbor from one of the south-facing balconies. I suspect that it will be the only one entering the bay for quite some time. Keep an eye out."

With that, he spun on his heel to leave. He didn't need to look behind to see that his guards followed.

As the count and his retinue disappeared out of sight, Dwapek dipped his head in appreciation. "That wasn't an *awful* plan there, Aynward"—he grinned—"for a princeling. A lot better than what most of these other bumbling idiots could have contrived. It's a shame those two have such an icy past."

Aynward and Kyllean exchanged a glance, then Aynward finally said, "Huh?"

Dwapek gave Aynward an appraising look. "Oh, never mind that. Not my story to tell. Let's just say that Kubal took the life of someone very dear to Gornstein, and the count returned the favor before striking a deal. I don't recommend bringing it up with him. He gets a bit testy about it. What's important is that I'm giving you a rarer gift than the blue sapphire I wear around my neck. I'm giving you *a compliment*. You may yet make a reasonable leader someday. Of course, after the stunt you just pulled in hopping from that ship, your father may never give you the chance. Shame. Then again, trees do grow on rocky shoals."

Aynward's excitement that he had finally done *something* right was trampled by Dwapek's finishing remarks. When his father found out from Dolme what he had done, that he had risked his own safety to go look for a friend, he would be lucky to be allowed out of the palace at all once he returned home.

Counselor Dwapek announced, "Well, I must be attending to some business of my own. Don't do anything too foolish. I hope to see you again, all three of you." He departed without another word.

Kyllean, Minathi, and Aynward decided to take the count's advice to wait for sight of their ship from the balcony of one of the top-floor guest rooms.

From their high vantage on the southwest corner of the palace, they could see the entire bay as well as the trail of refugees exiting the city in the opposite direction. They looked like birds attempting to fly into the wind, some unseen force slowing their progress. These people were leaving their homes, likely never to return; their reluctance was no surprise.

Aynward turned back to study the docks, and noted the five vessels he knew to be Kubal's ships. He bristled as he considered the selfishness of the thieving enterprise. That hundreds would likely die for the sake of preserving this man's coffers. He was about to say as much when Minathi asked, "What are the Lugienese colors?"

"Huh?" responded Kyllean and Aynward together.

"The Lugienese. What color do they wear?" There was fear in her voice. Aynward followed her line of sight.

Kyllean answered slowly, "Red?"

Aynward confirmed. "Uh-huh . . ." He saw what she saw, and felt his pulse quicken. "Guys, I don't know how, but I think those are Lugienese soldiers."

The line of refugees was still moving out of the city, but those in the front were no longer moving forward. They became a growing cluster, and some were trying to turn around. In front of them, just beyond the forest that marked the edge of the farmland, was a thin line of crimson. Men were pouring out of the wagon trail and into the clearing on either side.

Kyllean said, "How did they get here ahead of their own ships?" The question didn't matter. They were here, and that meant the people trying to flee had nowhere to go.

None of the soldiers had moved to strike. They seemed to be awaiting orders. But the line of refugees had backed away from the thickening wall of enemy soldiers.

Aynward's attention returned to the bay. The Lugienese navy couldn't be far behind. The city could end up trapped, and if so, that meant dead. The Lugienese had taken only the prisoners required to sail their stolen vessels; they slaughtered every remaining soul in their conquest of the Palpanese Union.

"Guys, I think we need to get down to the pier *now*."

A loud voice from behind startled them all. "No."

## CHAPTER 119

# SINDRI

INDRI STOOD IMPATIENTLY AT THE pier where Gornstein's last ship was supposed to arrive. The bustle of the docks region had slowed; however, there were still a handful of ship-hands scrambling to load people, supplies, or both. A little boy ran straight into her, almost knocking her into the water.

"Hey, watch—"

The boy scrabbled back to his feet and continued to run toward the nearest ship. He glanced back, and she saw pure terror in his eyes. He shouted, "Lugienese! Lugienese in the city!"

Sindri turned to give Draílock a quizzical look. Were there more Klerósi priests in the city? Why had they decided to finally reveal themselves?

Draílock and Arella shared a look of their own. Neither one seemed overly concerned, not until the second scream came, followed by a trail of refugees. They all headed for the nearest boat still docked at the pier, a stampede of frantic chaos.

Draílock said, "Something is *very* wrong."

Sindri was staring out into the harbor, praying their ship would arrive in time. If the Lugienese had somehow landed on the other side of the bay, there was no barrier on that side of the city. No wall. This was a merchant city, not a fortification designed to withstand an assault of ground troops. She didn't know how many Lugienese there were, or how long it might take them to pick their way to the dock, but she felt sweat gathering on her brow, along with a cold chill that caused her to shudder.

Out of the corner of her eye, she saw something far more frightening than the presence of Lugienese in the area. The blue amulet around Draílock's neck had begun to glow. Sindri had hoped that the ground troops would be sent in first with the priests far behind. That would give Sindri and the others time to escape. That had been a hopeless wish. Knowing the number of priests at their disposal to assist in an invasion, she was petrified.

Draílock held out a hand. He seemed to reach out toward some distant, unseen object in the sea. Did he sense the ship that would carry them to safety? She saw a shape emerge from the west, where the bay opened. Strange that it came from the west, but that didn't matter; it was here. She felt a twinge of excitement, of hope. Here was their salvation. She prayed it would arrive before the enemy tore through the city.

Arella turned to Draílock, a grim expression taking control of her small features. She, too, was reaching out a hand. Then she let it drop. "They are here."

Something about the way they looked at each other told Sindri they were not referring to the ship that was supposed to carry them to safety. All three stared out into the bay as ship after ship slowly took form. The first few had red sails, but others following retained the colors and flag of whatever Palpanese city had previously operated the ship. The Lugienese had been more concerned with stealth and speed than uniformity. They would have plenty of time to refit the ships after their enemies were dead.

Sindri watched them draw nearer in dread. Complete and utter dread.

## CHAPTER 120

# AYNWARD

AYNWARD, KYLLEAN, AND MINATHI TURNED to see Counselor
Dwapek standing behind them, Gervais by his side, and, to
Aynward's complete surprise, behind them stood a very wet Counselor
Dolmuevo. His mouth was a flat line. There was no rebuke in his expres-
sion, only determination. The rebuke, Aynward knew, would come later.
For now, they needed to escape the city. Alive.

Dwapek spoke. "The Lugienese have arrived."

*No kidding, that's why we need to get to the docks and get the heck out
of here.*

As if reading his mind, Dwapek pointed out toward the docks.
Aynward turned his head to look and went cold. It was as if the act of
Dwapek speaking it had made it so. Aynward saw the Lugienese ships;
dozens more of them. They seemed to have materialized from nowhere.

"We're all going to die, aren't we?" asked Kyllean, his voice both
crass and comedic at the same time. How Kyllean was able to retain
even a hint of joviality in the face of death was beyond Aynward.

Dwapek glared at them all one by one, then said, "If you start doing
as you're told, you may yet escape."

Kyllean chuckled. "Obedience is generally disagreeable with my already weak stomach, but if our survival is tied to it, I suppose . . ." Before he could execute a kneeling gesture, Minathi struck him hard in the ribs with an elbow. "Shut up!"

"Ow! What was that—"

"What do we need to do?" she asked.

Dwapek almost smiled. "Follow me. We'll have to move quickly, but I made arrangements for just such an inspired event of idiocy."

They followed him down until they reached the ground floor of the palace. Dwapek eyed Gervais and said, "Take the tunnels to the cove, I'll be along shortly. There is something I must do before leaving." Gervais nodded his understanding, then waved a hand for the others to follow.

Aynward turned back to see Dwapek heading out the main entrance leading to the palace walls and the city, which would soon be under siege. *What in the world is he doing going out into that mess?* Aynward also thought of the count, who had just headed to the docks to prepare for the arrival of a ship that would be too late. He too must know of the tunnels to the cove, but would he be able to make it there in time? How many people in the city would die today? The thought sobered him.

As they entered the network of tunnels, Kyllean asked Gervais, "How many of these things does he have sprouting out from the palace? Is this Gornstein guy part mole?"

Gervais didn't answer. Aynward just looked at his friend and shook his head in disbelief. Kyllean was the only one able to summon a jocular view of the situation; perhaps that was simply how he dealt with fear. Then again, he behaved that way no matter the situation. It inspired and aggravated Aynward all at once.

A portion of the tunnel looked vaguely familiar, but perhaps that was because it was underground and dark like the rest. The passage seemed to be descending, and he knew he'd not been in this particular stretch when he noted the long curve they took. It was slight, but it went on for minutes, a slow arc to the left. Their time in the tunnel seemed to last for hours, but that was probably because all Aynward could think about was Dwapek's warning that the Lugienese might find the cove they were heading for before they got there. Would they emerge from the tunnel to find dozens of Lugienese wielders ready to strike them down? Aynward started to feel claustrophobic. Each means of escape seemed to close in as they neared, the Lugienese a snake slowly constricting the city until it suffocated.

Gervais paused at a dead end that they all knew was not a dead end. The spy depressed the appropriate spaces on the wall and the door began to shake. It opened to reveal dim, natural light, an improvement from the torch they had been following. The smell of salt and the sound of water echoing through the space were encouraging. The tunnel had led them to a coastal cave.

"They must have a boat close by," said Aynward to himself as much as Gervais, who had been reluctant to answer any questions along the way. They followed him out of the dark tunnel and around a bend to an opening that led to the surface.

Gervais took them over a small, forested hill to a hidden cove, protected from view by two adjacent peninsulas. In the cove floated a schooner; Aynward had sailed a few in Salmune Lake, but he had never seen this particular design. He felt his immediate fears retreat as he approached the vessel, knowing for certain that his two classmates were safe. He still worried about the count and Counselor Dwapek, but after seeing the invading foot soldiers and the sails of the enemy ships filling the main harbor, he felt relieved to be leaving the place.

As they approached the schooner, Gervais waved and yelled out to the man on the deck leaning casually on the mast. "Ahoy! We come on behalf of Counselor Dwapek!"

The man did not respond. There was a bit of wind, but Aynward thought the man should have been able to hear. Then he wondered about the rest of the crew. Were they all sleeping? There should have been more.

"Something is wrong," said Dolme from behind.

Kyllean shrugged, appearing doubtful. "They probably just had too much to drink while waiting for Counselor Dwapek. You know how sailors are."

Gervais grabbed Kyllean's sleeve. "He's right—get back to the tunnel, *now*."

That's when the first arrow struck, followed by a loud cry from Minathi.

## CHAPTER 121

# SINDRI

**D**RAÍLOCK RAN; SINDRI AND ARELLA followed. They were like salmon trying to swim upstream. Those people who had been unable to get out of the city before the Lugienese arrived now rushed toward the docks hopelessly pursuing escape by sea. Booking passage was no longer a consideration. This was an emergency. The city was under attack.

Sindri, Arella, and Draílock were all breathing heavily by the time they made it to Draílock's home by the university. Arella let out a sigh of relief at the sound of the latch above them closing off the tunnel to the city above.

"What have of we to do now?" panted Sindri, wondering how they would get out of the city now that both means of escape had been pre-empted by the Lugienese.

Still labored in his breathing, Draílock simply said, "Follow me."

"What plan have of you now? Do you wish of us to wait below ground for the Lugienese to finish the death of all the people and hope they leave of the city when they finish?"

Arella had lit a torch for them while Draílock worked on something in the wall. With her face illuminated by the flames' orange glow, she said, "We will be leaving the city. Counselor Dwapek made arrangements of his own to escape from the city. He wished to remain here until the invasion began."

Shocked, Sindri asked, "This half-man has of the half-brain? Why does he think to—"

"His reasons are his own. But the Lugienese are here now, and Dwapek does not know that we're coming so we need to get there before he leaves."

A portion of the wall disappeared and torchlight revealed a new corridor. Draílock set off at a brisk pace, enough so that his breathing remained ragged and even the younger Sindri and Arella were disinclined to waste breath speaking. The gravity of the situation only added to the foreboding silence.

When daylight finally broke through the opening in the stone tunnel, the sound of shouting and the clang of steel gave pause to all three. "What now happens?" asked Sindri, worried.

"Something bad," was all Draílock had to say as he stepped hurriedly into the sunlit cave. Sindri heard the sound of water nearby. Draílock turned and said, "The count is in trouble!" The two sorcerers darted around the bend into an opening in the cavern that led to the outside. They almost tripped over a dark form just near the opening. As Sindri caught up, she saw that it was one of the girls from that class with the half-man. She was holding her leg, an arrow protruding from the calf. It did not appear to be a lethal wound, but she was no doubt in pain.

"Get back," echoed a male voice from outside. Draílock and Arella both obediently slipped back into the cavern, trailed by Aynward, Gervais, and Kyllean. A loud cry from outside announced that one of the ringing steel objects had met flesh. Then a different cry sounded.

An older man holding a sword stumbled into the cavern, he too sporting an arrow, but this one had entered his stomach. The blood didn't take long to color the clothes around it a deep crimson. Draílock yelled, "Where is the count?"

Aynward didn't answer, rushing over to the injured man. "Dolme!"

The man reached down, snapped off the end of the arrow, and pushed Aynward away, turning back to defend the opening. "Stay back!" he yelled.

"Dolme! You're hurt." He looked to Gervais and said, "Help me get him off his feet."

The other boy, Kyllean, took his place in the doorway while Aynward and Gervais pulled a reluctant Dolme inside and to the ground. Kyllean suddenly dove away from the door as an arrow skidded harmlessly against the stone floor. The clatter of feet announced that whoever was outside was on their way inside. Kyllean had scrambled back upright and took a swing at the leg of the first soldier to enter the cavern. The man went down with a shout, but four others pushed their way in behind him, sword and shields at the ready.

Sindri pulled her daggers from hiding and moved to help Kyllean.

Draílock repeated, "Where is the count?"

Minathi replied through gritted teeth, "He was headed to the docks just before we came here."

Draílock half turned to go back to the tunnel, then shook his head and drew a short and slightly curved sword from within the folds of his robe. This surprised Sindri: how had she not noticed the sword and, more important, why didn't he simply use his magic?

Kyllean proved to be lethal with his sword, dispatching two Lugienese soldiers before Draílock or Sindri was close enough to show concern for their own safety. So far, five men in the red of Klerós's army had pushed their way into the space but Sindri could see that there were more.

Sindri twirled the daggers in her hands, an old habit that returned with the prospect of using them again. The nearest soldier attacked just as they returned to her grip. Her body knew what to do before she had time to think. She stepped aside the blow, the blade in her left hand brushing the soldier's steel harmlessly away. He had hoped to cleave her in half, but her movement, in addition to his expectation that he would make contact with something more than air, exposed the side of his body that was not protected by a shield. This allowed the sharp object in Sindri's other hand to find its way into the man's side. He gasped, hunching over enough for her to bring her knee to his face. Her other dagger caught his throat as the man's face flew from the nose-shattering strike. Her steel's contact with the throat wasn't as clean as Sindri had hoped, but the spray of blood told her she had done well enough.

She immediately stepped over his fallen body to greet her next victim.

## CHAPTER 122

# AYNWARD

AYNWARD COMMANDED, "JUST—JUST, DON'T MOVE."
Dolme glared at Aynward and struggled back to his feet, ripping himself free of Gervais's grip. "I'm going to fight," growled Dolme. Aynward let out a grunt of frustration in response, knowing there was no convincing the old man, and no time to argue.

Gervais quickly added, "I will be no help in this fight. I'll see what I can do for Minathi's wound."

Aynward nodded to Gervais, then turned, and drew his own sword just as a man broke free of the line held by Kyllean, Draílock, Arella, and Sindri.

By the time he met his attacker, the Lugienese in the cavern outnumbered their own, but if they could limit the Lugienese advance to the narrow opening, they at least had a chance. Well, maybe not a chance, but they'd be able to kill more of them. Based on what he had seen while they fled back toward the cavern from the cove, they were flanked by at least two dozen enemy soldiers. The addition of Sindri and her companions may have extended their lives a few minutes, but it wouldn't be enough.

As he readied an attack on the nearest enemy soldier, the robed man yelled to the petite woman who was dressed similarly, "No magic!"

If they were magicians, why in Tecuix's name would they not use that power? *We're all going to die.*

Aynward blocked his opponent's first two attempts to separate his head from his body. The Lugienese swords were shorter and thinner than his broadsword, and he immediately recognized the disadvantage while fighting in such tight quarters. Kyllean wielded a scimitar, and seemed to flow in and out of the enemies' reach, leaving a line of blood nearly everywhere he moved. Aynward could not boast the same level of success. He found himself fighting on his heels. He needed more space, but that would undermine the strategy of keeping these men contained. He needed to get his hand on one of the shorter Lugienese swords. That meant he needed to kill one of them.

His current opponent's attacks were perfunctory, and Aynward began to feel out the many counterattacks available to him with a broadsword. He cursed his luck as he realized that before he could finish the job, he would have to give ground. Taking a few measured, defensive steps back, he almost tripped over Minathi, who still sat propped against the wall. *Gods! A little help would be great right about now.* He needed to dispose of this man quickly to close the gap he had left in front of the cavern opening.

Assuming his high guard stance, he brandished the broadsword the way it was meant to be used. He felt liberated by the higher ceiling. Aynward blocked another enemy attack, but could now respond in kind. He slammed the sword down on his opponent's shield. This knocked the man off balance, and Aynward gave him no time to reestablish his footing. He swung again, this time connecting with the man's sword, and then again and again, forcing the man to defend. Aynward knew that after a few more strikes, he would make contact with flesh. But his next foray was stunted when his backswing struck the ceiling, which allowed the man to parry and riposte. Aynward felt a burning sensation radiate from his side. He gritted his teeth and growled.

Energized by the sight of blood, the man came in for another attack. Aynward gave ground once more. But with the space, he was able to return to utilizing the strengths of the heavier, longer-reach of his weapon. Timing his adversary's increasingly predictable movements, he stepped in as the man made a diagonal attack, blocking it close to the hilt of his sword. He threw his weight into this movement, pushing the man back to give way for a powerful swing at his exposed legs. Aynward had used this move many times while training, but never with a real sword. His blade sank into flesh and the man cried out in pain, falling to the ground, cowering behind his shield. Aynward pulled the sword back and began a brutal series of downward strikes on the shield until again finding flesh. This time the man stopped moving when he was done.

Aynward froze. He had never killed before. He felt no remorse, but the realization still shattered his focus. He saw the man's arm relax in death, hand falling slightly open, his sword free for the taking. He should have immediately stooped to pick it up, but he hesitated, and then noticed something else.

Another Lugienese soldier didn't fill in to replace the fallen man. They had formed a wall of shields, protecting those behind them. They waited where they were as Kyllean and the others continued with their opponents.

Aynward watched Kyllean dance his way inside of his foe's reach then elbow the man in the nose before stepping back to tear open his stomach with his blade. Dolme fought equally well in spite of the wound to his abdomen. But when Dolme finished battering his enemy to the ground, he too stumbled back as if struck. Aynward ran over and caught him before he fell.

Seeing Dolme up close, it was a wonder the man had been standing at all, let alone fighting. Both of his legs now sported deep cuts, and the bleeding from his midsection showed no signs of stopping. Then, for the first time, Aynward saw fear in his counselor's expression. But that wasn't right. It wasn't fear: it was the empty expression of someone on the verge of—

Dolme's body sagged and Aynward lowered him to the ground. His breathing was ragged, but he was alive for now. Aynward's attention was torn away as he noted the dwindling clang of steel against steel. Draílock and Arella had both slain their Lugienese opponents, while Sindri battled a single man.

Yet the remaining Lugienese had not begun a new assault.

*What are they waiting for?*

Then he saw it. *Oh no.* The interlocking wall of shields lowered as the men holding them crouched. Behind them four others with bows appeared, arrows nocked, strings drawn. This time there was nowhere to hide.

## CHAPTER 123

# SINDRI

SINDRI FELT THE FAMILIAR STING of fatigue in her lungs, but her training as a priestess of Klerós had been rigorous, not only in spell casting, but also in her mastery of the body. These soldiers had received less, of that she was certain. These were infantrymen: expendable. Nevertheless she and her allies were outnumbered.

Her most recent enemy had stopped his awkward attempts to kill her, appearing content to keep her at arm's length. This made the work with her daggers far more challenging. Her fighting style was designed to take advantage of close quarters. The man had abruptly decided to give her a wide berth. She had killed two others already, so she could hardly blame him.

One of the Lugienese soldiers shouted, "Take aim!"

That's when she saw the line of shields and the archers behind them.

"Fire!"

She dove, expecting to feel the bite of an arrow. Instead she felt the tingling sensation of magical energy.

Draílock yelled, "'Rella! No!"

"Yes," Arella responded through gritted teeth.

All four arrows clicked against the ceiling and dropped to the ground harmlessly. Then a wave of power struck the Lugienese in the cavern, knocking them off their feet. Another sweep of her hand and the men slammed against the far wall—shields, swords, bows, and bodies all landing in one heap with shouts of pain. Another blast of energy sent the line of soldiers in the tunnel leading out of the cavern tumbling back on top of one another.

Arella finally spoke again, but her breaths were ragged. "We can't just die here waiting for Dwapek. He'll sense that we used magic and know our time is short."

She staggered, but managed to stay on her feet. Sindri didn't know exactly how much ateré magic one could wield, but she knew the limitations of bone mass degradation. Arella wasn't wearing much jewelry to protect against this side effect.

Draílock rose to his feet, scowling. "If we're going to make our presence known to the enemy, we may as well make sure none of their friends are left to help when they arrive."

He stomped toward the exit, outside of which remained at least ten Lugienese still waiting to kill them, that is, if they hadn't all fled the scene. One of the men within the tumble of bodies attempted to rise, but without sparing him a glance, Draílock flung out a hand and the man cried out and fell, permanently unmoving.

Then the hair on Sindri's neck rose and she knew there was another wielder, this one Lugienese. She saw the red robe flow into the cavern like blood leaking from the surface. The arrogance was unmistakable.

"They have a user of the magic!" Her warning came just as the jolt of energy sliced the air directly toward Draílock. "Nooo!" Sindri cried.

Maybe her warning saved him, maybe he simply *was* that good, but he cast the magical blow aside. The force struck the far wall in an explosion of dust and rubble. "I hope you brought more," he snarled. Then he sprinted forward with surprising speed, pulling his blade as he lunged to meet his foe, but that was just an act. He shot a dart of magic at the ceiling, just enough to cause a spray of pebbles. A distraction.

The coordinated attack seemed almost rehearsed. Out of the corner of her eye, Sindri saw Arella roll to the side and fire her own blast of energy, which in the man's disoriented state he was unable to stop. Draílock's own attack hit the man square in the chest. The two forces sent him tumbling into the wall beside the opening from which he had emerged. He did not get up.

Draílock continued forward. He didn't spare the Klerósi wizard so much as a glance as he strode out of the cavern. "We need to get on the boat and ready it to sail."

Sindri stood and brushed off the dust and dirt from her clothes; the red stains, some of them her own, would have to stay for now. Blood lust still protected her from the pain she knew would follow. Aynward and Gervais helped carry the now unconscious man who had taken an arrow to the stomach earlier, while Kyllean helped the injured girl from class whose wounds seemed far less severe.

By the time they reached the surface, the bodies of several Lugienese soldiers littered the ground; all but one had been extinguished. Draílock was holding the fabric around the remaining man's neck, and spoke to him in a quiet voice. The man gave Draílock an angry smile, then spit blood in his face. The wizard plunged his small dagger into the man's chest, before turning to face the others. "We need to find their ship. It can't be far. They certainly didn't walk here through the forest. I must ensure that we aren't followed."

Arella said, "I'll come with you, just in case—"

"No. You need to be here. There might be others, and if they have any priests, you're the only hope."

"But—"

"No."

Arella threw up her arms in frustration but didn't make another move toward him. "Hurry."

He turned without another word, trotting out of sight in the direction of the Lugienese soldiers' corpses. By the pattern of their final resting places, it was evident they had tried to escape to their ship.

When Sindri and the others reached the small, hidden beach, Aynward and Gervais lowered the injured man to the sand. Then Aynward sat and slipped off his boots, explaining, "The Lugienese killed the crew before ambushing us. I'll swim out to pull the anchor so we can drag the ship in." No one objected. They were all in some way wounded, exhausted, or both.

The vessel in the water wasn't large, but it would easily hold their current number twice over.

Minutes later, Sindri felt it again: *magic*. She could sense that it was far away, perhaps Draílock fighting, but what unnerved her was recognizing that some of the magic was of Klerós's power. That distinct familiarity to the air made her hunger for her old powers. Then the ground beneath them shook and Sindri looked to Arella to see if she had felt the same thing. Her blue amulet was glowing. Had Draílock found enemy priests onboard the other ship?

"We have need of more speed!" said Sindri.

The water was shallow enough for them to board without having to swim. Working together, they quickly hoisted the two conscious, but injured members of their group before depositing them belowdeck where they could rest and heal, gods willing. The man with the arrow through his abdomen did not look well.

Sindri was pulled out of the waist-deep water by Aynward's surprisingly powerful arm. Then a familiar voice cut the air behind them. "We need to go, *right now!*"

They all turned to see Count Gornstein, trailed by seven of his personal guard, all of them bloodied and battered and filthy. They splashed through the water as if the enemy were hot in pursuit; perhaps they were. This caused Sindri's heart to pound faster than she thought possible.

Gornstein climbed up and glanced around the deck. "Where's the crew Dwapek hired to man the ship?"

"Dead," replied Aynward, letting go of Sindri's hand. "Lugienese."

The Count nodded and continued to survey the situation as the last of his men boarded. "Where's Draílock?"

Arella answered, "Disposing of the Lugienese ship that brought the mess of Lugienese soldiers you passed in the cavern. Wanted to be sure we aren't pursued."

"Good idea, but we can't wait much longer for him to return. They'll be sending another ship now that Dwapek collapsed the tunnel."

Arella spun around at hearing that. "Where *is* Dwapek?"

Gornstein shook his head. "He remained behind to ensure we made it out alive. A dozen priests followed us into the tunnel."

"But—"

"It was the only way. He chose his path."

Arella became a sail without wind. She said in a cracked voice, "He may yet survive. He's very resourceful."

Gornstein nodded in agreement, but his eyes said he didn't believe her words. And neither did she.

## CHAPTER 124

# AYNWARD

AYNWARD BLINKED AWAY TEARS. DWAPEK'S death was *wrong*. The half-man had saved an undeserving Aynward countless times since arriving. He had also caused an unwitting Aynward to finally face his own flaws, flaws that he now realized Dolme had been trying to eradicate all along. With attempts coming from someone so familiar, Aynward had rebuffed them all and even scorned his childhood counselor for trying.

Aynward escaped belowdeck to avoid being caught in this moment of emotional weakness. Instead of regaining his composure as he had intended, the scene below tore his remaining poise asunder. Dolme lay there pale, feeble, and utterly helpless. Aynward had lived out dozens of brutal acts of revenge in his mind, with Dolme at the center of each macabre scene. In every one, Aynward towered over the defeated counselor in triumph, but it all felt so wrong now that the man lay so close to death on account of Aynward's reckless actions. It was *he* who caused Dolme to risk his own life, fleeing the safety of the outgoing ship to do his duty in spite of Aynward's treatment of him. Would Aynward have done the same if the roles were reversed?

Aynward tore open Dolme's tunic to have a better look at the arrow wound. There was so much blood that he had to take off his own shirt to sop up the blood. Deep red blood continued to ooze from all around the shaft. He was no medic, but he knew the bleeding needed to be stopped.

Count Gornstein's voice tore Aynward from his self-loathing. "Do either of you know your way around a ship?"

The count had slipped belowdeck to rally capable hands. Kyllean was on the other side of the cabin looking after Minathi's wound, and responded first. "I spent a fair amount of my childhood on the water."

Aynward's mouth was dry. "Me, too." It didn't even sound like his own voice. He was glad for a distraction, however. Perhaps the cloud of regret that loomed over him would be cast aside, even if only for a while.

"Then I need both of you on deck now. My guards are fine men, but they're soldiers; they don't know a lick about seamanship. They're pushing us out now, but I need real sailors if we're going to get to safety. We're not out of the water yet."

Kyllean turned and raised a finger to object. "Um . . ."

Gornstein frowned. "You know what I mean." Shaking his head, he returned up the ladder.

Aynward looked around and spotted Gervais huddled in the corner beside a crate of supplies. "Gervais! Come here, hurry. Hold this here. Keep pressure on the wound until I get back. Come on!"

Gervais did as he was asked.

Aynward moved to the ladder but turned back before beginning the climb. He couldn't bear the thought of losing Dwapek and Dolme in the same day. Dolme and he had a strained relationship to be certain, but that didn't mean he wanted the man dead, and certainly not as a direct result of something Aynward had done. He yelled up to the count, "Someone needs to help Gervais tend to Dolme's wounds."

The count directed one of his guards to do so. Then he added, "Once I know we're safely out of danger, we'll have Draílock and Arella do what they can to heal him."

Aynward's eyes widened. "Draílock?"

Gornstein answered quickly, "He returned just as we were pushing off. He's at the bow, keeping watch for any other danger from the shore."

The next minutes were consumed by the many tasks associated with setting their course. There were plenty enough men on board to handle the vessel, but too few with enough ship experience to be of much use. Aynward found himself running around the deck like a chambermaid on the morning of the solstice celebration back home. But the price of falling behind here was higher than the displeasure of a master. The price here would be capture and death.

Aynward should not have been surprised by Gornstein's quick take-over as captain, vaguely recalling the story of the count's rise to power on the seas, but to see it in person impressed him. Orders flowed from his lips like a man who had never set foot on dry land. The ship picked up speed as they exited the cove, more of the canvas sheets growing taught with the power of the wind behind them.

Then Aynward saw two larger ships—galleons!—on a collision course with their schooner. The red sails of the Lugienese foreshadowed the blood they would shed.

Count Gornstein saw the ships, too. He yelled, "Prepare to jibe!"

Aynward and the sparse few others who understood what that meant went to work. He followed the order, but he didn't understand exactly what the count intended to accomplish. They were turning the ship to travel parallel to the shoreline instead of out to sea. This move pointed them in the direction of the approaching Lugienese ships. He would have thought they might turn away from the enemy, not toward them.

The crew executed the task, and the ship adjusted course, now fully engaged by the wind toward their new destination. *Our ship is not going to fare as well as the galleons in a head-on collision.*

Aynward tied the last knot for their current course then walked over to where the count stood, peering out at the enemy who was a mere thousand paces away. "What's your plan here? We can't survive a collision with either of those ships."

The count's expression was one of deep concentration. "We won't need to."

Then Draílock yelled, "They've got a wizard."

Suddenly one of their smaller canvas sails was struck by an unseen force, snapping the rope that held it in place. Two of Gornstein's guards were thrown off deck, crashing into the water behind the ship.

Gornstein yelled back to Draílock, "Protect us from them, for the love of life, protect us!"

Arella was at Draílock's side. Both of their amulets were glowing bright enough to shine above the light of the midday sun. "We're trying!"

Another blast of energy struck the water beside the boat; a spray hit the deck, but did no damage this time. "We won't be able to hold off this wizard for long. This would be much easier if we were moving *away* from the ships, not *toward* them!"

"Keep that wizard busy!" barked the count. "Just a little more time!"

Another burst of energy came at their ship. The Lugienese had already managed to take out one of their smaller sails.

Yet another bolt of energy slammed into their ship, detaching a few more ropes. It did minimal damage besides, but they were getting closer. They would have no schooner left in a matter of moments. But then the enemy ship lurched violently and the sound of exploding wood resonated across the water. Several of the priests standing at the deck rail on the ship's bow hurtled forward, crashing headfirst into the water below.

The count barked the orders to change course, and Aynward clung to the rail as their schooner began to turn away from a dangerous underwater shoal. He heard Kyllean scream at the top of his lungs, "Woo-hoo! Take that, ya bunch of fanatic degenerates! Yeahhh!" Cheers echoed from others onboard as they watched the other ship meet the same fate, attacked by some unseen enemy below the surface.

Their own ship leveled out and the count gave a new set of orders. Sails and jib were adjusted to point them toward the safety of the eastern isles city of Tung.

Kyllean yelled out again, "Gornstein, I don't know how you knew, but you're a genius!"

The count lowered his ordinarily guarded expression for an instant, revealing a wide and sinister grin. "I wasn't always a count."

Aynward's own excitement was short-lived. *Dolme!* He ran to where Draílock stood. "You've got to help Counselor Dolme." The wizard looked near to death himself: pale, gaunt, and sweating profusely. He looked like a man who had just returned from an entire day trapped inside one of the steam caves that Scritlandians loved. Aynward's eyes searched for the other wizard—*what was her name?*

"I'll do what I can," Draílock said.

"Thank you. C'mon, this way."

Aynward led him down the ladder and turned to see Dolme's abandoned form.

Gervais sat beside him with his back against the wall, hands completely bloodstained and the soldier who had been sent to tend him was nowhere to be seen.

Aynward rushed to Dolme's side. The once proud warrior lay prostrate, his ordinary sense of dignity gone. His eyes were still closed. Aynward laid his head against Dolme's chest to listen for his heart, but heard nothing. Pulling his head away, he resorted to shaking the man back to consciousness, back to life. Dolme didn't respond.

"No. Dolme, Draílock is here to heal you. Come on."

Aynward attempted to pull him into a seated position, but the body didn't cooperate. His head went sideways and his body slumped back down as the blood-soaked shirt slid from Aynward's grasp.

"He's gone, Aynward." Gervais's voice was tired and weak, but also confident.

"But he—he can't be. He just needs some help. Draílock. Do some of your wizardly stuff. He's okay."

The sorcerer bent down and felt the man's neck then slowly shook his head. "I'm sorry, Aynward. The man is right, there's nothing I can do."

Aynward said nothing further for a long time. Draílock placed a hand on his shoulder and gave a light squeeze. Everyone remained silent in deference to the deceased while Aynward stayed kneeling beside his former counselor's lifeless body, knowing he was the one responsible.

Eventually people began slowly moving about the room, but they were distant, like a dream.

At some point Kyllean had come down, though Aynward couldn't recall when. He approached and knelt alongside Aynward. "I'm sorry. I know you two didn't always get along, but he was still your counselor."

Not knowing what to say, Aynward just shook his head slowly.

Kyllean finally stood and started toward Minathi but paused as he passed Draílock. "Say, Draílock is it? Have we met, like before all of this? Before Brinkwell?"

"Oh, I very much doubt that." Draílock patted Kyllean on the shoulder. "Trauma does funny things to the mind. See to your friends and get some rest." Then the mage ascended the ladder to the deck as Kyllean shrugged and sat beside the recovering Minathi.

The room returned to silence and Aynward was glad for it. He needed to mourn and he did so unashamedly, tears flowing beyond his ability to control. Not because he had lost someone he cared deeply about. He couldn't lie to himself about that. He had hated the man. He cried because he lost someone he knew he *should* have cared deeply about and hadn't. Someone who died trying to protect a person who hated him. Dolme didn't have to come back for him. He shouldn't have come back for him. But he did. His sense of honor would not have allowed for less. Dolme died because Aynward was an arrogant fool.

Aynward finally turned away from the dead man. He walked to the ladder and climbed to the deck. He walked to the stern and gazed out over the water to the west. Black smoke rose from the place on the horizon where Brinkwell used to be. He stood there for a long time.

A shape materialized to his left. Aynward glanced over to see who it was, then back to the destruction in the distance. The spray of salt water, sweat, and even blood caused the translucent Lugienese hair to glitter in the sunlight.

Sindri took a place beside him but didn't say a word. She hadn't been belowdeck, but she seemed to sense his emotional state. She stood and stared out in the same direction; out at the destruction wrought by her own people. The disgraced priestess had been forced to kill several of her own that day. He hadn't considered how difficult that must have been for her.

The feeling of loss slipped from Aynward's grasp, and he found himself gripping the rail harder, his fingernails trying to penetrate the wood. His head warmed and he realized his grief was becoming something else. Dolme's death was his fault, he recognized this, but the blame did not rest on his shoulders alone. He felt the seeds of a deep brooding begin their gestation in his heart. But he wasn't the only one who had lost today.

After a few more minutes of silence, he finally said, "I'm sorry about your friend." He didn't know exactly what had happened with their search, but he knew that the boy wasn't with them now, and that meant he would likely soon die, if he still lived at all. Sindri just nodded. Looking out at the distant carnage brought about another wave of deep-seated anger in Aynward. Through clenched teeth, he said, "The Lugienese *will* pay."

Sindri slowly turned to face him, and Aynward met her gaze. There were none of the expected tears in her eyes, yet neither was there malice. Her eyes were simply hard, or perhaps determined. He realized then that she was holding out a closed fist. She slowly opened it to reveal a small black object. It moved, and he blinked. Had he imagined that? It moved again. Leaning in closer to get a better looked, he asked, "Is that a . . . is that a cricket?"

He looked up to find Sindri's eyes fixed upon his. She reached out and took his hand in hers. There was nothing romantic about her expression, or the way she held his hand. Instead she peered so deeply into his eyes that he wondered if she wasn't staring through him entirely. She guided his hand to rest beneath her other hand, holding it between hers, all three now cupping the insect. His gaze remained on her, but he could see a bead of sweat move from her forehead and down the side of her face. Then he felt a slight tingling sensation run slowly up his arm. He shuddered. The tingle was so feeble he thought he imagined it, or that it was one of those things people speak of when a man and woman—that thought snapped in half. Sindri brought their hands down. The cricket remained suspended in the air.

Aynward wanted to recoil, but her eyes had returned to his, holding him in place.

He broke away from her stare to see the black cricket turning over in the air as if floating in a jar of water.

Then she spoke, her voice a contradiction of calm and menace as she said, "I have the promise to find Kibure, and make punishment of the women of the cloaks gray. Then I will kill every Lugienese of the Kleról. None will have of life." When her expression finally slipped, she wore a sinister grin.

Aynward simply smiled back and, for once, remained silent.

## CHAPTER 125

# GROBENNAR

MAZI GROBENNAR STOOD POISED ATOP the palace wall overlooking the fallen city of Brinkwell. The sounds of slaughter rang with vibrancy, the city was finished. He would wait here in triumph for Magog to enter the city. He had instructed a retinue of soldiers to spread the word that the palace had been taken, and that Mazi Grobennar awaited the God-king's arrival to hand over the city as an offering.

He wished he could have rejoiced more fully in the victory. The work he had been sent to accomplish had been won with minimal casualties. And yet he looked down at his hands and saw only blood. Not since the birth of the prophesied redeemer had he committed such an act. But in the moment just before his escape from their lair, he knew Baghel could not be allowed to survive. If he had lived to describe the prisoner they'd lost, Magog might have guessed Grobennar's failure. It had been the only way to ensure that this portion of the story went untold. He still had to explain how all three of the other priests had perished, but he would think of something. After all, there was no one alive to contest his word.

*"Oh, stop being so melancholy. You are the hero who took Brinkwell!"* Jaween remarked. *"Oooh, and I sense—yes. The boy whose mind you delved*

*back in that village, a friend of the enemy. Your priests brought him here after all! He will add great value to our plans. We should keep that boy close at hand."*

Grobennar ignored Jaween, insomuch as he could ignore the spirit, but he did force himself to puff out his own chest in defiance of the recent setback. Jaween was right about one thing: there was indeed much for which to be grateful. The last few days had entailed more than simply caretaking his now-lost quarry. He had acquired the means to orchestrate yet another, greater victory on behalf of his king. He knew exactly where and how to contact Kubal when the time came, as well as the other spy; this one poised to strike at the heart of their next foe. *I'd like to see Rajuban spin that!*

Grobennar stood proud as a sea of red-robed figures flowed toward the palace like an all-consuming river. And leading the current was no ordinary man. No, this was Klerós's appointed lieutenant on Doréa, his king, the Emperor, Magog.

As he drew near, Grobennar found himself suddenly kneeling, as if gravity itself increased by mere proximity to this being's presence. But Grobennar was struck by more than just Magog's powerful bearing. The moons had only turned a few times since he had last seen the Emperor, but the continued consumption of souls, and the resulting transformation, was remarkable. Entire swaths of Magog's face now glinted red in the light, glowing embers of power. Where before there had been mere isolated growths of shimmering scale, it was now difficult to discern any spaces of visible skin. It was both terrible and beautiful.

*Who could look upon this being and doubt the power of Klerós? No one.*

So when the full voice of his king told him to rise, he did so without hesitation.

In spite of the overwhelming presence of his master, Mazi Grobennar stood valiant, welcoming him in shared glory. A strong wind caused Grobennar's recently donned cape to billow like a banner raised in triumph. Mazi Grobennar considered his successes here in Brinkwell, and those he knew were yet to come, and smiled. He began for the first time since his fall from grace to envision his place beside the God-king, bathed in the blood of their enemies, Klerós light illuminating the both of them.

His smile broadened as he noted that Rajuban was nowhere to be seen in this vision.

# CHAPTER 126

# KIBURE

KIBURE SLUMPED AS THE MAGICAL bonds holding him in place were released. The cloaked women who had carried him away from the Lugienese priests had refused to heed his cries that they go back for Sindri.

His weak body turned to see the thin crease on the horizon where the city of Brinkwell had become host to the Lugienese horde. Sindri, he knew, would be among the fallen. He mourned the loss of yet another person he had come to trust, another person he might have called a friend.

Without turning away from the somber sight, he asked, "Where are you taking me?"

They had ignored all of his questions thus far, but finally one of the pale-skinned women responded in heavily accented Lugienese, "East. We go east. To defeat darkness, we first return to home. We teach you many things."

Kibure felt a chill come over him as he finally made the connection. *My nightmares.* This was the woman whose voice he had heard in his nightmare weeks earlier. She had warned against entering the world of dream while in the Lugienese Empire, not that he had been able to

615

control it at the time. These women had been waiting for his arrival. Somehow they had known he would come to Brinkwell. It was also one of these women who he had seen during his most recent visit to the world of dream, the dream that had ended in his capture by the Klerósi priests. The figure had worn a shimmering cloak much like that which these women all wore. He opened his mouth to speak but something stole his words—the all too familiar sound of a raaven's coo.

Kibure gasped and turned to see a raaven, this one distinguished by a white mark above its eyes. This was decidedly not Rave. But—he shoved his confusion aside when a similar sound floated to his ears, this one farther away. Kibure looked around—there! A dark shape emerged from belowdeck.

Rave—his Rave!—zipped toward him and collided with his chest, then scrambled up to his shoulder to curl around his neck.

Kibure laughed. In spite of everything that had befallen him, he sensed something he had never before felt. It was unexplainable; he knew nothing of his new captors, but he felt it all the same: he felt safe.

## CHAPTER 127

# SINDRI

INDRI OPENED HER EYES AND shook off the haze of sleep. She looked up slowly, allowing her vision to return to focus. She saw Arella sitting up in her hammock staring back at her, a pensive expression struggling to overcome one of confusion.

"You were radiating ateré magic as you slept," said the young sorceress, the tone of her voice matching her countenance of perplexity.

Sindri shrugged. "I was having of the queerest dream."

"Oh?"

Sindri recalled the odd dream then said, "I was of this same ship, but I hear of no sound, and—"

Sindri stopped speaking as a troubling thought occurred; the memory of a young, frightened boy waking within a cage, radiating magic beyond his understanding. Her dream was just as he had described. Then another memory flashed across her mind's eye with an icy chill. Her brother. The brother she had abandoned. He too had complained of inexplicable nightmares. And now . . .

"Sindri?"

Sindri was speechless but for one word, a word she could never have imagined might apply to her. It came out as a choked whisper, but the question boomed through her like a gong.

"Tazamine? I am tazamine."

READ ON FOR A SNEAK PEEK OF

# THE
# OTHER
# WAY

## PASSAGE TO DAWN: BOOK TWO

We hope you have enjoyed *The Other Magic,* the first book in the *Passage to Dawn* series. We're pleased to present you with a sneak peek of *The Other Way,* the second book in the series.

Visit **www.DerrickSmythe.com** and sign up to receive updates about this and other future projects.

# AYNWARD

THE IMPOSING OAK DOOR SWUNG soundlessly to reveal the enormous study connected to his father's bedchamber. Like the rest of the palace architecture, the room was circular. Leather-bound books and scrolls lined the walls, while the rest of the room remained bare, with the exception of a Kingdom tapestry, and a Scritlandian runner in Kingdom blue and white leading directly to the mohagany desk in the center. The space was lit by a window with tall curtains on either side, and—something new: a dozen chairs formed a half-circle with the desk at its head. This is interesting, thought Aynward. Has Father been holding meetings with his advisers right here in his personal study? That would be yet another sign of . . . concern? Fear? Paranoia?

To Aynward's surprise, his father rose from his seated position as the door closed behind. Then he rounded the desk and moved forward. Aynward noted that the King's stride remained regal in spite of the outward signs of age. His hair was still long, accentuated by a sharp widow's peak, and his face held its usual iron expression.

King Lupren's deep voice echoed around the study as he closed the gap between them. "Son, it is very good to see you returned and in one piece."

"Yes, well—" Aynward was without a witty retort, especially as his father's arms opened for an embrace. The King's strong arms pulled him in, though Aynward's confusion made his own movements perfunctory. Once separated, the King's stony face managed to form a slight smile. Another rarity. Everything at the dinner the evening before had been so formal. The King had hardly acknowledged Aynward. Aynward had assumed this was because he didn't wish to berate his son in front of the guests.

"If the reports are to be believed, you survived quite an ordeal, and not without some manner of heroics, if perhaps a foolhardy decision to remain behind in the first place."

What is going on here? wondered a befuddled Aynward. "I must admit, Father, I was expecting a bit more of a—stern homecoming."

"Yes, well, I can't honestly say that I expected to receive word from the Count of Brinkwell singing your praises. But your new counselor, Gervais, has corroborated these accounts. Son, I was hesitant to send you away as I did, but I was just as reluctant to keep you here in Salmune. It seems Brinkwell managed to carve a good man out of you after all, though the circumstances surrounding this experience are regrettable."

Aynward attempted to respond, but his bewilderment choked his words. "I—"

As he opened his mouth again, he felt a lump develop in his throat. "I—I believe much of the credit goes to the late Counselor Dolm—Dolmuevo."

The King placed a hand upon Aynward's shoulder and shook his head. "He was a decent man, but in the end, it was greed that caused his death, not you."

Aynward leaped back in shock. "What? What are you talking about? He was killed in the defense of my life. He didn't have to come back for me."

"Aynward, perhaps you should sit down."

The King walked back to his desk and gestured for Aynward to sit in the seat closest, facing him at an uncomfortable angle.

His father spoke again. "Aynward, it was uncovered that Counselor Dolmuevo returned for you in order to deliver you to the Lugienese. He was tasked with ensuring that you remain behind, but alive. We suspect you would have been held for ransom by the Lugienese."

Aynward could not believe what he was hearing. "No. There is no way Dolme would have betrayed the Kingdom. He was one of the most loyal men I have ever known!"

The King lowered his head with a sad expression, or perhaps one of pity, as he said, "Son. We have letters confirming his involvement with the Lugienese. I'm sorry. I, too, was skeptical, but it is the truth."

Aynward scrutinized Dolme's every action through this new lens, looking for proof that the accusations were false, but everything Dolme had done seemed to fit. Everything except—

"But how could he have known I would jump from that first ship? How would he have delivered me if I were safely ferried away?"

His father just shook his head slowly. "He knew you too well, Aynward. Why do you think your friend's name wasn't on the list for your ship? Was that an honest oversight, or could it have been a calculated move to keep you in the city long enough for the Lugienese to arrive?"

No. This just can't be.

"Listen, son. None of this is your fault. In fact, whatever guilt you were carrying over his death can be cast aside. He was a traitor. The gods delivered their justice. And I fear he was not the only traitor in our midst."

Aynward could hardly comprehend what he was hearing. "I just— he seemed so . . ."

Aynward's statement trailed as movement to his right caught his attention. A dark shape emerged from behind the dark-blue curtains. It was so unexpected that Aynward hardly registered what he was seeing. The shape wore all black, and carried a sword!

Aynward sprang to his feet. "Father! Behind you!"

The shadowy figure was already upon the King, slashing just as he spun to face the danger.

The King's movement saved him from a fatal blow, but the blade still cut away the King's mobility with a deep slash to the thigh, a spray of blood trailing the shimmering steel of the blade. King Lupren remained upright, one knee on the stone floor, the other leg helping him balance. Aynward was only two strides away. He let out a bellow, hoping to draw the assassin's attention away from the King.

King Lupren let out a grunt of pain as his arm deflected the swing of steel away from his body. The assassin was not dissuaded, flowing directly into his next swing. This one missed as his father hobbled into the open space between the window and his desk. "Guards!" he yelled. "Aynward, run!"

Help would not be here in time. His father was weaponless and bleeding from two serious gashes. Aynward was also without a means of defense, but he couldn't stand by and watch his father be cut to pieces.

King Lupren's movements became those of grace in spite of his injuries. He dodged several more attacks, moving with speed that seemed to defy natural law. The assassin too seemed taken aback, tilting his head to the side after a string of completely missed attacks. How is he doing that? Aynward had never seen his father, or anyone, move like this. Aynward had stopped where he was, mesmerized by the spectacle. His father might just last long enough for the guards to arrive.

Then the assassin growled and his attack lost its graceful flow, taking on a brutality, a blood lust that could no longer be predicted like the movements of a trained swordsman. This time even the unnatural speed of his father's defenses was not enough as the two bodies collided. Out of this tangle, the King was knocked to the floor, a deep gash in his other leg rendering him completely immobile.

Aynward started forward again, but the assassin must have heard his footfalls for he turned and swung.

Aynward came to a halt just in time—the metal hissing as it passed mere inches from his throat. The figure immediately closed the gap and swung again. This time Aynward had no doubt that he would die. He just hoped help would arrive in time to save his father. "Guards!" he yelled. "Guards!" Where are they?

The blade arced down and across on its way to cleave his chest, but the assassin spun away. Aynward stood frozen in disbelief, unprepared for the assassin's foot which then took him square in the chest. Aynward's body struck the hard cold floor followed by a sound that stole his breath: a groan of pain from his father. It was a dignified sound, the sound of a great man, a proud man, but a dying man. Aynward rolled to his stomach, then crawled to his knees, ready to take his turn at death when he heard the clang of steel upon stone.

Looking up, he saw the assassin dart for the window. It swung open soundlessly. Aynward jumped to his feet to give chase but the assassin was too quick. Aynward arrived just in time to see the cutthroat land far below. Then with a flick of his wrist, the snare holding the rope to the stone fell loose. There was no chasing this man, not unless Aynward could fly.

Aynward rushed to his father, whose breathing was ragged. He lay on his back, blood oozing from his chest.

"Father . . ." Aynward whispered, pulling him close, cradling his head. He didn't know what else to do. The King tried to sit up, but lacked the strength.

The King spoke, but his words were garbled by blood. "Betrayal. More betrayal. Your—"

A crimson river flowed from his open mouth, choking his speech.

Then the door to the study burst open and guards rushed in, swords at the ready. They were breathing heavily, followed by an imposing figure dressed in formal military garb, heir to the throne, the King Apparent, Perja.

Aynward's eldest brother stared down at him, then pointed. "Guards, seize the assassin."

Aynward didn't understand what was happening. Not until he spotted the sword the assassin had left behind. His sword. The blade was still slick with the crimson blood of his father…

# ABOUT THE AUTHOR

**D**ERRICK SMYTHE HAS BEEN FASCINATED with all things elvish, dwarvish, and magical since his days of running through the woods with sharpened sticks in defense of whatever fortification he and his brothers had built that summer. After consuming nearly every fantasy book he could find, he was driven to begin work on one of his own. When he isn't dreaming up new stories, he can be spotted hiking in the Adirondack Mountains or traveling the world. He currently resides near his hometown in upstate New York with his enchanting wife, ethereal daughters, and his faithful-if-neurotic Australian Shepherd, Magnus.

Derrick's debut novel, *The Other Magic,* is the award-winning first installment of his *Passage to Dawn* series, an epic fantasy set in the World of Doréa.

To learn more about Derrick and *The Other Magic* visit:
Website: derricksmythe.com
Facebook: derricksmythe.author
Email: author@derricksmythe.com

Made in the USA
Monee, IL
06 December 2021

84037896R10370